George MacDonald

The Parish Papers

Three Complete Novels in One

Edited for Today's Reader by Dan Hamilton

ChariotVictor
PUBLISHING
A Division of Cook Communications

Victor Books is an imprint of ChariotVictor Publishing,
a division of Cook Communications, Colorado Springs, Colorado 80918
Cook Communications, Paris, Ontario
Kingsway Communications, Eastbourne, England

Annals of a Quiet Neighborhood was first published in 1866 as a magazine serial in England, and as a Victor Book in 1985.

The Seaboard Parish was first published in England in 1868, and as a Victor Book in 1985.

The Vicar's Daughter was first published in England in 1872, and as a Victor Book in 1985.

ISBN 1-56476-618-7

Contents

INTRODUCTION

George MacDonald (1824–1905), a Scottish preacher, writer, and public figure, is most well known today for his children's books—*At the Back of the North Wind*, *The Princess and the Goblin*, *The Princess and Curdie*—and his fantasies *Lilith* and *Phantastes*. These five books have seldom been out of print since their first publication.

But MacDonald's literary legacy encompasses far more than fantasies. His more than fifty books include poetry, theology, literary criticism, plays, short stories, sermons, historical novels, and a wonderful series of mystery-romance-adventure novels.

His works placed him in the same literary realm as Charles Dickens, Wilkie Collins, William Thackeray, and Thomas Carlyle. He numbered among his friends Lewis Carroll, Mark Twain, Lady Byron, and John Ruskin, and was partially to thank for the publication of Carroll's Alice in Wonderland.

Modern writers such as C.S. Lewis and Madeleine L'Engle have acknowledged their debt to MacDonald. Phantastes was a turning point in Lewis' conversion, and Lewis regarded this man (whom he never met) as his spiritual master; he declared later in his life that he had never written a book without quoting from MacDonald.

❖ ❖ ❖

MacDonald's books should be read in the original versions, wherever patience and availability permit. In the years since the first publication of this edition, several small publishing houses have reprinted original editions; the undiluted MacDonald is no longer so scarce or so dear.

One of the finest American collections of his works is open to the public: The Wade Collection, Wheaton College, Wheaton, Illinois. The Wade Collection also houses many of the works and memorabilia of G.K. Chesterton, C.S. Lewis, J.R.R. Tolkien, Owen Barfield, and Dorothy L.

Sayers, and has established side collections of Madeleine L'Engle, Frederick Buechner, and other worthy modern writers.

The George MacDonald Society continues to organize and share a wealth of information on MacDonald and his world. This group publishes the newsletter Orts *and the annual* North Wind; *membership information may currently be obtained from*

Membership Secretary
61 Longdales Road
Lincoln, England
LN2 2JS

FOREWORD

Writing styles change. Good stories don't.

The first statement explains why George MacDonald's novels are not widely read these days. The second statement explains why they should be.

The three books which comprise *The Parish Papers (Annals of a Quiet Neighborhood, The Seaboard Parish,* and *The Vicar's Daughter)* were not written as "historical novels"—they were contemporary magazine serials as first published between 1866 and 1872. This trilogy was reprinted in numerous editions throughout his lifetime, but after MacDonald died in Surrey in 1905, his fiction began a slow fade from the public eye. Old copies of the books traded hands quietly over the ensuing years, but no attempt was made to reprint them.

This edited version of the three novels began in 1982—more than 100 years after the first publication. Although I had long been aware of the existence of MacDonald's twenty-nine novels for adults, I had never seen a copy for sale. Then, in a used bookstore in the wilds of Vermont, I encountered a first American edition of *Annals of a Quiet Neighborhood*—and paid without tremor or regret the full marked price: 35 cents Seldom has my money been better invested.

My wife, Elizabeth, and I began reading, and were immediately charmed. Buried among the debris of an outmoded and difficult literary style was an absolutely readable and relevant mystery/romance/adventure novel. True to the literary conventions of his age (which held that any novel worth reading would occupy no less than three thick volumes) MacDonald wrote at great length about small events, and used the events as springboards for doctrinal digressions and religious rhapsodizing. Many of these descriptions, dialectics, and dissertations, while fascinating in themselves, do nothing to advance the story and are not crucial to the main spiritual impact of the book.

Our immediate conclusion was that these stories still deserve to be in the hands of readers. So we edited *A Quiet Neighborhood* and eventually its sequels, striving to achieve a balance between brevity and breadth that would be economical to print, interesting to the modern reader, and faithful to the heart of MacDonald's vision. We do not pretend that these versions are better than the originals—merely shorter, more affordable, and easier to read. We have clarified language that has changed in the last hundred years, and have corrected a few editorial errors left over from the serial publication. The excesses of the Victorian style have been trimmed away—but none, I hope, of MacDonald's jewels have perished along with the trivia.

In preparing these books, we have learned much from our immersion in MacDonald's godly wisdom and charming storytelling. May the reader find the same joy in these pages

Dan Hamilton
Indianapolis, Indiana
July 1996

A Quiet Neighborhood

Contents

ONE
Despondency and Consolation

I was thirty when I was made a vicar—an age at which a man might be expected to begin to grow wise—but even then I had much to learn. For then I only felt that a man had to take up his cross, whereas now I know that a man has to follow Him, and that makes an unspeakable difference.

I remember the first evening—a Saturday—in my new vicarage. I had never been there before. The weather was depressing, and grave doubts as to my place in the Church kept rising and floating about like the rain clouds. Not that I doubted the Church—I only doubted myself. Were my motives pure? What were my motives? I did not know, and therefore could not answer for their purity. Had I any right to be in the Church—to be eating her bread and drinking her wine—without knowing whether I was fit to do her work? What good might I look for as the result of my labor? How could I hope to help men live with the sense of the kingdom of heaven about them, and the expectation of something glorious at hand just outside that invisible door between the worlds? I desired to do some work worth calling work, and I did not see how to begin.

The only answer I could find was that the Church is part of God's world. He made men to work, and work of some sort must be done by every honest man. Somehow I had found myself working in the Church. I did not know that I was more fit for any other work. There was work here which I could do. With God's help, I would try to do it well.

This resolution brought me some relief, but I was still depressed. I was not married then, and firmly believed I never should be married—not from any ambition of self-denial, nor from any notion that God takes pleasure in being a hard master. But there was a lady . . . I had been refused a few months before, which I think was the best thing ever to happen to me, except one.

And so I was still depressed. For is it not depressing when the rain is falling and the steam is rising? When the river is crawling along muddily, and the horses stand stock-still with their spines in a straight line from their ears to their lowered tails?

Even so, I took my umbrella and went out, for I wanted to do my work well. I would go and fall in love, if I could, with the country round about. In my first step beyond my own gate, I was up to my ankles in mud.

I had not gone far before the rain ceased, though it was still gloomy. The road soon took a sharp turn to pass along an old stone bridge that spanned the water with a single fine arch. Through the arch I could see the swollen river stretching through the meadows, its banks bordered with pollards—poplars whose lower branches have been trimmed away, leaving only a curious crown of leaves at the very top of the tree. Now pollards always made me miserable. In the first place, they look ill-used. In the next place, they look tame. In the third place, they look ugly. I had not then learned to honor them on the ground that they do not yield to the adversity of their circumstances. If they must be pollards, they still will be trees, and what they may not do with grace, they will yet do with bounty. Their life bursts forth, despite all that is done to repress and destroy their individuality. When you have once learned to honor anything, love is not very far off. But as I had not yet learned to honor pollards, they made me more miserable than I already was.

I stood on the bridge and, looking up and down the river through the misty air, saw two long rows of these pollards diminishing till they vanished in both directions. The sight of them took from me all power of enjoying the water beneath me, the green fields around me, or even the beauty of the little bridge, although all sorts of bridges have been a delight to me. For I am one of those who never get rid of their infantile predilections, and to have once enjoyed making a mud bridge is to enjoy all bridges forever.

I saw a man coming along the road beyond, but I turned my back to the road, leaned my arms on the parapet of the bridge, and stood gazing where I saw no visions—namely, at those very pollards. I heard the man's footsteps coming up the crown of the arch, but I would not turn to greet him. I was in a selfish humor—surely, if ever one man ought to greet another, it was on such a comfortless afternoon. The footsteps stopped behind me, and I heard a voice, "I beg yer pardon, Sir, but be you the new vicar?"

I turned instantly and answered, "I am. Do you want me?"

Before me stood a tall old man with his hat in his hand. He smoothed his short gray hair over his forehead as he stood. His face was hued red-brown from much exposure to the weather. There was a certain look of roughness (without hardness) in it, which spoke of endurance rather than resistance, although he could evidently set his face as a flint. His features were large and a little coarse, but the smile that parted his lips when he spoke shone in his gray eyes as well, and lighted up a countenance in which a man might trust. "I wanted to see yer face, Sir, if you'll not take it amiss."

"Certainly not," I answered, pleased with the man's address, as he stood square before me, looking as modest as he was fearless. "The sight of a man's face is what everybody has a right to—but, for all that, I should like to know why you want to see my face."

"Why, Sir, you be the new vicar. You kindly told me so when I axed you."

"Well, then, you'll see my face on Sunday in church—that is, if you happen to be there."

"Yes, Sir. But you see, Sir, on the bridge here, the parson is the parson like, and I'm Old Rogers. And I looks in his face, and he looks in mine, and I says to myself, 'This is my parson.' But o' Sundays he's nobody's parson. He's got his work to do, and it mun be done, and there's an end on't."

That there was a real idea in the old man's mind was considerably clearer than his logic.

"Did you know parson that's gone, Sir? He wur a good parson. Many's the time he come and sit at my son's bedside—him that's dead and gone—for a long hour, on a Saturday night too. And then, when I see him up in the desk the next mornin', I'd say to myself, 'Old Rogers, that's the same man as sat by your son's bedside last night. Think o' that, Old Rogers!' But he didn't seem to have the same cut, somehow, and he didn't talk a bit the same. And when he spoke to me after sermon, in the churchyard, I was always of a mind to go into the church again and look up to the pulpit to see if he wur really out ov it, for this warn't the same man, you see. I always likes parsons better out o' the pulpit, and that's how I come to want to make you look at me, Sir, instead o' the water down there, afore I see you in the church tomorrow mornin'."

The old man laughed a kindly laugh, but he had set me thinking, and I did not know what to say. So, after a short pause, he resumed, "You'll be thinking me a queer kind of a man, Sir, to speak to my betters before my betters speaks to me. But mayhap you don't know what a parson is to us poor folk that has ne'er a friend more larned than theirselves but the parson. And, besides, Sir, I'm an old salt—an old man-o'-war's man—and I've been all round the world, and I ha' been in all sorts o' company, pirates and all, and I ain't a bit frightened of a parson. No—I love a parson, Sir. He's got a good telescope, and he gits to the masthead, and he looks out. And he sings out, 'Land ahead!' or 'Breakers ahead!' and gives directions accordin'. Only I can't always make out what he says. But when he shuts up his spyglass, and comes down to the riggin', and talks to us like one man to another, then I don't know what I should do without the parson. Good evenin' to you, Sir, and welcome to Marshmallows."

The pollards did not look half so dreary. The river began to glimmer a little, and the old bridge became an interesting old bridge. I had found a friend already, that is, a man to whom I might possibly be of some use. I had learned something from him too, and I resolved to try all I could to be the same man out of the pulpit that I was in it—seeing and feeling the realities of the unseen. And in the pulpit I would be the same as I was out of it—taking facts as they are, and dealing with things as they show themselves in the world.

Before I left the bridge, the sun burst his cloudy bands and blazed out as if he had just risen from the dead, instead of being just about to sink into the grave. The whole sweep of the gloomy river answered him in gladness, and the wet leaves of the pollards quivered and glanced. The meadows offered up their perfect green, fresh and clear out of the trouble of the rain; and away in the distance, upon a rising ground covered with trees, glittered a weathercock. And when the sun had gone below the horizon, and the fields and the river were dusky once more, there the weathercock glittered still over the darkening earth, a symbol of that faith which is "the evidence of things not seen." I stood up and wandered off the bridge and along the road. I had not gone far before I passed a house, out of which came a young woman leading a little boy. They came after me, the boy gazing at the red and gold and green of the sunset sky. As they passed me, the child said, "Auntie, I think I should like to be a painter."

"Why?" returned his companion.

"Because then," answered the child, "I could help God paint the sky."

What his aunt replied I do not know, but I went on answering him myself all the way home. Did God care to paint the sky of an evening, that a few of His children might see it? And should I think my day's labor lost if it wrought no visible salvation in the earth?

But was the child's aspiration in vain? Could I tell him God did not want his help to paint the sky? True, he could mount no scaffold against the glowing west. But might he not, with his little palette and brush, make his brothers and sisters see what he had seen? Might he not help God to paint this glory of vapor and light inside the minds of His children? Ah! If any man's work is not *with* God, its results shall be burned, ruthlessly burned, because it is poor and bad.

"So, for my part," I said to myself, "if I can put one touch of a rosy sunset into the life of any man or woman of my parish, I shall feel that I have worked with God. He is in no haste, and if I do what I may in earnest, I need not mourn if I work no great work in the earth. Let God make His sunsets—I will mottle my little fading cloud. Such be my ambition! So shall I scale the rocks in front, not leave my name carved upon those behind me."

I could not fail to see God's providence in this, that on my first attempt to find where I stood, and while I was discouraged, I should fall in with these two—an old man whom I could help and a child who could help me—the one opening an outlet for my labor and my love, and the other reminding me of the highest source of the most humbling comfort—that in all my work I might be a fellow worker with God.

TWO

My First Sunday at Marshmallows

The next morning I read prayers and preached. Never before had I enjoyed so much the petitions of the Church, which Richard Hooker calls "the sending of angels upward," or the reading of the lessons, which he calls "the receiving of angels descended from above." And whether from the newness of the parson, or the love of the service, certainly a congregation more intent or more responsive a clergyman will hardly find. But it was different in the afternoon. The people had dined, and the usual somnolence followed, nor could I find it in my heart to blame men and women who worked hard all the week for being drowsy on the day of rest. So I curtailed my sermon as much as I could, omitting page after page of my manuscript. When I came to a close, I was rewarded by agreeable surprise upon the faces round me. I resolved that in the afternoons, at least, my sermons should be as short as heart could wish.

But that afternoon there was one man of the congregation who was neither drowsy nor inattentive. I glanced toward him repeatedly and not once did I find his eyes turned away from me.

There was a small loft in the west end of the church in which stood a little organ whose voice, weakened by years of praising and possibly of neglect, had yet among a good many tones that were rough, wooden, and reedy, a few remaining mellow notes. Now this little loft was something larger than was just necessary for the organ and its ministrants, and a few of the parishioners chose to sit there. On this occasion there was but one man there.

The space below this gallery was not included in the part of the church used for the service. It was claimed by the gardener of the place—the sexton—to hold his gardening tools. There were a few ancient wood carvings lying in it, very brown in the dusky light. There were also some broken old headstones, and the kindly spade and pickaxe.

Rising against a screen which separated this mouldy portion of the church from the rest was an old monument of carved wood, once brilliantly painted, but now all bare and worn. Its gablet was on a level with the rail of the organ loft, and over it appeared the face of the man. It was a very remarkable countenance—pale and very thin, without any hair except for thick gray eyebrows that far overhung keen, questioning eyes. Short bushy hair, gray, not white, covered a well-formed head, with a high, narrow forehead. As I have said, those keen eyes looked at me all through the sermon, though I did not meet their owner until later.

My vestry door opened upon a little group of graves—poor graves without headstone or slab. Good men must have preceded me here, else the poor would not have lain so near the chancel and the vestry door. All about and beyond were stones, with here and there a monument. Mine was a large parish, and there were old and rich families in it, more of which buried their dead here than assembled their living. But close by the vestry door there was this little billowy lake of grass, and at the end of the narrow path leading from the door was the churchyard wall. But I would not creep out the back way from my people. That way might do very well to come in by; but to go out, I would use the door of the people. So I went along the church, and out by the door in the north side into the middle of the churchyard.

It lay in bright sunshine. All the rain and gloom were gone. "If one could only bring this glory of sun and grass into one's hopes for the future!" I thought, and looking down, I saw the little boy who aspired to paint the sky looking up in my face with mingled confidence and awe.

"Do you trust me, my little man?" thought I. "You shall trust me, then. But I won't be a priest to you. I'll be a big brother."

So I stooped and lifted the child and held him in my arms. And the little fellow looked at me one moment longer, and then put his arms gently round my neck. And so we were friends. I set him down, for I shuddered at the idea of the people thinking that I was showing off the clergyman. I looked at the boy. He did not say a word, but walked away to join his aunt, who was waiting for him at the gate of the churchyard. He kept his head turned toward me, and so stumbled over the grave of a child. As he fell in the hollow on the other side, I ran to pick him up. His aunt reached him at the same moment.

"O thank you, Sir!" she said, with an earnestness which seemed to me disproportionate to the deed, and carried him away with a deep blush over all her countenance.

The old man-of-war's man was waiting at the churchyard gate. His hat was in his hand, and he gave a pull to the short hair over his forehead, as if he would gladly take that off too, to show his respect for the new parson. I held out my hand gratefully, but could not close it around the hard unyielding mass of fingers. He did not know how to shake hands and left it all to me, but pleasure sparkled in his eyes.

"My old woman would like to shake hands with you, Sir," he said.

Beside him stood his old woman in a portentous bonnet. Beneath the gay yellow ribbons appeared a dusky old wrinkled face with a pair of keen black eyes, where the best beauty—that of loving-kindness—triumphed.

"I shall be in to see you soon," I said, as I shook hands with her. "I shall find out where you live."

"Down by the mill," she said, "close by it, Sir. There's one bed in our garden that always thrives, in the hottest summer, by the splash from the mill."

"Ask for Old Rogers, Sir," said the man. "Everybody knows Old Rogers. But if Your Reverence minds what my wife says, you won't go wrong. When you find the river, it takes you to the mill, and when you find the mill, you find the wheel. And when you find the wheel, you haven't far to look for the cottage, Sir. It's a poor place, but you'll be welcome."

THREE

My First Monday at Marshmallows

The next day I expected visitors from among my rich. It is fortunate that English society regards the parson as a gentleman, else he would have little chance of being useful to the upper classes. But I wanted to get a good start and see some of my poor before my rich came to see me. So, after breakfast on that lovely Monday in the beginning of autumn, I walked out to the village. I strove to dismiss from my mind every feeling of doing duty, of performing my part, and all that. I had a horror of becoming a moral policeman as much as of "doing church." I would simply enjoy the privilege of ministering. But, as no servant has a right to force his service, so I would be the neighbor only until such time as the opportunity of being the servant should show itself.

The village was as irregular as a village should be, partly consisting of those white houses with black intersecting parallelograms which still abound in some regions of our island. Just in the center, however, clustered about a house of red brick, rose a group of buildings which seemed part of some old and larger town. But round any one of three visible directions were stacks of wheat and a farmyard, while in another direction the houses went straggling away into a wood that looked very like the beginning of a forest.

From the street, the poplar-bordered stream was here and there just visible. I did not like to have it between me and my village. I could not help preferring that homely relation in which the houses are built up like swallow's nests onto the very walls of the cathedrals themselves, to the arrangement here where the river flowed between the church and the people. A little way beyond the far end of the village appeared an iron gate of considerable size, dividing a lofty stone wall. Upon the top of one of the stone pillars supporting the gate stood a creature of stone, terrible enough for antediluvian heraldry.

As I passed along the street, my eye was caught by the window of a little shop, in which were arranged strings of beads and elephants of gingerbread.

It was a window much broader than it was high, divided into lozenge-shaped panes. I thought to make a visit by going in and buying something. But I hesitated, because I could not think of anything I was in want of—at least that I was likely to encounter here. To be sure, I wanted a copy of Bengel's *Gnomon*, but I was not likely to find that. I wanted the fourth plate in the third volume of Law's *Bohme*, but that was not likely either. I did not care for gingerbread, and I had no little girl to take home beads to.

But why should I not go in but with a likely errand? For this reason: there are dissenters everywhere, and I could not tell but I might be going into the shop of a dissenter. Now, though nothing would have pleased me better than that all the dissenters should return to their old home in the Church, I could not endure the suspicion of canvassing or using any personal influence. Whether they returned or not—and I did not expect many would—I hoped still to stand toward every one of them as the parson of the parish, that each one might feel certain that I was ready to serve him or her at any hour. In the meantime, I could not help hesitating.

Then the door opened and out came the little boy whom I had already seen twice, and who was therefore one of my oldest friends in the place. He came across the road to see me, took me by the hand, and said, "Come and see Mother."

"Is this your mother's shop?"

"Yes."

I said no more, but accompanied him.

The place was half a shop and half a kitchen. A yard or so of counter stretched inward from the door, just as a hint to those who might be intrusively inclined. Beyond this, by the chimney corner, sat the mother, who rose as we entered. She was one of the most remarkable women I had ever seen. Her face was absolutely white except her lips and a spot upon each cheek, which glowed with a deep carmine. You would have said she had been painting, and painting very inartistically, so little was the red shaded into the surrounding white. Now this was certainly not beautiful, but when I got used to her complexion, I saw that the form of her features was quite beautiful. She might indeed have been lovely but for a certain hardness which showed through the beauty. Her teeth were firmly closed and, taken with the look of the eyes and forehead, hers seemed the expression of a constant and bitter self-command. There were marks of ill health upon her as well. Her large dark eyes were burning as if the lamp of life had broken and the oil was blazing. But her manner was perfectly, almost dreadfully, quiet. Her voice was soft, low, book-proper, and chiefly expressive of indifference. She spoke without looking me in the face, but did not seem either shy or ashamed. Her figure was remarkably graceful, though too worn to be beautiful. Here was a strange parishioner for me—in a country shop too!

The little fellow shrunk away through a half-open door that revealed a stair behind.

"What can I do for you, Sir?" said the mother. She stood on the other side of the little counter, prepared to open box or drawer at command.

"To tell the truth, I hardly know," I said. "I am the new vicar—but I do not think that I should have come in to see you just today, if it had not been that your little boy there asked me to come in and see his mother."

"He is too ready to make advances to strangers, Sir."

"Oh, but I am not a stranger to him. I have met him twice before. He is a little darling. I assure you he has quite gained my heart."

No reply for a moment. Then just, "Indeed!" and nothing more. A tobacco jar on a shelf rescued me from the most pressing portion of the perplexity—namely, what to say next.

"Will you give me a quarter of a pound of tobacco?" I said.

The woman turned, took down the jar, weighed out the quantity, wrapped it, and took the money, all without one other word than "Thank you, Sir," which was all I could return, with the same addition of "Good morning."

I walked away with my parcel in my pocket. The little boy did not show himself again, although I had hoped to find him outside.

I set out for the mill, which I had already learned was on the village side of the river. Coming to a lane leading down to the river, I followed it and then walked up a path outside the row of pollards, through a lovely meadow where brown and white cows were eating the thick deep grass. Beyond the meadow, a wood on rising ground paralleled the river. The river flowed slowly on my right. Still swollen, it was of a clear brown, in which you could see the browner trout darting with such a slippery gliding that the motion seemed the result of will, without any such intermediate and complicated arrangement as brain and nerves and muscles. The water beetles went spinning about and one dragonfly made a mist about him with his long wings. The sun hung in the sky over all, pouring down life, shining on the roots of the willows, lighting up the black head of the water rat, glorifying the green lake of the grass, and giving to the whole an utterance of love and hope and joy which was, to him who could read it, a more certain and full revelation of God than any display of power in thunder, avalanche, or stormy sea.

I soon came within sound of the mill. Presently, crossing the stream that flowed back to the river after having done its work on the corn, I came in front of the building and looked over the half-door into the mill. The floor was clean and dusty. A few full sacks, tied at the mouth, stood about—they always look to me as if Joseph's silver cup were just inside. In the corner the flour was trickling down out of two wooden spouts into a wooden receptacle below. The whole place was full of its own faint but pleasant odor. No man was visible. The spouts went on pouring the slow torrent of flour as if everything could go on of itself with perfect propriety. I could not even see how a man could get at the stones that I heard grinding away above, except he went up the rope that hung from the ceiling. So I walked round the corner of the place and found myself in the company of the waterwheel, mossy and green with ancient waterdrops, furred and overgrown and lumpy. It was going round—slowly, indeed, and with the gravity of age, but doing its work—and casting its loose drops in a gentle rain upon a little plot of Master Rogers' garden, which was therefore full of moisture-loving flowers.

Beside the flowerbeds stood a dusty young man, talking to a young woman with a rosy face and clear honest eyes. The moment they saw me they parted. The young man came across the stream at a step, and the young woman went up toward the cottage.

"That must be Old Rogers' cottage," I said to the miller.

"Yes, Sir," he answered, looking a little sheepish.

"Was that his daughter—that nice-looking young woman you were talking to?"

"Yes, Sir, it was." And he stole a shy, pleased look at me out of the corners of his eyes.

"It's a good thing," I said, "to have an honest, experienced old mill like yours, that can manage to go on of itself for a little while now and then."

This gave a great help to his budding confidence. He laughed. "Well, Sir, it's not very often it's left to itself. Jane isn't at her father's above once or twice a week, at most."

"She doesn't live with them, then?"

"No, Sir. You see they're both hearty, and they ain't over well-to-do, and Jane lives up at the Hall, Sir. She's upper housemaid and waits on one of the young ladies. Old Rogers has seen a great deal of the world, Sir."

"So I imagine. I am just going to see him. Good morning."

I jumped across the stream and went up a little gravel walk to the cottage door. It was a sweet place to live in, with honeysuckle growing over the house, and the soft sounds of the mill wheel ever in its little porch and about its windows.

The door was open, and Dame Rogers came from within to meet me. She welcomed me, and led the way into her little kitchen. As I entered, Jane went out at the back door. But it was only to call her father, who presently came in.

"I'm glad to see ye, Sir. This pleasure comes of having no work today. After harvest there come slack times for the likes of me. People don't care about a bag of old bones when they can get hold of young men. Well, well, never mind, old woman. The Lord'll take us through somehow. When the wind blows, the ship goes; when the wind drops, the ship stops; but the sea is His all the same, for He made it; and the wind is His all the same too."

He spoke in the most matter-of-fact tone, unaware of anything poetic in what he said. To him it was just common sense.

"I am sorry you are out of work," I said. "But my garden is sadly out of order, and I must have something done to it. You don't dislike gardening, do you?"

"Well, I bean't a right good hand at garden work," answered the old man, with some embarrassment.

There was more in this than met the ear, but what I could not conjecture. I would press the point a little. So I took him at his own word.

"I won't ask you to do any of the more ornamental part," I said, "only plain digging and hoeing."

"I would rather be excused, Sir."

"I am afraid I made you think—"

"I thought nothing, Sir. I thank you kindly, Sir."

"I assure you I want the work done, and I must employ someone else if you don't undertake it."

"Well, Sir, my back's bad now—no, Sir, I won't tell a story about it. I would just rather not, Sir."

"Now," his wife broke in, "now, Old Rogers, why won't 'ee tell the parson the truth, like a man, downright? If ye won't I'll do it for 'ee. The fact is, Sir," she went on, turning to me, "the fact is, that the old parson's man for that kind o' work was Simmons, t'other end of the village. And my man is so afeard o' hurtin' e'er another, that he'll turn the bread away from his own mouth and let it fall in the dirt."

"Now, now, old 'oman, don't 'ee belie me. I'm not so bad as that. You see, Sir, I never was good at knowin' right from wrong like. I never was good, that is, at tellin' exactly what I ought to do. So, when anything comes up, I just says to myself, 'Now, Old Rogers, what do you think the Lord would best like you to do?' And as soon as I ax myself that, I know directly what I've got to do, and then my old woman can't turn me no more than a bull. But, you see, I daren't, Sir, once I axed myself that."

"Stick to that, Rogers," I said.

"Besides, Sir," he went on, "Simmons wants it more than I do. He's got a sick wife, and my old woman, thank God, is hale and hearty. And there is another thing besides, he might take it hard of you, Sir, and think it was turning away an old servant like. And then, he wouldn't be ready to hear what you had to tell him, and might, mayhap, lose a deal o' comfort. And that I would take worst of all, Sir."

"Well, well, Rogers, Simmons shall have the job."

"Thank ye, Sir," said the old man.

I rose to go. As I reached the door, I remembered the tobacco in my pocket. I had not bought it for myself. I never could smoke.

"You smoke, don't you, Rogers?" I said.

"Well, Sir, I can't deny it. It's not much I spend on baccay, anyhow, is it, Dame?"

"No, that it bean't," answered his wife.

"You see, Sir," he went on, "sailors learns many ways they might be better without. I used to take my pan o' grog with the rest of them, but I gave that up, 'cause as how I don't want it now."

" 'Cause as how," interrupted his wife, "you spend the money on tea for me instead. You wicked old man to tell stories."

"Well, I takes my share of the tea, old woman, and I'm sure it's a deal better for me. But, to tell the truth, Sir, I was a little troubled in my mind about the baccay, not knowing whether I ought to have it or not. For you see, the parson that's gone didn't more than half like it. Not as he said anything, for I was an old man. But I did hear him give a thunderin' broadside to a young chap i' the village he come upon with a pipe in his mouth. So I was in two minds whether I ought to go on with my pipe or not."

"And how did you settle the question, Rogers?"

"Why, I followed my own old chart, Sir."

"Quite right. One mustn't mind too much what other people think."

"That's not exactly what I mean, Sir. I mean that I said to myself, 'Now, Old Rogers, what do you think the Lord would say about this here baccay business?' "

"And what did you think He would say?"

"Why, Sir, I thought He would say, 'Old Rogers, have yer baccay—only mind ye don't grumble when you ain't got none.' "

Something in this touched me more than I can express. No doubt it was the simple reality of the relation in which the old man stood to his Father in heaven that made me feel as if the tears would come. "And this is the man," I said to myself, "whom I thought to teach! Well, the wisest learn most, and I may be useful to him after all."

As I said nothing, the old man resumed, "For you see, Sir, it is not always a body feels he has a right to spend his ha'pence on baccay, and sometimes, too, he ain't got none to spend."

"In the meantime," I said, "here is some that I bought for you as I came along. I hope you find it good. I am no judge."

The old sailor's eyes glistened with gratitude. "Well, who'd ha' thought it? You didn't think I was beggin' for it, Sir, surely?"

"You see I had it for you in my pocket."

"Well, that is good o' you, Sir."

"Why, Rogers, that'll last you a month!" exclaimed his wife.

"Six weeks at least, Wife," he answered. "And ye don't smoke yourself, and yet ye bring baccay to me!"

I went away resolved that Old Rogers should have no chance of "grumbling" for want of tobacco, if I could help it.

FOUR

The Coffin

As I went through the village, I explored a narrow lane striking off to the left. It led up to one side of the large house of which I have already spoken. As I came near, I smelt a delightful smell—that of fresh deals under the hands of the carpenter. If I were idling, that scent would draw me across many fields. I heard the sound of a saw, so I drew near, feeling as if the Lord might be working there at one of His own benches. And when I reached the door, there was my palefaced hearer of Sunday afternoon sawing a board for a coffin lid. As my shadow fell across and darkened his work, he lifted his head and saw me.

He stood upright from his labor and touched his old hat with a proud (rather than courteous) gesture. And I could not believe that he was glad to see me, although he laid down his saw and advanced to the door. It was the gentleman in him, not the man, that sought to make me welcome, hardly caring whether I saw through the ceremony or not. True, there was a smile on his lips, but the smile of a man who cherishes a secret grudge. So the smile seemed tightened, and stopped just when it was about to become hearty and begin to shine.

"I am glad I have happened to come upon you by accident," I said.

He smiled as if he did not quite believe in the accident, and considered it a part of the play between us that I should pretend it. I hastened to add, "I was wandering about the place, making some acquaintance with it, when I came upon you quite unexpectedly. I saw you in church on Sunday afternoon."

"I know you saw me, Sir," he answered, with a motion as if to return to his work, "but to tell the truth, I don't go to church very often."

I did not quite know whether to take this as proceeding from an honest fear of being misunderstood, or from a sense of being in general superior to all that sort of thing. But it would be of no good to pursue the inquiry directly. I looked, therefore, for something to say. "Your work is not always pleasant," I said, looking at the unfinished coffin.

"Well, there are unpleasant things in all trades," he answered, with an increase of bitterness in his smile.

"I didn't mean," I said, "that the work was unpleasant, only sad. It must always be painful to make a coffin."

"A joiner gets used to it, Sir, as you do to the funeral service. But, for my part, I don't see why it should be considered so unhappy for a man to be buried. This isn't such a good job, after all, this world, Sir, you must allow."

"Neither is that coffin," said I, by a sudden inspiration.

The man seemed taken aback. He looked at the coffin and then looked at me. "Well, Sir," he said, after a short pause which no doubt seemed long, "I don't see anything amiss with the coffin. I don't say it'll last till doomsday, as the gravedigger said to Hamlet; but you see, Sir, it's not finished yet."

"Thank you," I said. "That's just what I meant. You thought I was hasty in my judgment of your coffin, whereas I only said of it knowingly what you said of the world thoughtlessly. How do you know that the world is finished any more than your coffin? And how dare you say that it is a bad job?"

The same respectfully scornful smile passed over his face, as to say, "Ah! it's your trade to talk that way, so I must not be too hard on you."

"At any rate, Sir," he said, "whoever made it has taken long enough about it, a person would think, to finish anything he ever meant to finish."

"One day is with the Lord as a thousand years, and a thousand years as one day," I said.

"That's supposing," he answered, "that the Lord did make the world. For my part, I am half of a mind that the Lord didn't make it at all."

"I am very glad to hear you say so," I answered.

Hereupon I found that we had changed places a little. He looked up at me, and the smile of superiority was no longer there. I was in danger of being misunderstood, so I proceeded at once. "Of course, it seems to me better that you should not believe God had done a thing, than that you should believe He had not done it well."

"Ah, I see, Sir. Then you will allow there is some room for doubting whether He made the world at all?"

"Yes, for I do not think an honest man, as you seem to me to be, would be able to doubt without any room whatever. That would be only for a fool. But it is just possible, as we are not perfectly good ourselves. You'll allow that, won't you?"

"That I will, Sir. God knows."

"Well, I say, as we're not quite good ourselves, it's just possible that things may be too good for us to do them the justice of believing in them."

"But there are things, you must allow, so plainly wrong!"

"So much so, both in the world and in myself, that it would be to me torturing despair to believe that God did not make the world, for then, how would it ever be put right? Therefore I prefer the theory that He has not done making it yet."

"But mightn't God have managed it without so many slips in the making? I should think myself a bad workman if I worked after that fashion."

"I do not believe there are any slips. You know you are making a coffin, but are you sure you know what God is making of the world?"

"That I can't tell, of course, nor anybody else."

"Then you can't say that what looks like a slip is really a slip, either in the design or in the workmanship. You do not know what end He has in view, and you may find someday that those slips were just the straight road to that very end."

It is a principle of mine never to push anything over the edge. When I am successful in any argument, my one dread is of humiliating my opponent. When a man reasons for victory and not for the truth in the other soul, he is sure of just one ally—the devil. The defeat of the intellect is not the object in fighting with the sword of the Spirit, but rather the acceptance of the heart. Therefore, I drew back. "May I ask for whom you are making that coffin?"

"For a sister of my own, Sir."

"I'm sorry to hear that."

"There's no occasion. I can't say I'm sorry, though she was one of the best women I ever knew."

"Why are you not sorry, then? Life's a good thing in the main, you will allow."

"Yes, when it's endurable at all. But to have a brute of a husband coming home at any hour, drunk on the money she had earned by hard work, was enough to take more of the shine out of things than churchgoing on Sundays could put in again. I'm as glad as her husband that she's out of his way at last."

"How do you know he's glad of it?"

"He's been drunk every night since she died."

"Then he's the worse for losing her?"

"He may well be. Crying like a hypocrite too over his own work!"

"A fool he must be—a hypocrite, perhaps not. A hypocrite is a terrible name to give. Perhaps her death will do him good."

"He doesn't deserve to be done any good to. I would have made this coffin for him with a world of pleasure."

"I never found that I deserved anything, not even a coffin. The only claim that I could ever lay to anything was that I was very much in want of it."

The old smile returned, as if to say, "That's your little game in the church." But I resolved to try nothing more with him at present. "This has been a fine old room once," I said, looking round the workshop.

"You can see it wasn't a workshop always, Sir. Many a grand dinner party has sat down in this room when it was in its glory. The owners little thought it would come to this—a coffin on the spot where the grand dinner was laid for them and their guests! But there is another thing about it that is odder still: my son is the last male—"

Here he stopped suddenly and his face grew very red. As suddenly he resumed, "I'm not a gentleman, Sir, but I will tell the truth. My son's not the last male descendant."

Here followed another pause. While I looked at him, I was reminded of someone else I knew, though I could not in the least determine who that might be.

"It's very foolish of me to talk so to a stranger," he resumed.

"It is very kind and friendly of you," I said. "And you yourself belong to the old family that once lived in this old house?"

"It would be no boast to tell the truth, Sir, even if it were a credit to me, which it is not. That family has been nothing but a curse to ours."

I noted that he spoke of that family as different from his, and yet implied that he belonged to it. The explanation would come in time. But the man was again silent, planing away at the lid of his sister's coffin.

"I am sure there must be many a story to tell about this old place, if only there were someone to tell them," I said at last, looking round the room once more. "I think I see the remains of paintings on the ceiling."

"You are sharp-eyed, Sir. My father says they were plain enough in his young days."

"Is your father alive, then?"

"That he is, Sir—past ninety and hearty too—though he seldom goes out of doors now. Will you go upstairs and see him? He has plenty of stories to tell about the old place, before it began to fall to pieces, like."

"I won't go today," I said, partly to secure an excuse for calling again soon. "I expect visitors myself, and it is time I were at home. Good morning."

"Good morning, Sir."

I was certain of understanding this man when I had learned something of his history. A man may be on the way to the truth just in virtue of his doubting. Lord Bacon says, "So it is in contemplation: if a man will begin with certainties, he shall end in doubts; but if he will be content to begin with doubts, he shall end in certainties." This man's doubt was evidently real, and that was much in his favor. And I could see that he was a thinking man—just one of the sort I thought I should get on with in time. At all events, here was another strange parishioner. And who could it be that he was like?

FIVE
Visitors from the Hall

When I came near my own gate, I found a carriage standing there, and a footman ringing the bell. It was an old-fashioned carriage, with two white horses who were yet whiter by age than by nature. They looked as if no coachman could get more than three miles an hour out of them, they were so fat and knuckle-kneed. I reached the door just as my housekeeper was pronouncing me absent. There were two ladies in the carriage, one old and one young.

"Ah! Here is Mr. Walton," said the old lady, in a serene voice with a clear hardness in its tone. I held out my hand to aid her descent. She had pulled off her glove to get a card out of her card case, and so put the tips of two old fingers, worn very smooth as if polished with feeling what things were like, upon the palm of my hand. I then offered my hand to her companion, a girl about fourteen, who jumped down beside her with a smile. As I followed them into the house, I took their card from the housekeeper's hand and read *Mrs. Oldcastle* and *Miss Gladwyn.*

When they were seated in the drawing room, I said to the lady, "I remember seeing you in church on Sunday morning. It is very kind of you to call so soon."

"You will always see me in church," she returned, with a stiff bow, and an expansion of deadness on her face, which I interpreted as an assertion of dignity.

"Except when you have a headache, Grannie," said Miss Gladwyn, with an arch look first at her grandmother and then at me. "Grannie has bad headaches sometimes."

The deadness melted a little from Mrs. Oldcastle's face as she turned with a half smile to her grandchild and said, "Yes, Pet. But you know that cannot be an interesting fact to Mr. Walton."

"I beg your pardon, Mrs. Oldcastle," I said. "A clergyman ought to know the troubles of his flock, and sympathy is one of the first demands he ought to be able to meet. I know what a headache is."

The former expression, or rather nonexpression, returned, this time unaccompanied by a bow. "I trust, Mr. Walton, that I am above any morbid necessity for sympathy. But, as you say, among the poor of your flock, it is very desirable that a clergyman should be able to sympathize."

"It's quite true what Grannie says, Mr. Walton, though you mightn't think it. When she has a headache, she shuts herself up in her own room, and doesn't even let me come near her—nobody but Sarah—and how she can prefer her to me, I'm sure I don't know." And here the girl pretended to pout, but with a sparkle in her bright gray eyes.

"The subject is not interesting to me, Pet. Pray, Mr. Walton, is it a point of conscience with you to wear the surplice when you preach?"

"Not in the least," I answered. "I think I like it rather better on the whole. But that's not why I wear it."

"Never mind Grannie, Mr. Walton. I think the surplice is lovely. I'm sure it's much like the way we shall be dressed in heaven, though I don't think I shall ever get there, if I must read the good books Grannie reads."

"I don't know that it is necessary to read any good books but *the* Good Book," I said.

"There, Grannie!" exclaimed Miss Gladwyn, triumphantly. "I'm so glad I've got Mr. Walton on my side!"

"Mr. Walton is not so old as I am, my dear, and has much to learn yet."

I could not help feeling a little annoyed (which was very foolish, I know), and said to myself, "If it's to make me like you, I had rather not learn anymore!" but I said nothing aloud.

"Have you a headache today, Grannie?"

"No, Pet. Be quiet. I wish to ask Mr. Walton why he wears the surplice."

"Simply," I replied, "because I was told the people had been accustomed to it under my predecessor."

"But that can be no good reason for doing what is not right—that people have been accustomed to it."

"But I don't allow that it's not right. I think it is a matter of no consequence whatever. If I find that the people don't like it, I will give it up with pleasure."

"You ought to have principles of your own, Mr. Walton."

"I hope I have! And one of them is not to make mountains of molehills, for a molehill is not a mountain. A man ought to have too much to do in obeying his conscience and keeping his soul's garments clean, to mind whether he wears black or white when telling his flock that God loves them, and that they will never be happy till they believe it."

"They may believe that too soon."

"I don't think anyone can believe the truth too soon."

A pause followed, during which it became evident to me that Miss Gladwyn saw fun in the whole affair and was enjoying it thoroughly. Mrs. Oldcastle's face, on the contrary, was illegible. She resumed in a measured, still voice which she meant to be meek, I dare say, but which was really authoritative, "I am sorry, Mr. Walton, that your principles are so loose and unsettled. You will see my honesty in saying so when you find that objecting to the surplice, as I do on Protestant grounds, I yet warn you against making any change because you may discover that your parishioners are against it. You have no idea, Mr. Walton, what inroads Radicalism, as they call it, has been making in this neighborhood. It is quite dreadful. Everybody, down to the poorest, claiming a right to think for himself and set his betters right! There's one worse than any of the rest—but he's no better than an atheist—a carpenter of the name of Weir, always talking to his neighbors against the proprietors and the magistrates, and the clergy too, Mr. Walton, and the game laws, and what not. And if you once show them that you are afraid of them by going a step out of your way for their opinion about anything, there will be no end to it. The beginning of strife is like the letting out of water, as you know. *I* came to hear of it through my daughter's maid, a decent girl of the name of Rogers, and born of decent parents, but unfortunately attached to the son of one of your churchwardens, who has put him into that mill on the river."

"Who put him in the mill?"

"His own father, to whom it belongs."

"Well, it seems to me a very good match for her."

"Yes, indeed, and for him too. But his foolish father thinks the match below him, as if there was any difference between the positions of people in that rank of life! Everyone seems striving to tread on the heels of everyone else, instead of being content with the station to which God has called them. I am content with mine. I had nothing to do with putting myself there. Why should they not be content with theirs? They need to be taught Christian humility and respect for their superiors. That's the virtue most wanted at present. The poor have to look up to the rich—"

"That's right, Grannie! And the rich have to look down on the poor."

"No, my dear, I did not say that. The rich have to be kind to the poor."

"But, Grannie, why did you marry Mr. Oldcastle? Uncle Stoddart says you refused ever so many offers when you were a girl."

"Uncle Stoddart has no business to be talking about such things to a chit like you," returned the grandmother, smiling, however, at the charge which so far certainly contained no reproach.

"And Grandpa was the ugliest and the richest of them all, wasn't he, Grannie? And Colonel Markham the handsomest and the poorest?"

A flush of anger crimsoned the old lady's pale face. It looked dead no longer. "Hold your tongue," she said. "You are rude."

And Miss Gladwyn did hold her tongue but nothing else, for she was laughing all over.

The relation between these two was evidently a very odd one. It was clear that Miss Gladwyn was a spoiled child, though I could not help thinking her very nicely spoiled, as far as I saw. The old lady persisted in regarding her as a cub, although her claws had grown quite long enough to be dangerous. Certainly, if things went on thus, it was pretty clear which of them would soon have the upper hand, for Grannie was vulnerable and Pet was not.

But her granddaughter's tiger-cat play drove the old lady nearer to me. She rose and held out her hand, saying with some kindness, "Take my advice, my dear Mr. Walton, and don't make too much of your poor or they'll soon be too much for you to manage. Come, Pet, it's time to go home to lunch. And for the surplice, take your own way and wear it. I shan't say anything more about it."

"I will do what I can see to be right in the matter," I answered as gently as I could, for I did not want to quarrel with her, although I thought her both presumptuous and rude.

"I'm on your side, Mr. Walton," said the girl, with a sweet comical smile, as she squeezed my hand once more.

I led them to the carriage, and it was with a feeling of relief I saw it drive off.

The old lady certainly was not pleasant. She had a white smooth face over which the skin was drawn tight, gray hair, and rather lurid hazel eyes. I felt a repugnance toward her that was hardly to be accounted for by her arrogance to me, or by her superciliousness to the poor, although either would have accounted for much of it. I confess that I have not yet learned to bear presumption and rudeness with all the patience and forgiveness with which I ought by this time to be able to meet them. And as to the poor, I am afraid I was always in some danger of being a partisan of theirs against the rich, and that a clergyman ought never to be. Indeed, the rich have more need of the care of the clergyman than the others, seeing that the rich shall scarcely enter into the kingdom of heaven, and the poor have all the advantage over them in that respect.

"Still," I said to myself, "there must be some good in the woman—she can not be altogether so hard as she looks, else how should that child dare to take the liberties of a kitten with her? She doesn't look to me like one to make game of! However, I shall know a little more about her when I return her call, and I will do my best to keep on good terms with her."

I took down a volume of Plato to comfort me, and sat down in an easy chair beside the open window of my study. I began to feel as if a man might be happy, even if a lady had refused him. And there I sat, gazing out on the happy world, when a gentle wind came in as if to bid me welcome. I thought of the wind that blows where it wills, and I thanked God for the Life whose story and words are in that best of books, the Bible.

I prayed that He would make me able to speak good common heavenly sense to my people, and forgive me for feeling so cross and proud toward the unhappy old lady—for I was sure she was not happy—and make me into a rock which swallowed up the waves of wrong in its great caverns and never threw them back to swell the commotion of the angry sea whence they came. Ah! To annihilate wrong in this way—to say, "It shall not be wrong against me, so utterly do I forgive it!" Perhaps, however, the forgiveness of the great wrongs is not so true as it seems. For do we not think it is a fine thing to forgive such wrongs, and so do it rather for our own sakes than for the sake of the wrongdoer? It is dreadful not to be good, and to have bad ways inside one.

Such thoughts passed through my mind. And once more the great light went on with regard to my office, namely, that just because I was parson to the parish I must not be *the person* to myself. Therefore I prayed God to keep me from feeling stung and proud, however anyone might behave to me, for all my value lay in being a sacrifice to Him and the people.

So, when Mrs. Pearson knocked at the door, and told me that a lady and gentleman had called, I shut my book which I had just opened, and kept down as well as I could the rising grumble of the inhospitable Englishman who is apt to be forgetful to entertain strangers, at least in the parlor of his heart. And I cannot count it perfect hospitality to be friendly and plentiful toward those whom I have invited to my house, while I am cold and forbidding to those who have not that claim on my attention.

I went and received Mr. and Miss Boulderstone, who left me a little fatigued but in no way sore or grumbling. They only sent me back with additional zest to my Plato, of which I enjoyed a hearty page or two before anyone else arrived. The only other visitors I had that day were Dr. Duncan, a retired navy surgeon who practiced in the neighborhood, and Mr. Brownrigg, the church-warden.

Except Mr. and Miss Boulderstone, I had not yet seen any common people. They were all decidedly uncommon and, as regards most of them, I could not think I should have any difficulty in preaching to them. There was some good in preaching to a man like Weir or Old Rogers, but whether there was any good in preaching to a woman like Mrs. Oldcastle I did not know.

The evening I thought I might give to my books, and thus end my first Monday in my parish, but as I said, Mr. Brownrigg called and stayed a whole weary hour talking about matters quite uninteresting—such as the impeccable lineage of the pigs he nurtured. Really he was not an interesting man: short, broad, stout, red-faced, with an immense amount of mental inertia discharging itself in constant lingual activity about little nothings. Indeed, when there was no new nothing to be had, the old nothing would do over again to make fresh fuss about. But if I attempted to convey a thought into his mind which involved his moving round half a degree from where he stood, and looking at the matter from a new point, I found him utterly, totally impenetrable.

I could not help observing that his cheeks rose from the collar of his green coat, his neck being invisible. The conformation was just what he himself delighted to contemplate in his pigs, to which his resemblance was greatly increased by unwearied endeavors to keep himself close shaved. I could not help feeling anxious about his son and Jane Rogers. He gave a quantity of gossip about various people, evidently anxious that I should regard them as he regarded them; but in all he said concerning them, I could scarcely detect one point of significance as to character or history. I was very glad indeed when the waddling of hands—for handshaking—was over, and he was safely out of the gate. He had kept me standing on the steps for a full five minutes, and I did not feel safe from him till I was once more in my study with the door shut.

In the days following I found my poor who I thought must be somewhere, seeing the Lord had said we should have them with us always. There was a workhouse in the village, but there were not a great many in it. The poor who belonged to the place were kindly enough handled and were not too severely compelled to go into the house, though I believe in this house they would have been more comfortable than they were in their own houses.

Then I began to think it better to return Mrs. Oldcastle's visit, though I felt greatly disinclined to encounter that tight-skinned nose again, and that mouth whose smile had no light in it, except when it responded to some nonsense of her granddaughter's.

SIX
Oldcastle Hall

About noon on a lovely autumn day I set out for Oldcastle Hall. I walked over the old gothic bridge with a heart strong enough to meet Mrs. Oldcastle without flinching. I might have to quarrel with her—I could not tell; she certainly was neither safe nor wholesome. But this I was sure of, that I would not quarrel with her without being quite certain that I ought. I wish it were never one's duty to quarrel with anybody, I do so hate it. But not to do it sometimes is to smile in the devil's face, and that no one ought to do.

The woods on the other side of the river from my house, toward which I was now walking, were somber and rich like a life that has laid up treasure in heaven. I came nearer and nearer to them through the village, and approached the great iron gate with the antediluvian monsters on the top of its stone pillars. And awful monsters they were—are still! But they let me through very quietly, notwithstanding their evil looks: I thought they were saying to each other across the top of the gate, "Never mind—he'll catch it soon enough."

I wandered up the long winding road through the woods flanking the meadow. These woods smelt so sweet—their dead and dying leaves departing in sweet odors—that they quite made up for the absence of the flowers. And the wind—no, there was no wind, there was only a memory of wind that woke now and then in the bosom of the wood—shook down a few leaves, like the thoughts that flutter away in sighs, and then was still again. Up the slope of the hillside, the trees rose like one great rainbow-billow of foliage—bright yellow, rusty red, fading bright green, and all shades of brown and purple. Multitudes of leaves lay on the sides of the path, so many that I returned to my old childish amusement of walking in them without lifting my feet, driving whole armies of them rustling before me.

At length the road brought me up to the house. It did not look such a large house as I have since found it to be, and it certainly was not an interesting house from the outside, though its surroundings of green grass and trees were beautiful. Indeed, the house itself tried hard to look ugly, failing only because of the kind foiling of its efforts by the Virginia creepers and ivy. But there was one charming group of old chimneys belonging to some portion behind, which indicated a very different, a very much older face upon the house, a face that had passed away to give place to this.

Once inside, I found there were more remains of the olden time than I had expected. I was led up one of those grand, square oak staircases which look like a portion of the house to be dwelt in, and not like a ladder for getting from one part to another. On the top was a fine expanse of landing, from which I was led toward the back of the house by a narrow passage, and shown into a small, dark, oak drawing room with a deep stone-mullioned window. Here I found Mrs. Oldcastle reading one of the cheap and gaudy religious books of the day. She rose and received me, and having motioned me to a seat, began to talk about the parish. I perceived at once from her tone that she recognized no other bond of connection between us but the parish.

"I hear you have been most kind in visiting the poor, Mr. Walton. You must take care that they don't take advantage of your kindness, though. I assure you, you will find some of them very grasping indeed. And you need not expect that they will give you the least credit for good intentions."

"I have seen nothing yet to make me uneasy on that score. But certainly my testimony is of no weight yet."

"Mine is. I have proved them. The poor of this neighborhood are very deficient in gratitude."

"Yes, Grannie—"

I started, but when I looked round in the direction whence the voice came, the words that followed were all rippled with sweet amusement. "Yes, Grannie, you are right. You remember how Dame Hope wouldn't take the money offered her, and dropped such a disdainful curtsy. It was so greedy of her, wasn't it?"

"I am sorry to hear of any disdainful reception of kindness," I said.

"Yes, and she had the coolness, within a fortnight, to send up to me and ask if I would be kind enough to lend her half a crown for a few weeks."

"And then it was your turn, Grannie! You sent her five shillings, didn't you? Oh, no, I am wrong. That was the other woman."

"Indeed, I did not send her anything but a rebuke. I told her that it would be a very wrong thing in me to contribute to the support of such an evil spirit of unthankfulness as she indulged in. When she came to see her conduct in its true light, and confessed that she had behaved very abominably, I would see what I could do for her."

"And meantime she was served out, wasn't she? With her sick boy at home, and nothing to give him?" said Miss Gladwyn.

"She made her own bed and had to lie on it."

"Don't you think a little kindness might have had more effect in bringing her to see that she was wrong?" I countered.

"Grannie doesn't believe in kindness except to me—dear old Grannie! She spoils me. I'm sure I shall be ungrateful someday, and then she'll begin to read me long lectures and prick me with all manner of headless pins. But I won't stand it, I can tell you, Grannie! I'm too much spoiled for that."

Mrs. Oldcastle was silent, why I could not tell, except it was that she knew she had no chance of quieting the girl in any other way.

(Later, I inquired of the Dame Hope and found that there had been a great misunderstanding, as I had suspected. She was really in no want at the time, and did not feel that it would be quite honorable to take money which she did not need. She had refused it, not without feeling that it was more pleasant to refuse than to accept from such a giver. Some stray sparkle of that feeling, discovered by the keen eye of Miss Gladwyn, may have given that appearance of disdain to her curtsy. When, however, her boy in service was brought home ill, she had sent to ask for what she now required on the very ground that it had been offered to her before. The misunderstanding had arisen from the total incapacity of Mrs. Oldcastle to enter sympathetically into the feelings of one as superior to herself in character as she was inferior in worldly condition.)

I wished to change the subject. "This is a beautiful old house," I said. "There must be strange places about it."

Mrs. Oldcastle had not time to reply, or at least did not reply, before Miss Gladwyn said, "O Mr. Walton, have you looked out the window yet? You don't know what a lovely place this is, if you haven't." She emerged from a recess in the room, a kind of dark alcove. I followed her to the window. "There!" she said, holding back one of the dingy heavy curtains with her small childish hand.

And there indeed I saw an astonishment. I had approached the house by a gentle slope, which certainly was long and winding, but had occasioned no feeling in my mind that I had reached any considerable height. And I had come up that one beautiful staircase, no more, and yet now when I looked from this window I found myself on the edge of a precipice. Below the house on this side lay a great wooded hollow. The sides were all rocky and steep, with here and there slopes of green grass. And down in the bottom, in the center of the hollow, lay a pool of water. I knew it only by its slaty shimmer through the fading green of the treetops between me and it.

"There!" again exclaimed Miss Gladwyn, "isn't that beautiful? But you haven't seen the most beautiful thing yet. Grannie, where's—ah! There she is! There's Auntie! Don't you see her down there, by the side of the pond? That pond is a hundred feet deep. If Auntie were to fall in, she would be drowned before you could jump down to get her out. Can you swim?"

Before I had time to answer, she was off again. "Don't you see Auntie down there?"

"No, I don't see her. I have been trying very hard, but I can't."

"Well, I dare say you can't. Nobody, I think, has eyes but myself. Do you see a big stone by the edge of the pond, with another stone on the top of it, like a big potato with a little one grown out of it?"

"No."

"Well, Auntie is under the trees across from that stone. Do you see her yet?"

"No."

"Then you must come down with me, and I will introduce you to her. She's much the prettiest thing here, much prettier than Grannie."

Here she looked over her shoulder at Grannie who, instead of being angry, only said, without even looking up from the book, "You are a saucy child."

Miss Gladwyn laughed merrily. "Come along," she said, and seizing me by the hand, led me out of the room, down a back staircase, across a piece of grass, and then down a stair in the face of the rock toward the pond below. The stair went in zigzags and, although rough and dangerous, was protected by an iron balustrade.

"Isn't your grandmamma afraid to let you run up and down here, Miss Gladwyn?" I said.

"Me?" she exclaimed, apparently in the utmost surprise. "That would be fun! For, you know, if she tried to hinder me—but she knows it's no use. I taught her that long ago, ten years at least. I ran away and they thought I had drowned myself in the pond. And I saw them all the time, poking with a long stick in the pond which, if I had been drowned there, never could have brought me up, for it is a hundred feet deep, I am sure. I hurt my sides trying to keep from screaming with laughter! I heard one say to the other, 'We must wait till she swells and floats!' "

"Dear me, what a peculiar child!" I thought. And yet somehow, whatever she said, even when she was most rude to her grandmother, she was never offensive. No one could have helped feeling all the time that she was a little lady. I thought I would venture a question with her. I stood at a turn of the zigzag, and looked down into the hollow, still a good way below us, where I could now distinguish the form, on the opposite side of the pond, of a woman seated at the foot of a tree and stooping forward over a book.

"May I ask you a question, Miss Gladwyn?"

"Yes, twenty if you like, but I won't answer one of them till you give up calling me Miss Gladwyn. We can't be friends, you know, so long as you do that."

"What am I to call you, then? I never heard you called by any other name than Pet, and that would hardly do, would it?"

"Oh, just fancy if you called me Pet before Grannie! That's Grannie's name for me, and nobody dares to use it but Grannie, not even Auntie. Between me and you, Auntie is afraid of Grannie. I can't think why. I never was afraid of anybody except, yes, a little afraid of Old Sarah. She used to be my nurse, you know, and Grandmamma and everybody are afraid of her, and that's just why I never do one thing *she* wants me to do. It would never do to be afraid of her, you know. There's Auntie, you see, down there just where I told you before."

"Oh, yes, I see her now. What does your aunt call you, then?"

"Why, what you must call me—my own name, of course."

"What is that?"

"Judy." She said it in a tone which seemed to indicate surprise that I should not know her name—perhaps read it on her face—as one ought to know a flower's name by looking at it. But she added instantly, glancing up in my face most comically, "I wish yours was Punch."

"Why, Judy?"

"It would be such fun, you know."

"Well, it would be odd, I must confess. What is your Auntie's name?"

"Oh, such a funny name—much funnier than Judy—Ethelwyn. It sounds as if it ought to mean something, doesn't it?"

"Yes. It is an Anglo-Saxon word, without doubt."

"What does it mean?"

"I'm not sure. I will try to find out when I go home, if you would like to know."

"Yes, that I should. I should like to know everything about Auntie. Ethelwyn. Isn't it pretty?"

"So pretty that I should like to know something more about Aunt Ethelwyn. What is her other name?"

"Why, Ethelwyn Oldcastle, to be sure. What else could it be?"

"Why, for anything I knew, Judy, it might have been Gladwyn. She might have been your father's sister."

"Might she? I never thought of that. Oh, I suppose that is because I never think about my father. And now I do think of it, I wonder why nobody ever mentions him to me, or my mother either. But I often think Auntie must be thinking about my mother. Something in her eyes, when they are sadder than usual, seems to remind me of my mother."

"You remember your mother, then?"

"No, I don't think I ever saw her. But I've answered plenty of questions, haven't I? I assure you, if you want to get me on to the catechism, I don't know a word of it. Come along."

I laughed.

"What?" she said, pulling me by the hand, "you a clergyman, and laugh at the catechism! I didn't know that."

"I'm not laughing at the catechism, Judy. I'm only laughing at the idea of putting catechism questions to you."

"You know I didn't mean it," she said, with some indignation.

"I know now," I answered. "But you haven't let me put the only question I wanted to put."

"What is it?"

"How old are you?"

"Twelve. Come along." And away we went down the rest of the stairs. When we reached the bottom, a winding path led us through the trees to the side of the pond, and along to the other side. And the thought struck me, why was it that I have never seen this aunt with the lovely name at church? Was she going to be another strange parishioner? There she sat, intent on her book. As we drew near she looked up and rose, but did not come forward.

"Aunt Wynnie, here's Mr. Walton," said Judy.

I lifted my hat and held out my hand. Before our hands met, however, a tremendous splash reached my ears from the pond. I started round. Judy had vanished. I had my coat half off, and was rushing to the pool, when Miss Oldcastle stopped me, her face unmoved except by a smile, saying, "It's only one of that frolicsome child's tricks, Mr. Walton. It is well for you that I was here, though. Nothing would have delighted her more than to have you in the water too."

"But," I said, "where is she?"

"There," returned Miss Oldcastle, pointing to the pool, in the middle of which arose a heaving and bubbling, and presently the laughing face of Judy.

"Why don't you help me out, Mr. Walton? You said you could swim."

"No, I did not," I answered. "You talked so fast, you did not give me time to say so."

"It's very cold," she returned.

"Come out, Judy dear," said her aunt. "Run home, and change your clothes. There's a dear."

Judy swam to the opposite side, scrambled out, and was off like a spaniel through the trees and up the stairs, dripping and raining as she went.

"You must be very much astonished at the little creature, Mr. Walton. There never was a child so spoiled, and never a child on whom it took less effect. I suppose such things do happen sometimes. She really is a good girl—though Mamma, who has done all the spoiling, will not allow me to say she is good."

Here followed a pause for, Judy disposed of, what should I say next? And the moment her mind turned from Judy, I saw a certain stillness—not a cloud, but the shadow of a cloud—come over Miss Oldcastle's face, as if she too found herself uncomfortable, and did not know what to say next. I tried to get a glance at the book in her hand, for I should know something about her at once if I could only see what she was reading. She never came to church, and I wanted to arrive at some notion of the source of her spiritual life, for that she had such, a single glance at her face was enough to convince me. This made me even more anxious to see the book. But I could only discover that it was an old book in very shabby binding, not in the least like the books that young ladies generally have in their hands.

The two young ladies were not alike. Judy was rosy, gray-eyed, auburn-haired, sweet-mouthed. She had confidence in her chin, assertion in her nose, defiance in her eyebrows, and honesty and friendliness over all her face. No one, evidently, could have a warmer friend, and to an enemy she would be dangerous no longer than a fit of passion might last. There was nothing acrid in her and the reason, I presume, was that she had never yet hurt her conscience. (That is a very different thing from saying she had never done wrong.) She was not tall, even for her age, and just a little too plump for the immediate suggestion of grace. She would have been graceful except that impulse was always predominant, giving a certain jerkiness, like the hopping of a bird, instead of the gliding of one motion into another, such as you might see in the same bird on the wing.

There is one of the ladies. But the other—how shall I attempt to describe her?

The first thing I felt was that she was a lady-woman, and to feel that is almost to fall in love at first sight. She was graceful, rather slender, rather tall, and quite blue-eyed. But it was not upon that occasion that I found out the color of her eyes. I was so taken with her whole that I knew nothing about her parts. Yet she was blue-eyed, indicating northern extraction some centuries back perhaps. That blue was the blue of the sea that had sunk through the eyes of some sea-rover's wife and settled in those eyes of her child to be born when the voyage was over. It had been dyed so deep that it had never been worn from the souls of the race since. Her features were regular, delicate, and brave. After the grace, the dignity was the next thing I came to discover. And the only thing I did not like, I discovered last. For when the shine of the courtesy with which she received me had faded away, a certain look of negative haughtiness, of withdrawal (if not of repulsion) took its place. It was a look of consciousness of her own high breeding, a pride—not of life but of circumstance of life—which disappointed me in the midst of so much that was very lovely. Her voice was sweet, and her speech slow without drawling, and I could have fancied a tinge of sadness in it.

"This is a most romantic spot, Miss Oldcastle," I said, "and as surprising as it is romantic. I could hardly believe my eyes when I looked out of the window and saw it."

"Your surprise was the more natural in that the place itself is not natural. It *looks* pretty, but it does not have a very poetic origin. It is nothing but the quarry out of which the house was built."

"It seems to me a much more poetic origin than any convulsion of nature. From that buried mass of rock has arisen this living house, with its histories of ages and generations, and—"

Here I saw her face grow almost pallid, but her large blue eyes were still fixed on mine.

"And it seems to me," I went on, "that such a chasm is therefore more poetic. Human will, human thought, human hands in human labor and effort, have all been employed to build this house, making beautiful not only the house but also the place whence it came. It stands on the edge of its own origin, generation to generation in the same place."

Her face had grown still paler, and her lips moved as if she would speak, but no sound came from them.

"I am afraid you feel ill, Miss Oldcastle."

"Not at all," she answered quickly. She drew herself up a little haughtily, so I drew back to the subject of our conversation.

"But I can hardly think," I said, "that all this mass of stone could be required to build the house, large as it is. A house is not solid, you know."

"No," she answered. "The original building was more of a castle, with walls and battlements. I can show you the old foundations, and the picture too, of what the place used to be. We are not what we were then. Many cottages have been built out of this old quarry, though not a stone has been taken from it for fifty years. Let me show you one thing, Mr. Walton, and then I must leave you."

"Do not let me detain you. I will go at once," I said, "though, if you would allow me, I should be more at ease if I might see you safe at the top of the stair first."

She smiled. "I am not ill, but I have duties to attend to. Let me show you this, and then you shall go back with me." She led the way to the edge of the pond and looked into it. I followed and gazed down into its depths till my sight was lost in them. I could see no bottom to the rocky shaft.

"There is a strong spring down there," she said. "Is it not a dreadful place? Such a depth!"

"Yes," I answered, "but it has not the horror of dirty water. It is clear as crystal. How does the surplus escape?"

"On the opposite side of the hill you came up, there is a well with a strong stream from it into the river."

"I almost wonder at your choosing such a place to read."

"Judy has taken all that away. Nothing in nature is strange to Judy! Look down into the water on this side. Do you see anything there against the wall of the pond?"

"I see a kind of arch or opening in the side," I answered.

"Do you also see a little barred window there, in the face of the rock, through the trees? It is the window of a little room in the rock, from which a stair leads through the rock to a sloping passage. That is the end of it you see under the water."

"Provided, no doubt," I said, "in case of siege, to procure water."

"Most likely, but not, therefore, confined to that purpose. There are more dreadful stories than I can bear to think of—" here she paused abruptly, and began anew—"as if that house had brought death and doom out of the earth with it. There was an old burial ground here before the Hall was built."

"Have you ever been down the stair you speak of?" I asked.

"Only part of the way," she answered. "But Judy knows every step of it. If it were not that the door at the top is locked, she would have dived through that archway now, and been in her own room in half the time. The child does not know what fear means."

We moved away from the pond, toward the side of the quarry and up the open-air staircase. Miss Oldcastle accompanied me to the room where I had left her mother, and took her leave with merely a bow of farewell. I saw the old lady glance sharply from her to me, as if she were jealous of what we might have been talking about.

"Grannie, are you afraid Mr. Walton has been saying pretty things to Aunt Wynnie? I assure you he is not of that sort. But he would have jumped into the pond after me and got his death of cold if Auntie would have let him. It *was* cold. I think I see you dripping now, Mr. Walton." There she was in her dark corner, coiled up on a couch and laughing heartily, but all as if she had done nothing extraordinary. And by her own notions and practices, what she had done was not in the least extraordinary.

Disinclined to stay any longer, I shook hands with the grandmother (with a certain invincible sense of slime) and with the grandchild (with a feeling of mischievous health, as if the girl might soon corrupt the clergyman into a partnership in pranks as well as in friendship). She followed me out of the room and danced before me down the oak staircase, clearing the portion from the first landing at a bound, turning and waiting for me. I came very deliberately, feeling the unsure contact of sole and wax. As soon as I reached her, she said in a half whisper, reaching up toward me on tiptoe, "Isn't she a beauty?"

"Who, your grandmamma?" I returned.

She gave me a little push, her face glowing with fun. But I did not expect she would take her revenge as she did. "Yes, of course," she answered, quite gravely. "Isn't she a beauty?" Then she burst into loud laughter, opened the hall door for me, and let me go without another word.

I went home very quietly, stepping with curious care over the yellow and brown leaves that lay in the middle of the road.

SEVEN

The Bishop's Basin

I have never sat down with my parishioners without finding that they actually possess a history, the most marvelous and important fact to a human being. And I have come to the conclusion, not that this was an extraordinary parish of characters, but that every parish must be extraordinary from the same cause.

The people among whom I had been today belonged in a romantic story. The Hall would hardly come into my ideas of a country parish at all. All that had happened since I looked out of the window in the old house might have been but a dream. That wooded dell was much too large for a quarry. And that madcap girl who flung herself into the pond! And was that a real book that the lady with the sea-blue eyes was reading? A commonplace book would not have been her companion at the bottom of a quarry. And that terrible pool and subterranean passage—what had their story to do with this broad daylight and dying autumn leaves? No doubt there had been such places and no doubt there were such places somewhere yet—this was one of them. But, somehow or other, it would not fit well.

I took the impression off by going to see Weir, the carpenter's old father. I found the carpenter busy as usual, working now at a window sash. "Just like life," I thought. "The other day he was closing in the outer darkness, and now he is letting in the light."

"It's a long time since you was here last, Sir," he said, but without a smile.

"Well," I answered, "I wanted to know something about all my people before I paid a second visit to any of them."

"All right, Sir. Don't suppose I meant to complain. Only to let you know you was welcome, Sir."

"To tell the truth, for I don't like pretenses, my visit today was more to your father. I ought to have called upon him before, only I was afraid of seeming to intrude upon you, seeing we don't exactly think the same way about some things."

A smile lighted up his face, and his answer fixed his smile in my memory. "You made me think, Sir, that perhaps, after all, we were much of the same way of thinking, only perhaps you was a long way ahead of me."

Now our opinions could hardly do more than come within sight of each other. But what he meant was right enough—the man had regard for the downright honest way of things, and I hoped that I too had such a regard, and that the road lay open for further and more real communion between us in time to come.

"My father will be delighted to see you, I know, Sir. He can't get so far as the church on Sundays, but you'll find him much more to your mind than me. He's been putting ever so many questions to me about the new parson. I've never told him that I'd been to church since you came—I suppose from a bit of pride, because I had so long refused to go—but I don't doubt some of the neighbors have told him, for he never speaks about it now. I know he's been looking out for you, and I fancy he's begun to wonder that the parson was going to see everybody but him. It will pleasure him, Sir, for he don't see a great many to talk to."

Weir led the way through the shop and up a back stair into a large room over the workshop. There were bits of old carving about the whitewashed walls of the room. At one end stood a bed with chintz curtains and a warm-looking counterpane of rich but faded embroidery. There was a bit of carpet by the bedside, and another bit in front of the fire, and there the old man sat in a high-backed chair. He managed to rise, though bent nearly double, and tottered a few steps to meet me. He held out a thin, shaking hand and welcomed me with an air of kindly breeding rare in his station in society.

"I'm blithe to see ye, Sir," said he. "Sit ye down, Sir." He pointed to his own easy chair.

"No, Mr. Weir," I said. "The Bible tells us to rise up before the aged, not to turn them out of their seats."

"It would do me good to see you sitting in my cheer, Sir. The pains that my son Tom there takes to keep it up as the old man may want it! It's a good thing I bred him to the joiner's trade, Sir. Sit ye down, Sir. The cheer'll hold ye, though I warrant it won't last that long after I be gone home. Sit ye down, Sir."

Thus entreated, I hesitated no longer, but took the old man's seat. His son brought another chair for him, and he sat down opposite the fire and close to me. Thomas went back to his work, leaving us alone.

"Ye've had some speech wi' my son Tom," said the old man, the moment he was gone, leaning a little toward me. "It's main kind o' you, Sir, to take up kindly wi' poor folks like us."

"You don't say it's kind of a person to do what he likes best," I answered. "Besides, it's my duty to know all my people."

"Oh, yes, Sir, I know that. But there's a thousand ways ov doing the same thing. I ha' seen folks, parsons and other, 'at made a great show ov bein' friendly to the poor, ye know, Sir, and all the time you could see, or tell without seein', that they didn't much regard them in their hearts, but it was a sort of accomplishment for them to be able to talk to the poor after their own fashion. But the minute an ould man sees you, Sir, he believes that you mean it, Sir, whatever it is, for an ould man somehow comes to know things like a child. They call it a second childhood, don't they, Sir? And there are some things worth growin' a child again to get hould of again."

"I only hope what you say may be true—about me, I mean."

"Take my word for it, Sir. You have no idea how that boy of mine, Tom there, did hate all the clergy till you come. Not that he's any way favorable to them yet, only he'll say nothin' again' you, Sir. He's got an unfortunate gift o' seein' all the faults first—and when a man is that way given, the faults always hides the other side, so that there's nothing but faults to be seen."

"But I find Thomas quite open to reason."

"That's because you understand him, Sir, and know how to give him his head. He tould me of the talk you had with him. You don't bait him, you don't say, 'You must come along wi' me,' but you turn and goes along wi' him. He's not a bad fellow at all, is Tom, but he will have the reason for everythink. Now I never did want the reason for everythink. I was content to be tould a many things. But Tom, you see, he was born with a sore bit in him somewheres, I don't rightly know wheres—and I don't think he rightly knows himself."

"You might give him time, for he doesn't feel at home yet. And how can he, when he doesn't know his own father?"

"I don't rightly understand you," said the old man, looking bewildered and curious.

"Till a man knows that he is one of God's family, living in God's house, with God upstairs as it were, while he works or plays below stairs, he can't feel comfortable. For a man could not be made that should stand alone like some of the beasts. A man must feel a head over him, because he's not enough to satisfy himself, you know. Thomas just wants to feel that there is a loving Father over him, who is doing things well and right."

"Ah, Sir, I fancied that you were just putting your finger upon the sore place in Tom's mind. There's no use in keeping family misfortunes from a friend like you, Sir. That boy has known his father all his life, but I was nearly half his age before I knew mine."

"Then your father and mother—" I said, and hesitated.

"Were never married, Sir," said the old man, promptly. "I couldn't help it. And I'm no less the child of my Father in heaven for it. If He hadn't made me, I couldn't ha' been their son, so that He had more to do wi' the makin' o' me than they had. I do love my mother, and I'm so sorry for my father that I love him too, Sir. And if I could only get my boy Tom to think as I do, I would die like a psalm tune on an organ, Sir."

"But it seems strange," I said, "that your son should think so much of what is so far gone by. Surely he would not want another father than you, now."

"There has been other things to keep his mind on the old affair. We have had the same misfortune all over again among the young people, and my boy Tom has a sore heart."

(I had already learned that the strange handsome woman in the little shop was the daughter of Thomas Weir, and that she was neither wife nor widow. It was a likeness to her little boy that had affected me so pleasantly when I first saw Thomas, his grandfather, and now the likeness to his great-grandfather made the other fact clear. But yet I was haunted with a flickering sense of a third likeness, which I could not identify.)

"Perhaps," I said, "he may find some good come out of that too. If we do evil that good may come, the good we looked for will never come thereby. But once evil is done, we may humbly look to Him who brings good out of evil, and wait. Is your granddaughter Catharine in bad health? She looks so delicate."

"She always had an uncommon look, but what she looks like now I don't know. I hear no complaints. But she has never crossed this door since we got her set up in that shop. She never comes near her father or her sister, though she would let them go and see her. I'm afraid Tom has been rather unmerciful with her. If ever he put a bad name upon her in her hearing, she wouldn't be likely to forget it. I don't believe they do more nor nod to one another when they meet in the village. There's some people made so hard that they never can forgive anythink."

"How did she get into the trouble? Who is the father of her child?"

"That no one knows for certain, though there be suspicions, and one of them no doubt correct. But I believe fire wouldn't drive his name out at her mouth, for I know my lass."

I asked no more questions, but after a short pause the old man went on.

"I sha'n't soon forget the night I first heard about my father and mother. That was a night! The wind was roaring like a mad beast about the house—not here, Sir, but the great house over the way."

"You don't mean Oldcastle Hall?"

" 'Deed I do, Sir," returned the old man. "This house here belonged to the same family at one time, though when I was born it was another branch of the family that lived in it, but even then it was something on to the downhill road."

"But," I said, fearing he might have turned aside from a story worth hearing, "do go on. The wind was blowing?"

"Eh, Sir, it was roaring—mad with rage. It would come down the chimley like out of a gun, and blow the smoke and a'most the fire into the middle of the housekeeper's room. I called the housekeeper Auntie, then, and didn't know a bit that she wasn't my aunt really. And she said, 'It was just such a night as this, leastways it was snow and not rain that was comin' down, as if the Almighty was a-going to spend all His winter stock at once.'

" 'What happened such a night, Auntie?' I said.

" 'Ay, my lad,' said she, 'ye may well ask. None has a better right. You happened, that's all. And you certainly wasn't wanted. It's my fault, if it be fault, that you're sitting there now, and not lying at the bottom of the Bishop's Basin.'

"I said, feeling cold and small, as if I had no right to be there, 'But who wanted to drown me?'

" 'It was, I make no doubt, though I can't prove it—it was your father.'

"I felt the skin go creepin' together on my head, and I couldn't speak.

" 'And now,' she said, 'it's time you knew all about it. Poor Miss Wallis! I'm no aunt of yours, though I love you dearly, because I loved your mother. She was a beauty, and better than she was beautiful. The only wrong thing she ever did was to trust your father. But I'll give you the story right through.

" 'Miss Wallis' mother and father died early, and she was left alone, and she came to us to be a governess. She never got on well with the children, for they were young and self-willed and rude, and would not learn to do as they were bid. She was a sweet creature, that she was, but nobody took any notice or care of her. The children were kept away with her in the old house, and my lady wasn't one to take trouble about anybody. And so, when the poor thing was taken with a dreadful cold, which was no wonder if you saw the state of the window in the room she had to sleep in, it fell to me to look after her. It would have made your heart bleed to see the poor thing flung all of a heap on her bed, blue with cold and coughing.

" 'I had to nurse her for a fortnight before she was able to do anything again, though she didn't shirk her work. It was a heartsore to me to see the poor young thing, with her sweet eyes and pale face, talking away to those children that were more like wildcats than human beings. She used to come see me evenings, and sit there without speaking, her thin white hands folded in her lap and her eyes fixed on the fire. I used to wonder what she could be thinking about.

" 'And then Miss Oldcastle, who had been at school, came home, and we had a great deal of company and visitors, and your mother's health began to come back.

" 'But then I had a blow, Samuel. It was a lovely spring night, just after the sun was down, and I wanted a drop of milk fresh from the cow, so I went through the kitchen garden to the shippen. But who was at the other end of the path but Miss Wallis, walking arm-in-arm with Captain Crowfoot who was just home from India. He was about three and thirty, a relation of the family, and the only son of Sir Giles Crowfoot. As sure as judgment no good could come of it, for the captain had not the best of characters, though he was a great favorite with everybody that knew nothing about him. He was a fine, manly, handsome fellow with a smile that, as people said, no woman could resist, though that same smile was the falsest of all the false things about him. All the time he was smiling, you would have thought he was looking at himself in a glass.

" 'They came close past me, and never saw me. At least, if he saw me he took no notice, for I don't suppose that the angel with the flaming sword would have put him out. I know she didn't see me, for her face was down, burning and smiling at once.

" 'And it was days before I saw her again. She came to my room, and without a moment of parley I said to her, "Oh, my dear, what was that wretch Captain Crowfoot saying to you?"

" ' "What have you to say against Captain Crowfoot?" says she, quite sharp-like and scornful.

" 'He was said to have gathered a power of money in India, and I don't think he would have been the favorite he was with my lady if he hadn't. Reports were about, too, of the way he had made the money—some said by robbing the poor heathen creatures, and some said speculating in horses and other things. And this one of his own servants told me, not thinking any harm or shame of it. The captain had quarreled with a young ensign in the regiment, and the captain first thrashed him most unmercifully, and then called him out for a duel. And the poor fellow could scarcely see out of his eyes, and certainly couldn't take anything like an aim. And he shot him dead, did Captain Crowfoot.

" 'So I poured out all I had against him in one breath. She turned awful pale, and shook from head to foot, and said, "I don't believe one word of it. But I'll ask him next time I see him." I knew he would not make any fuss that might bring it out in the air, and I hoped it might lead to a quarrel between them. And the next time I met her, she passed me with a nod just, and a blush instead of a smile. I knew that villain had gotten a hold of her. I could only cry, and that I did.

" 'The captain came and went for months, stopping a week each time, and came again in the autumn for the shooting and began to make up to Miss Oldcastle who had grown a fine young woman by that time. And Miss Wallis began to pine, and before long I was certain she was in a consumption. But she never spoke a word about herself or the captain.

" 'Then came the news that the captain and Miss Oldcastle were to be married in the spring. Miss Wallis took to her bed, and my lady wanted to send her away, but Miss Oldcastle spoke up for her, for she had ne'er a home to go to. I said I would take all the care and trouble of her, and my lady promised, and the poor thing was left alone. Not a word would she speak, even to me, though every moment I could spare I was with her. One day she threw her arms about my neck, and burst into a terrible fit of crying. I put my arms around her and lifted her up, and then I understood her plight, and I said, "I know now, my dear. I'll do all I can for you." It was well for her that she could go to her bed, and I thought she might die before there was any need for further concealment. But people in that condition seldom die, they say, till all is over—and she lived on, though getting weaker.

" 'The wedding day was fixed at the captain's next visit, and after that a circumstance came about that made me uneasy. A foreign servant had been constantly attending the captain. I never could abide the snake-look of the fellow, nor the noiseless way he went about the house. But this time the captain had a foreign servant-woman with him as well. The captain went away, and left the servant-woman behind, for the wedding was to take place in three weeks. Meantime poor Emily—Miss Wallis—grew fast worse. And now, with the wedding, I could see yet less of her than before, and when Miss Oldcastle sent the foreign servant to ask if she could sit with the poor girl, I did not know how to object, though I did not at all trust her. I longed to have the wedding over, that I might get rid of the servant, and take her place, and get everything prepared. The captain arrived, and his man with him. And twice I came upon the two servants in close conversation.

" 'Well, the wedding day came. The people went to church, and while they were there a terrible storm of wind and snow came on, such that the horses would hardly face it. The captain was going to take his bride home, but the storm got so dreadful no one could leave the house. The wind blew for all the world just as it blows this night, only it was snow in its mouth and not rain.

" 'After dinner was over and the ladies were gone to the drawing room, and the gentlemen had been sitting over their wine for some time, the butler, William Weir, came to my room looking scared. "Lawks, William!" says I, "whatever is the matter with you?"

" ' "Well," says he, "it's a strange wedding, it is! There's the ladies all alone in the drawing room, and the gentlemen calling for more wine, and cursing and swearing awful to hear. Swords'll be drawn afore long. And I don't a'most like goin' down them stairs alone in sich a night, ma'am. Would you mind coming with me?"

" ' "Dear me, William," says I, "a pretty story to tell your wife"—she was my own half-sister and younger than me—"that you wanted an old body like me to go and take care of you in your own cellar. But I'll go with you for, to tell the truth, it's a terrible night." And so down we went and brought up six bottles more of the best port. And I really didn't wonder, when I was down there and heard the dull roar of the wind against the rock below, that William didn't much like to go alone. When he went back with the wine, the captain said, "William, what kept you so long? Mr. Centlivre says that you were afraid to go down into the cellar."

" 'Before William could reply, Sir Giles said, "A man might well be afraid to go anywhere alone on a night like this." Whereupon the captain swore that he would go down the underground stair, and into every vault on the way, for the wager of a guinea. And a few minutes after, they were all at my door, demanding the key of the room at the top of the stair. I was just going up to see poor Emily, and I gave the captain the key, wishing with all my heart he might get a good fright for his pains. He took a jug with him, to bring some water from the well as proof he had been down. The rest went with him into the little cellar room, but wouldn't stop there, they said it was so cold. They all came into my room, where they talked as gentlemen wouldn't do if the wine hadn't got uppermost.

" 'It was some time before the captain returned. He looked as if he had got the fright I wished him. The candle in his lantern was out, and there was no water in the jug. "There's your guinea, Centlivre," says he, throwing it on the table. "You needn't ask me any questions, for I won't answer one of them."

" ' "Captain," says I, as they turned to leave the room, "I'll just hang up the key again."

" 'He started, and searched his pockets all over for it. "I must have dropped it," says he, "but it's of no consequence. You can send William for it in the morning. It can't be lost."

" 'All this time I couldn't get to see Emily. As often as I looked from my window, I saw her old west turret out there. Now I had told that servant that if anything happened, or she was worse, she must put the candle on the window, and I would come directly. But the blind was drawn down, so I thought all was right. And what with the storm keeping Sir Giles and more that would have gone home, there was no end of work and contrivance, for we were nothing too well provided with blankets and linen in the house. There was always more room than money in it.

" 'So it was past twelve before they had all gone to bed—the bride and the bridegroom in the crimson chamber, of course. At last I crept into Emily's room. There was no light there, and my own candle had blown out. I spoke, but no one answered. Then I heard such a shriek from the crimson chamber that it made me all creep like worms. Doors were opened, and lights came out, with everybody looking terrified. And the door of the crimson chamber opened too, and the captain bawled out to know what was the matter—though I'm certain the cry came from that room and that he knew more about it than anyone else did. I got a light and ran back, and there was Emily lying white and motionless. A baby had been born, but no baby was to be seen. Though she was still warm, your mother was quite dead.

" 'Then I saw it all. Without waiting to be afraid, I ran to the underground stairs, and found the door standing open. I had not gone down more than three turnings, when I heard a cry, and just about halfway down, there lay a bundle in a blanket. And how you ever got over the state I found you in, Samuel, I can't think. But I caught you up and ran to my room and locked the door, and did the best for you I could. The breath wasn't out of you, though it well might have been. And then I laid you before the fire, and by that time you had begun to cry a little. I wrapped you up in a blanket and made my way with you to Mrs. Wier. William opened the door to me, and saw the bundle in my arms. "Mrs. Prendergast," says he, "I didn't expect it of you."

" ' "Hold your tongue," I said. "You would never talk such nonsense if you had the grace to have any of your own." I went into the bedroom and shut the door and left him out there in his shirt. My sister and I soon got everything arranged, and before morning I had made all tidy. Your poor mother was lying as sweet a corpse as ever an angel saw, and no one could say a word against her. She was buried down there in the churchyard, close by the vestry door,' said my aunt, Sir, and all our family have been buried there since, my son Tom's wife among them, Sir."

"But what was that cry in the house?" I asked. "And what became of the servant-woman?"

"The woman was never seen again, and what that cry was my aunt never would say. She seemed to know, although Captain and Mrs. Crowfoot denied all knowledge of it. But the lady looked dreadful, she said, and was never well again, and died at the birth of her first child. That was the present Mrs. Oldcastle's father, Sir."

"But why should the woman have left you on the stair, instead of drowning you in the well at the bottom?"

"There was some mystery about that. All my aunt would say was, 'The key was never found, Samuel. I had to get a new one made.' So I was brought up as her nephew, though people were surprised that William Weir's wife should have a child, and nobody know she was expecting.

"Well, with all the reports of the captain's money, none of it showed in this old place, which began to crumble away. If it hadn't been a well-built place to begin with, it wouldn't be standing now. It's very different now. Why, all behind was a garden with terraces and fruit trees and flowers to no end. I remember it as well as yesterday—nay, a great deal better, for I don't remember yesterday at all."

His story interested me greatly, but only tended to keep up the sense of distance between my experience at the Hall and the work I had to do among my other people.

I left the old man with thanks and walked home thinking of many things. I shut myself up in my study and tried in vain to read a sermon of Jeremy Taylor. I fell fast asleep over it, and woke refreshed.

EIGHT
What I Preached

During the suffering and disappointment at which I have already hinted, I sought consolation from the New Testament. To my surprise, I discovered that I could not read the Epistles at all—I did not then care an atom for the theology which had interested me before. Now that I was in trouble, what to me was that philosophical theology? All reading of the Book is not reading of the Word. It was Jesus Christ, and not theology, that filled the hearts of the men who wrote those Epistles—Jesus Christ, whom I found not in the Epistles but in the Gospels. And until we understand the Gospel, the good news of Jesus Christ—until we understand Him, until we have His Spirit—all the Epistles are to us a sealed book.

The Gospels then took hold of me as never before. I found out that I had known nothing at all—that I had only a certain surface knowledge which tended to ignorance, because it fostered the delusion that I did know. Know that Man, Christ Jesus? Ah! Lord, I would go through fire and water to sit at Thy table in Thy kingdom, but dare I say now I *know* Thee?

I found, as I read, that His very presence in my thoughts smoothed the troubled waters of my spirit, so that even while the storm lasted, I was able to walk upon them to go to Him. And when those waters became clear, I most rejoiced in their clearness because they mirrored His form.

And therefore, when I was once more in a position to help my fellows, what could I want to give them but the Saviour Himself? I took the story from the beginning and told them about the Baby. And I followed the life on, trying to show them how He felt, what His sayings meant, as far as I understood them myself. Where I could not understand them, I just told them so and said I hoped for more light by and by, because I knew that only as I did my duty would light go up in my heart. And I told them that if they would try to do their duty, they would find more understanding than from any explanation I could give them.

And so I went on from Sunday to Sunday. The number of people who slept grew fewer and fewer, until at last it was reduced to Mr. Brownrigg and an old washerwoman. She stood so much all the week that sitting down was like going to bed, and she never could do it without going to sleep. I therefore called on her every Monday morning, and had five minutes' chat with her as she stood at her washtub, thinking that if I could once get her interested, she might be able to keep awake a little while at the beginning of the sermon. I never got so far as that, however. The only fact that showed me I had made any impression upon her, beyond the pleasure she always manifested when I appeared, was that whereas all my linen had been very badly washed at first, a decided improvement took place after a while, gradually extending itself till even Mrs. Pearson was unable to find any fault with the sleepy woman's work.

For Mr. Brownrigg, I am not sure that the sense of any one sentence ever entered into his brain—I dare not say his mind or heart.

Before long I was also sure of seeing the pale face of Thomas Weir perched, like that of a man beheaded for treason, upon the gablet of the old tomb. I continued to pay him visits. The man was no more an atheist than David was when he saw the wicked spreading like a green bay tree and was troubled at the sight. He only wanted a God in whom he could trust. And if I succeeded at all in making him hope that there might be such a God, it is to me one of the most precious seals of my ministry.

It was getting very near Christmas, and there was one person whom I had never yet seen at church—Catharine Weir. I had told my housekeeper to buy whatever she could from her, instead of going to the larger shop in Marshmallows. Mrs. Pearson had grumbled a good deal, saying how could the things be so good out of a poky shop like that? But I told her I did not care if the things were not quite as good. It would be of more consequence to Catharine to have the custom, than it would be to me to have the sugar in my morning tea one or even two shades whiter.

So I had kept up a connection with her, although I saw that any attempt at conversation was so distasteful to her that it must do harm until something should have brought about a change in her feelings, though what feeling wanted changing I could not at first tell. I came to the conclusion that she had been wronged, and that this wrong, operating on a nature similar to her father's, had drawn all her mind to brood over it. The world itself would seem then to have wronged her, and to speak of religion would only rouse her scorn, and make her feel as if God Himself, if there were a God, had wronged her too. Evidently she had that peculiarity of being unable, once possessed by one set of thoughts, to get rid of them again or to see anything except in the shadow of these thoughts. I had no doubt that she was ashamed in the eyes of society, and that this prevented her from appearing where it was unnecessary, especially in church.

I could do nothing more than wait for a favorable opportunity. I could invent no way of reaching her yet, for I had found that kindness to her boy was regarded as an insult to her. I should have been greatly puzzled to account for his being such a sweet little fellow, had I not known that he was with his aunt and grandfather a great deal.

I should also say that on three occasions before Christmas I had seen Judy look grave. She was always quite well-behaved in church, though restless. But on these occasions she was not only attentive, but grave.

On the other hand, I never saw Mrs. Oldcastle change countenance or expression in church.

NINE
The Organist

I should explain that on the afternoon of my second Sunday at Marshmallows, I had been standing in the churchyard, casting a long shadow in the light of the declining sun. I was reading the inscription upon an old headstone, when I heard a door open and shut again before I could turn. I saw at once that it must have been a little door in the tower, almost concealed from where I stood by a deep buttress. I had never seen the door open, and had never inquired about it, supposing it led merely into the tower.

After a moment it opened again, and out came a man whom no one could pass without looking after him. Tall and strongly built, he had the carriage of a military man, a large face with regular features, and large clear gray eyes. His beard, which descended halfway down his breast, would have been white as snow except for a slightly yellowish tinge. His eyebrows were very dark, just touched with the frost of winter. His hair, too, as I saw when he lifted his hat, was still wonderfully dark. His clothes were all black, very neat and clean but old-fashioned, bearing signs of use and time and careful keeping. It flashed into my mind that this must be the organist who played so remarkably. I would have spoken to him, but something in the manner in which he bowed to me prevented me, and I let him go.

The sexton came out directly after, and I asked him who the gentleman was.

"That is Mr. Stoddart, Sir," he answered. "He's played our organ for the last ten years, ever since he come to live at Oldcastle Hall."

And then it dawned that I heard Judy mention her Uncle Stoddart. But how could he be her uncle? "Is he a relation of the family?" I asked.

"He's a brother-in-law, I believe, of the old lady, Sir—been in the military line in the Indies or somewhere."

Although I had intended to inquire after Mr. Stoddart when I left the vicarage to go to the Hall, and had even thought of him when sitting with

Mrs. Oldcastle, I never thought of him again after going with Judy, and I left the house without having made a single inquiry after him.

And now, after all this time, I resolved to call on him the following week, and did. When I rang the doorbell at the Hall and inquired for Mr. Stoddart, the butler stared at me, and answered with some hesitation, "Mr. Stoddart never calls upon anyone, Sir."

"I am not complaining of Mr. Stoddart," I answered, wishing to put the man at his ease.

"But nobody calls upon Mr. Stoddart," he returned.

"That's very unkind of somebody, surely," I said.

"But he doesn't want anybody to call upon him, Sir."

"Ah! that's another matter. I didn't know that. However, as I have come without knowing his dislike, perhaps you will take him my card, and say that I should like to thank him in person for his exquisite voluntary on the organ last Sunday."

"I will try, Sir," he answered. "But won't you come upstairs, Sir, while I take this to Mr. Stoddart?"

"No, I thank you," I answered. "I came to call upon Mr. Stoddart only, and I will wait here in the hall."

The man withdrew, and I sat down on a bench and amused myself with looking at the portraits about me. One particularly pleased me. It was the portrait of a young woman, very lovely but with an expression both sad and scared. It was remarkably like Miss Oldcastle. (I learned afterward that it was the portrait of Mrs. Oldcastle's grandmother, that very Mrs. Crowfoot mentioned in Weir's story. It had been made about six months after her marriage, and about as many before her death.)

The butler returned with a request to follow him. He led me up the grand staircase, through a passage, up a narrow staircase, across a landing, then up a straight, steep, narrow stair. At the top I found myself in a small cylindrical lobby, papered in blocks of stone and lighted by a conical skylight. There was no door to be seen. My conductor gave a push against the wall. Certain blocks yielded, and others came forward. A door revolved on central pivots, and we were admitted to a chamber crowded with books from floor to ceiling. From the center of the ceiling radiated a number of strong beams supporting bookshelves. On each side of those I passed under, I could see the gilded backs of books standing together.

"How does Mr. Stoddart reach those books?" I asked my conductor.

"I don't exactly know, Sir," whispered the butler. "I believe, however, he does not use a ladder."

There was no one in the room, and I saw no entrance but that by which we had entered. The next moment, however, a nest of shelves revolved in front of me, and there stood Mr. Stoddart with outstretched hand.

"You have found me at last, Mr. Walton, and I am glad to see you," he said.

He led me into an inner room, much larger than the one I had passed through.

"I am glad," I replied, "that I did not know your unwillingness to be intruded upon. Had I known it, I should have been yet longer a stranger to you."

"You are no stranger to me. I have heard you read prayers, and I have heard you preach."

"And I have heard you play, so you are no stranger to me either."

"I must say about this report of my unsociable disposition that I encourage it, but I am very glad to see you, notwithstanding. I was so bored with visits after I came—visits which were to me utterly uninteresting—that I was only too glad when the unusual nature of some of my pursuits gave rise to the rumor that I was mad. The more people say I am mad, the better pleased I am, so long as they are satisfied with my own mode of shutting myself up, and do not attempt to carry out any fancies of their own in regard to my personal freedom."

Like the outer room, this one was full of books from floor to ceiling.

"What a number of books you have!" I observed.

"Not a great many," he answered. "But they are almost personal acquaintances, as I have bound a couple of hundred or so of them myself. I don't think you could tell the work from a tradesman's. I'll give you a guinea for the poor box if you pick out three of my bindings consecutively."

I accepted the challenge. I could not bind a book but I consider myself to have a keen eye for the outside finish. After looking over the backs of a great many, I took one down, examined a little further, and presented it.

"You are right. Now try again."

Again I was successful, although I doubted.

"And now for the last," he said.

Once more I was right.

"There is your guinea," said he, a little mortified.

"No," I answered, "I do not feel at liberty to take it because, to tell the truth, the last was a mere guess."

Mr. Stoddart looked relieved. "You are more honest than most of your profession," he said. "But I am far more pleased to offer you the guinea upon the smallest doubt of you having won it."

"I have no claim upon it."

"What! Couldn't you swallow a small scruple like that for the sake of the poor even? Well, I don't believe you could. Oblige me by taking this guinea for your poor. But—I am glad you weren't sure of that last book."

I took the guinea, and put it in my purse.

"But," he resumed, "you won't do, Mr. Walton. You're not fit for your profession. You won't tell a lie for God's sake. You won't dodge about a little to keep all right between Jove and his weary parishioners. You won't cheat a little for the sake of the poor! You wouldn't even bamboozle a little at a bazaar!"

"I should not like to boast of my principles," I answered. "But assuredly

I would not favor a fiction to keep a world out of hell. The hell that a lie would keep any man out of is doubtless the very best place for him to go to. It is truth, yes, *The Truth* that saves the world."

"You are right, I dare say. You are more sure about it than I am, though."

"Let us agree where we can first of all, and that will make us able to disagree, where we must, without quarreling."

"Good," he said. "Would you like to see my workshop?"

"Very much indeed," I answered.

He pushed a compartment of books. It yielded, and we entered a small closet. In another moment I found myself rising, and in yet a moment we were on the floor of an upper room.

"What a nice way of getting upstairs!" I said.

"There is no other way to this room," answered Mr. Stoddart. "I built it myself and there was no room for stairs. This is my shop. Here I read anything I want to read, write anything I want to write, bind my books, invent machines, and amuse myself generally. Take a chair."

I obeyed and began to look about me. There were many books in detached bookcases, and various benches against the walls between—one a bookbinder's, another a carpenter's. A third had a turning lathe, and a fourth had an iron vice fixed on it. And there were several tables of chemical apparatus—flasks, retorts, sand baths, and such, while in a corner stood a furnace.

"What an accumulation of ways and means you have about you," I said, "and all, apparently, to different ends."

"All to the same end, if my object were understood. I have theories of education. I think a man has to educate himself into harmony. Therefore, he must open every possible window by which the influences of the All may come in upon him. I do not think any man complete without a perfect development of his mechanical faculties, for instance."

"I do not object to your theory, provided you do not put it forward as a perfect scheme of human life. If you did, I should have some questions to ask you about it, lest I should misunderstand you."

He smiled what I took for a self-satisfied smile. There was nothing offensive in it, but it left me without anything to reply to. No embarrassment followed, however, for a rustling motion in the room attracted my attention, and I saw, to my surprise and confusion, Miss Oldcastle. She was seated in a corner, reading from a quarto lying upon her knees.

"Oh! You didn't know my niece was here? I forgot her when I brought you up, else I would have introduced you."

"That is not necessary, Uncle," said Miss Oldcastle, closing her book.

I was by her instantly. She slipped the quarto from her knee and took my offered hand.

"Are you fond of old books?" I said.

"Some old books," she answered.

"May I ask what you were reading?"

"I will answer you—under protest," she said with a smile. "It is a volume of Jakob Bohme."

"I bought his works as I passed through London last, and found that one of the plates is missing from my copy."

"Which plate is it? It is not very easy, I understand, to procure a perfect copy. One of my uncle's sets has no two volumes bound alike. Each must have belonged to a different set."

"I can't tell you what the plate is. But there are only three of those very curious unfolding ones in my third volume, and there should be four."

"I should always like things to be perfect myself," she returned.

"Doubtless," I answered, and thought it better to try another direction. "How is Mrs. Oldcastle?" I asked, feeling the inner reproach of hypocrisy.

"Quite well, thank you," she answered, in a tone of indifference, which either implied that she saw through me or shared my indifference.

"And Miss Judy?" I inquired.

"A little savage, as usual."

"Not the worse for her wetting, I hope."

"Oh! Dear no. There never was health to equal that child's. It belongs to her savage nature."

"I wish some of us were more of savages, then," I returned, for I saw signs of exhaustion in her eyes which moved my sympathy.

"You don't mean me, Mr. Walton, I hope, for if you do I assure you your interest is quite thrown away. Uncle will tell you I am as strong as an elephant." But a shadow passed over her face, as though she felt she ought not to be the subject of conversation.

When I glanced away from Miss Oldcastle in slight embarrassment, I saw Judy in the room. Miss Oldcastle rose and said, "What is the matter, Judy?"

"Grannie wants you," said Judy.

As Miss Oldcastle left the room, Judy turned to me.

"How do you do, Mr. Walton?" she said.

"Quite well, thank you, Judy," I answered. "Your uncle admits you to his workshop, then?"

"Yes, indeed. He would feel rather dull, sometimes, without me. Wouldn't you, Uncle Stoddart?"

"Just as the horses in the field would feel dull without the gadfly, Judy," said Mr. Stoddart.

Judy was gone in a moment, leaving Mr. Stoddart alone with me. He had been busy at one of his benches, filing away at a piece of brass for a very curious machine. He turned and said to me, "I wonder what speech I shall make next, to drive *you* away, Mr. Walton."

"I am not so easily got rid of, Mr. Stoddart," I answered. "And as for taking offense, I don't like it, and therefore I never take it. But tell me what you are doing now."

"I have been working for some time at an attempt after perpetual motion, but, I must confess, I have not yet succeeded." He threw down his file on the bench. "But this, you will allow, would have made a very pretty machine."

"Pretty, I will allow," I answered, "as distinguished from beautiful, for I can never dissociate beauty from use."

"You say that! With all the poetic things you say in your sermons! For I am a sharp listener, and none the less such for that you do not see me. I have a loophole for seeing you. I flatter myself that I am the only person in the congregation on a level with you. I cannot contradict you, and you cannot address me."

"Do you mean, then, that whatever is poetical is useless?" I asked.

"Do you assert that whatever is useful is beautiful?" he retorted.

"Whatever subserves a noble end must in itself be beautiful."

"Then a gallows must be beautiful because it subserves the noble end of ridding the world of malefactors?" he returned promptly.

"I do not see anything noble in the end," I answered. "If the machine got rid of malefaction, it would indeed have a noble end. But if it only compels it to move on, as a constable does, from this world into another, I do not, I say, see anything so noble in that end. The gallows cannot be beautiful, for an inevitable necessity is very different from a noble end. To cure the diseased mind is the noblest of ends. To make the sinner forsake his ways, and the unrighteous man his thoughts, is the loftiest of designs. But to punish him for being wrong, however necessary it may be for others, cannot be called noble. But I ask you a question now: what is the immediate effect of anything poetic upon your mind?"

"Pleasure," he answered.

"And is pleasure good or bad?"

"Sometimes the one, sometimes the other."

"In itself?"

"I should say bad."

"I should not."

"Are you not, by your very profession, more or less an enemy of pleasure?"

"On the contrary, I believe that pleasure is good, and does good, and urges to good. Care is the evil thing."

"Strange doctrine for a clergyman."

"Now, do not misunderstand me, Mr. Stoddart. That might not hurt you, but it would distress me. Pleasure obtained by wrong is poison and horror. But it is not the pleasure that hurts; it is the wrong that is in it that hurts—the pleasure hurts only as it leads to more wrong. If you could make everybody happy, half the evil would vanish from the earth."

"Then why does not God destroy evil, at such a cheap and pleasant rate?"

"Because He wants to destroy all the evil, not the half of it, and destroy it so that it shall not grow again, which it would be sure to do very soon if it had no antidote but happiness. As soon as men got used to happiness, they would begin to sin again, and so lose it all."

But here I saw that I had lost Mr. Stoddart, so I went back to the original question.

"If I say poetic things in the pulpit, it is because true things come to me in poetic forms. Therefore, I am free to say as many poetic things as shall be of the highest use, namely to embody and reveal the true."

There was no satisfactory following out of the argument on either side. I don't like argument, and I don't care for victory. If I had my way, I would never argue, but only set forth what I believe, and so leave it to work its own way.

I thought it was time for me to take leave. But I could not bear to run away with the last word, as it were, so I said, "You put plenty of poetry yourself into that voluntary you played last Sunday. I am so much obliged to you for it!"

"Oh! that fugue. You liked it, did you?"

"More than I can tell you."

"Shall I tell you what I was thinking of while playing that fugue?"

"I should like to hear."

"I had been thinking, while you were preaching, of the many fancies men had worshiped for the truth—now following this, now following that, ever believing they were on the point of laying hold upon her, and going down to the grave as empty-handed as they came. Multitudes followed where nothing was to be seen, with arms outstretched in all directions, some clasping vacancy to their bosoms, some reaching on tiptoe over the heads of their neighbors, and some with hanging heads, and hands clasped behind their backs, retiring hopeless from the chase."

"Strange!" I said, "for I felt so full of hope while you played!"

"The multitude was full of hope, vain hope, to lay hold upon the truth. And you, being full of the main expression, and in sympathy with it, did not heed the undertones of disappointment, or the sighs of those who turned their backs on the chase. Just so it is in life."

"I am no musician," I returned, "to give you a musical counter to your picture. But I see a man tilling the ground in peace, and the form of Truth standing behind him, and folding her wings closer and closer over and around him as he works on at his day's labor."

"Very pretty," said Mr. Stoddart, and said no more.

"Suppose," I went on, "that a person knows that he has not laid hold on the truth—is that sufficient ground for his making any further assertion than that he has not found it?"

"No. But if he has tried hard and has not found anything that he can say is true, he cannot help thinking that most likely there is no such thing."

"Suppose," I said, "that nobody has found the truth. Is that sufficient ground for saying that nobody ever will find it? Or that there is no such thing as truth to be found? Are the ages so nearly done that no chance remains? Surely, if God has made us to desire the truth, He has some truth to cast into the gulf of that desire. Shall God create hunger and no food? But possibly a man may be looking the wrong way for it. You may be using the microscope when you ought to open both eyes and lift up your head. Or a man may be finding some truth which is feeding his soul when he does not think he is finding any. You know *The Faerie Queene.* Think how long the Red-cross Knight traveled with the Lady Truth without learning to believe in her, and how much longer still without ever seeing her face. For my part, may God give me strength to follow till I die. Only I will venture to say this, that it is not by any agony of the intellect that I expect to discover truth."

"But does not," he asked, gently lowering his eyes upon mine after a moment's pause, "does not your choice of a profession imply that you have, and hold, and therefore teach the truth?"

"I profess only to have caught glimpses of her white garments—those, I mean, of the abstract truth of which you speak. But I have seen that which is eternally beyond her—the ideal in the real, the living truth. Not the truth that I can *think,* but the truth that thinks itself, that thinks me, that God has thought, that God is, the truth being true to itself, and to God, and to man—Christ Jesus, my Lord, who knows and feels and does the truth. I have seen Him, and I am both content and unsatisfied, for in Him are hid all the treasures of wisdom and knowledge. Thomas à Kempis said, 'He to whom the eternal Word speaks is set free from a press of opinions.' "

I rose and held out my hand to Mr. Stoddart. He rose likewise and took it kindly, conducted me to the room below and, ringing the bell, committed me to the care of the butler.

As I approached the gate I met Jane Rogers coming back from the village. I stopped and spoke to her. Her eyes were very red.

"Nothing amiss at home, Jane?" I said.

"No, Sir, thank you," answered Jane, and burst out crying.

"What is the matter, then? Is your—"

"Nothing's the matter with nobody, Sir."

"Something is the matter with you."

"Yes, Sir. But I'm quite well."

"I don't want to pry into your affairs—but if you think I can be of any use to you, mind you come to me."

"Thank you kindly, Sir," said Jane. Dropping a curtsy, she walked on with her basket.

I went to her parents' cottage. As I came near the mill, the young miller was standing in the door with his eyes fixed on the ground, while the mill went on hopping behind him. But when he caught sight of me, he turned and went in, as if he had not seen me.

"Has he been behaving ill to Jane?" thought I.

As he evidently wished to avoid me, I passed the mill without looking in at the door, and went on to the cottage where I lifted the latch and walked in. Both the old people were there, and both looked troubled, though they welcomed me none the less kindly.

"I met Jane," I said, "and she looked unhappy, so I came on to hear what was the matter."

"You oughtn't to be troubled with our small affairs," said Mrs. Rogers.

"If the parson wants to know, why the parson must be told," said Old Rogers, smiling cheerily, as if he at least would be relieved by telling me.

"I don't want to know," I said, "if you don't want to tell me. But can I be of any use?"

"I don't think you can, Sir, leastways I'm afraid not," said the old woman.

"I am sorry to say, Sir, that Master Brownrigg and his son has come to words about our Jane, and it's not agreeable to have folks' daughter quarreled over in that way," said Old Rogers. "What'll be the upshot of it I don't know, but it looks bad now. For the father he tells the son that if ever he hears of him saying one word to our Jane, out ov the mill he goes, as sure as his name's Dick. Now it's rather a good chance, I think, to see what the young fellow's made of, Sir. So I tells Mrs. Rogers here, and so I told Jane, but neither of 'em seems to see the comfort of it somehow. But the New Testament do say a man shall leave father and mother, and cleave to his wife."

"But she ain't his wife yet," said Mrs. Rogers to her husband, whose drift was not yet evident.

"No more she can be, 'cept he leaves his father for her."

"And what'll become of them then, without the mill?"

"You and me never had no mill, yet here we be, very nearly ripe now, ain't us, Wife?"

"Medlar-like, Old Rogers, I doubt—rotten before we're ripe," replied his wife.

"Nay, nay, old 'oman. Don't 'e say so. The Lord won't let us rot before we're ripe, anyhow. That I be sure on."

"But, anyhow, it's all very well to talk. Thou knows how to talk, Rogers. But how will it be when the children comes, and no mill?"

"To grind 'em in, old 'oman?"

I was listening with real interest and much amusement, and Mrs. Rogers turned to me.

"I wish you would speak a word to Old Rogers, Sir. He never will speak as he's spoken to. He's always overmerry or overserious. He either takes me up short with a sermon, or he laughs me out of countenance."

Now I was pretty sure that Rogers' conduct was simple consistency, and that the difficulty arose from his always acting upon the plainest principles of truth and right. His wife, good woman—for the bad leaven of the Pharisees could not rise much in her somehow—was always reminding him of certain precepts of behavior to the oblivion of principles. "A bird in the hand is worth two in the bush," "Marry in haste, repent in leisure," and "When want comes in at the door, love flies out at the window," were among her favorite sayings, although not one of them was supported by her own experience. She had married in haste herself and never, I believe, had once thought of repenting of it, although she had had more than the requisite leisure for doing so. And many was the time that want had come in at her door, and the first thing it always did was to clip the wings of love and make him less flighty, and more tender and serviceable. So I could not even pretend to read her husband a lecture.

"He's a curious man, Old Rogers," I said, "but as far as I can see, he's in the right of the main. Isn't he, now?"

"Oh, yes, I dare say. I think he's always right about the rights of the thing, you know. But a body may go too far that way. It won't do to starve, Sir."

"I don't think anyone can go too far in the right way."

"That's just what I want my old 'oman to see, and I can't get it into her, Sir. If a thing's right, it's right, and if a thing's wrong, why, wrong it is. The helm must either be to starboard or port, Sir."

"But why talk of starving?" I said. "Can't Dick work? Who could think of starting that nonsense?"

"Why, my old 'oman here. She wants 'em to give it up and wait for better times. The fact is, she don't want to lose the girl."

"But she hasn't got her at home now."

"She can have her when she wants her though, leastways after a bit of warning, whereas, if she was married, and the consequences a follerin' at her heels, like a man-o'-war with her convoy, she would find she was chartered for another port, she would."

"Well, you see, Sir, Rogers and me's not so young as we once was, and we're likely to be growing older every day. And if there's a difficulty in the way of Jane's marriage, why, I take it as a godsend."

"How would you have liked such a godsend, Mrs. Rogers, when you were going to be married to your sailor here? What would you have done?"

"Why, whatever he liked, to be sure. But then, you see, Dick's not my Rogers."

"But your daughter thinks about him the same way you did about this dear old man when he was young."

"Young people may be in the wrong. I see nothing in Dick Brownrigg."

"But young people may be right sometimes, and old people may be wrong sometimes."

"I can't be wrong about Rogers."

"No, but you may be wrong about Dick."

"Don't you trouble yourself about my old 'oman, Sir. She allus was awk'ard in stays, but she never missed them yet. When she's said her say, round she comes in the wind like a bird, Sir."

"There's a good old man to stick up for your old wife!" she said. "Still, I say they may as well wait a bit. It would be a pity to anger the old gentleman."

"What does the young man say to it?" I asked.

"Why, he says like a man he can work for her as well's the mill, and he's ready, if she is."

"I am very glad to hear such a good account of him. I shall look in and have a little chat with him. Good morning, Mrs. Rogers."

"I'll see you across the stream, Sir," said the old man, following me out of the house.

"You see, Sir," he resumed, as soon as we were outside. "I'm always afeard of taking things out of the Lord's hands. It's the right way, surely, that when a man loves a woman, and has told her so, he should act like a man, and do as is right. And isn't that the Lord's way? And can't He give them what's good for them? Mayhap they won't love each other the less in the end if Dick has a little bit of hard work. I wouldn't like to anger the old gentleman, as my wife says, but if I was Dick, I know what I would do. But don't 'e think hard of my wife, Sir, for I believe there's a bit of pride in it. She's afeard of bein' supposed to catch at Richard Brownrigg because he's above us, you know, Sir, and I can't altogether blame her, only we ain't got to do with the look o' things, but with the things themselves."

"I understand you quite, and I'm very much of your mind. You can trust me to have a little chat with him, can't you?"

"That I can, Sir."

I bade him good-day, jumped across the stream, and went into the mill, where Richard was tying the mouth of a sack as gloomily as the brothers of Joseph must have tied their sacks after his silver cup had been found.

"Why did you turn away from me as I passed half an hour ago, Richard?" I said cheerily.

"I beg your pardon, Sir. I didn't think you saw me."

"But supposing I hadn't? But I won't tease you. I know all about it. Can I do anything for you?"

"No, Sir. You can't move my father. It's no use talking to him. He never hears a word anybody says. He never hears a word you say o' Sundays, Sir. He won't even believe the newspaper about the price of corn. It's no use talking to him, Sir."

"You wouldn't mind if I were to try?"

"No, Sir. You can't make matters worse. No more can you make them any better, Sir."

"I don't say I shall talk to him, but I may, if I find a fitting opportunity."

"He's always worse—more obstinate—that is, when he's in a good temper. So you may choose your opportunity wrong. But it's all the same. It can make no difference."

"What are you going to do, then?"

"I would let him do his worst. But Jane doesn't like to go against her mother. I'm sure I can't think how she should side with my father against both of us. He never laid her under any such obligation, I'm sure."

"There may be more ways than one of accounting for that. You must mind, however, and not be too hard on your father. You're quite right in holding fast to the girl, but mind that vexation does not make you unjust."

"I wish my mother were alive. She was the only one that ever could manage him. How she contrived to do it nobody could think—but manage him she did, somehow or other."

"I dare say he prides himself on not being moved by talk. But has he ever had a chance of knowing Jane, of seeing what kind of girl she is?"

"He's seen her over and over."

"But seeing isn't always believing."

"It certainly isn't with him."

"If he could only know her! But don't you be too hard on him. And don't do anything in a hurry. Give him a little time, you know. Mrs. Rogers won't interfere between you and Jane, I am pretty sure. But don't push matters till we see. Good-by."

"Good-by, and thank you kindly, Sir. Ain't I to see Jane in the meantime?"

"If I were you, I would make no difference. See her as often as you used, which I suppose was as often as you could. I don't think that her mother will interfere. Her father is all on your side."

I called on Mr. Brownrigg but, as his son had forewarned me, I could make nothing of him. He didn't see, when the mill was his property and Dick was his son, why he shouldn't have his way with them. His son might marry any lady in the land, and he wasn't going to throw himself away.

All my missiles of argument were lost, as it were, in a bank of mud. My experience in the attempt, however, did a little to reconcile me to his going to sleep in church, for I saw that it could make little difference whether he was asleep or awake. He, and not Mr. Stoddart in his organ sentry box, was the only person whom it was absolutely impossible to preach to. I might preach *at* him, but *to* him—no.

TEN

My Christmas Party

As Christmas drew near, my heart glowed with gladness, and the question came pressingly—could I not do something to make it more truly a holiday of the Church for my parishioners? That most of them would have a little more enjoyment on it than they had all the year through, I had ground to hope. But I wanted to connect this gladness in their minds with its source, the love of God manifested in the birth of the Son of man. But I would not interfere with the Christmas Day at home. I resolved to invite my parishioners to spend Christmas Eve at the vicarage.

I therefore had a notice affixed to the church door, and resolved to send out no personal invitations, so that I might not give offense by accidental omission. The only person thrown into perplexity by this mode of proceeding was Mrs. Pearson.

"How many am I to provide for, Sir?" she asked, with an injured air.

"For as many as you ever saw in church at one time," I said. "And if there should be too much, why, so much the better. It can go to make Christmas Day the merrier at some of the poorer houses."

She looked discomposed, for she was not of an easy temper. But she never *acted* from her temper—she only *looked* or *spoke* from it. "I shall want help," she said at length.

"As much as you like, Mrs. Pearson. I can trust you entirely."

Her face brightened, and the end showed that I had not trusted her amiss.

I was a little anxious about the result of the invitation, partly because it indicated the amount of confidence my people placed in me. But, although no one said a word to me about it beforehand except Old Rogers, as soon as the hour for the party arrived, the people began to come. And the first I welcomed was Mr. Brownrigg.

I had had all the rooms on the ground floor prepared for their reception. Tables of provision were set out in every one of them. My visitors had tea or coffee and plenty of bread and butter when they arrived. The more solid supplies were reserved for the later part of the evening. I soon found myself with enough to do. But before long I had a very efficient staff—for, after having had occasion once or twice to mention something of my plans for the evening, I found my labors gradually diminish, and yet everything seemed to go right. Good Mr. Boulderstone, in one part, had cast himself into the middle of the flood of people, and stood there immovable both in face and person, turning its waters toward the barn. In the barn, Dr. Duncan was doing his best, and that was simply something first-rate, to entertain the people till all should be ready. From a kind of instinct, and almost without knowing it, these gentlemen had taken upon them to be my staff, and very grateful I was.

When I came and saw the goodly assemblage, I could not help rejoicing that my predecessor had been so fond of farming that he had rented land and built this large barn, so I might make a hall to entertain my friends. For how can a man be *the person* of a parish if he never entertains his parishioners? And really, though it was lighted only with candles round the walls, and I had not been able to do much for the decoration of the place, I thought it looked very well, and my heart was glad—just as if the Babe had been coming again to us that same night. And is He not always coming to us afresh in every childlike feeling that awakes in the hearts of His people?

It was amusing to watch Mr. Boulderstone's honest though awkward endeavors to be at ease with everyone. Dr. Duncan was just a sight worth seeing. Very tall and stately, he was talking now to this old man, now to that young woman, and every face toward which he turned glistened. There was no condescension about him. He was as polite and courteous to the one as to another, and the smile that every now and then lighted up his old face was genuine and sympathetic. No one could have known by his behavior that he was not at court.

I felt more certain than ever that a free mingling of all classes would do more than anything else toward binding us all into a wise, patriotic nation, and keep down that foolish emulation which makes one class ape another from afar. It would refine the roughness of the rude, and enable the polished to see that public matters might also be committed into the hands of the honest workman.

There was no one there to represent Oldcastle Hall. And Catharine Weir was likewise absent. But how could I have everything a success at once?

After we had spent awhile in pleasant talk, and when I thought nearly all were with us, I got up on a chair and said, "Kind friends, I am very grateful to you for honoring my invitation as you have done. Permit me to hope that this meeting will be the first of many, and that it may grow the yearly custom in this parish of gathering in love and friendship upon Christmas Eve. When God comes to man, man looks round for his neighbor. When man departed from God in the Garden of Eden, the only man in the world ceased to be the friend of the only woman in the world. Instead of seeking to bear her burden, he became her accuser to God, in whom he saw only the Judge, unable to perceive that the infinite love of the Father had come to punish him in tenderness and grace. But when God in Jesus comes to men, brothers and sisters spread forth their arms to embrace each other, and so to embrace Him. We all need to become little children like Him, to cease to be careful about many things, and trust in Him, seeking only that He should rule, and that we should be made good like Him. What else is meant by, 'Seek ye first the kingdom of God and His righteousness, and all these things shall be added unto you'? Instead of doing so, we seek the things God has promised to look after for us, and refuse to seek the thing He wants us to seek—a thing that cannot be given us except we seek it. But tonight, at least, let all unkind thoughts, all hard judgments of one another, all selfish desires after our own way, be put from us, that we may welcome the Babe into our very bosoms, so that when He comes among us He may not be troubled to find that we are quarrelsome, and selfish, and unjust."

I came down from the chair, and shook hands with Mr. Brownrigg, and there was some meaning in the grasp with which he returned mine.

First of all, we sang a hymn about the Nativity, and then I read an extract from a book of travels, describing the interior of an Eastern cottage, probably much resembling the inn in which our Lord was born, the stable being scarcely divided from the rest of the house. I felt that to open the inner eyes even of the brain, enabling people to see in some measure the reality of the old lovely story, might help to open the yet deeper spiritual eyes which alone can see the meaning and truth dwelling in and giving shape to the outward facts. And the extract was listened to with all the attention I could wish, except, at first, from some youngsters at the farther end of the barn who became, however, perfectly still as I proceeded.

After this followed conversation, during which I talked a good deal to Jane Rogers, paying her particular attention indeed, with the hope of a chance of bringing old Mr. Brownrigg and her together in some way.

"How is your mistress, Jane?" I said.

"Quite well, Sir, thank you. I only wish she was here."

"I wish she were. But perhaps she will come next year."

"I think she will. I am almost sure she would have liked to come tonight, for I heard her say—"

"I beg your pardon, Jane, for interrupting you, but I would rather not be told anything you may have happened to overhear," I said, in a low voice.

"O Sir," returned Jane, blushing a dark crimson, "it wasn't anything in particular."

"Still, if it was anything on which a wrong conjecture might be built"—I wanted to soften it to her—"it is better that one should not be told it. Thank you for your kind intention, though. And now, Jane," I said, "will you do me a favor?"

"That I will, Sir, if I can."

"Sing that Christmas carol I heard you sing last night to your mother."

"I didn't know anyone was listening, Sir."

"I know you did not. I came to the door with your father, and we stood and listened."

She looked very frightened. But I would not have asked her had I not known that she could sing like a bird. "I am afraid I shall make a fool of myself," she said.

"We should all be willing to run that risk for the sake of others," I answered.

"I will try, then, Sir."

So she sang, and her voice soon silenced the speech all round.

"You have quite a gift of song, Jane," I said.

"My father and mother can both sing."

Mr. Brownrigg was seated on the other side of me, listening with some interest. His face was ten degrees less stupid than it usually was. I fancied I saw even a glimmer of some satisfaction in it. I turned to Old Rogers.

"Sing us a song, Old Rogers," I said.

"I'm no canary at that, Sir, and, besides, my singing days be over. I advise you to ask Dr. Duncan there. He can sing."

I rose and said to the assembly, "My friends, if I did not think God was pleased to see us enjoying ourselves, I should have no heart for it myself. I am going to ask our dear friend Dr. Duncan to give us a song. If you please, Dr. Duncan."

"I am very nearly too old," said the doctor, "but I will try."

His voice was certainly a little feeble, but the song was not much the worse for it, and genuine applause followed. I turned to Miss Boulderstone, from whom I had borrowed a piano, and asked her to play a country dance for us. But first I said—not getting up on a chair this time—"Some people think it is not proper for a clergyman to dance. I mean to assert my freedom from any such law. If our Lord chose to represent, in His Parable of the Prodigal Son, the joy in heaven over a repentant sinner by the figure of 'music and dancing,' I will hearken to Him rather than to men, be they as good as they may."

For I had long thought that the way to make indifferent things bad was for good people not to do them.

And, so saying, I stepped up to Jane Rogers, and asked her to dance with me. She blushed so dreadfully that, for a moment, I was almost sorry I had asked her. But she put her hand in mine at once—and if she was a little clumsy, she yet danced very naturally—an honest girl, and friendly to me in her heart.

But to see the faces of the people! While I had been talking, Old Rogers had been drinking in every word. To him it was milk and strong meat in one. But now his face shone with a father's gratification besides. And Richard's face was glowing too. Even old Mr. Brownrigg looked with a curious interest upon us, I thought.

Meantime Dr. Duncan was dancing with one of his own patients, old Mrs. Trotter, to whose wants he ministered far more from his table than from his surgery. I have known that man, hearing of a case of want, to send the fowl he was about to dine upon, untouched, to those whose necessity was greater than his.

And Mr. Boulderstone had taken out old Mrs. Rogers, and young Mr. Brownrigg had taken Mary Weir. Thomas Weir did not dance at all, but looked on kindly.

"Why don't you dance, Old Rogers?" I said, as I placed his daughter in a seat beside him.

"Did you ever see an elephant go up the futtock shrouds?"

"No, I never did."

"I thought you must, Sir, to ask me why I don't dance. You won't take my fun ill, Sir? I'm an old man-o'-war's man, you know, Sir."

"I should have thought, Rogers, that you would have known better by this time than make such an apology to me."

"God bless you, Sir. An old man's safe with you—or a young lass either, Sir," he added, turning with a smile to his daughter.

I turned and addressed Mr. Boulderstone. "I am greatly obliged to you, Mr. Boulderstone, for the help you have given me this evening. I've seen you talking to everyone, just as if you had to entertain them all."

"Well, I thought it wasn't a time to mind one's p's and q's exactly, and it's wonderful how one gets on without them. I hate formality myself."

The dear fellow was the most formal man I had ever met.

"Why don't you dance, Mr. Brownrigg?"

"Who'd care to dance with me, Sir? I don't care to dance with an old woman, and a young woman won't care to dance with me."

"I'll find you a partner, if you will put yourself in my hands."

"I don't mind trusting myself to you, Sir."

So I led him to Jane Rogers. She stood up in respectful awe before the master of her destiny. There were signs of calcitration in the church warden when he saw where I was leading him. But when he saw the girl stand trembling before him, whether it was that he was flattered by the signs of his own power, accepting them as homage, or that his hard heart actually softened a little, I cannot tell, but after a perceptible hesitation he said, "Come along, my lass, and let's have a hop together."

She obeyed very sweetly.

"Don't be too shy," I whispered to her as she passed me.

And the church warden danced very heartily with the lady's-maid.

I then asked him to take her into the house and give her something to eat in return for her song. He yielded somewhat awkwardly, and what passed between them I do not know. But when they returned, she seemed less frightened, and when the company was parting, I heard him take leave of her with the words, "Give us a kiss, my girl, and let bygones be bygones."

Which I heard with delight. For had I not been a peacemaker? And should I not feel blessed? But the understanding was brought about simply by making people meet—compelling them, as it were, to know something of each other.

I took care that we should have dancing in moderation. Indeed, we had only six country dances during the evening. And between the dances I read two or three of Wordsworth's ballads to them. For I thought if I could get them to like poetry and beautiful things in words, it would not only do them good, but would help them to see what is in the Bible, and therefore to love it more. For I never could believe that a man who did not find God in other places, as well as in the Bible, would ever find Him there at all. And I have always thought that to find God in other books enables us to see clearly that He is more in the Bible than in any other book, or all other books put together.

After supper we had a little more singing. And, to my satisfaction, nothing came to my eyes or ears during the whole evening that was undignified or ill-bred. Of course, I knew that many of them must have two behaviors, and that now they were on their good behavior. But I thought the oftener such were put on their good behavior, the more it would give them the opportunity of finding out how nice it was. It might make them ashamed of the other at last.

Before we parted I gave each guest a sheet of Christmas carols, gathered from the older portions of our literature. For to my mind, most of the modern hymns are neither milk nor meat but mere wretched imitations. There were a few curious words and idioms in these, but I thought it better to leave them as they were. They might set them inquiring, and give me an opportunity of interesting them further, sometime or other, in the history of a word; in their ups and downs of fortune, words fare very much like human beings.

ELEVEN

My Christmas Sermon

I never asked questions about the private affairs of any of my parishioners, except if they individually asked me for advice. Hence, I believe, they became the more willing that I should know. But I heard a good many things, notwithstanding, for I could not be constantly closing lips as I had done with Jane Rogers. Among other things, I learned that Miss Oldcastle went most Sundays to the neighboring town of Addicehead to church. Now I had often heard of the ability of the rector, and although I had never met him, I was prepared to find him a cultivated if not an original man. Yet I confess that I heard this news with a pang, which I discovered to be jealousy. It was no use asking myself why I should be jealous; there the ugly thing was. So I went and told God I was ashamed, and begged Him to deliver me from the evil, because His was the kingdom and the power and the glory. And He took my part against myself, for He waits to be gracious.

But there was one stray sheep of my flock that appeared in church for the first time on the morning of Christmas Day—Catharine Weir. She did not sit beside her father, but in the most shadowy corner of the church, yet near the organ loft. She could have seen her father if she had looked up, but she kept her eyes down the whole time, and never even lifted them to me. The spot on one cheek was much brighter than that on the other, and made her look very ill.

I took my text from the Sermon on the Mount—St. Matthew the sixth chapter, and part of verses twenty-four and twenty-five: " 'Ye cannot serve God and mammon. Therefore I say unto you, Take no thought for your life.'

"When the Child whose birth we celebrate grew up to be a Man, He said this. Did He mean it? He meant it altogether and entirely. When people do not understand what the Lord says, instead of searching deeper for a meaning which will be evidently true and wise, they comfort themselves by thinking He could not have meant it altogether, and so leave it. Or they think that if He did mean it, He could not expect them to carry it out. Let it not be so with us this day. Let us seek to find out what our Lord means, that we may do it.

"*Mammon,* you know, means *riches.* Now, riches are meant to be the slave—not even the servant of man, and not the master. If a man serve his own servant—anyone who has no just claim to be his master—he is a slave. But here he serves his own slave.

"But how can a man *serve* riches? Why, when he says to riches, 'Ye are my god.' When he feels he cannot be happy without them. When he schemes, and dreams, and lies awake thinking about them. When he will not give to his neighbor for fear of becoming poor himself. When he wants to have more—and to know he has more—than he can need. When he honors those who have money because they have money, or when he honors in a rich man what he would not honor in a poor man. Still more when his devotion to his god makes him oppressive to those over whom his wealth gives him power, or when he becomes unjust in order to add to his stores.

"How will it be with such a man when he finds that the world has vanished, and he is alone with God? There lies the body in which he used to live. He cannot now even try to bribe God with a check. The angels will not bow down to him. And the poor souls of hades, who envied him the wealth they had lost before, rise up as one man to welcome him, rejoicing in the mischief that has befallen him, and saying, 'Art thou also become one of us?' He can no longer deceive himself in his riches. And so even in hell he is something nobler than he was on earth, for he worships his riches no longer. He cannot. He curses them.

"Terrible things to say on Christmas Day! But if Christmas Day teaches us anything, it teaches us to worship God and not mammon, to worship Spirit and not matter, to worship love and not power.

" 'Ye cannot serve God and mammon. Therefore I say unto you, Take no thought for your life.'

"Why are you to take no thought? Where are you now, poor man? Brooding over the frost? Will it harden the ground so that the God of the sparrows cannot find food for His sons? Where are you now, poor woman? Sleepless over the empty cupboard and tomorrow's dinner, because you have no bread? Have you forgotten the five loaves among the five thousand, and the fragments that were left? Oh ye of little faith!

"But I may be too hard upon you. I know well that our Father sees a great difference between the man who is anxious about his children's dinner (or even about his own) and the man who is only anxious to add another ten thousand pounds to his much goods laid up. But you ought to find it easy to trust in God for your daily bread.

"But how is the work of the world to be done, if we take no thought? We are nowhere told not to take thought. We *must* take thought—but what about? Why, about our work. What are we not to take thought about?

Why, about life. The one is our business, the other God's. A man's business is just to do his duty. God takes upon Himself the feeding and the clothing. Will the work of the world be neglected if a man thinks of his work, his duty, God's will to be done, instead of what he is to eat and drink and how he is to be clothed?

"I *should* like to know a man who just minded his duty and troubled himself about nothing, who did his own work and did not interfere with God's. How nobly he would work—not for reward but because it was the will of God! What peace would be his! What a friend he would be! How sweet his sympathy! And his mind would be so clear he would understand everything. His eye being single, his whole body would be full of light. No fear of his ever doing a mean thing—he would die in a ditch rather. It is this fear of want that makes men do mean things. They are afraid to part with their precious lord—mammon. He gives no safety against such a fear. One of the richest men in England is haunted with the dread of the workhouse.

"But I think I hear my troubled friend who does not love money—and yet cannot trust in God out and out—I hear her say, 'I believe I could trust Him for myself, but it is the thought of my children that is too much for me.' Ah! Woman! She whom the Saviour praised so pleasedly was one who trusted Him for her daughter. 'Be it unto thee even as thou wilt.' Do you think you love your children better than He who made them? Is not your love what it is because He put it into your heart first? You did not create that love. God sent it. He loves them a thousand times better than you do—be sure of that.

"But don't we see people die of starvation sometimes? Yes. But if you did your work in God's name and left the rest to Him, that would not trouble you. You would say, 'If it be God's will that I should starve, I can starve as well as another.' And your mind would be at ease. 'Thou wilt keep him in perfect peace whose mind is stayed on Thee, because he trusteth in Thee.' Of that I am sure. It may be good for you to go hungry and barefoot, but it must be utter death to have no faith in God. We do not know why here and there a man may be left to die of hunger, but I do believe that they who wait upon the Lord shall not lack any good. What it may be good to deprive a man of till he knows and acknowledges whence it comes, it may be still better to give him when he has learned that every good and every perfect gift is from above, and cometh down from the Father of lights.

"It has been well said that no man ever sank under the burden of the day. It is when tomorrow's burden is added to the burden of today that the weight is more than a man can bear. If you find yourselves so loaded, remember: it is your own doing, not God's. He begs you to leave the future to Him, and mind the present. What more or what else could He do to take the burden off you? Money in the bank wouldn't do it. He cannot do tomorrow's business for you beforehand to save you from fear about it. What else is there but to tell you to trust in Him? Walk without fear, full of hope and courage, and strength to do His will, waiting for the endless good which He is always giving as fast as He can get us able to take it in.

"Pain and hunger are evils, but if faith in God swallows them up, do they not so turn into good? I say they do. I have never been too hungry, but I have had trouble which I would gladly have exchanged for hunger and cold and weariness. Some of you have known hunger and cold and weariness. Do you not join with me to say, 'It is well, and better than well, whatever helps us know the love of Him who is our God'?

"And this One is the Baby whose birth we celebrate this day. Was this a condition to choose—that of a baby? Did He not thus cast the whole matter at once upon the hands and heart of His Father? Sufficient unto a baby's day is the need thereof; he toils not, neither does he spin, and yet he is fed and clothed and loved and rejoiced in.

"But let us look at what will be more easily shown, how, namely, He did the will of His Father, and took no thought for the morrow after He became a man. Remember how He forsook His trade when the time came for Him to preach. Preaching was not a profession then. There were no monasteries or vicarages or stipends then. Yet witness for the Father the garment woven throughout—the ministering of women, the purse in common! Hardworking men and rich ladies were ready to help Him, and did help Him with all that He needed. Did He then never want? Yes, once at least, for a little while only.

"He was hungered in the wilderness. 'Make bread,' said Satan. 'No,' said our Lord. He could starve, but He could not eat bread that His Father did not give Him, even though He could make it Himself. He had come hither to be tried. But when the victory was secure, lo! the angels brought Him food from His Father. Which was better, to feed Himself or be fed by His Father? He sought the kingdom of God and His righteousness, and the bread was added unto Him.

"Do you feel inclined to say in your hearts, 'It was easy for Him to take no thought, for He had the matter in His own hands'? But there is nothing very noble in a man's taking no thought, except it be from faith. If there were no God to take thought for us, we should have no right to blame anyone for taking thought. You may fancy the Lord had His own power to fall back upon. But that would have been to Him the one dreadful thing—that His Father should forget Him! No power in Himself could make up for that. He feared nothing for Himself, and never once employed His divine power to save Himself from His human fate. Let God do that for Him if He saw fit. To fall back on Himself, God failing Him—that would be to declare heaven void, and the world without a God. He did not come into the world to take care of Himself.

"His need was not to be fed and clothed, but to be one with the Father, to be fed by His hand, clothed by His care. This was what the Lord wanted, and what we too often need without wanting it. He never once used His power for Himself. God would mind all that was necessary for

Him, and our Lord would mind the work His Father had given Him to do. And, my friends, this is the secret of a blessed life, the one thing every man comes into this world to learn. With what authority it comes to us from the lips of Him who knew all about it, and ever did as He said!

"Now you see that He took no thought for the morrow. And in the name of the Holy Child Jesus, I call upon you, this Christmas Day, to cast care to the winds, and trust in God; to receive the message of peace and goodwill to men; to yield yourselves to the Spirit of God, that you may be taught what He wants you to know; to remember that the one gift promised without reserve to those who ask it—the one gift worth having, the gift which makes all other gifts a thousandfold in value—is the gift of the Holy Spirit, the Spirit of the Child Jesus, who will take of the things of Jesus and show them to you, make you understand them, so that you shall see them to be true, and love Him with all your heart and soul, and your neighbors as yourselves."

I had more than ordinary attention during my discourse. At one point I saw the bent head of Catharine Weir sink yet lower upon her hands. After a moment, however, she sat more erect than before, though she never lifted her eyes to meet mine. She was not present to my mind when I spoke the words that so far had moved her. Indeed, had I thought of her, I could not have spoken them.

As I came out of the church, my people crowded about me with outstretched hands and good wishes. One woman, the aged wife of a more aged laborer, called from the outskirts of the little crowd. "May the Lord come and see ye every day, Sir. And may ye never know the hunger and cold as me and Tomkins has come through."

"Amen to the first of your blessing, Mrs. Tomkins, and hearty thanks to you. But I daren't say Amen to the other part of it after what I've been preaching, you know."

"But there'll be no harm if I say it for ye, Sir?"

"No, for God will give me what is good, even if your kind heart should pray against it."

"Ah! Sir, ye don't know what it is to be hungry *and* cold."

"Neither shall you anymore, if I can help it."

"God bless ye, Sir. But we're pretty tidy just now."

When I reached my own study I sat down by a blazing fire. Let me, if I may, be ever welcomed to my room in winter by a glowing hearth, in summer by a vase of flowers. If I may not, let me then think how nice they would be and bury myself in my work.

I soon fell into a dreamy state (which a few mistake for thinking, because it is the nearest approach they ever make to it) and in this reverie I kept staring about my bookshelves. I am very fond of books. Do not mistake me. I do not mean that I love reading. I hope I do. That is no fault—a virtue rather than a fault. But, as the old meaning of the word *fond* was foolish, I use that word: I am foolishly fond of the bodies of books as distinguished from their souls. I do not say that I love their bodies as divided from their souls—I should not keep a book for which I felt no respect or had no use. But I delight in seeing books about me, books even of which there seems to be no prospect that I shall have time to read a single chapter. I confess that if they are nicely bound, so as to glow and shine in a firelight, I like them ever so much the better. I suspect that by the time books (which ought to be loved for the truth that is in them) come to be loved as articles of furniture, the mind has gone through a process which the miser's mind goes through—that of passing from the respect of money because of what it can do, to the love of money because it is money. I have not yet reached the furniture stage, and I do not think I ever shall. I would rather burn them all.

The thought suddenly struck me that I had promised Judy to find out what her aunt's name meant in Anglo-Saxon. I got down my dictionary and discovered that Ethelwyn meant Home-Joy or Inheritance. A lovely meaning.

And I went off into another reverie for my half hour. Then I got up and filled my pockets with little presents for my poor people, and set out to find them in their homes. Several families had asked me to take my Christmas dinner with them but, not liking to be thus limited, I had answered each that I would not, if they would excuse me, but would look in some time or other in the course of the evening.

I was variously received, but always with kindness. Mrs. Tomkins looked as if she had never seen so much tea together before, though there was only a couple of pounds of it. Her husband received a pair of warm trousers none the less cordially that they were not quite new, the fact being that I found I did not myself need such warm clothing this winter as I had needed last. I did not dare to offer Catharine Weir anything, but I gave her little boy a box of watercolors in remembrance of the first time I saw him, though I said nothing about that. His mother did not thank me. She told little Gerard to do so, however, and that was something. And, indeed, the boy's sweetness would have been enough for both.

When I reached Old Rogers' cottage, I found not merely Jane there with her father and mother (which was natural on Christmas Day, with no company at the Hall) but my little Judy as well.

"Why, Judy!" I exclaimed, "you here?"

"Yes. Why not, Mr. Walton?" she returned, holding out her hand.

"I know no reason why I shouldn't see a Sandwich Islander here. Yet I might express surprise if I did find one, might I not?"

Judy pretended to pout, and muttered something about comparing her to a cannibal. But Jane took up the explanation.

"Mistress had to go off to London with her mother today, Sir, quite unexpected, on some banking business, I fancy, from what I—I beg your pardon, Sir. They're gone anyhow, whatever the reason may be, and so I came to see Father and Mother, and Miss Judy would come with me."

"She be very welcome," said Mrs. Rogers.

"How could I stay up there with Sarah? I wouldn't be left alone with her for the world. She'd have me in the Bishop's Pool before you came back, Janey dear."

"That wouldn't matter much to you, would it, Judy?" I said.

"She's a white wolf, that old Sarah, I know!" was all her answer.

"But what will the old lady say when she finds you brought the young lady here?" asked Mrs. Rogers.

"I didn't bring her, Mother. She would come."

"Had they actually to go away on the morning of Christmas Day?" I said.

"They went anyhow, whether they had to do it or not, Sir," answered Jane.

"Aunt Ethelwyn didn't want to go till tomorrow," said Judy. "She said something about coming to church this morning, but Grannie said they must go at once. It was very cross of old Grannie. Think what a Christmas Day is to me without Auntie, and with Sarah! But I don't mean to go home till it's quite dark. I mean to stop here with dear Old Rogers—that I do."

The latch was gently lifted, and in came young Brownrigg, so I thought it was time to leave my best Christmas wishes and take myself away. Old Rogers came with me to the millstream as usual.

"It 'mazes me, Sir," he said, "a gentleman o' your age and bringin'-up, to know all that you tould us this mornin'. It 'ud be no wonder, now, for a man like me, come to be the shock o' corn fully ripe—leastways yallow and white enough outside, if there bean't much more than milk inside it yet—it'ud be no mystery for a man like me, who'd been brought up hard, and tossed about well nigh all the world over—why, there's scarce a wave on the Atlantic but knows Old Rogers!

"It 'ud be a shame of a man like me not to know as you said this morning, Sir—leastways I don't mean able to say it right off as you do, Sir. But not to know it, after the Almighty had been at such pains to beat it into my hard head just to trust in Him and fear nothing and nobody—captain, bosun, devil, sunk rock, or breakers ahead, but just to mind Him and stand by the wheel, or hang on for that matter. For, you see, what does it signify whether I go to the bottom or not, so long as I didn't skulk? Or rather," and here the old man took off his hat and looked up, "so long as the Great Captain has His way, and things is done to His mind? But how ever a man like you, goin' to the college, and readin' books, and warm o' nights, and never knowin' what it was to be downright hungry, how ever you come to know all those things is just past my comprehension, except by a double portion o' the Spirit, Sir. And that's the way I account for it, Sir.

"I had to learn it all without book, as it were, though you know I had my old Bible that my mother gave me, and without that I should not have learned it at all."

"You have had more of the practice, and I more of the theory, but if we had not had both, we should neither of us have known anything about the matter. I never was content without trying at least to understand things—and if they are practical things, and you try to practice them at the same time as far as you do understand them, there is no end to the way in which the one lights up the other. I suppose that is how, without your experience, I have more to say about such things than you could expect. The only difference is that though I've got my clay and my straw together, and they stick pretty well as yet, my brick is not half so well baked as yours, old friend, and it may crumble away yet, though I hope not."

"I pray God to make both our bricks into stones of the New Jerusalem, Sir. I think I understand you quite well. To know about a thing is of no use except you do it. Besides, as I found out when I went to sea, you never can know a thing till you do it, though I thought I had a tidy fancy about some things beforehand. It's better not to be quite sure that all your seams are caulked, and so to keep a lookout on the bilge pump—isn't it, Sir?"

During most of the conversation we were standing by the mill water which was half frozen over. The ice from both sides came toward the middle, leaving an empty space between, along which the dark water showed itself, hurrying away as if in fear of its life from the white death of the frost. The wheel stood motionless, and the drip from the mill over it in the sun had frozen the shadow into icicles, making the wheel look like its own gray skeleton. The sun was getting low, and I should want all my time to see my other friends before dinner, for I would not willingly offend Mrs. Pearson on Christmas Day by being late.

"I must go, Old Rogers," I said, "but I will leave you something to think about till we meet again. Find out why our Lord was so much displeased with the disciples, whom He knew to be ignorant men, not knowing what He meant when He warned them against the leaven of the Pharisees. I want to know what you think about it. You'll find the story told both in the sixteenth chapter of St. Matthew and the eighth of St. Mark."

"Well, Sir, I'll try, that is, if you will tell me what you think about it afterward, so as to put me right if I'm wrong."

"Of course I will, if I can find out an explanation to satisfy me. But it is not at all clear to me now. In fact, I do not see the connecting links of our Lord's logic in the rebuke He gives them."

"How am I to find out then, Sir, knowing nothing of logic at all?" said the old man, his rough worn face summered over with his childlike smile.

"There are many things which a little learning, while it cannot really hide them, may make you less ready to see all at once," I answered, shaking hands with Old Rogers, and then springing across the rock with my carpetbag in my hand.

By the time I had got through the rest of my calls, the fogs were rising from the streams and the meadows to close in upon my first Christmas Day in my own parish. How much happier I was than when I came such a few months before! The only pang I felt that day was as I passed the monsters on the gate leading to Oldcastle Hall. Should I be honored to help only the poor of the flock? Was I to do nothing for the rich, for whom it is so hard to enter into the kingdom of heaven?

To these people at the Hall I did not seem acceptable. I might in time do something with Judy, but the old lady was still so dreadfully repulsive to me that it troubled my conscience to feel how I disliked her. Mr. Stoddart seemed nothing more than a dilettante in religion as well as in the arts and sciences—music always excepted. I did not understand Miss Oldcastle yet—and she was so beautiful! I thought her more beautiful every time I saw her. But I never appeared to make the least progress toward any real acquaintance with her thoughts and feelings. I longed to do something for these rich of my flock, for it was dreadful to think of their being poor inside, if not outside.

Perhaps I ought to have been as anxious about poor Farmer Brownrigg as about the beautiful lady. But the farmer had given me good reason to hope for some progress in him, after the way he had given in about Jane Rogers. Positively I had caught his eye during the sermon that very day. And we are nowhere told to love everybody alike, only to love everyone who comes within our reach as ourselves.

I made Mrs. Pearson sit down with me to dinner, for Christmas Day was not a time to dine alone. Ever since, I have had my servants dine with me on Christmas Day.

When we had finished our dinner, and I was sitting alone drinking a cup of tea before going out again, Mrs. Pearson came in and told me that little Gerard Weir wanted to see me. The little fellow entered, looking very shy, and clinging first to the door and then to the wall.

"Come, my dear boy," I said, "and sit down by me." He came directly and stood before me.

"Please, Sir," he said, putting his hand in his pocket, "Mother gave me some goodies, and I kept them till I saw you come back, and here they are, Sir."

I said, "Thank you," and I ate them up, every one of them, that he might see me at them before he left the house. And the dear child went off radiant.

Then I went out again, and made another round of visits. Those whom I could not see that day I saw on the following days between it and the new year, and so ended my Christmas holiday with my people.

TWELVE

The Avenue

After Christmas I found myself in closer relationship to my parishioners. I visited, of course, at the Hall, as at the farmhouse in the country and the cottages in the village. I did not come to like Mrs. Oldcastle better, and there was one woman in the house whom I disliked still more—that Sarah whom Judy had called in my hearing a white wolf. Her face was yet whiter than that of her mistress, only it was not smooth like hers—its whiteness came apparently from smallpox which had so thickened the skin that no blood could shine through. I seldom saw her—only, indeed, caught a glimpse of her now and then as I passed through the house.

Nor did I make much progress with Mr. Stoddart. He always had something friendly to say, and some theosophical theory to bring forward. He was a great reader of mystical books, and yet the man's nature seemed cold. It was sunshiny, but not sunny. His intellect was rather a lambent flame than genial warmth. He could make things, but he could not grow anything. And when I came to see that he had had more than anyone else to do with the education of Miss Oldcastle, I understood her a little better. For to teach speculation instead of devotion, mysticism instead of love, word instead of deed, is surely repressive to the nature meant for sunbright activity. My chief perplexity continued to be how he could play the organ as he did.

I have not much more to tell about this winter. As out of a whole changeful season only one day will cling to the memory, so of that winter nothing more of nature or human nature occurs to me worth recording. I will pass on to the summer season, though the early spring will detain me with the relation of a single incident.

I was on my way to the Hall to see Mr. Stoddart. I wanted to ask him whether something could not be done beyond his exquisite playing to rouse the sense of music in my people. Now I had, I confess, little hope of moving Mr. Stoddart in the matter; but if I should succeed, I thought it would do him good to mingle with his humble fellows in the attempt to do them a trifle of good.

It was just beginning to grow dusk. The wind was blustering in gusts among the trees. There was just one cold bar of light in the west, and the east was one gray mass, while overhead the stars were twinkling. The grass and all the ground about the trees was very wet. The time seemed more dreary somehow than the winter. Rigor was past, and tenderness had not come, for the wind was cold without being keen, and whirled about me as if it wanted me to join in its fierce play.

Suddenly I saw, in a walk that ran along the avenue, Miss Oldcastle struggling against the wind. I had supposed her with her mother in London, whither their journeys had been not infrequent since Christmas. And why should she be fighting with the wind, so far from the house, with only a shawl drawn over her head?

Passing between two great tree trunks, I was by her side in a moment. But the noise of the wind prevented her from hearing my approach, and when I uttered her name, she started violently and, turning, drew herself up very haughtily, in part to hide her tremor.

"I beg your pardon," I said. "I have startled you dreadfully."

"Not in the least," she replied, but without moving, and still with a curve in her form like the neck of a frayed horse.

"I was on my way to call on Mr. Stoddart," I said.

"You will find him at home, I believe."

"I fancied you and Mrs. Oldcastle in London."

"We returned yesterday."

Still she stood as before. I made a movement in the direction of the house. She seemed as if she would walk in the opposite direction.

"May I not walk with you to the house?"

"I am not going in just yet."

"Are you protected enough for such a night?"

"I enjoy the wind."

I bowed and walked on. What else could I do?

I cannot say that I enjoyed leaving her behind me in the gathering dark, the wind blowing her about with no more reverence than if she had been a bush of privet. Nor was it with a light heart that I bore her repulse as I slowly climbed the hill to the house.

Sarah opened the glass door, her black, glossy, restless eyes looking out of her white face from under the gray eyebrows. I knew at once by her look beyond me that she had expected to find me accompanied by her young mistress. I did not volunteer any information.

As I had feared, I found that, although Mr. Stoddart seemed to listen with some interest to what I said about the music in the church, I could not bring him to the point of making any practical suggestion, or of responding to one made by me, and I left with the conviction that he would do nothing to help me. Yet during the whole of our interview he had not opposed a single word I said. He was like clay too much softened with water to keep the form into which it has been modeled. He would take some kind of form easily, and lose it yet more easily. I did not show all my dissatisfaction, however, for that would only have estranged us. It is not required, nay, it may be wrong, to show all we feel or think. What is required of us is *not* to show what we do *not* feel or think, for that is to be false.

I left the house in a gloomy mood. I know I ought to have looked up to God and said, "These things do not reach to Thee, my Father. Thou art ever the same. I rise above my small as well as my great troubles by remembering Thy peace, and Thy unchangeable godhood to me and all Thy creatures." But I did not come to myself all at once. The thought of God had not come, though it was sure to come. I was brooding over the littleness of all I could do, and feeling that sickness which sometimes will overtake a man in the midst of the work he likes best, when the unpleasant parts of it crowd upon him and his own efforts—especially those made from the will without sustaining impulse—come back upon him with a feeling of unreality, decay, and bitterness, as if he had been unnatural and untrue, and putting himself in false relations by false efforts for good. I know this all came from selfishness—thinking about myself instead of about God and my neighbor. But so it was. And I was walking down the avenue, now very dark, with my head bent to the ground. I started at the sound of a woman's voice and, looking up, saw by the starlight the dim form of Miss Oldcastle before me.

She spoke first.

"Mr. Walton, I was very rude to you. I beg your pardon."

"Indeed, I did not think so. I only thought what a blundering, awkward fellow I was to startle you as I did. You have to forgive me."

"I fancy"—and here I know she smiled—"I fancy I have made that even, for you must confess I startled you now."

"You did, but in a very different way. I annoyed you with my rudeness. You only scattered a swarm of bats that kept flapping their skinny wings in my face."

"What do you mean? There are no bats at this time of year."

"Not outside. In 'winter and rough weather' they creep inside, you know."

"Ah! I ought to understand you. But I did not think you were ever like that. I thought you were too good."

"I wish I were. I hope to be someday. I am not yet, anyhow. And I thank you for driving the bats away."

"You make me the more ashamed of myself to think that perhaps my rudeness had a share in bringing them. Yours is, no doubt, thankless labor sometimes."

She seemed to make the last remark just to prevent the conversation from returning to her as its subject.

The wind rose again with a gush in the trees. Was it fancy? Or, as the wind moved the shrubbery, did I see a white face? And could it be the White Wolf?

I spoke aloud, "But it is cruel to keep you standing here in such a night. You must be a real lover of nature to walk in the dark wind."

"I like it. Good night."

So we parted. I gazed into the darkness after her, though she disappeared at the distance of a yard or two. I would have stood longer, had I not still suspected the proximity of Judy's Wolf, which made me turn and go home.

I met Miss Oldcastle several times before the summer, but her old manner remained, or rather had returned, for there had been nothing of it in the tone of her voice in that interview, if interview it could be called where neither could see more than the other's outline.

THIRTEEN
Young Weir

By slow degrees the summer bloomed. Green came instead of white, rainbows instead of icicles. I often wandered in the fields and woods, with a book in my hand at which I often did not look the whole day, and which yet I liked to have with me. And I seemed somehow to come back with most on those days in which I did not read. I prepared almost all my sermons that summer in the open country, but had another custom before I preached them—to spend the Saturday evening not in my study but in the church. It was always clean and ready for me after midday, so that I could be alone there as soon as I pleased.

This fine old church was not the expression of the religious feeling of my time. There was a gloom about it—a sacred gloom, I know, and I loved it—but such gloom was not in my feeling when I talked to my flock. The place soothed me, tuned me to a solemn mood of gentle gladness; but, had I been an architect, and had I had to build a church, I am certain it would have been very different from this. For I always found the open air the most genial influence upon me. Our Lord seemed so much to delight in the open air, and late in the day, as well as early in the morning, He would climb the mountain to be alone with His Father.

I therefore sought to bridge this difference, to find an easy passage between the open air and the church, so as to bring into the church the fresh air and the gladness over all. I thought my sermon over again in the afternoon sun slanting through the stained window, pacing up and down the solemn old place, hanging my thought here on a cricket, there on a corbel, and now on the gable point over which Weir's face would gaze next morning. And when the next day came, I found the forms around me so interwoven with the forms of my thought, that I felt almost like one of the old monks who had built the place.

One lovely Saturday, I had been out all morning. I had my Greek Testament with me, and I read when I sat and thought when I walked. I was planning to preach about the cloud of witnesses and explain this did not mean persons looking at our behavior—as if any addition could be made to the awfulness of the fact that the eye of God was upon us—but witnesses to the truth, people who did what God wanted them to do, come of it what might, whether a crown or a rack, scoffs or applause. When I came home I had an early dinner, and then betook myself to my Saturday resort.

All through the slowly fading afternoon, the autumn of the day when the colors are richest and the shadows long and lengthening, I paced my solemn, old-thoughted church. Sometimes I sat in the pulpit, looking on the ancient walls which had grown up under men's hands that men might be helped to pray, and I thought how many witnesses to the truth had knelt in those ancient pews. And my eye was caught by a yellow light that gilded the apex of the font cover, which had been wrought like a flame or a bursting blossom, and then by a red light all over a white marble tablet in the wall—the red of life and the cold hue of the grave. And this red light did not come from any work of man, but from the great window of the west, which little Gerard Weir wanted to help God to paint. And I lingered on till the night had come—till the church only gloomed about me and had no shine—and then I found my spirit burning up the clearer, as a lamp which has been flaming all the day with light unseen becomes a glory in the room when the sun is gone down.

At length I felt tired and would go home. Yet I lingered for a few moments in the vestry, thinking what hymns would harmonize best with the things I wanted to make my people think about. It was now quite dark out-of-doors. Suddenly I heard a moan and a sob. I listened, but heard nothing more, and concluded I had deceived myself. So I left the church by my vestry door and took my way along the path through the clustered graves.

Again I heard a sob. This time I was sure of it. And there lay something dark upon one of the grassy mounds. I approached it, but it did not move. I spoke. "Can I be of any use to you?" I said.

"No," returned an almost inaudible voice.

Though I did not know whose was the grave, I knew that no one had been buried there very lately, and if the grief were for the loss of the dead, it was more than probably aroused to fresh vigor by recent misfortune. I stopped and, taking the figure by the arm, said, "Come with me, and let us see what can be done for you."

Then I saw that it was a youth, perhaps scarcely more than a boy. And as soon as I saw that, I knew that his grief could hardly be incurable. He returned no answer, but rose at once to his feet and submitted to be led away. I took him the shortest road to my house through the shrubbery, brought him into the study, made him sit down in my easy chair and rang for lights and wine, for the dew had been falling heavily and his clothes were quite dank. But when the wine came he refused to take any.

"But you want it," I said.

"No, Sir, I don't, indeed."

"Take some for my sake, then."

"I would rather not, Sir."

"Why?"

"I promised my father a year ago, when I left for London, that I would not drink anything stronger than water. I can't break my promise now."

"That wasn't your father's grave I found you upon, was it?"

"No, Sir, it was my mother's. You know my father very well, Thomas Weir."

"Ah! He told me he had a son in London. Then what is the matter? Your father is a good friend of mine and would tell you you might trust me."

"I don't doubt it, Sir. But you won't believe me any more than my father."

The boy was of middle size but evidently not full grown. His dress was very decent. His face was pale and thin, and revealed a likeness to his father. He had blue eyes that looked full at me and, as far as I could judge, an honest and sensitive nature. I was therefore emboldened to press for his story.

"I cannot promise to believe whatever you say. But if you tell me the truth, I like you too much already to be in great danger of doubting you, for you know the truth has a force of its own."

"I thought so till tonight," he answered. "But if my father would not believe me, how can I expect you to do so, Sir?"

"Your father may have been too much troubled by your story to do it justice. It is not a bit like your father to be unfair."

"No, Sir. And so much the less chance of your believing me."

Somehow his talk prepossessed me still more in his favor, and I became more and more certain that he would yet tell me the truth. "Come, try me," I said.

"I will, Sir. But I must begin at the beginning."

"Begin where you like. I have nothing more to do tonight, and you may take what time you please. But I will ring for tea first, for I daresay you have not made any promise about that."

A faint smile flickered on his face. He was evidently beginning to feel a little more comfortable.

"When did you arrive from London?" I asked.

"About two hours ago, I suppose."

"Bring tea, Mrs. Pearson, and that cold chicken and ham, and plenty of toast. We are both hungry." Mrs. Pearson gave a questioning look at the lad and departed to do her duty.

When she returned with the tray and we were left alone, I would not let him say a word till he had made a good meal. Few troubles will destroy a growing lad's hunger; indeed, it has always been to me a marvel how the feelings and the appetite affect each other.

After the tea things had been taken away, I put the candles out, for I thought that he might find it easier to tell his story in the moonlight. So, sitting by the window, he told his tale. The moon lighted up his pale face as he told it and gave a wild expression to his eyes.

He had, he told me, filled a place in the employment of Messrs. Bates and Co., large silk mercers, linen drapers, etc., etc., in London. His work at first was to accompany one of the carts which delivered purchases, but they took him at length into the shop to wait behind the counter. This he did not like so much but, as it was considered a rise in life, he made no objection to the change.

He seemed to himself to get on pretty well. He soon learned all the marks on the goods understood by the shopmen, and within a few months believed that he was found generally useful. He had as yet no distinct department allotted to him, but was moved from place to place as business might demand.

"I confess," he said, "that I was not always satisfied with what was going on about me. I could not help doubting if everything was done on the square, as they say. But nothing came plainly my way, and so I could honestly say it did not concern me. But one day while I was showing a lady some handkerchiefs, she said she did not believe they were French cambric. Knowing little about it, I said nothing. But happening to look up, I caught sight of the shopwalker—the man who shows customers where to go for what they want and sees that they are attended to. He was a fat man, dressed in black, with a great gold chain which they say in the shop is only copper gilt. He was standing staring at me. From that day I often caught him watching me, as if I had been a customer suspected of shoplifting. I only thought he was disagreeable, and tried to forget him.

"The day before yesterday, two ladies, an old lady and a young one, came into the shop, and wanted to look at some shawls. I am sure the two were Mrs. and Miss Oldcastle of the Hall. They wanted to buy a cashmere for the young lady. I showed them some but they wanted better. I brought the best we had. They asked the price and I told them. They said they were not good enough and wanted to see some more. I told them they were the best we had. They looked at them again, said the shawls were not good enough, and left the shop without buying a thing. I proceeded to take the shawls upstairs again and, as I went, I passed the shopwalker whom I had not observed. 'You're for no good, young man!' he said, with a nasty sneer.

" 'What do you mean by that?' I asked, for his sneer made me angry.

" 'You'll know before tomorrow,' he answered, and walked away.

"That same evening, as we were shutting up shop, I was sent for to the manager's room. The moment I entered, he said, 'You won't suit us, young man, I find. You had better pack up your box tonight, and be off tomorrow. There's your quarter's salary.'

" 'What have I done?' I asked in astonishment, and yet with a vague suspicion.

" 'It's not what you've done, but what you won't do,' he answered. 'Do you think we can afford to keep you here and pay you wages to send people away from the shop without buying? If you do, you're mistaken. You may go.'

" 'But what could I do?' I said. 'I suppose that spy. . . .'

" 'Now, now, young man, none of your sauce!' said Mr. Barlow. 'Honest people don't think about spies.'

" 'I thought it was for honesty you were getting rid of me,' I said.

"Mr. Barlow rose to his feet, his lips white, and pointed to the door. 'Take your money and be off. And mind you don't refer to me for a character. After such impudence I couldn't in conscience give you one.' Then, calming down a little when he saw I turned to go, 'You had better take to your hands again, for your head will never keep you. There, be off!' he said, pushing the money toward me and turning his back to me. I could not touch it.

" 'Keep the money, Mr. Barlow,' I said. 'It will make up for what you've lost by me.' And I left the room at once.

"While I was packing my box, one of my chums came in, and I told him all about it. He laughed and said, 'What a fool you are, Weir! You'll never make your daily bread. If you knew what I know, you'd have known better. Mr. Barlow was serving some ladies himself. They wanted the best Indian shawl they could get. None of those he showed them were good enough, for the ladies really didn't know one from another. They always go by the price you ask, and Mr. Barlow knew that well enough. He sent me upstairs for the shawls, and as I brought them he said, "These are the best imported, Madam." There were three ladies, and one shook her head, and another shook her head, and they all shook their heads. And then Mr. Barlow was sorry that he had said they were the best. But you won't catch him in a trap. He's too old a fox for that. He looked close down at the shawls, as if he were shortsighted, though he could see as far as any man. "I beg your pardon, ladies," said he, "you're right. I am quite wrong. What a stupid blunder to make! And yet they did deceive me. Here, Johnson, take these shawls away. I will fetch the thing you want myself, ladies." He chose out three or four shawls, of the nicest patterns, from the very same lot, marked in the very same way, folded them differently, and gave them to me to carry down. "Now, ladies, here they are!" he said. "These are quite a different thing, as you will see—and, indeed, they cost half as much again." In five minutes they bought two of them, and paid just half as much more than he asked for them the first time. That's Mr. Barlow! And that's what you should have done if you had wanted to keep your place.' But I assure you, Sir, I could not help being glad to be out of it."

"But there is nothing in all this to be miserable about," I said. "You did your duty."

"It would be all right, Sir, if Father believed me. I don't want to be idle, I'm sure."

"Does your father think you do?"

"I don't know what he thinks. He won't speak to me. I told my story—as much of it as he would let me, at least—but he wouldn't listen to me. He only said he knew better than that. I couldn't bear it. He always was rather hard on us. I'm sure if you hadn't been so kind to me, Sir, I don't know what I should have done by this time. I haven't another friend in the world."

"Yes, you have. Your Father in heaven is your friend."

"I don't know that, Sir. I'm not good enough."

"That's quite true. But you would never have done your duty if He had not been with you. Everything good comes from the Father of lights. Everyone who walks in any light walks in His light, for there is no light—only darkness—from below. Man, apart from God, can generate no light."

"I think I understand. But I didn't feel good at all in the matter. I didn't see any other way of doing."

"So much the better. We ought never to feel good. We are but unprofitable servants at best. There is no merit in doing your duty; you would have been a poor wretched creature not to do as you did. And now, instead of making yourself miserable over the consequences of it, you ought to bear them like a man, with courage and hope, thanking God that He has made you suffer for righteousness' sake and denied you the success and the praise of cheating. I will go to your father at once and find out what he is thinking about it, for no doubt Mr. Barlow has written to him with his version of the story. Perhaps he will be more inclined to believe you when he finds that I believe you."

"Oh, thank you, Sir!" cried the lad, and jumped up from his seat to go with me.

"No," I said, "you had better stay where you are. I shall be able to speak more freely if you are not present. Here is a book to amuse yourself with. I do not think I shall be long gone."

But I was longer gone than I thought I should be.

When I reached the carpenter's house I found, to my surprise, that he was still at work. By the light of a single tallow candle beside him on the bench, he was plowing away at a groove. He looked up, but, without even greeting me, dropped his pale face again and went on with his work.

"What!" I said, cheerily. "Working so late?"

"Yes, Sir."

"It is not unusual with you, I know."

"It's all a humbug!" he said fiercely, but coldly. He stood erect from his work, and turned his white face full on me, though his eyes dropped. "It's all a humbug, and I don't mean to be humbugged anymore. Tell me that a God governs the world! What have I done, to be used like this?"

I thought with myself how I could retort for his young son: "What has he done to be used like this?" I could only stand and wait. "It would be wrong in me to pretend ignorance," I said. "I know all about it."

"He has been to you, has he? But you don't know all about it, Sir. The impudence of the young rascal! Me to be treated like this! One child a. . . ." Here came a terrible break in his speech. But he tried again. "And the other a. . . . " Instead of finishing the sentence he drove his plow fiercely through the groove, splitting off some inches of the wall of it at the end.

"If anyone has treated you so," I said, "it must be the devil, not God."

"But if there were a God, He could have prevented it all."

"Mind what I said to you once before—He hasn't done yet. And there is another enemy in His way as bad as the devil—ourselves. When people want to walk their own way without God, God lets them try it. And then the devil gets a hold of them. But God won't let him keep them. As soon as they are 'wearied in the greatness of their way,' they begin to look about for a Saviour. And then they find God ready to pardon, ready to help, not breaking the bruised reed but leading them to His own self manifest. God is tender—just like the prodigal son's father—only with this difference, that God has millions of prodigals, and never gets tired of going out to meet them and welcome them back, every one as if he were the only prodigal son He had ever had. There's a Father indeed! Have you been such a father to your son?"

"The prodigal didn't come with a pack of lies. He told his father the truth, bad as it was."

"How do you know that your son didn't tell you the truth? All the young men that go from home don't do as the prodigal did. Why should you not believe what he tells you?"

He handed me a letter. I took it and read:

"Sir—It has become our painful duty to inform you that your son has this day been discharged from our employment, his conduct not being such as to justify the confidence hitherto reposed in him. It would have been contrary to the interests of the establishment to continue him longer behind the counter, although we are not prepared to urge anything against him beyond the fact that he has shown himself absolutely indifferent to the interests of his employers. We trust that the chief blame will be found to lie with certain connections of a kind easily formed in large cities, and that the loss of his situation here may be punishment sufficient, if not for justice, yet to make him consider his ways and be wise. We enclose his quarter's salary, which the young man rejected with insult, and we remain, etc., Bates and Co."

"And," I exclaimed, "this is what you found your judgment of your own son upon! You reject him unheard, and take the word of a stranger! I don't wonder you cannot believe in your Father when you behave so to your son. I don't say your conclusion is false—though I don't believe it—but I do say the grounds you go on are anything but sufficient."

"You don't mean to tell me that a man of Mr. Barlow's standing, who manages one of the largest shops in London, and whose brother is mayor of Addicehead, would slander a poor lad like that!"

"O you mammon-worshiper!" I cried. "Because a man runs one of the largest shops in London, and his brother is mayor of Addicehead, you take his testimony and refuse your son's! I did not know the boy till this evening—but I call upon you to bring back to your memory all that you have known of him from his childhood, and then ask yourself whether there is not at least as much probability of his having remained honest as of the master of a great London shop being infallible in his conclusions."

The pale face of the carpenter was red as fire, for he had been acting contrary to all his own theories of human equality, and that in a shameful manner. Still, whether convinced or not, he would not give in. He only drove away at his work, which he was utterly destroying. His mouth was closed tight, and his eyes gleamed over the ruined board with a light which seemed to have more obstinacy in it than contrition.

"Ah, Thomas!" I said, "if God had behaved to us as you have behaved to your boy—be he innocent, be he guilty—there's not a man or woman of all our lost race would have returned to Him from the time of Adam till now. I don't wonder that you find it difficult to believe in Him."

And with those words I left the shop, determined to overwhelm the unbeliever with proof, and put him to shame before his own soul whence, I thought, would come even more good to him than to his son. For there was a great deal of self-satisfaction mixed up with the man's honesty, and the sooner that had a blow the better. It was pride that lay at the root of his hardness. He visited the daughter's fault upon thc son. His daughter had disgraced him—her he had never forgiven—and now his pride flung his son out after her upon the first suspicion. His imagination had filled up all the blanks in the wicked insinuations of Mr. Barlow. His pride paralyzed his love. He thought more about himself than about his children. It was a lesser matter that they should be guilty than that he, their father, should be disgraced.

Thinking over all this, and forgetting how late it was, I found myself halfway up the avenue of the Hall. I wanted to find out whether the ladies were Mrs. and Miss Oldcastle. What a point if they were! I should not then be satisfied except I could prevail on Miss Oldcastle to accompany me to Thomas Weir. So eager was I that it was not till I stood before the house that I saw clearly the impropriety of attempting anything further that night. One light only was burning, and that on the first floor.

As I turned to go down the hill again, I saw a corner of the blind drawn aside, and a face peeping out—whose, I could not tell. This was uncomfortable, for what could be taking me there at such a time? But I walked steadily away, certain I could not escape recognition, and determining to refer to this ill-considered visit when I called again.

I lingered on the bridge as I went home. Not a light was to be seen in the village except one over Catharine Weir's shop. There were not many restless souls in my parish, not so many as there ought to be. Yet gladly would I see the troubled in peace—not a moment, though, before their troubles should have brought them where the weary and heavy-laden can alone find rest to their souls.

I had little immediate comfort to give my young guest, but I had plenty of hope. I told him he must stay in the house tomorrow, for it would be better to have the reconciliation with his father over before he appeared in public.

So the next day neither Weir was at church.

As soon as the afternoon service was over, I went to the Hall and was shown into the drawing room. It looked down upon the lawn, where Mrs. Oldcastle sat reading. A little way off sat Miss Oldcastle, with a book on her knee, but her gaze fixed on the landscape before her. I caught glimpses of Judy flitting among the trees, never a moment in one place.

Fearful of having an interview with the old lady alone, which was not likely to lead to what I wanted, I stepped out on the terrace, and thence down the steps to the lawn below. The servant had just informed Mrs. Oldcastle of my visit when I came near. She drew herself up in her chair, and evidently chose to regard my approach as an intrusion.

"I did not expect a visit from you today, Mr. Walton, you will allow me to say."

"I am doing Sunday work," I answered. "Will you kindly tell me whether you were in London on Thursday last? But stay—allow me to ask Miss Oldcastle to join us."

Without waiting for an answer, I went to Miss Oldcastle and begged her to come and listen to something in which I wanted her help. She rose courteously, though without cordiality, and accompanied me to her mother who sat with perfect rigidity watching us.

"Again let me ask," I said, "if you were in London on Thursday?"

Though I addressed the old lady, the answer came from her daughter. "Yes, we were."

"Were you in Bates and Co.'s, in Dublin Street?"

But now, before Miss Oldcastle could reply, her mother interposed. "Are we charged with shoplifting, Mr. Walton? Really, one is not accustomed to such cross-questioning, except from a lawyer."

"Have patience with me for a moment," I returned. "I am not going to be mysterious for more than two or three questions. Please tell me whether you were in that shop or not."

"I believe we were," said the mother.

"Yes, certainly," said the daughter.

"Did you buy anything?"

"No. We—" Miss Oldcastle began.

"Not a word more," I exclaimed, eagerly. "Come with me at once."

"What do you mean, Mr. Walton?" said the mother, with a sort of cold indignation, while the daughter looked surprised, but said nothing.

"I beg your pardon for my impetuosity, but much is in your power at this moment. The son of one of my parishioners has come home in trouble. His father, Thomas Weir—"

"Ah!" said Mrs. Oldcastle, in a tone considerably at strife with refinement. But I took no notice.

"His father will not believe his story. The lad thinks you are the ladies whom he was serving when he got into trouble. I am so confident he tells the truth, that I want Miss Oldcastle to be so kind as to accompany me to Weir's house—"

"Really, Mr. Walton, I am astonished at your making such a request!" exclaimed Mrs. Oldcastle. "To ask Miss Oldcastle to accompany you to the dwelling of the ringleader of all the *canaille* of the neighborhood!"

"It is for the sake of justice," I interposed.

"That is no concern of ours. Let them fight it out between them. I am sure any trouble that comes of it is no more than they all deserve. A low family—men and women!"

"I assure you, I think very differently. However, neither your opinion nor mine has anything to do with the matter." Here I turned to Miss Oldcastle and went on. "It is a chance which seldom occurs in one's life, Miss Oldcastle—a chance of setting wrong right by a word. As a minister of the Gospel of truth and love, I beg you to assist me with your presence to that end."

I would have spoken more strongly, but I knew that her word given to me would be enough without her presence. At my last words, Mrs. Oldcastle rose to her feet, her face whiter than usual.

"You dare to persist! You take advantage of your profession to drag my daughter into a vile dispute between people of the lowest class—against the positive command of her only parent! Have you no respect for her position in society? For her sex? *Mister Walton,* you act in a manner unworthy of your cloth."

I had stood with as much self-possession as I could muster, and I believe I should have borne it all quietly but for that last word. If there is one epithet I hate more than another, it is that execrable word *cloth* used for the office of a clergyman.

"Madam," I said, "I owe nothing to my tailor, but I owe God my whole being, and my neighbor all I can do for him. 'He that loveth not his brother is a murderer,' or murderess, as the case may be."

At the word *murderess,* her face became livid and she turned without reply. By this time her daughter was halfway to the house. She followed her. And here was I left to go home, with the full knowledge that, partly from trying to gain too much, and partly from losing my temper, I had at best a mangled and unsatisfactory testimony to carry back to Thomas Weir.

I walked away, round the end of the house and down the avenue, and the farther I went the more mortified I grew. It was not merely the shame of losing my temper, though that was a shame—and with a woman too, merely because she used a common epithet!—but I saw that it must appear very strange to the carpenter that I had not learned anything decisive in the matter. It only amounted to this—that Mrs. and Miss Oldcastle were in the shop on the very day on which Weir was dismissed. It proved that so much of what he had told me was correct, nothing more.

In fact, I had lost all the certain good of my attempt, in part from the foolish desire to produce a conviction *of* Weir, rather than *in* Weir, which should be triumphant and melodramatic, and—must I confess it?—should punish him for not believing in his son when I did, forgetting in my selfishness that not to believe in his son was unspeakable punishment enough.

I felt humiliated, and humiliation is a very different condition of mind from humility. Humiliation no man can desire, for it is shame and torture. Humility is the true, right condition of humanity—peaceful, divine. And yet a man may gladly welcome humiliation when it comes, if he finds that it has turned him right round, with his face away from pride and toward humility. To me there came an effective dissolution of the bonds both of pride and humiliation, and I became nearly as anxious to heal Weir's wounded spirit as I was to work justice for his son.

I was still walking slowly, with burning cheek and downcast eyes, away from the great house (which seemed to be staring after me down the avenue with all its window-eyes) when suddenly my deliverance came. At a sharp turn, where the avenue changed into a winding road, Miss Oldcastle stood waiting for me, the glow of haste upon her cheek, and the firmness of resolution upon her lips.

"Mr. Walton, what do you want me to do? I would not willingly refuse, if it is, as you say, my duty to go with you."

"I cannot be positive about that," I answered. "I think I put it too strongly. But it would be a considerable advantage, I think, if you would go with me and let me ask you a few questions in the presence of Thomas Weir."

"I will go."

"A thousand thanks. But how did you manage to—" Here I stopped, not knowing how to finish the question.

"You are surprised that I came, notwithstanding Mamma's objection to my going? Do you think obedience to parents is to last forever? The honor is, of course. But I am surely old enough to be right in following my conscience at least."

"You mistake me. That is not the difficulty at all. Of course you ought to do what is right against the highest authority on earth, which I take to be the parental. What I am surprised at is your courage."

"Not because of its degree, only that it is mine!" And she sighed. She was quite right, and I did not know what to answer. "I know I am cowardly. But, if I cannot dare, I can bear. Is it not strange? With my mother looking at me, I dare not say a word, dare hardly move against her will. And it is not always a good will. I cannot honor my mother as I would. But the moment her eyes are off me I can do anything, knowing the consequences perfectly, and just as regardless of them. Once she kept me shut up in my room, and sent me only bread and water, for a whole week to the very hour. Not that I minded that much, but it will let you know a little of my position in my own home. That is why I walked away before her. I saw what was coming."

And Miss Oldcastle drew herself up with more expression of pride than I had yet seen in her, revealing to me that perhaps I had misunderstood the source of her apparent haughtiness. I could not reply for indignation. My silence must have been the cause of what she said next.

"Ah! You think I have no right to speak so about my own mother! Well! But indeed I would not have done so a month ago."

"If I am silent, Miss Oldcastle, it is that my sympathy is too strong. There are mothers and mothers, and for a mother not to be a mother is too dreadful." She made no reply. "Perhaps—and I shall feel more honest when I have said it—the only thing I feel should be altered in your conduct is that you should dare your mother. Do not think that my meaning is a vulgar one. If it were, I should at least know better than to utter it to you. What I mean is that you ought to be able to be and do the same before your mother's eyes that you are and do when she is out of sight."

"I *know* that. I know it *well*. But you do not know what a spell she casts upon me, how impossible it is to do as you say."

"Difficult, I allow. Impossible, not. You will never be free till you do."

We walked in silence for some minutes. At length she said, "My mother's self-will amounts to madness, I do believe. I have yet to learn where she would stop of herself."

"All self-will is madness," I returned. "To want one's own way, just and only because it is one's own way, is the height of madness."

"Perhaps. But when madness has to be encountered as if it were sense, it makes it no easier to know that it is madness."

"Does your uncle give you no help?"

"He is as frightened of her as I am! He dares not even go away. He did not know what he was coming to when he came to Oldcastle Hall. Dear Uncle! I owe him a great deal. But for any help of that sort, he is of no more use than a child. I believe Mamma looks upon him as half an idiot. He can do anything or everything but help one to live, to *be* anything. O me! I *am* so tired!" And the proud lady burst out crying.

By this time we were at the gate, and as soon as we had passed the guardian monstrosities, we found the open road an effectual antidote to tears. When we came within sight of the old house where Weir lived, Miss Oldcastle became again a little curious as to what I required of her.

"Trust me," I said. "There is nothing mysterious about it. Only I prefer the truth to come out fresh in the ears of the man most concerned."

"I do trust you," she answered. And we knocked at the house door.

Thomas Weir himself opened the door, with a candle in hand. He looked very much astonished to see his lady visitor. He asked us in, politely enough, and ushered us into the large room upstairs. There sat the old man, as I had first seen him, by the side of the fire. He received us with more than politeness—with courtesy—and I could not help glancing at Miss Oldcastle to see what impression this family of "low, freethinking republicans" made upon her. It was easy to discover that the impression was of favorable surprise. But I was as much surprised at her behavior as she was at theirs. Not a haughty tone was to be heard in her voice, not a haughty movement to be seen in her form. She accepted the chair offered her and sat down by the fireside, perfectly at home, only that she turned toward me, waiting for what explanation I might think proper to give.

Before I had time to speak, however, old Mr. Weir broke the silence. "I've been telling Tom, Sir, as I've told him many a time afore, as how he's a deal too hard with his children."

"Father!" interrupted Thomas angrily.

"Have patience a bit, my boy," persisted the old man, turning again toward me. "Now, Sir, he won't even hear young Tom's side of the story, and I say that boy won't tell him no lie if he's the same boy he went away."

"I tell you, Father," again began Thomas, but this time I interposed, to prevent useless talk beforehand.

"Thomas," I said, "listen to me. I have heard your son's side of the story. Because of something he said, I went to Miss Oldcastle and asked her whether she was in that shop last Thursday. That is all I have asked her, and all she has told me is that she was. I know no more than you what she is going to reply to my questions now, but I have no doubt her answers will correspond to your son's story."

I then put my questions to Miss Oldcastle, whose answers amounted to this: that they had wanted to buy a shawl; that they had seen none good enough; that they had left the shop without buying anything; and that they had been waited upon by a young man who, while perfectly polite and attentive to their wants, did not seem to have the ways or manners of a London shoplad. And that was all.

"I think, Mr. Walton, if you have done with me, I ought to go home now," said Miss Oldcastle.

"Certainly," I answered. "I will take you home at once. I am greatly obliged to you for coming."

"Indeed, Sir," said the old man, rising with difficulty, "we're obliged to both you and the lady more than we can tell. To take such a deal of trouble for us! But you see, Sir, you're one of them as thinks a man's got his duty to do one way or another, whether he be clergyman or carpenter. God bless you, Miss. You're of the right sort, which you'll excuse an old man, Miss, as'll never see ye again till ye've got the wings as ye ought to have."

Miss Oldcastle smiled very sweetly and answered nothing, but shook hands with them both and bade them good-night. Weir could not speak a word—he could hardly even lift his eyes. But a red spot glowed on each of his pale cheeks, making him look very like his daughter Catharine, and I could see Miss Oldcastle wince and grow red too with the grip he gave her hand. But she smiled again none the less sweetly.

"I will see Miss Oldcastle home, and then go back to my house and bring the boy with me," I said as we left.

It was some time before either Miss Oldcastle or I spoke. The sun was setting, the sky, the earth, and the air were lovely with rosy light, and the world full of that peculiar calm which belongs to the evening of the day of rest. Surely the world ought to wake better on the morrow.

"Not very dangerous people, those, Miss Oldcastle," I said at last.

"I thank you very much for taking me to see them," she returned, cordially.

"You won't believe all you may happen to hear against the working people now?"

"I never did."

"There are ill-conditioned, cross-grained, low-minded, selfish, unbelieving people among them. God knows it. But there are ladies and gentlemen among them too."

"That old man is a gentleman."

"He is. And the only way to teach them all to be such is to be such to them. The man who does not show himself a gentleman to the working people—why should I call them the poor? Some of them are better off than many of the rich, for they can pay their debts and do it—"

I had forgot the beginning of my sentence.

"You were saying that the man who does not show himself a gentleman to the poor—"

"Is no gentleman at all, only a gentle without the man; and if you consult my namesake, old Izaak, you will find what that is."

"I will look. I know your way now. You won't tell me anything I can find out for myself."

"Is it not the best way?"

"Yes. Because, for one thing, you find out so much more than you look for."

"Certainly that has been my own experience."

"I am very glad you asked me to go tonight."

"If people only knew their own brothers and sisters, the kingdom of heaven would not be far off."

I do not think Miss Oldcastle quite liked this, for she was silent thereafter. And we had now come close to the house.

"I wish I could help you," I said.

"In what?"

"To bear what I fear is waiting you."

"I told you I was equal to that. It is where we are unequal that we want help. You may have to help me someday—who knows?"

I left her most unwillingly on the porch, though rejoicing in my heart over her last words. (Although I do happen to know how she fared that night after I left, the painful record is not essential to my story.)

Later, when young Tom and I came to his father's house and entered the room, his grandfather rose and tottered to meet him. His father made one step toward him and then hesitated. Of all conditions of the human mind, that of being ashamed of himself must have been the strangest to Thomas Weir. His fall had been from the pinnacle of pride. I call it Thomas Weir's fall, for surely to behave in an unfatherly manner to both daughter and son—the one sinful, and therefore needing the more tenderness; the other innocent, and therefore claiming justification—and to do so from pride, and hurt pride, was fall enough. And now, if he was humbled in the one instance, there would be room to hope he might become humble in the other. But I had soon to see that for a time, his pride, driven from his entrenchment against his son, only retreated with all its forces into the other against his daughter.

Before a moment had passed, however, justice overcame so far that he held out his hand and said, "Come, Tom, let bygones be bygones."

But I stepped between. "Thomas Weir," I said, "I have too great a regard for you—and you know I dare not flatter you—to let you off this way, or rather leave you to think you have done your duty when you have not done the half of it. You have done your son a wrong, a great wrong. How can you claim to be a gentleman—I say nothing of being a Christian, for there you make no claim—if, having done a man wrong you don't beg his pardon?"

He did not move a step. But young Tom stepped hurriedly forward and, catching his father's hand in both of his, cried out, "My father shan't beg my pardon. I beg yours, Father, for everything I ever did to displease you, but I wasn't to blame in this. I wasn't, indeed."

"Tom, I beg your pardon," said the hard man, overcome at last. "And now, Sir," he added, turning to me, "will you let bygones be bygones between my boy and me?" There was just a touch of bitterness in his tone.

"With all my heart," I replied. "But I want just a word with you in the shop before I go."

"Certainly," he answered, stiffly.

"Thomas, my friend," I said, when we got into the shop, laying my hand on his shoulder, "will you after this say that God has dealt hardly with you? There's a son to give thanks for on your knees! Thomas, you have a strong sense of fair play in your heart, and you give fair play neither to your own son nor yet to God Himself. You close your doors and brood over your own miseries and the wrongs people have done you—whereas, if you would but open those doors, you might come out unto the light of God's truth, and see that His heart is as clear as sunlight toward you. You won't believe this, and therefore you can't quite believe that there is a God at all. If you would but let Him teach you, you would find your perplexities melt away like the snow in the spring, till you could hardly believe you had ever felt them. No arguing will convince you of a God, but let Him once come in, and all argument will be tenfold useless to convince you that there is no God. Give God justice. Try Him as I have said. Good night."

He did not return my farewell with a single word, but the grasp of his strong rough hand was earnest and loving. I felt that it was better I could not see his face in the dark.

I went home as peaceful in my heart as the night whose curtains God had drawn about the earth.

FOURTEEN
My Pupil

In the middle of the following week I was returning from a visit I had made to Tomkins and his wife, when I met Dr. Duncan.

"Well, Dr. Duncan," I said, "busy as usual fighting the devil?"

"Ah! My dear Mr. Walton," returned the doctor—and a kind word from him went a long way into my heart—"I know what you mean. You fight the devil from the inside, and I fight him from the outside. My chance is a poor one."

"It would be, perhaps, if you were confined to outside remedies. But what an opportunity your profession gives you of attacking the enemy from the inside as well! And you have this advantage over us, that no man can say it belongs to your profession to say such things, and therefore disregard them."

"Ah! Mr. Walton, I have too great a respect for your profession to dare interfere with it. The doctor in *Macbeth,* you know, could

> Not minister to a mind diseased,
> Pluck from the memory a rooted sorrow,
> Raze out the written troubles of the brain,
> And with some sweet oblivious antidote
> Cleanse the stuff'd bosom of that perilous stuff
> Which weighs upon the heart."

"What a memory you have! But do you think I can do that anymore than you?"

"You know the best medicine to give, anyhow. I wish I always did. But you see we have no *theriaca* now."

"Well, we have. For the Lord says, 'Come unto Me and I will give you rest.' "

"There! I told you! That will meet all diseases."

"There comes to my mind a line of Chaucer. You have mentioned *theriaca* and I quoted our Lord's words. Chaucer brings the two together, for the word *triacle* is merely a corruption of *theriaca,* the unfailing cure for everything. 'Crist, which that is to every harm triacle.' "

"That is in Chaucer?"

"Yes. In the *Man of Law's Tale.*"

"I have just come from referring to the passage I quoted from Shakespeare. And I mention that because I want to tell you what made me think of the passage: I have been to see Catharine Weir. I think she is not long for this world. She has a bad cough, and her lungs are going."

"I am not surprised. But I do wish I had got a hold of her before, that I might be of some use to her now. Is she in immediate danger?"

"No, but I have no expectation of her recovery. Very likely she will just live through the winter and die in the spring. Those patients so often go as the flowers come! All her coughing, poor woman, will not cleanse *her* stuffed bosom either. For that perilous stuff weighs on her heart as well as on her lungs."

"Ah, dear! What is it, Doctor, that weighs upon her heart? Is it shame, or what is it? She is so uncommunicative that I hardly know anything at all about her yet."

"I cannot tell. She has the faculty of silence."

"If she would talk at all, one would have a chance of knowing something of the state of her mind, and so might give her some help."

"Perhaps she will break down all at once and open her mind to you. I have not told her she is dying. I think a medical man ought at least to be quite sure before he dares to say such a thing. I have known a long life injured, to human view at least, by the medical verdict in youth of imminent death."

"Certainly one has no right to say what God is going to do with anyone till he knows it beyond a doubt. Illness has its own peculiar mission, independent of any association with coming death, and may often work better when mingled with the hope of life. But could you not suggest something, Dr. Duncan, to guide me in trying to do my duty by her?"

"I cannot. We don't know what she is thinking. How can I prescribe without some diagnosis? I do not think anything will save her life, as we say; but you have taught us to think of the life that belongs to the spirit as the life, and I do believe confession would do everything for that."

"Yes, if made to God. But I will grant that communication of one's sorrows or sins to a wise brother of mankind may help to deepen confession to the Father in heaven. But we must not hurry things. She will perhaps come to me of herself before long. But I will call and inquire after her."

We parted, and I went at once to Catharine Weir's shop. She received me much as usual, which was hardly to be called receiving at all. Her eyes were full of a stony brilliance, and the flame of the consuming fire glowed upon her cheeks more brightly than ever. Her hand trembled, but her demeanor was perfectly calm.

"I am sorry to hear you are complaining, Miss Weir," I said.

"I suppose Dr. Duncan told you so, Sir. But I am quite well. I did not send for him. He called of himself, and wanted to persuade me I was ill."

I understood that she felt injured by his interference. "You should attend to his advice, though. He is a prudent man, and not in the least given to alarming people without cause."

She returned no answer. So I tried another subject. "What a fine fellow your brother is! Has your father found another place for him yet?"

"I don't know. My father never tells me any of his doings."

"But don't you go and talk to him sometimes?"

"No. He does not care to see me."

"I am going there now. Will you come with me?"

"Thank you. I never go where I am not wanted."

"But it is not right that father and daughter should live as you do. Suppose he may not have been so kind to you as he ought, you should not cherish resentment against him for it. That only makes matters worse, you know."

"I never said that he had been unkind to me."

"And yet you let every person in the village know it."

"How?" Her eyes had no longer the stony glitter.

"You are never seen together. You scarcely speak when you meet. Neither of you crosses the other's threshold."

"It is not my fault."

"It is not all your fault, I know. But do you think you can go to a heaven at last where you will be able to keep apart from each other, he in his house and you in your house, without any sign that it was through this father on earth that you were born into the world which the Father in heaven redeemed by the gift of His own Son?"

She was silent. After a pause, I went on. "I believe in my heart that you love your father. I could not believe otherwise of you. And you will never be happy till you have made it up with him. Have you done him no wrong?"

At these words her face turned white with anger—all but those spots on her cheekbones, which shone out in dreadful contrast to the deathly paleness of the rest of her face. Then the returning blood surged violently from her heart, and the red spots were lost in one crimson glow. She opened her lips to speak but, changing her mind, turned and walked haughtily out of the shop and closed the door behind her.

I waited, hoping she would recover herself and return; but, after ten minutes had passed, I thought it better to go away.

As I had told her, I was going to her father's shop. There I was received very differently. There was a certain softness in the manner of the carpenter, with the same heartiness in the shake of his hand which had accompanied my last leave-taking. I had purposely allowed ten days to elapse before I called again, to give time for the unpleasant feelings associated with my interference to vanish. And now I had something in my mind about young Tom.

"Have you got anything for your boy yet, Thomas?"

"Not yet, Sir. There's time enough. I don't want to part with him just yet. There he is, taking his turn at what's going. Tom!"

And from the farther end of the large shop, where I had not observed him, now approached young Tom, looking quite like a workman in his canvas jacket.

"Well, Tom, I am glad to find you can turn your hand to anything."

"I must be a stupid, Sir, if I couldn't handle my father's tools," returned the lad.

"I don't know that quite. My father is a lawyer, and I never could read a chapter in one of his books."

"Perhaps you never tried, Sir."

"Indeed I did, and no doubt I could have done it if I had made up my mind to it. But I never felt inclined to finish the page. And that reminds me why I called today. Thomas, I know that lad of yours is fond of reading. Can you spare him from his work for an hour or so before breakfast?"

"Tomorrow, Sir?"

" 'Tomorrow, and tomorrow, and tomorrow,' " I answered, "and there's Shakespeare for you."

"Of course, Sir, whatever you wish," said Thomas, with a perplexed look, in which pleasure seemed to long for confirmation.

"I want to give him some direction in his reading. When a man is fond of any tools, and can use them, it is worthwhile showing him how to use them better."

"Oh, thank you, Sir!" exclaimed Tom, his face beaming with delight.

"That is kind of you, Sir! Tom, you're a made man!" cried the father.

"So," I went on, "if you will let him come to me for an hour every morning, till he gets another place, say from eight to nine, I will see what I can do for him."

Tom's face was as red with delight as his sister's had been with anger. And I left the shop somewhat consoled for the pain I had given Catharine, which grieved me without making me sorry that I had occasioned it.

I had intended to try to do something from the father's side toward a reconciliation with his daughter, but I saw I had blocked up my own way. I could not bear to offer to bribe him. The first impression would be that I had a professional end to gain—that the reconciling of father and daughter was a sort of parish business of mine, and that I had smoothed the way to it by offering a gift. This was just what would irritate such a man, and I resolved to bide my time.

When Tom came, I asked him if he had read any Wordsworth. I always give people what I like myself, because that must be wherein I can best help them. I was anxious, too, to find out what he was capable of.

I therefore chose one of Wordsworth's sonnets, the one entitled, "Composed During a Storm," telling him to let me know when he considered that he had mastered the meaning of it. It was fully half an hour before Tom rose. I had not been uneasy about the experiment after ten minutes had passed, and after that time was doubled I felt certain of some measure of success. It was clear that Tom did not understand the sonnet at first, but I was delighted that he at least knew that he did not know, for that is the very next step to knowing.

"Well, Tom," I said, "have you made it out?"

"I can't say I have, Sir. I'm afraid I'm very stupid, for I've tried hard. I must just ask you to tell me what it means. But I must tell you one thing, Sir. Every time I read it over—twenty times, I dare say—I thought I was lying on my mother's grave, as I lay that terrible night. And then, at the end, there you were standing over me and saying, 'Can I do anything to help you?' "

I was struck with astonishment. For here in a wonderful manner I saw the imagination outrunning the intellect and manifesting to the heart what the brain could not yet understand. There was a hidden sympathy of the deepest kind between the life experience of the lad and the embodiment of such life experience on the part of the poet. He went on. "I am sure, Sir, I ought to have been at my prayers then, but I wasn't, so I didn't deserve you to come. But don't you think God is sometimes better to us than we deserve?"

"He is just everything to us, Tom, and we don't and can't deserve anything. Now I will try to explain the sonnet to you."

I had always had an impulse to teach, but not for the teaching's sake—for the attempt to fill skulls with knowledge had always been to me a desolate dreariness. But the moment I saw a sign of hunger, an indication of readiness to receive, I was invariably seized with a kind of passion for giving. I now proceeded to explain the sonnet as well as I could.

Tom said, "It is very strange, Sir. But, now that I have heard you say what the poem means, I feel as if I had known it all the time, though I could not say it."

Here at least was no common mind. The hour before breakfast extended into two hours after breakfast as well. Nor did this take up too much of my time, for the lad was capable of doing a great deal for himself under the sense of help at hand. His father, so far from making any objection to the arrangement, was delighted with it. Nor do I believe that the lad did less work in the shop for it—I learned he worked regularly till eight o'clock every night.

I had the lad fresh in the morning, clearheaded, with no mists from the valley of labor to cloud the heights of understanding. From the exercise to the mind it was a pleasant and relieving change to turn to bodily exertion. I am certain that he both thought and worked better, because he both thought and worked. But it would have been quite a different matter if he had come to me after the labor of the day. He would not then have been able to think nearly so well. Labor, sleep, thought, labor again, seems to me to be the right order.

Having exercised him in the analysis of literature—I mean helped him to take them to pieces that, putting them together again, he might see what kinds of things they were—I resolved to try something fresh with him.

By the end of three months, my pupil, without knowing any other Latin author, was able to read any part of the first book of the *Aeneid*—to read it tolerably in measure, and to enjoy the poetry of it—and this not without a knowledge of the declensions and conjugations. As to the syntax, I made the sentences themselves teach him that. As an end, all this was of no great value. But as a beginning it was invaluable, for it made and kept him hungry for more. In most modes of teaching, the beginnings are such that, without pressure, no boy will return to them.

Through the whole of that summer and the following winter I went on teaching Tom Weir. His father, though his own book learning was but small, had enough insight to perceive that his son was something out of the common, and that any possible advantage he might lose by remaining in Marshmallows was considerably more than balanced by the instruction from the vicar.

FIFTEEN

Dr. Duncan's Story

On the second Sunday after that—which was surprising to me when I considered our last parting—Catharine Weir was again in church.

I was endeavoring to enforce the Lord's Prayer by making them think about the meaning of the words they were so familiar with. I had come to the petition, "Forgive us our debts, as we forgive our debtors," with which I naturally connected the words of our Lord that follow: "For if ye forgive men their trespasses, your Heavenly Father will also forgive you; but if ye forgive not men their trespasses, neither will your Father forgive your trespasses." I tried to show that even were it possible with God to forgive an unforgiving man, the man himself would not be able to believe that God did forgive him, and therefore he could get no comfort, or help, or joy of any kind from the forgiveness. Hatred or revenge or contempt, or anything that separates us from man, separates us from God too. To the loving soul alone does the Father reveal Himself, for love alone can understand Him. It is the peacemakers who are His children.

This I said, thinking of no one more than another of my audience. But as I closed my sermon, I could not help fancying that Mrs. Oldcastle looked at me with more than her usual fierceness. I forgot all about it, however, for I never seemed to myself to have any hold of, or relation to, that woman. When I called upon her next, after the interview last related, she behaved much as if she had forgotten all about it, which was not likely.

In the end of the week after that sermon, I was passing the Hall gate on my usual Saturday walk, when Judy saw me and came out of the lodge. "Mr. Walton," she said, "how could you preach at Grannie as you did last Sunday?"

"I did not preach at anybody, Judy."

"O Mr. Walton!"

"You know I didn't, Judy. You know that if I had, I would not say I had not."

"Yes, yes, I know that perfectly," she said, seriously, "but Grannie thinks you did."

"How do you know that?"

"I can read her face—not so well as plain print, but as well as what Uncle Stoddart calls black letter, at least. I know she thought you were preaching at her, and her face said, 'I shan't forgive you, anyhow. I never forgive, and I won't for all your preaching.' That's what her face said."

"I am sure she would not say so, Judy."

"Oh, no, she would not say so. She would say, 'I always forgive, but I never forget.' That's a favorite saying of hers."

"But, Judy, don't you think it is rather hypocritical of you to say all this to me about your grandmother when she is so kind to you, and you seem such good friends with her?"

She looked up in my face with an expression of surprise.

"It is all true, Mr. Walton," she said.

"Perhaps. But you are saying it behind her back."

"I will go home and say it to her face directly." And she turned to go.

"No, no, Judy, I did not mean that," I said, taking her by the arm.

"I won't say you told me to do it. I thought there was no harm in telling you. Grannie is kind to me, and I am kind to her. But Grannie is afraid of my tongue, and I mean her to be afraid of it. It's the only way to keep her in order. Darling Aunt Wynnie! It's all she's got to defend her. If you knew how Grannie treats her sometimes, you would be cross with her yourself, Mr. Walton, for all your goodness and your white surplice."

And to my yet greater surprise, the wayward girl burst out crying and, breaking away from me, ran through the gate and out of sight among the trees, without once looking back.

I pursued my walk, my meditations somewhat discomposed. Would she go home and tell her grandmother what she had said to me? And, if she did, would it not widen the breach beyond which Ethelwyn stood, out of the reach of my help?

I walked quickly on to leave the little world of Marshmallows behind me, and be alone with nature and my Greek Testament. Hearing the sound of horse hooves on the road, I glanced up and saw a young man approaching upon a good serviceable hack. He turned into my road and passed me. He was pale, with a dark mustache, and large dark eyes; sat his horse well and carelessly; had fine features of the type commonly considered Grecian, but thin, and expressive chiefly of conscious weariness. He wore a white hat with crepe upon it, white gloves, and long, military boots. All this I caught as he passed me. I saw him stop at the lodge of the Hall, ring the bell, and then ride through the gate. I confess I did not quite like this, but I got over the feeling so far as to be able to turn to my Testament when I had crossed the stile.

I came home another way, after one of the most delightful days I had ever spent. Having reached the river in the course of my wandering, I came down the side of it toward Old Rogers' cottage, loitering and looking, quiet in heart and soul and mind, because I had committed my cares to Him who careth for us. I was gazing over the stump of an old pollard on which I was leaning, down on a great bed of white water lilies that lay on the broad slow river, here broader and slower than in most places. And then came a hand on my shoulder and, turning, I saw the gray head and white smock of my friend Old Rogers, and I was glad that he loved me enough not to be afraid of the parson and the gentleman.

"I've found it, Sir, I do think," he said, his brown furrowed old face shining.

"Found what, Old Rogers?" I returned.

"Why He was displeased with the disciples for not knowing what He meant about the leaven of the Pharisees. It was all dark to me for days. For it appeared to me very nat'ral that, seeing they had no bread in the locker, and hearing tell of leaven which they weren't to eat, they should think it had summat to do with their having none of any sort. But He didn't seem to think it was right of them to fall into the blunder. For why then? A man can't be always right. He may be like myself, a foremastman with no schoolin' but what the winds and the waves puts into him, and I'm thinkin' those fishermen the Lord took to so much were something o' that sort. 'How could they help it?' I said to myself, Sir. And from that I came to ask myself, 'Could they have helped it?' If they couldn't, He wouldn't have been vexed with them. And all at once, Sir, this mornin', it came to me. And when I saw you, Sir, a readin' upon the lilies, I couldn't help runnin' out to tell you. Isn't it a satisfaction, Sir, when yer dead reckonin' runs ye right in betwixt the cheeks of the harbor? I see it all now."

"Well, I want to know, Old Rogers. I'm not so old as you, and so I may live longer; and every time I read that passage, I should like to be able to say to myself, 'Old Rogers gave me this.' "

"I only hope I'm right, Sir. It was just this: their heads was full of their dinner because they didn't know where it was to come from. If their hearts had been full of the dinner He gave to the five thousand hungry men, women, and children, they wouldn't have been uncomfortable about not having a loaf. And so they wouldn't have been set upon the wrong tack when He spoke about the leaven of the Pharisees and Sadducees, and they would have known in a moment what He meant."

"You're right! You must be right, Old Rogers. It's as plain as possible!" I cried, rejoicing at the man's insight. "Thank you. I'll preach about it tomorrow. I thought I had got my sermon, but I was mistaken; you had got it."

But I was mistaken again. I had not got my sermon yet.

I walked with him to his cottage and left him, after a greeting with the "old woman." Passing then through the village, and seeing by the light of her candle Catharine Weir behind her counter, I went in. I thought Old Rogers' tobacco must be nearly gone, and I might safely buy some more.

Catharine's manner was much the same as usual. But, as she was weighing my purchase, she broke out all at once, "It's no use your preaching at me, Mr. Walton. I cannot, I will not forgive. I will do anything but forgive. And it's no use."

"It is not I that say it, Catharine. It is the Lord Himself. And I was not preaching at you. I was preaching to you as much as to anyone there, and no more. Just think of what He says, not what I say."

"I can't help it. If He won't forgive me, I must go without it. I can't forgive."

I saw that good and evil were fighting in her, and felt that no words of mine could be of further avail at the moment. The words of our Lord had laid hold of her and that was enough for this time. All I could venture to say was, "I won't trouble you with talk, Catharine. Our Lord wants to talk to you. It is not for me to interfere. But please remember, if ever you think I can serve you in any way, you have only to send for me."

She murmured a mechanical thanks and handed me my parcel. I paid for it, bade her good-night, and left the shop.

"O Lord," I said in my heart, as I walked away, "what a labor Thou hast with us all! Shall we ever, someday, be all and quite, good like Thee? Help me. Fill me with Thy light, that my work may all go to bring about the gladness of Thy kingdom."

And now I found that I wanted very much to see my friend Dr. Duncan. He received me with stately cordiality, and a smile that went further than all his words of greeting.

"Come, now, Mr. Walton, I am just going to sit down to my dinner, and you must join me. I think there will be enough for us both. There is, I believe, a chicken for us, and we can make up with cheese and a glass of my own father's port. He was fond of port, though I never saw him with one glass more than the registered tonnage. He always sat light on the water."

We sat down to our dinner, so simple and so well-cooked that it was just what I liked. We chattered away concerning many things, and I happened to refer to Old Rogers.

"What a fine old fellow that is!" said Dr. Duncan.

"Indeed he is," I answered. "He is great comfort and help to me. I don't think anybody but myself has an idea what there is in that old man."

"The people in the village don't quite like him though, I find. He is too ready to be down on them when he sees things going amiss. The fact is, they are afraid of him."

"Something as the Jews were afraid of John the Baptist, because he was an honest man and spoke not merely his own mind, but the mind of God in it."

"Just so. I believe you're quite right. Do you know, the other day, happening to go into Weir's shop to get him to do a job for me, I found him and Old Rogers in an argument? Keen as Weir was, and far surpassing

Rogers in correctness of speech, and precision as well, the old sailor carried too heavy metal for the carpenter. It evidently annoyed Weir, but such was the good humor of Rogers, that he could not, for very shame, lose his temper."

"I know how he would talk exactly," I returned. "He has a kind of loving banter with him that is irresistible to any man with a good heart. I am very glad to hear there is anything like communion begun between them. Weir will get good from him."

"My man-of-all-work is going to leave me. I wonder if the old man would take his place."

"I do not know whether he is fit for it. But of one thing you may be sure—if Old Rogers does not honestly believe he is fit for it, he will not take it. And he will tell you why too."

"Of that, however, I think I may be a better judge than he. There is nothing to which a good sailor cannot turn his hand, whatever he may think himself. It is not like a routine trade. Things are never twice the same at sea. The sailor has a thousand chances of using his judgment—if he has any to use—and that Old Rogers has in no common degree, so I should have no fear of him. If he won't let me steer him, you must put your hand to the tiller for me."

"I will do what I can," I answered, "for nothing would please me more than to see him in your service. It would be much better for him, and his wife too, than living by uncertain jobs as he does now."

(The result was that Old Rogers consented to try for a month. But when the end of the month came, nothing was said on either side, and the old man remained. And I could see several little new comforts about the cottage, in consequence of the regularity of his wages.)

At length I brought my conversation with Dr. Duncan around to my interview with Catharine Weir.

"Can you understand," I said, "a woman finding it so hard to forgive her own father?"

"Are you sure it is her father?"

"Surely she has not this feeling toward more than one. That she has it toward her father, I know."

"I don't know," he answered. "I have known resentment preponderate over every other feeling and passion—in the mind of a woman too. I once heard of a good woman who cherished this feeling against a good man because of some distrustful words he had once addressed to her. She had lived to a great age, and was expressing to her clergyman her desire that God would take her away—she had been waiting a long time. The clergyman, a very shrewd as well as devout man, and not without a touch of humor, said, 'Perhaps God doesn't mean to let you die till you've forgiven Mr. Maxwell.' She was as if struck with a flash of thought, sat silent during the rest of his visit. When the clergyman called the next day, he found Mr. Maxwell and her talking together very quietly over a cup of tea. And she hadn't long to wait after that, I was told, but was gathered to her fathers—or went home to her children, whichever is the better phrase."

"I wish I had your experience, Dr. Duncan," I said.

"I have not had so much experience as a general practitioner, because I have been so long at sea. But I am satisfied that until a medical man knows a good deal more about his patient than most medical men give themselves the trouble to find out, his prescriptions will partake a good deal more than necessary of haphazard. As to this question of obstinate resentment, I know one case in which it is the ruling presence of a woman's life—the very light that is in her is resentment."

"Tell me something about her."

"I will. But even to you I will mention no names. I was called to attend a lady at a house where I had never yet been."

"Was it in—?" I began, but checked myself. Dr. Duncan smiled and went on without remark. I could see that he told his story with great care, lest he should let anything slip that might give a clue to the place or people.

"I was led up into an old-fashioned, richly furnished room. A great wood fire burned on the hearth. The bed was surrounded with heavy dark curtains. In the bed lay one of the loveliest young creatures I had ever seen and, one on each side, stood two of the most dreadful-looking women I have ever beheld. Still as death they stood, while I examined my patient, with moveless faces, one as white as the other. One was evidently mistress, and the other the servant. The latter looked more self-contained than the former, but less determined and possibly more cruel. That both could be unkind was plain enough. There was trouble and signs of inward conflict in the eyes of the mistress. The maid gave no sign of any inside to her at all, but stood watching her mistress. A child's toy was lying in the corner of the room.

"I found the lady very weak and very feverish—a quick, feeble pulse, and a restlessness in her eye which I felt contained the secret of her disorder. She kept glancing toward the door, which would not open for all her looking, and I heard her once murmur to herself, 'He won't come!' I prescribed for her as far as I could venture, but begged a word with her mother. She went with me into an adjoining room.

" 'The lady is longing for something,' I said, not wishing to be so definite as I could have been.

"The mother made no reply. I saw her lips shut yet closer than she had before.

" 'She is your daughter, is she not?'

" 'Yes,' very decidedly.

" 'Could you not find out what she wishes?'

" 'Perhaps I could guess.'

" 'I do not think I can do her any good till she has what she wants.'

" 'Is that your mode of prescribing, Doctor?' she said, tartly.

" 'Yes, certainly,' I answered, 'in the present case. Is she married?'

" 'Yes.'

" 'Has she any children?'

" 'One daughter.'

" 'Let her see her, then.'

" 'She does not care to see her.'

" 'Where is her husband?'

" 'Excuse me, Doctor. I did not send for you to ask questions, but to give advice.'

" 'And I came to ask questions, in order that I may give advice. Do you think a human being is like a clock that can be taken to pieces, cleaned, and put together again?'

" 'My daughter's condition is not a fit subject for jesting.'

" 'Certainly not. Send for her husband or the undertaker, whichever you please,' I said, forgetting my manners and my temper together, for I was more irritable then than I am now, and there was something so repulsive about the woman that I felt as if I was talking to an evil creature that, for her own ends, was tormenting the dying lady.

" 'I understood you were a gentleman of experience and breeding.'

" 'I am not in question, Madam. It is your daughter. She must see her husband if it be possible.'

" 'It is not possible.'

" 'Why?'

" 'I say it is not possible, and that is enough. Good morning.'

"I could say no more at that time. I called the next day. She was just the same, only that I knew she wanted to speak to me, and dared not because of the presence of the two women. Her troubled eyes searched mine for pity and help, and I could not tell what to do for her. There are, indeed, strongholds of injustice and wrong into which no law can enter to help.

"One afternoon, about a week after my first visit, I was sitting by her bedside, wondering what could be done to get her out of the clutches of these tormentors who were consuming her in the slow fire of her own affections. I heard a faint noise, a rapid foot in the house so quiet before—heard doors open and shut, then a dull sound of conflict of some sort. Presently a quick step came up the oak stair. The face of my patient flushed, and her eyes gleamed as if her soul would come out of them. Weak as she was, she sat up in bed, and the two women darted from the room.

" 'My husband!' said the girl, for indeed she was little more in age. 'They will murder him.'

"I heard a cry, and what sounded like an inarticulate imprecation, but both from a woman's voice. Then a young man, as fine a fellow as I ever saw—palefaced, dressed like a gamekeeper but evidently a gentleman—walked quietly into the room. The two women followed in fierce wrath, as red as he was white. He came round the bed, and she fell into his embrace.

"I had gone to the mother. 'Let us have no scene now,' I said, 'or her blood will be on your head.'

"She took no notice of what I said, but stood silently glaring, not gazing, at the pair. I feared an outburst and had resolved, if it came, to carry her at once from the room.

"But in a moment more the young man lifted up his wife's head. Seeing the look of terror in his face, I hastened to him, and lifting her from him, laid her down, dead. Disease of the heart, I believe.

"The mother burst into a shriek—not of horror or grief or remorse, but of deadly hatred. 'Look at your work!' she cried to him as he stood gazing in stupor on the face of the girl. 'You said she was yours, not mine. Take her. You may have her now you have killed her.'

" 'He may have killed her, but you have murdered her, Madam,' I said, as I took the man by the arm, and led him away, yielding like a child. But the moment I got him out of the house, he gave a groan and broke away from me. I heard the gallop of a horse, and saw him tearing away at full speed along the London road. I never heard more of him or of the story."

(I could hardly doubt whose was the story I had heard. Things which seem as if they could not happen in a civilized country and a polished age, are proved as possible as ever where the heart is unloving, the feelings unrefined, self the center, and God nowhere in the man or woman's vision. The terrible things that one reads in old histories or in modern newspapers were done by human beings, not by demons.

(I did not let my friend know that I knew what he concealed, and indeed knew all the story:

(Dorothy—*the gift of God,* a wonderful name, to be so treated, faring in this, however, like many other of God's gifts—Dorothy Oldcastle was the eldest daughter of Jeremy and Sibyl Oldcastle, and the sister, therefore, of Ethelwyn. Her father, an easygoing man entirely under the dominion of his wife, died when Dorothy was about fifteen. Her mother sent her to school, with especial recommendation to the care of a clergyman in the neighborhood, though the mother paid no attention to what our Lord or His apostles said, nor indeed seemed to care to ask herself if what she did was right.

(Dorothy was there three or four years. She and the clergyman's son fell in love with each other. The mother heard of it and sent for her home. She had other views for her. Of course, in such eyes, a daughter's fancy was a thing to be sneered at. But she found, to her fierce disdain, that she had not been able to keep all her beloved obstinacy to herself—she had transmitted a portion of it to her daughter. But in the daughter it was combined with noble qualities and, ceasing to be the evil thing it was in her mother, became an honorable firmness, rendering her able to withstand her mother's stormy importunities. Thus Nature had begun to right herself—the right in the daughter turning to meet and defy the wrong in the mother—and that in the same strength of character which the mother had misused for evil and selfish ends. And thus the bad breed was broken. She was and would be true to her love. The consequent scenes were dreadful. The spirit, but not the will of the girl, was all but broken. She felt that she could not sustain the strife long.

(The young man had procured a good appointment in India, whither he must sail within a month. The end was that Dorothy left her mother's house. Mr. Gladwyn was waiting for her near, and conducted her to his father who had constantly refused to aid Mrs. Oldcastle by interfering in the matter. They were married the next day by the clergyman of a neighboring parish. But almost immediately she was taken so ill that it was impossible for her to accompany her husband and she was compelled to remain behind, hoping to join him the following year.

(Before the time arrived, she gave birth to my little friend Judy, and her departure was again delayed, probably by the early stages of the disease of which she died. Then, just as she was about to set sail for India, news arrived that Mr. Gladwyn had had a sunstroke, and would come home as soon as he was able. So, instead of going to join him, she must wait where she was.

(His mother had been dead for some time. His father was found dead in his chair soon after the news of the illness of his son, and so the poor young creature was left alone with her child, without money, and in weak health. The old man had left nothing behind him but his furniture and books, and nothing could be done in arranging his affairs till the arrival of his son. Mrs. Oldcastle wrote, offering her daughter all that she required in her old home.

(She had not been more than a few days in the house before her mother began to tyrannize over her as in old times, and although Mrs. Gladwyn's health was evidently failing in consequence, Mrs. Oldcastle either did not see the cause, or could not restrain her evil impulses. At length the news arrived of Mr. Gladwyn's departure for home. Perhaps then, for the first time, the temptation entered the mother's mind to take her revenge, by making her daughter's illness a pretext for refusing him admission to her presence. She told her she should not see him till she was better; persisted in her resolution after his arrival; and effected, by the help of Sarah, that he should not gain admittance to the house. It was only by the connivance of Ethelwyn, then a girl about fifteen, that he was admitted by the underground entrance.

(What a horror of darkness seemed to hang over that family! What deeds of wickedness! But the horror came from within—selfishness and fierceness of temper were its source—no unhappy doom. The worship of one's own will fumes out around the being an atmosphere of evil, an altogether abnormal condition of the moral firmament, out of which will break the very flames of hell.)

I had very little time for the privacy of the church that night. Dark as it was, however, I went in before I went home. I groped my way into the pulpit, and sat down in the darkness and thought. The words of Dr. Duncan had opened up a good deal to me. Yet my personal interest in his story did not make me forget poor Catharine Weir and the terrible sore in her heart. And I saw that of herself she would not, could not, forgive to all eternity—that all the pains of hell could not make her forgive—for it was a divine glory to forgive and must come from God. And thinking of Mrs. Oldcastle, I saw that in ourselves we could be sure of no safety, not from the worst and vilest sins. Only by being filled with a higher spirit than our own are we, or can we be, safe from this eternal death of our being. This spirit was fighting the evil spirit in Catharine Weir—how was I to urge her to give ear to the good? If will would but side with God, the forces of self, deserted by their leader, must soon quit the field, and the woman—the kingdom within her no longer torn by conflicting forces—would sit quiet at the feet of the Master. Might she not be roused to utter one feeble cry to God for help? That would be one step toward the forgiveness of others. To ask something for herself would be a great advance in such a proud nature as hers, and to ask good heartily is the very next step to giving good heartily.

Many thoughts such as these passed through my mind, chiefly associated with her, for I could not think how to think about Mrs. Oldcastle yet. And I kept lifting up my heart to the God who had cared to make me, and then drew me to be a preacher to my fellows, and had surely something to give me to say to them. Might not my humble ignorance work His will, though my wrath could not work His righteousness? And I descended from the pulpit thinking with myself, "Let Him do as He will. Here I am. I will say what I see. Let Him make it good."

SIXTEEN
The Organ

The next morning I spoke about the words of our Lord:

"If ye then, being evil, know how to give good gifts to your children, how much more shall your Heavenly Father give the Holy Spirit to them that ask Him!"

When I rose in the reading desk, I saw Catharine Weir and Mrs. Oldcastle and Judy, all looking me in the face. To my surprise and discomposure, Miss Oldcastle was there for the first time. And by her side was the gentleman whom the day before I had encountered on horseback. He sat carelessly, easily, contentedly—indifferently. I could not help seeing that he was always behind the rest of the congregation, as if he had no idea of what was coming next, or did not care to conform.

Gladly would I have shunned the necessity of preaching that was laid upon me. "But," I said to myself, "shall the work given me to do fail because of my perturbation of spirit? No harm is done, though I suffer, but much harm if one tone fails of its force because I suffer." I therefore prayed God to help me, and looking to Him for aid, I cast my care upon Him, kept my thoughts strenuously away from that which discomposed me, and never turned my eyes toward the Oldcastle Hall pew from the moment I entered the pulpit. Partly, I presume, from the freedom given by the sense of irresponsibility for the result, I being weak and God strong, I preached, I think, a better sermon than I had ever preached before. But when I got into the vestry I found that I could scarcely stand for trembling. I must have looked ill, for my attendant got me a glass of wine without even asking, although it was not my custom to take any there.

I recovered in a few moments from my weakness but, altogether disinclined to face any of my congregation, I went out at my vestry door and home through the shrubbery, a path I seldom used because it had a separatist look about it. When I got to my study, I threw myself on a couch and fell fast asleep. How often in trouble have I had to thank God for sleep as one of His best gifts! And how often, when I have awaked refreshed and calm, have I thought of poor Sir Philip Sidney who, dying slowly and patiently in the prime of life and health, was sorely troubled in his mind to know how he had offended God because, having prayed earnestly for sleep, no sleep came in answer to his cry!

I woke just in time for my afternoon service, and the peace in my heart was a marvel and a delight. I felt almost as if I were walking in a blessed dream from a world of serener air than ours.

I found, after I was already in the reading desk, that I was a few minutes early. With bowed head, I was simply living in the consciousness of the presence of a supreme quiet, when the first low notes of the organ broke upon my stillness with the sense of a deeper delight. Never before had I felt the triumph of contemplation in Handel's rendering of "I Know That My Redeemer Liveth." And through it all ran a cold silvery quiver of sadness, like the light in the east after the sun is gone down, which would have been pain but for the golden glow of the west. Before the music ceased, it crossed my mind that I had never before heard that organ utter the language of Handel. But I had no time to think more about it just then, for I rose to read the words of our Lord, "I will arise and go to My Father."

There was no one in the Hall pew. Indeed, it was a rare occurrence if anyone was in that pew in the afternoon.

But, for all the quietness of my mind during that evening service, I fell ill before I went to bed, and awoke in the morning with a headache which increased along with other signs, until I thought it better to send for Dr. Duncan. I am not so much an imbecile as to suppose that a history of the following six weeks would be interesting. I suffered that long from low fever, and several more weeks passed during which I was unable to meet my flock. Thanks to the care of Mr. Brownrigg, a clever young man in priest's orders at Addicehead kindly undertook my parish duties for me, and thus relieved me of all anxiety.

SEVENTEEN
Judy's News

I have reason to fear that during my illness, when I was light-headed from fever, I may have talked a good deal of nonsense about Miss Oldcastle. I remember that I was haunted with visions of magnificent conventual ruins which I had discovered and had wandered through at my own lonely will. Within was a labyrinth of passages in the walls, and long corridors and sudden galleries. Through these I was ever wandering, ever discovering new rooms, new galleries, new marvels of architecture, yet ever disappointed and ever dissatisfied, because I knew that in one room somewhere in the forgotten mysteries of the pile sat Ethelwyn reading, never lifting those sea-blue eyes of hers from the great volume on her knee, reading every word, slowly turning leaf after leaf. I knew that she would sit there reading till every leaf in the huge volume was turned, and she came to the last and read it from top to bottom, down to the *finis* and the urn with a weeping willow over it, when she would close the book with a sigh, lay it down on the floor, rise and walk slowly away forever. I knew that if I did not find her before that terrible last page was read, I should never find her at all, but have to go wandering alone all my life through those dreary galleries and corridors, with only one hope left—that I might yet, before I died, find the "palace chamber far apart," and see the forsaken volume lying on the floor where she had left it, and the chair beside it on which she had sat so long waiting for someone in vain.

And perhaps to words spoken under these impressions may partly be attributed the fact (which I knew nothing of till long afterward) that the people of the village began to couple my name with that of Miss Oldcastle.

When all this vanished from me in the returning wave of health that spread through my weary brain, I was yet left anxious and thoughtful. There was no one from whom I could ask information about the family at the Hall, so that I was just driven to the best thing—to try to cast my care upon Him who cared for my care. How often do we look upon God as our last and feeblest resource! We go to Him because we have nowhere else to go. And then we learn that the storms of life have driven us not upon the rocks but into the desired haven.

One day when I was sitting reading in my study, who should be announced but my friend Judy!

"O dear Mr. Walton, I am so sorry! I haven't had a chance of coming to see you before, though we've always managed—I mean Auntie and I—to hear about you. I would have come to nurse you, but it was no use thinking of it."

I smiled as I thanked her.

"Ah! You think, because I'm such a tomboy, that I couldn't nurse you? I only wish I had had a chance of letting you see. I am so sorry for you!"

"But I'm nearly well now, Judy, and I have been taken good care of. But now I want to hear how everybody is at the Hall."

"What, Grannie and the Wolf and all?"

"As many as you please to tell me about."

"Well, Grannie is gracious to everybody but Auntie."

"Why isn't she gracious to Auntie?"

"I don't know. I only guess."

"Is your visitor gone?"

"Yes, long ago. Do you know, I think Grannie wants Auntie to marry him, and Auntie doesn't quite like it. But he's very nice. He's so funny. He'll be back again soon, I dare say. I don't quite like him—not so well as you by a whole half, Mr. Walton. I wish you would marry Auntie, but that would never do. It would drive Grannie out of her wits."

To stop her and hide some confusion, I said, "Now tell me about the rest of them."

"Sarah comes next. She's as white and as wolfy as ever. Mr. Walton, I hate that woman. She walks like a cat. I am sure she is bad."

"Did you ever think, Judy, what an awful thing it is to be bad? If you did, I think you would be so sorry for her, you could not hate her."

At the same time, knowing what I knew, and remembering that impressions can date from farther back than the conscious memory can reach, I was not surprised to hear that Judy hated Sarah, though I could not believe that in such a child the hatred was of the most deadly description.

"I am afraid I must go on hating in the meantime," said Judy. "I wish someone would marry Auntie and turn Sarah away. But that couldn't be, so long as Grannie lives."

"How is Mr. Stoddart?"

"That's one of the things Auntie said I was to be sure to tell you."

"Then your aunt knew you were coming to see me?"

"Oh, yes, I told her. Not Grannie, you know. You mustn't let it out."

"I shall be careful. How is Mr. Stoddart, then?"

"Not well at all. He was taken ill before you, and has been in bed and by the fireside ever since. Auntie doesn't know what to do with him, he is so out of spirits."

"If tomorrow is fine, I shall go and see him."

"Thank you. I believe that's just what Auntie wanted. He won't like it at first, I dare say. But he'll come to, and you'll do him good. You do everybody good you come near."

"I wish that were true, Judy. I fear it is not. What good did I ever do you?"

"Do me?" she exclaimed, half angry at the question. "Don't you know I have been an altered character ever since I knew you?" And here she laughed, leaving me in absolute ignorance of how to interpret her. But presently her eyes grew clearer, and I could see the slow film of a tear gathering. "Mr. Walton," she said, "I have been trying not to be selfish. You have done me that much good."

"I am very glad, Judy. Don't forget who can do you all good. There is One who can not only show you what is right, but make you able to do and be what is right."

Judy did not answer, but sat looking fixedly at the carpet. She was thinking though, I saw.

"Who has played the organ, Judy, since your uncle was taken ill?" I asked at length.

"Why, Auntie, to be sure. Didn't you hear?"

"No," I answered, turning almost sick at the idea of having been away while she was giving voice and expression to the dear asthmatic old pipes. Think of her there, and me here!

"Then," I said to myself, "it must have been she that played 'I Know That My Redeemer Liveth!' And, instead of thanking God for that, here I am murmuring that He did not give me more! And this child has just been telling me that I have taught her to try not to be selfish."

"When was your uncle taken ill?"

"I don't exactly remember. But you will come and see him tomorrow? And then we shall see you too, for we are always in and out of his room just now."

"I will come if Dr. Duncan will let me. Perhaps he will take me in his carriage."

"No, no. Don't you come with him. Uncle can't bear doctors. He never was ill in his life before, and he behaves to Dr. Duncan just as if he had made him ill. I wish I could send the carriage for you. But I can't, you know."

"Never mind, Judy. I shall manage somehow. What is the name of the gentleman who was staying with you?"

"Don't you know? Captain George Everard. He would change his name to Oldcastle, you know."

What a foolish pain, like a spear thrust, they sent through me—those words spoken in such a taken-for-granted way!

"He's a relation, on Grannie's side mostly, I believe. But I never could understand the explanation. All the husbands and wives in our family, for a hundred and fifty years, have been more or less cousins, or half-cousins, or second or third cousins. Captain Everard has what Grannie calls a neat little property somewhere in Northumberland. His second brother is dead, and the eldest is something worse for the wear, as Grannie says, so that the captain comes just within sight of the coronet of an old uncle who ought to have been dead long ago. Just the match for Auntie!"

"But you say Auntie doesn't like him."

"Oh, but you know that doesn't matter," returned Judy, with bitterness. "What will Grannie care for that? It's nothing to anybody but Auntie, and she must get used to it. Nobody makes anything of her."

"How were you able to get here today?" I asked, as she rose to go.

"Grannie is in London, and the wolf is with her. Auntie wouldn't leave Uncle."

"They have been a good deal in London of late, have they not?"

"Yes. They say it's about money of Auntie's. But I don't understand. I think it's that Grannie wants to make the captain marry her, for they sometimes see him when they go to London."

It was only after she had gone that I thought how astounding it would have been to me to hear a girl of her age show such an acquaintance with worldliness and scheming, had I not been personally so much concerned about one of the objects of her remarks. It was a satisfaction to think that the aunt had such a friend and ally in her wild niece. Evidently she had inherited her father's fearlessness, and if only it should turn out that she had likewise inherited her mother's firmness, she might render the best possible service to her aunt.

EIGHTEEN
The Invalid

The following day being very fine, I walked to Oldcastle Hall, but much slower than I was willing. I found to my relief that Mrs. Oldcastle had not yet returned. I was shown at once to Mr. Stoddart's library, where I found the two ladies in attendance upon him. He was seated by a splendid fire in the most luxurious of easy chairs, with his furred feet buried in the long hair of the hearthrug. He looked worn and peevish, and all the placidity of his countenance had vanished. The smooth expanse of forehead was drawn into fifty wrinkles, like a sea over which the fretting wind has been blowing. Nor was it only suffering that his face expressed. He looked like a man who strongly suspected that he was ill-used.

"You are well off, Mr. Stoddart," I said, "to have two such nurses."

"They are very kind," sighed the patient.

Aunt and niece rose and left the room quietly.

"Do you suffer much, Mr. Stoddart?"

"Much weariness worse than pain. I could welcome death."

"I do not think, from what Dr. Duncan says of you, that there is reason to apprehend more than a lingering illness," I said, to try him, I confess.

"I hope not, indeed," he exclaimed angrily, sitting up in his chair. "What right has Dr. Duncan to talk of me so?"

"To a friend, you know," I returned, apologetically, "who is much interested in your welfare."

"Yes, of course. So is the doctor. A sick man belongs to you both by prescription."

Satisfied that, ill as he was, he might be better if he would, I asked, "Do you remember how Ligarius, in *Julius Caesar,* discards his sickness?"

" 'I am not sick, if Brutus have in hand any exploit worthy the name of honor.'

"I want to be well because I don't like to be ill. But what there is in this foggy, swampy world worth being well for, I'm sure I haven't found out yet."

"If you have not, it must be because you have never tried to find out. But I'm not going to attack you when you are not able to defend yourself. We shall find a better time for that. But can't I do something for you? Would you like me to read to you for half an hour?"

"No, thank you. The girls tire me out with reading to me. I hate the very sound of their voices."

"I have today's *Times* in my pocket."

"I've heard all the news already."

"Then I think I shall only bore you if I stay."

He made no answer. I rose. He returned my "Good morning" as if there was nothing good in the world, least of all this same morning.

I found the ladies in the outer room. Judy was on her knees on the floor occupied with a long row of books. And then I learned the secret—how Mr. Stoddart reached the volumes arranged in the ceiling beams. Judy rose from the floor, and proceeded to put in motion a mechanical arrangement concealed in one of the bookshelves along the wall. There were strong cords reaching from the ceiling, and attached to the shelf, or rather long box (open sideways), which contained the books.

"Do take care, Judy," said Ethelwyn. "You know it is very venturous of you to let that shelf down, when Uncle is as jealous of his books as a hen of her chickens. I oughtn't to have let you touch the cords."

"You couldn't help it, Auntie dear, for I had the shelf halfway down before you saw me," returned Judy, proceeding to raise the books to their usual position under the ceiling.

But in another moment, either from Judy's awkwardness or from the gradual decay and final fracture of some cord, down came the whole shelf with a thundering noise, and the books were scattered about the floor. The door of the inner room opened and Mr. Stoddart appeared. His brow was already flushed, but when he saw the condition of his books, he broke out in a passion to which he could not have given way but for the weak state of his health.

"How *dare* you?" he said, with terrible emphasis on the word *dare*. "Judy, I beg you will not again show yourself in my apartment till I send for you."

"And then," said Judy, leaving the room, "I am not in the least likely to be otherwise engaged."

"I am very sorry, Uncle," began Miss Oldcastle.

But Mr. Stoddart had already retreated and banged the door behind him. So Miss Oldcastle and I were left standing together amid the ruins. She glanced at me with a distressed look. I smiled. She smiled in return.

"He will be sorry when he comes to himself," I said, "so we must take his repentance now, and think nothing more of the matter than if he had already said he was sorry. Besides, when books are in the case, I, for one, must not be too hard on my unfortunate neighbor."

"Thank you, Mr. Walton, for taking my uncle's part. He has been very good to me, and dear Judy is provoking sometimes. I am afraid I help to spoil her, but you would hardly believe how good she really is, and what a comfort she is to me."

"I think I understand Judy," I replied, "and I shall be mistaken if she does not turn out a very fine woman. The marvel to me is that, with all the various influences among which she is placed here, she is not seriously spoiled after all. I have the greatest regard for, and confidence in, my friend Judy."

Ethelwyn—Miss Oldcastle, I should say—gave me such a pleased look that I was well recompensed for my defense of Judy.

"Will you come with me," she said, "for our talk may continue to annoy Mr. Stoddart."

"I am at your service," I returned, and followed her from the room.

"Are you still as fond of the old quarry as you used to be, Miss Oldcastle?" I said, as we caught a glimpse of it from the window of a long passage.

"I am. I go there most days. I have not been today, though. Would you like to go down?"

"Very much," I said.

"Ah! I forgot, though. You must not go: it is not a fit place for an invalid."

"I cannot call myself an invalid now."

"Your face, I am sorry to say, contradicts your words." And she looked so kindly at me that I almost broke into thanks for the mere look. "And indeed," she went on, "it is too damp down there, not to speak of the stairs."

By this time we had reached the little room in which I was received the first time I visited the Hall. There we found Judy.

"If you are not too tired already, I should like to show you my little study. It has, I think, a better view than any other room in the house," said Miss Oldcastle.

"I shall be delighted," I replied.

"Come, Judy," said her aunt.

"You don't want me, I am sure, Auntie."

"I do, Judy, really. You mustn't be cross to us because Uncle has been cross to you. Uncle is not well, you know, and isn't a bit like himself. And you know you should not have meddled with his machinery."

And Miss Oldcastle put her arm round Judy and kissed her, whereupon Judy jumped from her seat, threw her book down, and ran to one of the several doors that opened from the room. This disclosed a little staircase, almost like a ladder, that wound about up to a charming little room, whose window looked down upon the Bishop's Basin, glimmering slaty through the tops of the trees between. It was paneled in dark oak, like the room below, but with more carving. Just opposite the window was a small space of brightness formed by the backs of nicely bound books. Seeing that these attracted my eye, Miss Oldcastle said, "Those are almost all gifts from my uncle. He is really very kind. You will not think of him as you have seen him today?"

"Indeed I will not," I replied.

"Do sit down," said Miss Oldcastle. "You have been very ill, and I could do nothing for you who have been so kind to me." She spoke as if she had wanted to say this.

"I only wish I had a chance of doing anything for you," I said, as I took a chair near the window. "But if I had done all I ever could hope to do, you have repaid me long ago, I think."

"How? I do not know what you mean, Mr. Walton. I have never done you the least service."

"Tell me first, did you play the organ in church that afternoon when—after—before I was taken ill—I mean the same day you had—a friend with you in the pew in the morning?"

I daresay my voice was as irregular as my construction. I ventured just one glance. Her face was flushed. But she answered me at once, "I did."

"Then I am in your debt more than you know or I can tell you."

"Why, if that is all, I have played the organ every Sunday since Uncle was taken ill," she said, smiling.

"I know that now, but I did not know it. It is only for what I heard that I mean now to acknowledge my obligation. Tell me, Miss Oldcastle, what is the most precious gift one person can give another?"

She hesitated; and I, fearing to embarrass her, answered for her.

"It must be something imperishable in its own nature. If, instead of a gem, or even of a flower, we could cast the gift of a lovely thought into the heart of a friend, that would be giving as the angels, I suppose, must give. But you did more and better for me than that. I had been troubled all the morning, and you made me know that 'my Redeemer liveth.' I did not know you were playing, mind, though I felt a difference. You gave me more trust in God, and what other gift so great could one give? I think that last impression, just as I was taken ill, must have helped me through my illness. Often, when I was most oppressed, that song would rise up in the troubled air of my mind, sung by a voice which, though I never heard you sing, I never questioned to be yours."

She turned her face toward me: those sea-blue eyes were full of tears.

"I was troubled myself," she said, with a faltering voice, "when I sang—I mean played—that. I am so glad it did somebody good! I fear it did not do me much. I will sing it to you now, if you like."

And she rose to get the music. But that instant Judy, who had left the room, bounded into it with the exclamation, "Auntie, Auntie, here's Grannie!"

Miss Oldcastle turned pale. I confess I felt embarrassed, as if I had been caught in something underhand.

"Is she come in?" asked Miss Oldcastle, trying to speak with indifference.

"She is just at the door—must be getting out of the fly now. What shall we do?"

"What do you mean, Judy?" said her aunt.

"Well, you know, Auntie, as well as I do, that Grannie will look as black as a thundercloud to find Mr. Walton here, and if she doesn't speak as loud, it will only be because she can't. I don't care for myself, but you know on whose head the storm will fall. Do, dear Mr. Walton, come down the back stairs. Then she won't be a bit the wiser. I'll manage it all."

Here was a dilemma for me—either to bring suffering on her, to save whom I would have borne any pain, or to creep out of the house as if I were and ought to be ashamed of myself. Miss Oldcastle, however, did not leave it to me to settle the matter.

"Judy, for shame to propose such a thing to Mr. Walton! I am very sorry that he may chance to have an unpleasant meeting with Mamma, but we can't help it. Come, Judy, we will show Mr. Walton out together."

"It wasn't for Mr. Walton's sake," returned Judy, pouting. "You are very troublesome, Auntie. Mr. Walton, she is so hard to take care of! And she's worse since you came. I shall have to give her up someday. Do be generous, Mr. Walton, and take my side—that is, Auntie's."

"I am afraid, Judy, I must thank your aunt for taking the part of my duty against my inclination. But this kindness, at least," I said to Miss Oldcastle, "I can never hope to return."

It was a stupid speech, but I could not be annoyed that I had made it.

"All obligations are not burdens to be got rid of, are they?" she replied, with a sweet smile on her pale, troubled face. I was more moved for her, deliberately handing her over to the torture for the truth's sake, than I care to confess.

Miss Oldcastle led the way down the stairs; I followed, and Judy brought up the rear. The affair was not so bad as it might have been. I insisted on going out alone and met Mrs. Oldcastle in the hall only. She held out no hand to greet me. I bowed, and said I was sorry to find Mr. Stoddart so far from well.

"I fear he is far from well," she returned, "certainly, in my opinion, too ill to receive visitors."

So saying, she bowed and passed on. I turned and walked out, not ill-pleased with my visit.

From that day I recovered rapidly, and the next Sunday had the pleasure of preaching to my flock. Mr. Aikin, the gentleman already mentioned as doing duty for me, read prayers. I took for my subject one of our Lord's miracles of healing and tried to show my people that all healing, and all kinds of healing, come as certainly and only from His hand as those instances in which He put forth His bodily hand and touched the diseased and told them to be whole.

And as they left the church the organ played, " 'Comfort ye, comfort ye My people,' saith your God."

I tried hard to prevent my new feelings from so filling my mind as to make me fail of my duty toward my flock. I said to myself, "Let me be the more gentle, the more honorable, the more tender toward these my brothers and sisters, for they are her brothers and sisters too." I wanted to do my work the better that I loved her.

Thus week after week passed, with little that I can remember worthy of record. I seldom saw Miss Oldcastle, and during this period never alone.

I could not venture more until she had seen more of me, and how to enjoy her society while her mother was so unfriendly, I did not know. I feared that to call oftener might only prevent me from seeing her at all, and I could not tell how far such measures might expedite the event I most dreaded, or add to the discomfort to which Miss Oldcastle was already so much exposed. Meantime I heard nothing of Captain Everard, and the comfort that flowed from such a negative source was yet of a very positive character. I was in some measure deterred from making further advances by the thought that her favor for Captain Everard might be greater than Judy had represented it. I had always shrunk from rivalry of every kind—it was, somehow, contrary to my nature. Besides, Miss Oldcastle was likely to be rich someday—apparently had money of her own even now—and I writhed at the thought of being supposed to marry for money. "Ah! you see!" they would say. "That's the way with the clergy! They talk about poverty and faith, pretending to despise riches and to trust in God, but just put money in their way, and what chance will a poor girl have beside a rich one! It's all very well in the pulpit. It's their business to talk so. But does one of them believe what he says or at least act upon it?"

I mention this only as a repressing influence, to which I certainly should not have been such a fool as to yield, had I seen the way otherwise clear. For a man, by showing how to use money, or rather by simply using money aright, may do more good than by refusing to possess it if it comes to him in an entirely honorable way. But I felt sure—(if I should be so blessed as to marry Miss Oldcastle)—that the poor of my own people would be those most likely to understand my position and feelings, and least likely to impute to me worldly motives.

Ethelwyn played the organ still, but I never made any attempt to see her as she came in or went from the organ loft. She seemed, by some intuition, to know the music I liked best, and great help she often gave me by so uplifting my heart upon the billows of the organ harmony.

So the time went on. I called once or twice upon Mr. Stoddart, and found him, as I thought, better. But he would not allow that he was. Dr. Duncan said he was better, and would be better still if he would only believe it and exert himself.

NINETEEN
Mood and Will

Winter came apace, with its fogs, and dripping boughs, and sodden paths, and rotting leaves, and rains, and skies of weary gray, but also with its fierce red suns, and delicate ice over prisoned waters, and white chaotic snowstorms. And when the hard frost came, it brought Mr. Stoddart to my door.

He entered my room with something of the countenance Naaman must have borne after his flesh had come again like the flesh of a little child. He did not look ashamed, but his pale face looked humbled and distressed. Its somewhat self-satisfied placidity had vanished, and instead of the usual diffused geniality, it now showed traces of feeling and plain signs of suffering. I seated him comfortably by the fire and began to chat.

"The cold weather, which makes so many invalids creep into bed, seems to have brought you out into the air, Mr. Stoddart," I said.

"I feel just as if I were coming out of a winter. Don't you think illness is a kind of human winter?"

"Certainly, more or less stormy. With some, a winter of snow and hail and piercing winds; with others, of black frosts and creeping fogs, with now and then a glimmer of the sun."

"The last is more like mine. I feel as if I had been in a wet hole in the earth. Mr. Walton, I will explain myself. I have come to tell you how sorry and ashamed I am that I behaved so badly to you every time you came to see me."

"Oh, nonsense!" I said. "It was your illness, not you."

"At least, my dear sir, the facts of my behavior did not really represent my feelings toward you."

"I know that as well as you do. Don't say another word about it. You had the best excuse of being cross. I should have had none for being offended."

"It was only the outside of me."

"Yes, yes, I acknowledge it heartily."

"But that does not settle the matter between me and myself, Mr. Walton, although, by your goodness, it settles it between me and you. It is humiliating to think that illness should so completely overcrow me that I am no more myself—lose my hold, in fact, of what I call me—so that I am almost driven to doubt my personal identity.

"I have labored much to withdraw my mind from the influence of money and ambition and pleasure, and to turn it to the contemplation of spiritual things. Yet on the first attack of a depressing illness, I ceased to be a gentleman, I was rude to ladies who did their best and kindest to serve me, and I talked to the friend who came to cheer and comfort me as if he were an idle vagrant. I am ashamed that it should be possible for me to behave so and am humiliated to have no assurance that I should not again behave in the same manner, should my illness return."

"I understand perfectly what you mean, for I fancy I know a little more of illness than you do. Shall I tell you where the fault of your self-training lies?"

"That is just what I want. The things which it pleased me to contemplate, when I was well, gave me no pleasure when I was ill. Nothing seemed the same."

"If we were always in a right mood, there would be no room for the exercises of the will: we should go by mood and inclination only. Where you have been wrong is that you influence your feelings only by thought and argument with yourself, and not also by contact with your fellows. Besides myself and the two ladies, you have hardly a friend in this neighborhood. One friend cannot afford you half enough experience to teach you the relations of life and human needs. At best, under such circumstances, you can only have right theories; practice for realizing them in yourself is nowhere—'but if a man love not his brother whom he hath seen, how can he love God whom he hath not seen?' To love our neighbor is a great help toward loving God. How this love is to come about without relations, I do not see. And how without this love we are to bear up against the thousand irritations of our unavoidable human relations, I cannot tell either."

"But," returned Mr. Stoddart, "I have true regard for you, and some friendly communication with you. If human contact were what is required in my case, how should I fail just with respect to the only man with whom I hold such?"

"Because the relations in which you stood with me were those of the individual, not of the race. You like me because I am fortunate enough to please you—to be a gentleman, I hope—to be a man of some education, and capable of understanding what you tell me of your plans and pursuits. But you do not feel any relation to me on the ground of my humanity—that God made me and therefore I am your brother. It is not because we grow out of the same stem, but merely because my leaf is a little like your own that you draw to me. Disturb your liking, and your love vanishes."

"You are severe."

"I don't mean really vanishes, but disappears for the time. Yet you will confess you have to wait till it comes back again of itself."

"Yes, I confess. To my sorrow, I find it so."

"Let me tell you the truth, Mr. Stoddart. You seem to me to have been only a dilettante or amateur in spiritual matters. Do not imagine I mean hypocrite. Very far from it. The word *amateur* itself suggests a real interest, though it may be superficial. But in relations one must be *all* there. You have taken much interest in unusual forms of theory, and in mystical speculations, to which in themselves I make no objection. But to be content with those, instead of knowing God Himself, or to substitute a general amateur friendship toward the race for the love of your neighbor, is a mockery which will always manifest itself to an honest mind like yours in such failure and disappointment in your own character as you are now lamenting, if not in some mode far more alarming, because gross and terrible."

"Am I to understand you, then, that relations with one's neighbors ought to take the place of meditation?"

"By no means. They ought to go side by side, if you would have at once a healthy mind to judge, and the means of either verifying your speculations or discovering their falsehood."

"But where am I to find such friends besides yourself with whom to hold spiritual communion?"

"It is the communion of spiritual deeds—deeds of justice, of mercy, of humility, the kind word, the cup of cold water, the visitation in sickness, the lending of money—not spiritual conference or talk. The latter will come of itself where it is natural. You would soon find that it is not only to those whose spiritual windows are of the same shape as your own that you are neighbor; there is one poor man in my congregation who knows more, *practically,* of spirituality of mind than any of us. Perhaps you could not teach him much, but he could teach you. At all events, our neighbors are just those round about us. And the most ignorant man in a little place like Marshmallows, one like you ought to know and understand, and have some good influence upon. He is your brother whom you are bound to care for and elevate—not socially but in himself—if it be possible. Never was there a more injurious mistake than to say it is the business of only the clergy to care for souls."

"But that would leave me no time for myself."

"Would that be no time for yourself spent in leading a noble, Christian life? In verifying the words of our Lord by doing them? In building your house on the rock of action instead of the sands of theory? You would find health radiating into your own bosom, healing sympathies springing up in the most barren acquaintance, channels opening for the inrush of truth into your own mind, and opportunities afforded for the exercise of that self-discipline, the lack of which led to the failures which you now bemoan. Some of your speculations would fall into the background simply because the truth, showing itself grandly true, had so filled and occupied your mind that it left no room for anxiety about such questions. Nothing so much as humble ministrations to your neighbors will help you to that perfect love of God which casteth out fear. Nothing but the love of God—that God revealed in Christ—will make you able to love your neighbor aright. And the Spirit of God will by these loves strengthen you to believe in the light even in the midst of darkness; to hold the resolution formed in health when sickness has altered the appearance of everything around you; and to feel tenderly toward your fellow, even when you yourself are dejected or in pain. But, I fear I have transgressed the bounds of all propriety. I can only say I have spoken in proportion to my feeling of its weight and truth."

"I thank you heartily," returned Mr. Stoddart, rising. "I promise you to think over what you have been saying. I hope to be in the organ loft next Sunday."

So he was. And Miss Oldcastle was in the pew with her mother. Nor did she go anymore to Addicehead to church.

TWENTY

The Devil in Thomas Weir

As the winter went on, it was sad to look on the slow decline of Catharine Weir. It seemed as if the dead season was dragging her to its bosom, to lay her among the leaves of past summers. She was still to be found in the shop, or appeared in it as often as the bell rang to announce a customer, but she was terribly worn, and her step indicated much weakness. Nor had the signs of restless trouble diminished. There was the same dry, fierce fire in her eyes, the same forceful compression of her lips, the same evidences of brooding over some absorbing thought or feeling. She seemed to me, and to Dr. Duncan as well, to be dying of resentment. Would nobody do anything for her? Would not her father help her? He was grown more gentle now, as Christian principles and feelings had begun to rise and operate in him. And surely the influence of his son must by this time have done something not only to soften his character generally, but to appease the anger he had cherished toward the one ewe-lamb, against which—having wandered away into the desert place—he had closed and barred the door of the sheepfold. I would go and see him, and see what could be done for her.

(When I thought of a thing and had concluded it might do, I seldom put off the consequent action. I found I was wrong sometimes, and that the particular action did no good; but thus movement was kept up in my operative nature, preventing it from sinking toward inactivity. Besides, to find out what will *not* do is a step toward finding out what will do, and an unsuccessful attempt may set something in motion that *will* help.)

A red, rayless sun was looking through the frosty fog of the winter morning as I walked across the bridge to find Thomas Weir in his workshop. The poplars stood all along the dark, cold river like goblin sentinels, with black heads upon which the long hair stood on end. Nature looked like a life out of which the love had vanished. I turned from it and hastened on.

Young Tom was busy working with a spokeshave at the spoke of a cartwheel. How curiously the smallest visual fact will sometimes keep its place in the memory, when it cannot, with all earnestness of endeavor, recall a far more important fact!

"A cold morning, Thomas," I called from the door.

"I can always keep myself warm, Sir."

"What are you doing, Tom?" I said, going up to him first.

"A little job for myself, Sir. I'm making a few bookshelves."

"I want to have a little talk with your father. Just let me have half an hour."

"Yes, Sir, certainly."

I went to the other end of the shop for, curiously, although father and son were on the best of terms, they always worked as far from each other as the shop would permit, and it was a very large room.

"It is not easy always to keep warm through and through, Thomas," I said.

I suppose my tone revealed to his quick perceptions that "more was meant than met the ear." He looked up from his work, his tool filled with an uncompleted shaving.

"And when the heart gets cold," I went on, "it is not easily warmed again. The fire's hard to light there, Thomas."

Still he looked at me, stopped over his work, apparently with a presentiment of what was coming.

I continued, "I fear there is no way of lighting it again, except the blacksmith's way."

"Hammering the iron till it is red-hot, you mean, Sir?"

"I do. When a man's heart has grown cold, the blows of affliction must fall thick and heavy before the fire can light it. When did you last see your daughter Catharine, Thomas?"

His head dropped, and he began to work as if for bare life. Not a word came from the form now bent over his tool, as if he had never lifted himself up since he first began in the morning. I could just see that his face was deadly pale, and his lips compressed like those of one of the violent who take the kingdom of heaven by force. He went on working till the silence became so lengthened that it seemed settled into the endless. I felt embarrassed. To break a silence is sometimes as hard as to break a spell. What Thomas would have done or said if he had not had this safety valve of bodily exertion, I cannot even imagine.

"Thomas," I said, at length, laying my hand on his shoulder, "you are not going to part company with me, I hope?"

"You drive a man too far, Sir, and I don't know that I oughtn't to be ashamed of it. But you don't know where to stop. A man must be at peace somewhen."

"The question is, Thomas, whether I would be driving you on or back. You and I too must go on or back. I want to go on, myself, and to make you go on too. I don't want to be parted from you now or then."

"That's all very well, Sir, and very kind, I don't doubt. But, as I said afore, a man must be at peace somewhen."

"Peace! I trust in God we shall both have it one day, somewhen, as you say. Have you this peace so plentifully now that you are satisfied? You will never get it but by going on."

"I do not think there is any good in stirring a puddle. Let bygones be bygones. You make a mistake, Sir, in rousing an anger which I would willingly let sleep."

"Better a wakeful anger and a wakeful conscience with it, than an anger sunk into indifference and a sleeping dog of conscience that will not bark. To have ceased to be angry is not one step nearer to your daughter. Better strike her, abuse her, with the chance of a kiss to follow. Ah! Thomas, you are like Jonah with his gourd."

"I don't see what that has to do with it."

"I will tell you. You are fierce in wrath at the disgrace to your family. Your pride is up in arms. You don't care for the misery of your daughter who, the more wrong she has done, is the more to be pitied by a father's heart. The wrong your daughter has done you care nothing about, or you would have taken her to your arms years ago, in the hope that the fervor of your love would drive the devil out of her and make her repent. I say it is not the wrong but the disgrace you care for. The gourd of your pride is withered, and yet you will water it with your daughter's misery."

"Go out of my shop," he cried, "or I may say what I should be sorry for."

I turned at once and left him. I found young Tom round the corner, leaning against the wall, reading his Virgil.

"Don't speak to your father for a while, Tom," I said. "I've put him out of temper. He will be best left alone."

He looked frightened.

"There's no harm done, Tom, my boy. I've been talking to him about your sister. He must have time to think over what I have said to him. Be as attentive to him as you can."

"I will, Sir."

I had called up all the man's old misery, set the wound bleeding again. Shame was once more wide awake and tearing at his heart. That his daughter should have done so! For she had been his pride. She had been the belle of the village, had been apprenticed to a dressmaker in Addicehead and had, after a year and a half, returned with child. The fact of Addicehead being a garrison town had something to do with her fate. In springtime, when flowers were loveliest and hope was strongest for summer, her life was changed into a dreary, windswept, rain-sodden moor. The man who can accept such a sacrifice from a woman—much less will it from her—is as contemptible as the pharisee who, with his long prayers, devours the widow's house. He leaves her desolate while he walks off free.

But Catharine never would utter a word to reveal the name or condition of him by whom she had been wronged. To his child, as long as he drew his life from her, she behaved with strange alternations of dislike and passionate affection, after which season the latter began to diminish in violence, and the former to become more fixed. By the time I had made their acquaintance, her feelings seemed to have settled into what would have been indifference, but for the constant reminder of her shame and wrong which his very presence was.

The child had been born under her father's roof. What a wretched time it must have been for both her and her father until she left his house!

TWENTY-ONE

The Devil in Catharine Weir

About this time my father was taken ill, and several journeys to London followed. I had a half sister, about half my own age, whose anxiety during my father's illness rendered my visits more frequent than perhaps they would have been. But my sister was right in her anxiety: my father grew worse, and in December he died. I will not eulogize one so dear to me. That he was no common man will appear from his unconventionality and justice in leaving his property to my sister, saying in his will that he had done all I could require of him in giving me a good education and that men having means in their power which women had not, it was unjust to the latter to make them (without a choice) dependent upon the former. After the funeral, my sister begged me to take her with me. So, after arranging affairs, we set out and reached Marshmallows on New Year's Day.

My sister being so much younger than myself, her presence in my house made very little change in my habits. She came into my ways without any difficulty, and soon I began to find her of considerable service among the poor and sick of my flock, the latter class being more numerous this winter, on account of the greater severity of the weather.

I now began to note a change in the habits of Catharine Weir. As far as I remember, I had never up to this time seen her out of her own house, except in church, at which she had been a regular attendant for many weeks. Now, however, I began to meet her when and where I least expected—I do not say often, but so often as to make me believe she wandered about frequently. It was always at night, however, and always in stormy weather. The marvel was not that a sick woman could be there—for a sick woman may be able to do anything—but that she could do so more than once. At the same time, I began to miss her from church.

I had naturally a predilection for rough weather. I think I enjoyed fighting with a storm in winter nearly as much as lying on the grass under a beech tree in summer. There is a pleasure of its own in conflict, and I have always experienced a certain indescribable exaltation even in struggling with a well-set, thoroughly roused storm of wind and snow or rain. I was now quite well, and had no reason to fear bad consequences from the indulgence of this surely innocent form of the love of strife.

One January afternoon, just as twilight was folding her gray cloak about her, I felt as if the elements were calling me, and I rose to obey the summons. My sister was, by this time, so accustomed to my going out in all weathers that she troubled me with no expostulation. My spirits began to rise the moment I was in the wind. Keen and cold and unsparing, it swept through the leafless branches around me with a different hiss for every tree that bent and swayed and tossed in its torrent. I made my way to the gate and out upon the road and then, turning to the right, away from the village. I sought a kind of common, open and treeless, the nearest approach to a wind-swept moor in the county.

I had walked with my head bent low against the blast for the better part of a mile, fighting for every step of the way. I came to a deep-cut opening at right angles from the road, whence at some time or other a large quantity of sand had been carted. I turned into it to recover my breath, and to listen to the wind in its fierce rush over the common. I was startled by such a moan as seemed about to break into a storm of passionate cries, but was followed by the words, "O God! I cannot bear it longer! Hast Thou no help for me?"

I knew that Catharine Weir was beside me, though I could not see where she was. In a moment more, however, I thought I could distinguish her figure crouching in an attitude of abandoned despair, the body bent forward over the drawn-up knees, and the face thus hidden even from the darkness. I resolved to make an attempt to probe the evil to its root, though I had but little hope of doing any good. I went near her with the words, "God has, indeed, help for His own offspring. Has He not suffered that He might help? But you have not yet forgiven."

When I began to speak she gave a slight start—she was far too miserable to be terrified at anything. Before I had finished, she stood erect on her feet, facing me, with the whiteness of her face glimmering through the blackness of the night.

"I ask Him for peace," she said, "and He sends me more torment."

"If we had what we asked for always, we should too often find it was not what we wanted, after all."

"You will not leave me alone," she said. "It is too bad."

Poor woman! It was well for her she could pray to God in her trouble, for she could scarcely endure a word from her fellowman. Despairing before God, she was fierce as a tigress to her fellow-sinner who would stretch a hand to help her out of the mire, and set her beside him on the rock which he felt firm under his own feet.

"I will not leave you alone, Catharine," I said. "Scorn my interference as you will. I have yet to give an account of you—and I have to fear lest my

Master should require your blood at my hands. I did not follow you here, but I have found you here, and I must speak."

All this time the wind was roaring overhead. But in the hollow was stillness, and I was so near that I could hear every word she spoke in her low, compressed tone.

"Have you a right to persecute me," she said, "because I am unhappy?"

"I have a right and more—a duty to aid your better self against your worse. You, I fear, are siding with your worse self."

"You judge me hard. I have had wrongs that—"

And here she stopped in a way that let me know she could say no more.

"That you have had wrongs, and bitter wrongs, I do not for a moment doubt. And him who has done you most wrong you will not forgive."

"No."

"No, not even for the sake of Him who, hanging on the tree—after all the bitterness of blows and whipping and derision and rudest gestures and taunts, even when the faintness of death was upon Him—cried to His Father to forgive their cruelty? He asks you to forgive the man who wronged you, and you will not—not even for Him? O Catharine, Catharine!"

"It is very easy to talk, Mr. Walton," she returned, with forced but cool scorn.

"Tell me then," I said, "have *you* nothing to repent of? Have *you* done no wrong in this miserable matter?"

"I do not understand you, Sir," she said, freezingly.

"Catharine Weir," I said, "did not God give you a house to keep fair and pure for Him? Did you keep it such?"

"He told me lies," she cried fiercely, with a cry that seemed to pierce the storm and rise toward the everlasting justice. "He lied and I trusted. For his sake I sinned, and he threw me from him."

"You gave him what was not yours to give. What right had you to cast your pearl before a swine? But dare you say it was all for his sake you did it? Was it all self-denial? Was there no self-indulgence?"

She made a broken gesture of lifting her hands to her head, let them drop by her side, and said nothing.

"You knew you were doing wrong. You felt it even more than he did, for God made you with a more delicate sense of purity, with a womanly foreboding of disgrace to help you to hold your cup of honor steady, which yet you dropped on the ground. Do not seek refuge in the cant about a woman's weakness. A woman is just as strong as she will be. And now, instead of humbling yourself before your Father in heaven, whom you have wronged more even than your father on earth, you rage over your injuries and cherish hatred against him who wronged you. But I will go yet further and show you, in God's name, that you wronged your seducer, for you were his keeper, as he was yours. What if he had found a noble-hearted girl, who also trusted him entirely just until she knew she ought not to listen to him a moment longer—who, when his love showed itself less than human, caring but for itself, rose in the royalty of her maidenhood, and looked him in the face—would he not have been ashamed before her and so before himself, seeing in the glass of her dignity his own contemptibleness? But instead of such a woman, he found you who let him do as he would. No redemption for him in you. And now he walks the earth the worse for you, defiled by your spoil, glorying in his poor victory over you, despising all women for your sake, unrepentant and proud, ruining others the easier that he has already ruined you."

"He does! He does!" she shrieked. "But I will have my revenge. I can and I will!"

And, darting past me, she rushed out into the storm. Her dim shape went down the wind before me into the darkness. I followed in the same direction, fast and faster, for the wind was behind me, and a vague fear which ever grew in my heart urged me to overtake her. What had I done? To what had I driven her? All I had said was true, and I had spoken from motives which I could not condemn. "Poor sister," I thought, "was it for me thus to reproach thee who hadst suffered already so fiercely? If the Spirit speaking in thy heart could not win thee, how should my words of hard accusation, true though they were, every one of them, rouse in thee anything but the wrath that springs from shame? Should I not have tried again, and yet again, to waken thy love? And then a sweet and healing shame, like that of her who bathed the Master's feet with her tears, would have bred fresh love, and no wrath."

But I answered myself that my heart had not been the less tender toward her for that I had tried to humble her, for it was that she might slip from under the net of her pride. Even when my tongue spoke the hardest things I could find, my heart was yearning over her.

The wind fell a little as we came near the village, and the rain began to come down in torrents. Suddenly, her strength giving way, she fell to the earth with a cry. I was beside her in a moment. She was insensible. I did what I could for her, and in a few minutes she began to come to.

"Where am I? Who is it?" she asked listlessly.

When she found who I was, she made a great effort to rise and succeeded.

"You must take my arm," I said, "and I will help you to the vicarage."

"I will go home," she answered.

"Lean on me now, at least, for you must get somewhere."

"What does it matter?" she said, in a tone of despair that went to my very heart.

A wild half cry, half sob followed, and then she took my arm and said nothing more. Nor did I trouble her with any words, except, when we reached the gate, to beg her to come into the vicarage instead of going home. But she would not listen to me, and so I took her home.

She pulled the key of the shop from her pocket. Her hand trembled so that I took it from her and opened the door. A candle was flickering on the counter, and stretched out there lay little Gerard, fast asleep.

"Ah! Little darling!" I said in my heart, "this is not much like painting the sky yet. But who knows?" And as I uttered the commonplace question in my mind, in my mind it was suddenly changed for the answer was, "God."

I lifted the little fellow in my arms. He had fallen asleep weeping, and his face was dirty and streaked with the channels of his tears. Catharine stood with the candle in her hand, waiting for me to go. But, without heeding her, I bore my child to the door that led to their dwelling. I had never been up those stairs before and, therefore, knew nothing of the way. But, without offering any opposition, his mother followed and lighted my way. What a sad face of suffering and strife it was upon which that dim light fell! She set the candle down upon the table of a small room at the top of the stairs, which might have been comfortable enough but that it was neglected and disordered. I saw that her child did not sleep with her, for his crib stood in a corner of their sitting room.

I sat down on a haircloth couch and proceeded to undress little Gerard, trying not to wake him. In this I was almost successful. Catharine stood staring at me without saying a word. She looked dazed, perhaps from the effects of her fall, but she did bring me his nightgown. Just as I had finished putting it on and was rising to lay him in his crib, he opened his eyes and looked at me. Then he gave a hurried look round for his mother, and threw his arms about my neck and kissed me. I laid him down, and the same moment he was fast asleep. In the morning it would not be even a dream to him.

"Now," I thought, "you are safe for the night, poor fatherless child. Even your mother's hardness will not make you sad now. Perhaps the Heavenly Father will send you loving dreams."

I turned to Catharine and bade her good-night. Instead of returning my leave-taking, she said, "Do not fancy you will get the better of me, Mr. Walton, by being kind to that boy. I will have my revenge, and I know how. I am only waiting my time. When he is just going to drink, I will dash it from his hand. I will. At the altar I will."

Her eyes were flashing almost with madness, and she made fierce gestures with her arm. I saw that argument was useless.

"You loved him once, Catharine," I said. "Love him again. Love him better. Forgive him. Revenge is far worse than anything you have done yet."

"What do I care? Why should I care?" And she laughed terribly.

I made haste to leave the room and the house. I lingered outside, however, for nearly an hour, lest she should do something altogether insane. But at length I saw the candle appear in the shop, which was some relief to my anxiety. Reflecting that her one consuming thought of revenge was some security for her conduct otherwise, I went home.

That night my own troubles seemed small to me, and I did not brood over them at all. My mind was filled with the idea of the sad misery which that poor woman was, and I prayed for her as a desolate human world whose sun had deserted the heavens, whose fair fields, rivers, and groves were hardening into the frost of death. "If I am sorrowful," I said, "God lives, nonetheless. And His will is better than mine, yea, is my hidden and perfected will. In Him is my life. His will be done. What, then, is my trouble compared to hers? I will not sink into it and be selfish."

In the morning my first business was to inquire after her. I found her in the shop, looking very ill, and obstinately reserved. Gerard sat in a corner, looking as far from happy as a child of his years could look. As I left the shop, he crept out with me.

"Gerard, come back," cried his mother.

"I will not take him away," I said.

The boy looked up in my face, as if he wanted to whisper to me, and I stooped to listen.

"I dreamed last night," said the boy, "that a big angel with white wings came and took me out of my bed, and carried me high, high up—so high that I could not dream anymore."

"We shall be carried up so high one day, Gerard, my boy, that we shall not want to dream anymore, for we shall be carried up to God Himself. But, until then, you should go back to your mother."

He obeyed at once, and I went on through the village.

TWENTY-TWO

The Devil in the Vicar

I wanted just to pass the gate and look up the road toward Oldcastle Hall. I thought to see nothing but the empty road between the leafless trees, lying there like a dead stream that would not bear me on to the "sunny pleasure dome with caves of ice" that lay beyond. But just as I reached the gate, Miss Oldcastle came out of the lodge, where I learned afterward the woman who kept the gate was ill.

When she saw me she stopped, and I entered hurriedly and addressed her. But I could say nothing better than the merest commonplaces, for her old manner, a certain coldness shadowed with haughtiness, had returned. This was somehow blended with the sweetness in her face and the gentleness of her manners—there the opposites were, and I could feel them both. There was likewise a certain drawing of herself away from me which checked the smallest advance on my part, so that I bade her good-morning and went away, feeling like "a man forbid"—as if I had done her some wrong and she had chidden me for it. What a stone lay in my breast! I could hardly breathe for it. What could have caused her to change her manner toward me? I had made no advance and could not have offended her. But there I stood enchanted, and there she floated away between the trees, till she turned the slow sweep and I, breathing deep as she vanished from my sight, turned likewise and walked back the dreary way to the village. And now I knew that I had never been more miserable in my life before—and I knew too that I had never loved her as I did now.

But I would continue to try to do my work as if nothing had happened. So I went on to fulfill the plan with which I had left home, including, as it did, a visit to Thomas Weir, whom I had not seen in his shop since he had ordered me out of it. This was more accidental than intentional. I was pleased to find that my words had had force enough to rouse his wrath. Anything rather than indifference! That the heart of the honest man would in the end right me, I could not doubt. In the meantime I would see whether a friendly call might not improve the state of affairs. Till he yielded to the voice within him, however, I could not expect that our relation to each other would be restored. As long as he resisted his conscience, and knew that I sided with his conscience, it was impossible that he should regard me with peaceful eyes.

I found him busy, as usual, for he was one of the most diligent men I have ever known. But his face was gloomy, and I thought or fancied that the old scorn had begun once more to usurp the expression of it. Young Tom was not in the shop.

"It is a long time since I saw you, now, Thomas."

"I can hardly wonder at that," he returned, as if he were trying to do me justice; but his eyes dropped, and he resumed his work and said no more. I thought it better to make no reference to the past.

"How is Tom?" I asked.

"Well enough," he returned. Then, with a smile of peevishness not unmingled with contempt, he added, "He's getting too uppish for me. I don't think the Latin agrees with him."

I could not help suspecting at once how the matter stood, namely, that the father, unhappy in his conduct to his daughter, and unable to make up his mind to do right with regard to her, had been behaving captiously and unjustly to his son, and so had rendered himself more miserable than ever.

"Perhaps he finds it too much for him without me," I said, evasively, "but I called today partly to inform him that I am quite ready now to recommence our readings together, after which I hope you will find the Latin agrees with him better."

"I wish you would let him alone, Sir—I mean, take no more trouble about him. You see I can't do as you want me. I wasn't made to go another man's way, and so it's very hard—more than I can bear—to be under so much obligation to you."

"But you mistake me altogether, Thomas. It is for the lad's own sake that I want to go on reading with him, and hope you won't interfere between him and any use I can be of to him. I assure you, to have you go my way instead of your own is the last thing I could wish, though I confess I do wish very much that you would choose the right way for your own way."

He made me no answer but maintained a sullen silence.

"Thomas," I said, at length, "I had thought you were breaking every bond of Satan that withheld you from entering into the kingdom of heaven. But I fear he has strengthened his bands, and holds you now as much a captive as ever. It is not even your own way you are walking in, but his."

"It's no use your trying to frighten me. I don't believe in the devil."

"It is God I want you to believe in, and I am not going to dispute with you about whether there is a devil. In a matter of life and death, we have no time for settling every disputed point."

"Life or death! What do you mean?"

"I mean that whether you believe there is a devil or not, you *know* there is an evil power in your mind dragging you down. I am not speaking in generalities. I mean *now,* and you know as to what I mean it. And if you yield to it, that evil power will drag you down to death. It is a matter of life or death, not of theory about the devil."

"Well, I always did say that if you once give a priest an inch, he'll take an ell, and I am sorry I forgot it for once."

Having said this, he shut up his mouth in a manner that indicated plainly enough he would not open it again for some time. This, more than his speech, irritated me, and with a mere "Good morning," I walked out of the shop.

No sooner was I in the open air than I knew that I too—I as well as poor Thomas Weir—was under a spell; knew that I had gone to him before I had recovered sufficiently from the mingled disappointment and mortification of my interview with Miss Oldcastle; that while I spoke to him I was not speaking with a whole heart; that I had been discharging a duty as if I had been discharging a musket; that, although I had spoken the truth, I had spoken it ungraciously and selfishly.

I could not bear it. I turned and went back into the shop.

"Thomas, my friend," I said, holding out my hand, "I beg your pardon. I was wrong. I spoke to you as I ought not. I was troubled in my own mind, and that made me lose my temper and be rude to you, who are far more troubled than I. Forgive me!"

He did not take my hand at first, but stared at me as if he supposed that I was backing up what I had said last with more of the same sort. But by the time I had finished he saw what I meant. His countenance altered, and he looked as if the evil spirit were about to depart from him. He held out his hand, gave mine a great grasp, dropped his head, went on with his work without a word.

I went out of the shop once more, but in a greatly altered mood.

On the way home, I tried to find out how it was that I had that morning failed so signally. I had little virtue in keeping my temper, because it was naturally very even. Therefore, I had the more shame in losing it. I had borne all my uneasiness about Miss Oldcastle without, as far as I knew, transgressing in this fashion till this very morning.

Till this morning I had experienced no personal mortification with respect to Miss Oldcastle. It was not the mere disappointment of having no more talk with her—for the sight of her was a blessing I had not in the least expected—but the fact that she had repelled or seemed to repel me. And thus I found that self was at the root of the wrong I had done. I ought to have been as tender as a mother over her wounded child. Something was wrong when one whose special business it was to serve his people, in the name of Him who was full of grace and truth, made them suffer because of his own inward pain.

No sooner had I settled this in my mind than my trouble returned with a sudden pang. Had I actually seen her that morning, and spoken to her, and left her with a pain in my heart? What if that face of hers was doomed ever to bring with it such a pain—to be ever to me no more than a lovely vision radiating grief? If so, I would endure in silence and as patiently as I could, trying to make up for the lack of brightness in my own fate by causing more brightness in the fate of others.

That moment I felt a little hand poke itself into mine. I looked down, and there was Gerard Weir looking up in my face. I found myself in the midst of the children coming out of school, for it was Saturday, and a half holiday. He smiled up in my face, and I smiled in his. And so, hand in hand, we went on to the vicarage where I gave him up to my sister. But I cannot convey any notion of the quietness that entered my heart with the grasp of that childish hand. I think it was the faith of the boy in me that comforted me; but I could not help thinking of the words of our Lord about receiving a child in His name, and so receiving Him.

By the time we reached the vicarage my heart was very quiet. As the little child held my hand, so I seemed to be holding God's hand. A sense of heart-security, as well as soul-safety, awoke in me, and I said to myself, "Surely He will take care of my heart as well as of my mind and my conscience." For one blessed moment I seemed to be at the very center of things, and I thought I then knew something of what the Apostle Paul meant when he said, "Your life is hid with Christ in God."

I had not had my usual ramble this morning and was otherwise ill-prepared for Sunday, so I went early into the church. But, finding that the sexton's wife had not yet finished lighting the stove, I sat down to wait by my own fire in the vestry.

I was very particular in having the church well warmed before Sunday. I think some parsons must neglect this on principle, because warmth may make a weary creature go to sleep here and there about the place—as if any healing doctrine could enter the soul while it is on the rack of the frost. The clergy should see—for it is their business—that their people have no occasion to think of their bodies at all while they are in church. They have enough ado to think of the truth. When our Lord was feeding even their bodies, He made them all sit down on the grass. It is worth noticing that there was much grass in the place—a rare thing, I should think, in those countries—and therefore, perhaps, it was chosen by Him for their comfort in feeding their souls and bodies both. One of the reasons why some churches are the least likely places for anything good to be found is that they are as wretchedly cold to the body as they are to the soul—too cold every way for anything to grow in them. Edelweiss, "noblewhite," as they call a plant growing under the snow on some of the Alps, could not survive the winter in such churches. There is small welcome in a cold house, and the clergyman, who is the steward, should look to it. It is for him to give his Master's friends a welcome to his Master's house, for the welcome of a servant is precious, and nowadays very rare.

I went into the old church, which looked as if it were quietly waiting for its people. As if, having gathered a soul of its own out of the generations that have worshiped here for so long, it had feeling enough to grow hungry for a psalm before the end of the week.

To my amazement and delight the old organ woke up and began to think aloud. It began to sigh out the "Agnes Dei" of Mozart's *Twelfth Mass* upon the air of the still church. How could it be? I know now, and I guessed then, though I took no step to verify my conjecture, for I felt that I was upon my honor. I sat in one of the pews and listened till the old organ sobbed itself into silence. Then I heard the steps of the sexton's wife vanish from the church, heard her lock the door, and I knew I was alone in the ancient pile, with the twilight growing thick about me; and I felt like Sir Galahad when, after the "rolling organ harmony," he heard "wings flutter, voices hover clear."

I lingered on long in the dark church and there I made my sermon for the next morning. Its original germ, its concentrated essence of sermon, was in these four verses:

Had I the grace to win the grace
Of some old man complete in lore,
My face would worship at his face,
Like childhood seated on the floor.

Had I the grace to win the grace
Of childhood, loving, shy, apart,
The child should find a nearer place,
And teach me resting on my heart.

Had I the grace to win the grace
Of maiden living all above,
My soul would trample down the base,
That she might have a man to love.

A grace I have no grace to win
Knocks now at my half-open door:
Ah, Lord of glory, come Thou in,
Thy grace divine is all and more.

I told my people that God had created all our worships, reverences, tendernesses, loves. That they had come out of His heart and were put into us because they were in Him first. That all we could imagine of the wise, the lovely, the beautiful, was in Him, only infinitely more than we could imagine or understand. That in Him was all the wise teaching of the best man and more; all the grace, gentleness, and truth of the best child and more; all the tenderness and devotion of the truest woman and more. Therefore, we must be all God's, and all our aspirations, all our worships, all our honors, all our loves, must center in Him.

TWENTY-THREE

An Angel Unawares

I resolved on Monday to have the long country walk I had been disappointed of on Saturday. It was such a day as seems impossible to describe except in negatives. It was not stormy, it was not rainy, it was not sunshiny, it was not snowy, it was not frosty, it was not foggy, it was not clear—it was nothing but cloudy and quiet and cold, and generally ungenial, with just a puff of wind now and then. It was an exact representation of my own mind and heart. The summer was thousands of miles off on the other side of the globe. Ethelwyn seemed millions of miles away. The summer might come back but she never would come nearer. The whole of life appeared faint and foggy. I seemed to have done no good. I had driven Catharine Weir to the verge of suicide, while at the same time I could not restrain her from the contemplation of some dire revenge. I had lost the man upon whom I had most reckoned as a seal of my ministry, namely, Thomas Weir. True, there was Old Rogers, but Old Rogers was just as good before I found him. I could not dream of having made him any better. And so I went on brooding over all the disappointing portions of my labor, all the time thinking about myself instead of God and the work that lay for me to do in the days to come.

"Nobody," I said, "but Old Rogers understands me. Nobody would care, as far as my teaching goes, if another man took my place from next Sunday forward." And for Miss Oldcastle, her playing "Agnus Dei"—even if she intended that I should hear it—indicated at most that she thought she had gone too far and been unkind that morning, or perhaps was afraid lest she should be accountable for any failure I might make in my Sunday duties, and therefore felt bound to do something to restore me.

Unconsciously choosing the dreariest path, I wandered up the side of the slow black river, caring for nothing. The first miserable afternoon at Marshmallows looked now as if it had been the whole of my coming relation to the place seen through a reversed telescope. And here I was in it now.

When I came to the bridge I wanted to cross—a wooden one—I found that the approach to it had been partly undermined and carried away; for here the river had overflowed its banks in one of the late storms, and all about the place was still very wet and swampy. I could therefore get no farther in my gloomy walk, and so turned back upon my steps. Scarcely had I done so when I saw a man coming toward me upon the river walk. I could not mistake him at any distance—Old Rogers.

"Well, Old Rogers," I said, trying to speak cheerfully, "you cannot get much farther this way, without wading a bit, at least."

"I don't want to go no farther now, Sir. I came to find you. I told Master I wanted to leave for an hour or so. He allus lets me do just as I like."

"But how did you know where to find me?"

"I saw you come this way. You passed me right on the bridge, and didn't see me, Sir. So says I to myself, 'Old Rogers, summat's amiss wi' Parson today. He never went by me like that afore. This won't do. You just go and see.' So I went home and told Master, and here I be, Sir. And I hope you're noways offended with the liberty of me."

"Did I really pass you on the bridge?" I said, unable to understand it.

"That you did, Sir. I knowed Parson must be a goodish bit in his own in'ards afore he would do that."

"I needn't tell you that I didn't see you."

"I could tell you that, Sir. I hope there's nothing gone main wrong, Sir. Miss is well, Sir?"

"Quite well, I thank you. No, my dear fellow, nothing's gone main wrong, as you say. Some of my running tackle got jammed a bit, that's all. I'm a little out of spirits, I believe."

"Well, Sir, don't think I want to get aboard your ship, except you fling me a rope. There's a many things you mun ha' to think about that an ignorant man like me couldn't take up if you was to let 'em drop. And being a gentleman, I do believe, makes the matter worse betuxt us. And there's many a thing that no man can go talkin' about to any but only the Lord Himself. Still, you can't help us poor folks seeing when there's summat amiss, and we can't help havin' our own thoughts anymore than the sailor's jackdaw that couldn't speak. And sometimes we may be nearer the mark than you would suppose, for God has made us all of one blood, you know."

"What are you driving at, Old Rogers?" I said, with a smile, which was none the less true that I suspected he had read some of the worst trouble of my heart. For why should I mind an honorable man like him knowing what oppressed me, though I should not choose to tell it to any but one?

"I want—with the clumsy hand of a rough old tar, with a heart as soft as the pitch that makes his hand hard—to trim your sails a bit, Sir, and help you to lie a point closer to the wind. You're just not close-hauled, Sir."

"Say on, Old Rogers. I will listen with all my heart, for you have a good right to speak."

And Old Rogers spoke thus:

"Oncet upon a time we were becalmed in the South Seas—and weary work it wur, a doin' of nothin' from day to day. But when the water began to come up thick from the bottom of the water casks, it was wearier a deal. Then a thick fog came on, as white as snow a'most, and we couldn't see more than a few yards ahead or on any side of us. But the fog didn't keep the heat off—it only made it worse, and the water was fast going done. The men, some of them, were half mad with thirst. The captain took to his berth, and several of the crew to their hammocks, for it was just as hot on deck as anywhere else. The mate lay on a spare sail on the quarterdeck, groaning. I had a strong suspicion that the barque was drifting, and hove the lead again and again, but could find no bottom. Some of the men got hold of the spirits, and that didn't quench their thirst. It drove them clean mad. I had to knock one of them down myself with a capstan-bar, for he ran at the mate with his knife. At last I began to lose all hope. And still I was sure the barque was slowly drifting. My head was like to burst, and my tongue was like a lump of holystone in my mouth. Well, one morning, I had just, as I thought, lain down on the deck to breathe my last, hoping I should die, when all at once the fog lifted like the foot of a sail. I sprung to my feet. There was the blue sky overhead, but the terrible burning sun was there. A moment more, and a light air blew on my cheek, and turning my face to it as if it had been the very breath of God, I saw an island within half a mile, and the shine of water on the face of a rock on the shore. I cried out, 'Land on the weather-quarter! Fresh water in sight!' A boat was lowered, and in a few minutes we were lying, clothes and all, in a little stream that came down from the hills above.

"There's just as many good days as bad ones—as much fair weather as foul. And if a man keeps up heart, he's all the better for that, and none the worse when the evil day does come. As if there was any chance about what the days would bring forth. No, my lad," said the old sailor, assuming the dignity of his superior years under the inspiration of the truth, "neither boast, nor trust, nor hope in the morrow. Boast and trust and hope in God, for thou shalt yet praise Him, who is the health of thy countenance and thy God."

I could but hold out my hand. I had nothing to say, for he had spoken to me as an angel of God.

The old man was silent for some moments; his emotion needed time to still itself again. Nor did he return to the subject. He held out his hand once more, saying, "Good day, Sir. I must go back to my work."

"I will go back with you."

And so we walked back side by side to the village, but not a word did we speak to the other till we parted upon the bridge where we had first met. Old Rogers went to his work, and I lingered upon the bridge. I leaned upon the low parapet and looked up the stream as far as the mists would permit.

Then I turned and looked down the river crawling out of sight. Then I looked to the left, and there stood my old church, quiet in the dreary day. I turned to the right and saw, as on that first afternoon, the weathercock that watched the winds over the stables at Oldcastle Hall. It caught just one glimpse of the sun through some rent in the vapors, and flung it across to me amidst the general dinginess of the hour.

TWENTY-FOUR
Two Parishioners

My parish was a large one. I have mentioned but one of the great families in it, and confined my recollections entirely to the village and its immediate neighborhood. The houses of most of the gentlefolk lay considerably apart from the church and from each other. Many of them went elsewhere to church, and I did not feel bound to visit those. Still, there were one or two families which I would have visited oftener had I had a horse. Before the winter was over I did buy a gray mare, partly to please Dr. Duncan (who urged me to do it for my health); partly because I could then do my duty better; and partly, I confess, from having been very fond of an old gray mare of my father's.

I mounted her to pay a visit to two rich maiden ladies, the Misses Jemima and Hester Crowther, who came to the services most Sundays when the weather was favorable. I had, however, called upon them only once.

I was shown with much ceremony by a butler (apparently as old as his livery of yellow and green) into the presence of the two ladies, one of whom sat in state reading a volume of the *Spectator*. She—Miss Hester—was very tall and as square as the straight long-backed chair upon which she sat. A fat asthmatic poodle lay at her feet upon the hearthrug. The other—Miss Jemima, a little, lively, gray-haired creature, who looked like a most ancient girl whom no power would ever make old—was standing upon a high chair, cooing to a cockatoo in a gilded cage. As I entered the room, the latter lady all but jumped from her perch with a merry, wavering laugh, and advanced to meet me.

"Jonathan, bring the cake and wine," she cried to the retreating servant.

Hester rose with a solemn stiff-backedness, which was more amusing than dignified, and extended her hand as I approached her, without moving from her place.

"We were afraid, Mr. Walton," said Jemima, "that you had forgotten we were parishioners of yours."

"That I could hardly do," I answered, "seeing you are such regular attendants at church. But I confess I have given you ground for your rebuke, Miss Jemima. I bought a horse the other day, and this is the first use I have put her to."

"We're charmed to see you. It is very good of you not to forget such uninteresting girls as we are."

"You forget, Jemima," interposed her sister, "that time is always on the wing. I should have thought we were both decidedly middle-aged, though you are the elder by I will not say how many years."

"All but ten years, Hester. I remember rocking you in your cradle scores of times. But somehow, Mr. Walton, I can't help feeling as if she were my elder sister. She is so learned, and I don't read anything but the newspapers."

"And your Bible, Jemima. Do yourself justice."

"That's a matter of course, Sister. But this is not the way to entertain Mr. Walton."

"The gentlemen used to entertain the ladies when I was young, Jemima. I do not know how it may have been when you were."

"Much the same, I believe, Sister. But if you look at Mr. Walton, I think you will see that he is pretty much entertained as it is."

"I agree with Miss Hester," I said. "It is the duty of gentlemen to entertain ladies, but it is so much the kinder of ladies when they surpass their duty and condescend to entertain gentlemen."

"What can surpass duty, Mr. Walton?" asked Hester. "I confess I do not agree with your doctrines upon that point. I hope you will not think me rude, but it always seems to me that your congregation is chiefly composed of the lower classes, who may be greatly injured by such a style of preaching. I must say I think so, Mr. Walton. Only perhaps you are one of those who think a lady's opinion on such matters is worth nothing."

"On the contrary, I respect an opinion just as far as the lady or gentleman who holds it seems to me qualified to have formed it first. But you have not yet told me what you think so objectionable in my preaching."

"You always speak as if faith in Christ was something greater than duty. Now I think duty the first thing."

"I quite agree with you, Miss Hester. How can I, or any clergyman, urge a man to that which is not his duty? But tell me, is not faith in Christ a duty? Where you have mistaken me is that you think I speak of faith as higher than duty, when indeed I speak of faith as higher than any *other* duty. It is the highest duty of man. I do not say the duty he always sees clearest, or even sees at all. But when a duty becomes the highest delight of a man, the joy of his very being, he no more thinks or needs to think about it as a duty. What would you think of the love of a son who, when an appeal was made to his affections, should say, 'Oh, yes, I love my mother dearly: it is my duty, of course'?"

"That sounds very plausible but still I cannot help feeling that you preach faith and not works. I do not say that you are not to preach faith, but you know that faith without works is dead."

"Now, really, Hester," interposed Miss Jemima, "I should have said that Mr. Walton was constantly preaching works. He's always telling you to do something or other. I know I always come out of the church with something on my mind, and I've got to work it off somehow before I'm comfortable."

And here Miss Jemima got up on the chair, and began to flirt with the cockatoo once more, but only in silent signs.

I cannot quite recall how this part of the conversation drew to a close. But I will tell a fact or two about the sisters which may explain their different notions of my preaching. Miss Hester scarce left the house, but spent almost the whole of her time in reading small dingy books of eighteenth-century literature. Somehow or other, respectability—in position, in morals, in religion, in conduct—was everything. The consequence was that her very nature was old-fashioned and had nothing in it of that lasting youth which is the birthright of every immortal being.

Miss Jemima, on the contrary, whose eccentricities did not lie on the side of respectability, had gone on shocking the stiff proprieties of her younger sister till she could be shocked no more. She had had a severe disappointment in youth, and had not only survived it but had saved her heart alive out of it, losing only any remnant of selfish care about herself. She now spent that love, which had before been concentrated upon one object, upon every living thing that came near her. She was very odd—with her gray hair, her clear gray eyes with wrinkled eyelids, her light step, her laugh at once girlish and cracked, darting in and out of the cottages, scolding this matron with a smile lurking in every tone, hugging that baby, boxing the ears of the other little tyrant, forgiving this one's rent, and threatening that other with awful vengeances—but it was a very lovely oddity. Their property was not large, and she knew every living thing on the place down to the dogs and pigs. And Miss Jemima, as the people always called her, was the actual queen of the neighborhood—for, though she was the very soul of kindness, she was determined to have her own way and had it.

The one lady did nothing but read, and considered that I neglected the doctrine of works as the seal of faith. The other was busy helping her neighbors from morning to night, and found little in my preaching except incentive to benevolence.

Then Miss Hester made the following further criticism on my pulpit labors:

"You are too anxious to explain everything, Mr. Walton."

What she said looks worse on paper than it sounded from her lips. She was a gentlewoman, and her tone had much to do with the impression made.

"Where can be the use of trying to make uneducated people see the grounds of everything?" she said. "It is enough that this or that is in the Bible."

"Yes, but there is just the point. What is in the Bible? Is it this or that?"

"You are their spiritual instructor: tell them what is in the Bible."

"But you have just been objecting to my mode of representing what is in the Bible."

"It will be so much worse if you add argument to convince them of what is incorrect."

"I doubt that. Falsehood will expose itself the sooner that dishonest argument is used to support it."

"You cannot expect them to judge what you tell them."

"The Bible urges us to search and understand."

"For those whose business it is, like yourself."

"Do you think, then, that the church consists of a few privileged to understand, and a great many who cannot understand and therefore need not be taught?"

"I said you had to teach them."

"But to teach is to make people understand."

"Why don't you try your friend Mrs. Oldcastle? It might do her a little good," said Miss Hester.

"I should have very little influence with Mrs. Oldcastle if I were to make the attempt. And I am not called upon to address my flock individually upon every point of character."

"I thought she was an intimate friend of yours."

"Quite the contrary. We are scarcely friendly."

"I am very glad to hear it," said Miss Jemima, who had been silent during the little controversy that her sister and I had been carrying on. "We have been quite misinformed. We thought we might have seen more of you if it had not been for her. And as very few people of her own position in society care to visit her, we thought it a pity she should be your principal friend in the parish."

"Why do they not visit her more?"

"There are strange stories about her, which it is well to leave alone. They are getting out of date too. But she is not a fit woman to be regarded as the clergyman's friend. There!" said Miss Jemima, as if she had wanted to relieve her bosom of a burden.

"I think, however, her religious opinions would correspond with your own, Mr. Walton," said Miss Hester.

"Possibly," I answered, with indifference. "I don't care much about opinion."

"Her daughter would be a nice girl, I fancy, if she weren't kept down by her mother. She looks scared, poor thing! And they say she's not quite—you know," said Miss Jemima, and gently tapped her head with a forefinger. I laughed. I thought it was not worthwhile to champion Miss Oldcastle's sanity.

"They are, and have been, a strange family as far back as I can remember, and my mother used to say the same. I am glad she comes to our church now. You mustn't let her set her cap at you, though. It wouldn't do at all. She's pretty enough too!"

"Yes," I returned, "she is rather pretty. But I don't think she looks as if she had a cap to set at anybody."

I rose to go, for I did not relish the present conversation.

I rode home slowly, brooding on the lovely marvel that out of such a rough, ungracious stem as the Oldcastle family should have sprung such a delicate, pale, winter-braved flower as Ethelwyn. I prayed that I might rescue her from that ungenial soil.

TWENTY-FIVE
Satan Cast Out

I was within a mile of the village, returning from my visit to the Misses Crowther. My horse, which was walking slowly along the soft side of the road, lifted her head and pricked up her ears at the sound of approaching hooves. The riders soon came in sight—Miss Oldcastle, Judy, and Captain Everard. Miss Oldcastle I had never seen on horseback before. Judy was on a little white pony she used for galloping about the fields near the Hall. The captain was laughing and chatting gaily, now to the one, now to the other. I lifted my hat to Miss Oldcastle, without drawing bridle, and went on. The captain returned my salutation, and likewise rode on. I could just see, as they passed me, that Miss Oldcastle's pale face was flushed even to scarlet, but she only bowed and kept alongside of her companion. About twenty yards farther, I heard the clatter of Judy's pony behind me, and up she came at full gallop.

"Why didn't you stop to speak to us, Mr. Walton?" she said. "I pulled up, but you never looked at me. We shall be cross all the rest of the day because you cut us so. What have we done?"

"Nothing, Judy, that I know of," I answered, trying to speak cheerfully. "But I do not know your companion, and I was not in the humor for an introduction."

She looked hard at me with her keen gray eyes, and I felt as if the child was seeing through me. "I don't know what to make of it, Mr. Walton. You're very different, somehow, from what you used to be. There's something wrong somewhere. I only wish I could do something for you."

I felt the child's kindness, but could only say, "Thank you, Judy. I am sure I should ask you if there were anything you could do for me. But you'll be left behind."

"No fear of that. My Dobbin can go much faster than their big horses. But I see you don't want me, so good-by."

She turned her pony's head as she spoke, jumped the ditch at the side of the road, and flew after them along the grass like a swallow. I likewise roused my horse and went off at a hard trot, with the vain impulse to shake off the tormenting thoughts that crowded me like gadflies. But this day was to be one of more trial still.

As I turned the corner into a street of the village, young Tom Weir was at my side. His face was pale, and he had evidently been watching for me.

"What is the matter, Tom?" I asked, in some alarm.

I could see his bare throat knot and relax, like the motion of a serpent before he could utter the words, "Kate has killed her little boy, Sir." He followed this with a stifled cry and hid his face in his hands.

"God forbid!" I exclaimed, and struck my heels in my horse's sides, nearly overturning poor Tom in my haste. "Come after me, Tom," I said, "and take the mare home."

Had I had a share, by my harsh words, in driving the woman beyond the bounds of human reason and endurance?

Before I reached the door I saw a little crowd of the villagers, mostly women and children, gathered about it. I got off my horse, and gave her to a woman to hold for Tom. With a little difficulty, I prevailed on the rest to go home, and not add to the confusion and terrors by the excitement of their presence. I entered the shop and, locking the door behind me, went up to the room above.

I found no one there. On the hearth and in the fender lay two little pools of blood. All in the house was utterly, dreadfully still. I went to the only other door, peeped in, and entered. On the bed lay the mother, white as death, but with her black eyes wide open, staring at the ceiling. On her arm lay little Gerard, just as white, except where the blood had flowed from the bandage down his deathlike face.

When Catharine caught sight of me, she showed no surprise or emotion of any kind. Her lips uttered the words, "I have done it at last. I am ready. Take me away. I shall be hanged. I don't care. I confess it. Only don't let the people stare at me."

Her lips went on moving, but I could hear no more, till suddenly she broke out in a cry of agony, "Oh! My baby! My baby!"

I heard a loud knocking at the shop door and went down to see who was there. I found Thomas Weir accompanied by Dr. Duncan. We went up together to Catharine's room. Thomas said nothing, and I found it difficult even to conjecture from his countenance what thoughts were passing through his mind.

Catharine looked from one to another of us as if she did not know the one from the other. She made no motion to rise from her bed, nor did she utter a word, although her lips would now and then move as if molding a sentence. When Dr. Duncan, after looking at the child, proceeded to take him from her, she gave him one imploring look and yielded with a moan, then began to stare hopelessly at the ceiling again. The doctor carried the child into the next room, and the grandfather followed.

"You see what you have driven me to!" cried Catharine, the moment I was left alone with her. "I hope you are satisfied."

The words went to my very soul. But when I looked at her, her eyes were wandering about over the ceiling, and I thought it better to leave her and join the others in the sitting room. The first thing I saw there was Thomas on his knees, with a basin of water, washing away the blood of his grandson from his daughter's floor. The very sight of the child had hitherto been nauseous to him, and his daughter had been beyond the reach of his forgiveness. Here was the end of it—the blood of the one shed by the hand of the other, and the father of both on his knees wiping it up. The blood flowed from a wound on the boy's head, evidently occasioned by a fall upon the fender, where the blood lay both inside and out.

In a few minutes Dr. Duncan said, "I think he'll come round."

"Will it be safe to tell his mother so?" I asked.

"I think you may."

I hastened to her room. "Your little darling is not dead, Catharine. He is coming to."

She threw herself off the bed at my feet, caught them round with her arms, and cried, "I will forgive him. I will do anything you like. I forgive George Everard. I will go and ask my father to forgive me."

I lifted her in my arms—how light she was!—and laid her again on the bed, where she lay sobbing and weeping. I went to the other room. Little Gerard opened his eyes and closed them again as I entered.

I beckoned to Thomas. "She wants to ask you to forgive her. Do not, in God's name, wait till she asks you, but go and tell her that you forgive her."

"I dare not say I forgive her," he answered. "I have more need to ask her to forgive me."

I took him by the hand and led him into her room. She feebly lifted her arms toward him. Not a word was said on either side. I left them in each other's embrace. The hard rocks had been struck with the rod, and the waters of life had flowed forth from each and had met between.

When I rejoined Dr. Duncan, I found little Gerard asleep and breathing quietly. "What do you know of this sad business, Mr. Walton?" said the doctor.

"I should like to ask the same question of you," I returned. "Young Tom told me that his sister had murdered the child. That is all I know."

"His father told me the same, and that is all I know. Do you believe it?"

"We have no evidence. We must wait till she is able to explain the thing herself."

"I believe," said Dr. Duncan, "that she struck the child, and that he fell upon the fender."

(As far as Catharine could later account, this was the truth. She could not remember with any clearness what had happened. All she remembered was that she had been more miserable than ever in her life before; that the child had come to her, as he seldom did, with some childish request or other; that she felt herself seized with intense hatred of him; and the next thing she knew was that his blood was running in a long red finger toward her. Then she knew what she had done, though not how she had done it. She remembered nothing more that happened till she lay weeping with the hope that the child would yet live. In the illness that followed, I more than once saw her shudder while she slept, dreaming what her waking memory had forgotten, and once she started awake, crying, "I have murdered him again!")

When Thomas came from his daughter's room, he looked like a man from whom the bitterness of evil had passed away. His face had that childlike expression in its paleness, and the tearfulness without tears haunted his eyes.

"She is asleep," he said.

"You and I must sit with them tonight, Thomas. You'll attend to your daughter, if she wants anything, and I know this little darling won't be frightened if he comes to himself and sees me beside him."

"God bless you, Sir," said Thomas, fervently. (And from that hour to this there has never been a coolness between us.)

"A very good arrangement," said Dr. Duncan, "only I feel as if I ought to have a share in it."

"No, no," I said. "We do not know who may want you. Besides, we are both younger than you."

"I will come over early in the morning, then, and see how you are going on."

I went home to tell my sister and arrange for the night. We carried back with us things to make the two patients comfortable. As regarded Catharine, now that she would let her fellows help her, I was anxious that she should feel that love about her which she had so long driven from her door. I wanted her to read the love of God in the love that even I could show her. And my heart still smote me for the severity with which I had spoken the truth to her.

I took my place beside Gerard, and watched through the night. The little fellow repeatedly cried out in that terror which is so often the consequence of the loss of blood, but when I laid my hand on him, he smiled without waking and lay quite still again for a while. Once or twice he woke up and looked so bewildered that I feared delirium, but a bit of jam comforted him, and he fell fast asleep again. He did not seem even to have a headache from the blow.

But when I was left alone with the child, seated in a chair by the fire—my only light—how my thoughts rushed upon the facts bearing on my own history which this day had brought before me! Horror it was to think of Miss Oldcastle as even riding with the seducer of Catharine Weir! There was torture in the thought of his touching her hand, and to think that before the summer came once more, he might be her husband! Was it fair to let her marry such a man in ignorance? Would she marry him if she knew what I knew of him? Could I speak against my rival? Blacken him even with the truth—the only defilement that can really cling? Could I, for my own dignity, do so? And was she therefore to be sacrificed in ignorance? Might not someone else do it instead of me? But, if I set it agoing, was it not precisely the same thing as if I did it myself, only more cowardly? There was but one way of doing it, and that was with the full and solemn consciousness that it was and must be a barrier between us forever. If I could give her up fully and altogether, then I might tell her the truth. But how bitter to cast away my chance!

Then came another bitter and wicked thought—my own earnestness with Catharine Weir, in urging her to forgiveness, would bear a main part in wrapping up in secrecy that evil thing which ought not to be hid. For had she not vowed to denounce the man at the very altar? Had not the revenge which I had ignorantly combatted been my best ally? And for one brief, black, wicked moment I repented that I had acted as I had. The next I was on my knees by the side of the sleeping child and repenting back again in shame and sorrow. Then came the consolation that if I suffered hereby, I suffered from doing my duty, and that was well.

Scarcely had I seated myself again by the fire when the door of the room opened softly, and Thomas appeared. "Kate wants to see you," he said.

I rose at once. "Perhaps, then, you had better stay with Gerard."

"I will, Sir, for I think she wants to speak to you alone."

I entered her chamber. A candle stood on a chest of drawers, and its light fell on her face. Her eyes glittered, but the fierceness was gone, and only the suffering remained. I drew a chair beside her and took her hand.

"I want to tell you all," she said. "He promised to marry me. I believed him. But I did very wrong. And I have been a bad mother, for I could not keep from seeing his face in Gerard's. Gerard was the name he told me to call him when I had to write to him, and so I named the little darling Gerard. How is he, Sir?"

"Doing nicely," I replied. "I do not think you need be at all uneasy about him now."

"Thank God! I forgive his father now with all my heart. I feel it easier since I saw how wicked I could be myself, and I feel it easier, too, that I have not long to live. I forgive him with all my heart, and I will take no revenge. I have never told anyone yet who he is, but I will tell you. His name is George Everard—Captain Everard. I came to know him when I was apprenticed at Addicehead. I would not tell you, Sir, if I did not know that you will not tell anyone. I saw him yesterday, and it drove me wild. But it is all over now. My heart feels so cool now. Do you think God will forgive me?"

Without one word of my own, I took out my pocket Testament and read these words, "For if ye forgive men their trespasses, your Heavenly Father will also forgive you."

Then I read to her, from the seventh chapter of St. Luke, the story of the woman who was a sinner, and came to Jesus in Simon's house. When I had finished, I found that she was gently weeping, and so I left her and resumed my place by the boy. I told Thomas that he had better not go near her just yet. So we sat in silence together for a while, during which I felt so weary and benumbed that I fell asleep in my chair. I suddenly returned to consciousness at a cry from Gerard. He was fast asleep, but standing on his feet in his crib, pushing with his hands from before him, as if resisting someone, and crying, "Don't—don't. Go away! Mammy! Mr. Walton!"

I took him in my arms and kissed him and laid him down again, and he lay still.

Thomas came again into the room. "I am sorry to be so troublesome, Sir," he said, "but my poor daughter says there is one thing more she wants to say to you."

I returned at once. As soon as I entered the room she said eagerly, "I forgive him. I forgive him with all my heart—but don't let him take Gerard."

I assured her I would do my best to prevent any such attempt on his part, and making her promise to try to go to sleep, left her once more. Nor was either of the patients disturbed again during the night. Both slept, as it appeared, refreshingly.

In the morning the old doctor made his welcome appearance, and pronounced both quite as well as he had expected to find them. He sent young Tom to take my place, and my sister to take the father's. It was of no use trying to go to sleep, so I set out for a walk.

TWENTY-SIX

The Man and the Child

It was a fine frosty morning, which overcame in a great measure my depression. I sought the rugged common where I had met Catharine Weir in the storm and darkness. I reached the same chasm where I had sought a breathing space that night, and sat down upon a block of sand which the frost had detached from the wall above.

I found my mind relieved by the fact that I had urged Catharine to a confession. It was, however, a confession which I was not, could not be, at liberty to disclose. Disclosed by herself, it would have been the revenge from which I had warned her and, at the same time, my deliverance. I was relieved; at first by this view of the matter, because I might thus keep my own chance of some favorable turn, whereas, if I once told Miss Oldcastle, I must give her up forever. But my love did not long remain skulking thus behind the hedge of honor. I saw that I was unworthy of loving her, for I was willing to risk her well-being for the chance of my own happiness, a risk which involved infinitely more wretchedness to her than the loss of my dearest hopes to me. It is one thing for a man not to marry the woman he loves, and quite another thing for a woman to marry a man she cannot even respect. And that I had given her up first could never be known even to her in this world.

I was sitting in the hollow when I heard the sound of horses' hooves in the distance, and felt a foreboding of what would appear. I was only a few yards from the road upon which the sand-cleft opened, and could see a space of it sufficient to show the persons even of rapid riders. The sounds drew nearer. I could distinguish the step of a pony and the steps of two horses besides. Up they came and swept past—Miss Oldcastle upon Judy's pony, Mr. Stoddart upon her horse, with the captain upon his own. How grateful I felt to Mr. Stoddart! And the hope arose in me that he had accompanied them at Miss Oldcastle's request.

Miss Oldcastle caught a glimpse of me, and even in the moment ere she vanished, I fancied I saw the lily-white grow rosy-red. But it must have been fancy, for she could hardly have been quite pale upon horseback on such a keen morning.

I could not sit any longer. As soon as I ceased to hear the sound of their progress, I rose and walked home, much quieter in heart and mind than when I set out.

As I entered by the nearer gate of the vicarage, I saw Old Rogers enter by the farther. He did not see me, but we met at the door.

"I'm in luck," he said, "to meet you just coming home. How's poor Miss Weir today, Sir?"

"She was rather better this morning, but I greatly doubt if she will ever get up again. That's between us, you know. Come in."

"Thank you, Sir. I wanted to have a little talk with you. You don't believe what they say—that she tried to kill the poor little fellow?" he asked, as soon as the door was closed behind us.

"If she did, she was out of her mind for the moment. But I don't believe it."

And thereupon I told him what both his master and I thought about it, but I did not tell him what she had said.

"That's just what I came to myself, Sir, turning the thing over in my old head. But there's dreadful things done in the world, Sir. There's my daughter been a telling me—"

I was instantly breathless with attention. What he chose to tell me I felt at liberty to hear, though I would not have listened to Jane herself, still in her place of attendance upon Miss Oldcastle.

"—that the old lady up at the Hall there is tormenting the life out of that daughter of hers—she don't look much like hers, do she, Sir?—wanting to make her marry a man of her choosing. I saw him go past o' horseback with her yesterday, and I didn't more than half like the looks of him. He's too like a fair-spoken captain I sailed with once, what was the hardest man I ever sailed with. His own way was everything, even after he saw it wouldn't do. Now don't you think, Sir, somebody or other ought to interfere? It's as bad as murder, that, and anybody has a right to do summat to perwent it."

"I don't know what can be done, Rogers. I can't interfere."

The old man was silent. Evidently he thought I might interfere if I pleased. I could see what he was thinking. Possibly his daughter had told him something more than he chose to communicate to me. I could not help suspecting the mode in which he judged I might interfere. But I had no plain path to follow.

"Old Rogers," I said, "I can almost guess what you mean. But I am in more difficulty with regard to what you suggest than I can easily explain to you. I need not tell you, however, that I will turn the whole matter over in my mind."

"The prey ought to be taken from the lion somehow, if it please God," returned the old man, solemnly. "The poor young lady keeps up as well as she can before her mother, but Jane do say there's a power o' crying done in her own room."

Partly to hide my emotion, partly with the resolve to do something, I said, "I will call on Mr. Stoddart this evening. I may hear something from him to suggest a mode of action."

"I don't think you'll get anything worthwhile from Mr. Stoddart. He takes things a deal too easy like. He'll be this man's man and that man's man both at oncet. I beg your pardon, Sir. But he won't help us."

"That's all I can think of at present, though," I said, whereupon the man-of-war's man, with true breeding, rose at once and took a kindly leave.

I was in the storm again. She suffering, resisting, and I standing aloof! But what could I do? She had repelled me—she would repel me. She had said that the day might come when she would ask help from me, but she had made no movement. Just to do something, I would go and see Mr. Stoddart that evening. I was sure to find him alone, for he never dined with the family, and I might possibly catch a glimpse of Miss Oldcastle.

I found little Gerard so much better, though very weak, and his mother so quiet, that I might safely leave them to the care of Mary and her brother Tom. So there was something off my mind.

The heavens were glorious with stars, but I did not care for them. Let them shine—they could not shine into me. I tried to lift my eyes to Him who is above the stars, and yet how much sustaining I got from that region, I cannot tell. But somehow things did seem a little more endurable before I reached the house.

I was passing across the hall, following the "Wolf" to Mr. Stoddart's room, when the drawing room door opened and Miss Oldcastle came half out. Seeing me, she drew back instantly. A moment after, however, I heard the sound of her dress following us. Light as was her step, every footfall seemed to be upon my heart. I did not dare to look round. Soon, however, the silken vortex of sound behind me ceased as she turned aside in some other direction. I passed on to Mr. Stoddart's room.

He received me kindly, as he always did, but his smile flickered uneasily. He seemed in some trouble, and yet pleased to see me.

"I am glad you have taken to horseback," I said. "It gives me hope that you will be my companion sometimes when I make a round of my parish. I should like you to see some of our people. You would find more in them to interest you than perhaps you would expect."

I thus tried to seem at ease, as I was far from feeling.

"I am not so fond of riding as I used to be," he said.

"Did you like the Arab horses in India?"

"Yes, after I got used to their careless ways. That horse you must have seen me on the other day is very nearly a pure Arab. He belongs to Captain Everard and carries Miss Oldcastle beautifully. I was quite sorry to take him from her, but it was her own doing. She would have me go with her. I think I have lost much firmness since I was ill."

"If the loss of firmness means the increase of kindness, I do not think you will have to lament it," I answered. "Does Captain Everard make a long stay?"

"He stays from day to day. I wish he would go. I don't know what to do. Mrs. Oldcastle and he form one party, Miss Oldcastle and Judy another, and each is trying to gain me over. I don't want to belong to either. If they would only let me alone."

"What do they want of you, Mr. Stoddart?"

"Mrs. Oldcastle wants me to use my influence with Ethelwyn to persuade her to behave differently to Captain Everard. The old lady has set her heart on their marriage, and Ethelwyn, though she dares not break with him, yet keeps him somehow at arm's length. Then Judy is always begging me to stand up for her aunt. But what's the use of my standing up for her if she won't stand up for herself? She never says a word to me about it herself. It's all Judy's doing. How am I to know what she wants?"

"I thought you said just now she asked you to ride with her?"

"So she did, but nothing more. She did not even press it, only the tears came in her eyes when I refused and I could not bear that, so I went against my will. I don't want to make enemies. I am sure I don't see why she should stand out. He's a very good match in point of property, and family too."

"Perhaps she does not like him?" I forced myself to say.

"Oh! I suppose not, or she would not be so troublesome. But she could arrange all that if she were inclined to be agreeable to her friends. After all I have done for her! Well, one must not look to be repaid for anything one does for others."

And what had this man done for her, then? He had, for his own amusement, taught her Hindustan; he had given her some insight into the principles of mechanics; and he had roused in her some taste for the writings of the mystics. But for all that regarded the dignity of her humanity and her womanhood, if she had had no teaching but what he gave her, her mind would have been merely "an unweeded garden that grows to seed." And now he complained that in return for his pains she would not submit to the degradation of marrying a man she did not love, in order to leave him in the enjoyment of his own lazy and cowardly peace. Really, he was a worse man than I had thought him. Clearly he would not help to keep her in the right path, not even interfere to prevent her from being pushed into the wrong one. But perhaps he was only expressing his own discomfort, not giving his real judgment, and I might be censuring him too hardly.

"What will be the result, do you suppose?" I asked.

"I can't tell. Sooner or later she will have to give in to her mother. She might as well yield with a good grace."

"She must do what she thinks is right," I said. "And you, Mr. Stoddart, ought to help her to do what is right. You surely would not urge her to marry a man she does not love."

"Well, no, not exactly. And yet society does not object to it. It is an acknowledged arrangement, common enough."

"Society is scarcely an interpreter of the divine will. Society will honor vile things so long as the doer has money sufficient to clothe them in a grace not their own. There is God's way of doing everything in the world, up to marrying, or down to paying a bill."

"Yes, yes, I know what you would say, and I suppose you are right. I will not urge any opinion of mine. Besides, we shall have a respite soon, for he must join his regiment in a day or two."

It was some relief to hear this, and I presently took my leave. As I walked through one of the long, dimly lighted passages, I started at Judy's light touch on my arm.

"Dear Mr. Walton—" she said, and stopped, for at the same moment Sarah appeared at the end of the passage and said,

"Miss Judy, your grandmamma wants you."

Judy took her hand from my arm, and with an almost martial stride approached Sarah and stood before her defiantly.

"Sarah," she said, "you know you are telling me a lie. Grannie does not want me. You have not been in the dining room since I left it one moment ago. Do you think, you bad woman, I am going to be afraid of you? I know you better than you think. Go away directly, or I will make you."

She stamped her little foot, and Sarah turned and walked away without a word.

As valuable as propriety of demeanor is, truth of conduct is infinitely more precious. In the face of her courage and uprightness, I could not rebuke her for her want of decorum. When I joined her she put her hand in mine, and so walked with me down the stair and out at the front door.

"You will take cold, Judy, going out like that," I said.

"I am in too great a passion to take cold," she answered. "But I have no time to talk about that creeping creature. Auntie doesn't like Captain Everard, and Grannie insists that she shall have him, whether she likes him or not. Now do tell me what you think."

"I do not quite understand you, my child."

"I know Auntie would like to know what you think, but she will never ask you herself. So *I* am asking you whether a lady ought to marry a gentleman she does not like, to please her mother."

"Certainly not, Judy. It is often wicked, and at best a mistake."

"Thank you, Mr. Walton. I will tell her. She will be glad to hear that you say so, I know."

"Mind you tell her you asked me, Judy. I should not like her to think I had been interfering, you know."

"Yes, yes, I know quite well. I will take care. Thank you. He's going tomorrow. Good night."

She bounded into the house again, and I walked away down the avenue. I saw and felt the stars now, for hope had come again in my heart, and I thanked the God of hope. "Our minds are small because they are faithless," I said to myself. "If we had faith in God, our hearts would share in His greatness and peace, for we should not then be shut up in ourselves, but would walk abroad in Him." And with a light step and a light heart I went home.

TWENTY-SEVEN

Old Mrs. Tomkins

Very severe weather came, and much sickness followed, chiefly among the poorer people who can so ill keep out the cold. Yet some of my well-to-do parishioners, including Mr. Boulderstone, were laid up likewise. I had grown quite attached to Mr. Boulderstone by this time, not because he was what is called interesting, for he was not; not because he was clever, for he was not; not because he was well-read, for he was not; not because he was possessed of influence in the parish, though he had that influence; but simply because he was true. He was what he appeared, felt what he professed, and did what he said—appearing kind, and feeling and acting kindly. Such a man is rare and precious, were he as stupid as the Welsh giant in "Jack the Giant-killer." I could never see Mr. Boulderstone a mile off but my heart felt the warmer for the sight. Even in his great pain he seemed to forget himself as he received me, and to gain comfort from my mere presence. I could not help regarding him as a child of heaven, to be treated with the more reverence that he had the less aid to his goodness from his slow understanding.

But I could not help feeling keenly the contrast when I went from his warm, comfortable, well-defended chamber to the Tomkins' cottage and found it lying open and bare to the enemy. What holes and cracks there were about the door, through which the fierce wind rushed into the room to attack the aged feet and hands and throats! There were no defenses of threefold draperies, and no soft carpet on the brick floor—only a small rug which my sister had carried them, laid down before a weak little fire that seemed to despair against the cold. True, we had had the little cottage patched up. The two Thomas Weirs had been at work upon it in the first of the cold weather this winter, but it was like putting the new cloth on the old garment, for fresh places had broken out. Although Mrs. Tomkins had fought the cold well with what rags she could spare, such razor-edged winds are hard to keep out. And here she was now, lying in bed and breathing hard, like the sore-pressed garrison which had retreated to its last defense in the keep of the castle. Poor old Tomkins sat shivering over the little fire.

"Come, come, Tomkins, this won't do," I said. "Why don't you burn your coals in weather like this?" It made my heart ache to see the little heap in a box hardly bigger than the chest of tea my sister brought from London with her. I threw half of it on the fire at once.

"Deary me, Mr. Walton, you *are* wasteful, Sir. The Lord never sent His good coals to be used that way."

"He did, though, Tomkins," I answered. "And He'll send you a little more this evening, after I get home. Keep yourself warm, man. This world's cold in winter, you know."

"Indeed, Sir, I know that, and I'm like to know it worse afore long. She's going," he said, pointing toward the bed where his wife lay.

I went to her. I had seen her several times within the last few weeks, but had observed nothing to make me consider her seriously ill. I now saw at a glance that Tomkins was right: she had not long to live.

"I am sorry to see you suffering so much, Mrs. Tomkins," I said.

"I don't suffer so very much, Sir, though, to be sure, it be hard to get the breath into my body. And I do feel cold-like, Sir."

"I'm going home directly, and I'll send you down another blanket. It's much colder today than it was yesterday."

"It's not weather-cold, Sir, wi' me. It's grave-cold, Sir. Blankets won't do me no good, Sir. I can't get it out of my head how perishing cold I shall be when I'm under the mound, though I oughtn't to mind it when it's the will o' God. It's only till the resurrection, Sir."

"But it's not the will of God, Mrs. Tomkins."

"Ain't it, Sir? Sure I thought it was."

"You believe in Jesus Christ, don't you, Mrs. Tomkins?"

"That I do, Sir, with all my heart and soul."

"Well, He says that whosoever liveth and believeth in Him shall never die."

"But you know, Sir, everybody dies. I *must* die and be laid in the churchyard, Sir. And that's what I don't like."

"But I say that is all a mistake. *You* won't die. Your body will die, and be laid away out of sight, but you will be awake, alive, more alive than you are now, a great deal."

(It is a great mistake to teach children that they have souls. Then they think of their souls as of something which is not themselves. For what a man *has* cannot be himself. Hence, when they are told that their souls go to heaven, they think of their selves as lying in the grave. They ought to be taught that they have bodies, and that their bodies die while they themselves live on. Then they will not think, as old Mrs. Tomkins did, that they will be laid in the grave. We talk as if we *possessed* souls instead of *being* souls, whereas we should teach our children to think no more of their bodies when they are dead than they do of their hair when it is cut off, or of their old clothes when they have done with them.)

"But you will be with God in your Father's house, you know. And that is enough, is it not?"

"Yes, surely, Sir. But I wish you was to be there by the bedside of me when I was a dyin'. I can't help bein' summat skeered at it. It don't come nat'ral to me, like. I ha' got used to this old bed here, cold as it has been—many's the night—wi' my good man there by the side of me."

"Send for me, Mrs. Tomkins, any moment, day or night, and I'll be with you directly."

"I think, Sir, if I had a hold ov you i' the one hand, and my man there, the Lord bless him, i' the other, I could go comfortable."

"I'll come the minute you send for me—just to keep you in mind that a better friend than I am is holding you all the time, though you mayn't feel His hands."

"But I can't help thinking, Sir, that I wouldn't be troublesome. He has such a deal to look after! And I don't see how He can think of everybody, at every minute, like. I don't mean that He will let anything go wrong, but He might forget an old body like me for a minute, like."

"You would need to be as wise as He is before you could see how He does it. But you must believe more than you can understand. It would be unreasonable to think that He must forget because you can't understand how He could remember. I think it is as hard for Him to forget anything as it is for us to remember everything, for forgetting comes of weakness, and from our not being finished yet, and He is all strength and all perfection."

"Then you think, Sir, He never forgets anything?"

I knew by the trouble that gathered on the old woman's brow what kind of thought was passing through her mind, but I let her go on. She paused for one moment only, and then resumed, much interrupted by the shortness of her breathing.

"When I was brought to bed first," she said, "it was o' twins, Sir. And oh! It was *very* hard. As I said to my man after I got my head up a bit, 'Tomkins,' says I, 'you don't know what it is to have two on 'em cryin' and cryin', and you next to nothin' to give 'em, till their cryin' sticks to your brain, and ye hear 'em when they're fast asleep, one on each side o' you. Would you believe it, Sir, I wished 'em dead? Just to get the wailin' of them out o' my head, I wished 'em dead. In the courtyard o' the squire's house, where my Tomkins worked on the home-farm, there was an old draw-well. It wasn't used, and there was a lid to it, with a hole in it, through which you could put a good big stone. And Tomkins once took me to it and put a stone in, and told me to hearken. And I hearkened, but I heard nothing, as I told him so. 'But,' says he, 'hearken, Lass.' And in a little while there comes a blast o' noise from somewheres. 'What's that, Tomkins?' I said. 'That's the stone,' says he, 'a strikin' on the water down that there well.' And I turned sick at the thoughts of it. And it's down there that I wished the darlin's that God had sent me, for there they'd be quiet."

"Mothers are often a little out of their minds at such times, Mrs. Tomkins, and so were you."

"I don't know, Sir. But I must tell you another thing. The Sunday afore that, the parson had been preachin' about 'Suffer little children,' you know, Sir, 'to come unto Me.' I suppose that was what put it in my head. But I fell asleep wi' nothin' else in my head but the cries o' the infants and the sound o' the stone in the draw-well. And I dreamed that I had one o' them under each arm, cryin' dreadful, and was walkin' across the court the way to the draw-well, when all at once a man come up to me and held out his hands, and said, 'Gie me my childer.' And I was in a terrible fear. And I gave him first one and then the t'other, and he took them, and one laid its head on one shoulder of him, and t'other upon t'other, and they stopped their cryin', and fell fast asleep. And away he walked wi' them into the dark, and I saw him no more. And then I awoke cryin', and I didn't know why. And I took my twins to me, and my breasts was full, and my heart was as full o' love to them, and they hardly cried worth mentionin' again. But afore they was two years old, they both died o' the brown chytis, Sir—and I think that He took them."

"He did take them, Mrs. Tomkins, and you'll see them again soon."

"But, if He never forgets anything—"

"I didn't say that. I think He can do what He pleases. And if He pleases to forget anything, then He can forget it. And I think that is what He does with our sins—that is, after He has got them away from us, once we are clean from them altogether. It would be a dreadful thing if He forgot them before that and left them sticking fast to us and defiling us. How then should we ever be made clean? What else does the Prophet Isaiah mean when he says, 'Thou hast cast my sins behind Thy back'? Is not that where He chooses to not see them anymore?"

"They are good words, Sir. I could not bear Him to think of me and my sins both at once."

The old woman lay quiet after this, relieved in mind, though not in body. I hastened home to send some coals and other things, and then call upon Dr. Duncan, lest he should not know that his patient was worse.

From Dr. Duncan's I went to see old Samuel Weir, who likewise was ailing. I found him alone, in bed under the old embroidery. He greeted me with a withered smile, sweet and true, though no flash of white teeth broke forth to light up the welcome of the aged head.

"Are you not lonely, Mr. Weir?"

"No, Sir. I don't know as ever I was less lonely. I've got my stick, you see, Sir," he said, pointing to a thorn-stick which lay beside him.

"I do not quite understand you," I returned, knowing that the old man's sayings always meant something.

"You see, Sir, when I want anything, I've only to knock on the floor, and up comes my son out of the shop. And then again, when I knock at the door of the house up there, my Father opens it and looks out. So I have both my son on earth and my Father in heaven, and what can an old man want more?

"It's very strange," the old man resumed, after pause, "but as I lie here I begin to feel a child again. They say old age is a second childhood. Before I grew so old, I used to think that meant only that a man was helpless and silly again, as he used to be when he was a child. I never thought it meant that a man felt like a child again, as lighthearted and untroubled as I do now."

"Well, I suspect that is not what people do mean when they say so. But I am very glad—you don't know how pleased it makes me to hear that you feel so. I will hope to fare in the same way when my time comes."

"Indeed, I hope you will, Sir. Just before you came in now, I had quite forgotten that I was a toothless old man, and thought I was lying here waiting for my mother to come in and say good-night to me before I went to sleep. Wasn't that curious, when I never saw my mother, as I told you before, Sir? But I have no end of fancies. There's one I see often—a man down on his knees at that cupboard nigh the floor there, searching and searching for somewhat; and I wish he would just turn round his face once for a moment that I might see him. I have a notion it's my own father."

"How do you account for that fancy, now, Mr. Weir?"

"I've often thought about it, Sir, but I never could account for it. I'm none willing to think it's a ghost. I've turned out that cupboard over and over, and there's nothing there I don't know."

"You're not afraid of it, are you?"

"No, Sir. Why should I be? I never did it no harm. And God can surely take care of me from all sorts."

I came simply to the conclusion that when he was a child, he had peeped in at the door of the same room where he now lay, and had actually seen a man in the position he described, half in the cupboard, searching for something. His mind had kept the impression after the conscious memory had lost its hold of the circumstance. It was a glimpse out of one of the many stories which haunted the old place.

A week had elapsed from the night I had sat up with Gerard Weir, and it did not seem likely his mother would ever rise from her bed again. On a Friday I went to see her just as the darkness was beginning to gather. The fire of life was burning itself out fast. It glowed on her cheeks, it burned in her hands, it blazed in her eyes—but the fever had left her mind. That was cool, oh, so cool now! Those fierce tropical storms of passion had passed away, and nothing of life was lost. Revenge had passed away, but revenge is of death and deadly. Forgiveness had taken its place, and forgiveness is the giving, and so the receiving of life. Gerard, his little head starred with sticking plaster, sat on her bed, happy over a spotted wooden horse with cylindrical body and jointless legs. But he dropped it when he saw me and flung himself upon my neck. Catharine's face gleamed with pleasure.

"Dear boy!" I said, "I am very glad to see you so much better." For this was the first time he had shown such a revival of energy. He had been quite sweet when he saw me but, until this evening, listless.

"Yes," he said, "I am quite well now." And he put his hand up to his head.

"Does it ache?"

"Not much now. The doctor says I had a bad fall."

"So you had, my child. But you will soon be well again."

The mother's face was turned aside, yet I could see one tear forcing its way from under her closed eyelid.

"Oh, I don't mind it," he answered. "Mammy is so kind to me! She lets me sit on her bed as long as I like."

"That is nice. But just run to Auntie in the next room. I think your mammy would like to talk to me for a little while."

The child ran off with overflowing obedience.

"I can even think of *him* now," said the mother, "without going into a passion. I hope God will forgive him. *I* do. I think He will forgive me."

"Did you ever hear," I asked, "of Jesus refusing anybody that wanted kindness from Him? He wouldn't always do exactly what they asked Him, because that would sometimes be of no use and would sometimes even be wrong—but He never pushed them away from Him, never repulsed their approach to Him. For the sake of His disciples, He made the Syro-Phoenician woman suffer a little while, but only to give her praise afterward and a wonderful granting of her prayer."

She said nothing for a little while, then murmured, "Shall I have to be ashamed to all eternity? I do not want to be ashamed. Shall I never be like other people—in heaven I mean?"

"If He is satisfied with you, you need not think anything more about yourself. If He lets you kiss His feet, you won't care about other people's opinions of you, even in heaven. But things will go very differently there from here, for everybody there will be more or less ashamed of himself, and will think worse of himself than of anyone else. If trouble about your past life were to show itself on your face there, they would all run to comfort you, telling you that you must think about yourself as He thinks about you. What He thinks is the rule, because it is the infallible right way. Leave all that to Him who has taken away our sins, and do not trouble yourself anymore about it. Such thoughts will not come to you at all when you have seen the face of Jesus Christ."

"Will He let us tell Him anything we please?"

"He lets you do that now; surely He will not be less our God and our Friend there."

"Oh, I don't mind how soon He takes me now! Only there's that poor child that I've behaved so badly to! I wish I could take him with me. I have no time to make it up to him here."

"You must wait till he comes there. He won't think hardly of you. There's no fear of that."

"What will become of him though? I can't bear the idea of burdening my father with him."

"Your father will be glad to have him, I know. He will feel it a privilege to do something for your sake, and the boy will do him good. If he does not want him, I will take him myself."

"Oh! Thank you—thank you, Sir." A burst of tears followed.

"He has often done me good," I said.

"Who, Sir—my father?"

"No. Your son."

"I don't quite understand what you mean, Sir."

"I mean just what I say. His words and behavior have both roused and comforted my heart again and again."

"To think of your saying that! The poor little innocent! Then it isn't all punishment?"

"If it were *all* punishment, we should perish utterly. He is your punishment—but look in what a lovely loving form your punishment has come, and say whether God has been good to you or not."

"If I had only received my punishment humbly, things would have been very different now. But I do take it—at least, I want to take it—just as He would have me take it. I will bear anything He likes. I suppose I must die?"

"I think He means you to die now. You are ready, I think. You have wanted to die for a long time, but you were not ready before."

"And now I want to live for my boy. But His will be done."

"Amen. There is no better prayer in the universe."

She lay silent. Mary tapped at the chamber door. "If you please, Sir, here's a little girl come to say that Mrs. Tomkins is dying and wants to see you."

"Then I must say good-night to you, Catharine. I will see you tomorrow morning. Think about old Mrs. Tomkins—she's a good old soul. When you find your heart drawn to her in the trouble of death, then lift it up to God for her, that He will please to comfort and support her and make her happier than health, stronger than strength, taking off the old worn garment of her body, and putting upon her the garment of salvation which will be a grand new body, like that the Saviour had when He rose again."

"I will try. I will think about her."

For I thought this would help to prepare her for her own death. In thinking lovingly about others, we think healthily about ourselves. And the things she thought of for the comfort of Mrs. Tomkins would return to comfort her in her own end.

TWENTY-EIGHT

Calm and Storm

Again and again I was sent for to say farewell to Mrs. Tomkins, and again and again I returned home leaving her asleep, and for the time better. But on a Saturday evening young Tom came to me with the news that Catharine seemed much worse. I sent Tom on before and followed alone.

It was a brilliant starry night—no moon, no clouds, no wind, nothing but stars seeming to lean down toward the earth. It was, indeed, a glorious night—that is, I knew it was though I did not feel it. For the death, which I went to be near, came with a strange sense of separation between me and the nature around me. Here was death and there shone the stars.

I had very little knowledge of death. I had never yet seen a fellow creature—even my father—die. And the thought was oppressive to me. "To think," I said to myself, as I walked over the bridge to the village street, "to think that the one moment the person is here and the next, who shall say where? We know nothing of the region beyond the grave. Not even our risen Lord thought fit to bring back from Hades any news for the human family standing and straining their eyes after their brothers and sisters who have vanished in the dark. Surely it is well, all well, although we know nothing save that our Lord has been there, knows all about it, and does not choose to tell us." And so the oppression passed from me, and I was free.

But little as I knew of death, I was certain, the moment I saw Catharine, that the veil that hid the "silent land" from her had begun to lift. For a moment I almost envied her, that she was so soon to see and know that after which our blindness and ignorance are always wondering and hungering. She could hardly speak. She looked more patient than calm. There was no light in the room but that of the fire. Thomas sat by the hearth with the child on his knee. Gerard's natural mood was so quiet and earnest that the solemnity about him did not oppress him. He looked as if he were present at some religious observance of which he felt more than he understood, and he was no more disquieted at the presence of death than the stars were.

And this was the end of the lovely girl—to leave the fair world still young because a selfish man had seen that she was fair! No time can change the relation of cause and effect. The poison that operates ever so slowly is yet poison and yet slays. And that man was now murdering her, with weapon long-reaching from the past. But no, thank God! This was not the end of her. Though there is woe for that man by whom the offense comes, yet there is provision for the offense. There is One who brings light out of darkness, joy out of sorrow, humility out of wrong. Back to the Father's house we go with the sorrows and sins which we gathered and heaped upon our weary shoulders, and an Elder Brother—different from that angry one who would not receive the prodigal—takes the burden from our shoulders, and leads us into the presence of the Good.

She put out her hand feebly and let it lie in mine. When I sat down by her bedside, she closed her eyes and said nothing. Her father was troubled, though his was a nature that ever sought concealment for its emotion. Gerard clambered up on my knee and laid his little hand upon his mother's. She opened her eyes, looked at the child, shut them again, and tears came out from between the closed lids.

"Has Gerard ever been baptized?" I asked her.

Her lips indicated a no.

"Then I will be his godfather, and that will be a pledge to you that I will never lose sight of him."

She pressed my hand, and the tears came faster.

Believing with all my heart that the dying should remember their dying Lord, and that the "Do this in remembrance of Me" can never be better obeyed, we kneeled. Then Thomas and I and Tom and Mary partook with the dying woman of the signs of that death wherein our Lord gave Himself entirely to us. Upon what that bread and that wine mean—the sacrifice of our Lord—the whole world of humanity hangs, for it is the redemption of men.

After she had received the holy sacrament, she lay still as before. I heard her murmur once, "Lord, I do not deserve it, but I do love Thee," and about two hours after, she quietly breathed her last. We all kneeled, and I thanked aloud the Father of us that He had taken her to Himself. Gerard had fallen fast asleep on his aunt's lap, and was now in his bed. Surely he slept a deeper sleep than his mother's, for had she not awakened even as she fell asleep?

When I came out once more, I knew better what the stars meant. They looked to me now as if they knew all about death, and therefore could not be sad to the eyes of men.

When I returned home, my sister told me that Old Rogers had called and seemed concerned not to find me at home. He would have gone to find me, my sister said, had I been anywhere but by a deathbed. He would not leave any message, however, saying he would call in the morning.

I thought it better to go to his house. The stars were still shining as brightly as before, but a strong foreboding of trouble filled my mind, and once more the stars were far away. I could give no reason for my sudden fearfulness save this—that as I went to Catharine's house I had passed Jane Rogers on her way to her father's and, having just greeted her, had gone on. But, as it came back to me, she had looked at me strangely, and now her father had been to seek me. It must have something to do with Miss Oldcastle.

But it was past eleven when I came to the dark, still cottage, and I could not bring myself to rouse the weary man from his bed. So I turned and lingered by the old mill, and pondered on the profusion of strength that rushed past the wheel away to the great sea, doing nothing. "Nature," I thought, "does not demand that power should always be force. Power itself must repose. He that believes shall not make haste, says the Bible. But power needs strength to be still. Is my faith not strong enough to be still?" I looked up to the heavens once more, and the quietness of the stars seemed to reproach me. "We are safe up here," they seemed to say. "We shine, fearless and confident. We cannot fall out of His safety. Lift up your eyes on high and behold! Who hath created these things, that bringeth out our host by number? He calleth us all by name."

The night was very still and there was, I thought, no one awake within miles of me. The stars seemed to shine into me the divine reproach of those glorious words. "O my God!" I cried, and fell to my knees by the mill door.

I tried to say more to Him—but what that was ought not, cannot, be repeated to another.

When I opened my eyes, I saw the door of the mill was open too, and there in the door, his white head glimmering, stood Old Rogers, with a look on his face as if he had just come down from the mount. I started to my feet with that strange feeling of something like shame that seizes one at the very thought of other eyes than those of the Father. The old man came forward and bowed his head, but would have passed me without speech. I could not bear to part with him thus.

"Won't you speak to me, Old Rogers?" I said.

He turned at once with evident pleasure. "I beg your pardon, Sir. I was ashamed of having intruded on you, and I thought you would rather be left alone. I thought—I thought," hesitated the old man, "that you might like to go into the old mill, for the night's cold out o'doors."

"Thank you, Rogers. I won't now. I thought you had been in bed. How do you come to be out so late?"

"You see, Sir, when I'm in any trouble, it's no use to go to bed. I can't sleep. I only keep the old 'oman wakin'. And the key o' the mill allus hangin' at the back o' my door, and knowin' it to be a good place to—to—shut the door in, I came out as soon as she was asleep. I little thought to see you, Sir."

"I came to find you, not thinking how the time went. Catharine Weir is gone home."

"Poor woman. And perhaps something will come out now that will help us."

"I do not quite understand you," I said, with hesitation.

But Rogers made no reply.

"I am sorry to hear you are in trouble tonight. Can I help you?" I resumed.

"If you can help yourself, Sir, you can help me. But I have no right to say so. Only, if a pair of old eyes be not blind, a man may pray to God about anything he sees. I was prayin' hard about you in there, Sir, while you was on your knees o' the other side o' the door."

I could partly guess what the old man meant, and I could not ask him for further explanation.

"What did you want to see me about?" I inquired.

He hesitated for a moment.

"I dare say it was very foolish of me, Sir. But I just wanted to tell you that our Jane was down here from the Hall this arternoon—"

"I passed her on the bridge. Is she quite well?"

"Yes, yes, Sir. You know that's not the point."

The old man's tone seemed to reprove me for vain words, and I held my peace.

"The captain's there again."

An icy spear seemed to pass through my heart. I could make no reply, but turned away from the old man without a word. He made no attempt to detain me.

The first I remember after that, I was fighting with the wind of a gathering storm, out upon the common where I had dealt so severely with her who had this very night gone to a waveless sea. Is it the sea of death? No. The sea of life—a life too keen, too refined for our senses to know it and therefore we call it death, because we cannot lay hold upon it.

Next I found myself standing at the iron gate of Oldcastle Hall. I knew that I was there only when first I stood in the shelter of one of those great pillars and the monster on its top. I pushed the gate open and entered. The wind was roaring in the trees as I think I have never heard it roar since—the hail clashed upon the bare branches and twigs and mingled an unearthly hiss with the roar. The house stood like a tomb—dark, silent, without one dim light to show that sleep and not death ruled within. I passed round to the other side, but dared not stop to look up at the back of the house. I went on to the staircase in the rock and, by its rude and dangerous steps, descended to the little grove below. Here the wind roared overhead, yet could not reach me. But my heart was a well in which a storm boiled and raged, and all that was over my head was peace itself compared to what I felt. I sat down at the foot of a tree where I had first seen Miss Oldcastle reading, and then I looked up to the house. Yes, there was a light there! It must be in her window. She then could not rest anymore than I. Sleep was driven from her eyes because she must wed the man she would not, while sleep was driven from mine because I could not marry the woman I would. But was that all of it? Gladly would I have given her up forever to redeem her from such a bondage. "But it would be to marry another someday," suggested the tormentor within. And then the storm, which had a little abated, broke out afresh in my soul. But before I rose from her seat I was ready even for that—if only I might deliver her. Glancing once more at the dull light in her window, I rose and almost felt my way to the stair, and climbed again into the storm.

But I was quieter now, and able to go home. It must have been nearly morning when I reached my house.

When I fell asleep I dreamed I was again in the old quarry staring into the deep well. Mrs. Oldcastle was murdering her daughter in the house above, while I was spellbound where I should see her body float into the well from the subterranean passage. But as a white hand and arm appeared in the water below me, sorrow and pity more than horror broke the bonds of sleep, and I awoke to less trouble than that of my dreams, only because that which I feared had not yet come.

TWENTY-NINE

A Sermon to Myself

Such a Sabbath morn! The day seemed all wan and weeping and gray with care. The wind dashed itself against the casement, laden with soft heavy sleet. The first thing I knew when I awoke was the raving of that wind. I could lie in bed not a moment longer. But how was I to do the work of my office? When a man's duty looks like an enemy, dragging him into the dark mountains, he has no less to go with it than when, like a friend with loving face, it offers to lead him along green pastures by the river's side. I had little power over my feelings. I could not prevent my mind from mirroring the nature around me, but I could address myself to the work I had to do. "My God!" was all the prayer I could pray before breakfast. But He knew what lay behind the utterance.

But how was I to preach? The subject on which I was pondering when young Weir came to me had retreated into the far past, on the far side of that black night. To speak upon that would have been vain, for I had nothing to say on the matter now. I could not even recall what I had thought and felt. I felt ashamed of yielding to personal trouble when the truths of God were all about me, although I could not feel them. Might not some hungry soul go away without being satisfied because I was faint and downhearted?

Then I remembered a sermon I had once preached upon the words of St. Paul: "Thou therefore which teachest another, teachest thou not thyself?" And I said to myself, "Might I not try the other way now, and preach to myself? In teaching myself, might I not teach others?" All this passed through my mind as I sat in my study after breakfast, within an hour of churchtime.

I took my Bible, read and thought, and found myself in my vestry not quite unwilling to read the prayers and speak to my people. There were very few present. The day was violently stormy and, to my relief, the Hall pew was empty. Instead of finding myself a mere minister to the prayers of others, I found as I read that my heart went out in crying to God for the divine presence of His Spirit. And if I thought more of myself in my prayers than was well, yet as soon as I was converted, would I not strengthen my brethren? And the sermon I preached was that which the stars had preached to me and thereby driven me to my knees. I took for my text, "The glory of the Lord shall be revealed."

I preached to myself that the power of God is put side by side with the weakness of men—not that He may glory over His feeble children, but that He may say, "You will never be strong but with *My* strength, and that you can get only by trusting in Me. Look how strong I am. You wither like the grass. Do not fear; let the grass wither. Lay hold of My Word, and that will be life in you that the withering wind cannot reach. I am coming with My strong hand to do My work—to feed My flock like a shepherd, to gather the lambs with My arm and carry them in My bosom, and to gently lead those who are with young. I come to you with help. Look at the stars I have made—I know every one of them. Not one goes wrong, because I keep them right. I give *power* to the *faint,* and plenty of strength to them that have no might."

"Thus," I went on to say, "God brings His strength to destroy our weakness by making us strong. This is a God indeed! Shall we not trust Him?" And then I tried to show that it is in the commonest troubles of life, as well as in spiritual fears and perplexities, that we are to trust in God. For God made the outside as well as the inside, and when outside things such as pain or difficulties in money, are referred to God and His will, they too become spiritual affairs; for nothing in the world can appear commonplace or unclean to the man who sees God in everything.

All the time I was speaking, the rain, mingled with sleet, was dashing against the windows. The wind was howling over the graves all about, but the dead were not troubled by the storm. Over my head a sparrow flitted from beam to beam, taking refuge in the church till the storm should cease. "This," I said aloud, "is what the church is for: as the sparrow finds there is a house from the storm, so the human heart escapes thither to hear the still small voice of God, when its faith is too weak to find Him in the storm." A dim watery gleam fell on the chancel floor, and the comfort of the sun awoke in my heart. I received that pale sunray of hope as comfort for the race, and for me as one of the family—even as the rainbow that was set in the cloud—a promise of light for them that sit in darkness.

I descended from the pulpit comforted by the sermon I had preached to myself. But I felt justified in telling my people that in consequence of the continued storm (for there had been no more sunshine than just that watery gleam), there would be no service in the afternoon.

The people were very slow in dispersing. There was so much putting on of clogs, gathering up of skirts over the head, and expanding of umbrellas (although worse than useless in the violent wind), that the porches were crowded. I lingered with these.

"I am sorry you will have such a wet walk home," I said to the wife of the shoemaker, a sweet little wizened creature with more wrinkles than hair.

"It's very good of you to let us off this afternoon, Sir. Not as I minds the wet—it finds out the holes in people's shoes, and gets my husband more work." Nor was there anything necessarily selfish in her response, for if there are holes in people's shoes, the sooner they are found out the better.

Mr. Stoddart, whose love for the old organ had been stronger than his dislike to the storm, approached me.

"I never saw you down in the church before, Mr. Stoddart," I said, "though I have heard you often enough. You use your own private door always."

"I thought to go that way now, but there came such a fierce burst of wind and rain in my face that my courage failed me, and I turned back, like the sparrow, for refuge."

"A thought strikes me," I said. "Come home with me and have some lunch, and then we will go together to see some of my poor people. I have often wished to ask you."

His face fell. "It is such a day!" he answered, but not positively refusing.

"So it was when you set out this morning," I returned, "but you would not deprive us of the aid of your music for the sake of a charge of wind and a rattle of raindrops."

"But I shan't be of any use. You are going, and that is enough."

"I beg your pardon. Your very presence will be of use. Nothing yet given him or done for him by his fellow ever did any man so much good as the recognition of the brotherhood by the common signs of friendship and sympathy. The best good of given money depends on the degree to which it is the sign of that friendship and sympathy. Our Lord did not make little of visiting: 'I was sick, and ye visited Me.' 'Inasmuch as ye did it not to one of the least of these, ye did it not to Me.' "

"But I cannot pretend to feel any interest. Why then should I go?"

"To please me, your friend. That is a good human reason. You need not say a word—you must not pretend anything. Go as my companion, not as their visitor. Will you come?"

"I suppose I must."

"Thank you. You will help me, for I seldom have a companion."

So, when the storm-fit had abated for the moment, we hurried to the vicarage, had a good though hasty lunch, and set out for the village. The rain was worse than ever. There was no sleet, and the wind was not cold, but the windows of heaven were opened.

"Don't you find some pleasure in fighting the wind?" I said.

"I have no doubt I should," answered Mr. Stoddart, "if I thought I were going to do any good. But, to tell the truth, I would rather be by my own fire, with my folio Dante on the reading desk."

"Well, I would rather help the poorest woman in creation than contemplate the sufferings of the greatest and wickedest."

"There are two things you forget," returned Mr. Stoddart. "First, that the works of Dante are not nearly occupied with the sufferings of the wicked. And next, that what I have complained of in this expedition—a wild-goose chase, were it not your doing—is that I am not going to help anybody."

"You would have the best of the argument entirely," I replied, "if your expectation were correct."

We had come within a few yards of the Tomkins' cottage, which lay low down toward the river, and I saw that the water was at the threshold. I turned to Mr. Stoddart who, to do him justice, had not yet grumbled in the least.

"Perhaps you had better go home, after all," I said, "for you must wade into Tomkins' if you go at all. Poor old man! What can he be doing, with his wife dying and the river in his house?"

"You have constituted yourself my superior officer, Mr. Walton. I never turned my back on my leader yet, though I confess I wish I could see the enemy a little clearer."

"There is the enemy," I said, pointing to the water and walking into it.

Mr. Stoddart followed me without a moment's hesitation.

When I opened the door, I saw a small stream of water running straight to the fire on the hearth, which it had already drowned. The old man was sitting by his wife's bedside. Life seemed rapidly going from the old woman. She lay breathing very hard.

"Oh, Sir," said the old man, as he rose, almost crying, "you've come at last!"

"Did you send for me?" I asked.

"No, Sir. I had nobody to send. Leastways I asked the Lord if He wouldn't fetch you. I been prayin' hard for you for the last hour. I couldn't leave her to come for you. And I do believe the wind 'ud ha' blown me off my two old legs."

"Well, I am come, you see. I would have come sooner, but I had no idea you would be flooded."

"It's not that I mind, Sir, though it *is* cold sin' the fire went out. But she *is* goin' now, Sir. She ha'n't spoken a word this two hours and more, and her breathin's worse and worse. She don't know me now, Sir."

A moan of protestation came from the dying woman.

"She does know you, and loves you too, Tomkins," I said. "And you'll both know each other better by and by."

The old woman made a feeble motion with her hand. I took it in mine. It was cold and deathlike. The rain was falling in large slow drops from the roof onto the bedclothes. But she would be beyond the reach of all storms before long, and it did not matter much.

"If you can find a basin or plate, Mr. Stoddart, put it to catch the drop here," I said, for I wanted to give him the first chance of being useful.

"There's one in the press there," said the old man, rising feebly.

"Keep your seat," said Mr. Stoddart. "I'll get it." And he got a basin from the cupboard and put it on the bed to catch the drop.

The old woman held my hand in hers, but by its motion I knew she wanted something, and I made her husband take hold of her other hand. This seemed to content her. So I went and whispered to Mr. Stoddart, who stood looking on, "You heard me say I would visit some of my sick people this afternoon. You must go instead of me and tell them that I cannot come, because old Mrs. Tomkins is dying—but I will see them soon."

He seemed rather relieved at the commission. I gave him the necessary directions to find the cottages, and he left me. He was one of those men who make excellent front-line men, but are quite unfit for officers. He did what he was told without flinching, but he had to be told.

(This was the beginning of a relation between Mr. Stoddart and the poor of the parish, a very slight one, indeed, for it consisted only in his knowing two or three of them, so as to ask after their health when he met them, and give them an occasional half crown. But it led to better things. I once came upon him in the avenue, standing in dismay over the fragments of a jug of soup which he had dropped. "What am I to do?" he said. "Poor Jones expects his soup today."

("Why, go back and get some more."

("But what will cook say?" He was more afraid of the cook than of a squadron of cavalry.

("Never mind the cook. Tell her you must have some more as soon as it can be got ready." He stood uncertain for a moment, and then his face brightened.

("I will tell her I want my soup. And I'll get out through the greenhouse and carry it to Jones."

("Very well," I said, "that will do capitally." And I went on, without determining whether the gift of his own soup arose more from love of Jones or fear of the cook.)

I resumed my seat by the bedside, where the old woman was again moaning. As soon as I took her hand she ceased, and so I sat till it began to grow dark.

"Are you there, Sir?" she would murmur.

"Yes, I am here. I have your hand."

"I can't feel you, Sir."

"But you can hear me, and you can hear God's voice in your heart. I am here, though you can't feel me; and God is here, though you can't see Him."

"Are you there, Tomkins?"

"Yes, my woman, I'm here," he answered, "but I wish I was there instead, wheresomever it be you're goin', old girl."

And all that I could hear of her answer was, "bym-by—bym-by."

Why should I linger over the deathbed of an illiterate woman, old and plain? Here was a woman with a heart like my own, who needed the same salvation I needed, to whom the love of God was the one blessed thing, who was passing through the same dark passage that the Lord had passed through before her, and that I had to pass through after her. And now her old age and plainness were about to vanish, and all that had made her youth attractive to Tomkins was about to return to her, only rendered tenfold more beautiful.

At length, after a long silence, the peculiar sounds of obstructed breathing indicated the end at hand. The jaw fell, and the eyes were fixed. The old man closed the mouth and the eyes of his old companion, weeping like a child, and I prayed aloud, giving thanks to God for taking her to Himself. It went to my heart to leave the old man alone with the dead, but it was better to let him be alone for a while.

I went to Old Rogers and asked him what was to be done.

"I'll go and bring him home, Sir, directly. He can't be left there."

"But how can you bring him in such a night?"

"Would your mare go with a cart, do you think?"

"Quite quietly. She brought a load of gravel from the common a few days ago. But where's a cart? I haven't got one."

"There's one at Weir's to be repaired, Sir. It wouldn't be stealing to borrow it."

How he managed with Tomkins I do not know. He only said afterward that he could hardly get the old man away from the body. When I went in the next day, I found Tomkins sitting disconsolate but comfortable in the easy chair by the fire. Mrs. Rogers was bustling about cheerily. The storm had died in the night, and the sun was shining. It was the first of the spring weather. The whole country was gleaming with water, which soon would sink away and leave the grass the thicker for its rising.

THIRTY
A Council of Friends

I was in danger of a return of my last attack. I had been sitting for hours in wet clothes, with my boots full of water, and now I had to suffer for it. But, as I was not to blame and had had no choice whether I should be wet or dry, I felt no depression at the prospect of illness. Indeed, I was too depressed from other causes to care much. I was unable to leave my bed, and knew that Captain Everard was at the Hall, and knew nothing besides. No voice reached me from that quarter any more than if Oldcastle Hall had been beyond the grave.

One pleasant thing happened. My sister came into my room and said that Miss Crowther had called and wanted to see me.

"Which Miss Crowther is it?" I asked.

"The little lady that looks like a bird, and chirps when she talks."

"You told her I had a bad cold, did you not?"

"Oh, yes. But she says if it is only a cold, it will do you no harm to see her."

"But you told her I was in bed, didn't you?"

"Of course. But it makes no difference. She says she's used to seeing sick folk in bed, and if you don't mind seeing her, she doesn't mind seeing you."

"Well, I suppose I must see her," I said.

So my sister made me a little tidier, and introduced Miss Crowther.

"O dear Mr. Walton, I am so sorry! But you're not very ill, are you?"

"I hope not, Miss Jemima. Indeed, I think I will get off easier than I expected."

"I am glad of that. Now listen to me. I won't keep you, and it is a matter of some importance. I hear that one of your people is dead, and has left a little boy behind her. Now I have been wanting for a long time to adopt a child—"

"But," I interrupted her, "what would Miss Hester say?"

"My sister is not so very dreadful as perhaps you think her, Mr. Walton.

Besides, when I do want my own way—which is not often, for there are not so many things worth insisting upon—I always have it. I stand upon my right of primogeniture. Well, I think I know something of this child's father. I am sorry to say I don't know much good of him, and that's the worst of the boy. Still—"

"The boy is an uncommonly sweet and lovable child, whoever was his father," I interposed.

"Then I am the more determined to adopt him. What friends has he?"

"He has a grandfather, and an uncle and aunt, and will have a godfather—me—in a few days, I hope."

"There will be no opposition on the part of the relatives, I presume?"

"I am not so sure of that. I fear I shall object for one, Miss Jemima."

"I didn't expect that of you, Mr. Walton, I must say." And there was a tremor in the old lady's voice more of disappointment and hurt than of anger.

"I will think it over, though, and talk about it to his grandfather, and we shall find out what's best. You must not think I should not like you to have him."

"Thank you, Mr. Walton. Then I won't stay longer now. But I warn you I will call again very soon, if you don't come to see me. Good morning."

And the dear old lady left me rather hurriedly, turning at the door, however, to add, "Mind, I've set my heart upon having the boy, Mr. Walton. I've seen him often."

What would have made her take such a fancy to the boy? Of course, I talked the matter over with Thomas Weir but, as I had suspected, I found that he was now unwilling to part with the boy.

At the very time Miss Jemima was with me (as I found out some years later), Old Rogers turned into Thomas Weir's workshop and said, "Don't you think, Mr. Weir, there's summat the matter wi' Parson?"

"Overworked," returned Weir. "He's lost two, ye see, and had to see them both safe over within the same day. He's got a bad cold besides. Have ye heard of him today?"

"Yes, he's badly, and in bed. But that's not what I mean. There's summat on his mind," said Old Rogers.

"Well, I don't think it's for you or me to meddle with Parson's mind," returned Weir.

"I'm not so sure o' that," persisted Rogers. "But if I had thought, Mr. Weir, as how you would be ready to take me up short for mentionin' of the thing, I wouldn't ha' opened my mouth to you about Parson—leastways about his in'ards. I means this—as how Parson's in love. There, that's paid out."

"Suppose he was, I don't see yet what business that is of yours or mine either."

"Well, I do. I'd go to Davie Jones for that man."

"But what can we do?" returned Weir. Perhaps he was less inclined to listen, seeing that he was busy with a coffin for his daughter.

"I tell you what, Mr. Weir, this here's a serious business, and it seems to me it's not shipshape o' you to go on with that plane o' yours when we're talkin' about Parson."

"Well, Old Rogers, I meant no offense. Here goes. Now, what have you to say? Though if it's offense to Parson you're speakin' of, I know, if I were Parson, who I'd think was takin' the greatest liberty, me wi' my plane, or you wi' your fancies."

"Belay there and hearken." So Old Rogers went into as many particulars as he thought fit to prove his suspicion.

"Supposing all you say, Old Rogers," remarked Thomas, "I don't yet see what we've got to do with it. Parson ought to know best what he's about."

"But my daughter tells me," said Rogers, "that Miss Oldcastle has no mind to marry Captain Everard, and she thinks if Parson would only speak out he might have a chance."

Weir made no reply and was silent so long, with his head bent, that Rogers grew impatient. "Well, Man, ha' you nothing to say now—not for your best friend—on earth, I mean—and that's Parson? It may seem a small matter to you, but it's no small matter to Parson."

"Small to me!" said Weir, and, taking up his tool—a constant recourse with him when agitated—he began to plane furiously.

Old Rogers now saw that there was more in it than he had thought, and he held his peace and waited. After a minute or two of fierce activity, Thomas lifted up a face more white than the deal-board he was planing, and said, "You should have come to the point a little sooner, Old Rogers."

He then laid down his plane and went out of the workshop, leaving Rogers standing there in bewilderment. But he was not gone many minutes. He returned with a letter in his hand. "There," he said, giving it to Rogers.

"I can't read hand o' write," returned Rogers. "I ha' enough ado with straight-foret print. But I'll take it to Parson."

"On no account," returned Thomas, emphatically. "That's not what I gave it you for. Neither you nor Parson has any right to read that letter. Can Jane read writing?"

"I don't know as she can. What makes lasses take to writin' is when their young man's over the seas, not in the mill over the brook."

"I'll be back in a minute," said Thomas, and taking the letter from Rogers' hand, he left the shop again.

He returned once more with the letter sealed up in an envelope and addressed to Miss Oldcastle.

"Now you tell your Jane to give that to Miss Oldcastle from me—mind, from me—and she must give it into her own hands, and let no one else see it. And I must have it again. Mind you tell Jane all that, Old Rogers. Can you trust her not to go talking about it?"

"I think I can. I ought to, anyhow. But she can't know anythink in the letter now, Mr. Weir."

"I know that, but Marshmallows is a talkin' place, and poor Kate ain't right out o' hearin' yet. You'll come and see her buried tomorrow, won't ye, Old Rogers?"

"I will, Thomas. You've had a troubled life but, thank God, the sun came out a bit before she died."

"That's true, Old Rogers. It's all right, I do think, though I grumbled long and sore. But Jane mustn't speak of that letter."

"No, that she shan't."

"I'll tell you someday what's in it, but I can't bear to talk about it yet." And so they parted.

I was too unwell either to bury my dead or to comfort my living the next Sunday. I got help from Addicehead, however, and the dead were laid aside in the ancient wardrobe of the tomb. They were both buried by my vestry door, Catharine in the grave of her mother (where I had found young Tom lying), and old Mrs. Tomkins on the other side of the path. On Sunday Rogers gave his daughter the letter, and she carried it to the Hall.

That night when her bell rang, Jane went up and found Miss Oldcastle so pale and haggard that she was frightened. She had thrown herself back on the couch, with her hands lying by her sides, as if she cared for nothing in this world or out of it. But when Jane entered, she started and sat up, and tried to look like herself.

"Here is a letter," said Jane, "that Mr. Weir the carpenter sent to you, Miss."

"What is it about, Jane?" she asked, listlessly.

Then a sudden flash broke from her eyes, and she held out her hand eagerly to take it. She opened it and read it with changing color, but when she had finished it her cheeks were crimson, and her eyes glowing like fire.

"The wretch!" she said, and threw the letter into the middle of the floor. Jane stooped to pick it up, but had hardly raised herself when the door opened, and in came Mrs. Oldcastle. The moment she saw her mother, Ethelwyn rose and, advancing to meet her, said, "Mother, I will *not* marry that man. You may do what you please with me, but I *will not.*"

"Heighho!" exclaimed Mrs. Oldcastle, with spread nostrils, and turning suddenly upon Jane, snatched the letter out of her hand.

She opened and read it, her face getting more still and stony as she read. Miss Oldcastle stood and looked at her mother with cheeks now pale, but with eyes still flashing. Her mother finished the letter and walked swiftly to the fire, tearing the letter as she went. She thrust it between the bars, pushing it in fiercely with the poker and muttering, "A vile forgery of those wretches! As if he would ever have looked upon one of *their* women! A low conspiracy to get money from a gentleman!"

And for the first time since she went to the Hall, Jane said, there was color in that dead white face. She turned once more upon Jane and screamed, "You leave the house—*this instant!*"

And she came from the fire toward Jane, whose absolute fear drove her from the room before she knew what she was about. The locking of the door behind her let her know that she had abandoned her young mistress, but it was too late. She lingered by the door and listened, but beyond the occasional hoarse tone of suppressed rage, she heard nothing. Then the lock suddenly turned, and she was surprised by Mrs. Oldcastle, for if she was not listening, she at least was where she had no right to be.

Opposite Miss Oldcastle's bedroom was another room, seldom used, the door of which was now standing open. Mrs. Oldcastle gave Jane a violent push into this room and shut the door and locked it. Jane examined the door to see if she could escape, but she found the lock at least as strong as the door. Being a sensible girl and self-possessed, as her parents' child ought to be, she made no noise, but waited patiently through the night. At length, hearing a step in the passage, she tapped gently at the door and called, "Who's there?"

The cook's voice answered her.

"Let me out," said Jane. "The door's locked."

The cook promised to get her out, but found no key. Meantime, all she could do was hand Jane a loaf of bread on a stick from the next window. Finally the door was unlocked, and she was left at liberty. Unable to find her young mistress, she packed her box and escaped to her father. As soon as she had told him her story, he came straight to me.

But Judy found me first.

THIRTY-ONE
The Next Thing

Judy hurriedly opened my study door and entered. She looked about the room with a quick glance to see that we were alone, then caught my hand in both of hers, and burst out crying.

"Why, Judy," I said, "what is the matter?"

But the sobs would not allow her to answer. I was frightened, and so stood silent, my chest feeling like an empty tomb waiting for death to fill it. With a strong effort, she checked the succession of her sobs and spoke, "They are killing Auntie! She looks like a ghost already."

"Tell me, Judy, what *can* I do for her?"

"You must find out, Mr. Walton. If you loved her as much as I do, you would find out what to do."

"But she will not let me do anything for her."

"Yes, she will. She says you promised to help her someday."

"Did she send you, then?"

"Oh, you exact people! You must have everything square and in print before you move. If it had been me now, wouldn't I have been off like a shot! Do get your hat, Mr. Walton."

"Then I will go at once."

In a moment we were in the open air. It was a still night, and a pale half-moon hung in the sky. I offered Judy my arm, but she took my hand, and we walked on through the village and out upon the road.

"Now, Judy," I said at last, "tell me what they are doing to your aunt."

"I don't know what they are doing. But I am sure she will die. She is as white as a sheet and will not leave her room. Grannie must have frightened her dreadfully. Everybody is frightened at her but me, and I begin to be frightened too. And what will become of Auntie then?"

"But what can her mother do to her?"

"I don't know. I think it is her determination to have her own way that makes Auntie afraid she will get it somehow—and she says now she will rather die than marry Captain Everard. No one is allowed to wait on her but Sarah, and what has become of Jane I don't know. I haven't seen her all day, and the servants are whispering together more than usual. Auntie won't eat what Sarah brings her, I am sure, else I should almost fancy she was starving herself to death to keep clear of that Captain Everard."

"Is he still at the Hall?"

"Yes. But I don't think it is altogether his fault. Grannie won't let him go. I don't believe he knows how determined Auntie is not to marry him. To be sure, though Grannie never lets her have more than five shillings at a time, she will be worth something when she is married."

"Nothing can make her worth more than she is, Judy," I said, perhaps with some discontent in my tone.

"That's as you and I think, Mr. Walton, not as Grannie and the captain think at all. I dare say he would not care much more than Grannie whether she was willing or not, so long as she married him."

"But, Judy, we must have some plan laid before we reach the Hall, else my coming will be of no use."

"Of course. I know how much I can do, and you must arrange the rest with her. Auntie and the captain will be at dinner. I will take you to the little room upstairs, the octagon just under Auntie's room. I will leave you there, and tell Auntie that you want to see her."

"But, Judy—"

"Don't you want to see her, Mr. Walton?"

"Yes, I do, more than you can think."

"Then I will tell her so."

"But will she come to me?"

"I don't know. We have to find that out."

"Very well. I leave myself in your hands."

I was now perfectly collected. Judy and I scarcely spoke from the moment we entered the gate till I found myself at a side door. Judy went in and opened it and led me along a passage and up a stair into the little drawing room. There was no light. She led me to a seat at the farther end and, opening a door beside me, left me in the dark.

There I sat so long that I fell into a fit of musing. Castle after castle I built up; castle after castle fell to pieces in my hands. Suddenly from out of the dark a hand settled on my arm. I looked up and could just see the whiteness of Ethelwyn's face. She said in a broken half-whisper, "Will you save me, Mr. Walton?"

I reached for her hand and held it. All my trembling was gone in a moment, and the suppressed feelings of many months rushed to my lips. What I said I do not know, but I know that I told her I loved her. And she did not draw her hand from mine, even as I said, "If all I am, all I have will save you—"

"But I am saved already," she interposed, "if you love me, for I love you."

And for some moments there were no words to speak. Holding her hand,

I was conscious only of God and her. At last I said, "There is no time now but for action. You should go with me at once. Will you come home to my sister? Or I will take you wherever you please."

"I will go with you anywhere you think best. Only take me away."

"Put on your bonnet, then, and a warm cloak, and we will settle it as we go."

She had scarcely left the room when Mrs. Oldcastle came to the door. "Sarah, bring candles," she said, "and tell Captain Everard to come to the octagon room." Then she continued to herself, "Where can that little Judy be? The child gets more and more troublesome, I do think. I must take her in hand."

How was I to let her know that I was there? To announce yourself to a lady by a voice out of the darkness, or to wait for her to discover you where she thought she was quite alone—neither is a pleasant way of presenting yourself. But I was helped out once more by that blessed little Judy.

"Here I am, Grannie," she said. "But I won't be taken in hand by you or anyone else. I tell you that, so mind. And Mr. Walton is here too, and Aunt Ethelwyn is going with him."

"What do you mean, you silly child?"

"I mean what I say," and "Miss Judy speaks the truth," fell together from her lips to mine.

"Mr. Walton," began Mrs. Oldcastle, indignantly, "it is scarcely like a gentleman to come where you are not wanted—"

Here Judy interrupted her. "I beg your pardon, Grannie, Mr. Walton was wanted—very much wanted. I fetched him."

But Mrs. Oldcastle went on, unheeding, "—and to be sitting in my room in the dark too!"

"That couldn't be helped, Grannie. Here comes Sarah with candles."

"Sarah," said Mrs. Oldcastle, "ask Captain Everard to be kind enough to step this way."

"Yes, Ma'am," answered Sarah, with an untranslatable look at me as she set down the candles.

We could now see each other. Knowing words to be but idle breath, I did not complicate matters by speech, but stood silent, regarding Mrs. Oldcastle. She did not flinch, but returned my look with one both haughty and contemptuous. In a few moments Captain Everard entered, bowed slightly, and looked to Mrs. Oldcastle as if for an explanation, whereupon she spoke, but to me. "Mr. Walton," she said, "will you explain to Captain Everard to what we owe the *unexpected* pleasure of a visit from you?"

"Captain Everard has no claim to any explanation from me. To you, Mrs. Oldcastle, I would have answered, had you asked me, that I was waiting for Miss Oldcastle."

"Pray inform Miss Oldcastle, Judy, that Mr. Walton insists upon seeing her at once."

"That is quite unnecessary. Miss Oldcastle will be here presently," I said.

Mrs. Oldcastle, livid with wrath, walked toward the door beside me. I stepped between her and it, and said, "Pardon me, Mrs. Oldcastle. That is the way to Miss Oldcastle's room. I am here to protect her."

Without saying a word, she turned and looked at Captain Everard. He advanced with a long stride of determination. But then the door behind me opened, and Miss Oldcastle appeared in her bonnet and shawl, carrying a small bag in her hand. She put her hand on my arm and stood fronting the enemy with me. Judy was on my right, her eyes flashing and her cheeks red, prepared to do battle.

"Ethelwyn, go to your room instantly, I *command* you," said her mother, and she approached to remove her hand from my arm. I put my other arm between her and her daughter.

"No, Mrs. Oldcastle," I said, "you have lost all a mother's rights by ceasing to behave like a mother. Miss Oldcastle will never more do anything in obedience to your commands, whatever she may do in compliance with your wishes."

"Allow me to remark," said Captain Everard, with attempted nonchalance, "that that is strange doctrine for your cloth."

"So much the worse for my cloth, then," I answered, "and the better for yours, if it leads you to act more honorably."

He smiled haughtily, and gave a look of dramatic appeal to Mrs. Oldcastle.

"At least," said that lady, "do not disgrace yourself, Ethelwyn, by leaving this house in this unaccountable manner at night and on foot. If you *will* leave the protection of your mother's roof, wait at least till tomorrow."

"I would rather spend the night in the open air than pass another night under your roof, Mother. You have been a strange mother to me—and to Dorothy too!"

"At least do not put your character in question by going in this unmaidenly fashion. People will talk to your prejudice—and Mr. Walton's too."

Ethelwyn smiled. She was now as collected as I was, seeming to have cast off all her weakness. She knew her mother too well to be caught by the change in her tone. She answered nothing, but only looked at me. So I said, "They will hardly have time to do so, I trust, before it will be out of their power. It rests with Miss Oldcastle herself to say when that shall be."

As if she had never suspected that such was the result of her scheming, Mrs. Oldcastle's demeanor changed utterly. She made a spring at her daughter and seized her by her arm.

"Then I forbid it," she screamed, "and I *will* be obeyed. I stand on my rights. Go to your room, you minx."

"There is no law, human or divine, to prevent her from marrying whom she will," I said. "How old are you, Ethelwyn?"

"Twenty-seven," answered Miss Oldcastle.

"Is it possible you can be so foolish, Mrs. Oldcastle, as to think you have any hold on your daughter's freedom? Let her go."

But she kept her grasp.

"You hurt me, Mother," said Miss Oldcastle.

"Hurt you! You smooth-faced hypocrite, I will hurt you, then!"

But I took Mrs. Oldcastle's arm in my hand, and she let go her hold.

"How dare you touch a woman!" she said.

"Because she has so far ceased to be a woman as to torture her own daughter."

Here Captain Everard stepped forward, saying, "The riot act ought to be read, I think. It is time for the military to interfere."

"Well put, Captain Everard," I said. "Our side will disperse if you will only leave room for us to go."

"Possibly *I* may have something to say in the matter."

"Say on."

"This lady has jilted me."

"Have you, Ethelwyn?"

"I have not."

"Then, Captain Everard, you lie."

"You dare to tell me so?" And he strode a pace nearer.

"It needs no daring. I know you too well, and so does another who trusted you and found you as false as hell."

"You presume on your cloth, but—" he said, lifting his hand.

"You may strike me, presuming on my cloth," I answered, "and I will not return your blow. Insult me as you will, and I will bear it. Call me coward, and I will say nothing. But lay one hand on me to prevent me from doing my duty, and I will knock you down—or find you more of a man than I take you for."

Conscience—or something not so good—made a coward of him, and he turned on his heel. "I really am not sufficiently interested in the affair to oppose you. You may take the girl. Both your cloth and the presence of ladies protect your insolence. I do not like brawling where one cannot fight. You shall hear from me before long, Mr. Walton."

"No, Captain Everard, I shall not hear from you. I know that of you which, even on the code of the duelist, would justify any gentleman in refusing to meet you. Stand out of my way!"

I advanced with Miss Oldcastle on my arm, and he drew back. As we reached the door, Judy bounded after us, threw her arms round her aunt's neck, then round mine, kissing us both, and returned to her place on the sofa. Mrs. Oldcastle gave a scream and sunk fainting on a chair—a last effort to detain her daughter. Miss Oldcastle would have returned, but I would not permit her.

"No," I said, "she will be better without you. Judy, ring the bell for Sarah."

"How dare you give orders in my house?" exclaimed Mrs. Oldcastle, sitting bolt upright in the chair and shaking her fist at us. Then assuming the heroic, she added, "From this moment she is no daughter of mine. Nor can you touch one farthing of her money, Sir. You have married a beggar after all, and that you'll both know before long."

"Thy money perish with thee!" I said, and repented the moment I had said it. It sounded like an imprecation, and I had no correspondent feeling—after all, she was the mother of my Ethelwyn. But the allusion to money made me so indignant that the words burst from me before I could consider their import.

The cool wind greeted us like the breath of God as we left the house and closed the door behind us. The moon was shining alone in the midst of a lake of blue. We had not gone far from the house when Miss Oldcastle began to tremble violently. When we reached the vicarage, I gave her in charge to my sister while I went for Dr. Duncan.

THIRTY-TWO
Old Rogers' Thanksgiving

I found Dr. Duncan seated at his dinner, which he left immediately when he heard that Miss Oldcastle needed his help. I told him as we went what had befallen at the Hall. He listened with the interest of a boy reading a romance, asking twenty questions about the particulars. Then he shook me warmly by the hand, saying, "You have fairly won her, Walton, and I am glad of it. She is well worth all you must have suffered. Perhaps this will remove the curse from that wretched family. You have saved her from a fate worse than her sister's."

"I fear she will be ill, though," I said, "after all that she has gone through." But even I did not suspect how ill she would be.

An excited Old Rogers arrived and was shown into the study, where I allowed him to tell out his daughter's story without interruption. He ended by saying, "Now, Sir, you really must do summat. This won't do in a Christian country. We ain't aboard ship here with a nor'easter a-walkin' the quarterdeck."

"There's no occasion, my dear old fellow, to do anything."

He was taken aback. "Well, I don't understand you, Mr. Walton. You're the last man I'd have expected to hear argufy for faith without works. It's right to trust in God, but if you don't stand to your halliards, your craft'll miss stays, and your faith'll be blown out of the boltropes in the turn of a marlinspike."

I suspect there was some confusion in the figure, but the old man's meaning was plain enough. Nor would I keep him in a moment more of suspense. "Miss Oldcastle is in the house, Old Rogers," I said.

"What house, Sir?" returned the old man, his gray eyes opening wider as he spoke.

"This house, to be sure."

I shall never forget the look he cast upward to the Father. And never shall I find one who will listen to my story with more interest than Old Rogers did, as I recounted the adventures of the evening. There were few to whom I could have told them; to Old Rogers I felt that it was right and natural and dignified to tell the story even of my love's victory.

He rose, took my hand, and said, "Mr. Walton, you *will* preach now. I thank God for the good we shall all get from the trouble you have gone through."

"I ought to be the better for it," I answered.

"You *will* be the better for it," he returned. "I've allus been the better for any trouble as ever I had to go through. I couldn't quite say the same for every bit of good luck I had—leastaways I consider trouble the best luck a man can have. And I wish you a good-night, Sir. Thank God! Again."

My design had been to go at once to London and make preparation for as early a wedding as Miss Oldcastle would consent to, but now life and not marriage was the question. Dr. Duncan looked very grave, and all his encouragement did not amount to much. There was such a lack of vitality about her! Her life was nearly quenched from lack of hope, and her whole complaint appeared in excessive weakness. Finding that she fainted after every little excitement, I left her for four weeks entirely to my sister and Dr. Duncan. It was long before I could venture to stay in her room more than a minute or two, but by the summer she was able to be wheeled into the garden in a chair.

I had some painful apprehensions as to the treatment Judy herself might meet with from her grandmother, and had been doubtful whether I ought not to have carried her off as well as her aunt. But Judy came often to the vicarage, and on her first visit to Ethelwyn (which was the next day) she set my mind at rest.

"But does your grannie know where you are?" I had asked her.

"So well, Mr. Walton," she replied, "that there was no occasion to tell her. Why shouldn't I rebel as well as Aunt Wynnie, I wonder?" she added, looking archness itself.

"How does she bear it?"

"Bear what, Mr. Walton?"

"The loss of your aunt."

"You don't think Grannie cares about that, do you? She's vexed enough at the loss of Captain Everard. Do you know, I think he had too much wine yesterday, or he wouldn't have made quite such a fool of himself."

"I fear he hadn't had quite enough to give him courage, Judy. I dare say he was brave enough once, but a bad conscience soon destroys a man's courage."

"Why do you call it a bad conscience, Mr. Walton? I should have thought that a bad conscience was one that would let a girl go on anyhow and say nothing about it to make her uncomfortable."

"You are quite right, Judy. That is certainly the worst kind of conscience. But tell me, how does Mrs. Oldcastle bear it?"

"Grannie never says a word about you, or Auntie either."

"But you said she was vexed: how do you know that?"

"Because ever since the captain went away this morning, she won't speak a word even to Sarah."

"Are you not afraid of her locking you up someday or other?"

"Not a bit of it. Grannie won't touch me. And you shouldn't tempt me to run away from her like Auntie. I won't. Grannie is a naughty old lady, and I don't believe anybody loves her but me—certainly not Sarah. Therefore, I can't leave her, and I won't leave her, Mr. Walton, whatever you may say about her."

"Indeed, I don't want you to leave her, Judy."

(And Judy did not leave her as long as she lived, and the old lady's love to that child was one redeeming point in her fierce character. And a quarrel took place between that old woman and Sarah, which I regarded as a hopeful sign. And once she folded her granddaughter in her arms and wept long and bitterly. Perhaps the thought of her dying child came back upon her, along with the reflection that the only friend she had was the child of that marriage which she had persecuted to dissolution. Only a few years passed, however, before her soul was required of her. And to this day, Judy has never heard how her old grannie treated her mother.)

THIRTY-THREE
Tom's Story

It was summer when Ethelwyn and I were married. She was now quite well, and no shadow hung upon her half-moon forehead. We went for a fortnight into Wales, and then returned to the vicarage and the duties of the parish, in which she was quite ready to assist me. She saw that the best thing she could do for our parishioners was to help me—to serve me and not them.

I began to arrange my work again, and it came to my mind that I had been doing very little for Tom Weir. I could not blame myself much for this, and I was sure neither he nor his father blamed me at all. I called him to my house the next morning and proceeded to acquaint myself with what he had been doing. I found that he had made considerable progress both in Latin and mathematics, and I resolved that I would now push him a little. I found this only brought out his mettle, and his progress was extraordinary.

Although I carefully abstained from making the suggestion to him, I was more than pleased when I discovered that he would gladly give himself to the service of the church. At the same time, I felt compelled to be cautious, in fear that the prospect of the social elevation involved might be a temptation to him, as it has been to many a man of humble birth. However, as I continued to observe him closely, my conviction was deepened that he was rarely fitted for ministering to his fellows. And I found that Thomas, so far from being unfavorably inclined to the proposal, was prepared to spend the few savings of his careful life upon Tom's education. To this, however, I could not listen, because there was his daughter Mary, and his grandchild too, for whom he ought to make what little provision he could.

I therefore took the matter in my own hands, and managed (at less expense than most suppose) to maintain my young friend at Oxford till such time as he gained a fellowship. I felt justified in doing so, as someday Mrs. Walton would inherit the Oldcastle property. Certain other moneys of hers were now in the trust of her mother and two gentlemen in London, though she could not touch it as long as her mother lived and chose to refuse her the use of it. But I did not lose a penny, for of the very first money Tom received after his fellowship, he brought the half to me, and eventually repaid me every shilling. As soon as he was in deacon's orders he came to assist me as curate, and I found him a great help and comfort.

But, in looking back and trying to account for the snare into which I fell, I see plainly enough that I thought too much of what I had done for Tom, and too little of the honor God had done me in allowing me to help Tom. I took the throne over him, not consciously, but still with a contemptible condescension of heart that the nature in me called only fatherly friendship.

One evening a gentle tap came at my door, and Tom entered. He looked pale and anxious and uncertain in his motions.

"What is the matter, Tom?" I asked.

"I wanted to say something to you, Sir," answered Tom.

"Say on," I returned cheerily.

"It is not easy to say, Sir," rejoined Tom, with a faint smile. "Miss Walton, Sir—"

"Well, what of her? There's nothing happened to her? She was here a few minutes ago—"

Here a suspicion of the truth flashed on me and struck me dumb. I am now covered with shame to think how it swept away for the moment all my fine theories about the equality of men in Christ. How could Tom Weir, whose father was a joiner, who had been a lad in a London shop himself, dare to propose marrying my sister? Instead of thinking of what he really was, my regard rested upon this and that stage through which he had passed to reach his present condition. In fact, I regarded him rather as of my making than of God's.

I have known good people who were noble and generous toward their so-called inferiors, and full of the rights of the race, until it touched their own family, and just no longer. Yea, I, when Tom Weir wanted to marry my sister, judged according to appearances in which I did not even believe, and judged not righteous judgment.

What answer I returned to Tom I hardly know. I remember that the poor fellow's face fell, and that he murmured something which I did not heed. And then I found myself walking in the garden under the great cedar, having stepped out of the window almost unconsciously and left Tom standing there alone. It was very good of him ever to forgive me.

Wandering about in the garden, my wife saw me from her window and met me as I turned a corner in the shrubbery.

"What is the matter with you?" she asked.

"Oh, not much," I answered, "only that Weir has been making me feel rather uncomfortable."

"What has he been doing?" she inquired, in some alarm. "It is not possible he has done anything wrong."

My wife trusted him as much as I did.

"No-o-o," I answered, "not anything exactly wrong."

"It must be very nearly wrong to make you look so miserable."

I began to feel ashamed and more uncomfortable. "He has fallen in love with Martha," I said, "and I fear he may have made her fall in love with him too."

My wife laughed merrily. "What a wicked curate!"

"Well, but you know it is not exactly agreeable."

"Why?"

"You know well enough."

"I am not going to take it for granted. Is he not a good man, and well educated?"

"Yes."

"Is he not clever, and a gentleman?"

"One of the cleverest fellows I ever met, and I have no fault to find with his manners."

"Nor with his habits or his ways of thinking?" my wife went on.

"No. But, Ethelwyn, you know what I mean quite well. His family, you know—"

"Well, is his father not a respectable man?"

"Oh, yes, certainly. Thoroughly respectable."

"He wouldn't borrow money of his tailor instead of paying for his clothes, would he?"

"Certainly not."

"And if he were to die today, he would carry no debts to heaven with him? Does he bear false witness against his neighbor?"

"No."

"Well, I think Tom very fortunate in having such a father. I wish my mother had been as good."

"That is all true, and yet—"

"And yet, suppose a young man you liked had a fashionable father who had ruined half a score of tradespeople—would you object to him because of his family?"

"Perhaps not."

"Then, with you, position outweighs honesty, in fathers, at least."

To this I was not ready with an answer, and my wife went on. "Do you know why I would not accept your offer of taking my name when I should succeed to the property?"

"You said you liked mine better," I answered.

"So I did. But I did not tell you that I was ashamed that my good husband should take a name which for centuries had been borne by hard-hearted, worldly-minded people, who were neither gentle nor honest, nor high-minded."

"Still, Ethelwyn, you know there is something in it, though it is not easy to say what. And you avoid that. I suppose Martha has been talking you over to her side."

"For the first time, I am almost ashamed of you," my wife said with a shade of solemnity. "And I will punish you by telling you the truth. Do you think I had nothing of that sort to get over when I began to find that I was thinking a little more about you than was convenient under the circumstances? Your manners, though irreproachable, just had not the tone that I had been accustomed to. There was a diffidence about you also that did not at first advance you in my regard."

"Yes, yes," I answered, a little piqued, "I have no doubt you thought me a boor. But it is quite bad enough to have brought you down to my level, without sinking you still lower now."

"Now there you are wrong, and that is what I want to show you. I found that my love to you would not be satisfied with simply making an exception in your favor. I must see what force there really was in the notions I had been bred in."

"Ah!" I said, "I see. You looked for a principle in what you had thought was an exception."

"Yes," returned my wife, "and I soon found one. The next step was to throw away all false judgment in regard to such things. Would you hesitate a moment between Tom Weir and the dissolute son of an earl?"

"You know I would not."

"Well, just carry out the considerations that suggests."

"But his sister?"

"You were preaching last Sunday about the way God thinks of things, and you said that was the only true way of thinking about them. Would the Mary who poured the ointment on the head of Jesus have refused to marry a good man because he was the brother of that Mary who poured it on His feet? Have you thought what God would think of Tom for a husband to Martha?"

I did not answer, and when I lifted my eyes from the ground, thinking Ethelwyn stood beside me, she was gone. I was ashamed to follow and find her, so I got my hat instead and strolled out.

What was it that drew me toward Thomas Weir's shop? It must have been incipient repentance—a feeling that I had wronged the man. But just as I turned the corner, and the smell of the wood reached me, the picture so often associated in my mind with such a scene of human labor rose before me. I saw the Lord of Life bending over His bench, fashioning some lowly utensil for a housewife of Nazareth. And He would receive payment for it too, for He, at least, could see no disgrace in the order of things that His Father had appointed. It is the vulgar mind that looks down on the earning and worships the inheriting of money.

And the thought sprung up at once in my mind, "If I ever see our Lord face to face, how shall I feel if He says to me, 'Didst thou do well to murmur that thy sister espoused a certain man, for that in his youth he had earned his bread as I earned Mine? Where was then thy right to say unto Me, Lord, Lord?' "

I hurried into the workshop. "Has Tom told you about it?" I said.

"Yes, Sir. And I told him to mind what he was about, for he was not a gentleman, and you was, Sir."

"I hope I am. And Tom is as much a gentleman as I have any claim to be."

Thomas Weir held out his hand. "Now, Sir, I do believe you mean in my shop what you say in your pulpit, and there is *one* Christian in the world at least. But what will your good lady say? She's higher born than you—no offense, Sir."

"Ah! Thomas, you shame me. I am not so good as you think me. It was my wife that brought me to reason about it."

"God bless her."

"Amen. I'm going to find Tom."

At the same moment Tom entered the shop, with a very melancholy face. He started when he saw me and looked confused.

"Tom, my boy," I said, "I behaved very badly to you. I am sorry for it. Come back with me and have a walk with my sister. I don't think she'll be sorry to see you." His face brightened up at once, and we left the shop together.

Tom was the first to speak. "I know, Sir, how many difficulties my presumption must put you in."

"Not another word about it, Tom. You are blameless. I wish I were. Take my sister, in God's name, Tom, and be good to her."

Tom went to find Martha, and I to find Ethelwyn.

"It is all right," I said, "even to the shame I feel at having needed your reproof."

"Don't think of that. God gives us all time to come to our right minds, you know," answered my wife.

"But how did you get on so far ahead of me?"

Ethelwyn laughed. "Why," she said, "I only told you back again what you have been telling me for the last seven or eight years."

So to me the message had come first, but my wife had answered first with the deed.

Next to her and my children, Tom has been my greatest comfort for many years. He is still my curate, and I do not think we shall part till death separates us for a time. He has distinguished himself in the literary world, and when I read his books, I am yet prouder of my brother-in-law. My sister is worth twice what she was before.

Thomas Weir is now too old to work any longer. His father is dead, and Thomas occupies his chair in the large room of the old house. The workshop I have turned into a schoolroom. A great part of Tom's time is devoted to the children, for he and I agree that the pastoral care ought to be equally divided between the sheep and the lambs.

Jane Rogers was married to young Brownrigg about a year after we were married. Old Brownrigg is all but confined to the chimney corner now, and Richard manages the farm, though not quite to his father's satisfaction, of course. The old mill has been superseded by one of new and rare device (built by Richard), but the cottage where Old Rogers and his woman lived has slowly moldered back to the dust, for the old people have been dead for years.

Often in the summer, as I go to or come from the vestry, I sit down for a moment on the turf that covers my old friend Rogers, and think that this body of mine is everyday moldering away, till it shall fall a heap of dust into its appointed place. But what is that to me? It is to me the drawing nigh of the fresh morning of life when I shall be young and strong again, glad in the presence of the wise and beloved dead, and unspeakably glad in the presence of God.

I am seated now in that little octagonal room overlooking the Hall quarry, with its green lining of trees and its deep central well. It is my study now. My wife is not yet too old to prefer her old little room, although the stair is high and steep. Nor do I object, for I see her the oftener.

And Ethelwyn bends her smooth forehead over me—for she has a smooth forehead still. One of the good things that come of being married is that there is one face which you can still see the same through all the shadows which years have gathered and heaped upon it. No, I have a better way of putting it: there is one face whose final beauty you can see the more clearly as the bloom of youth departs, and the loveliness of wisdom and the beauty of holiness take its place.

I myself am getting old—faster and faster. When my voice quavers, I feel that it is mine and not mine, that it just belongs to me like my watch which does not run well now, though it did thirty years ago. And my knees shake—even walking across the floor of my study—like that old mare of my father's, which came at last to have the same weakness in her knees that I have in mine. But these things are not me, I say. I *have* them, and please God, shall soon have better. For, of all children, how can the children of God be old?

The
Seaboard Parish

Contents

PROLOGUE

I am seated once again at my writing table in the little octagonal room, which I have made my study because I like it best. It is rather a shame, for my books cover every foot of the old oak paneling. But they make the room all the more pleasant, and after I am gone, there is the old oak, none the worse, for anyone who prefers it to books.

My story will be rather about my family than myself now. What was once one, and had become two, is now seven. Ethelwyn—or Wynnie—is the eldest, and is named, of course, after her mother. Constance—Connie—followed her, and after that Dorothy, whom we often call Dora. And our two boys, Harry and Charlie, came to us last.

I intend to relate the history of one year during which I took charge of a friend's parish, while my brother-in-law, Thomas Weir, took the entire charge of Marshmallows.

ONE

Constance's Birthday

It was a custom with my family that each of the children, as his or her birthday came round, should be king or queen for that day and—subject to the veto of Father and Mother—should have everything his or her own way. Let me say for them, however, that in the matter of choosing the dinner—the royal prerogative—it was almost invariably the favorite dishes of others that were chosen, and not those especially agreeable to the royal palate. (Members of families where children have not been taught that the great privilege of possession is the right to bestow, may regard this as an improbable assertion.) But there was always the choice of some individual treat, determined solely by the preference of the individual in authority.

And Constance, for her eighteenth birthday, had chosen "a long ride with Papa."

On her birthday morning, a lovely October day with a golden east and clouds of golden foliage, there came yet an occasional blast of wind which smelt of winter. However, I do not think Connie felt it at all as she stood on the steps in her riding habit, waiting for the horses. She had been at school for two years and had been home a month that very day. She was as fresh as the young day, for we were early people. Breakfast and prayers were over, and it was nine o'clock.

"O Papa! Isn't it jolly?" she said, merrily.

"Very jolly indeed, my dear," I answered, delighted to hear the word from the lips of my gentle daughter. She very seldom used slang, and when she did, she used it like a lady.

She was rather little, but so slight that she looked tall. She was fair in complexion, with her mother's blue eyes and long, dark, wavy hair. She was generally playful and took greater liberties with me than any of the others, but on the borders of her playfulness there was a fringe of thoughtfulness. She enjoyed life like a bird—her laugh was merry and her heart was careless. Her sweet soprano voice rang through the house as she sang snatches of songs—now a street tune from a London organ, now an air from Handel or Mozart. She would sometimes tease her older sister about her anxious and solemn looks, for Wynnie had to suffer for her grandmother's sins against my wife, and she came into the world with a troubled heart.

"Where shall we go, Connie?" I asked, the same moment as the sound of the horses' hooves reached us.

"Would it be too far to go to Addicehead?"

"It is a long ride."

"Too much for the pony?"

"No, not at all. I was thinking of you, not the pony."

"I'm quite as able to ride as the pony is to carry me, Papa. And I want to get something for Wynnie. Do let us go."

"Very well, my dear," I said, and raised her to the saddle—if I may say *raised,* for no bird ever hopped more lightly from one twig to another than she sprang from the ground to her pony's back. In a moment I was beside her, and away we rode.

The shadows were still long, and the dew still pearly on the spiders' webs, as we trotted out of our own grounds into a lane that led away toward the high road. Our horses were fresh and the air was exciting, so we turned from the hard road into the first suitable field and had a gallop to begin with. Constance was a good horsewoman, for she had been used to the saddle longer than she could remember. She was now riding Sprite, a tall well-bred pony, with plenty of life—rather too much, I sometimes thought when I was out with Wynnie, but I never thought so when I was with Constance. Another field or two quieted both animals, and then we began to talk.

"You are quite a woman now, Connie, my dear," I said.

"Quite an old grannie, Papa," she answered.

"Old enough to think about what's coming next," I said.

"O Papa! And you are always telling us that we must not think about the morrow, or even the next hour. But, then, that's in the pulpit," she added, with a sly look up at me from under the drooping feather of her pretty hat.

"You know very well what I mean," I answered. "And I don't say one thing in the pulpit and another out of it."

She was at my horse's shoulder with a bound, as if Sprite had been of one mind and one piece with her. She was afraid she had offended me and looked up at me anxiously.

"Oh, thank you, Papa!" she said, when I smiled. "I thought I had been rude. I didn't mean it. But I do wish sometimes you wouldn't explain things so much. I seem to understand you while you are preaching, but when I try the text by myself, I can't make anything of it, and I've forgotten every word you've said."

"Perhaps that is because you have no right to understand it."

"I thought we all had a right to understand every word of the Bible."

"If we can. But last Sunday, for instance, I did not expect anybody there to understand a certain bit of my sermon, except your mamma and Thomas Weir."

"How funny! What part was it?"

"Oh, I'm not going to tell you. You have no right to understand it. But tell me what you are so full of care about, and perhaps I can help you there."

"Well, you often say that half the misery in this world comes from idleness, and that you do not believe that God could have intended that women, any more than men, should have nothing to do. Now what am I to do? What have I been sent into the world for? I don't see it, and I feel very useless and wrong sometimes. I don't want to stay at home and lead an easy, comfortable life, when there are so many to be helped everywhere in the world."

"Is there anything better in doing something where God has not placed you, than in doing it where He has placed you?"

"No, Papa. But my sisters are quite enough for all you have for us to do at home. Is nobody ever to go away to find the work meant for her? But you won't think that I *want* to get away from home, will you?"

"No, my dear. I believe that you are thinking about duty. What God may hereafter require of you, you must not give yourself the least trouble about. Everything He gives you to do, you must do as well as ever you can. That is the best possible preparation for what He may want you to do next. If people would but do what they have to do, they would always find themselves ready for what comes next.

"But there is one more thing. It is not your moral nature alone you ought to cultivate. You ought to make yourself as worth God's making as you possibly can. Now I am a little doubtful whether you keep up your studies at all."

She shrugged her shoulders playfully, looking up into my face again. "I don't like dry things, Papa "

"Nobody does."

"Nobody? How do the grammars and history books come to be written, then?"

"Those books are exceedingly interesting to the people who make them. Dry things are just things that you do not know enough about to care for. And all you learn at school is nothing to what you have to learn."

"Must I go all over my French grammar again?" she sighed. "Oh, dear! I hate it so."

"If you will tell me something you like, Connie instead of something you don't like, I may be able to give you advice Is there nothing you are fond of?"

"I don't remember much in the way of schoolwork that I really liked. I did what I had to. But there was one thing I liked—the poetry we had to learn once a week. But I suppose gentlemen count that silly, don't they?"

"On the contrary, I would make that liking the foundation of all your work. Besides, I think poetry the grandest thing God has given us, though perhaps we might not agree about *what* poetry was a special gift of God. Most poetry is very thin, and it is time you had done with thin things, however good they may be. I must take you in hand myself, and see what I can do for you. I hold that whatever mental food you take should be just a little too strong for you. That implies trouble, necessitates growth, and involves delight."

"I shan't mind how difficult it is if you help me, Papa."

We went on talking a little more in the same way, and at length fell into silence—a very happy one on my part. I was more than delighted to find that my child was following after the truth, wanting to do what was right in the voice of her own conscience and the light of that understanding which is the candle of the Lord.

We were going at a gentle trot along a woodland path—a brown, soft, shady road, nearly five miles from home. Our horses scattered the withered leaves that lay thick upon it, between the underwood and the few large trees that had been lately cleared from the place. There were many piles of sticks about, and a great log lying here and there along the side of the path. One tree had been struck by lightning and had stood till the frosts and rains had bared it of its bark. Now it lay white as a skeleton by the side of the path and was, I think, the cause of what followed.

All at once Sprite sprang to the other side of the road, shying sideways. Then, rearing and plunging, he threw Connie from the saddle across one of the logs, and then bolted away between the trees. I slid from my horse, and was by Connie's side in an instant. She lay motionless; her eyes were closed, and when I took her up in my arms she did not open them. I laid her on the moss, and got some water and sprinkled her face. Then she revived a little, but fainted again in pain.

Very shortly, a woodsman came up and asked how he could help. He had been cutting firewood at a little distance, and had seen the pony careering through the woods. I told him to ride my horse to Oldcastle Hall and ask Mrs. Walton to come with the carriage as quickly as possible. "Tell her," I said, "that her daughter has had a fall from her pony and is rather shaken. Ride as hard as you can go."

The man was off in a moment, and there I sat watching my poor child. She had come to, but complained of much pain in her back and found that she could not move. Her face was dreadfully pale and looked worn with a month's illness. All my fear was for her spine.

At length the carriage came, as fast as the road would allow, with the woodsman on the box directing the coachman. My wife got out, as pale as Constance, but quiet and firm. She asked no questions; there was time enough for that afterward. She had brought plenty of cushions and pillows, and though we did all we could to make an easy couch for the poor girl, she moaned dreadfully as we lifted her into the carriage. We did our best to keep her from being shaken, but those few miles were the longest journey I ever made in my life.

When we reached home, we found that Wynnie had readied a room on the ground floor for her sister, and we were glad indeed not to have to carry her up the stairs. Before my wife had left, she had sent the groom for aid, and a young doctor named Turner was waiting for us when we arrived. He had settled at Marshmallows as general practitioner a year or two before. He immediately began to direct her care, and helped us lay her on a mattress. It was painfully clear to all that her spine was seriously injured, and that she probably had years of suffering before her.

I left her at last, with her mother seated by her bedside, and found Wynnie and Dora seated on the floor outside, one weeping on each side of the door. I called them into my study and said to them, "My darlings, this is very sad, but you must remember that it is God's will. As you would both try to bear it cheerfully if it had fallen to your lot to bear, you must try to be cheerful even when it is your sister's part to endure."

"O Papa! Poor Connie!" cried Dora, and burst into fresh tears. Wynnie said nothing, but knelt down by my knee and laid her cheek upon it.

"Shall I tell you what Constance said to me just before I left the room?" I asked.

"Please do, Papa."

"She whispered, 'You must try to bear it, all of you, as well as you can. I don't mind it very much, only for you.' So, you see, if you want to make her comfortable, you must not look gloomy and troubled. Sick people like to see cheerful faces about them. I am sure Connie will not suffer nearly so much if she finds that she does not make the household gloomy.

"We will do all we can, will we not," I went on, "to make her as comfortable as possible? You, Dora, must attend to your little brothers, so that your mother may not have too much there to think about."

They would not say much, but they both kissed me and went away.

My wife and I watched by Connie's bedside on alternate nights, until the pain had so far subsided, and the fever was so far reduced, that we could allow Wynnie to take some care of her. Connie's chief suffering came from keeping nearly one position on her back, and from the external bruises and consequent swelling of her muscles.

It soon became evident that Connie's new room was like a new and more sacred heart to the house. At first it radiated gloom to the remotest corners, but soon rays of light began to mingle with the gloom. Bits of news were carried from there to the servants in the kitchen, in the garden, in the stable, and over the way to the home farm. Even in the village, and everywhere over the parish, I was received more kindly and listened to more willingly, because of the trouble my family and I were in. In the house, although we had never been anything else than a loving family, it was easy to discover that we all drew more closely together in consequence of our common anxiety.

Previous to this, it had been no unusual thing to see Wynnie and Dora impatient with each other, for Dora was wild and somewhat lawless, though profoundly affectionate. She rather resembled her cousin, Judy, whom she called Aunt Judy, and with whom she was naturally a great favorite. Wynnie, on the other hand, was sedate and rather severe, more severe, I must in justice say, with herself than with anyone else. It was soon evident not only that Wynnie had grown more indulgent to Dora's vagaries, but that Dora was more submissive to Wynnie, while the younger children began to obey their eldest sister willingly, keeping down their effervescence inside and letting it off only out-of-doors.

TWO
The Sick Chamber

In the course of a month, Connie's pain was greatly reduced but the power of moving her limbs had not yet begun to show itself.

One day she received me with a happy smile, put out her thin white hand, took mine and kissed it, and said, "Papa," with a lingering on the last syllable.

"What is it, my pet?" I asked.

"I am so happy!"

"What makes you so happy?" I asked again.

"I don't know," she answered. "I haven't thought about it yet. But everything looks so pleasant around me. Is it nearly winter yet, Papa? I've forgotten all about how the time has been going."

"It is almost winter, my dear. There is hardly a leaf left on the trees—just two or three disconsolate yellow ones that want to get away down to the rest. They flutter and try to break away, but can't."

"That is just as I felt. I wanted to die and get away, for I thought I should never be well again, and I should be in everybody's way."

"Well, my darling, we are in God's hands. We shall never get tired of you, and you must not get tired of us. Would you get tired of nursing me, if I were ill?"

"O Papa!" And the tears began to gather in her eyes.

"Then you must think we are not able to love so well as you."

"I know what you mean. I did not think of it that way. I was only thinking how useless I was."

"There you are quite mistaken, my dear. No living creature ever was useless. You've plenty to do."

"But what have I got to do? I don't feel able for anything," she said, and again the tears came to her eyes, as if I had been telling her to get up and she could not.

"A great deal of our work," I answered, "we do without knowing what it is. But I'll tell you what you have to do: you have to believe in God, and in everybody in this house."

"I do, I do. But that is easy," she returned.

"And do you think that the work God gives us to do is never easy? Jesus says His yoke is easy, His burden light. People sometimes refuse to do God's work just because it is easy. Sometimes this is because they cannot believe that easy work is His work, and so they accept it with half a heart and do it with half a hand. But, however easy any work may be, it cannot be well done without taking thought about it. And such people, instead of taking thought about their work, generally take thought about the morrow, in which no work can be done any more than in yesterday. Do you remember our talk on that dreadful morning? You wanted something to do, and so God gave you something to do."

"Lying in bed and doing nothing!"

"Yes. Just lying in bed and doing His will."

"If I could but feel that I was doing His will!"

"When you do it, then you will feel you are doing it."

"I know you are coming to something, Papa. Please make haste."

"You must say to God something like this: 'O Heavenly Father, I have nothing to offer Thee but my patience. I will bear Thy will, and so offer my will a burnt offering unto Thine. I will be as useless as Thou pleasest.' Depend on it, my darling, in the midst of all the science about the world and its ways, and all the ignorance of God and His greatness, the man or woman who can thus say, 'Thy will be done,' with the true heart of surrender, is nearer the secret of things than the geologist and theologian."

She held up her mouth to kiss me, but did not speak, and I left her and sent Dora to sit with her.

In the evening, when I went into her room again, having been out in my parish all day, I began to unload my budget of small events. Indeed, we all came in like pelicans with stuffed pouches to empty them in her room, as if she had been the only young one we had, and we must cram her with news.

After I had done talking, she said, "And you have been to the school too, Papa?"

"Yes. I go to the school almost every day."

"You'll have to take up my teaching soon, as you promised—you know, Papa—just before Sprite threw me."

"Certainly, my dear, and I will begin to think about it at once."

She was quite unable for any kind of work such as she would have me commence with her, but I used to take something to read to her every now and then, and always after our early tea on Sundays. And it was in part the result of Connie's wish that it became the custom to gather in her room on Sunday evenings.

This custom began one Sunday evening as I was sitting beside Constance's bed. The twilight had deepened nearly into night, and the curtains had not yet been drawn. There was no light in the room but that of the fire. Now Constance was in the way of asking what kind of day or night it was, for there was never a girl more a child of nature than she.

"What is it like, Papa?"

"It is growing dark," I answered. "It is a still evening, and what they call a black frost. The trees are standing as still as if they were carved out of stone, and would snap off everywhere if the wind were to blow. The ground is dark, and as hard as cast iron. A gloomy night, rather—it looks as if there were something on its mind that made it sullenly thoughtful. But the stars are coming out one after another overhead, and the sky will be awake soon. Strange, the life that goes on all night, is it not? The life of owlets and mice and beasts of prey and bats and stars," I said, with no very categorical arrangement, "and dreams and flowers that don't go to sleep like the rest, but send out their scent all night long. Only those are gone now. There are no scents abroad, not even of the earth, in such a frost as this."

"Don't you think it looks sometimes, Papa, as if God turned His back on the world, or went farther away from it for a while?"

"Tell me a little more what you mean, Connie."

"Well, this night now, this dark, frozen, lifeless night, which you have been describing to me, isn't like God at all, is it?"

"No, it is not. I see what you mean now."

"It is just as if He had gone away and said, 'Now you shall see what you can do without Me.' "

"Something like that. But I think the English people enjoy the changeful weather of their country much more than those who have fine weather constantly. It is not enough to satisfy God's goodness but that He should make us able to enjoy them as richly as He gives them. Now can you tell me anything in history that confirms what I have been saying?"

"I don't know anything about history, Papa. The only thing that comes into my head is what you were saying yourself the other day about Milton's blindness."

"Ah, yes. I had not thought of that. I believe that God wanted a grand poem from that man, and therefore blinded him that he might be able to write it."

"It was rather hard for poor Milton, though, wasn't it, Papa?"

"Wait till *he* says so, my dear. We are sometimes too ready with our sympathy, and think things a great deal worse than do those who have to undergo them. Who would not be glad to be struck with such blindness as Milton's?"

"Those who do not care about his poetry, Papa," answered Constance, with a deprecatory smile.

"Well said. And to such it never can come. But, if it please God, you shall love Milton before you are about again. You can't love one you know nothing about."

"I have tried to read him a little. I am only sorry that I am not capable of appreciating him."

"There you are wrong again. I think you are quite capable, but you cannot appreciate what you have never seen. You have a figure before you in your fancy which is dry, and which you call Milton. But it is not Milton, any more than your Dutch doll was your Aunt Judy, even though you named her so. But here comes your mamma—and I haven't said what I wanted to say yet."

"But surely, Harry, you can say it all the same," said my wife. "I will go away if you can't."

"I can say it all the better, my love. Come and sit down here beside me. I was showing Connie that a gift has sometimes to be taken away before we can know what it is worth, and so receive it right.

"As long as our Lord was with His disciples, they could not see Him right—He was too near them. Too much light, too many words, too much revelation, blinds or stupefies. They loved Him dearly, and yet often forgot His words almost as soon as He said them. He could not get it into them, for instance, that He had not come to be a king. Whatever He said, they shaped it over again after their own fancy. Their minds were full of their own worldly notions of grandeur and command. Therefore He was taken away, that His Spirit might come into them—that they might receive the gift of God into their innermost being. After He had gone from their sight, they looked all around—down in the grave and up in the air—and did not see Him anywhere. And when they thought they had lost Him, He came to them again from the other side—from the inside. And His words came back to them, no longer as they had received them, but as He meant them. They were then always saying to each other, 'You remember how. . . . whereas before they had been always staring at each other with astonishment while He spoke to them. So after He had gone away, He was really nearer to them than before.

"And so the world and all its beauty has come nearer to you, my dear, just because you are separated from it for a time."

"Thank you, dear Papa. I do like to get a little sermon all to myself now and then. But should we not know Jesus better now if He were to come and let us see Him, as He came to the disciples so long ago?"

"As to the time, it makes no difference whether it was last year or two thousand years ago. The whole question is how much we understand—and understanding, obey Him. And I do not think we should be any nearer *than* if He came amongst us bodily again. If we should, He would come."

"Shall we never, never, never see Him?"

"That is quite another thing, my Connie. That is the heart of my hopes by day and my dreams by night. To behold the face of Jesus seems to me the one thing to be desired. The pure in heart shall see God. The seeing of Him will be the sign that we are like Him, for only by being like Him can we see Him as He is. But when we shall be fit to look Him in the face, God only knows."

"Papa, could we, who have never seen Him, know Him better than the disciples?"

"Certainly."

"O Papa! Is it possible? Then why don't we?"

"Because we won't take the trouble. Whoever wants to learn must pray and think and, above all, obey—that is, simply do what Jesus says."

There followed a little silence, and I could hear my child sobbing. And the tears stood in my wife's eyes—tears of gladness to hear her daughter's sobs.

"I'll try, Papa," Connie said at last. "But you will help me?"

"Next Sunday. You have plenty to think about till then."

"But," said my wife, "don't you think, Connie, this is too good to keep all to ourselves? Don't you think we ought to have Wynnie and Dora in?"

"Yes, yes, Mamma. Do let us have them in. And Harry and Charlie too."

"It would be all the better for us to have them," said Ethelwyn smiling.

"How do you mean, my dear?"

"Because you will say things more simply if you have them by you. Besides, you always say such things to children as delight grown people, though they could never get them out of you."

"Well," I said, "I don't mind them coming in, but I don't promise to say anything directly to them. And you must let them go away the moment they wish it."

"Certainly," answered my wife. And so the matter was arranged.

THREE
A Sunday Evening

On the following Sunday evening when I went into Connie's room with my Bible in my hand, I found all our little company assembled. There was a glorious fire, for it was very cold, and the little ones were seated on the rug before it, one on each side of their mother. Wynnie sat by the farther side of the bed (for she always avoided any place or thing she thought another might like), and Dora sat by the chimney corner.

"The wind is very high, Papa," said Constance, as I seated myself beside her. "I am afraid I do like it when it roars like that in the chimneys, and shakes the windows with a great rush. I feel so safe in the very jaws of danger."

"But tell me, Connie," I said, "why you are *afraid* you enjoy hearing the wind about the house."

"Because it must be so dreadful for those who are out in it."

"Perhaps not quite so bad as we think. You must not suppose that God has forgotten them, or cares less for them than for you because they are out in the wind."

"But if we thought like that, Papa," said Wynnie, "shouldn't we come to feel that their sufferings were none of our business?"

"If our benevolence rests on the belief that God is less loving than we, it will come to a bad end before long, Wynnie. Then your kindness would be such that you should cease to help those whom you could help! Either God intended that there should be poverty and suffering, or He did not. If He did not intend it, then we should sell everything that we have and give it away to the poor."

"Then why don't we?" said Wynnie.

"Because that is not God's way, and we should do no end of harm by so doing. We should make so many more of those who will not help themselves, who will not be set free from themselves by rising above themselves. We are not to gratify our own benevolence at the expense of its object, not to save our own souls by putting other souls into more danger than God meant for them."

"It sounds a hard doctrine from your lips, Papa," said Wynnie.

"Many things will sound hard in so many words. If people should have everything they want, then everyone ought to be rich. There was once a baby born in a stable, because His poor mother could get no room in a decent house. Had God forsaken them? Would they not have been more comfortable somewhere else? Ah! If the disciples had only been old enough, and had known that He was coming, would they not have gotten everything ready for Him? They would have clubbed their little savings together and worked day and night, and some rich women would have helped them, and they would have dressed the baby in fine linen, and got Him the richest room their money would buy, and they would have made the gold that the wise men brought into a crown for His little head, and would have burnt frankincense before Him. And so our Manger Baby would have been taken away from us. No more the stable-born Saviour, no more the poor Son of God born for us all, as strong, as noble, as loving, as worshipful, as beautiful as He was poor! And we should not have learned that God does not care for money; or that if He does not give us more of it, it is not that it is scarce with Him, or that He is unkind, but that He does not value it. He sent His own Son not merely to be brought up in the house of the carpenter in a little village, but to be born in a stable of a village inn. We need not suppose, then, because a man sleeps under a haystack, and is put in prison the next day, that God does not care for him."

"But why did Jesus come so poor, Papa?"

"That He might be just a human baby; that He might not be distinguished by this or that accident of birth; that He might have nothing but a mother's love to welcome Him, and so belong to everybody; that from the first He might show that the kingdom and favor of God lie not in these external things at all. Had Jesus come among the rich, riches would have been more worshiped than ever. See how so many who count themselves good Christians honor possession and family and social rank. Even in the services of the church, they will accumulate gorgeousness and cost."

"But are we not to serve Him with our very best?" asked my wife.

"Yes, with our very hearts and souls, with our wills, with our absolute being. But all external things should be in harmony with the spirit of His revelation. And if God chose that His Son should visit the earth in homely fashion, in homely fashion likewise should be everything that enforces and commemorates that revelation. All church forms should be on the other side from show and expense. Let the money go to build decent houses for God's poor, not to give them His holy bread and wine out of silver and gold and precious stones. I would send all the church plate to fight the devil with his own weapons in our overcrowded cities and in our villages where the husbandmen are housed like swine, by giving them room to be clean and to breathe decent air from heaven. When the people find the clergy thus in earnest, they will follow them fast enough, and the money will come in like salt and oil upon the sacrifice."

"There is one thing," said Wynnie, after a pause, "that I have often thought about. Why was it necessary for Jesus to come as a Baby? He could not do anything for so long."

"First, Wynnie, all of us come as babies, and whatever was human must be His. And are you sure that He could not do anything for so long? Does a baby do nothing? Ask Mamma there. Is it for nothing that the mother lifts up such heartfuls of thanks to God for the baby on her knee? Is it nothing that the baby opens such fountains of love in almost all the hearts around? Was not Jesus going to establish the reign of love in the earth? How could He do better than begin from babyhood? He had to lay hold of the heart of the world; how could He do better than begin with His mother's? Charlie, wouldn't you have liked to see the little Baby Jesus?"

"Yes. I would have given Him my white rabbit with the pink eyes."

"That is what the great painter Titian must have thought, Charlie, for he has painted Him playing with a white rabbit."

"I would have carried Him about all day," said Dora, "as a baby brother."

"Did He have any brother or sister to carry Him about, Papa?" asked Harry.

"No, my boy, for He was the eldest. But you may be sure He carried about His brothers and sisters who came after Him."

"Wouldn't He take care of them, just!" said Charlie.

"I wish I had been one of them," said Constance.

"You are one of them."

Then we sang a child's hymn, and the little ones went to bed. Constance was tired now, and leaving her with Wynnie, we too went to bed.

About midnight my wife and I awoke together. The wind was still raving about the house, with lulls between its charges.

"There's a child crying!" said my wife, starting up.

I sat up too, and listened. "It is some creature, I grant."

"It is an infant," insisted my wife. "It can't be either of the boys."

We were out of bed in a moment and into our clothes. I got a lantern, hurried out, and listened. I heard it, but not as clearly as before, and set out as well as I could judge in the direction of the sound. I found nothing, for my lantern lighted only a few yards around me, and the strong wind threatened to blow it out. My wife was by my side, all the mother awake in her bosom.

Another wail reached us from a thicket at one corner of the lawn. "There it is!" Ethelwyn cried, as the feeble light of the lantern fell on a dark bundle under a bush—the poor baby of some tramp, rolled up in a dirty, ragged shawl and tied round with a bit of string. It gave another pitiful wail, and Ethelwyn caught it up and ran off to the house with it, up to her own room where the fire was not yet out.

"Run to the kitchen, Harry, and get some hot water."

By the time I returned with the hot water, she had taken off the child's covering, and was sitting with it wrapped in a blanket, before the fire. The little thing was as cold as a stone, and now silent and motionless. We had found it just in time. It was a girl—not more than a few weeks old, we agreed. Her little heart was still beating feebly, and we had every hope of her recovery. And we were not disappointed, for she began to move her little legs and arms with short, convulsive movements.

"Do you know where the dairy is, Harry?" asked my wife. "Bring a little of this night's milk and some more hot water. I've got some sugar here. I wish we had a bottle."

I executed her commands faithfully. By the time I returned, the child was lying on her lap, clean and dry. Ethelwyn went on talking to her, and praising her as if she had not only been the finest specimen of mortality in the world, but her own child to boot. She got her to take a few spoonfuls of milk and water, and then the little thing fell fast asleep.

She gave me the child, and going to a wardrobe in the room, brought out some night things and put them on her. I could not understand in the least why the sleeping darling must be endued with a little chemise and flannel and nightgown, and I do not know what all, requiring a world of nice care, and a hundred turnings to and fro, when it would have slept just as well (and I think much more comfortably) if laid in soft blankets and well covered over. I had never ventured to interfere with any of my own children, devoutly believing that there must be some hidden feminine wisdom in the whole process. But now that I had begun to question, I found that my opportunity had long gone by, if I had ever had one.

We went to bed again, and the forsaken child lay in Ethelwyn's bosom. So we had another child in the house, and nobody else knew anything about it. The household had never been disturbed by the going and coming. We had a good laugh over the whole matter, and then Ethelwyn fell to crying. "Pray for the poor thing, Harry," she sobbed.

I knelt down, and said, "O Lord our Father, this is as much Thy child and as certainly sent to us as if she had been born of us. Help us to keep the child for Thee. Take Thou care of Thy own, and teach us what to do with her, and how to order our ways toward her."

Then I said to Ethelwyn, "I dare say the little thing will sleep till morning, and I am sure I shall if she does. Good night, my love. You are a true mother."

"I am half asleep already, Harry. Good night," she returned.

I knew nothing more about anything till I woke in the morning, except that I had a dream. I found myself in a pleasant field full of daisies and white clover. The sun was setting. The wind was going one way and the shadows another. I saw a long, rather narrow stone lying a few yards from me. I wondered how it could have come there, for there were no mountains or rocks near—the field was part of a level country. I sat astride it and watched the setting of the sun. Somehow I fancied that its light was more sorrowful than the light of the setting sun should be, and I began to feel very heavy at heart. No sooner had the last brilliant spark of its light vanished, than I felt the stone under me begin to move. With the inactivity of a dreamer, however, I did not care to rise, but wondered only what would come next. My seat, after several strange tumbling motions, seemed to rise into the air a little way, and then I found that I was astride a gaunt, bony horse, a skeleton horse almost, only he had gray skin on him. He began, apparently with pain, as if his joints were all but too stiff to move, to go forward in the direction in which he found himself.

I kept my seat. Indeed, I never thought of dismounting—I was going on to meet what might come. Slowly, feebly, trembling at every step, the strange steed went; and as he went his joints seemed to become less stiff, and he went a little faster. The pleasant field vanished, and we were on the borders of a moor. Straight forward the horse carried me, and the moor grew very rough, and he went stumbling dreadfully, but always recovering himself. We reached a low, broken wall, over which he half walked, half fell into what was plainly a neglected ancient graveyard. The mounds were low and covered with rank grass. In some parts, hollows had taken the place of mounds. Gravestones lay in every position except the level or the upright, and broken masses of monuments were scattered about. My horse bore me into the midst of it, and there, slow and stiff as he had risen, he lay down again.

Once more I was astride a long narrow stone—an ancient gravestone (which I knew well) in a certain Sussex churchyard—the top of it carved into the rough resemblance of a human skeleton, that of a man, tradition said, who had been killed by a serpent that came out of a bottomless pool in the next field. How long I sat there I do not know, but at last the dawn grew against the horizon. But it was a wild dreary dawn, a blot of gray first, which then stretched into long lines of dreary yellow and gray, looking more like a blasted and withered sunset than a fresh sunrise. And well it suited that waste, wide, deserted churchyard—if churchyard I ought to call it where no church was to be seen, only a vast hideous square of graves.

I took special notice of one old grave, the flat stone of which had been broken in two and sunk in the middle. The crack in the middle closed, then widened again as the two halves of the stone were lifted up and flung outward, like the two halves of a folding door. From the grave rose a little child, smiling such perfect contentment as if he had just come from kissing his mother. His little arms had flung the stones apart, and they remained outspread for a moment as if blessing the sleeping people. Then he came toward me with the same smile and took my hand. I rose and he led me away over another broken wall toward the hill that lay before us. And as we went, the sun came nearer; the pale yellow bars flushed into orange and rosy red, till at length the edges of the clouds were swept with an agony of golden light which even my dreamy eyes could not endure, and I awoke weeping for joy.

This woke my wife who asked in some alarm, "What is the matter?"

So I told her my dream, and how in my sleep my gladness had overcome me.

"It was this little darling that set you dreaming so," she said, and turning, put the baby in my arms.

FOUR
The New Baby

I will not attempt to describe the astonishment of the members of our household as the news of the child spread. Charlie was heard shouting across the stableyard to his brother, "Harry! Harry! Mamma has a new baby. Isn't it jolly?"

"Where did she get it?"

"In the parsley bed, I suppose," answered Charlie, and was nearer right than usual.

Every one of our family hugged her first, and then asked questions. (And that, I say, is the right way of receiving every good gift of God.)

The truth soon became known over the parish and then, strange to relate, we began to receive visits of condolence. How that baby was frowned upon, and how it had heads shaken over it, just because she was not Ethelwyn's baby!

"Of course, you'll give the information to the police," said one of my brethren who had the misfortune to be a magistrate as well.

"Why?" I asked.

"Why! That they may discover the parents, to be sure."

"Wouldn't it be as hard a matter to prove the parentage, as it would be easy to suspect it?" I asked. "And just think what it would be to give the baby to a woman who not only did not want her, but who was not her mother. If her own mother came to claim her now, I don't say I would refuse her, but I should think twice about giving her up, after the mother had abandoned her for a whole night in the open air. In fact, I don't want the parents."

"But you don't want the child."

"How do you know that?"

"Oh! Of course, if you want to have an orphan asylum of your own, no one has the right to interfere. But you ought to consider other people."

"That is just what I thought I was doing," I answered.

He went on without heeding my reply, "We shall all be having babies left at our doors, and some of us are not so fond of them as you are. Remember, you are your brother's keeper."

"And my sister's too," I answered. "And if the question lies between keeping a big burly brother like you, and a tiny, wee sister like that, I venture to choose for myself."

"She ought to go to the workhouse," said the magistrate—a friendly, good-natured enough man in ordinary—and rising, he took his hat and departed. (This man had no children, so he was not so much to blame.)

Some of Ethelwyn's friends were no less positive about their duty. I happened to go into the drawing room during the visit of Miss Bowdler.

"But my dear Mrs. Walton," she was saying, "soon all the tramps in England will be leaving babies at your door."

"The better for the babies," I interposed, laughing.

"Depend upon it, you'll repent it."

"I hope I shall never repent of anything but what is bad."

"It's not a thing to be made game of!"

"Certainly not. The baby shall be treated with the utmost respect in this house."

This lady was one of my oldest parishioners, and took liberties for which she had no justification, with an unhesitating belief in the superior rectitude of whatever came into her own head. When she was gone, my wife said, with a half-anxious and half-comic look, "But it *would* be rather alarming if this were to get abroad. We couldn't go out the door without being in danger of stepping on another abandoned baby."

"He who sent us this one can surely prevent any more from coming than He wants to come. If you believe that God sent this one, that is enough for the present. If He should send another, we should know that we had to take it in."

Before three months had passed, even Miss Bowdler had to admit that Theodora—for we turned the name of my youngest daughter upside down for her—"was a proper child." To none, however, did she seem to bring so much delight as to Constance. Oftener than not, when I went into Connie's room, I found the sleepy useless little thing lying beside her on the bed, and her staring at the baby with such loving eyes! How it began, I do not know, but it came at last to be called "Connie's Dora" or "Miss Connie's baby" all over the house, and nothing pleased Connie better. Not till she saw this did her old nurse take quite kindly to the infant. She had regarded her as an interloper who had no right to the tenderness which was lavished upon her. However, she had no sooner given in than the baby began to grow dear to her as well.

But before Theodora was three months old, anxious thoughts began to intrude into my mind, all centering round the question: in what manner was the child to be brought up?

FIVE
Tales of Two Boys

During all this time Connie made no very perceptible recovery—of her bodily powers, I mean—for her heart and mind advanced remarkably. We continued to hold our Sunday evening assemblies in her room.

One evening I read to them the story of the Boy Jesus in the temple. I sought to make the story more real to them by dwelling a little on the growing fears of His parents as they went from group to group of their friends, tracing back the road toward Jerusalem, and asking every fresh company they knew if they had seen their Boy, till at length they were in great trouble when they could not find Him even in Jerusalem. Then came the delight of His mother when she did find Him at last, and His answer to what she said.

At that point Wynnie said, "That has always troubled me, Papa. I feel as if Jesus spoke unkindly to His mother when He said that to her."

I read again for them the words, "How is it that ye sought Me? Wist ye not that I must be about My Father's business?" And I sat silent for a while.

"Why don't you speak, Papa?" said Harry.

"I am sitting wondering at myself, Harry," I said. "I remember quite well that those words troubled me once as they now trouble you. But when I read them over now, they seemed to me so lovely that I could hardly read them aloud. I can hardly see now the hurt or offense the words gave me. I understand them now, and I did not understand them then. I once took them as uttered with a tone of reproof; now I hear them as uttered with a tone of loving surprise."

"But how could He be surprised at anything?" said Connie. "If He was God, He must have known everything."

"He tells us Himself that He did not know everything. He said once that even He did not know one particular thing—only the Father knew it."

"But how could that be if He is God?"

"Since Jesus was a real man, and no mere appearance of a man, is it any wonder that, with a heart full to the brim of the love of God, He should be for a moment surprised—surprised that His mother should not have taken it as a matter of course that if He was not with her, He must be doing something His Father wanted Him to do? For His answer means just this: 'Why did you look for Me? Didn't you know that I must of course be doing something My Father had given Me to do?' A good many things had passed before then, which ought to have been sufficient to make Mary conclude that her missing Boy must be about God's business somewhere. If her heart had been as full of God and God's business as His was, she would not have been in the least uneasy about Him. And here is the lesson of His whole life: it was all His Father's business."

"But we have so many things to do that are not His business," said Wynnie, with a sigh of oppression.

"Not one, my darling. If anything is not His business, you not only do not have to do it, but you ought not to do it."

"I wish He would tell me something to do," said Charlie. "Wouldn't I do it!"

I made no reply, but waited for an opportunity which I was pretty sure was at hand, while I carried the matter a little further.

"But listen to this, Wynnie," I said. " 'And He went down with them, and came to Nazareth, and was subject unto them.' Was that not His Father's business too? Was it not also doing the business of His Father in heaven to honor His father and His mother, though He knew that His days would not be long in that land? But I am afraid I have wearied you children, and so, Charlie, my boy, perhaps you should go to bed."

But Charlie was very comfortable on the rug before the fire, and did not want to go. First one shoulder went up, and then the other, and the corners of his mouth went down, as if to keep the balance true, and he did not move to go. I gave him a few moments to recover himself, but, as the black frost still endured, I thought it was time to hold up a mirror to him. (When he was a very little boy he was much in the habit of getting out of temper, and then as now, he made a face that was hideous to behold. To cure him of this, I used to make him carry a little mirror about his neck that it might be always at hand for showing him to himself—a sort of artificial conscience.)

"Charlie," I said, "a little while ago you were wishing that God would give you something to do. And now when He does, you refuse at once, without even thinking about it."

"How do you know that God wants me to go to bed?" said Charlie, with something of surly impertinence.

"I know that God wants you to do what I tell you, and to do it pleasantly. Do you think the Boy Jesus would have put on such a face as that—I wish I had the little mirror to show it to you—when His mother told Him it was time to go to bed?"

And now Charlie began to look ashamed. I left the truth to work in him, because I saw it was working. Had I not seen that, I should have compelled him to go at once, that he might learn the majesty of law. I went on talking to the others. In the space of not more than one minute, he rose and came to me, looking both good and ashamed, and held up his face to kiss me, saying, "Good night, Papa." I bade him good night, and kissed him more tenderly than usual, that he might know all was right between us. I required no formal apology, no begging of my pardon, as some parents think right. It seemed enough to me that his heart was turned. For it is a terrible thing to risk changing humility into humiliation.

SIX
Theodora

On the following Monday morning I set out to visit one or two people whom the severity of the weather had kept from church on Sunday. The last severe frost of the season was possessing the earth. The sun was low in the wintry sky, and a very cold mist up in the air hid it from the earth. I was walking along a path in a field close by a hedge, and as I was getting over a stile, whom should I see in the next field along the footpath, but Miss Bowdler? I prepared myself to meet her in the strength of good humor.

"Good morning, Miss Bowdler," I said.

"Good morning, Mr. Walton," she returned. "I am afraid you thought me impertinent the other week—but you know by this time it is only my way."

"As such I take it," I answered, with a smile.

She did not seem quite satisfied that I did not defend her from her own accusation. But, as it was a just one, I could not do so. Therefore she went on to repeat the offense by way of justification.

"It was all for Mrs. Walton's sake. You ought to consider her, Mr. Walton. She has quite enough to do with that dear Connie, who is likely to be an invalid all her days—too much to take the trouble of a beggar's brat as well."

"Has Mrs. Walton been complaining to you about it, Miss Bowdler?" I asked.

"Oh, dear, no!" she answered. "She is far too good to complain of anything. That's just why her friends must look after her a bit, Mr. Walton."

"Then I beg you won't speak disrespectfully of my little Theodora."

"Oh, dear me! No. Not at all. I don't speak disrespectfully of her."

"Even amongst the class of which she comes, 'a beggar's brat' would be regarded as bad language."

"I beg your pardon, I'm sure, Mr. Walton! But if you will take offense. . . . "

"I do take offense. And you know there is One who has given especial warning against offending the little ones."

Miss Bowdler walked away in high displeasure—let me hope in conviction of sin as well. (She did not appear in church for the next two Sundays. Then she came again, but called very seldom at the Hall after this. I believe my wife was not sorry.)

Before I reached home I had at last a glimpse of the right way of bringing up Theodora. I found my wife in Connie's room and asked Ethelwyn to walk out with me.

"I can't just this moment," she answered, "for there is no one at liberty to stay with Connie."

"Oh, never mind me, Mamma," said Connie, cheerfully. "Theodora will take care of me." And she looked fondly at the child fast asleep at her side.

"There!" I said. And both looked up surprised, for neither knew what I meant. "I will tell you afterward," I said, laughing. "Come along."

Ethel put on her hooded cloak, and we went out together. I told her about Miss Bowdler, and what she had said. Ethelwyn was very angry at her impertinence.

"She seems to think," she said, "that she was sent into the world to keep other people right instead of herself. I am very glad you set her down."

"Oh, I don't think there's much harm in her," I returned, which was easy generosity, seeing my wife was taking my part. "Indeed, I am not sure that we are not both considerably indebted to her, for it was after I met her that a thought came into my head as to how we ought to raise Theodora."

"Still troubling yourself about that?"

"There's one thing we have both made up our minds about, that there is to be no concealment with the child. God's fact must be known by her. It would be cruel to keep the truth from her, even if it were not sure to come upon her with a terrible shock some day. She must know from the first that she came out of the shrubbery. That's settled, is it not?"

"Certainly."

"Now, are we bound to bring her up exactly as our own, or are we not?"

"We are bound to do as well for her as for our own."

"Assuredly. So here is my proposition: to bring up little Theodora as a servant to Constance."

My wife laughed. "Well," she said, "for one who says so much about not thinking of the morrow, you do look rather far forward."

"Not with any anxiety, however, if only I know that I am doing right."

"But just think—the child is only about three months old."

"Well, Connie will be none the worse that she is being trained for her. I don't say that she is to commence her duties at once."

"But Connie may be at the head of a house of her own long before that."

"The training won't be lost to the child though. But I fear that Connie will never be herself again, for Turner does not give much hope."

"Oh! Harry, Harry, don't say so. I can't bear it. To think of the darling child lying like that all her life!"

"It is sad, indeed, but no such awful misfortune, surely. Haven't you seen the growth of that child's nature since her accident? Ten times rather would I have her lying there, such as she is, than have her well and strong and silly."

"Yes, but she needn't have been like that. Wynnie never will."

"Well, God does all things not only well, but best, absolutely best. But just think what it would be in any circumstances to have a maid that had begun to wait upon her from the first days that she was able to toddle after something to fetch."

"Won't it be like making a slave of her?"

"Won't it be like giving her a divine freedom from the first? The lack of service is the ruin of humanity."

"But we can't train her then like one of our own."

"Why not? Could we not give her all the love and all the teaching?"

"Because it would not be fair to give her the education of a lady, and then make a servant of her."

"You forget that the service would be part of her training from the first, and she would know no change of position in it. When we tell her that she was found in the shrubbery, we will add that we think God sent her to take care of Constance. You cannot have perfect service except from a lady. It is not education that unfits for service—it is the want of it. Connie loves the child; the child will love Connie and find delight in serving her like a little cherub. Train Theodora as a holy child-servant, and there will be no need to restrain any impulse of wise affection from pouring itself forth upon her. We would then love and honor her far more than if we made her just like one of our own."

"But what if she should turn out utterly unfit for it?"

"Ah! Then would come an obstacle. But it will not come till that discovery is made."

"But if we should be going wrong all the time?"

"Now there comes the kind of care that never troubles me. We ought always to act on the ideal—it is the only safe ground of action."

"Well, I will think about it, Harry. There is time enough."

"Plenty. And if a thing be good, the more you think about it, the better it will look. Its real nature will go on coming out and showing itself."

Only two days later my wife said to me, "I am more than reconciled to your plan, Harry. It seems to me delightful."

SEVEN

An Invitation

I have not mentioned Weir or my sister in connection with the accident, and for a very good reason—I had given them both a long holiday. Martha had been ill, and because there was some fear for her lungs, a winter in the south of France had been strongly recommended. They had decided to go (partly at my insistence), and had left in October, before the accident. My sister had grown almost quite well by the beginning of the following April, and I was not sorry to think that I should soon have a little more leisure for my small literary pursuits—to my own enrichment, and consequently, to the good of my parishioners and friends.

In the beginning of that same April, I received a letter from an old college friend of mine. His name was David Shepherd—a good name for a clergyman. As soon as I had read the letter, I went to find my wife.

"Here is Shepherd," I said to her, "with a clerical sore throat, and forced to give up his duty for at least a long summer. He asks me whether, as I have a good curate, it might not suit me to take my family to his place in his absence. He assures me I should like it, and that it would do us all good. His house, he says, is large enough to hold us, and he knows I should not like to be without duty wherever I was. And so on. Read the letter for yourself, and turn it over in your mind. Weir will come back so fresh and active that it will be no oppression to him to take the duty here. I will run and ask Turner whether it would be safe to move Connie, and whether the sea air would be good for her."

"One would think you were only twenty, Harry, you make up your mind so quickly and are in such a hurry."

The fact was, a vision of the sea had rushed in upon me. It was many years since I had seen the sea, and the thought of looking on it once more, in its most glorious show—the Atlantic itself, with nothing between us and America but the round of the ridgy water—had excited me so that my wife's reproof (if reproof it was) was quite necessary to bring me to my usually quiet and sober senses. I laughed, begged her pardon, and set off to see Turner.

"What do you think, Turner?" I said, and told him the case.

He looked rather grave. "When would you think of going?" he asked.

"About the beginning of June."

"Nearly two months," he said, thoughtfully. "And Miss Connie was not the worse for getting on the sofa yesterday? And no increase of pain since?"

"No. And no again."

He thought again. Although young, he was a careful man. "It is a long journey."

"She could make it by easy stages."

"It would certainly do her good to breathe the sea air and have such a thorough change in every way. I think, if you can get her up every day between now and then, we shall be justified in trying it at least. The sooner you get her out-of-doors the better too, but the weather is scarcely fit for that yet."

"Could you manage, supposing we make the experiment, to accompany us the first stage or two?"

"Very likely. I cannot tell beforehand."

I returned to my wife and found her in Connie's room. "Well, my dear," I said, "what do you think of it?"

"Of what?" she asked.

"Why, of Shepherd's letter, of course," I answered.

"I've been ordering the dinner since, Harry."

"The dinner!" I returned, with some show of contempt, for I knew my wife was only teasing me. "What's the dinner to the Atlantic?"

"What do you mean by the Atlantic, Papa?" said Connie, from whose roguish eyes I could see that her mother had told her all about it, and that she would get up, if only she could.

"The Atlantic, my dear, is the name given to that portion of the waters of the globe which divides Europe from America. I will fetch you the *Universal Gazetteer,* if you would like to consult it on the subject."

"O Papa!" laughed Connie. "You know what I mean."

"Yes, and you know what I mean too, you squirrel!"

"But you really do mean, Papa," she said, "that you will take me to the Atlantic?"

"If you will only oblige me by getting well enough to go as soon as possible."

The poor child half rose on her elbow, but sank back again with a moan, which I took for a cry of pain. I was beside her in a moment. "You have hurt yourself!"

"Oh, no, Papa. I felt for the moment as if I could get up if I liked. But I soon found that I hadn't any back or legs. Oh! What a plague I am to you!"

"On the contrary, you are the nicest doll in the world, Connie. One always knows where to find you."

She half laughed and half cried, and the two halves made a very bewitching whole.

"But," I went on, "I mean to try whether you won't bear moving. One thing is clear, I can't go without it. Do you think you could be got on the sofa today without hurting you?"

"I am sure I could, Papa. I feel better today. Mamma, do send for Susan, and get me up before dinner."

When I went in later, I found her lying on the couch, propped up with pillows, and looking out the window over the lawn at the back of the house. A smile hovered about her bloodless lips, and the blue-gray of her eyes looked sunny. Her white face showed the whiter because her dark brown hair was all about it.

"I have been trying to count the daisies on the lawn," she said.

"What a sharp sight you must have, child!"

"I see them all as clear as if they were enameled on that table before me."

I was not so anxious to get rid of the daisies as some people are. Neither did I keep the grass quite so close shaved.

"But," she went on, "I could not count them, for it gave me the fidgets in my feet. Isn't it wonderful?"

"Enough to go on my knees and thank God. I take it as a sign of the beginning of your recovery."

She lay very still. Only the tears rose slowly and lay shimmering in her eyes. "O Papa!" she said. "To think of ever walking out with you again, and feeling the wind on my face!"

"I think you might have half that pleasure at once," I answered.

I opened the window, let the spring air gently move her hair for one moment, and then shut it again. Connie breathed deep, and said after a little pause, "I had no idea how delightful it was. To think that I have been in the way of breathing that every moment for so many years, and have never thought about it!"

"I suspect we shall find someday that the loss of the human paradise consists chiefly in the closing of our eyes, that far more of it than people think remains about us still, only we are so filled with foolish desires and evil cares, that we cannot see or hear, cannot even smell or taste the pleasant things around us. Shall I tell you what such a breath of fresh air makes me think of?"

"It comes to me," said Connie, "like forgiveness when I was a little girl and was naughty. I used to feel just like that."

"Once when I was a young man, long before I saw your mamma, I had gone out for a long walk along some high downs. I had been working rather hard at Cambridge, and the life seemed to be all gone out of me. Though my holidays had come, they did not feel quite like the holidays. Even when walking along those downs, with the scents of sixteen grasses in my brain, with just enough of a wind to stir them up and set them in motion, I could not feel at all. I remembered something of what I had used to feel in such places, but instead of believing in that, I doubted now whether it had not been all a trick.

"I was walking along with the sea behind me. It was a warm, cloudy day—no sunshine. All at once I turned, and there lay the gray sea, but not as I had seen it last. Now it was dotted, spotted, and splashed all over with drops, pools, and lakes of light, of all shades of depth, from a light shimmer of tremulous gray through a translucent green half-light. There was no sun on me, but there were breaks in the clouds over the sea, and I could see the long lines of the sun rays descending on the waters like rain. I questioned the past no more. The present seized upon me, and I knew that the past was true, and that nature was more lovely, more awful in her loveliness, than I could grasp. It was a lonely place! I fell on my knees, and worshiped the God who made the glory and my soul."

While I spoke Connie's tears had been flowing quietly.

"And Mamma and I were making fun while you were seeing such things as those!" she said, pitifully.

"You didn't hurt them one bit, my darling—neither Mamma nor you. Your merriment only made me enjoy it more. And, Connie, I hope you will see the Atlantic before long."

"O Papa! Do you think we shall really go?"

"I do. I am going to write to Shepherd, my dear, that I will take his parish in hand. If I cannot go myself, I will find someone, so that he need not be anxious."

EIGHT
Connie's Dream

Dr. Turner, being a good mechanic as well as surgeon, proceeded to invent and construct a kind of litter. It could be placed in our carriage for Connie to lie on, and from that lifted and placed in the railway carriage. He had repeatedly laid Connie on it before he was satisfied that the arrangement was successful. But at length she declared it was perfect, and that she would not mind being carried across the Arabian Desert on a camel's back with that under her.

As the season advanced she continued to improve. I shall never forget the first time she was carried out on the lawn. If you can imagine an infant coming into the world capable of the observation and delight of a child of eight or ten, you will have some idea of how Connie received the new impressions of everything around her. They were almost too much for her at first, however. She who used to scamper about like a wild thing on her pony now found the delight of a breath of wind almost more than she could bear. There on the lawn she closed her eyes, and a smile flickered about her mouth, and two great tears crept softly out from under her eyelids and sank down her cheeks.

She lay so that she faced a rich tract of gently receding upland, plentifully wooded to the horizon's edge. Through the wood peeped the white and red houses of a little hamlet, with the square tower of its church rising above the trees. It was morning in early summer, when the leaves were not quite full-grown, and their shining green was as pure as the blue of the sky. The air was warm, with no touch of bitterness, and it filled the lungs with the reviving as of a draught of cold water. A lark was scattering bright beads of ringing melody straight down upon our heads. A little stream scampered down the slope of the lawn from a well in the stableyard. White clouds floated in the majesty of silence across the blue deeps of the heavens.

We had fastened the carriage umbrella to Connie's sofa, so that it should shade her. "Papa," said Connie at length, and I was beside her in a moment. Her face looked almost glorified with delight: there was a hush of that awe upon it which is perhaps one of the deepest kinds of delight. She put out her thin white hand, took hold of a button of my coat, drew me down toward her, and said in a whisper, "Don't you think God is here, Papa?"

"Yes, I do, my darling," I answered.

"Doesn't He enjoy this?"

"Yes, my dear. He wouldn't make us enjoy it if He did not. It would be to deceive us to make us glad and blessed, if our Father did not care about it or how it came to us. At least it would amount to making us no longer His children."

"I am so glad you think so. I shall enjoy it so much more now." She could hardly finish her sentence, but burst out sobbing, so we left her to quiet herself. The emotion passed off in a summer shower, and soon her face was shining just like a wet landscape after the sun comes out. In a little while, she was merry—merrier than ever before.

"Look at that comical sparrow," she said. "Look how he cocks his head first on one side and then on the other. Does he want us to see him? Is he bumptious or what?"

"I hardly know, my dear. I think sparrows are like schoolboys, and I suspect that if we understood the one class thoroughly, we should understand the other. But I confess I do not yet understand either."

"Perhaps you will when Charlie and Harry are old enough to go to school," said Connie.

"It is my only chance of making any true acquaintance with the sparrows," I answered. "Look at them now!" I exclaimed, as a little crowd of them suddenly appeared and exploded in unintelligible excitement. After some fluttering of wings and pecking, they all vanished except two which walked about in a dignified manner, apparently trying to ignore each other.

"I think it was a political meeting of some sort," said Connie, as she laughed merrily.

"Well, they have this advantage over us," I answered, "that they get through their business with considerably greater expedition than we get through ours."

A short silence followed, during which Connie lay contemplating everything. "What do you think we girls are like, then, Papa?" she asked at length. "Don't say you don't know, now."

"I ought to know something more about you than I do about schoolboys. And I think I do know a little about girls, though they puzzle me a good deal sometimes. I know what a greathearted woman is, Connie."

"You can't help doing that, Papa," interrupted Connie, adding with her old roguishness, "but you mustn't pass yourself off for only knowing that. By the time Dora is grown up, your skill will be tried."

"I hope I shall understand her then, and you too, Connie."

A shadow, just like the shadow of one of those white clouds above us, passed over her face, and she said, trying to smile, "I shall never grow up, Papa. If I live, I shall only be a girl, at best—a creature you can't understand."

"On the contrary, Connie, I think I understand you almost as well as I do Mamma. But there isn't so much to understand yet as there will be."

Her merriment returned. "Tell me what girls are like, then, or I shall sulk all day because you say there isn't so much in me as in Mamma."

"Well, if boys are like sparrows, then girls are like swallows. Did you ever watch them before rain, Connie, skimming about over the lawn but never alighting? You never see them grubbing after worms. Nothing less than things with wings like themselves will satisfy them. They will be obliged to the earth only for a little mud to build themselves nests with. For the rest, they live in the air, and on the creatures of the air. And then, when they fancy the air begins to send little shoots of cold through their warm feathers, they vanish. They won't stand it. They're off to a warmer climate, and you never know till you find they're not there anymore. There, Connie!"

"I don't know, Papa, whether you are making game of us or not. If you are not, then I wish all you say were quite true of us. If you are, then I think it is quite like you to be satirical."

"I am no believer in satire, Connie. And I didn't mean any.

"The swallows are lovely creatures, and there would be no harm if the girls were a little steadier than the swallows. Further satire than that I am innocent of."

"I don't mind that much, Papa. Only I'm steady enough—and no thanks to me for it," she added with a sigh.

"Connie," I said, "it's all for the sake of your wings that you're kept in your nest."

She did not stay out long this first day, but the next morning she was brighter and better, and longing to get up and go out again. When she was once more on the lawn, in the midst of the world of light, she said to me, "Papa, I had such a strange dream last night. It was dreadful at first, and delightful afterward. I dreamed I was lying quite still, without breathing even, with my hands straight down by my sides and my eyes closed. I knew that if I opened them I should see nothing but the inside of the lid of my coffin. I did not mind it much at first, for I was very quiet, and not uncomfortable. Everything was as silent as it should be, for I was ten feet under the surface of the earth in the churchyard. Old Rogers was not far from me on one side, and that was a comfort, only there was a thick wall of earth between. But as the time went on, I began to get uncomfortable. I could not help thinking how long I should have to wait for the resurrection. Somehow I had forgotten all that you teach us about that. Perhaps it was a punishment—the dream—for forgetting it."

"Silly child! Your dream is far better than your reflections."

"Well, I got very tired, and wanted to get up, oh, so much! I tried, but I could not move, and at last I burst out crying. I was ashamed of crying in my coffin, but I couldn't bear it any longer. I thought I was quite disgraced, for everybody was expected to be perfectly quiet and patient down there. But the moment I began to cry, I heard a sound—the sound of spades and pickaxes. And then—it was so strange—I was dreadfully frightened at the idea of the light and the wind, and of the people seeing me in my coffin and my nightdress. And I tried to persuade myself that it was somebody else they were digging for, or that they were only going to lay another coffin over mine. And I thought that if it was you, Papa, I shouldn't mind how long I lay there, for I shouldn't feel a bit lonely. But the sounds came on, nearer and nearer, and at last a pickaxe struck with a blow that jarred me through, upon the lid right over my head.

" 'Here she is, poor thing!' I heard a sweet voice say.

" 'I am so glad we've found her,' said another voice.

" 'She couldn't bear it any longer,' said a third voice, more pitiful than the others. 'I heard her first,' it went on. 'I was away up in Orion, when I thought I heard a woman crying that oughtn't to be crying. And I stopped and listened. And I heard her again. Then I knew that it was one of the buried ones, and that she had been buried long enough, and was ready for the resurrection. So as any business can wait except that, I flew here and there till I fell in with the rest of you.'

"They cleared away the earth and stones from the top of my coffin. And I lay trembling and expecting every moment to be looked at, like a thing in a box as I was. But they lifted me, coffin and all, out of the grave, then they set it down, and I heard them taking the lid off. But after the lid was off, it did not seem to make much difference to me. I could not open my eyes, but I heard whispering about me. Then I felt warm, soft hands washing my face, and then I felt wafts of wind coming on my face, and thought they came from the waving of wings. And when they had washed my eyes, the air came on them, so sweet and cool! And I opened them, and I was lying here on this couch, with butterflies and bees flitting and buzzing about me, the brook singing somewhere near me, and a lark up in the sky. But there were no angels—only plenty of light and wind and living creatures. And I don't think I ever knew before what happiness meant. Wasn't it a resurrection, Papa, to come out of the grave into such a world as this?"

"Indeed it was, my darling, and a very beautiful and true dream. There is no need for me to moralize it to you. No dream of such delight can come up to the sense of fresh life and being that we shall have, when we put on the higher body, after this one is worn out and cast aside. The very ability of the mind to dream such things, whether of itself or by some inspiration of the Almighty, is proof of our capacity for them—a proof, I think, that for such things we were made. Here comes the chance for faith in God, the confidence in His being and perfection, that He would not have made us capable without meaning to fill that capacity. If He is able to make us capable, that is the harder half done already. The other He can easily do. And if He is love, He will do it. You should thank God for that dream, Connie."

"I was afraid to do that, Papa."

"That is to fear that there is one place to which you might flee, where God would not find you—the most terrible of all thoughts."

"Where do you mean, Papa?"

"Dreamland, my dear. If it is right to thank God for a beautiful thought—I mean a thought of strength and grace giving you fresh life and hope—then why should you be less bold to thank Him when such thoughts arise in the plainer shape of dreams?"

NINE
The Journey

For more than two months Charlie and Harry had been preparing for the journey. The moment they heard of it, they began to accumulate and pack stores both for the transit and the sojourn. First of all there was an extensive preparation of ginger beer, consisting (as I was informed in confidence) of brown sugar, ground ginger, and cold water. This store was exhausted and renewed about twelve times before the day of departure, when they remembered with dismay that they had drunk the last drop two days before, and there was none in stock.

Then there was a wonderful and more successful hoarding of marbles, carefully deposited in one of the many divisions of a huge old hair trunk, with its multiplicity of boxes and cupboards and drawers and trays and slides. In this same box was stowed also a quantity of hair—the gleanings of all the horsetails upon the premises. This was for making fishing tackle, with a vague notion on the part of Harry that it was to be employed in catching whales and crocodiles.

Then all their favorite books were stowed away in the same chest—including a packet of a dozen penny books from *Jack the Giant Killer* down to *Hop o' My Thumb.* Harry could not read these, and Charlie not very well, but they put confidence in them notwithstanding, in virtue of the red, blue, and yellow prints. Then there was a box of sawdust, a huge ball of string, a rabbit's skin, a Noah's ark, an American clock that refused to go—for all the variety of treatment they gave it—a box of lead soldiers, and twenty other things, amongst which was a huge gilt ball having an eagle of brass with outspread wings on the top of it.

Great was their consternation and dismay when they found that this trunk could not be taken with us to the station. Knowing well how little they would miss it, and with what shouts of discovery they would greet the forgotten treasure when they returned, I insisted on the lumbering article being left in peace. So that, as a man goes treasureless to his grave—whatever he may have accumulated before the fatal moment—

they had to set off for the far country without chest or ginger beer—but not so desolate and unprovided for as they imagined. The abandoned treasure was forgotten the moment the few tears it had occasioned were wiped away.

It was the loveliest of mornings when we started our journey. The sun shone, the wind was quiet, and everything was glad. The swallows were twittering from the corbels of the dear old house.

"I'm sorry to leave the swallows behind," said Wynnie, as she stepped into the carriage after her mother. Connie was already there, eager and stronghearted for the journey.

We set off. Connie was delighted with everything, especially with all forms of animal life and enjoyment that we saw on the road. She seemed eager to enter into the spirit of the cows feeding in the meadows, of the donkeys eating by the roadside, of the horses we met trudging along the road with wagon or cart behind them. I sat by the coachman, so I could see Connie's face by the slightest turning of my head. A fleet of ducklings in a pool, paddling along under the convoy of the parent duck, attracted her.

"Look—look. Isn't that delicious?" she cried.

"I don't think I should like it though," said Wynnie. "To be in the water and not feel wet. Those feathers!"

"They feel it with their legs and their webby toes," said Connie. "And if you were a duck, you would feel the good of your feathers in winter, when you got into your cold morning bath."

We had to pass through the village to reach the railway station. Almost everyone was out to bid us good-by. I stopped the carriage to speak a word to one of my people, and the same instant there was a crowd of women about us. But Connie was the center of all their regards, for they hardly looked at the rest of us.

After we had again started, our ears were invaded with shouts from the post chaise behind us, in which Charlie and Harry were yelling in the exuberance of their gladness. Dora, more staid as became her years, was trying to act the matron with them in vain, and Old Nursey had too much to do with Miss Connie's baby to heed what the young gentlemen were about, so long as noise was all the mischief.

"Good-by, Marshmallows," they were shouting at the top of their voices, as if they had just been released from a prison where they had spent a wretched childhood. As it could hardly offend anybody's ears on the open country road, I allowed them to shout till they were tired, which condition fortunately arrived before we reached the station. I always sought to give them as much liberty as could be afforded them.

At the station we found Weir and my sister (looking well again) waiting to see us off. Turner was likewise there, and ready to accompany us a good part of the way. But beyond his valuable assistance in moving Connie, no occasion arose for the exercise of his professional skill. She bore the journey wonderfully, slept not infrequently, and only at the end showed herself wearied. We stopped three times on the way, first at Salisbury, where the streams running through the street delighted her. There we remained one whole day, but sent the children and Walter and the other servants (all but my wife's maid) on before us. This left us more at our ease, and at Exeter we stopped only for the night.

Here Turner left us. Connie looked a little out of spirits after his departure, but soon recovered. The next night we spent at a small town on the borders of Devonshire, which was the limit of our railway traveling. Here we remained for another whole day, for the remnant of the journey across part of Devonshire and Cornwall to the shore was a good five hours' work. We started about eleven o'clock. Connie was quite merry, for the air was thoroughly warm, and we had an open carriage with a hood. Wynnie sat opposite her mother, Dora and Eliza the maid in the rumble, and I by the coachman. The road being very hilly, we had four horses—and with four horses, sunshine, a gentle wind, hope, and thankfulness, who would not be happy?

I must have been the very happiest of the party myself. And ought I not to have been happy when all who were with me were happy? My Ethelwyn's face was bright with the brightness of a pale silvery moon that has done her harvest work and, a little weary, lifts herself again into the deeper heavens from stooping toward the earth. Wynnie's face was bright with the brightness of the morning star, ever growing pale and faint over the amber ocean that brightens at the sun's approach, for to Wynnie life looked severe and somewhat sad in its light. Connie's face was bright with the brightness of a lake in the rosy evening, content to be still and mirror the sunset.

We stopped once, and Connie begged to be carried into the parlor of the little inn, that she might see the china figures that were certain to be on the chimney piece, as indeed they were. She drank a whole tumbler of new milk before we lifted her to carry her back. Leaving, we came upon a wide, high moorland country, the roads of which were lined with gorse in full golden bloom, while patches of heather all about were showing their bells, though not yet in their autumnal outburst of purple fire. Here I began to be reminded of Scotland, in which I had traveled a good deal in my younger years. The farther I went, the stronger I felt the resemblance to be. The look of the fields, the stone fences that divided them, the shape and color and materials of the houses, the aspect of the people, the feeling of the air and of the earth and sky generally, made me imagine myself in a milder and more favored Scotland. The west wind was fresh, but had none of that sharp edge which one can so often detect in otherwise warm winds blowing under a hot sun.

Though she had already traveled many miles, Connie brightened up within a few minutes after we reached this moor. And we had not gone much farther before a shout informed us that keen-eyed little Dora had discovered the Atlantic, blue and bright, through a dip in the high coast. We soon lost sight of it again, but in Connie's eyes it seemed to linger still. Their blue seemed to be the very reflection of the sea. Ethelwyn's eyes were full of it too, as she also expected the ocean. Down the winding of a gradual slope interrupted by steep descents, we approached this new chapter in our history.

We came again upon a few trees here and there, all with their tops cut off in a plane inclined upward away from the sea. For the sea winds, like a sweeping scythe, bend the trees toward the land, and keep their tops mown with their sharp rushing, keen with salt spray from the crests of the broken waves. Then we passed through some ancient villages, with streets narrow and steep and sharp-angled, that needed careful driving and the frequent pressure of the brake on the wheel.

At length we descended a sharp hill, reached the last level, drove over a bridge and down the line of the stream, over another wooden drawbridge, and along the side of a canal in which lay half a dozen sloops and schooners. Then came a row of pretty cottages, then a gate and an ascent, and the sight of Charlie and Harry shouting and scampering along the top of a stone wall to meet us. A moment after, we drew up at a long porch, leading through the segment of a circle to the door of the rectory. The journey was over. We alighted in the little village of Kilkhaven, in the county of Cornwall.

TEN
Kilkhaven

First of all, we carried Connie into her room, the best in the house, of course. She did seem tired now, and no wonder. After dinner, she fell fast asleep on the sofa, and Wynnie on the floor beside her. The drive and the sea air had had the same effect on both of them. What a wonderful satisfaction it may give to a father and mother to see this or that child asleep! When parents see their children asleep (especially if they have been suffering in any way) they breathe more freely. A load is lifted off their minds; their responsibility seems over; the children have gone back to their Father, and He alone is looking after them for a while.

Now, I had not been comfortable about Wynnie for some time. There was something amiss with her. She seemed constantly more or less dejected, as if she had something to think about that was too much for her, although I believe now that she had not quite enough to think about. She did not look quite happy, did not always meet a smile with a smile, looked almost reprovingly upon the frolics of her little brothers. And though kindness itself when any real hurt or grief befell them, she had reverted to her old, somewhat dictatorial manner. She was service itself, only service without the smile which is the flame of the sacrifice and makes it holy. So Ethelwyn and I were both a little uneasy about her, for we did not understand her.

As I stood regarding my sleeping Wynnie, she suddenly opened her eyes and started to her feet, with the words, "I beg your pardon, Papa," looking almost guiltily round her, and putting up her hair hurriedly as if she had committed an impropriety in being caught untidy. This was a fresh sign of a condition of mind that was not healthy.

"My dear," I said, "what do you beg my pardon for? I was so pleased to see you asleep! And you look as if you thought I were going to scold you."

"O Papa," she said, laying her head on my shoulder, "I am afraid I must be very naughty. I so often feel now as if I were doing something wrong, or rather as if you would think I was doing something wrong. I am sure there must be something wicked in me somewhere, though I do not clearly know what it is. When I woke up now, I felt as if I had neglected something, and you had come to find fault with me. Is there anything, Papa?"

"Nothing whatever, my child. But you cannot be well if you feel like that."

"I am perfectly well, so far as I know. I was so cross to Dora today! Why shouldn't I feel happy when everybody else is? I must be wicked, Papa."

"My dear child," I said, "we must all pray to God for His Spirit, and then we shall feel as we ought to feel. It is not easy for anyone to tell himself how he ought to feel at any given moment, and still less to tell another how he ought to feel. Get your bonnet, Wynnie, and come out with me. We are going to explore a little of this desert island on which we have been cast."

When we left the door of the house, we went up the few steps of a stair leading to the downs. The ground underfoot was green and soft and springy, and sprinkled all over with the bright yellow flowers that live amidst the short grasses of the downs. I stood up, stretched out my arms, threw back my shoulders and my head, and filled my chest with a draught of the delicious wind. Wynnie stood apparently unmoved, thoughtful, and turning her eyes here and there.

"This makes me feel young again," I said.

"I wish it would make me feel old then," said Wynnie.

"What do you mean, my child?"

"Because then I should have a chance of knowing what it is like to feel young," she answered rather enigmatically.

I did not reply. We were walking up the brow which hid the sea from us. The smell of the down-turf was indescribable in its homely delicacy, and by the time we had reached the top, almost every sense was filled with its own delight. The top of the hill was the edge of the great shore-cliff, and the sun was hanging on the face of the mightier sky-cliff opposite. The sea stretched for visible miles and miles along the shore on either hand, its wide blue mantle fringed with lovely white wherever it met the land. The sense of space—of mighty room for life and growth—filled my soul, and I thanked God in my heart. I turned and looked at Wynnie, standing pleased but listless amidst that which lifted me into the heaven of the Presence.

"Don't you enjoy all this grandeur, Wynnie?"

"I told you I was very wicked, Papa."

"And I told you not to say so, Wynnie."

"You see I cannot enjoy it, Papa. I wonder why it is."

"I suspect it is because you haven't room, Wynnie. It is not because you are wicked, but because you do not know God well enough, and therefore your being, which can only live in Him, is 'cabined, cribbed, confined, bound in.' It is only in Him that the soul has room. The secret of your own heart you can never know, but you can know Him who knows its secret."

I paused to breathe the fragrant sea air. "Look up, my darling, see the heavens and the earth. You do not feel them, and I do not call upon you to feel them. It would be both useless and absurd to do so. But just let them look at you for a moment. Then tell me whether it must not be a blessed life that creates such a glory as this."

She stood silent for a moment, looked up at the sky, looked round on the earth, looked far across the sea to the setting sun, and then turned her eyes upon me. They were filled with tears, but whether from feeling or sorrow that she could not feel, I would not inquire. I made haste to speak again.

"Do not say it is too high for you. God made you in His own image, and therefore capable of understanding Him. For this He sent His Son, that They might come into you, and dwell with you. Till They do so, the temple of your soul is vacant. There is no light behind the veil, and no cloudy pillar over it, and the priests—your thoughts and feelings and loves and desires—moan and are troubled, for where is the work of the priests when God is not there? But do not think that I blame you, Wynnie, for feeling sad. I take it rather as the sign of large life in you—that you will not be satisfied with small things. I do not know when or how it may please God to give you the quiet of mind that you need, but it is to be had, and you must go on doing your work and trusting in God. Tell Him to look at your sorrow. Ask Him to come and set it right, making the joy go up in your heart by His presence. Till He lays His hand on your head, you must be content to wash His feet with your tears."

Whatever the immediate occasion of her sadness, such was its only real cure. Nothing would do finally but God Himself.

We walked on together. Wynnie made me no reply, but clung to my arm. We walked a long way by the edge of the cliffs, beheld the sun go down, and then turned for home. When we reached the house, Wynnie left me, saying only, "Thank you, Papa. I think it is all true. I will try to be a better girl."

I went straight to Connie's room, where she was lying as I saw her last, looking out of her window.

"Connie," I said, "Wynnie and I have had such a treat—such a glorious sunset!"

"I've seen a little of the light of it on the waves in the bay there, but the high ground kept me from seeing the sunset itself. Did it set in the sea?"

"You do want the *General Gazetteer,* after all, Connie. Is that water the Atlantic, or is it not? And if it be, where on earth could the sun set but in it?"

"Of course, Papa. What a goose I am! But don't make game of me, *please.* I am too deliciously happy to be made game of tonight."

"I won't make game of you, my darling. I will tell you about the sunset, the colors of it, at least. This must be one of the best places in the whole world to see sunsets."

"But you had no tea, Papa. I thought you would come and have your tea with me. But you were so long that Mamma would not let me wait any longer."

"Oh, never mind the tea, my dear. But Wynnie has had none. You've a tea caddy of your own, haven't you?"

"Yes, and a teapot, and there's the kettle on the hob—for I can't do without a little fire in the evenings."

"Then I'll make some tea for Wynnie and myself, and tell you at the same time about the sunset. I never saw such colors—translucent green on the horizon, a broad band. Then came another broad band of pale rose, and above that the sky's own eternal blue. I never saw the green and blue divided and harmonized by the rose before. It was wonderful. If it is warm enough tomorrow, we will carry you out on the height, that you may see what the evening will bring."

"There are two things about sunsets," returned Connie, "that make me rather sad—about themselves, not about anything else. One thing is that we shall never, never, never see the same sunset again."

"That is true. But why should we? God does not care to do the same thing over again. When it is once done, it is done, and He goes on doing something new. For to all eternity, He never will have done showing Himself by new, fresh things. It would be a loss to do the same thing again."

"But that just brings me to my second trouble. The thing is lost. I forget it. Do what I can, I cannot remember sunsets. I try to fix them fast in my memory, but just as they fade out of the sky, so they fade out of my mind. Now, though I did not see this one, yet, after you have talked about it, I shall never forget it."

"They have their influence, and leave that far deeper than your memory—in your very being, Connie. But here comes Wynnie to see how you are. I've been making some tea for you, Wynnie, my love."

"Oh, thank you, Papa. I shall be so glad of some tea!" said Wynnie.

The same moment my wife came in. "Why didn't you send for me, Harry, to get your tea?"

"I did not deserve any, seeing I had disregarded proper times and seasons. And I knew you were busy."

"I have been superintending the arrangement of bedrooms, and the unpacking, and twenty different things," said Ethelwyn. "We shall be so comfortable! It is such a curious house! Have you had a nice walk?"

"Mamma, I never had such a walk in my life," returned Wynnie. "You would think the shore had been built for the sake of the show—just for a platform to see the sunsets. And the sea! But the cliffs will be rather dangerous for the children."

"I have just been telling Connie about the sunset. She could see something of the colors on the water, but not much more."

"O Connie, it will be so delightful to get you out! Everything is so big! And such room everywhere!" said Wynnie. "Even though," she continued thoughtfully, "it must be awfully windy in winter."

ELEVEN
More About Kilkhaven

Our dining room was one story below the level at which we had entered the parsonage, for the house was built into the face of the cliff, just where it sunk nearly to the shores of the bay. At dinner, on the evening of our arrival, I kept looking from the window and saw first a little garden mostly in turf, and then a low stone wall. Beyond, over the top of the wall, was the blue water of the bay—then beyond the water, all alive with light and motion, the rocks and sand hills of the opposite side of the little bay. Not a quarter of a mile across, I could likewise see where the shore went sweeping out and away to the north, with rock after rock standing far into the water, as if gazing over the awful wild, where there was nothing to break the deathly waste between Cornwall and Newfoundland. If I moved my head a little to the right, I saw, over the top of the low wall, the slender yellow masts of a schooner. We must, I thought, be on the very harbor quay.

When I came down to breakfast in the same room the next morning, I stared. The blue had changed to yellow. The life of the water was gone. Nothing met my eyes but a wide expanse of dead sand across the bay to the hills opposite. From the look of the rocks, from the perpendicular cliffs on the coast, I had concluded that we were on the shore of a deep-water bay. It was high water then, and now I looked over a long reach of sands, on the far border of which the white fringe of the waves was visible. Beyond the fringe lay the low hill of the Atlantic. To add to my confusion, there was no schooner near the wall. I went out to look, and saw in a moment how it was.

"Do you know, my dear," I said to my wife, "we are just at the mouth of that canal we saw as we came along? There are gates and a lock just outside there. The schooner that was under this window last night must have gone in with the tide. She is laying in the basin above now."

"Oh, yes, Papa," Charlie and Harry broke in together. "We saw it go up this morning. We've been out ever so long. It was so funny," Charlie went on—everything was funny with Charlie—"to see it rise up like a jack-in-the-box, and then slip into the quiet water through the other gates!"

After breakfast we had prayers as usual, and after a visit to Connie, I went out for a walk to explore the neighborhood and find the church. The day was glorious. I wandered along a green path in the opposite direction from our walk the evening before, with a fir-wood on my right hand and a belt of feathery tamarisks on my left. Behind lay gardens sloping steeply to a lower road, where a few pretty cottages stood.

Turning a corner, I came suddenly in sight of the church on the green down above me—a sheltered yet commanding situation. For, while the hill rose above it, protecting it from the east, it looked down the bay, and the Atlantic lay open before it. All the earth seemed to lie behind it, and all its gaze to be fixed on the symbol of the infinite. It stood as the church ought to stand, leading men up the mount of vision to the verge of the eternal, to send them back with their hearts full of the strength that springs from hope, by which alone the true work of the world can be done. And when I saw it, I rejoiced to think that once more I was favored with a church that had a history.

I looked about for some cottage where the sexton might live, and spied a slated roof nearly on a level with the road, a little distance in front of me. Before I reached it, however, an elderly woman came out and approached me. She was dressed in a white cap and dark-colored gown. On her face lay a certain repose which attracted me—she looked as if she had suffered but had consented to it, and therefore could smile. Her smile was near the surface, and a kind word would be enough to draw it up from the well where it lay shimmering—you could always see the smile there, whether it was born or not.

She drew near me, as if to pass me, and she would have done so had I not spoken. I think she came toward me to give me the opportunity of speaking if I wished, but she would not address me.

"Good morning," I said. "Can you tell me where to find Mr. Coombes, the sexton?"

"Well, Sir," she answered, with a gleam of the smile brightening beneath her old skin, "I be all the sexton you be likely to find this mornin'. My husband, he be gone out to see one o' Squire Tregarva's hounds as was took ill last night. So if you want to see the old church, Sir, you'll have to be content with an old woman to show you."

"I shall be quite content, I assure you," I answered.

"I have the key in my pocket, Sir, for I thought that would be what you'd be after. For mayhap, says I to myself, he be the gentleman as be come to take Mr. Shepherd's duty for him. Be ye now, Sir?"

All this was said in a slow, sweet, subdued tone, nearly of one pitch. She claimed the privilege of age with a kind of mournful gaiety, but was careful not to presume upon it, and was therefore as gentle as a young girl.

"Yes," I answered. "My name is Walton. I have come to take the place of my friend Shepherd and, of course, I want to see the church."

"Well, she be a bee-utiful old church. Some things, I think, grow more beautiful the older they grows. But it ain't us, Sir."

"I'm not so sure of that," I said. "What do you mean?"

"Well, Sir, there's my little grandson in the cottage there—he'll never be so beautiful again. Them children du be the loves. But we all grows uglier as we grows older. Churches don't seem to."

"I'm not so sure about all that," I said again.

"They did say, Sir, that I was a pretty girl once. I'm not much to look at now." And she smiled with gracious amusement. If there was any vanity left in this memory of her past loveliness, it was as sweet as the memory of old fragrance in the withered leaves of the roses.

"But it du not matter, du it, Sir? Beauty is only skin-deep."

"I don't believe that," I answered. "Beauty is as deep as the heart at least."

"Well, to be sure, my old husband du say I be as handsome in his eyes as ever I be. But I beg your pardon, Sir, for talkin' about myself. I believe it was the old church—she set us on to it."

"The old church didn't lead you into any harm then," I answered. "The beauty that is in the heart will shine out of the face again someday—be sure of that. After all, there is just the same kind of beauty in a good old face that there is in an old church. You can't say the church is so trim and neat as it was the day that the first blast of the organ filled it as with a living soul. The carving is not quite so sharp, the timbers are not quite so clean, and there is a good deal of mold and worm-eating and cobwebs about the old place. Yet both you and I think it more beautiful now than it was then. Well, it is the same with an old face. It is stained and weather-beaten and worn, but the wrinkles and the brownness can't spoil it. A light shines through it all—that of the indwelling Spirit. I wish we all grew old like the old churches."

She did not reply, but I saw in her face that she understood. We had been walking very slowly, had passed through the quaint lych-gate, and now the old woman had the key in the lock of the door, whose archway was figured and fashioned with a dozen curiously carved moldings.

TWELVE

The Old Church

The awe that dwells in churches fell upon me as I crossed the threshold—an awe I never fail to feel, for the air of petition and of holy need seems to linger in the place. A flush of subdued glory invaded my eyes from the chancel—all the windows were of richly stained glass, and the roof of carved oak was lavishly gilded. There were carvings on the ends of the benches all along the aisle on both sides, and supporting arches of different fashion on the opposite sides. The pillars were of coarse country granite, each a single chiseled stone with chamfered sides.

Walking softly through the ancient house, I came at length into the tower, the basement of which was open and formed part of the body of the church. There hung many ropes through the holes in a ceiling above, as I would have expected, for bell ringing was encouraged and indeed practiced by my friend Shepherd.

My guide was seated against the south wall of the tower, on a stool, I thought, or small table. While I was wandering about the church she had taken some socks and wires out of her pocket and was now knitting busily. How her needles did go! Her eyes never regarded them, however, but fixed on the slabs a yard or two from her feet, seemed to be gazing far out to sea. To try her, I took for the moment the position of an accuser.

"So you don't mind working in church?" I said.

She instantly rose. Her eyes turned from the far sea waves to my face, and light came out of them. With a smile she answered, "The church knows me, Sir."

"But what has that to do with it?"

"I don't think she minds it. We are told to be diligent in business, you know, Sir."

"Yes, but it does not say in church and out of church. You could be diligent somewhere else, couldn't you?"

As soon as I said this, I began to fear she would think I meant it. But she only smiled and said, "It won't hurt she, Sir, and my good man, who does all he can to keep her tidy, is out at toes and heels, and if I don't keep he warm he'll be laid up, and then the church won't be kep' nice till he's up again."

"But you could have sat down outside—there are some nice gravestones near—and waited till I came out."

"But what's the church for, Sir? The sun's werry hot today, and Mr. Shepherd, he say that the church is like the shadow of a great rock in a weary land. So you see, if I was to sit out in the sun, instead of comin' in here to the cool o' the shadow, I wouldn't be takin' the church at her word. It does my heart good to sit in the old church. There's a something do seem to come out o' the old walls and settle down like the cool o' the day upon my old heart that's nearly tired o' crying, and would fain keep its eyes dry for the rest o' the journey. My knitting won't hurt the church and, bein' a good deed, it's none the worse for the place. If He was to come by wi' the whip o' small cords, I wouldn't be afeard of His layin' it upo' my old back. Do you think He would, Sir?"

I made haste to reply, more delighted with the result of my experiment than I cared to let her know. "Indeed I do not. I was only talking and testing. It is only the selfish, cheating, or ill-done work that the church's Master drives away. All our work ought to be done in the shadow of the church."

"I thought you be only having a talk about it, Sir," she said, smiling her sweet old smile. "Nobody knows what this old church is to me."

"You have had a family?" I asked.

"Thirteen," she answered. "Six boys and seven maidens."

"Why, you are rich!" I returned. "And where are they all?"

"Four maidens be lying in the churchyard, Sir, and two be married, and one be down in the mill, there."

"And your boys?"

"One of them be lyin' beside his sisters—drownded afore my eyes, Sir. Three o' them be at sea, and two o' them in it."

At sea! I thought. What a wide *where*, and so vague to the imagination! How a mother's thoughts must go roaming about the waste to find them!

"It be no wonder, be it, that I like to creep into the church with my knitting? Many's the stormy night, when my husband couldn't keep still, but would be out on the cliffs or on the breakwater, for no good in life, but just to hear the roar of the waves that he could only see by the white of them, with the balls o' foam flying in his face in the dark—many's the night I have left the house after he was gone, with this blessed key in my hand, and crept into the old church here, and sat down, and hearkened to the wind howling about the place. The church windows never rattle, Sir. Somehow, I feel safe in the church."

"But if you had sons at sea," said I, again wishing to draw her out, "it would not be of much good to you to feel safe yourself, so long as they were in danger."

"Oh! Yes it be, Sir. What's the good of feeling safe yourself but it let you know other people be safe too? It's when you don't feel safe yourself that you feel other people ben't safe."

"But," I said, "some of your sons *were* drowned, for all you say about their safety."

"Well, Sir," she answered with a sigh, "I trust they're none the less safe for that. It would be a strange thing for an old woman like me, well-nigh threescore and ten, to suppose that safety lay not in being drownded. Why, they might ha' been cast on a desert island, and wasted to skin and bone, and got home again wi' the loss of half the wits they set out with. Wouldn't that ha' been worse than being drownded right off? And that wouldn't ha' been the worst, either. The church she seemed to tell me all the time, that for all the roaring outside, there be really no danger after all. What matter if they go to the bottom? What is the bottom of the sea, Sir? You bein' a clergyman can tell that. I shouldn't ha' known it if I hadn't had boys o' my own at sea. But *you* can tell, though you ain't got none there."

She was putting her parson to his catechism. "The hollow of His hand," I said.

"I thought you would know it," she returned, with a little glow of triumph in her tone. "Well, then, that's just what the church tells me, when I come in here in the stormy night. I bring my knitting then too, for I can knit in the dark as well as in the light almost. And when they come home, if they do come home, they're none the worse that I went to the old church to pray for them. There it goes roaring about them, poor dears, all out there—and their old mother sitting still as a stone almost in the quiet old church, a-caring for them. And then it do come across me, Sir, that God be a-sitting in His own house at home, hearing all the noise and all the roaring in which His children are tossed about in the world, watching it all, letting it drown some o' them and take them back to Him, and keeping it from going too far with others of them that are not quite ready for that same. I have my thoughts, you see, though I be an old woman, and not nice to look at."

I had come upon a genius. How nature laughs at our schools sometimes! For life is God's school, and they that will listen to the Master there will learn at God's speed. For one moment, I am ashamed to say, I was envious of Shepherd. And I repined that, now that old Rogers was gone, I had no such glorious old stained-glass window in my church to let in the eternal upon my light-thirsty soul.

"You are very nice to look at," I said. "You must not find fault with the work of God, because you would like better to be young and pretty than to be as you now are. Time and time's rents and furrows are all His making and His doing. God makes nothing ugly."

"Are you quite sure of that, Sir?"

I paused, and the thought of certain animals flashed into my mind, and I could not insist that God never made anything ugly.

"No, I am not sure," I answered. For any pretense of knowing more than I did know seemed repugnant to the spirit and mind of the Master. "But if He does," I went on to say, "it must be that we may see what it is like, and therefore not like it."

Then I turned the conversation to the sort of stool or bench on which my guide had been sitting. It was curiously carved in old oak, very much like the ends of the benches and bookboards.

"What is that you are sitting on?" I asked. "A chest?"

"It be here when we come to this place, and that be nigh fifty years agone. But what it be, you'll be better able to tell than I be, Sir."

"Perhaps a chest for holding the Communion plate in old time," I said. "But how should it then come to be banished to the tower?"

"No, Sir, it can't be that. It be some sort of ancient musical piano, I be thinking."

I stooped and saw that its lid was shaped like the cover of an organ. With some difficulty I opened it, and there was a row of huge keys, fit for the fingers of a Cyclops. I pressed upon them, one after another, but no sound followed. They were stiff to the touch, and once down, so they mostly remained until lifted again. There were a dozen little round holes in the fixed part of the top, which might afford some clue to the mystery of its former life. I glanced up at the holes in the ceiling through which the bell ropes went and spied two or three thick wires hanging through the same ceiling close to the wall, and right over the box with the keys. The vague suspicion of a discovery dawned upon me.

"Have you the key of the tower?" I asked.

"No, Sir. But I'll run home for it at once," she answered. And rising, she went out in haste.

Run! thought I, looking after her. ***It is a word of the will and the feeling, not of the body.*** But I was mistaken. The dear old creature had no sooner got outside of the churchyard than she did run, and ran well too. I was on the point of starting after her, to prevent her from hurting herself, but reflected that her own judgment ought to be as good as mine.

I sat down on her seat, awaiting her reappearance, and gazed at the ceiling. There I either saw, or imagined I saw, signs of openings corresponding in number and position with those in the lid. In about three minutes the old woman returned; she was panting but not distressed, and she held a great crooked old key in her hand.

"You shouldn't run like that. I am in no hurry."

"Be you not, Sir? I thought, by the way you spoke, you be taken with a longing to get a-top o' the tower, and see all about you like. Fond as I be of the old church, I du feel sometimes as if she'd smother me, and then nothing will do but I must get at the top of the old tower. And then, what with the sun, if there be any sun, and what with the fresh air, which there always be up there, Sir—it du always be fresh up there, Sir," she repeated, "and I come back down again blessing the old church for its tower."

As she spoke she was toiling up the winding staircase after me, where there was just room enough for my shoulders to get through. As I ascended, I was thinking of what she had said. Strange to tell, the significance of the towers or spires of our churches had never been clear to me before. True, I was quite awake to their significance, at least to that of the spires, as fingers pointing ever upward to

> . . . regions mild of calm and serene air,
> Above the smoke and stir of this dim spot,
> Which men call Earth.

Yet I had never thought of their symbolism as lifting one up above the church itself into a region where no church is wanted, because the Lord God Almighty and the Lamb are the temple of it. Happy church, indeed, if it destroys the need of itself by lifting men up into the eternal kingdom!

In the ascent I forgot all about the special object for which I had requested the key of the tower, and led the way myself up to the summit, and stepped out of a little door. And there, filling the west, lay the ocean beneath, with a dark curtain of storm hanging over part of its horizon. On the other side was the peaceful solid land, with its numberless shades of green, its heights and hollows, its farms and wooded vales, its scattered villages and country dwellings. Beyond lay the blue heights of Dartmoor. The old woman stood beside me, silently enjoying my enjoyment, with a smile that seemed to say, in kindly triumph, "Was I not right about the tower and the wind that dwells among its pinnacles?"

There were a good many trees in the churchyard, and as I looked down, their rich foliage hid all the graves directly below me, except a single flat stone looking up through an opening in the leaves, which seemed to have been just made for it to see the top of the tower. Upon the stone a child was playing with a few flowers, not once looking up to the tower. I turned to the eastern side, and looked over upon the church roof. It lay far below—looking very narrow and small but long, with the four ridges of four steep roofs stretching away to the eastern end.

When I turned to look down again, the little child was gone. Some butterfly fancy had seized her, and she was away. A little lamb was in her place, nibbling at the grass that grew on the side of the next mound.

Reentering by the angels' door to descend the narrow corkscrew stair, so dark and cool, I caught a glimpse of a tiny maidenhair fern growing out of the wall. I stopped and said, "I have a sick daughter at home, or I wouldn't rob your tower of this lovely little thing."

"Well, Sir, what eyes you have! I never saw the thing before. Do take it home to Miss. It'll do her good to see it. I be main sorry to hear you've got a sick maiden."

I succeeded with my knife in getting out all the roots without hurting them, and said, "She can't even sit up and must be carried everywhere."

"Poor dear! Everyone has their troubles, Sir. The sea's been mine."

She continued talking and asking kind questions about Connie as we went down the stair. Not till she opened a little door was I reminded of my first object in ascending the tower. For this door revealed a number of bells hanging in silent power in the brown twilight of the place. I entered carefully, for there were only some planks laid upon the joists to keep one's feet from going through the ceiling. My conjecture about the keys below was correct. The small iron rods I had seen hung down from this place. There were more of them hanging above, and there was yet enough mechanism remaining to prove that those keys (by means of the looped and cranked rods) had been in connection with hammers which struck the bells, so that a tune could be played upon them.

"A clever blacksmith, now," I said to myself, "could repair all this, and Shepherd could play a psalm tune to his parish when he pleased. I will see what can be done." I left the abode of the bells and descended to the church. Then I bade Mrs. Coombes good-morning (promising to visit her soon in her own house), and bore home to Connie the fern from the lofty wall.

THIRTEEN

Connie's Watchtower

Our "new" house was one of those that have grown, rather than being built after a straight-up-and-down model of uninteresting convenience. The builders must have had some plan—good, bad, or indifferent—but that plan they had left far behind. And now the fact that they have a history is plainly written on their aspect. These are the houses which fairies used to haunt, and hence perhaps the sense of soothing comfort which pervades us when we cross their thresholds. You do not know, the moment you have cast a glance about the hall, where the dining room, drawing room, and best bedroom are. You have it all to find out. It had formerly been a kind of manor house, though the germ cell of it was a cottage of the simplest sort. It had grown by the addition of other cells, till it had reached the development in which we found it.

The dining room was almost on the level of the shore—indeed, some of the flat stones that coped the low wall in front of it were thrown into the garden by the waves before the next winter. But Connie's room looked out on a little flower garden almost on the downs, sheltered only a little by the rise of a short grassy slope above it. This, however, left open the prospect from her window down the bay and out to sea.

To reach this room I had to go up but one simple cottage stair, for the door of the house entered on the first floor. The room had a large bay window, and in this window Connie was lying on her couch, with the lower sash wide open. There the breeze entered, smelling of seaweed tempered with sweet grasses and the wall- flowers and stocks that were in the little plot under it. I thought I could see an improvement in her already. Certainly she looked very happy.

"O Papa!" she said. "Isn't it delightful?"

"What is, my dear?"

"Oh, everything. The wind, and the sky, and the sea, and the smell of the flowers. Do look at that seabird. His wings are like the barb of a terrible arrow. How he goes undulating, neck and body, up and down as he flies! I never felt before that a bird moves his wings. It always looked as if the wings flew with the bird. But I see the effort in him. He chooses and means to fly, and so he does it. It makes one almost reconciled to the idea of wings. Do angels have wings, Papa?"

"It is generally so represented, I think, in the Bible. But whether it is meant as a natural fact about them, is more than I take upon me to decide. But wings are very beautiful things, and I do not exactly see why you should need reconciling to them."

Connie gave a little shrug of her shoulders. "I don't like the notion of them growing out at my shoulder blades. And however would you get on your clothes? If you put them over your wings, they would be of no use, and would make you humpbacked besides. And if you did not, everything would have to be buttoned round their roots. You could not do it yourself, and even on Wynnie I don't think I could bear to touch the things—I don't mean the feathers, but the skinny, folding-up bits of them."

I laughed at her fastidious fancy.

"Papa," she said, "would you like to have wings?"

"I should like to fly like a bird, to swim like a fish, to gallop like a horse, and to creep like a serpent. But I suspect the good of all these is to be had without doing any of them. I mean by a perfect sympathy with the creatures that do these things. What it may please God to give to ourselves, we can quite comfortably leave to Him.

"Now, Connie, what would you think about getting out?"

"Think about it, Papa! I have been thinking about it ever since daylight."

"I will go and see what your mother is doing then, and if she is ready to go out with us."

In a few moments all was arranged. Walter and I lifted Connie and sofa and all out over the windowsill. We carried her high enough on the down for her to see the brilliant waters lying many feet below her, with the seabirds winging their undulating way between heaven and ocean. It is when first you have a chance of looking a bird in the face on the wing that you know what the marvel of flight is. There it hangs or rests, borne up, as far as any can witness, by its own will alone. One of those barb-winged birds rested over my head, regarding me from above, as if I might afford some claim to his theory of treasure trove.

Connie lay silent a long time. At length I spoke. "Are you longing to be running about amongst the rocks, my Connie?"

"No, Papa, not a bit. I don't know how it is, but I don't think I ever wished much for anything I knew I could not have. I am enjoying everything more than I can tell you. I wish Wynnie were as happy as I am."

"Why? Do you think she's not happy, my dear?"

"That doesn't want any thinking, Papa. You can see that."

"You're right, Connie. What do you think is the cause of it?"

"I think it is because she can't wait. She's always going out to meet things, and then when they're not there waiting for her, she thinks they're nowhere. But I always think her way is finer than mine. If everybody were like me, there wouldn't be much done in the world, would there, Papa?"

"At all events, my dear, your way is wise for you, and I am glad you do not judge your sister."

"Judge Wynnie, Papa! That would be cool impudence. She's worth ten of me.

"Don't you think, Papa," she added, after a pause, "that if Mary had said the smallest word against Martha, as Martha did against Mary, Jesus would have had a word to say on Martha's side next?"

"Indeed I do, my dear. And I think that Mary did not sit very long without asking Jesus if she mightn't go and help her sister. There is but one thing needful—that is, the will of God. When people love that above everything, they soon come to see that there are two sides to everything else, and that only the will of God gives fair play to both."

Another silence followed before Connie spoke. "Is it not strange, Papa, that the only thing here that makes me want to get up is nothing of all the grand things round about me? Do you see down there, away across the bay amongst the rocks at the other side, a man sitting sketching?"

I looked for some time before I could discover him.

"Your sight is good, Connie. I see the man, but I could not tell what he was doing."

"Don't you see him lifting his head every now and then for a moment, and then keeping it down for a longer while?"

"I cannot distinguish that. But then I am rather shortsighted, you know."

"Then I wonder how you see so many little things that nobody else seems to notice, Papa."

"That is because I have trained myself to observe. The power in the sight is of less consequence than the habit of seeing. But you have not yet told me what it is that makes you desirous of getting up."

"I want to look over his shoulder, and see what he is doing. Is it not strange that in the midst of all this beautiful plenty, I should want to rise to look at a few lines and scratches, or smears of color, upon a bit of paper?"

"No, it is not strange. There a new element of interest is introduced—the human."

"I think I understand you, Papa. But look a little farther off. Don't you see a lady's bonnet over the top of another rock? I do believe that's Wynnie. I know she took her box of watercolors out with her this morning, just before you came home. Dora went with her."

"Can't you tell by her ribbons, Connie? You seem sharpsighted enough to see her face if she would show it. I don't even see the bonnet. If I were like some people I know . . . but here comes Mamma at last."

Connie's face brightened as if she had not seen her mother for a fortnight. "Mamma, don't you think that's Wynnie's bonnet over that black rock there, just beyond where you see that man drawing?"

"You absurd child! How should I know Wynnie's bonnet at this distance?"

"Can't you see the little white feather you gave her out of your wardrobe just before we left? She put it in this morning before she went out."

"I think I do see something white. But I want you to look out there, toward what they call the Chapel Rock, at the other end of that long mound they call the breakwater. You will soon see a boat full of the coast guard. I saw them just as I left the house. Their officer came down with his sword, and each of the men had a cutlass. I wonder what it can mean."

We looked. But before the boat made its appearance, Connie cried out, "Look! That big boat rowing for the land, away northward there!"

I turned my eyes in the direction she indicated, and saw a long boat with some half-dozen oars, full of men rowing hard, apparently for some spot on the shore at a considerable distance to the north of our bay.

"Ah!" I said, "That boat has something to do with the coast guard and their cutlasses. You'll see that as soon as they get out of the bay, they will row in the same direction."

So it was. Our boat appeared presently, and made full speed after the other boat.

"Surely they can't be smugglers," I said. "I thought all that was over and done with."

In the course of another twenty minutes, both boats had disappeared behind the headland to the northward. I went to fetch Walter, and we carried Connie back. She had not been in the shadow of her own room five minutes before she was fast asleep.

It was nearly time for our early dinner. We always dined early when we could, that we might eat along with our children.

"Oh! We've seen such a nice gentleman!" said Dora, becoming lively under the influence of her soup.

"Have you, Dora? Where?"

"Sitting on the rocks, making a portrait of the sea."

"What makes you say he was a nice gentleman?"

"He had such beautiful boots!" answered Dora, at which there was a great laugh about the table.

"Oh! We must run and tell Connie that," said Harry. "It will make her laugh."

"What will you tell Connie, then, Harry?"

"Oh, what was it, Charlie? I've forgotten."

Another laugh followed at Harry's expense now, and we were all very merry when Dora, who sat opposite to the window, called out clapping her hands, "There's Niceboots again! There's Niceboots again!"

The same moment the head of a young man appeared over our wall by the entrance of the canal. I saw at once that he must be more than ordinarily tall to show his face, for he was not close to the wall. His was a dark countenance, with a long beard—a noble, handsome face, a little sad, with downbent eyes which, released from their more immediate duty toward nature, had now bent themselves upon the earth.

"He is a fine-looking fellow," said I, "and ought, with that face and head, to be able to paint good pictures."

"I should like to see what he has done," said Wynnie, "for, by the way we were sitting, I should think we were attempting the same thing."

"And what was that, Wynnie?" I asked.

"A rock," she answered, "that you could not see from where you were sitting. I saw you on the top of the cliff."

"Connie said it was you, by your bonnet. She too was wishing she could look over the shoulder of the artist at work beside you."

"Not beside me. There were yards and yards of solid rock between us."

"Space, you see, in removing things from the beholder, seems always to bring them nearer to each other, and the most differing things are classed under one name by the man who knows nothing about them. But what sort of rock were you trying to draw?"

"A strange looking, conical rock that stands alone in front of one of the ridges that project from the shore into the water. Three seabirds with long white wings were flying about it, and the little waves of the rising tide were beating themselves against it and breaking in white splashes. So the rock stood between the blue and white below and the blue and white above."

"Now, Dora," I said, "do you see why I want you to learn to draw? Look how Wynnie sees things. That is, in great measure, because she draws things, and has learned to watch in order to find out. It is a great thing to have your eyes open."

Dora's eyes were large, and she opened them to their full width, as if she would take in the universe at their little doors.

"Now let us go up to Connie, and tell her about the rock and everything else you have seen since you went out. We are all her messengers, sent out to discover things and bring back news of them."

After a little talk with Connie, I retired to the study, which was on the same floor as her room, completing, indeed, the whole of that part of the house. It had a roof of its own, and stood higher up the rock than the rest of the dwelling. Here I began to glance over Shepherd's books. To have the run of another man's library, especially if it has been gathered by himself, is like having a pass key into the chambers of his thought. I found one thing plain enough, that Shepherd had kept up that love for older English literature which had been one of the cords to draw us together as students long ago. I had taken down a last century edition of the poems of the brothers Fletcher, and had begun to read a lovely passage in "Christ's Victory and Triumph" when a knock came at the door and Charlie entered, breathless with eagerness.

"There's the boat with the men with the swords in it, and another boat behind them, twice as big."

I hurried out and there, close under our windows, were the two boats we had seen in the morning, landing their crews on the little beach. The second boat was full of weather-beaten men, in all kinds of attire, some in blue jerseys, some in red shirts, some in ragged coats. One man, who looked their superior, was dressed in blue from head to foot.

"What's the matter?" I asked the officer.

"Vessel foundered, Sir," he answered. "Sprung a leak on Sunday morning. She was laden with iron, and in a heavy ground swell it shifted and knocked a hole in her. The poor fellows are worn out with the pump and rowing, upon little or nothing to eat."

They were trooping past us by this time, looking rather dismal, though not by any means abject.

"Where will they go now?"

"They'll be taken in by the people. We'll get up a little subscription for them, but they all belong to the society the sailors have for sending the shipwrecked to their homes, or where they want to go."

"Well, here's something to help," I said, handing him a coin from my pocket.

"Thank you, Sir. They'll be very glad of it. You are our new clergyman, I believe."

"Not exactly that. Only for a little while, till my friend Mr. Shepherd is able to come back to you."

"We don't want to lose Mr. Shepherd, Sir. He's what they call *high* in these parts, but he's a great favorite with all the poor people, because you see he understands them as if he was of the same flesh and blood with themselves—as, for that matter, I suppose we all are."

"If we weren't, there would be nothing to say at all. Will any of these men be at church tomorrow, do you suppose? I am afraid sailors are not much in the way of going to church."

"I am afraid not. You see they are all anxious to get home, and most likely they'll be traveling tomorrow. It's a pity. It would be a good chance for saying something to them. But I often think that sailors won't be judged exactly like other people. They're so knocked about, you see, Sir."

"Of course not. Nobody will be judged like any other body. To his own Master, who knows all about him, every man stands or falls. Depend upon it, God likes fair play far better than any sailor at all. But the question is this: shall we, who know what a blessed thing life is because we know what God is like, who can trust in Him with all our hearts because He is the Father of our Lord Jesus Christ, the friend of sinners, shall we not try all we can to let them know the blessedness of trusting in their Father in heaven? If we could only get them to say the Lord's Prayer, meaning it, think what that would be! Look here—this can't be called bribery, for they are in want of it, and it will show them I am friendly. Here's another sovereign. Give them my compliments, and say that if any of them happen to be in Kilkhaven tomorrow, I shall be quite pleased to welcome them to church. Tell them I will give them of my best there if they will come. Make the invitation merrily, you know. No long face and solemn speech. I will give them the solemn speech when they come to church. But even there I hope God will keep the long face from me. That is for fear and suffering, and the house of God holds the antidote against all fear and most suffering. But I am preaching my sermon on Saturday instead of Sunday, and keeping you from your ministration to your men."

"I will give them your message as near as I can," he said, and we shook hands and parted.

This was the first experience we had of the might and battle of the ocean. To our eyes it lay quiet as a baby asleep. On that Sunday morning there had been no commotion here. Yet now on the Saturday morning, home came the conquered and spoiled of the sea. As if with a mock, she takes all they have and flings them on shore again, with her weeds and her shells and her sand. There are few coasts on which the sea rages so wildly as this, where the whole force of the Atlantic breaks upon it. Even when all is still as a church on land, the storm which raves somewhere out upon the vast waste will drive the waves in upon the shore with such fury, that not even a lifeboat could make its way through the yawning hollows, and their fierce, shattered, and tumbling crests.

FOURTEEN

A Sermon for Sailors

I hoped that some of the shipwrecked mariners might be present in church that bright Sunday—my first in this seaboard parish—with the sea outside the church flashing in the sunlight.

While I stood at the lectern, I could see little of my congregation, partly from my being on a level with them, partly from the necessity for keeping my eyes and thoughts upon that which I read. However, when I rose from prayer in the pulpit, I saw that one long bench in the middle of the church was full of sunburnt men in torn and worn garments, the very men in whom we had been so much interested. Not only were they behaving with perfect decorum, but their rough faces wore an aspect of solemnity which I do not suppose was their usual aspect.

I gave them no text. I had one myself, which was the necessary thing, and they should have it soon enough.

"Once upon a time," I said, "a man went up a mountain and stayed there till it was dark. Now, a man who finds himself on a mountain as the sun is going down, especially if he is alone, makes haste to get down before it is dark. But this man went up when the sun was going down and continued there for a good long while after it was dark. He went because he wished to be alone. He hadn't a house of his own. He hadn't even a room of his own into which he could go. True, he had kind friends who would give him a bed; but they were all poor people, and their houses were small, and very likely they had large families, and he could not always find a quiet place to go. And I daresay, if he had had a room, he would have been a little troubled with the children constantly coming to find him. For however much he loved them—and no man was ever so fond of children as he was—he needed to be left quiet sometimes. So, on this occasion, he went up the mountain just to be quiet.

"For he had been talking with men all day, which tires and sometimes confuses a man's thoughts, and now he wanted to talk with God, for that makes a man strong, and puts all the confusion in order again. So he went to the top of the hill. That was his secret chamber. It had no door, but that did not matter—no one could see him but God. It was so quiet up there! The people had all gone away to their homes, and perhaps next day would hardly think about him at all, as they were busy catching fish, or digging their gardens, or making things for their houses. But he knew that God would not forget him the next day any more than this day, and that God had sent him not to be the king that these people wanted him to be, but their servant. So, to make his heart strong, he went up into the mountain alone to have a talk with his Father. I need not tell you who this man was—it was the King of men, the Servant of men, the Lord Jesus Christ, the everlasting Son of our Father in heaven.

"Now this mountain had a small lake at the foot of it. He had sent His usual companions away in their boat across this water to the other side, where their homes and families were. You must remember that it was a little boat—and there are often tremendous storms upon these small lakes with great mountains about them. For the wind will come all at once, rushing down through the clefts in as sudden a squall as ever overtook a sailor at sea. He saw them worn out at the oar, toiling in rowing, for the wind was contrary to them. He went straight down. Could not His Father help them out without Him? Yes. But He wanted to do it Himself, that they might see that He did it. Otherwise they could only have thought that the wind fell of itself and the waves lay down without cause, never supposing for a moment that their Master or His Father had had anything to do with it. They would have done just as people do now—they would think that the help comes of itself. So when He reached the border of the lake, He found the waves breaking furiously upon the rocks. But that made no difference to Him."

The mariners had been staring at me up to this point, leaning forward on their benches, for sailors are nearly as fond of a good yarn as they are of tobacco. (I heard afterward that they had voted parson's yarn a good one.)

"The companions of our Lord had not been willing to go away and leave Him behind. Now, they wished more than ever that He had been with them—not that they thought He could do anything with a storm, only that somehow they would have been less afraid with His face to look at.

"At length, when they were nearly worn out, taking feebler and feebler strokes, sometimes missing the water altogether, at other times burying their oars in it up to the handles, one of them gave a cry, and they all stopped rowing and stared, leaning forward to peer through the darkness. And through the spray, they saw, perhaps a hundred yards or so from the boat, something standing up from the surface of the water. It was a shape like a man, and they all cried out with fear, for they thought it must be a ghost."

How the faces of the sailors strained toward me at this part of the story!

"But then, over the noise of the wind and the waters came the voice they knew so well—'It is I. Be not afraid.' In the first flush of his delight, Peter felt strong and full of courage. 'Lord, if it be Thou,' he said, 'bid me come unto Thee on the water.' Jesus just said, 'Come!' and Peter scrambled over the gunwale on to the sea. But when he let go of his hold on the boat and began to look around him, and when he saw how the wind was tearing the water, and how it tossed and raved between him and Jesus, he began to be afraid. And as soon as he began to be afraid he began to sink; but he had just sense enough to cry out, 'Lord, save me.' And Jesus put out His hand, and took hold of him, and lifted him out of the water, and said to him, 'O thou of little faith, wherefore didst thou doubt?' And then they got into the boat, and the wind fell all at once and altogether.

"Now, do not think that Peter was a coward. It wasn't that he hadn't courage, but that he hadn't enough of it. And why was it that he hadn't enough of it? Because he hadn't faith enough. You would have thought that once he found himself standing on the water, he need not be afraid of the wind and the waves that lay between him and Jesus. You would have thought that the greatest trial of his courage was over when he got out of the boat, and that there was comparatively little more ahead of him. Yet the sight of the waves and the blast of the boisterous wind were too much for him. When he got out of the boat, and found himself standing on the water, he began to think much of himself for being able to do so, and fancy himself better and greater than his companions, and a special favorite of God. Now, there is nothing that kills faith sooner than pride. The two are directly against each other. The moment that Peter grew proud and began to think about himself instead of his Master, he began to lose his faith, and then he grew afraid, and then he began to sink, and that brought him to his senses. When he forgot himself and remembered his Master, the hand of the Lord caught him, and the voice of the Lord gently rebuked him for the smallness of his faith, asking, 'Wherefore didst thou doubt?'

"If the disciples had known that Jesus saw them from the top of the mountain and was watching them all the time, would they have been frightened at the storm? Suppose you were alone on the sea and expected your boat to be swamped any moment. If you saw that He was watching you from some lofty hilltop, would you be afraid? He might mean you to go to the bottom, you know. But would you mind going to the bottom with Him looking at you? I do not think I should mind it myself. But I must take care lest I be boastful like Peter.

"Why should we be afraid of anything with Him watching us? But we are afraid of Him instead, because we do not believe that He is what He says He is, the Saviour of men. We do not believe that what He offers us is salvation. We think it is slavery, and therefore we continue to be slaves. But, floating on the sea of your troubles, all kinds of fears and anxieties assailing you, is He not on the mountaintop? Sees He not the little boat of your fortunes tossed with the waves and the contrary wind? Do not think that the Lord sees and will not come. Down the mountain He will assuredly come, and you are now as safe in your troubles as the disciples were in theirs with Jesus looking on. They did not know it, but it was so—the Lord was watching them. And when you look back upon your past lives, cannot you see some instances of the same kind when you felt and acted as if the Lord had forgotten you, and you found afterward that He had been watching you all the time?

"You do not trust Him more because you obey Him so little. If you would only ask what God would have you to do, you would soon find your confidence growing. It is because you are proud and envious and greedy after gain, that you do not trust Him more. Ah! Trust Him to get rid of these evil things, and be clean and beautiful in heart.

"O sailors with me on the ocean of life, knowing that He is watching you from His mountaintop, will you do and say the things that hurt and wrong and disappoint Him? Sailors on the waters that surround this globe, He beholds you and cares for you and watches over you. Will you do that which is unpleasing, distressful to Him? Will you be irreverent, cruel, coarse? Will you say evil things, lie, and delight in vile stories and reports, with His eye on you, watching your ship on its watery ways, ever ready to come over the waves to help you? It is a fine thing, Sailors, to fear nothing. But it would be far finer to fear nothing because He is above all and over all and in you all. For His sake and for His love, give up everything bad, and take Him for your Captain. He will be both Captain and Pilot to you, and will steer you safe into the port of glory. Now to God the Father. . . ."

And so I preached that first Sunday morning, and followed it up with a short enforcement in the afternoon.

FIFTEEN
Another Sunday Evening

In the evening we met in Connie's room, as usual, to have our talk.

The window was open, and the sun was brilliant in the west. We sat a little aside out of his radiance, and let him look full into the room. Only Wynnie sat back in a dark corner, as if she would get out of his way. Below him the sea lay bluer than belief—blue with a delicate yet deep silky blue, with the brilliant white lines of its lapping on the high coast to the north.

We had just sat down when Dora broke out, "I saw Niceboots at church. He did stare at you, Papa, as if he had never heard a sermon before."

"I dare say he never heard such a sermon before!" said Connie, with the perfect confidence of inexperience and partiality, not to say ignorance, seeing she had not heard the sermon herself.

Here Wynnie spoke from her dark corner, apparently forcing herself to speak, and thereby giving what seemed an unpleasant tone to what she said. "Well, Papa, I don't know what to think. You are always telling us to trust in Him, but how can we if we are not good?"

"The first good thing you can do is to look up to Him. That is faith and the beginning of trust in Him."

"But it's no use sometimes."

"How do you know that?"

"Because you—I mean I—can't feel good, or care about it at all."

"But is that any ground for saying that it is no use—that He does not heed you? Does He disregard the look cast up to Him? Will He not help you until your heart goes with your will? He made Himself strong to be the helper of the weak, and He pities most those who are most destitute. And who are so destitute as those who do not love what they want to love?"

Connie, as if partly to help her sister, followed on the same side. "I don't know exactly how to say what I mean, Papa, but I wish I could get this lovely afternoon, all full of sunshine and blue, into unity with all that you teach us about Jesus Christ. I wish this beautiful day came in with my thought of Him, like the frame—gold and red and blue—that you have around that picture of Him at home. Why doesn't it?"

"You do not know Him well enough yet. You do not yet believe that He means you all gladness, heartily, honestly, thoroughly."

"And no suffering, Papa?"

"I did not say that, my dear. There you are on your couch and can't move. But He does mean you gladness, nonetheless. What a chance you have, Connie, of believing in Him, of offering upon His altar!"

"But," said my wife, "are not these feelings in a great measure dependent on the state of one's health? I find it so different when the sunshine is inside me as well as outside me."

"No doubt, my dear. But that is only the more reason for rising above all that. From the way some people speak of physical difficulties, you would think that they were not merely inevitable, which they are, but insurmountable, which they are not. That they are physical and not spiritual is not only a great consolation, but also a strong argument for overcoming them. For all that is physical is put—or is in the process of being put—under the feet of the spiritual. Do not mistake me. I do not say you can make yourself merry or happy when you are in a physical condition which is contrary to such mental condition. But you can withdraw from it, not all at once, but by practice and effort you can learn to withdraw from it, refusing to allow your judgments and actions to be ruled by it. 'What does that matter?' you will learn to say. 'It is enough for me to know that the sun does shine, and that this is only a weary fog round me for the moment. I shall come out into the light beyond presently.' The most glorious instances of calmness in suffering are thus achieved—that the sufferers really do not suffer, for they have taken refuge in the inner chamber. Out of the spring of their life, a power goes forth that quenches the flames of the furnace of their suffering.

"Still less is physical difficulty to be used as an excuse for giving way to ill temper and leaving ourselves to be tossed and shaken by every tremble of our nerves. That is as if a man should give himself into the hands and will and caprice of an organ-grinder to work on him, not with the music of the spheres but with the wretched growling of the streets."

"But Papa," said Wynnie, "you yourself excuse other people's ill temper on the very ground that they are out of health. Indeed," she went on, "I have heard you do so for myself when you did not know that I was within hearing."

"Yes, my dear, most assuredly. A real difference lies between excusing ourselves and excusing others. No doubt the same excuse is just for ourselves that is just for other people. But we can do something to put ourselves right. Where we cannot work—that is, in the life of another—we have time to make all the excuse we can. Nay, more—it is only justice there. We are not bound to insist on our own rights, even of excuse; the wisest thing often is to forego them. We are bound by heaven, earth, and hell, to give them to other people. But it would be a sad thing to have to think that when we found ourselves in ungracious condition, from whatever the cause, we had only to submit to it saying, 'It is a law of nature.' It may be a law of nature, but it must yet bow before the Law of the Spirit of Life."

A little pause followed. That Wynnie, at least, was thinking, her next question made evident.

"What you say about a law of nature and a Law of the Spirit makes me think again how Jesus' walking on the water has always been a puzzle to me."

"It could hardly be other, seeing that we cannot possibly understand it," I answered.

"But I find it so hard to believe. Can't you say something, Papa, to help me believe it?"

"I think if you admit what goes before, you will find there is nothing against reason in the story. If all things were made by Jesus, the Word of God, would it be reasonable that the water that He had created should be able to drown Him?"

"It might drown His body."

"It would if He had not the power over it still, to prevent it from laying hold of Him. But just think for a moment. God is a Spirit. Spirit is greater than matter. I suspect this miracle was wrought not through anything done to the water, but through the power of the Spirit over the body of Jesus. If we look at the history of our Lord, we shall find that true real human body as His was, it was yet used by His spirit after a fashion in which we cannot yet use our bodies."

"But then about Peter, Papa? What you have been saying will not apply to Peter's body, you know."

"I confess there is more difficulty there. But if you can suppose that such power were indwelling in Jesus, you cannot limit the sphere of its action. Peter's faith in Him brought even Peter's body within the sphere of the outgoing power of the Master. Do you suppose that because Peter ceased to be brave and trusting, therefore Jesus withdrew from him some sustaining power and allowed him to sink? I do not believe it. I believe Peter's sinking followed naturally. The pride of Peter had withdrawn him from the immediate spiritual influence of Christ, and had conquered his matter. Therefore, the Lord must come from His own height of safety above the sphere of the natural law, stretch out to Peter the arm of physical aid, lift him up, and lead him to the boat. The whole salvation of the human race is figured in this story. It is all Christ, my love. Does this help you to believe at all?"

"I think it does, Papa. But it wants thinking over a good deal."

"But there's one thing," said my wife, "that is more interesting to me than what you have been talking about. It is the other instances in the life of Peter in which you said he failed in a similar manner from pride or self-satisfaction."

"One, at least, seems to me very clear. You have often remarked to me, Ethelwyn, how little praise servants can stand—how almost invariably after you have commended the diligence or skill of any of your household, one of the first visible results was either a falling away in performance or an outbreak of self-conceit. Now you will see precisely the same kind of thing in Peter."

Here I opened my New Testament and read fragmentarily, " 'But whom say ye that I am? . . . Thou art the Christ, the Son of the living God. . . . Blessed art thou, Simon. . . . My Father hath revealed that unto thee. . . . I will give unto thee the keys of the kingdom of heaven. . . . I must suffer many things, and be killed, and be raised again the third day. . . . Be it far from Thee, Lord. This shall not be unto Thee. . . . Get thee behind Me, Satan. Thou art an offense unto Me.' Just contemplate the change here in the words of our Lord. 'Blessed art thou. . . . Thou art an offense unto Me.' The Lord had praised Peter. Peter grew self-sufficient, even to the rebuking of Him whose praise had so uplifted him. But it is ever so. A man will gain a great moral victory; glad first, then uplifted, he will fall before a paltry temptation.

"I have sometimes wondered whether his denial of our Lord had anything to do with his satisfaction with himself for making that onslaught upon the high priest's servant. It was a brave and faithful act to draw a single sword against a multitude. Peter had justified his confident saying that he would not deny Him. He was not one to deny his Lord—who had been the first to confess Him! Yet ere the cock had crowed, ere the morning had dawned, the vulgar grandeur of the palace of the high priest and the accusation of a maid-servant were enough to make him quail. He was excited before, and now he was cold in the middle of the night, with Jesus gone from his sight a prisoner.

"Alas, that the courage which had led him to follow the Lord should have thus led him but into the denial of Him! Yet why should I say *alas?* If the denial of our Lord lay in his heart a possible thing, only prevented by his being kept in favorable circumstances for confessing Him, it was a thousand times better that he should deny Him, and thus know what a poor weak thing that heart of his was, trust it no more, and give it up to the Master to make it strong and pure and grand. For such an end, the Lord was willing to bear all the pain of Peter's denial."

Here I ceased and, a little overcome, rose and retired to my own room. There I could only fall on my knees and pray that the Lord Christ, who had died for me, might have His own way with me—that it might be worth His while to have done what He did and what He was doing now for me. To my Elder Brother, my Lord and my God, I gave myself yet again, confidently, because He cared to have me and because my very breath was His. I would be what He wanted, who knew all about it and had done everything that I might be a son of God—a living glory of gladness.

SIXTEEN
Niceboots

The next morning the captain of the lost vessel called upon me early. He was a fine, honest-looking, burly fellow, dressed in blue from head to heel. I thought I had something to bring against him, and therefore I said to him, "They tell me, Captain, that your vessel was not seaworthy, and that you knew that."

"She was my own craft, Sir, and I judged her fit for several voyages more. If she had been A-1 she couldn't have been mine, and a man must do what he can for his family."

"But you were risking your life, you know."

"A few chances more or less don't much signify to a sailor, Sir. There ain't nothing to be done without risk. You'll find an old tub go voyage after voyage, and she beyond bail, and a clipper fresh off the stocks go down in the harbor. It's all in the luck, I assure you."

"Well, if it were your own life I should have nothing to say, seeing you have a family to look after. But what about the poor fellows who made the voyage with you—did they know what kind of vessel they were embarking in?"

"Wherever the captain's ready to go he'll always find men ready to follow him. Bless you, Sir, they never ask no questions. If a sailor was always to be thinking of the chances, he'd never set his foot offshore."

"Still I don't think it's right they shouldn't know."

"I daresay they knowed all about the brig as well as I did myself. You gets to know all about the craft just as you do about her captain. She's got a character of her own, and she can't hide it long, anymore than you can hide yours, Sir, begging your pardon."

"I daresay that's all correct, but still I shouldn't like anyone to say to me, 'You ought to have told me, Captain.' Therefore, I'm telling you, Captain, and now I'm clear. A glass of wine before you go?" I concluded, ringing the bell.

"Thank you, Sir. I'll turn over what you've been saying, and anyhow I take it kind of you."

So we parted. I have never seen him since and shall not, most likely, in this world. But he looked like a man who could understand why and wherefore I spoke as I did.

All the next week, I wandered about my parish, making acquaintance with different people in an outside sort of way, only now and then finding an opportunity of seeing into their souls. But I enjoyed endlessly the aspects of the country. It was not picturesque except in parts. There was a little wood and there were no hills, only undulations, though many of them were steep enough from a pedestrian's point of view. Neither were there any plains except high moorland tracts. But the impression of the whole country was large, airy, sunshiny, and it was clasped in the arms of the infinite, awful yet bountiful sea. The sea and the sky dwarfed the earth, made it of small account beside them, but who could complain of such an influence?

My children bathed in this sea every day, and gathered strength and knowledge from it. It was, as I have indicated, a dangerous coast to bathe on. The sweep of the tides varied with the sands that were cast up. There was sometimes a strong undertow, a reflux of the inflowing waters, quite sufficient to carry out into the great deep all those who could not swim well. But there was a fine, strong Cornish woman to take charge of the ladies and the little boys, and she, watching the ways of the wild monster, knew the when and the where and all about it.

Connie got out on the downs every day, and the weather continued superb. What rain there was fell at night, just enough for nature to wash her face with, and so look quite fresh in the morning. We contrived a dinner on the sands on the other side of the bay, for the Friday of this same week.

That morning rose gloriously. Harry and Charlie were turning the house upside down, to judge by their noise, long before I was in the humor to get up, for I had been reading late the night before. I never made much objection to mere noise, knowing that I could stop it the moment I pleased, and knowing too that so far from there being anything wrong in making a noise, the sea would make noise enough in our ears before we left Kilkhaven. But the moment that I heard a thread of whining or a burst of anger in the noise, I would interfere—treating these as things that must be dismissed at once.

So, far from seeking to put an end to the noise—I knew Connie did not mind it—I listened to it with a kind of reverence, as the outcome of a gladness which the God of joy had kindled in their hearts. Soon after, however, I heard certain dim growls of expostulation from Harry, and having ground for believing that the elder was tyrannizing the younger, I sent Charlie to find out where the tide would be between one and two o'clock, and Harry to run to the top of the hill, to find out the direction of the wind. Before I was dressed, Charlie was knocking at my door with the news that it would be half tide about one. Harry speedily followed with the discovery that the wind was northeast by southwest, which determined that the sun would shine all day.

As the dinner hour drew near, the servants went over, with Walter at their head, to choose a rock convenient for a table under the shelter of the rocks on the sands across the bay. And there, when Walter returned, we bore Connie, carrying her litter close by the edge of the retreating tide, which sometimes broke in a ripple of music under her, wetting our feet with an innocuous rush. The child's delight was extreme, as she thus skimmed the edge of the ocean, with the little ones gamboling about her, and her mamma and Wynnie walking quietly on the landward side, for she wished to have no one between her and the sea.

After scrambling with difficulty over some rocky ledges, and stopping, at Connie's request, to let her look into a deep pool in the sand, which somehow or other retained the water after the rest had retreated, we set her down near the mouth of a cave in the shadow of a rock. And there was our dinner nicely laid for us on a flat rock in front of the cave. The cliffs rose behind us, with curiously carved and variously angled strata. The sun in full splendor threw dark shadows on the brilliant yellow sand, more and more of which appeared as the bright blue water withdrew itself, now rippling over it as if to hide it all up again, now uncovering more as it withdrew for another rush. Before we had finished our dinner, the foremost wavelets appeared so far away over the plain of the sand, that it seemed a long walk to the edge that had been almost at our feet a little while ago. Between us and it lay a lovely desert of glittering sand.

When even Charlie and Harry had concluded that it was time to stop eating, we left the shadow and went out into the sun, carrying Connie and laying her down in the midst of "the ribbed sea sand," which was very ribby today. On a shawl a little way off from her lay the baby, crowing and kicking with the same jollity that had possessed the boys ever since the morning. I wandered about with Wynnie on the sands, picking up, amongst other things, strange creatures in thin shells ending in vegetablelike tufts. My wife sat on the end of Connie's litter, and Dora and the boys (a little way off) were trying how far the full force of three wooden spades could, in digging a hole in the sand, keep ahead of the water tumbling in. Behind, the servants were busy washing the plates in a pool and burying the fragments of the feast, for I made it a rule wherever we went that the fair face of nature was not to be defiled.

In our roaming, Wynnie and I approached a long low ridge of rock, rising toward the sea into which it ran. Crossing this, we came suddenly upon the painter whom Dora had called Niceboots, sitting with a small easel before him. We were right above him, and he had his back toward us, so that we saw at once what he was painting.

"O Papa!" cried Wynnie involuntarily, and the painter looked around.

"I beg your pardon," I said. "We came over from the other side and did not see you before. I hope we have not disturbed you much."

"Not in the least," he answered courteously, and rose as he spoke.

I saw that the subject on his easel suggested that of which Wynnie had been making a sketch, on the day when Connie first lay on the top of the opposite cliff. But he was not even looking in the same direction now.

"Do you mind having your work seen before it is finished?"

"Not in the least, if the spectators will remember that most processes have a seemingly chaotic stage," answered he.

I was struck with the mode and tone of the remark. "Here is no common man," I said to myself.

"I wish we could always keep that in mind with regard to human beings themselves, as well as their works," I said aloud.

The painter looked at me, and I looked at him.

"We speak each from the experience of his own profession, I presume," he said.

"But," I returned, glancing at his little picture in oils, "this must have long ago passed the chaotic stage."

"It is nearly as much finished as I care to make it," he returned. "I hardly count this work at all. I am chiefly amusing, or rather pleasing, my own fancy at present."

"Apparently," I remarked, "you had the conical rock outside the bay for your model, and now you are finishing it with your back turned toward it. How is that?"

"I will soon explain," he answered. "The moment I saw this rock it reminded me of Dante's Purgatory."

"Ah, you are a reader of Dante?" I asked. "In the original, I hope."

"Yes. A painter friend of mine, an Italian, set me going with that—and once going with Dante, nobody could well stop."

"That is quite my own feeling. Now, to return to your picture."

"Without departing at all from natural forms, I thought to make it suggest that Purgatorio to any who remembered the description given of the place. Of course, that thing there is a mere rock, yet it has certain mountain forms about it. I have put it at a much greater distance, you see, and have sought to make it look a solitary mountain in the midst of a great water. The circles of Purgatory are suggested without any artificial structure, and there are occasional hints at figures, which you cannot definitely detach from the rocks—which, you remember, were in one part full of sculptures. I have kept the mountain near enough to indicate the great expanse of wild flowers on the top, which the Lady of the Sacred Forest was so busy gathering. I want to indicate too the wind up there in the terrestrial paradise, ever and always blowing one way. You remember, Mr. Walton?

> An air of sweetness, changeless in its flow,
> With no more strength than in a soft wind lies,
> Smote peacefully against me on the brow.
> By which the leaves all trembling, levelwise,

Did every one bend thitherward to where
The high mount throws its shadow at sunrise.
(*Purgatorio,* Canto XXVIII)

"I thought you said you did not use translations?"

"I thought it possible that—Miss Walton—might not follow the Italian so easily."

"She won't lag far behind, I flatter myself," I returned. "Whose translation do you quote?"

He hesitated a moment, then said carelessly, "I have cobbled a few passages after that fashion myself."

"It has the merit of being near the original at least," I returned, "and that seems to me one of the chief merits a translation can possess."

"Then," the painter resumed, rather hastily, as if to avoid any further remark upon his verses, "you see those white things in the air above?" Here he turned to Wynnie. "Miss Walton will remember—I think she was making a drawing of the rock at the same time I was—how the seagulls or some such birds kept flitting about the top of it?"

"I remember quite well," answered Wynnie, with a look of appeal to me.

"Yes," I interposed, "my daughter spoke especially of the birds over the rock. She said the white lapping of the waves looked like the spirits trying to get loose, and the white birds like the foam that had broken its chains and risen in triumph into the air."

Here Mr. Niceboots (for as yet I did not know what else to call him) looked at Wynnie almost with a start. "How wonderfully that falls in with my fancy about the rock!" he said. "Purgatory indeed! With imprisoned souls lapping at its foot, and the free souls winging their way aloft in ether. Well, this world is a kind of purgatory anyhow, is it not, Mr. Walton?"

"Certainly it is. We are here tried as by fire, to see what our work is, whether wood, hay, stubble, or gold and silver and precious stones."

"You see," resumed the painter, "if anybody only glanced at my little picture, he would take those for seabirds. But if he looked into it and began to suspect me, he would find they were Dante and Beatrice on their way to the sphere of the moon."

"What is there in the world, that the spiritual man will not see merely the things of nature but the things of the spirit?"

"I am no theologian," said the painter, turning away somewhat coldly, I thought.

I could see that Wynnie was greatly interested in him. Perhaps she thought that here was some enlightenment of the riddle of the world for her, if she could but get at what he was thinking. She was used to my way of it; here might be something new.

"If I can be of any service to Miss Walton with her drawing, I shall be happy to do so," he said.

But his last gesture had made me a little distrustful of him, and I received his advances on this point with a coldness which I did not wish to make more marked than his own toward my last observation.

"You are very kind," I said, "but Miss Walton does not presume to be an artist."

I saw a slight shade pass over Wynnie's countenance. When I turned to Mr. Niceboots, a shade of a different sort was on his. Surely I had said something wrong to cast a gloom on two young faces. I made haste to make amends. "We are just going to have some coffee," I said. "Will you come and allow me to introduce you to Mrs. Walton?"

"With much pleasure," he answered. He was a finely built, black-bearded, sunburnt fellow, with clear gray eyes, a rather Roman nose, and good features generally. But there was an air of oppression, if not sadness, about him.

"But," I said, "how am I to effect an introduction, seeing I do not yet know your name?"

I had had to keep a sharp lookout on myself lest I should call him Mr. Niceboots. He smiled very graciously, and replied, "My name is Percivale—Charles Percivale."

"A descendant of Sir Percivale of King Arthur's Round Table?"

"I cannot count quite so far back as that," he answered, "I do come of a fighting race, but I cannot claim Sir Percivale."

We were now walking along the edge of the still retreating waves toward the group upon the sands, Mr. Percivale and I foremost, and Wynnie lingering behind.

"Oh, look, Papa!" she cried, from some little distance.

We turned and saw her gazing at something on the sand at her feet. Hastening back, we found it to be a little narrow line of foam bubbles, which the water had left behind on the sand, slowly breaking and passing out of sight. Why there should be foam bubbles there then, and not always, I do not know. But there they were—and such colors! Deep rose and grassy green and ultramarine blue and above all, one dark, yet brilliant and intensely burnished, metallic gold. All of them were of a solid-looking burnished color, like opaque body color laid on behind translucent crystal.

Those little ocean bubbles were well worth turning to see, and so I said to Wynnie. But, as we gazed, they went on vanishing, one by one. Every moment a heavenly glory of hue burst, and was gone.

We walked away again toward the rest of our party.

"Don't you think those bubbles more beautiful than any precious stones you ever saw, Papa?"

"Yes, my love, I think they are, except the opal. In the opal, God seems to have fixed the evanescent and made the vanishing eternal."

"And flowers are more beautiful than jewels?" she asked.

"Many—perhaps most flowers are," I granted.

"And did you ever see such curves and delicate textures anywhere else as in the clouds, Papa?"

"I think not. But what are you putting me to my catechism for in this way, my child?"

"O Papa, I could go on a long time with that catechism, but I will end with one question more, which you will perhaps find a little harder to answer. Only, I daresay you have had an answer for years, lest one of us should ask you someday."

"No, my love. I never got an answer ready for anything lest one of my children should ask me. But it is not surprising either that children should be puzzled about the things that have puzzled their father, or that by the time they are able to put the questions, he should have some sort of an answer to most of them. Go on with your catechism, Wynnie."

"It's not a funny question, Papa—it's a very serious one. I can't think why the unchanging God should have made all the most beautiful things wither and grow ugly, or burst and vanish, or die somehow and be no more. Mamma is not so beautiful as she once was, is she?"

"In one way no, but in another and better way much more so. But we will not talk about her kind of beauty just now: we will keep to the more material loveliness of which you have been speaking—though, in truth, no loveliness can be only material. I think it is because God loves beauty so much that He makes all beautiful things vanish quickly."

"I do not understand you, Papa."

"I will explain, if Mr. Percivale will excuse me."

"On the contrary, I am greatly interested, both in the question and the answer."

"Well, Wynnie, if the flowers were not perishable, we should cease to contemplate their beauty, for they should become commonplace and therefore dull. To compare great things with small, the flowers wither, the bubbles break, the clouds and sunsets pass, for the very same holy reason. Therefore, that we may always have them, and ever learn to love their beauty and yet more their truth, God sends the beneficent winter that we may think about what we have lost, and welcome them when they come again."

"I told you, Papa, you would have an answer ready, didn't I?"

"Yes, my child—but with this difference: I found the answer to meet my own necessities, not yours."

"And so you had it ready for me when I wanted it."

"Just so. That is the only certainty you have in regard to what you give away. No one who has not tasted it and found it good has a right to offer any spiritual dish to his neighbor."

Mr. Percivale took no part in our conversation. The moment I had presented him to Mrs. Walton and Connie, and he had paid his respects by a somewhat stately old-world obeisance, he merged the salutation into a farewell, and either forgetting my offer of coffee, or having changed his mind, he withdrew.

He was scarcely beyond hearing when Dora came up to me from her digging with an eager look on her sunny face.

"Hasn't he got nice boots, Papa?"

"Indeed, my dear, I am unable to support you in that assertion, for I never saw his boots."

"I did then," returned the child, "and I never saw such nice boots."

"I accept the statement willingly," I replied, and we heard no more of the boots, for his name was now substituted for his nickname. Nor did I see him again for some days, not till the next Sunday—though why he should come to church at all was something of a puzzle to me, especially when I knew him better.

SEVENTEEN
The Blacksmith

The next day I set out after breakfast to inquire about a blacksmith. It was not any blacksmith that would do. There was one in the village, but I found him an ordinary man who could shoe a horse and avoid the quick, but from whom any greater delicacy of touch was not to be expected. Inquiring further, I heard of a young smith in a hamlet a couple of miles distant, but still within the parish. In the afternoon I set out to find him. To my surprise he was a pale-faced, thoughtful-looking man, with a huge frame which appeared worn rather than naturally thin, and large eyes that looked at the anvil as if it were the horizon of the world. He had a horseshoe in his tongs when I entered. Notwithstanding the fire that glowed on the hearth, and the sparks that flew like a nimbus in eruption about his person, the place seemed very dark and cool to me, entering from the glorious blaze of the almost noontide sun. I could see the smith by the glow of his horseshoe, but all between me and the shoe was dark.

"Good morning," I said. "It is good to find a man by his work. I heard you half a mile off or so, and now I see you, but only by the glow of your work. It is a grand thing to work in fire."

He lifted his hammered hand to his forehead courteously, and as lightly as if the hammer had been the butt end of a whip. "I don't know if you would say the same if you had to work at it in weather like this," he answered.

"If I did not," I returned, "that would be the fault of my weakness."

"Well, you may be right," he rejoined with a sigh. Throwing the horseshoe on the ground, he let the hammer drop beside the anvil, and leaning against it, held his head for a moment between his hands and regarded the floor. "It does not much matter to me," he went on, "if I only get through my work and have done with it. No man shall say I shirked what I'd got to do. And then when it's over there won't be a word to say agen me, or—"

He did not finish the sentence.

"I hope you are not ill," I said.

He made no answer, but taking up his tongs caught with it from a beam one of a number of roughly finished horseshoes which hung there, and put it on the fire. While he turned it in the fire, and blew the bellows, I stood regarding him. "This man will do for my work," I said to myself, "though I should not wonder from the look of him if it was the last piece of work he ever did under the New Jerusalem."

The smith's words broke in on my meditations. "When I was a little boy," he said, "I once wanted to stay home from school. I had a little headache but nothing worth minding. I told my mother that I had a headache and she kept me, and I helped her at her spinning, which was what I liked best of anything. But in the afternoon the Methodist preacher came to see my mother. He asked what was the matter with me, and my mother answered that I had a bad head. He looked at me, and as my head was quite well by this time, I could not help feeling guilty. And he saw my look, I suppose, for I can't account for what he said any other way. He turned to me and said, solemnlike, 'Is your head bad enough to send you to the Lord Jesus to make you whole?' I could not speak a word, partly from bashfulness, I suppose, for I was but ten years old. So he followed it up, 'Then you ought to be at school.' I said nothing, because I couldn't. But never since then have I given in as long as I could stand. And I can stand now, and lift my hammer too," he said, as he took the horseshoe from the forge, laid it on the anvil, and again made a nimbus of coruscating iron.

"You are just the man I want," I said. "I've got a job for you, down to Kilkhaven."

"What is it, Sir? I should ha' thought the church was all spic and span by this time."

"I see you know who I am," I said.

"Of course I do," he answered. "I don't go to church myself, being brought up a Methodist, but anything that happens in the parish is known the next day all over it."

"You won't mind doing my job though you are a Methodist, will you?" I asked.

"Not I, Sir. If I've read right, it's the fault of the church that we don't pull alongside. You turned us out, Sir, we didn't go out of ourselves. At least, if all they say is true, which I can't be sure of you know, in this world."

"You are quite right there," I answered. "And in doing so, the church had the worst of it, as all that judge and punish their neighbors have. But you have been the worse for it too, all of which is to be laid to the charge of the church. For there is not one clergyman I know—mind, I say that I know—who would have made such a cruel speech to a boy as that the Methodist parson made to you."

"But it did me good, Sir."

"Are you sure of that? I am not. Are you sure, first of all, that it did not make you proud? Are you sure it has not made you work beyond your strength—I don't mean your strength of arm, for clearly that is all that could be wished—but of your chest, your lungs? Is there not some danger of your leaving someone who is dependent on you too soon unprovided for? Is there not some danger of your having worked as if God were a hard master? Of your having worked fiercely, indignantly, as if He wronged you by not caring for you, not understanding you?"

He returned me no answer, but hammered momentarily on his anvil. I thought it best to conclude the interview with business. "I have a delicate little job that wants nice handling, and I fancy you are just the man to do it to my mind," I said.

"What is it, Sir?" he asked, in a friendly enough manner.

"I would rather show it to you than talk about it," I returned.

"As you please, Sir. When do you want me?"

"The first hour you can come."

"Tomorrow morning?"

"If you feel inclined."

"For that matter, I'd rather go to bed."

"Come to me instead: it's light work."

"I will, Sir, at ten o'clock."

"If you please."

And so it was arranged.

EIGHTEEN
The Lifeboat

After breakfast and prayers the next day, I left for the church to await the arrival of the smith. In order to obtain entrance, I had to go to the cottage of the sexton. To reach the door, I crossed a hollow by a bridge built over what had once been the course of a rivulet from the heights above. Now it was a kind of little glen, grown with grass and wild flowers and ferns, and some of them rare and fine. The roof of the cottage came down to the road, but the ground behind fell suddenly away and left a bank against which the cottage was built.

Crossing a tiny garden by a flag-paved path, I entered the building and found myself in a waste-looking space that seemed to have forgotten the use for which it had been built. There was a sort of loft along one side of it, and it was heaped with indescribable lumber-looking stuff, with here and there a hint at possible machinery. (The place had been a mill for grinding corn, and its wheel had been driven by the stream which had run for ages in the hollow. But when the canal was built, the stream was turned aside to feed the canal, so that the mill fell into disuse and decay.) Crossing this floor, I entered another door, and turning sharp to the left, went down a few steps of a ladder stair, and after knocking my hat against a beam, emerged in a comfortable quaint little cottage kitchen.

The ceiling, which consisted only of the joists and the floorboards of the bedroom above, was so low that necessity, if not politeness, compelled me to take off my already bruised hat. Some of these joists were made further useful by supporting each a shelf, before which hung a little curtain of printed cotton, concealing the few stores and postponed eatables of the house, forming, in fact, both storeroom and larder of the family. On the walls hung several colored prints, and within a deep glazed frame the figure of a ship in full dress, carved in rather high relief in sycamore.

As I entered, Mrs. Coombes rose from a high-backed settle near the fire, and bade me good-morning with a curtsy.

"What a lovely day it is, Mrs. Coombes! It is so bright over the sea," I said, going on to the one little window which looked out on the great Atlantic, "that one almost expects a great merchant navy to come sailing into Kilkhaven, sunk to the water's edge with silks and ivory and spices and apes and peacocks, like the ships of Solomon that we read about."

"I know, Sir. When I was as young as you, I thought like that about the sea myself. Everything comes from the sea. For my boy Willie he du bring me home the beautifullest parrot and the talkingest you ever see, and a red shawl all worked over with flowers. He made that ship you see in the frame there, all with his own knife, out of a bit of wood that he got at the Marishes, as they calls it—a bit of an island somewheres in the great sea. And I thought like that till my third boy fell asleep in the wide water—for it du call it falling asleep, don't it, Sir?"

"The Bible certainly does," I answered.

"It's the Bible I be meaning, of course," she returned. "Well, after that I did begin to think about the sea as something that took away things and didn't bring them no more. And somehow or other she never looked so blue after that, and she gave me the shivers. But now she always looks to me like one o' the shining ones that come to fetch the pilgrims. You've heard tell of the *Pilgrim's Progress,* I daresay, among the poor people. They do say it was written by a tinker, though there be a power o' good things in it that I think the gentle folk would like if they knowed it."

"I do know the book—nearly as well as I know the Bible," I answered, "and the shining ones are very beautiful in it. I am glad you can think of the sea that way."

"It's looking in at the window all day as I go about the house," she answered, "and all night too when I'm asleep, and if I hadn't learned to think of it that way, it would have driven me mad, I do believe. I was forced to think that way about it, or not think at all. And that wouldn't be easy, with the sound of it in my ears the last thing at night and the first thing in the morning."

"The truth of things is indeed the only refuge from the look of things," I replied. "But I came for the key to the church, if you will trust me with it, for I have something to do there this morning. And the key of the tower as well, if you please."

With her old smile, ripened only by age, she reached the ponderous keys from the nail where they hung, and gave them into my hand. I left her in the shadow of her dwelling, and stepped forth into the sunlight.

The blacksmith was waiting for me at the church door. He was plainly far from well. There was a flush on his thin cheek, and his eyes had something of the far country in them—"the light that never was on the sea or shore." But his speech was cheerful, for he had been walking in the light of this world, and that had done something to make the light within him shine a little more freely.

"How do you find yourself today?" I asked.

"Quite well, Sir, thank you," he answered. "A day like this does a man good. But," he added, and his countenance fell, "the heart knoweth its own bitterness."

"It may know it too much," I returned, "just because it refuses to let a stranger meddle therein."

He made no reply. I turned the key in the great lock, and the iron-studded oak opened and let us into the solemn gloom.

It did not require many minutes to make the man understand what I wanted of him. "We must begin at the bells and work down," he said.

So we went up into the tower where, with the help of a candle, he made a good many measurements; found that carpenter's work was necessary; undertook the management of the whole; and in the course of an hour and a half went home to do what had to be done, assuring me that he had no doubt of bringing the job to a satisfactory conclusion.

"In a fortnight, I hope you will be able to play a tune to the parish, Sir," he added as he took his leave.

I resolved to know more of the man and find out his trouble, for I was certain there was a deep cause for his gloom.

As I left the churchyard, the sound of voices reached my ear. There, down below me, at the foot of the high bank on which I stood, lay a gorgeous shining thing upon the bosom of the canal, full of men and surrounded by men, women, and children delighting in its beauty. It was the lifeboat, but in its gorgeous colors red and white and green—it looked more like the galley that bore Cleopatra to Actium. Nor, floating so light on the top of the water, and broad in the beam, curved upward and ornamented, did it look at all formed to battle the elements. A pleasure boat it seemed, fit to be drawn by swans. Ten men sat on the thwarts, and one in the stern by the yet useless rudder, while men and boys drew the showy thing by a rope to the lockgates. The men in the boat wore blue jerseys, but you could see little of the color for the strange unshapely things that they wore above them, like armor cut out of a row of organ pipes. They were their cork jackets, for every man had to be made into a lifeboat himself.

They towed the shining thing through the upper gate of the lock, and slowly she sank from my sight, and for some moments was no more to be seen. All at once there she was beyond the lockhead, abroad and free, fleeting from the strokes of ten swift oars over the still waters of the bay toward the waves that roared farther out where the ground swell was broken by the rise of the sandy coast. There was no vessel in danger now; they were going out for exercise and show. It seemed all child's play for a time, but when they got among the broken waves, then it looked quite another thing. The motion of the waters laid hold upon her, and soon tossed her fearfully, now revealing the whole of her capacity on the near side of one of their slopes, now hiding her whole bulk in one of the hollows beyond. She, careless as a child in the troubles of the world, floated about with what appeared too much buoyancy for the promise of a safe return. Again and again she was driven from her course toward the low rocks on the other side of the bay, and again and again returned to disport herself like a sea animal, upon the backs of the wild bursting billows.

"Can she go no farther?" I asked of the captain of the coast guard, a man named Roxton, who was standing by my side.

"Not without some danger," he answered.

"What, then, must it be in a storm!"

"Then, of course," he returned, "they must take their chances. But there is no good in running risks for nothing. That swell is quite enough for exercise."

"But is it enough to accustom them to face the danger that will come?" I asked.

"With danger comes courage," said the old sailor.

While we spoke I saw on the pierhead the tall figure of Percivale looking earnestly at the boat. (He had been, I learned soon after, a crack oarsman at Oxford and had belonged to the University boat.)

In a little while the boat sped swiftly back, entered the lock, was lifted above the level of the storm-heaved ocean, and floated calmly up the smooth canal to the pretty little Tudor-fashioned house in which she lay.

All this time I had the keys in my hand, and now went back to the cottage to restore them to their place. When I entered, there was a young woman of sweet and interesting countenance talking to Mrs. Coombes. I had never yet seen the daughter who lived with her, and thought this was she.

"I've found your daughter at last then?" I said, approaching them.

"Not yet, Sir. She goes out to work, and her hands be pretty full at present. But this be almost my daughter," she added. "This is my next daughter, Mary Trehern, from the south. She's got a place nearby, to be near her mother that is to be, that's me."

Mary was hanging her head and blushing as the old woman spoke.

"I understand," I said. "And when are you going to get your new mother, Mary? Soon, I hope."

But she gave me no reply, only hung her head lower and blushed deeper.

Mrs. Coombes spoke for her. "She's shy, but if she was to speak her mind, she would ask you whether you wouldn't marry her and Willie when he comes home from his next voyage."

Mary's hands were trembling now, and she turned half away.

"With all my heart," I said.

The girl tried to turn toward me, but could not. I looked at her face a little more closely. Through all its tremor, there was a look of constancy that greatly pleased me. I tried to make her speak. "When do you expect Willie home?" I said.

She lifted a pair of soft brown eyes with one glance and a smile, and then sank them again.

"He'll be home in about a month," answered the mother. "She's a good ship he's aboard of, and makes good voyages."

"It is time then to think about the banns. Just come to me when you think it proper, and I will attend to it."

I thought I could hear a murmured "Thank you, Sir," from the girl, but I could not be certain. I shook hands with them, and went for a stroll on the other side of the bay.

NINETEEN
Mr. Percivale

I returned home and found my whole family about Connie's couch. With them was Mr. Percivale, who was showing her some sketches. Wynnie stood behind Connie, looking over her shoulder at the drawing in her hand.

My two daughters were talking away with the young man as if they had known him for years, and my wife was seated at the foot of the couch, apparently taking no exception to the suddenness of the intimacy.

"I think, though," Connie was saying, "it is only fair that Mr. Percivale should see *your* work, Wynnie."

"Then I will fetch my portfolio, if Mr. Percivale will promise to remember that I have no opinion of it. At the same time, if I could do what I wanted to do, I think I should not be ashamed of showing my drawings even to him." As Wynnie spoke, she turned and went back into the house to fetch some of her work. Now, had she been going on a message for me, she would have gone like the wind, but on this occasion she stepped along in a stately manner. And I could not help noting that Mr. Percivale's eyes also followed her. She was not long in returning, and came back with the same dignified motion.

"There is nothing really worth either showing or concealing," she said to Mr. Percivale, as she handed him the portfolio—to help himself, as it were. She then turned away, as if a little feeling of shyness had come over her, and began to look for something to do about Connie. I could see that, although she had hitherto been almost indifferent about the merit of her drawings, she had a newborn wish that they might not appear altogether contemptible in the eyes of Mr. Percivale. And Connie hastened to her sister's rescue.

"Give me your hand, Wynnie," said Connie, "and help me to move one inch farther on my side. I may move just that much on my side, mayn't I, Papa?"

"I think you had better not, my dear, if you can do without it," I answered, for the doctor's injunctions had been strong.

"Very well, Papa, but I feel as if it would do me good."

"Mr. Turner will be here next week, and you must try to stick to his rules till he comes to see you. Perhaps he will let you relax a little."

Connie smiled very sweetly and lay still, while Wynnie stood holding her hand.

Meantime, Mr. Percivale, having received the drawings, had walked away with them toward what they called the storm tower—a small building standing square to the points of the compass, with little windows from which the coast guard could see along the coast on both sides and far out to sea with their telescopes. This tower stood on the very edge of the cliff, but behind it was a steep descent, where he went round the tower and disappeared. He evidently wanted to make a leisurely examination of the drawings—somewhat formidable for Wynnie. It impressed me favorably that he was not inclined to pay a set of stupid and untrue compliments the instant the portfolio was opened, but, in order to speak what was real about them, would take the trouble to make himself acquainted with them.

I therefore strolled after him, seeing no harm in taking a peep at him while he was taking a peep at my daughter's mind. I went round the tower to the other side, and there saw him at a little distance below me, but farther out on a great rock that overhung the sea, connected with the cliff by a long narrow isthmus, a few yards lower than the cliff itself, and only just broad enough for a footpath along its top, and on one side going sheer down with a smooth hard rock face to the sands below. The other side was less steep, and had some grass on it. But the path was too narrow, and the precipice too steep for me. So I stood and saw him from the mainland—saw his head bent over the drawings; saw how slowly he turned from one to the other; saw how, after having gone over them once, he turned to the beginning and went over them again, even more slowly than before; saw how he turned back the third time. Then I went back to the group on the down, caught sight of Charlie and Harry turning heels over head down the slope, and found that my wife had gone home. Only Connie and Wynnie were left. The sun had disappeared under a cloud, the sea had turned a little slaty, and the wind had just the suspicion of an edge in it. And Wynnie's face looked a little cloudy too, I thought, and I feared that it was my fault.

"Run, Wynnie, and ask Mr. Percivale, with my compliments, to come and lunch with us," I said, more to let her see I was not displeased, however I might have looked, than for any other reason. She went, sedately as before.

Almost as soon as she was gone, I saw that I had put her in a difficulty. For I had discovered, very soon after coming to these parts, that her head was no more steady than mine upon high places. But if she could not cross that narrow and really dangerous isthmus, still less could she call across the chasm to a man she had seen but once. I therefore set off after her, leaving Connie lying in loneliness between the sea and the sky.

But when I got to the other side of the tower, instead of finding Wynnie standing hesitating on the brink of action, there she was on the rock beyond. Mr. Percivale had risen, and the next moment they turned to come back.

I stood trembling almost to see her cross the knife-back of that ledge. In the middle of the path—up to which point she had been walking with perfect steadiness and composure—she lifted her eyes, saw me, looked as if she saw a ghost, half lifted her arms, swayed as if she would fall, and indeed, was falling over the precipice, when Mr. Percivale caught her in his arms, almost too late for both of them. So nearly down was she already, that her weight bent him over the rocky side till it seemed as if he must yield, or his body snap. For he bent from the waist, and his feet kept hold on the ground. It was all over in a moment, and in another moment they were at my side—she with a wan, terrified smile, he in ruddy alarm. I was unable to speak and could only, with trembling steps, lead the way from the dreadful spot. Without a word they followed me.

Before we reached Connie, I recovered myself sufficiently to say, "Not a word to Connie," and they understood me. I told Wynnie to run to the house and send Walter to help me carry Connie home. Until Walter came, I talked to Mr. Percivale as if nothing had happened. He did not do as some young men, wishing to ingratiate themselves, would have done—he did not offer to help me carry Connie home. I saw that the offer rose in his mind, and that he repressed it. He understood that I must consider such a permission as a privilege not to be accorded to the acquaintance of a day, that I must know him better before I could again allow the weight of my child to rest upon his strength. But he responded to my invitation to lunch with us, and walked by my side as Walter and I bore the precious burden home.

During our meal, he made himself quite agreeable; he talked well on the topics of the day—not altogether as a man who had made up his mind, but as one who had thought about them and did not find it easy to come to a conclusion. His behavior was entirely that of a gentleman, and his education was good. But what I did not like was, that as often as the conversation made a bend in the direction of religious matters, he was sure to bend it away in some other direction. This, however, might have various reasons to account for it, and I would wait.

After lunch, as we rose from the table, he took Wynnie's portfolio from the side table where he had laid it, and with no more than a bow and thanks returned it to her. I thought she looked a little disappointed, though she said as lightly as she could, "I am afraid you have not found anything worthy of criticism in my poor attempts, Mr. Percivale."

"On the contrary, I shall be most happy to tell you what I think of them."

"I shall be greatly obliged to you," she said, "for I have had no help since I left school, except Mr. Ruskin's book called *Modern Painters*. Do you know the author, Mr. Percivale?"

"I wish I did. He has given me much help. I have such a respect for him that I always feel as if he must be right, whether he seems to me to be right or not. And if he is severe, it is with the severity of love that will speak only the truth."

This last speech fell on my ear like the tone of a church bell. *I've been waiting for that, my friend,* I thought, but I said nothing to interrupt.

He opened the portfolio on the side table, and placed a chair in front of it for my daughter. Then, seating himself by her side, but without the least approach to familiarity, he began to talk to her at length about her drawings, generally praising the feeling, but finding fault with the want of nicety in the execution.

"But," said my daughter, "it seems to me that if you get the feeling right, that is the main thing."

"So much the main thing," returned Mr. Percivale, "that any imperfection or coarseness or untruth which interferes with it becomes of the greatest consequence."

"But can it really interfere with the feeling?"

"Perhaps not with most people, simply because most people observe so badly that their recollections of nature are all blurred and blotted and indistinct, and therefore the imperfections do not affect them. But with the more cultivated, it is otherwise. It is for them you ought to work, for you do not thereby lose the others. Besides, the feeling is always intensified by the finish, for that belongs to the feeling too, and must have some influence even where it is not noted."

"But is it not a hopeless thing to attempt the finish of nature?"

"Not at all—to the degree, that is, in which you can represent anything else of nature. But in this drawing now you have nothing to hint at or recall the feeling of the exquisiteness of nature's finish. Why should you not at least have drawn a true horizon line there? Has the absolute truth of the meeting of sea and sky nothing to do with the feeling which such a landscape produces? I should have thought you would have learned that, if anything, from Mr. Ruskin."

Mr. Percivale spoke earnestly. Wynnie, either from disappointment or despair, probably from a mixture of both, apparently felt as if he was scolding her, and got cross. This was anything but dignified, especially with a stranger, and one who was doing his best to help her. Her face was flushed, and tears came in her eyes, and she rose, saying with a little choke in her voice, "I see it's no use in trying. I won't intrude anymore into things I am incapable of. I am much obliged to you, Mr. Percivale, for showing me how presumptuous I have been."

The painter rose as she rose, looking greatly concerned, but he did not attempt to answer her. Indeed, she gave him no time. He could only spring after her to open the door for her. A more than respectable bow as she left the room was his only adieu.

But when he turned his face again toward me, it expressed consternation. "I fear," he said, "I have been rude to Miss Walton, but nothing was farther—"

"I heard all you were saying, and you were not rude in the least. On the contrary, I consider you very kind to take the trouble with her you did. Allow me to make the apology for my daughter. She will recover from the disappointment of finding unexpected obstacles in the way of her favorite pursuit. She is only too ready to lose heart, and she paid too little attention to your approbation and too much to your criticism. She lost her temper, but more with herself and her poor attempts, I assure you, than with your remarks."

"But I must have been to blame if I caused any such feeling with regard to those drawings, for I assure you they contain great promise."

"I am glad you think so. That I should myself be of the same opinion can be of no consequence."

"Miss Walton at least sees what ought to be represented. All she needs is greater severity in the quality of representation. And that would have grown without any remarks from onlookers, but a friendly criticism opens the eyes a little sooner than they would have opened themselves. And time," he added, "is half the battle in this world. It is over so soon."

"No sooner than it ought to be," I rejoined.

"So it may appear to you," he returned. "Here I am nearly thirty, and have made no mark on the world yet."

"I don't know that that is of so much consequence," I said. "I have never hoped for more than to rub out a few of the marks already made."

"Perhaps you are right," he returned. "Every man has something he can do, and more, I suppose, that he can't do. But I have no right to turn a visit into a visitation. Will you please tell Miss Walton that I am very sorry I presumed on the privileges of a drawing master, and gave her pain. It was so far from my intention that it will be a lesson to me for the future."

With these words he took his leave, and I could not help being greatly pleased. He was clearly anything but a common man.

TWENTY
The Shadow of Death

When Wynnie appeared at dinner she looked ashamed of herself, and her face betrayed that she had been crying. But I said nothing, for I had confidence that all she needed was time to come to herself, that the voice that speaks louder than any thunder might make its stillness heard. And when I came home from my walk the next morning, I found Mr. Percivale once more in the group about Connie, and evidently on the best possible terms with all. The same afternoon Wynnie went out sketching with Dora. I had no doubt that she had made some sort of apology to Mr. Percivale, but I did not make the slightest attempt to discover what had passed between them. For though it is of all things desirable that children should be quite open with their parents, I was most anxious to lay upon them no burden of obligation. Therefore I trusted my child. And when I saw that she looked at me a little shyly when we next met, I only sought to show her the more tenderness and confidence, telling her all about my plans with the bells and my talks with the smith and Mrs. Coombes. She listened with interest, asking questions, and making remarks, but I still felt that there was the thread of a little uneasiness through the web of our talk. Yet it was for Wynnie to bring it out, not me.

And she did not leave it long. For as she bade me good-night in my study, she said suddenly, yet with hesitating openness, "Papa, I told Mr. Percivale that I was sorry I had behaved so badly about the drawings."

"You did right, my child," I replied. "And what did Mr. Percivale say?"

"He took the blame all on himself, Papa."

"Like a gentleman."

"But I could not leave it so, you know, Papa, because that was not the truth."

"Well?"

"I told him that I had lost my temper from disappointment—that I had thought I did not care for my drawings because I was so far from satisfied with them. But when he made me feel that they were worth nothing, then

I found from the vexation I felt that I had cared for them. But I think, Papa, I was more ashamed of having shown them, and vexed with myself, than cross with him. I was very silly."

"Well, and what did he say?"

"He began to praise them then. But you know I could not take much of that, for what could he do?"

"You might give him credit for a little honesty, at least."

"Yes, but things may be true in a way, you know, and not mean much."

"He seems to have succeeded in reconciling you to the prosecution of your efforts, however, for I saw you go out with your sketching apparatus this afternoon."

"Yes," she answered, shyly. "He was so kind, that somehow I got heart to try again. He's very nice, isn't he?"

My answer was not quite ready.

"Don't you like him, Papa?"

"Well—I like him—yes. But we must not be in haste with our judgments, you know. I have had very little opportunity of seeing into him. There is much in him that I like, but—"

"But what, please, Papa?"

"I can speak my mind to you, my child; he has a certain shyness of approaching the subject of religion. I have my fears lest he should belong to some school of a fragmentary philosophy which acknowledges no source of truth but the testimony of the senses and the deductions made therefrom by the intellect."

"But is not that a hasty conclusion, Papa?"

"That is a hasty question, my dear. I have come to no conclusion. I was only speaking confidentially about my fears."

"Perhaps, Papa, it's only that he's not sure enough and is afraid of appearing to profess more than he believes. I'm sure, if that's it, I have the greatest sympathy with him."

I looked at her, and saw the tears gathering fast in her eyes.

"Pray to God on the chance of His hearing you, my darling, and go to sleep," I said. "I will not think hardly of you because you cannot be so sure as I am. How could you be? You have not had my experience. Perhaps you are right about Mr. Percivale too. But it would be an awkward thing to get intimate with him, you know, and then find out that we did not like him after all. You couldn't like a man much, could you, who did not believe in anything greater than himself, anything marvelous, grand, beyond our understanding, who thought that he had come out of the dirt and was going back to the dirt?"

"I could, Papa, if he tried to do his duty notwithstanding, for I am sure *I* couldn't. I should cry myself to death."

"You are right, my child. I should honor him too. But I should be very sorry for him, for he would be so disappointed in himself." I do not know whether this was the best answer to make, but I had little time to think.

"But you don't know that he's like that."

"I do not, my dear. And more, I will not associate the idea with him till I know for certain. We will leave it to ignorant old people who lay claim to an instinct for theology to jump at conclusions, and reserve ours till we have sufficient facts from which to draw them. Now go to bed, my child."

"Good night then, dear Papa," she said, and left me with a kiss.

I was not altogether comfortable. I had tried to be fair to the young man both in word and thought, but I could not relish the idea of my daughter falling in love with him—which looked likely enough—before I knew more about him, and found that more hope-giving. There was but one rational thing left to do, and that was to cast my care on Him that careth for us, on the Father who loved my child more than I even could love her, and loved the young man too, and regarded my anxiety, and would take its cause upon Himself. After I had lifted up my heart to Him and was at ease, I read a canto of Dante's *Paradisio* and then went to bed.

As I went out for my walk the next morning, I caught sight of the sexton busily trimming some of the newer graves in the churchyard. I turned in through the nearer gate.

"Good morning, Coombes," I said.

He turned up a wizened, humorous, old face, the very type of a gravedigger; and with one hand leaning on the edge of the green mound where he had been cropping the too long and too thin grass, he touched his cap with the other and bade me a cheerful good-morning in return.

"You're making things tidy," I said.

"It take time to make them all comfortable, you see, Sir," he returned, taking up his shears again, and clipping away at the top and sides of the mound.

"You mean the dead, Coombes?"

"Yes, Sir, to be sure."

"You don't think it makes much difference to their comfort, do you, whether the grass is one length or another upon their graves?"

"Well, no, I don't suppose it makes much difference to them. But it look more comfortable, you know. And I like things to look comfortable. Don't you, Sir?"

"To be sure I do, Coombes. And you are quite right. The resting-place of the body, although the person it belonged to be far away, should be respected."

"That's what I think, though I don't get no credit for it. I do my best to make the poor things comfortable."

He seemed unable to rid his mind of the idea that the comfort of the departed was dependent upon his ministrations.

"The trouble I have with them sometimes! There's now this same one as lies here, old Jonathan Giles. He have the gout so bad! And just as I come within a couple o' inches o' the right depth, out come the edge of a great stone in the near corner at the foot of the bed. Thinks I, he'll never lie comfortable with that under his gouty toe. But the trouble I had to get out that stone! I du assure you, Sir, it took me nigh half the day. But this be one of the nicest places to lie in, all up and down the coast—a nice gravelly soil, dry, and warm, and comfortable. Them poor things as comes out of the sea must quite enjoy the change."

It was a grotesque and curious way for the humanity that was in him to find expression, but I did not like to let him go on thus. It was so much opposed to all that I believed and felt about the change from this world to the next!

"But, Coombes," I said, "why will you go on talking as if it made an atom of difference to the dead bodies where they were buried? They care no more about it than your old coat would care where it was thrown after you had done with it."

He turned and regarded his coat where it hung beside him on the headstone, shaking his head with a smile that seemed to doubt whether the said old coat would be altogether so indifferent to such treatment. Then he began to approach me from another angle—and I confess he had the better of me before I was aware of what he was about.

"The church of Boscastle stands high on the cliff. You've been to Boscastle, Sir?"

"Not yet, but I hope to go before the summer is over."

"Ah, you should see Boscastle, Sir. That's where I was born. And when I was a boy that church was haunted. It's a damp place, and the wind in it awful. I du believe it stand higher than any church in the country, and have got more wind in it of a stormy night than any church whatsomever. Well, they said it was haunted, and every now and then there was a knocking heard down below. And this always took place of a stormy night, as if there was some poor thing down in the low wouts," (for so he pronounced *vaults*) "and he wasn't comfortable and wanted to get out. Well, one fearful night the sexton went and took the blacksmith and a ship's carpenter, and they go together and they open one of the old family wouts that belongs to the Penhaligans, and they go down with a light. Now the wind was a-blowing all as usual, only worse than common. And there to be sure what do they see but the wout half full of seawater, and nows and thens a great spout coming in through a hole in the rock, for it was high water and a wind off the sea, as I tell you. And there was a coffin afloat on the water, and every time the spout come through, it set it knocking agen the side o' the wout, and that was the ghost."

"What a horrible idea!" I said, with a half-shudder at the unrest of the dead.

The old man uttered a queer long-drawn sound, neither a chuckle, a crow, nor a laugh, but a mixture of all three, and said, "I thought you would like to be comfortable then as well as other people, Sir."

I could not help laughing to see how the cunning old fellow had caught me. I have not yet been able to find out how much truth was in his story.

From the twinkle of his eye I cannot help suspecting that if he did not invent the tale, he embellished it. Neither could I help thinking with pleasure, as I turned away, how the merry little old man would enjoy telling his companions how he had posed the old parson. Very welcome was he to his laugh, for my part.

I gladly left the churchyard, with its sunshine above and its darkness below. I had to look up to the glittering vanes on the four pinnacles of the church tower, dwelling aloft in the clean sunny air, to get the feeling of the dark vault and the floating coffin and the knocking in the windy church out of my brain. But the thing that did free me was the reflection with what supreme disregard the disincarcerated spirit would look upon any possible vicissitudes of its abandoned vault. For the body of man's revelation becomes a vault, a prison, from which it must be freedom to escape at length. The house we like best would be a prison of awful sort if the doors and windows were all built up. Man's abode, as age begins to draw nigh, fares thus. Age is the mason that builds up the doors and the windows, and death is the angel that breaks the prison house and lets the captives free. Thus I got something out of the sexton's horrible story.

But before the week was over, death came near indeed. I had retired to my study after lunch and was dozing in my chair, for the day was hot, when Charlie rushed into the room with the cry, "Papa, Papa, there's a man drowning!"

I hurried down to the drawing room which looked out over the bay. I could see nothing but people running about on the edge of the quiet waves. No sign of human being was on the water, but one boat was coming out from the lock of the canal, and Roxton of the coast guard was running down from the tower on the cliff with ropes in his hand. He would not stop the boat even for the moment it would need to take him on board, but threw them in and urged them to haste.

I stood at the window and watched. Every now and then I fancied I saw something white heaved up on the swell of a wave, and as often was satisfied that I had but fancied it. The boat seemed to be floating about lazily, if not idly. The eagerness to help made it appear as if nothing was going on. Could it, after all, have been a false alarm? I watched, and still the boat kept moving from place to place, so far out that I could see nothing distinctly of the motions of its crew. At length a long white thing rose from the water slowly, and was drawn into the boat which was rowed swiftly to the shore. There was but one place fit to land upon—a little patch of sand under the window at which I stood, and immediately under our garden wall. There stood Roxton, earnest and sad, waiting to use—though without much immediate hope—every appliance so well known to him.

I will not linger over the sad details of the vain endeavor. The honored head of a family had departed, and left a good name behind him. But even in the midst of my poor attentions to the quiet, speechless pale-faced wife who sat at the head of the corpse, I could not help feeling anxious about the effect on Connie, for it was impossible to keep the matter concealed from her. The undoubted concern on the faces of the two boys was enough to reveal that something serious and painful had occurred, while my wife and Wynnie, and indeed the whole household, were busy in attending to every remotest suggestion of aid that reached them from the little crowd gathered about the body. The body was borne away, and I led the poor lady to her lodging, and remained there with her till she lay on the sofa and slept.

I left her with her son and her daughter, and returned to my own family. Had they only heard of the occurrence, it would have had little effect, but death had appeared to them. Everyone but Connie had seen the dead lying there, and before the day was over, I wished she had too. For I found from what she said at intervals, and from the shudder that now and then passed through her, that her imagination was at work, showing the horrors that belong to death, without the enfolding peace that accompanies the sight of the dead.

And now I became more grateful than ever for the gift of Theodora, for I felt no anxiety about Connie so long as she was with her. The presence even of her mother could not relieve her, for Ethelwyn and Wynnie were both clouded with the same awe, and its reflex in Connie was distorted by her fancy. But the sweet ignorance of the baby healed, for she appeared in her sweet merry ways—to the mood in which they all were—like a little sunny window in a cathedral crypt, telling of a whole universe of sunshine and motion beyond those oppressed pillars and low-groined arches.

But my wife suffered nearly as much as Connie. As long as she was going about the house or attending to the wants of her family, she was free. But no sooner did she lay her head on the pillow than in rushed the cry of the sea—fierce, unkind, craving like a wild beast. Again and again she spoke of it to me, for it came to her mingled with the voice of the tempter, saying, "Cruel chance," over and over again. For although the two words contradict each other when put together thus, each in its turn would assert itself.

"It is all fancy, my dear," I said to her. "There is nothing more terrible in this than in any other death. On the contrary, I can hardly imagine a less fearful one. A big wave falls on the man's head and stuns him, and without further suffering he floats gently out on the sea of the unknown."

But though she always seemed satisfied after any conversation of the sort, yet every night she would call out once and again, "Oh, that sea out there!" I was very glad indeed when Turner, who had arranged to spend a short holiday with us, arrived.

He was concerned at the news I gave him and counseled an immediate change, that time might, in the absence of surrounding associations, obliterate something of the impression that had been made. So we resolved to remove our household, for a short time, to some place not too far off to permit of my attending to my duties at Kilkhaven, but out of the sight and sound of the sea. It was Thursday when Mr. Turner arrived, and he spent the next two days in finding a suitable spot for us.

On the Saturday, the blacksmith was busy in the church tower, and I went to see how he was getting on.

"You had a sad business here last week," he said, after we had done talking about the repairs.

"A very sad business, indeed."

"It was a warning to us all."

"We may take it so," I returned. "But it seems to me that we are too ready to think of such remarkable things only by themselves, instead of being roused by them to regard everything, common and uncommon, as ordered by the same care and wisdom."

"One of our local preachers made a grand use of it."

I made no reply, so he resumed. "They tell me you took no notice of it last Sunday."

"I made no immediate allusion to it, certainly, but I preached under the influence of it. And I thought it better that those who could reflect on the matter should be thus led to think for themselves, than that they should be subjected to the reception of my thoughts and feelings about it. For in the main, it is life and not death that we have to preach."

"I don't quite understand you, Sir. But then you don't care much for preaching in your churches."

"Anyone who can preach what you call rousing sermons is considered a grand preacher amongst you Methodists, and there is a great danger of him being led thereby to talk more nonsense than sense. And then when the excitement goes off, there is no seed left in the soil to grow in peace, and they are always craving after more excitement."

"Well, there is the preacher to rouse them up again."

"And so they continue like children—the good ones, I mean—and have hardly a chance of making a calm, deliberate choice of that which is good. And those who have been only excited, and nothing more, are hardened and seared by the recurrence of such feeling as is neither aroused by truth nor followed by action."

"You'd daren't talk like that if you knew the kind of people in this country that the Methodists, as you call them, have got a hold of. They tell me it was like hell itself down in those mines before Wesley come among them."

"I should be a fool or a bigot to doubt that the Wesleyans have done incalculable good in the country. And that not alone to the people who never went to church. The whole Church of England is under obligation to Methodism such as no words can overstate."

"I wonder you can say such things against them then."

"I confess I do not know much about your clergy, for I have not had the opportunity. But I do know this, that some of the best and most liberal people I have ever known have belonged to your community."

"They do gather a deal of money for good purposes."

"Yes. But that is not what I meant by 'liberal.' It is far easier to give money than to be generous in judgment. I meant, by 'liberal,' able to see the good and true in people that differ from you, glad to be roused to the reception of truth in God's name from whatever quarter it may come, and not readily finding offense. But I see that I ought to be more careful, for I have made you misunderstand me."

"I beg your pardon, Sir. I was hasty. But I do think I am more ready to lose my temper since—"

Here he stopped. A fit of coughing came on, and was followed by what could only be the result of a rupture in the lungs. I insisted on his dropping his work and coming home with me, where I made him rest the remainder of the day and all Sunday, sending word to his mother that I could not let him go home.

When we left on the Monday morning, we took him with us in the carriage hired for the journey, and set him down at his mother's, apparently no worse than usual.

TWENTY-ONE
The Keeve

Leaving the younger members of the family at home with the servants, we set out for a farmhouse, some twenty miles off, which Turner had discovered for us. Through deep lanes with many cottages and here and there a very ugly little chapel, over steep hills (up which Turner and Wynnie and I walked), and along sterile moors we drove. We stopped often at roadside inns, to raise Connie and let her look about upon the extended prospect. On the way Turner warned us that we were not to expect a beautiful country, although the place was within reach of much that was remarkable. Therefore we were not surprised when we drew up at the door of a bare-looking house, with scarcely a tree in sight, and a stretch of undulating fields on every side.

"A dreary place in winter, Turner," I said. We had seen Connie comfortably deposited in the nice white-curtained parlor, smelling of dried roses even in the height of the fresh ones, and had strolled out while our tea-dinner was being got ready for us.

"No doubt of it, but just the place I wanted for Miss Connie," he replied. "We are high above the sea, and the air is very bracing and not too cold now. A month later I should not on any account have brought her here."

We all went to bed early and, for the first time for many nights, my wife said nothing about the crying of the sea. The following day Turner and I set out to explore the neighborhood. The rest remained quietly at home.

It was, as I have said, a high bare country. The fields lay side by side, parted from each other chiefly—as so often in Scotland—by walls of thin stone plates laid on their edges. In the middle of the fields came here and there patches of yet unreclaimed moorland.

Now in a region like this, beauty must be looked for below the surface. There is a probability of finding hollows of repose, sunken spots of loveliness hidden away—existent because they are below the surface, and not laid bare to the sweep of the cold winds that roam above.

When Turner and I set out that morning to explore, I expected to light upon some mine or other in which nature had hidden away rare jewels, but I was not prepared to find such as we did find. With our hearts full of a glad secret we returned home, but we said nothing about it, in order that Ethelwyn and Wynnie might enjoy the discovery even as we had.

There was another grand fact with regard to the neighborhood about which we judged it better to be silent for a few days. We were considerably nearer the ocean than my wife and daughters supposed, for we had made a great round in order to arrive from the landside. We were, however, out of the sound of its waves, which broke along the shore at the foot of tremendous cliffs. What cliffs they were, they would soon find.

"Now, Wynnie!" I said, after prayers the next morning, "you must come out for a walk as soon as ever you can get your bonnet on."

"But we can't leave Connie, Papa," objected Wynnie.

"Oh, yes, you can, quite well. There's Nursie to look after her. What do you say, Connie?"

"I am entirely independent of help from my family," returned Connie, grandiloquently. "I am a woman of independent means," she added. "If you say another word, I will rise and leave the room."

Then, her mood changing, she added, as if to suppress the tears gathering in her eyes, "I am the queen of luxury and self-will, and I won't have anybody come near me till dinnertime. I mean to enjoy myself."

So the matter was settled and we went out for our walk. Ethelwyn was not such a good walker as she had been; but even if she retained the strength of her youth, we should not have got on much the better for it, so often did she and Wynnie stop to grub ferns out of the chinks and roots of the stone walls.

At length, partly by the inducement I held out to them of a much greater variety of ferns where we were bound, I succeeded in getting them over two miles in little more than two hours. After passing from the lanes into the fields, we reached a very steep large slope with a delightful southern exposure, and covered with the sweetest down-grasses. It was just the place to lie in, as on the edge of the earth, and look abroad upon the universe of air and floating worlds.

"Let us have a rest here, Ethelwyn," I said. "I am sure this is much more delightful than uprooting ferns."

"What's that in the grass?" cried Wynnie.

I looked where she had indicated, and saw a slowworm, or blindworm, basking in the sun. I rose and went toward it.

"Here's your stick," said Turner.

"What for?" I asked. "Why should I kill it? It is perfectly harmless and, to my mind, beautiful."

I took it in my hands and brought it to my wife. She gave an involuntary shudder as it came near her.

"I assure you it is harmless," I said, "though it has a forked tongue." And I opened its mouth as I spoke. "I do not think the serpent form is essentially ugly."

"It makes me feel ugly," said Wynnie.

"I allow I do not quite understand the mystery of it," I said. "But you never saw lovelier ornamentation than these silvery scales, with all the neatness of what you ladies call a set pattern. And you never saw lovelier curves than this little patient creature makes with its long thin body."

"I wonder how it can look after its tail, it is so far off," said Wynnie.

"It does though, better than you ladies look after your long dresses. I wonder whether it is descended from creatures that once had feet, but did not make a good use of them. Perhaps they had wings, even, and would not use them at all, and so lost them. Its ancestors may have had poison fangs, but it is innocent enough. But it is a terrible thing to be all feet, is it not? There is an awful significance in the condemnation of the serpent—'On thy belly shalt thou go, and eat dust.' But it is better to talk of beautiful things. Let us go on."

They did not seem willing to rise. But the glen drew me, and I rose first, and on we went.

We turned down the valley in the direction of the sea. It was but a narrow cleft, and narrowed much toward a deeper cleft in which we now saw the tops of trees, and from which we heard the rush of water. Nor had we gone far in this direction before we came upon a gate in a stone wall, which led into what seemed a neglected garden. We entered and found a path turning and winding among small trees and luxuriant ferns. There were great stones, and fragments of ruins down toward the bottom of the chasm. The noise of falling water increased as we went on, and at length, after some scrambling and several sharp turns, we found ourselves with a nearly precipitous wall on each side, clothed with shrubs and ivy and creeping things of the vegetable world. Up this cleft there was no advance. The head of it was a precipice down which shot the stream from the vale above, pouring out of a deep slit it had itself cut in the rock as with a knife. Halfway down, it tumbled into a great basin of hollowed stone, and flowing from a chasm in its side (which left part of the lip of the basin standing like the arch of a vanished bridge) it fell into a black pool below, whence it crept as if stunned or weary down the gentle decline of the ravine. It was a little gem of nature, complete and perfect in effect, and the ladies were full of pleasure. Wynnie, forgetting her usual reserve, broke out in exclamations of delight.

We stood for a while regarding the ceaseless pour of the water down the precipice, full of force and purpose, here falling in great curls of green and gray, there rejoicing the next moment to find itself brought up boiling and bubbling in the basin to issue in the gathered hope of experience. Then we turned down the stream a little way, crossed it by a plank, and stood again to regard it from the opposite side. The whole affair was small—not more than about a hundred and fifty feet in height—but full of variety. I was contemplating it fixedly, when a little stifled cry from Wynnie made me start and look round. Her face was flushed, yet she was trying to look unconcerned.

"I thought we were quite alone, Papa," she said, "but I see a gentleman sketching."

I looked whither she indicated. A little way down, the bed of the ravine widened considerably, and was no doubt filled with water in rainy weather. Now it was swampy, full of reeds and willow bushes. But on the opposite side of the stream, with a little canal going all around it, lay a great flat rectangular stone, not more than a foot above the level of the water. On a campstool in the center of this stone sat a gentleman sketching. Wynnie recognized him at once. And I was annoyed, and indeed, angry, to think that Mr. Percivale had followed us here. But while I regarded him, he looked up, rose very quietly and, with his pencil in his hand, came toward us. With no nearer approach to familiarity than a bow, and no expression of either much pleasure or any surprise, he said, "I have seen your party for some time, Mr. Walton—since you crossed the stream—but I would not break your enjoyment with the surprise of my presence."

I answered with a bow, for I could not say with truth that I was glad to see him. He resumed, doubtless penetrating my suspicion, "I have been here almost a week. I certainly had no expectation of the pleasure of seeing you."

This he said lightly, though no doubt with the object of clearing himself. And I was, if not reassured, yet disarmed, by his statement, for I could not believe, from what I knew of him, that he would be guilty of such a white lie as many a gentleman would have thought justifiable on the occasion. Still, I suppose he found me a little stiff, for presently he said, "If you will excuse me, I will return to my work."

Then I felt as if I must say something, for I had shown him no courtesy during the interview. "It must be a great pleasure to carry away such talismans with you—capable of bringing the place back to your mental vision at any moment."

"To tell the truth," he answered, "I am a little ashamed of being found sketching here. Such bits of scenery are not my favorite studies. But it is a change."

"It is very beautiful here," I said.

"It is very pretty," he answered, "very lovely, if you will—not very beautiful, I think. I would keep that word for things of larger regard. Beauty requires width and here is none."

"Why, then, do you sketch such a place?"

"A very fair question," he returned, with a smile. "Just because it is soothing from the very absence of beauty. I would rather, however, if I were only following my taste, take the barest bit of the moor above, with a streak of the cold sky over it. That gives room."

"You would like to put a skylark in it, wouldn't you?"

"That I would, if I knew how. I see you know what I mean. But the mere romantic I never had much taste for, and I am not working now. I am only playing."

"With a view to working better afterward, I have no doubt."

"You are right there, I hope," was his quiet reply, as he turned and walked back to the island.

He had not made a step toward joining us, and had only taken his hat off to the ladies. He was gaining ground upon me rapidly.

"Have you quarreled with our new friend, Harry?" said my wife, as I came up to her. She was sitting on a stone. Turner and Wynnie were farther off toward the foot of the fall.

"Not in the least," I answered, slightly outraged by the question. "He is only gone to his work, which is a duty belonging both to the first and second tables of the Law."

"I hope you have asked him to come home to our early dinner, then," she rejoined.

"I have not. That remains for you to do. Come, I will take you to him."

Ethelwyn rose at once, put her hand in mine, and with a little help, soon reached the table rock. Percivale rose, and when she came near enough, held out his hand, and she was beside him in a moment. After the usual greetings, which on her part, although very quiet—like every motion and word of hers—were yet cordial and kind, she said, "When you get back to London, Mr. Percivale, might some friends of mine call at your studio to see your paintings?"

"With all my heart," answered Percivale. "I must warn you, however, that I have not much they will care to see. They will perhaps go away less happy than they entered. Not many people care to see my pictures twice."

"I would not send you anyone I thought unworthy of the honor," answered my wife.

Percivale bowed one of his stately, old-world bows, which I greatly liked.

"Any friend of yours—that is guarantee sufficient," he answered.

There was this peculiarity about any compliment Percivale paid, that you had not a doubt of its being genuine.

"Will you come and take an early dinner with us?" said my wife. "My invalid daughter will be very pleased to see you."

"I will with pleasure," he answered, but in a tone of some hesitation, as he glanced from Ethelwyn to me.

"My wife speaks for us all," I said. "It will give us all pleasure."

"We're not quite ready to go yet," said my wife, loath to leave the lovely spot. "What a curious flat stone this is!" she added.

"It is," said Percivale. "The man to whom the place belongs, a worthy yeoman of the old school, says that this wider part of the channel must have been the fishpond, and that the portly monks stood on this stone and fished in the pond."

"There was a monastery here?" I asked.

"Certainly. The ruins of the chapel are on the top, just above the fall—rather a fearful place to look down from. They say it had a silver bell in the days of its glory, which now lies in a deep hole under the basin, halfway between the top and the bottom of the fall. But the old man says that nothing will make him look, or let anyone else lift the huge stone. For he is much better pleased to believe that it may be there, than he would be to know it was not there. Certainly, if it were found, it would not be left there long."

As he spoke, he had turned toward his easel and hastily bundled up his things. He now led our party up to the chapel ruins, and thence down a few yards to the edge of the chasm, where the water fell headlong. I turned away with that fear of high places which is one of my many weaknesses, and when I turned again toward the spot, there was Wynnie on the very edge, looking over into the flash and tumult of the water below, but with a nervous grasp of the hand of Percivale, who stood a little farther back.

In going home, the painter led us by an easier way out of the valley, left his little easel and other things at a cottage, and then walked on in front between my wife and daughter, while Turner and I followed. He seemed quite at his ease with them, and plenty of talk and laughter rose on the way. I, however, was chiefly occupied with finding out Turner's impression of Connie's condition.

"She is certainly better," he said. "The pain is nearly gone from her spine, and she can move herself a good deal more than when she left. I do think she might be allowed a little more change of posture now."

"Then you have some hope of her final recovery?"

"I have hope, most certainly. But what is hope in me, you must not allow to become certainty in you. I am nearly sure, though, that she can never be other than an invalid."

"I am thankful for the hope," I answered. "For all true hope, even as hope, man has to be unspeakably thankful."

TWENTY-TWO

The Ruins of Tintagel

I was able to arrange a young visiting clergyman to take my duty for me the next Sunday in Kilkhaven. Turner and Wynnie and I walked together the two miles to the church nearest the farmhouse. It was a lovely morning, with just a tint of autumn in the air. But even that tint, though all else was of the summer, brought a shadow to Wynnie's face, and it was with a tremor that she spoke.

"I never know, Papa, what people mean by talking about childhood in the fond way they do. I never seem to have been a bit younger and more innocent than I am."

"Don't you remember a time, Wynnie, when the things about you—the sky and the earth, say—seemed to you much grander than they seem now? You are old enough to have lost something."

She thought for a little while before she answered. "My dreams were, I know. I cannot say so of anything else."

"Then you must make good use of your dreams, my child."

"Why, Papa?"

"Because they are the only memories of childhood you have left."

"How am I to make a good use of them? I don't know what to do with my silly old dreams." But she gave a sigh as she spoke that testified her silly old dreams had a charm for her still.

"If your dreams, my child, have ever testified to you of a condition of things beyond that which you see around you; if they have been to you the hints of a wonder and glory beyond what visits you now, you must not call them silly, for they are the scents of paradise. If you have had no childhood, permit your old father to say that it is this childhood after which you are blindly longing, without which you find that life is hardly to be endured. Thank God for your dreams, my child. In Him you will find that the essence of those dreams is fulfilled. We are saved by hope. Never man hoped too much, or repented that he had hoped. The plague is that we don't hope in God half enough."

We reached the church, where, if I found the sermon neither healing nor inspiring, I found the prayers full of hope and consolation. They at least are safe beyond human caprice, conceit, or incapacity. But I did think they were too long for any individual Christian soul to sympathize with or respond to from beginning to end. It is one thing to read prayers and another to respond, and I had very few opportunities of being in the position of the latter duty. I had had suspicions before—and now they were confirmed—that the present crowding of services was most inexpedient. And as I pondered on the matter, instead of trying to go on praying after I had already uttered my soul, I thought how our Lord had given us such a short prayer to pray, and I began to wonder when or how the services came to be so heaped the one on the back of the other as they now were. No doubt many people defended them; no doubt many people could sit them out, but how many people could pray from beginning to end of them? On this point we had some talk as we went home. Wynnie was opposed to any change of the present use on the ground that we should only have the longer sermons.

"Still," I said, "I do not think even that so great an evil. A sensitive conscience will not reproach itself so much for not listening to the whole of a sermon, as for kneeling in prayer and not praying. I think that after prayers are over, each man should be at liberty to go out and leave the sermon unheard, if he pleases. I think the result would be in the end a good one both for parson and people. It would break through the deadness of the custom. Many a young mind is turned for life against churchgoing, just by the feeling that he *must* do so and so, that he *must* go through a certain round of duty. It is willing service that the Lord wants. No forced devotions are either acceptable to Him, or other than injurious to the worshiper, if such we can call him."

After attending to my duties each of the two following Sundays at Kilkhaven, I returned on the Monday or Tuesday to the farmhouse. Turner left us in the middle of the second week, and we missed him much. It was some days before Connie was quite as cheerful again as usual. I do not mean that she was in the least gloomy—she was only a little less merry. Certainly she appeared to us to have made considerable progress. One evening, while we were still at the farm, she startled us by calling out suddenly, "Papa, Papa! I moved my big toe! I did indeed!"

We were all about her in a moment. But I saw that she was excited, and I said, as calmly as I could, "But, my dear, you are possessed of two big toes; which of them are we to congratulate on this first stride in the march of improvement?"

She broke out in the merriest laugh, and then looked puzzled. All at once she said, "Papa, it is very odd, but I can't tell which of them," and burst into tears. I was afraid that I had done her more harm than good.

"It is not of the slightest consequence, my child," I said. "You have had so little communication of late with the twins, that it is no wonder you should not be able to tell the one from the other."

She smiled again, but was silent, yet with shining face, for the rest of the evening. Our hopes took a fresh start, but we heard no more from her of her power over her big toe. As often as I inquired she said she was afraid she had made a mistake, for she had not had another hint of its existence. Still I thought it could not have been fancy, and I would cleave to my belief in the good sign.

Percivale called to see us several times, but always appeared anxious not to intrude more of his society upon us than might be agreeable. He grew in my regard, however, and at length I asked him if he would assist me in another surprise which I had meditated for my companions, and this time for Connie as well, and which I hoped would prevent the painful influences of the sea from returning upon them when they went back to Kilkhaven—they must see the sea from a quite different shore first. An early day was fixed for carrying out our project, and I proceeded to get everything ready.

On the morning of a glorious day of blue and gold, we set out for the little village of Trevenna. Connie had been out every day since she came, now in one part of the fields, now in another, enjoying the expanse of earth and sky, but she had had no drive, and consequently had seen no variety of scenery. Therefore, believing she was now thoroughly able to bear it, I quite reckoned of the good she would get from the inevitable excitement. We resolved, however, after finding how much she enjoyed the few miles' drive, that we would not demand more of her strength that day, and therefore put up at the little inn, where after ordering dinner, Percivale and I left the ladies, and sallied forth to reconnoiter.

We walked through the village and down the valley beyond, sloping steeply between hills toward the sea. But when we reached the mouth of the valley, we found that we were not yet on the shore, for a precipice lay between us and the little beach below. On the left a great peninsula of rock stood out into the sea, upon which rose the ruins of the keep of Tintagel; while behind on the mainland stood the ruins of the castle itself, connected with the other only by a narrow isthmus. We had read that this peninsula had once been an island, and that the two parts of the castle were formerly connected by a drawbridge.

Looking up at the great gap which now divided the two portions, it seemed at first impossible to believe that they had ever been thus united; but a little reflection cleared up the mystery. The fact was that the isthmus, of half the height of the two parts connected by it, had been formed entirely by the fall of portions of the rock and soil on each side into the narrow dividing space, through which the waters of the Atlantic had been wont to sweep. And now the fragments of walls stood on the very verge of the precipice, and showed that large portions of the castle itself had fallen into the gulf between.

We turned to the left along the edge of the rock, and so by a narrow path reached and crossed to the other side of the isthmus. We then found that the path led to the foot of the rock (the former island) of the keep, and thence in a zigzag up the face of it to the top. We followed it, and after a great climb reached a door in a modern battlement. Entering, we found ourselves on grass amidst ruins haggard with age. We turned and surveyed the path by which we had come. It was steep and somewhat difficult, but the outlook was glorious. It was indeed one of God's mounts of vision upon which we stood. The thought, "Oh that Connie could see this!" was swelling in my heart, when Percivale broke the silence—not with any remark on the glory around us, but with the commonplace question—"You haven't got your man with you, I think, Mr. Walton?"

"No," I answered, "we thought it better to leave him to look after the boys."

He was silent for a few minutes, while I gazed in delight.

"Don't you think," he said, "it would be possible to bring Miss Constance up here? It would delight her all the rest of her life."

"It would, indeed. But it is impossible."

"I do not think so, if you would allow me the honor to assist you. I think we could do it perfectly between us."

I was again silent for a while. Looking down on the way we had come, it seemed an almost dreadful undertaking. Percivale added, "As we shall come here tomorrow, we need not explore the place now. Shall we go down at once and observe the whole path with a view to carrying her up?"

"There can be no objection to that," I answered, as a little hope, and courage with it, began to dawn in my heart. "But you must allow it does not look very practical."

"Perhaps it would seem more so to you, if you had come up with the idea in your head all the way, as I did. Any path seems more difficult in looking back, than at the time when the difficulties themselves have to be met and overcome."

"Yes, but then you must remember that we have to take the way back whether or no, if we once take the way forward."

"True. And now I will go down with the descent in my head as well."

"Well, there can be no harm in reconnoitering it at least. Let us go."

"We can rest as often as we please," said Percivale, and turned to lead the way.

It certainly was steep and required care even in our own descent; but for a man who had climbed mountains, as I had done in my youth, it could hardly be called difficult even in middle age. By the time we had got again into the valley road, I was all but convinced of the practicality of the proposal. I was a little vexed, however, that a stranger should have thought of giving such pleasure to Connie, when the bare wish that she might have enjoyed it had alone arisen in my mind. I reflected that this was one of the ways in which we were to be weaned from the world and knit the faster to our fellows. For even the middle-aged, in the decay of their daring, must look to the youth which follow at their heels for fresh thought and fresh impulse.

By the time we reached home we had agreed to make the attempt. As soon as we had arrived at this conclusion, I felt so happy in the prospect that I grew quite merry, especially after we had further agreed that, both for the sake of her nerves and for the sake of the lordly surprise, we should bind Connie's eyes so that she should see nothing till we had placed her high in the castle ruins.

"What mischief have you two been about?" said my wife, as we entered our room in the inn, where the cloth was already laid for dinner. "You look just like two schoolboys who have been laying some plot and can hardly hold their tongues about it."

"We have been enjoying our little walk amazingly," I answered. "So much so, that we mean to set out for another the moment dinner is over."

"I hope you will take Wynnie with you, then."

"Or you, my love," I returned.

"No. I will stay with Connie."

"Very well. You and Connie too shall go out tomorrow, for we have found a place we want to take you to."

When dinner was over—and a very good dinner it was—Wynnie and Percivale and I set out again. For as Percivale and I came back in the morning, we had seen the church standing far aloft and aloof on the other side of the little valley, and we wanted to go to it. It was rather a steep climb, and Wynnie accepted Percivale's offered arm. I led the way, therefore, and left them to follow—not so far in the rear, however, but that I could take a share in the conversation. It was some little time before any arose, and it was Wynnie who led the way into it.

"What kinds of things do you like best to paint, Mr. Percivale?" she asked.

He hesitated. "I would rather you should see some of my pictures. I should prefer that to answering your question."

"But I have seen some of your pictures," she returned.

"Pardon me. Indeed you have not, Miss Walton."

"At least I have seen some of your sketches and studies."

"Some of my sketches. None of my studies."

"But you make use of your sketches for your pictures, do you not?"

"Never of such as you have seen. They are only a slight antidote to my pictures. But I would rather, I repeat, say nothing about my pictures till you see some of them."

"But how am I to have that pleasure, then?"

"You go to London, sometimes, do you not?"

"Very rarely. More rarely still when the Royal Academy is open."

"That does not much matter. My pictures are seldom to be found there."

"Do you not care to send them there?"

"I send one at least every year. But they are rarely accepted."

"Why?"

This was a very improper question, I thought, but if Wynnie had thought so she would not have put it.

He hesitated a little before he replied. "It is hardly for me to say why, but I cannot wonder much at it, considering the subjects I choose."

He said no more. And till we reached the church, nothing more of significance passed between them.

What a waste, bare churchyard that was! It had two or three lych gates, but they had no roofs. Not a tree stood in that churchyard. Rank grass was the sole covering of the soil heaved up with the dead beneath. The ancient church stood in the midst, with its low, strong, square tower, and its long narrow nave, the ridge bowed with age, like the back of a horse worn out in the service of man, and its little homely chancel, like a small cottage that had leaned up against its end for shelter from the western blasts. It was locked, and we could not enter. But of all world-worn, sad-looking churches, that one was the dreariest I had ever beheld. Surely it needed the Gospel of the resurrection fervently preached therein, to keep it from sinking to the dust with dismay and weariness. Near it was one huge mound of grass-grown rubbish, looking like the grave where some former church had been buried, when it could stand erect no longer before the onsets of Atlantic winds. I walked round and round it, gathering its architecture, and peeping in at every window I could reach. Suddenly I was aware that I was alone.

Returning to the other side, I found Percivale seated on the churchyard wall, next to the sea. It would have been less dismal had it stood immediately on the cliffs, but they were at some little distance beyond the bare downs and rough stone walls. He was sketching the place, and Wynnie stood beside him, looking over his shoulder. I did not interrupt him, but walked among the graves, reading the poor memorials of the dead and wondering how many of the words of laudation that were inscribed on their tombs were spoken of them while they were yet alive. I was yet wandering around and reading, and stumbling over the mounds, when my companions joined me, and without a word, we walked out of the churchyard. We were nearly home before one of us spoke.

"That church is oppressive," said Percivale. "It looks like a great sepulchre, a place built only for the dead—The Church of the Dead."

"It is only that it partakes with the living," I returned, "suffers with them the buffetings of life, outlasts them, but shows, like the shield of the Red-Cross Knight, the 'old dints of deep wounds.' "

"Still, is it not a dreary place to choose for a church to stand in?"

"The church must stand everywhere. There is no region into which it must not, ought not, enter. If it refuses any earthly spot, it is shrinking from its calling. This one stands high-uplifted, looking out over the waters as a sign of the haven from all storms, the rest in God. And down beneath lie the bodies of men—you saw the graves of some of them on the other side—flung ashore from the gulfing sea." Then I told them the conversation I had had with the sexton at Kilkhaven. "But," I went on, "these fancies are only the ghostly mists that hang about the eastern hills before the sun rises. We shall look down on all that with a smile, for the Lord tells us that if we believe in Him we shall never die."

By this time we were back once more with the others, and gave Connie an account of all we had seen.

TWENTY-THREE
The Surprise

The next day I awoke very early, full of anticipation for the attempt. I got up at once, found the weather most promising. After breakfast I went to Connie's room and told her that Mr. Percivale and I had devised a treat for her. Her face shone at once.

"But we want to do it our own way."

"Of course, Papa," she answered.

"Will you let us tie your eyes up?"

"Yes—and my ears and my hands too. It would be no good tying my feet, when I don't know one big toe from the other." And she laughed merrily.

"We'll try to keep up the talk all the way, so that you shan't weary of the journey."

"You're going to carry me somewhere with my eyes tied up. Oh! How jolly! And then I shall see something all at once! Jolly! Jolly!" she repeated. "Even the wind on my face would be pleasure enough for half a day. I shan't get tired so soon as you will—you dear, kind Papa! I am afraid I shall be dreadfully heavy. But I shan't jerk your arms much. I will lie so still!"

"And you won't mind letting Mr. Percivale help me carry you?"

"No. Why should I, if he doesn't mind it? He looks strong enough."

"Very well, then. I will send Mamma and Wynnie to dress you at once, and we shall set out as soon as you are ready."

She clapped her hands with delight, then caught me round the neck and gave me one of her best kisses, and began to call as loud as she could for her mamma and Wynnie to come and dress her.

It was indeed a glorious morning. The wind came in little wafts, like veins of cool, white silver amid the great warm, yellow-gold of the sunshine. The sea lay before us, a mound of blue closing up the end of the valley, and the hills lay like great green sheep, basking in the blissful heat. The gleam from the waters came up the pass and the grand castle crowned the left-hand steep, seeming to warm its old bones, like the ruins of some awful megatherium in the lighted air.

And of all this we talked to Connie as we went, and every now and then she would clap her hands gently in the fullness of her delight, although she beheld the splendor only as with her ears, or from the kisses of the wind on her cheeks. But, since her accident, she seemed to have approached the condition which Milton represents Samson as longing for in his blindness, wherein

> the sight should be "through all the parts diffused,
> That she might look at will through every pore."
> (*Samson Agonistes*)

I arranged with the rest of the company that the moment we reached the cliff over the shore and turned to cross the isthmus, they should no longer converse about the things around us, and that no exclamation of surprise or delight should break from them before Connie's eyes were uncovered. I said nothing about the difficulties of the way, that, seeing us take them as ordinary things, they might so take them too, and not be uneasy.

We never stopped till we reached the foot of the keep. There we set Connie down, to take breath and ease our arms before we began the arduous way.

"Now, now!" said Connie, eagerly, lifting her hands to her eyes.

"No, no, my love, not yet," I said, and she lay still again, only more eager than before.

"I am afraid I have tired out you and Mr. Percivale, Papa," she said.

Percivale laughed so amusedly, that she rejoined roguishly, "Oh, yes! I know every gentleman is a Hercules—at least he chooses to be considered one! But, notwithstanding my firm faith in the fact, I have a little womanly conscience left that is hard to hoodwink."

There was a speech for wee Connie to make! The best answer and the best revenge was to lift her and go on. This we did, trying to prevent the difference of level between us from tilting the litter too much for her comfort.

"Where are you going, Papa?" she said once, but without fear in her voice, as a little slip I made lowered my end of the litter suddenly. "You must be going up a steep place. Don't hurt yourself, dear Papa."

We had changed our positions and were now carrying her, head foremost, up the hill. Percivale led and I followed. Now I could see every change on her lovely face, and it made me strong to endure—for I did find it hard work, I confess, to get to the top. Percivale strode on as if he bore a feather behind him. I did wish we were at the top, for my arms began to feel like iron cables, stiff and stark. I was afraid of my fingers giving way, and my heart was beating uncomfortably too. But Percivale strode on unconcernedly, turning every corner of the zigzag where I expected to halt, and striding on again. But I held out, strengthened by the play on my daughter's face, delicate as the play on an opal—one that inclines more to the milk than the fire.

When at length we turned in through the gothic door in the battlement wall, and set our lovely burden down upon the grass, I said, "Percivale," forgetting the proprieties in the affected humor of being angry with him, so glad was I that we had her at length on the mount of glory, "why did you go on walking like a castle, and pay no heed to me?"

"You didn't speak, did you, Mr. Walton?" he returned, with just a shadow of solicitude in the question.

"No. Of course not," I rejoined.

"Oh, then," he returned, in a tone of relief, "how could I stop? You were my captain: how could I give in so long as you were holding on?"

I am afraid the "Percivale"—without the "Mister"—came again and again after this, though I pulled myself up for it as often as I caught myself.

"Now, Papa!" said Connie from the grass.

"Not yet, my dear. Wait till your mamma and Wynnie come. Let us go and meet them, Percivale."

"Oh, yes, do, Papa. Leave me alone here without knowing where I am or what kind of place I am in. I should like to know how it feels. I have never been alone in all my life."

"Very well, my dear," I said, and Percivale and I left her alone in the ruins.

We found Ethelwyn toiling up with Wynnie helping her.

"Dear Harry," she said, "how could you think of bringing Connie up such an awful place? I wonder you dared to do it."

"It's done, you see, Wife," I answered, "thanks to Mr. Percivale, who has nearly torn the breath out of me. But now we must get you up, and you will say that to see Connie's delight, not to mention your own, is quite wages for the labor."

"Isn't she afraid to find herself so high up?"

"She knows nothing about it yet."

"You do not mean you have left the child there with her eyes tied up!"

"We could not uncover them before you came. It would spoil half the pleasure."

"Do let us make haste then. It is surely dangerous to leave her so."

"Not in the least—but she must be getting tired of the darkness. Take my arm now."

"Don't you think Mrs. Walton had better take my arm?" said Percivale. "Then you can put your hand on her back, and help her a little that way."

We tried the plan and found it a good one, and soon reached the top. The moment our eyes fell on Connie, we could see that she had found the place neither fearful nor lonely. The sweetest ghost of a smile hovered on her pale face, which shone in the shadow of the old gateway of the keep with light from her own sunny soul. She lay in still expectation, as if she had just fallen asleep after receiving an answer to prayer.

But she heard our steps, and her face awoke. "Has Mamma come?"

"Yes, my darling. I am here," said her mother. "How do you feel?"

"Perfectly well, Mamma, thank you. Now, Papa!"

"One moment more, my love. Percivale?"

We carried her to the spot we had agreed on, and while we held her a little inclined that she might see the better, her mother undid the bandage from her head.

"Hold your hands over her eyes, a little way from them," I said to her as she untied the handkerchief, "that the light may reach them by degrees and not blind her."

Ethelwyn did so for a few moments, then removed them. Still, for a moment or two more, it was plain from Connie's look of utter bewilderment, that all was a confused mass of light and color. Then she gave a little cry, and to my astonishment, half rose to a sitting posture. One moment more, and she laid herself gently back, and tears glistened in her eyes and down each cheek.

And now I may tell of the glory that made her weep.

Through the gothic-arched door in the battlemented wall, Connie saw a great gulf at her feet, full to the brim of a splendor of light and color. Before her rose the great ruins of rock and castle: rough stone below, clear green grass above, even to the verge of the abrupt and awful precipice. At the foot of the rocks, hundreds of feet below, the blue waters broke white upon the dark gray sands, and all was full of the gladness of the sun overflowing in speechless delight. But the main marvel was the look sheer below into the abyss full of light and air and color, its sides lined with rock and grass, and its bottom lined with blue ripples and sand.

"O Lord God!" I said, almost involuntarily, "Thou art very rich. Thou art the one Poet, the one Maker. We worship Thee. Make our souls as full of glory in Thy sight as this chasm is to our eyes, glorious with the forms which Thou hast cloven and carved out of nothingness, and we shall be worthy to worship Thee, O Lord, our God." For I was carried beyond myself with delight, and with sympathy with Connie's delight and with the calm worship of gladness in my wife's countenance.

But when my eye fell on Wynnie, I saw trouble mingled with her admiration, a self-accusation, I think, that she did not and could not enjoy it more—and when I turned from her, there were the eyes of Percivale fixed on me in wonderment. For the moment I felt as David must have felt, when, in his dance of undignified delight that he had got the ark home again, he saw the contemptuous eyes of Michal fixed on him in the window. But I could not leave it so. I said to him, coldly, I daresay, "Excuse me, Mr. Percivale. I forgot for the moment that I was not amongst my own family."

Percivale took his hat off. "Forgive my seeming rudeness, Mr. Walton. I was half envying and half wondering. You would not be surprised at my unconscious behavior if you had seen as much of the wrong side of life as I have seen in London."

I had some idea what he meant, but this was no time to enter upon a discussion. I could only say, "My heart was full, Mr. Percivale, and I let it overflow."

"Let me at least share in its overflow," he rejoined, and nothing more passed on the subject.

For the next ten minutes we stood in absolute silence. We had set Connie down on the grass again, but propped up so that she could see through the doorway. And she lay in still ecstasy. But there was more to be seen ere we descended. There was the rest of the little islet with its crop of down-grass, on which the horses of all the knights of King Arthur's Round Table might have fed for a week—yes, a fortnight. There were the ruins of the castle so built of plates of the laminated stone of the rocks on which they stood, and so woven in with the outstanding rock themselves, that in some parts I found it impossible to tell which was building and which was rock—the walls seeming like a growth out of the island itself. But the walls were in some parts so thin that one wondered how they could have stood so long. They must have been built before the time of any formidable artillery—enough only for defense from arrows. But then the island was nowhere commanded, and its own steep cliffs would be more easily defended than any edifices on it. Clearly the intention was that no enemy should thereon find rest for the sole of his foot, for if he was able to land, farewell to the notion of any further defense.

Outside the walls there was the little chapel—such a tiny chapel! Little more than the foundation remained, with the ruins of the altar still standing, and outside the chancel, nestling by its wall, a coffin hollowed in the rock. The churchyard a little way off was full of graves which, I presume, would have vanished long ago were it not that the very graves were founded on the rock. There still stood old wornout headstones of thin slate, but no memorials were left. Then there was the fragment of an arched underground passage laid open to the air in the center of the islet; and last, and grandest of all, the awful edges of the rock, broken by time, and carved by the winds and the waters into grotesque shapes and threatening forms.

Over all the surface of the islet we carried Connie, and from three sides of this sea-fortress she looked abroad over "the Atlantic's level powers." Over the edge she gazed at the strange fantastic needle-rock, and round the corner she peeped to see Wynnie and her mother seated in what they call Arthur's Chair—a canopied hollow wrought in the plated rock by the mightiest of all solvents, air and water. At length it was time to leave, so we issued by the gothic door and wound away down the dangerous path to the safe ground below.

"I think we had better tie up your eyes again, Connie," I said.

"Why?" she asked, in wonderment. "There's nothing higher yet, is there?"

"No, my love. If there were, you would hardly be able for it today. It is only to keep you from being frightened at the precipice as you go down."

"But I shan't be frightened, Papa."

"How do you know that?"

"Because you are going to carry me."

"But what if I should slip? I might, you know."

"I don't mind. I shan't mind being tumbled over the precipice, if you do it. I shan't be to blame, and I'm sure you won't, Papa." Then she drew my head down and whispered in my ear, "If I get as much more by being killed, as I have got by having my poor back hurt, I'm sure it will be well worth it."

I tried to smile a reply, for I could not speak one. We took her just as she was and—with some tremor on my part, but not a single slip—we bore her down the winding path, her face showing all the time that, instead of being afraid, she was in a state of ecstatic delight. My wife, I could see, was nervous, and she breathed a sigh of relief when we were once more at the foot.

"Well, I'm glad that's over," she said.

"So am I," I returned as we set down the litter.

"Poor Papa! I've pulled his arms to pieces! And Mr. Percivale's too!"

Meantime, Wynnie had scrambled down to the shore and came running back to us out of breath with the news, "Papa! Mr. Percivale! There's such a grand cave down there! It goes right through under the island."

Connie looked so eager, that Percivale and I glanced at each other, and without a word, lifted her, and followed Wynnie. It was a little way, but very broken and difficult, but at length we stood in the cavern. What a contrast to the vision overhead—nothing to be seen but the cool, dark vault of the cave, long and winding, with the fresh seaweed lying on its pebbly floor, and its walls wet with the last tide. The forms of huge outlying rocks looked in at the farther end where the roof rose like a grand cathedral arch. Gleaming veins, rich with copper, dashed and streaked the darkness. The floor of heaped-up pebbles rose and rose within to meet the descending roof. It was like going down from paradise into the grave—but a cool, friendly, brown-lighted grave. Even in its darkest recesses there was a witness to the wind of God outside—an occasional ripple of shadowed light, from the play of the sun on the waves, that wandered across the jagged roof. But we dared not keep Connie long in the damp coolness, and we soon returned.

My family had now beheld the sea in such a different aspect that I no longer feared to go back to Kilkhaven. There we went three days after, and at my invitation, Percivale took Turner's place in the carriage.

TWENTY-FOUR

Joe and His Trouble

How bright the yellow shores of Kilkhaven looked after the dark sands of Tintagel! But how low and tame its highest cliffs, after the mighty rampart of rocks facing the sea! It was pleasant to settle down again, after a boisterous welcome by Dora and the boys. Connie's baby crowed aloud and stretched forth her chubby arms at the sight of her. And the dread vision of the shore receded far into the past.

I called at the blacksmith's house, and found that he was so far better as to be working at his forge again. His mother said he was used to such attacks and soon got over them, but I feared that they indicated an approaching breakdown.

"Indeed, Sir," she said, "Joe might be well enough if he liked. It's all his own fault."

"What do you mean?" I asked. "I cannot believe that your son is in any way guilty of his own illness."

"He's a well-behaved lad, my Joe," she answered, "but he hasn't learned what I had to learn long ago."

"What is that?" I asked.

"To make up his mind and to stick to it. To do one thing or the other."

She was a woman with a long upper lip and a judicial face, and as she spoke, her lip grew longer and longer. When she closed her mouth in resolution, that lip seemed to occupy two-thirds of all her face under her nose.

"And what is it he won't do?"

"I don't mind whether he does it or not, if he would only *make up his mind and stick to it!*"

"What is it you want him to do, then?"

"I don't want him to do it, I'm sure. It's no good to me—and wouldn't be much good to him, that I'll be bound. Howsomever, he must please himself."

I thought it not very wondrous that he looked gloomy, if there was no more sunshine for him at home than his mother's face indicated. I made no further attempt to question her.

In passing Joe's workshop, I stopped for a moment and made an arrangement to meet him at the church. Harry Cobb, his carpenter cousin, was to come with him.

The two soon arrived, and a small consultation followed. They had done a good deal in our absence, and little remained except to get the keys put to rights, and the rods attached to the cranks in the box.

The cousin was a bright-eyed, cherub-cheeked little man, with a ready smile and white teeth. I thought he might help me understand what was amiss in Joe's affairs, but I would not make the attempt except openly. I therefore said (half in a jocular fashion) as the gloomy smith was fitting one loop into another in two of his iron rods, "I wish we could get this cousin of yours to look a little more cheerful. You would think he had quarreled with the sunshine."

The carpenter showed his white teeth between his rosy lips. "Well, Sir, if you'll excuse me, you see my cousin Joe is not like the rest of us. He's a religious man, is Joe."

"But I don't see how that should make him miserable. It hasn't made me miserable."

"Ah, well," returned the carpenter, in a thoughtful tone, as he worked away gently to get the inside out of the oak chest without hurting it, "I don't say it's the religion, for I don't know, but perhaps it's the way he takes it up. He don't look after hisself enough. He's always thinking about other people, and if you don't look after yourself, why, who is to look after you? That's common sense, I think."

"But," I said, "if everybody would take Joe's way of it, there would then be no occasion for taking care of yourself."

"I don't see why."

"Why, because everybody would take care of everybody else."

"Not so well, I doubt."

"Yes, and a great deal better."

"At any rate, that's a long way off, and meantime, who's to take care of the odd man like Joe there, that don't look after hisself?"

"Why, God, of course."

"Well, there's just where I'm out. I don't know nothing about that branch, Sir."

I saw a grateful light mount up in Joe's gloomy eyes as I spoke thus upon his side of the question. He said nothing, however, and as his cousin volunteered no further information, I did not push the advantage.

At noon I made them leave their work and come home with me to have their dinner, for they hoped to finish the job before dusk. Harry Cobb and I dropped behind, and Joe walked on in front, apparently sunk in meditation.

Scarcely were we out of the churchyard, and on the road leading to the rectory, when I saw the sexton's daughter Agnes before us. She had almost come up to Joe before he saw her, for his gaze was bent on the ground, and he started. They shook hands in what seemed to me an odd and constrained, yet familiar fashion, and then stood as if they wanted to talk, but without speaking. Harry and I passed, both with a nod of recognition to the young woman. When we reached the turning that would hide them from our view, I looked back and there they were still standing. But before we reached the door of the rectory, Joe caught up with us.

There was something remarkable in the appearance of Agnes Coombes. She was about six and twenty, the youngest of the family, with a sallow, rather sickly complexion, somewhat sorrowful eyes, a rare and sweet smile, a fine figure, tall and slender, and a graceful gait. I now saw further into the smith's affairs.

After dinner, the men went back to the church and I went straight to the sexton's cottage. I found the old man seated at the window, with his pot of beer on the sill, and an empty plate beside it.

"Come in, Sir," he said, rising as I put my head in at the door. "The mis'ess ben't in, but she'll be here in a few minutes."

"Oh, it's of no consequence," I said. "Are they all well?"

"All comfortable, Sir. It be fine dry weather for them. It be in winter it be worst for them. There ben't much snow in these parts—but when it du come, that be very bad for them, poor things!"

Could it be that he was harping on the old theme again?

"But at least this cottage keeps out the wet," I said. "If not, we must have it seen to."

"This cottage du well enough. It'll last my time, anyhow."

"Then why are you pitying your family for having to live in it?"

"Bless your heart, Sir! It's not them. They du well enough. It's my people out yonder. You've got the souls to look after, and I've got the bodies, to be sure!"

The last exclamation was uttered in a tone of impatient surprise at my stupidity in giving all my thoughts and sympathies to the living, and none to the dead. (I pursued the subject no further, but as I lay in bed later that night, it began to dawn upon me as a lovable kind of hallucination in which the man indulged. He too had an office in the church of God, and he would magnify that office. He could not bear that there should be no further outcome of his labor—that the burying of the dead out of sight should be "the be-all and the end-all." When all others had forsaken the dead, he remained their friend, caring for what little comfort yet remained possible to them. It was his way of keeping up the relation between the living and the dead.) Finding I made no reply, he took up the word again.

"You've got your part, Sir, and I've got mine. You up in the pulpit, and I down in the grave. But it'll be all the same by and by."

"I hope it will," I answered. "But when you do go down into your own grave, you'll know a good deal less about it than you do now. You'll find you've got other things to think about. But here comes your wife. She'll talk about the living rather than the dead."

"That's natural, Sir. She brought 'em to life, and I buried 'em—at least the best part of 'em. If only I had the other two safe down with the rest!" He regarded his drowned boys as still tossed about in the weary wet cold ocean, and would have gladly laid them to rest in the warm dry churchyard.

He wiped a tear from the corner of his eye with the back of his hand, and saying, "Well, I must be off to my gardening," left me to his wife. I saw then that, humorist as the old man might be, his humor lay close about the wells of weeping.

"The old man seems a little out of sorts," I said to his wife.

"Well, Sir," she answered, with her usual gentleness, "this be the day he buried our Nancy, this day two years ago, and today Agnes be come home from her work poorly. The two things together, they've upset him a bit."

"I met Agnes coming this way. Where is she?"

"I believe she be in the churchyard. I've been to the doctor about her."

"I hope it's nothing serious."

"I hope not, Sir, but you see—four on 'em!"

"Well, she's in God's hands, you know."

"That she be, Sir."

"I want to ask you about something, Mrs. Coombes."

"What be that? If I can tell, I will, you may be sure."

"I want to know what's the matter with Joe Harper, the blacksmith."

"They du say it be consumption, Sir."

"But what has he got on his mind?"

"He's got nothing on his mind, Sir. He be as good a boy as ever, I assure you."

"There is something on his mind. He's not the man to be unhappy because he's ill. A man like him would not be miserable because he was going to die. It might make him look sad sometimes, but not gloomy."

"Well, Sir, I believe you to be right, and perhaps I know summat. I believe my Agnes and Joe Harper are as fond upon one another as any two in the county."

"Are they not going to be married then?"

"There be the pint, Sir. I don't believe Joe ever said a word o' the sort to Aggy. She never could ha' kep it from me."

"Why doesn't he then?"

"That's the pint again, Sir. All as knows him says it's because he be in such bad health, and he thinks he oughtn't to go marrying with one foot in the grave."

"What does your daughter think?"

"The same. And so they go on talking to each other, quiet-like, like old married folks, not like lovers at all. But I can't help fancying it have something to do with my Aggy's pale face."

"And something to do with Joe's pale face too, Mrs. Coombes," I said.

"Thank you. You've told me more than I expected. It explains everything. I must have it out with Joe now."

"Oh, deary me! Sir, don't go and tell him I said anything, as if I wanted him to marry my daughter."

"Don't you be afraid. I'll take good care of that. And don't fancy I'm fond of meddling with other people's affairs. But this is a case in which I ought to do something. Joe's a fine fellow."

"That he be, Sir. I couldn't wish a better for a son-in-law."

I put my hat on and went straight to the church. There were the two men working away in the shadowy tower, and there was Agnes beside, knitting like her mother, quiet and solemn, as if she were a long-married wife hovering about her husband at his work. Harry was saying something to her as I went in, but when they saw me they were silent, and Agnes left the church.

"Do you think you will get through tonight?" I asked.

"Sure of it, Sir," answered Harry.

And Joe responded, "You shouldn't be sure of anything, Harry. We are told in the New Testament that we ought to say 'If the Lord will.' "

"Now, Joe, you're too hard on Harry," I said. "You don't think that the Bible means to pull a man up every time like that, till he's afraid to speak a word? It was about a long journey and a year's residence that the Apostle James was speaking."

"But the principle's the same. Harry can no more be sure of finishing his work before it be dark, than those people could of their long journey."

"That is perfectly true. But you are taking the letter for the spirit. Religion does not lie in not being sure about anything, but in a loving desire that the will of God in the matter, whatever it may be, may be done. And if Harry has not learned yet to care about the will of God, what is the good of coming down upon him that way, as if that would teach him in the least. When he loves God, then, and not till then, will he care about His will. Nor does religion lie in saying, 'if the Lord will' every time anything is to be done. It is a most dangerous thing to use sacred words often, for it makes them so common. Our hearts ought to ever be in the spirit of those words, but our lips ought to utter them rarely. Besides, there are some things a man might be pretty sure the Lord wills."

"It sounds fine, Sir, but I'm not sure I understand you. It sounds to me like a darkening of wisdom."

I saw I had irritated him, and so had in some measure lost ground. But Harry struck in, "How can you say that now, Joe? I know what the parson means well enough, and everybody knows I ain't got half the brains you've got."

"The reason is, Harry, that he's got something in his head that stands in the way."

"And there's nothing in my head to stand in the way!" returned Harry, laughing.

I laughed too, and even Joe could not help a sympathetic grin. By this time it was getting dark.

"I'm afraid, Harry, after all, you won't get through tonight."

"I think so too. And there's Joe saying, 'I told you so,' over and over to himself, though he won't say it out like a man."

Joe answered only with another grin.

"Harry," I said, "you must come again on Monday. And on your way home just look in and tell Joe's mother that I have kept him over tomorrow. The change will do him good."

"No, Sir, that can't be. I haven't got a clean shirt."

"You can have a shirt of mine," I said. "But I'm afraid you'll want your Sunday clothes."

"I'll bring them for you, Joe, before you're up," interposed Harry. "And then you can go to church with Agnes."

Here was just what I wanted.

"Hold your tongue, Harry," said Joe angrily. "You're talking of what you don't know anything about."

"Well, Joe, I ben't a fool, even if I ben't so religious as you be. You ben't a bad fellow, though you be a Methodist, and I ben't a fool, though I be Harry Cobb. Nobody could help seeing the eyes you and Aggy make at each other, and why you don't port your helm and board her—I won't say it's more than I know, but I du say it be more than I think fair to the young woman."

"Hold your tongue, Harry."

"I've answered you, so no more at present. But I'll be over with your clothes afore you're up in the morning."

As Harry spoke he was busy gathering his tools. "They won't be in the way, will they?" he said, as he heaped them together in that farthest corner of the tower.

"Not in the least," I returned. "If I had my way, all the tools used in building the church should be carved on the posts and pillars of it to indicate the sacredness of labor. For a necessity of God is laid upon every workman as well as on the Apostle Paul. Only Paul saw it, and every workman doesn't, Harry."

"I like that way of it. I almost think I could be a little bit religious after your way of it, Sir."

"Almost, Harry?" growled Joe, not unkindly.

"Now you hold your tongue, Joe," I said. "Leave Harry to me. You may take him, if you like, after I've done with him."

Laughing merrily, but making no other reply than a hearty good-night, Harry strode away out of the church, and Joe and I went home together. When he had had his tea, I asked him to go out with me for a walk.

The sun was shining aslant upon the downs from over the sea. As we rose out of the shadowy hollow to the sunlit brow, I was a little in advance of Joe. Happening to turn, I saw the light full on his head and face, while the rest of his body had not yet emerged from the shadow.

"Stop, Joe," I said. "I want to see you so for a moment."

He stood—a little surprised.

"You look just like a man rising from the dead, Joe," I said. "Your head and face are full of sunlight, but the rest of your body is still buried in the shadow. Look—I will stand where you are now, and you come here. You will see what I mean."

We changed places. Joe stared for a moment, and then his face brightened. "I see what you mean," he said.

I stood up in the sunlight, so that my eyes caught only about half the sun's disc. Then I bent my face toward the earth.

"What part of me is the light shining on now, Joe?"

"Just the top of your head," answered he.

"There, then," I returned, "that is just what you are like—a man with the light on his head, but not on his face. And why not on your face? Because you hold your head down. To be frank with you, Joe, I do not see that light in your face. Therefore I think something must be wrong with you. Remember a good man is not necessarily in the right. Peter was a good man, yet our Lord called him Satan and meant it, of course, for He never said what He did not mean."

"How can I be wrong when all my trouble comes from doing my duty—nothing else, as far as I know?"

"Then," I replied, a sudden light breaking in on my mind, "I doubt whether what you suppose to be your duty can be your duty. If it were, I do not think it would make you so miserable."

"What is a man to go by, then? If he thinks a thing is his duty, is he not to do it?"

"Most assuredly, until he knows better. The supposed duty may be the will of God, or the invention of one's own fancy or mistaken judgment. A real duty is always something right in itself. The duty a man makes his for the time, by supposing it to be a duty, may be something quite wrong in itself. The duty of a Hindu widow is to burn herself on the body of her husband, but that duty lasts only till she sees that, not being the will of God, it is not her duty. It was the duty of the early hermits to encourage the growth of vermin upon their bodies, for they supposed that was pleasing to God—but they could not fare so well as if they had seen that the will of God was cleanliness. And there may be far more serious things done by Christian people against the will of God, in the fancy of doing their duty, than such a trifle as swarming with worms. In a word, thinking a thing is your duty makes it your duty only till you know better. And the prime duty of every man is to seek and find, that he may do the will of God."

"But how are you to know the will of God in every case?" asked Joe.

"By looking at the general laws of life, and obeying them—unless there be anything special in a particular case to bring it under a higher law."

"Ah! But that be just what there is here."

"Well, my dear fellow, that may be; but the special conduct may not be right for the special case. But it is of no use talking generals. Let us come to particulars. If you can trust me, tell me all about it, and we may be able to let some light in."

"I will turn it over in my mind, Sir, and if I can bring myself to talk about it, I will. I would rather tell you than anyone else."

I said no more. We watched a glorious sunset—there never was a grander place for sunsets—and went home.

TWENTY-FIVE
A Small Adventure

The next morning Harry came with the clothes, but Joe did not go to church. Neither did Agnes make an appearance that morning. They were, however, both present at the evening service.

When we came out of church, the sky was dark, covered with one cloud, and not a star cracked through. The wind was *gurly,* blowing cold from the sea. (I once heard that word in Scotland, and never forgot it.)

I have always had a certain peculiar pleasure in the surly aspects of nature. When I was a young man, this took form in opposition and defiance, but since I had begun to grow old, the form had changed into a sense of safety. So, after supper, I put on my greatcoat and traveling cap, and went out into the ill-tempered night.

I meant to stroll down to the breakwater. At the farther end of it, always covered at high water, was an outlying cluster of low rocks, in the heart of which the lord of the manor (a noble-hearted Christian gentleman of the old school) had constructed a bath of graduated depth—an open-air swimming pool, the only really safe place for men who were not swimmers to bathe. I was in the habit of bathing with my two little men there every morning.

The nearest way to the breakwater was, strangely, through Connie's room. By the side of her window was a narrow door communicating with a narrow, curving, wood-built passage, leading into a little wooden hut, the walls of which were formed of outside planks with the bark still on them. From this hut one or two little windows looked seaward, and a door led out on the bit of sward in which lay the flower bed under Connie's window. Then a door in the low wall and thick hedge led out on the downs, where a path wound along the cliffs that formed the side of the bay till, descending under the storm tower, it came out upon the root of the breakwater.

When I went into Connie's room, I found her lying in bed, a very picture of peace. But my entrance destroyed the picture.

"Papa," she said, "why have you got your coat on? Surely you are not going out tonight. The wind is blowing dreadfully."

"Not very dreadfully, Connie. It blew much worse the night we found your baby."

"But it is very dark."

"I allow that, but there is a glimmer from the sea. I am only going on the breakwater for a few minutes. You know I like a stormy night as much as a fine one."

"I shall be miserable till you come home, Papa."

"Nonsense, Connie. You don't think your father hasn't sense to take care of himself? Or rather, Connie, for I grant that is poor ground of comfort, you don't think I can go anywhere without my Father to take care of me?"

"But there is no occasion, is there, Papa?"

"Do you think I should be better pleased with my boys if they shrunk from everything involving the least possibility of danger because there was no occasion for it? That is just the way to make cowards. There is positively no ground for apprehension, and I hope you won't spoil my walk by the thought that my foolish little girl is frightened."

"I will be good—indeed I will, Papa," she said, holding up her mouth to kiss me.

I left through the wooden passage. The wind roared about the bark hut, shook it, and pawed it, and sang and whistled in the chinks of the planks. I went out and shut the door. That moment the wind seized upon me, and I had to fight with it. When I reached the path leading along the edge of the downs, I felt something lighter than any feather fly in my face. When I put up my hand, I found my cheek wet. They were flakes of foam, bubbles worked up into little masses of adhering thousands, which the wind blew off the waters and across the downs, carrying some of them miles inland.

Now and then a little rush of water from a higher wave swept over the top of the broad breakwater, as with head bowed sideways against the wind, I struggled along toward the rock at its end. But I said to myself, "The tide is falling fast, and salt water hurts nobody." And I struggled on over the huge rough stones of the mighty heap, outside which the waves were white with wrath, inside which they had fallen asleep, only heaving with the memory of their late unrest. I reached the tall rock at length, climbed the rude stair leading up to the flagstaff, and looked abroad into the thick dark. But the wind blew so strong on the top that I was glad to descend. The deathly waves rolled between me and the basin, where yesterday morning I had bathed in still water and sunshine with my boys. I wandered on and found a sheltered nook in a mass of rock where I sat with the wind howling and the waves bursting around me. There I fell into a sort of brown study—almost half asleep.

But I had not sat long before I came broad awake, for I heard voices, low and earnest. One I recognized as Joe's voice. The other was a woman's. In a lull of the wind, I heard the woman say (I could fancy with a sigh), "I'm sure you'll du what is right, Joe. Don't 'e think o' me, Joe."

"It's just of you that I do think, Aggy. You know it ben't for my sake. Surely you know that?"

There was no answer for a moment. I was doubting what I had best do—go away quietly or let them know I was there—when she spoke again. There was a momentary lull now in the noises of both wind and water, and I heard what she said well enough.

"It ben't for me to contradict you, Joe. But I don't think you be going to die. You be no worse than last year. Be you now, Joe?"

Once before, a stormy night and darkness had brought me close to a soul in agony. Then I was in agony myself, and now the world was all fair and hopeful around me. But here were two souls straying in a mist which faith might roll away and leave them walking in the light. The moment was come for me to speak.

"Joe!" I called out.

"Who's there?" he cried, and I heard him start to his feet.

"Only Mr. Walton. Where are you?"

"We can't be very far off," he answered, not in a tone of any pleasure.

I rose, and peering about through the darkness, found that they were a little higher up on the same rock by which I was sheltered.

"You mustn't think," I said, "that I have been eavesdropping. I had no idea anyone was near me till I heard your voices."

"I saw someone go up the Castle Rock," said Joe, "but I thought he was gone away again. It will be a lesson to me."

"I'm no telltale, Joe," I returned, as I scrambled up the rock. "You will have no cause to regret that I happened to overhear a little. I am sure you will never say anything you need be ashamed of. But what I heard was sufficient to let me into the secret of your trouble. Will you let me talk to Joe, Agnes? I've been young myself, and to tell the truth, I don't think I'm old yet."

"I am sure, Sir," she answered, "you won't be hard on Joe and me. I don't suppose there be anything wrong in liking each other, though we can't be . . . married."

She spoke in a low tone, and her voice trembled very much, yet there was a certain womanly composure in her utterance. "I'm sure it's very bold of me to talk so," she added, "but Joe will tell you all about it."

I was close beside them now, and fancied I saw through the dusk the motion of her hand stealing into his.

"Well, Joe, this is just what I wanted," I said. "A woman can be braver than a big smith sometimes. Agnes has done her part. Now you do yours, and tell me all about it."

No response followed my adjuration. I must help him.

"I think I know how the matter lies, Joe. You think you are not going to live long, and that therefore you ought not to marry. Am I right?"

"Not far off it, Sir," he answered.

"Now, Joe," I said, "can't we talk as friends about this matter? I have no right to intrude into your affairs—none in the least—except what friendship gives me. If you say I am not to talk about it, I shall be silent. To force advice upon you would be as impertinent as useless."

"My mind has been made up for a long time. What right have I to bring other people into trouble? But I take it kind of you, though I mayn't look overpleased. Agnes wants to hear your way of it. I'm agreeable."

This was not very encouraging, but I thought it sufficient ground for proceeding. "I suppose that you will allow that the root of all Christian behavior is the will of God?"

"Surely, Sir."

"Is it not the will of God then, that when a man and a woman love each other, they should marry?"

"Where there be no reasons against it."

"Of course. And you judge you see reason for not doing so, else you would?"

"I do see that a man should not bring a woman into trouble for the sake of being comfortable himself for the rest of a few weary days."

Agnes was sobbing gently behind her handkerchief. I knew how gladly she would be Joe's wife, if only to nurse him through his last illness.

"Not except it would make her comfortable too, I grant you, Joe. But listen to me. In the first place, you don't know, and you are not required to know, when you are going to die. In fact, you have nothing to do with it. Many a life has been injured by the constant expectation of death. It is life we have to do with, not death. The best preparation for the night is to work diligently while the day lasts. The best preparation for death is life. Besides, I have known delicate people who have outlived all their strong relations and have been left alone in the earth. Marriage and death are both God's will, and you have no business to set the one over against the other. For anything you know, the gladness and the peace of marriage may be the very means intended for your restoration to health and strength. I suspect your desire to marry, yet fighting against the idea that you ought not to marry, has a good deal to do with the state of health in which you now find yourself. If a man were happy, he would get over many things that he could not get over if he were miserable."

"But it's for Aggy. You forget that."

"I do not forget that. What right have you to seek for her another kind of welfare than you would have yourself? Are you to treat her as if she were worldly when you are not, to provide for her a comfort which you yourself would despise? Why should you not marry because you have to die soon? If you are thus doomed, which to me is by no means clear, why not have what happiness you may? You may find at the end of twenty years that here you are after all."

"And if I find myself dying at the end of six months?"

"Thank God for those six months. The whole thing, my dear fellow, is a want of faith in God. I do not doubt you think you are doing right, but, I repeat, the whole thing comes from want of faith in God. You will take things into your own hands and order them after a preventive and self-protective fashion, lest God should have ordained the worst for you—which is truly no evil, and would be best met by doing His will. Death is no more an evil than marriage is."

"But you don't see it as I do," persisted the blacksmith.

"Of course I don't. I think you see it as it is not."

He remained silent for a little. A shower of spray fell upon us. He started. "What a wave!" he cried. "That spray came over the top of the rock—we shall have to run for it!"

I fancied that he only wanted to avoid further conversation. "There's no hurry," I said. "It was high water an hour and a half ago."

"You don't know this coast, Sir," returned he, "or you wouldn't talk like that." As he spoke he rose. "For God's sake, Aggy!" he cried in terror, "Come at once! Every other wave be rushing across the breakwater as if it were on the level!"

He hurried back, caught her by the hand, and began to draw her along.

"Hadn't we better stay where we are?" I suggested.

"It's not the tide, Sir. It's a groundswell—from a storm somewhere at sea—and that never asks no questions about tide or no tide."

"Come along, then," I said. "But just wait one minute more. It is better to be ready for the worst."

I had seen a crowbar lying among the stones, and thought now it might be useful. I found it and gave it to Joe, then took the girl's disengaged hand. She thanked me in a voice perfectly calm and firm. Joe took the bar in haste, and drew Agnes toward the breakwater.

Any thought of real danger had not yet crossed my mind. But when I looked at the outstretched back of the breakwater, and saw a dim sheet of white sweep across it, I prepared myself for a struggle.

"Do you know what to do with the crowbar, Joe?" I asked, grasping my own stout oak stick more firmly.

"To stick between the stones and hold on. We must watch our time between the waves."

"You take the command then, Joe," I returned. "You see better than I do, and you know that raging wild beast there. I will obey orders, one of which will be not to lose hold of Agnes—eh, Joe?"

Joe gave a grim enough laugh in reply, and we started, he carrying his crowbar in his right hand against the advancing sea, and I my oak stick in my left toward the still water within.

"Quick march!" said Joe, and away we went. Now the back of the breakwater was very rugged, for it was formed of huge stones, with wide gaps between where the waters had washed out the cement and worn their edges. But what impeded our progress secured our safety.

"Halt!" cried Joe, when we were but a few yards beyond the shelter of the rocks. "There's a topper coming."

A huge wave rushed against the far outsloping base and flung its heavy top right over the middle of the mass, a score of yards in front of us.

"Now for it," cried Joe. "Run!"

We did run. In my mind there was just sense enough of danger to add to the pleasure of the excitement. I did not know how much danger there was. Over the rough worn stones we sped, stumbling.

"Halt!" cried the smith once more, and we did halt, but this time, as it turned out, in the middle front of the coming danger.

"God be with us!" I exclaimed, when the huge billow showed itself through the night. The smith stuck his crowbar between two great stones. To this he held on with one hand, and threw the other arm around Agnes' waist. I too had got my oak firmly fixed, held on with the other hand, and threw the other arm round Agnes. It took but a moment.

"Now then!" cried Joe. "Here she comes! Hold on, Sir. Hold on, Aggy!"

But when I saw the height of the water as it rushed on us, I cried out, "Down, Joe! Down on your face, and let it over us easy! Down, Agnes!"

They obeyed. We threw ourselves across the breakwater, with our heads to the coming foe, and I grasped my stick close to the stones. Over us burst the mighty wave, floating us up from the stones where we lay. But we held on, the wave passed, and we sprung gasping to our feet.

"Now, now!" cried Joe and I together and, heavy as we were, with the water pouring from us, we flew across the remainder of the heap and arrived, panting and safe, at the other end, ere one wave more had swept the surface. The moment we were in safety we turned and looked back, and saw a huge billow sweep the breakwater from end to end. We looked at each other for a moment without speaking.

"I believe, Sir," said Joe at length, with slow and solemn speech, "if you hadn't taken the command at that moment we should all have been lost. We were awfully near death."

"Nearer than you thought, Joe, and yet we escaped it. Things don't go all as we fancy, you see. Faith is as essential to manhood as foresight. Believe me, Joe. It is very absurd to trust God for the future, and not trust Him for the present. The man who is not anxious is the man most likely to do the right thing. He is cool and collected and ready. Our Lord told His disciples that when they should be brought before kings and rulers, they were to take no thought what answer they should make, for it would be given them when the time came."

We were climbing the steep path up the downs. Neither of my companions spoke.

"You have escaped one death together," I said. "Dare another."

Neither of them returned an answer. When we came near the parsonage, I said, "Now, Joe, you must go in and go to bed at once. I will take Agnes home. You can trust me not to say anything against you."

Joe laughed rather hoarsely, and replied, "As you please, Sir. Good night, Aggy. Mind you get to bed as soon as you can."

When I returned from giving Agnes over to her parents, I made haste to change my clothes and put on my warm dressing gown. (I may as well mention that not one of us was the worse for our ducking.) I then went up to Connie's room.

"Here I am to see you, Connie, quite safe."

"I've been lying listening to every blast of wind since you went out, Papa. But all I could do was trust in God."

"Do you call that *all,* Connie? Believe me, there is more power in that than any human being knows the tenth part of yet. It is indeed all."

I said no more then. Though I told my wife about it that night, we were well into another month before I told Connie.

When I left her, I went to Joe's room to see how he was, and found him having some gruel. I sat down on the edge of his bed, and said, "Well, Joe, this is better than under water. I hope you won't be the worse for it."

"I don't much care what comes of it—it will all be over soon."

"But you ought to care what comes of you, Joe. I will tell you why. You are an instrument out of which ought to come praise to God, and, therefore, you ought to care for the instrument."

"That way, yes, I ought."

"And you have no business to be like some children, who say, 'Mamma won't give me so and so,' instead of asking her to give it to them."

"I see what you mean. But, really, you put me out before the young woman. I couldn't say before her what I meant. Suppose, you know, Sir, there was to come a family. It might be, you know."

"Of course. What else would you have?"

"But if I was to die, where would she be then?"

"In God's hands, just as she is now."

"But I ought to take care that she is not left with a burden like that to provide for."

"O Joe! How little you know of a woman's heart! It would just be the greatest comfort she could have for losing you, that's all. Many a woman has married a man she did not care enough for, just that she might have a child of her own to let out her heart upon. I don't say that is right, you know, for such love cannot be perfect. A woman ought to love her child because it is her husband's more than because it is her own, and because it is God's more than either's. If Agnes really loves you, as no one can look in her face and doubt, she will be far happier if you leave her a child—yes, she will be happier if you only leave her your name for hers—than if you died without calling her your wife."

I took Joe's basin from him, and he lay down. He turned his face to the wall. I waited a moment, but finding him silent, bade him good-night, and left the room.

My words must have found their intended mark, for only a month after that storm-tossed night I married the two of them.

TWENTY-SIX
A Walk With My Wife

It was some time before we got the old church bells to work. The worst of it was to get the cranks, which at first required strong pressure on the keys, to work easily enough. But neither Joe nor his cousin spared any pains to perfect the attempt, and at length we succeeded. I took Wynnie down to the instrument, and she made the old tower discourse loudly and eloquently.

One of the nights after that I had a walk and a talk with my wife. It had rained a good deal during the day, but as the sun went down, the air began to clear. And when the moon shone out near the full, she walked the heavens, not "like one that hath been led astray," but as "queen and huntress, chaste and fair."

"What a lovely night it is!" said Ethelwyn, who had come into my study—where I always sat with unblinded windows that the night and her creatures might look in upon me—and she had stood gazing out for a moment.

"Shall we go for a little turn?" I said.

"I should like it very much," she answered. "I will go and put on my bonnet."

In a minute or two she looked in again, all ready. I rose, laid aside my Plato, and went with her. We turned our steps along the edge of the down, and descended upon the breakwater where we seated ourselves on the same spot where, in the darkness, I had heard the voices of Joe and Agnes. What a different night it was from that! The sea lay as quiet as if it could not move for the moonlight that lay upon it. The glory over it was so mighty in its peacefulness, that the wild element beneath was afraid to toss itself even with the motions of its natural unrest. The moon was like the face of a saint before which the stormy people have grown dumb. The rocks stood up solid and dark, and the pulse of the ocean throbbed against them with a lapping gush, soft as the voice of a passionate child soothed into shame of its vanished petulance. But the sky was the glory. Although no breath moved below, there was a gentle wind abroad in the upper regions.

We sat and watched the marvelous depth of the heavens, covered with a stately procession of ever-appearing and ever-vanishing cloud forms—great sculpturesque blocks of a shattered storm, the icebergs of the upper sea. These were not far off against a blue background, but floating near us in the heart of a blue-black space, gloriously lighted by a golden rather than a silvery moon.

At length my wife spoke. "I hope Mr. Percivale is out tonight," she said. "How he must be enjoying it if he is!"

"I wonder the young man is not returning to his professional labors," I said. "Few artists can afford such long holidays as he is taking."

"He is laying in stock, though, I suppose," she answered. "And he must paint better the more familiar he gets with the things God cares to fashion."

"Doubtless. But I am afraid the work of God he is chiefly studying at present is our Wynnie."

"Well, is she not a worthy object of his study?" returned Ethelwyn, looking up into my face with an arch expression.

"Doubtless, again. But I hope she is not studying him quite so much in her turn. I have seen her eyes following him about."

My wife made no answer for a moment. Then she said, "Don't you like him, Harry?"

"Yes. I like him very much."

"Then why should you not like Wynnie to like him?"

"I should like to be surer of his principles, for one thing."

"I should like to be surer of Wynnie's."

I was silent. Ethelwyn resumed, "Don't you think they might do each other good? They both love the truth, I am sure—only they don't perhaps know what it is yet. I think if they were to fall in love with each other, it would very likely make them both more desirous of finding it."

"Perhaps," I said at last. "But you are talking about awfully serious things, Ethelwyn."

"Yes, as serious as life," she answered.

"You make me very anxious," I said. "The young man has not, I fear, any means of gaining a livelihood for more than himself."

"Why should he, before he wanted it? I like to see a man who can be content with an art and a living by it."

"I hope I have not been to blame in allowing them to see so much of each other," I said, hardly heeding my wife's words.

"It came about quite naturally," she rejoined. "If you had opposed their meeting, you would have been interfering, just as if you had been Providence. And you would have only made them think more about each other."

"He hasn't said anything—has he?" I asked in positive alarm.

"Oh, dear no. It may be all my fancy. I am only looking a little ahead. I confess I should like him for a son-in-law. I approve of him," she added, with a sweet laugh.

"Well," I said, "I suppose sons-in-law are the possible, however disagreeable, results of having daughters." I tried to laugh, but hardly succeeded.

"Harry," said my wife, "I don't like you in such a mood. It is not like you at all. It is unworthy of you."

"How can I help being anxious when you speak of such dreadful things as the possibility of having to give away my daughter, my precious wonder that came to me through you out of the infinite—the tender little darling!"

" 'Out of the heart of God,' you used to say, Harry. Yes, and with a destiny He had ordained. It is strange to me how you forget your best and noblest teaching sometimes. You are always telling us to trust God. Surely it is a poor creed that will only allow us to trust in God for ourselves—a very selfish creed. There must be something wrong there. I should say that the man who can only trust God for himself is not half a Christian. Either he is so selfish that that satisfies him, or he has such a poor notion of God that he cannot trust Him with what most concerns him. The former is not your case, Harry. Is it the latter, then? For I must take my turn at the preaching sometimes, mayn't I, Dearest?"

She took my hand in both of hers, and the truth arose in my heart. I never loved my wife more than at that moment, but now I could not speak for other reasons. I saw that I had been faithless to my God, and the moment I could command my speech, I hastened to confess it.

"You are right, my dear," I said, "quite right. I have been wicked, for I have been denying my God. I have been putting my providence in the place of His, trying like an anxious fool to count the hairs on Wynnie's head, instead of being content that the grand, loving Father should count them. My love, let us pray for Wynnie, for what is prayer but giving her to God and His holy, blessed will?"

We sat hand in hand. Neither of us spoke aloud, but we spoke in our hearts to God, talking to Him about Wynnie. Then we rose together and walked homeward, still in silence. But my heart and hand clung to my wife as to the angel whom God had sent to deliver me out of the prison of my faithlessness. And as we went, lo, the sky was glorious again. It had faded from my sight, had grown flat as a dogma and uninteresting; the moon had been but a round thing with the sun shining upon it, and the stars were only minding their own business. But now the solemn march toward an unseen, unimagined goal had again begun. Wynnie's life was hid with Christ in God. Away strode the cloudy pageant with its banners blowing in the wind. Solitary stars, with all their sparkles drawn in, shone quiet as human eyes in the deep solemn clefts of dark blue air. The moon saw the sun, and therefore made the earth glad.

"You have been a moon to me this night, my wife," I said. "You were looking full at the truth, while I was dark. I saw its light in your face, and believed, and turned my soul to the sun. And now I am both ashamed and glad. God keep me from sinning so again."

"My dear husband, it was only a mood, a passing mood," said Ethelwyn, seeking to comfort me.

"It was a mood, and thank God, it is now past; but it was a wicked one. It was a mood in which the Lord might have called me a devil, as He did St. Peter. Such moods have to be grappled with and fought the moment they appear. They must not have their way for a single thought even."

"But we can't always help it, can we?"

"We can't help it out and out, because our wills are not yet free with the freedom God is giving us as fast as we will let Him. When we are able to will thoroughly, then we shall do what we will. At least, I think we shall. But there is a mystery in it God understands. All we know is that we can struggle and pray. But a mood is an awful oppression sometimes, when you least believe in it and most wish to get rid of it. It is like a headache in the soul."

"What *do* the people do who don't believe in God?" said Ethelwyn.

Then Wynnie, who had seen us pass the window, opened the door of the bark house for us. We passed into Connie's chamber and found her lying in the moonlight, gazing at the same heavens as had her father and mother.

TWENTY-SEVEN

Our Last Shore Dinner

The next day there was to be an unusually low tide about two o'clock, and we resolved to dine upon the sands. All morning the children were out playing on the threshold of old Neptune's palace—for in his quieter mood, he will, like a fierce mastiff, let children do with him what they will. I gave myself a whole holiday and wandered about on the shore. The sea was so calm, and the shore so gently sloping that you could hardly tell where the sand ceased and the sea began—the water sloped to such a thin pellicle, thinner than any knife edge, upon the shining brown sand, and you saw the sand underneath the water to such a distance out. Yet this depth, which would not drown a red spider, was the ocean.

In my mind I followed that bed of shining sand, bared of its hiding waters, out and out, till I was lost in an awful wilderness of chasms, precipices, and mountain peaks, in whose caverns the sea serpent may dwell with his breath of pestilence, and the kraken with "his scaly rind" may be sleeping "his ancient dreamless, uninvaded sleep."

I lifted my eyes and saw how the autumn sun hung above the waters, oppressed with a mist of his own glory. Far away to the left, a man who had been gathering mussels on a low rock—inaccessible save in such a tide—threw himself into the sea and swam ashore. Above his head the storm tower stood in the stormless air, and the sea glittered and shone. The long-winged birds knew not which to choose, the balmy air or the cool deep, now flitting like arrowheads through the one, now alighting eagerly upon the other, to forsake it anew for the thinner element. I thanked God for His glory.

"O Papa, it's so jolly! So jolly!" shouted the children as I passed them again.

"What is it that's so jolly, Charlie?" I asked.

"My castle," screeched Harry in reply, "only it's tumbled down. The water *would* keep coming in underneath."

"I tried to stop it with a newspaper," cried Charlie, "but it wouldn't. So we were forced to let it be, and down it went into the ditch."

"We blew it up rather than surrender," said Dora. "We did. Only Harry always forgets, and says the water did it."

I drew near the rock that held the bath. I had never approached it from this side before. It was high above my head, and a stream of water was flowing from it. I scrambled up, undressed and plunged into its dark hollow, where I felt like one of the sea beasts of which I had been dreaming, down in the caves of the unvisited ocean. But the sun was over my head, and the air with an edge of the winter was about me. I dressed quickly, descended on the other side of the rock, and wandered again on the sands to seaward of the breakwater. How different was the scene when a raving mountain of water filled all the hollow where I now wandered, and rushed over the top now so high above me, where I had to cling to its stones to keep from being carried off like a bit of floating seaweed! Here and there rose a well-known rock, but now changed in look by being lifted all the height between the base on the waters, and the second base in the sand.

But the chief delight of the spot, closed in by rocks from the open sands, was the multitude of fairy rivers that flowed across it to the sea. The gladness these streams gave me I cannot communicate. The tide had filled thousands of hollows in the breakwater, hundreds of cracked basins in the rock, huge sponges of sand. From all of these—from cranny and crack and oozing sponge—the water flowed in restricted haste back to the sea, tumbling in tiny cataracts down the faces of the rocks, bubbling from their roots as from wells, gathering in tanks of sand, and overflowing in broad, shallow streams, curving and sweeping in their sandy channels just like the great rivers of a continent—here spreading into smooth, silent lakes and reaches, here babbling along in ripples and waves innumerable. All their channels were of golden sand, and the golden sunlight was above and through and in them all: gold and gold met with the waters between. And all the ripples made shadows. The eye could not see the rippling on the surface, but the sun saw it, and drew it in shadowy motion upon the sand beneath—with gold burnished and trembling, melting, curving, blending, vanishing ever, ever renewed. It was as if all the watermarks upon a web of golden silk had been set in wildest yet most graceful motion. My eye could not be filled with seeing. I stood in speechless delight for a while, gazing at the "endless ending" which was "the humor of the game."

"Father," I murmured half aloud, "Thou alone art, and I am because Thou art. Thy will shall be mine."

I know that I must have spoken aloud, because I remember the start of consciousness and discomposure occasioned by the voice of Percivale greeting me.

"I beg your pardon," he added, "I did not mean to startle you, Mr. Walton. I thought you were only looking at Nature's childplay—not thinking."

"I know few things more fit to set one to thinking than what you have very well called Nature's childplay," I returned. "Is Nature very heartless now, do you think, to go on with this kind of thing at our feet, when away up yonder lies the awful London with so many sores festering in her heart?"

"You must answer your own question, Mr. Walton. You know I cannot. I confess I feel the difficulty deeply. I will go further and confess that the discrepancy makes me doubt many things I would gladly believe. I know *you* are able to distinguish between a glad unbelief and a sorrowful doubt."

"How will you go back to your work in London after seeing all this? Suppose you had had nothing here but rain and high winds and sea fogs, would you have been better fitted for doing something to comfort those who know nothing of such influences than you will be now? One of the most important qualifications of a sick nurse is a ready smile. A long-faced nurse in a sick room is a visible embodiment and presence of the disease against which the life of the patient is fighting in agony. What a power of life and hope has a woman—young or old, I do not care—with a face of the morning, a dress like the spring, and in her hand a bunch of wild flowers with the dew upon them! That is sympathy, not the worship of darkness. And she, looking death in the face with a smile, brings a little health, a little strength to fight, a little hope to endure, actually lapt in the folds of her gracious garments. For the soul itself can do more healing than any medicine, if it be fed with the truth of life."

"But is life such an affair of sunshine and gladness?"

"If life is not, then I confess all this show of Nature is worse than vanity; it is a vile mockery. Life is gladness; it is the death in it that makes the misery. But our Lord has conquered death—the moral death that He called the world—and Nature has God at her heart. God wears His singing robes in a day like this, and says to His children, 'Be not afraid: your brothers and sisters up there in London are in My hands; go and help them. I am with you. Bear to them the message of joy. Tell them to be of good cheer; I have overcome the world. Tell them to endure hunger and not sin, to endure passion and not yield, to admire and not desire. Sorrow and pain are serving My ends, for by them will I slay sin, and save My children.' "

"I wish I could believe as you do, Mr. Walton."

"I wish you could. But God will teach you if you are willing to be taught."

"I desire the truth, Mr. Walton."

"God bless you. God is blessing you," I said.

"Amen," returned Percivale devoutly, and we strolled away together in silence toward the cliffs, where the recession of the tide allowed us to get far enough away from the face of the rocks to see the general effect.

"Who could imagine, in weather like this, and with this baby of a tide lying behind us, low at our feet, that those grand cliffs before us bear on their front the scars and dints of centuries of passionate contest with this same creature that is at this moment unable to rock the cradle of an infant? Look behind you, at your feet, Mr. Percivale; look before you at the chasms, rents, caves, and hollows, of those rocks."

"I wish you were a painter, Mr. Walton," he said.

"And *I* wish I were," I returned. "At least, I know I should rejoice in it, if it had been given me to be one. But why do you say so now?"

"Because you have always some individual predominating idea, which would give interpretation to nature while it gave harmony, reality, and individuality to your representation."

"I know what you mean," I answered, "but I have no gift whatever in that direction. I have no idea of drawing, or of producing the effects of light and shade, though I think I have a little notion of color."

"Even so, I wish I could ask your opinion of some of my pictures."

"That I should never presume to give. I could only tell you what they made me feel or think. Some day I may have the pleasure of looking at them."

"May I offer you my address?" he said, and took a card from his pocketbook. "It is a poor place, but if you should happen to think of me when you are in London, I shall be honored by your paying me a visit."

"I shall be most happy," I returned, taking his card. "Did it ever occur to you, in reference to the subject we were upon a few moments ago, how little you can do without shadow in making a picture?"

"Little indeed," answered Percivale. "In fact, it would be no picture at all."

"I doubt if the world would fare better without its shadows."

"But it would be a poor satisfaction with regard to the nature of God, to be told that He allowed evil for artistic purposes."

"It would, indeed, if you regard the world as a picture. But if you think of His art as expended, not upon the making of a history or drama, but upon the making of an individual, a being, a character, then I think a great part of the difficulty vanishes. So long as a creature has not sinned, sin is possible to him. Does it seem inconsistent with the character of God that, in order that sin should become impossible, He should allow sin to come? That, in order that His creatures should choose the good and refuse the evil, in order that they might turn from sin with a perfect repugnance of the will, He should allow them to fall? That, in order that from being sweet childish children they should become noble, childlike men and women, He should let them try to walk alone? Why should He not allow the possible in order that it should become impossible?"

"I think I understand you," returned Percivale. "I will think over what you have said. These are very difficult questions."

As we spoke, we turned from the cliffs and wandered back across the salt streams to the sands beyond. From the direction of the house came a little procession of servants, with Walter at their head, bearing the preparations for our dinner over the gates of the lock, down the sides of the embankment of the canal, and across the sands.

"Will you join our early dinner?" I asked.

"I shall be delighted," he answered, "if you will let me be of some use first. I presume you mean to carry Connie out."

"Yes, and you shall help me carry her, if you will."

"That is what I hoped," said Percivale, and we went together toward the parsonage.

As we approached, I saw Wynnie sitting at the drawing room window, but when we entered the room, only my wife was there.

"Where is Wynnie?" I asked.

"She saw you coming," she answered, "and went to get Connie ready, for I guessed Mr. Percivale had come to help you carry her out."

But I could not help thinking there might be more than that in Wynnie's disappearance. *What if she should fall in love with him,* I thought, *and he should never say a word? That would be dreadful for us all.*

They had been repeatedly together of late, and if they did fall in love, it would be very natural on both sides. There was evidently a great mental resemblance between them, so that they could not help sympathizing with each other's peculiarities and would make a fine couple.

Why should not two such walk together along the path to the gates of the light? And yet I could not help some anxiety. I did not know anything of his history. I had no testimony concerning him from anyone who knew him, and his past life was a blank to me. His means of livelihood was probably insufficient—certainly, I judged, precarious; and his position in society—but there I checked myself. I had had enough of that kind of thing already.

All this passed through my mind in about three turns of the winnowing fan of thought. Mr. Percivale had begun talking to my wife, who took no pains to conceal that his presence was pleasant to her; and I went upstairs, almost unconsciously, to Connie's room.

When I opened the door, forgetting to announce my approach as I ought to have done, I saw Wynnie leaning over Connie, and Connie's arm round her waist. Wynnie started back, and Connie gave a little cry, for the jerk hurt her. Wynnie turned her head at Connie's cry, and I saw a tear on her face.

"My darlings, I beg your pardon," I said. "It was very stupid of me not to knock at the door."

Connie looked up at me with large eyes and said, "It's nothing, Papa. Wynnie is in one of her gloomy moods, and didn't want you to see her crying. She gave me a little pull, that was all. It didn't hurt me much, only I'm such a goose! I'm in terror before the pain comes. Look at me," she added. "I'm all right now." And she smiled in my face perfectly.

I turned to Wynnie, put my arm about her, kissed her cheek, and left the room. I looked round at the door, and saw that Connie was following me with her eyes, but Wynnie's were hidden in her handkerchief.

I went back to the drawing room, and in a few minutes Walter announced dinner. The same moment Wynnie came to say that Connie was ready. She did not lift her eyes, or approach to give Percivale any greeting, but went again as soon as she had given her message. I saw that he looked first concerned, and then thoughtful.

Percivale and I ascended to Connie's room. Wynnie was not there, but Connie lay, looking lovely, all ready for going. We lifted her, and carried her out the window and down by the path to the breakwater.

As we reached the breakwater, I found that Wynnie was following behind us. We stopped in the very middle of it and set Connie down, as if I wanted to take a breath. But I had thought of something to say to her, which I wanted Wynnie to hear without its being addressed to her.

"Do you see, Connie," I said, "how far off the water is?"

"Yes, Papa, it is a long way off. I wish I could get up and run down to it."

"You can hardly believe that all between, all those rocks, and all that sand, will be covered before sunset."

"I know it will be. But it doesn't *look* likely, does it, Papa?"

"Not in the least, my dear. Do you remember that stormy night when I came through your room to go out for a walk in the dark?"

"Remember it, Papa? I cannot forget it. Every time I hear the wind blowing when I wake in the night, I fancy you are out in it."

"Well, Connie, look down into the great hollow there, with rocks and sand at the bottom of it."

"Yes, Papa."

"Now, look over the side of your litter. You see these holes all about between the stones?"

"Yes, Papa."

"Well, one of these little holes saved my life that night, when the great gulf there was full of huge mounds of roaring water, rushing across this breakwater with force enough to sweep a whole cavalry regiment off its back."

"Papa!" exclaimed Connie, turning pale.

Then I told her all the story while Wynnie listened behind.

"Then I *was* right in being frightened!" cried Connie.

"You were right in trusting in God, Connie."

"But you might have been drowned, Papa!"

"Nobody has a right to say that anything might have been other than what has been. Before a thing has happened, we can say might or might not, but that has to do only with our ignorance. Think what a change, from the dark night and roaring water, to this fullness of sunlight and the bare sands with the water lisping on their edge away there in the distance. Now, troubles will come in life which look as if they would never pass away, just as the night and the storm look as if they would last forever. But the calm and the morning cannot be stayed, and the storm in its very nature is transient. The effort of Nature, as that of the human heart, ever is to return to its repose, for God is peace."

"But if you will excuse me, Mr. Walton," said Percivale, "you say that from your experience. But you can hardly expect experience to be of use to any but those who have had it. It seems to me that its influences cannot be imparted."

"That depends. Of course, as experience, it can have no weight with another, for it is no longer experience. One remove, and it ceases. But faith in the person who *has* experienced can draw over or derive some of its benefits to him who has the faith. Experience may thus, in a sense, be accumulated, and we may go on the fresh experience of our own. At least I can hope that the experience of a father may take the form of hope in the minds of his daughters. Hope never hurt anyone, never yet interfered with duty. It always strengthens to the performance of duty, gives courage and clears the judgment. St. Paul says we are saved by hope. Hope is the most rational thing in the universe. Even the ancient poets, who believed it was delusive, yet regarded it as an antidote given by the mercy of the gods against some of the least of life's ills."

"But they counted it delusive. A wise man cannot consent to be deluded."

"Assuredly not. The sorest truth rather than a false hope! But what is a false hope? Only one that ought not to be fulfilled. The old poets could give themselves little room for hope, and less for its fulfillment, for what were their gods? One thing I repeat—the waves that foamed across the spot where we now stand are gone away, have sunk, and vanished."

"But they will come again, Papa," faltered Wynnie.

"And God will come with them, my love," I said, as we lifted the litter.

In a few minutes more, we were all seated on the sand around a tablecloth spread upon it. The tide had turned, and the waves were creeping up over the level, soundless almost as thought, but it would be time to go home long before they had reached us. The sun was in the western half of the sky, and now and then a breath of wind came from the sea, with a slight saw-edge in it, but not enough to hurt. Connie could stand much more in that way now. And when I saw how she could move herself on her couch, hope for her kept fluttering joyously in my heart. I could not help fancying even that I saw her move her legs a little.

Charles and Harry were every now and then starting up from their dinner and running off with a shout, to return with apparently increased appetite for the rest of it. Neither their mother nor I cared to interfere with the indecorum. Wynnie was very silent, but looked more cheerful. Connie seemed full of quiet bliss. My wife's face was a picture of heavenly repose. The nurse was walking about with the baby, occasionally with one hand helping the other servants to wait upon us. They too seemed to have a share in the gladness of the hour and, like Ariel, did their spiriting gently.

"This is the will of God," I said, after the things were removed, and we had sat for a few moments in silence.

"What is the will of God, Harry?" asked Ethelwyn.

"Why, this, my love," I answered, "this living air and wind and sea and light and land all about us—this consenting, consorting harmony of Nature that mirrors a like peace in our souls. The perfection of such visions, the gathering of them all in one, was—is, I should say—in the face of Christ Jesus. You will say His face was troubled sometimes. Yes, but with a trouble that broke not the music but deepened the harmony. When He wept at the grave of Lazarus, you do not think it was for Lazarus himself, or for His own loss of him? That could not be, seeing He had the power to call him back when He would. The grief was for the poor troubled hearts left behind, to whom it was so dreadful because they had not faith enough in His Father, the God of life and love.

"It was the aching, loving hearts of humanity for which He wept—the hearts that needed God so awfully and could not yet trust Him. Their brother was only hidden in the skirts of their Father's garment, but they could not believe that. They said he was dead, lost, away, all gone, as the children say. And it was so sad to think of a whole world full of the grief of death, that He could not bear it without the human tears to help His heart, as they help ours.

"It was for our dark sorrows that He wept. But the peace could be no less plain on the face that saw God. Did you ever think of that wonderful saying, 'Again a little while, and ye shall see Me, because I go to the Father'? The heart of man would have joined the 'because I go to the Father' with the former result, the not seeing of Him. The heart of man is not able, without more and more light, to understand that all vision is in the light of the Father. Because Jesus went to the Father, the disciples saw Him tenfold more. His body was no longer before their eyes, but His very Being, His very Self was in their hearts—not in their affections only—in their spirits, their heavenly consciousness.

"People find it hard to believe grand things, but why? If there be a God, is it not likely everything ought to be grand, simple, and noble? The ages of eternity will go on showing that such they are and ever have been. God will yet be victorious over our wretched unbeliefs."

I was sitting facing the sea, but with my eyes fixed on the sand, boring holes in it with my stick, for I could talk better when I did not look at my familiar faces. (I did not feel thus in the pulpit. There I sought the faces of my flock to assist me in speaking to their needs.) As I drew near to the close of my last monologue, a colder and stronger blast from the sea blew in my face. I lifted my head, and saw that the tide had crept up a long way, and was coming in fast. A luminous fog had sunk down over that western horizon, had almost hidden the sun, had obscured half the sea, and destroyed all our hopes of a sunset. A certain commonplace veil had dropped over the face of nature, and the wind came in little bitter gusts across the dull waters.

It was time to lift Connie and take her home. We did so, and that was the last time we ate together on the open shore.

TWENTY-EIGHT
A Pastoral Visit

The next morning rose in a rainy mist, which the wind mingled with salt spray torn from the tops of the waves. Every now and then the wind blew a blast of larger drops against the window of my study with an angry clatter and clash, as if daring me to go out and meet its ire. Earth, sea, and sky were possessed by a gray spirit that threatened wrath.

The breakfast bell rang and I went down. Wynnie stood at the window, looking out upon the restless tossing of the waters, but with no despondent answer to the trouble of nature. On the contrary, her cheeks were luminous, and her eyes flashed. Had Percivale said something to her? Or had he just passed the window, and given her a look which she might interpret as she pleased? No, it was only that she was always more peaceful in storm than in sunshine. I said to myself: "She must marry a poor man someday. She is a creature of the north, not of the south; the hot sun of prosperity would wither her up. Give her a bleak hillside, with a glint or two of sunshine between the hailstorms, and she will live and grow. Give her poverty and love, and life will be interesting to her as a romance. Give her money and position and she will grow dull and haughty; she will believe in nothing that poet can sing or architect build. She will, like Cassius, 'scorn her spirit for being moved to smile at anything.' "

She turned and saw me, and came forward. "Don't you like a day like this, Papa?"

"I always have. And you take after me in that, as in a good many things besides. That is how I understand you so well."

"Do I really take after you, Papa? Are you sure that you understand me so well?" she asked, brightening up.

"Yes. And I know I do," I returned.

"Even better than I do myself?" she asked, with an arch smile.

"Considerably, if I mistake not."

"How delightful! To think that I am understood even when I don't understand myself!"

"But even if I am wrong, you are yet understood. The blessedness of life is that we can hide nothing from God. If we could hide anything from God, that hidden thing would by and by turn into a terrible disease. It is the sight of God that keeps and makes things clean. But as we are both fond of this kind of weather, what do you say to going out with me? I have to visit a sick woman."

"You don't mean Mrs. Coombes, Papa?"

"No, my dear. I did not hear she was ill."

"Oh, I daresay it is nothing much. Only Old Nursey said yesterday she was in bed with a bad cold."

"We'll call and inquire as we pass. I have just had a message from that cottage that stands all alone on the corner of Mr. Barton's farm—over the cliff, you know—that the woman is ill, and would like to see me. So the sooner we start, the better, that is, if you are inclined to go with me."

"How can you put an *if* to that, Papa? I shall have done my breakfast in five minutes, Papa. Oh! Here's Mamma. Mamma, I'm going out for a walk in the rain with Papa. You won't mind, will you?"

"I don't think it will do you any harm, my dear."

Wynnie left the room to put on her long cloak and her bonnet, and after that we went out into the weather. We called at the sexton's cottage and found him sitting gloomily by the low window, looking seaward.

"I hope your wife is not *very* poorly, Coombes," I said.

"No, Sir. She be very comfortable in bed. Bed's not a bad place to be in such weather," he answered, turning again a dreary look toward the Atlantic. "Poor things!"

"What a passion for comfort you have, Coombes! How does that come about, do you think?"

"I suppose I was made so."

"To be sure you were. God made you so."

"Surely. Who else?"

"Then I suppose He likes *making* people comfortable if He makes people *like* to be comfortable."

"It du look likely enough."

"Then when He takes it out of your hands, you mustn't think He doesn't look after the people you would make comfortable if you could."

"I must mind my work, you know."

"Yes, surely. And you mustn't want to take His out of His hands, and go grumbling as if you would do it so much better if He would only let you get *your* hand to it."

"I daresay you be right," he said. "I must just go and have a look about though. Here's Agnes. She'll tell you about her mother."

He took his spade from the corner and went out. He often brought his tools into the cottage, and he had carved the handle of his spade all over with the names of the people he had buried.

"Tell your mother, Agnes, that I will call in the evening and see her, if she would like to see me. We are going now to see Mrs. Stokes. She is very poorly, I hear."

Wynnie turned to me outside and said, "Let us go through the churchyard, Papa, and see what the old man is doing."

"Very well, my dear. It is only a few steps round."

"Why do you humor the sexton's foolish fancy so much, Papa? It is such nonsense! You taught us about the resurrection."

"Most certainly, my dear. But it would be of no use to try to get it out of his head by any argument. He has a kind of craze in that direction. To get people's hearts right is of much more importance than convincing their judgments. Right judgment will follow. All such fixed ideas should be encountered from the deepest grounds of truth, and not from the outsides of their relations. Coombes has to be taught that God cares for the dead more than he does, and therefore it is unreasonable for him to be anxious about them."

When we reached the churchyard, we found the old man kneeling on a grave before its headstone. It was very old, with a death's skull and crossbones carved upon the top of it in high relief. With his pocketknife, he was removing the lumps of green moss out of the hollows of the eyes of the carven skull. We did not interrupt him, but walked past with a nod.

Then we were on the downs, and the wind was buffeting us, and every other minute assailing us with a blast of rain. Wynnie drew her cloak closer about her, bent her head toward the blast, and struggled on bravely by my side. No one who wants to enjoy a walk in the rain must carry an umbrella—it is pure folly. We came to one of the stone fences, cowered down by its side for a few moments to recover our breath, and then struggled on again.

When we reached the house, I left Wynnie seated by the kitchen fire, and was shown into the room where Mrs. Stokes lay. She was a hard-featured woman, with cold, troubled black eyes that rolled restlessly about. She lay on her back, moving her head from side to side. She looked at me, and turned her eyes away toward the wall, and I guessed that something was on her mind. I approached the bedside and seated myself by it. I always do so at once, for the patient feels more at rest than if I stand up tall. I laid my hand on hers.

"Are you very ill, Mrs. Stokes?" I said.

"Yes, very," she answered with a groan. "It be come to the last with me."

"I hope not indeed, Mrs. Stokes. It's not come to the last with us, so long as we have a Father in heaven."

"Ah, but it be with me. He can't take any notice of the like of me."

"But indeed He does, whether you think it or not. He takes notice of every thought we think, and every deed we do, and every sin we commit."

I said the last words with emphasis, for I suspected something more than usual upon her conscience. She gave another groan, but made no reply. I therefore went on. "Our Father in heaven is not like some fathers on earth, who so long as their children don't bother them, let them do anything they like. He will not have us do what is wrong. He loves us too much for that."

"He won't look at me," she said, half murmuring, half sighing it out, so that I could hardly hear what she said.

"It is because He is looking at you that you are feeling uncomfortable," I answered. "He wants you to confess your sins. I don't mean to me, but to Himself—though if you would like to tell me anything, and I can help you, I shall be very glad. You know Jesus Christ came to save us from our sins, and that's why we call Him our Saviour. But He can't save us from our sins if we won't confess that we have any."

"I'm sure I never said but what I be a great sinner, as well as other people."

"You don't suppose that's confessing your sins?" I said. "I once knew a woman of very bad character, who allowed to me she was a great sinner. But when I said, 'Yes, you have done so and so,' she would not allow any of those deeds to be worthy of being reckoned amongst her sins. When I asked her what great sins she had been guilty of—seeing these counted for nothing—I could get no more out of her than that she was a great sinner, like other people, as you have been saying."

"I hope you don't be thinking I ha' done anything of that sort!" she said, with wakening energy. "No man or woman dare say I've done anything to be ashamed of."

"Then you've committed no sins," I returned. "But why did you send for me? You must have something to say to me."

"I never did send for you. It must ha' been my husband."

"Ah, then, I'm afraid I've no business here!" I returned, rising. "I thought you had sent for me."

She returned no answer. I hoped that by retiring I should set her thinking, and make her more willing to listen the next time I came. I think clergymen may do much harm by insisting when people are in a bad mood, as if they had everything to do, and the Spirit of God nothing at all. I bade her good-day, hoped she would be better soon, and returned to Wynnie.

As we walked home together, I said, "Mrs. Stokes had not sent for me herself, and rather resented my appearance. But I think she will send for me before many days are over."

TWENTY-NINE
The Sore Spot

We had a week of hazy weather after this, which I spent chiefly in my study and in Connie's room. A world of mist hung over the sea which, as if ill-tempered or unhappy, folded itself in its mantle, and lay still. It refused to hold any communion with mortals.

One morning Dora knocked at the door saying that Mr. Percivale had called, that Mamma was busy, and would I mind if she brought him up to the study.

"Not in the least, my dear," I answered, "I shall be very glad to see him."

"Unfavorable weather for your sacred craft, Percivale," I said, as he entered. "I presume you are thinking of returning to London now, as there seems so little to be gained by remaining here. When this weather begins to show itself, I could wish myself in my own parish. But I am sure the change, even through the winter, will be good for my daughter."

"I must be going soon," he answered. "But it would be too bad to take offense at the old lady's first touch of temper. I mean to wait and see whether we shall not have a little bit of St. Martin's Summer, as Shakespeare calls it, after which, hail London, queen of smoke and—"

"And what?" I asked, seeing he hesitated.

" 'And soap,' I was fancying you would say. For you never will allow the worst of things, Mr. Walton."

"No, surely I will not. For one thing, the worst has never been seen by anybody yet. We have no experience to justify it."

We were chatting in this loose manner, when Walter came to tell me that Mr. Stokes was asking for me. I went down to see him.

"My wife be very bad, Sir," he said. "I wish you could come and see her."

"Does she want to see me?" I asked.

"She's been more uncomfortable than ever since you were there last," he said.

"But," I repeated, "has she said she would like to see me?"

"I can't say it, Sir."

"Then *you* want me to see her?"

"Yes, Sir. But I be sure she do want to see you. I know her way, you see. She never would say she wanted anything in her life. She would always leave you to find it out. So I got sharp at that."

"And then, would she allow she had wanted it when you got it?"

"No, never. She be peculiar, my wife. She always be."

"Does she know that you have come to ask me now?"

"No."

"Have you courage to tell her?"

The man hesitated.

"If you haven't courage to tell her," I resumed, "I have nothing more to say. I can't go—or, rather, I will not go."

"I will tell her."

"Then tell her that I refuse to come until she sends for me herself."

"Ben't that rather hard on a dying woman?"

"I have my reasons. Except she send for me herself, the moment I go she will take refuge in the fact that she did not send for me. I know your wife's peculiarity too, Mr. Stokes."

"Well, I *will* tell her. It's time to speak my own mind."

"When she sends for me, if it be in the middle of the night, I shall be with her at once."

He left, and I returned to Percivale. We went on talking for some time. Indeed, we talked so long that the dinner hour was approaching, and one of the maids came with the message that Mr. Stokes had called again. I could not help smiling inwardly at the news. I went down at once, and found him smiling too.

"My wife do send me for you this time, Sir," he said. "Between you and me, I cannot help thinking she have something on her mind she wants to tell you."

"Why shouldn't she tell you, Mr. Stokes? That would be most natural. And then if you wanted any help about it, why, of course here I am."

"She don't think well enough of my judgment for that. And I daresay she be quite right. She always do make me give in before she have done talking. But she have been a right good wife to me."

"Perhaps she would have been a better wife if you hadn't given in quite so much. It is very wrong to give in when you think you are right."

"But I never be sure of it when she talk to me awhile."

"Ah, then, I have nothing to say, except that you ought to have been surer—*sometimes*. I don't say *always*."

"But she do want you very bad now, Sir. I don't think she'll behave to you as she did before. Do come."

"Of course I will—instantly."

I returned to the study, and said to Percivale, "I do not know how long I may have to be with the poor woman. Why don't you wait here and take my place at the dinner table? I promise not to depose you if I should return before the meal is over."

He thanked me very heartily. I showed him into the drawing room, told my wife where I was going, and not to wait dinner for me—I would take my chance—and joined Mr. Stokes.

"You have no idea, then," I said, after we had gone about half-way, "what makes your wife so uneasy?"

"No, I haven't," he answered. "Except it be," he resumed, "that she was too hard, as I thought, upon our Mary, when she wanted to marry beneath her, as my wife thought."

"How beneath her? Who was it she wanted to marry?"

"She did marry him. She has a bit of her mother's temper, you see, and she would take her own way."

"Ah! There's a lesson to mothers, is it not? If they want to have their own way, they mustn't give their own temper to their daughters."

"But how are they to help it?"

"Ah, how indeed? But what is your daughter's husband?"

"A laborer. He works on a farm out by Carpstone."

"But you have worked on Mr. Barton's farm for many years, if I don't mistake."

"I have. But I am a foreman now, you see."

"But you weren't so always, and your son-in-law, whether he works his way up or not, is, I presume, much where you were when you married Mrs. Stokes."

"True as you say. But it's not me that has anything to say about it. I never gave the man a nay. But you see my wife, she always do be wanting to get her head up in the world, and since she took to the shopkeeping—"

"The shopkeeping!" I said, with some surprise. "I didn't know that."

"Well, you see, it's only for a quarter or so out of the year. This is a favorite walk for the folks as comes here for the bathing—past our house, to see the great cave down below. And my wife she got a bit of a sign put up, and put a few ginger-beer bottles there in the window, and—"

"A bad place for the ginger beer," I said.

"They were only empty ones with corks and strings, you know. My wife she know better than to put the ginger beer its own self in the sun. But she do carry her head higher after that, and a farm-laborer was none good enough for her daughter."

"And hasn't she been kind to her since she married, then?"

"She's never done her no harm."

"But she hasn't gone to see her very often, or asked her to come and see you very often, I suppose."

"There's ne'er a one o' them crossed the door of the other," he answered, with some evident feeling of his own in the matter.

"Ah! But you don't approve of that yourself, Stokes?"

"Approve of it? No, Sir. I be a farm laborer once myself. But she take after her mother, she do. I don't know which of the two it is as does it, but there's no coming and going between Carpstone and this."

We were approaching the house. I told Stokes he had better let her know I was there. If she had changed her mind, it was not too late for me to go home again without disturbing her. He came back saying she was still very anxious to see me.

"Well, Mrs. Stokes, how do you feel today? You don't look much worse."

"I be much worse. You don't know what I suffer, or you wouldn't make so little of it. I be very bad."

"I know you are very ill, but I hope you are not too ill to tell me why you are so anxious to see me. You *have* something to tell me, I suppose."

With pale and deathlike countenance, she appeared to be fighting more with herself than with the disease which had nearly overcome her. The drops stood upon her forehead, and she did not speak.

"Was it about your daughter you wanted to speak to me?"

"No," she muttered. "I have nothing to say about my daughter. She was my own, and I could do as I pleased with her."

I thought that we must have a word about that by and by, but meantime she must relieve her heart of the one thing whose pressure she felt.

"Then," I said, "you want to tell me about something that was not your own?"

"Who said I ever took what was not my own?" she returned fiercely. "Did Stokes dare to say I took anything that wasn't my own?"

"No one has said anything of the sort. Only I cannot help thinking, from your own words and from your own behavior, that such must be the cause of your misery."

"It is very hard that the parson should think such things," she muttered again.

"My poor woman," I said, "you sent for me because you had something to confess to me. I want to help you, if I can. But you are too proud to confess it yet, I see. There is no use in my staying here, for it only does you harm. So I will bid you good-morning. If you cannot confess to me, confess to God."

"God knows it, I suppose, without that."

"Yes. But that does not make it less necessary for you to confess it. How is He to forgive you, if you won't allow that you have done wrong?"

"It be not so easy as you think. How would you like to say you had took something that was not your own?"

"Well, I shouldn't like it, certainly. But if I had it to do, I think I should make haste and do it, and so get rid of it."

"But that's the worst of it—I can't get rid of it."

"But," I said, laying my hand on hers, and trying to speak as kindly as I could, although her whole behavior would have been exceedingly repulsive but for her evidently great suffering, "you have now confessed taking something that did not belong to you. Why don't you summon courage and tell me all about it? I want to help you out of the trouble as easily as ever I can, but I can't if you don't tell me what you've got that isn't yours."

"I haven't got anything," she muttered.

"You had something then, whatever may have become of it now."

She was again silent.

"What did you do with it?"

"Nothing."

I rose and took up my hat. She stretched out her hand, as if to lay hold of me, with a cry, "Stop, stop. I'll tell you all about it. I lost it again. That's the worst of it. I got no good of it."

"What was it?"

"A sovereign," she said, with a groan. "And now I'm a thief, I suppose."

"No more a thief than you were before. Rather less, I hope. But do you think it would have been any better for you if you hadn't lost it, and had got some good of it, as you say?"

She was silent yet again.

"If you hadn't lost it, you would most likely have been a great deal worse for it than you are—a more wicked woman altogether."

"I'm not a wicked woman."

"It is wicked to steal, is it not?"

"I didn't steal it."

"How did you come by it, then?"

"I found it."

"Did you try to find out the owner?"

"No. I knew whose it was."

"Then it was very wicked not to return it. And, I say again, that if you had not lost the sovereign, you would have been most likely a more wicked woman than you are."

"It was very hard to lose it. I could have given it back. And then I wouldn't have lost my character as I have done this day."

"Yes, you could—but I doubt if you would."

"I would."

"Now, if you had it, you are sure you would give it back?"

"Yes, that I would," she said, looking me so full in the face that I was sure she meant it.

"How would you give it back? Would you get your husband to take it?"

"No! I wouldn't trust him."

"With the story, you mean? You do not wish to imply that he would not restore it."

"I don't mean that. He would do what I told him."

"How would you return it, then?"

"Make a parcel of it and send it."

"Without saying anything about it?"

"Yes. Where's the good? The man would have his own."

"No, he would not. He has a right to your confession, for you have wronged him. That would never do."

"You are too hard upon me." She began to weep angrily.

"Do you want to get the weight of this sin off your mind?"

"Of course I do. I am going to die. Oh, dear! Oh, dear!"

"That is just how I want to help you. You must confess, or the weight of it will stick there."

"But if I confess, I shall be expected to pay it back."

"Of course. That is only reasonable."

"But I haven't got it, I tell you. I have lost it."

"Have you not a sovereign in your possession?"

"No, not one."

"Can't you ask your husband to let you have one?"

"There! I knew it was no use. I knew you would only make matters worse. I do wish I had never seen that wicked money."

"You ought not to abuse the money. It was not wicked. You ought to wish that you had returned it. But that is no use. The thing is to return it now. Has your husband a sovereign?"

"No. He may ha' got one since I be laid up. But I never can tell him about it. And I should be main sorry to spend one of his hard earnings in that way, poor man."

"Well, I'll tell him. And we'll manage it somehow."

I thought for a few moments she would break out in opposition, but she hid her face with the sheet instead, and burst into a great weeping.

I took this as permission, and went to the door and called her husband. He came in looking scared. His wife did not look up, but lay weeping. I hoped much for her and him too from this humiliation before him, for I had little doubt she needed it.

"Your wife, poor woman," I said, "is in great distress because—I do not know when or how—she picked up a sovereign that did not belong to her, and instead of returning it, put it away somewhere, and lost it. This is what is making her so miserable."

"Deary me!" said Stokes, in the tone with which he would have spoken to a sick child. Going up to his wife he sought to draw down the sheet from her face, apparently that he might kiss her, but she kept tight hold of it, and he could not. "Deary me!" he went on. "We'll soon put that to rights. When was it, Jane, that you found it?"

"When we wanted so to have a pig of our own; and I thought I could soon return it," she sobbed from under the sheet.

"Deary me! Ten years ago! Where did you find it?"

"I saw Squire Tresham drop it, as he paid me for some ginger beer he got for some ladies that was with him. I do believe I should ha given it back at the time, but he made faces at the ginger beer, and said it was very nasty, and I thought, well, I would punish him for it."

"It was your temper that made a thief of you, then," I said.

"My old man won't be so hard on me as you. I wish I had told him first."

"I wish that too," I said, "were it not that I am afraid you might have persuaded him to be silent about it, and so have made him miserable and wicked too. But now, Stokes, what is to be done? This money must be paid. Have you got it?"

The poor man looked blank.

"She will never be at ease till this money is paid," I insisted.

"Well, I ain't got it, but I'll borrow it of someone. I'll go to master and ask him."

"No, my good fellow, that won't do. Your master would want to know what you were going to do with it, perhaps, and we mustn't let more people know about it than just ourselves and Squire Tresham. There is no occasion for that. I'll tell you what. I'll give you the money, and you must take it—or, if you like, I will take it to the squire—and tell him all about it. Do you authorize me to do this, Mrs. Stokes?"

"Please, Sir. It's very kind of you. I will work hard to pay you again, if it please God to spare me. I am very sorry I was so cross-tempered to you, but I couldn't bear the disgrace of it," she said from under the bedclothes.

"Well, I'll go," I said, "and as soon as I've had my dinner, I'll go over to Squire Tresham's, then come back tonight and tell you about it. And now I hope you will be able to thank God for forgiving you this sin. But you must not hide and cover it up, but confess it clean out to Him, you know."

She made me no answer, but went on sobbing.

I hastened home, and when I went into the dining room, I found that they had not sat down to dinner. I expostulated that it was against the rule of the house, when my return was uncertain.

"But, my love," said my wife, "why should you not let us please ourselves sometimes? Dinner is so much nicer when you are with us."

"I am very glad you think so," I answered. "But there are the children."

"The children have had their dinner."

"Always in the right, Ethelwyn—but there's Mr. Percivale."

"I never dine till seven o'clock—to save daylight," he said.

"Then I am beaten on all points. Let us dine."

During dinner I could scarcely help observing how Percivale's eyes followed Wynnie, or, rather, every now and then settled down upon her face. That she was aware, almost conscious of this, I could not doubt. One glance at her satisfied me of that. But certain words of the Apostle Paul kept coming again and again into my mind, for they were winged words those, and even when they did not enter, they fluttered their wings at my window: "Whatsoever is not of faith is sin." And I kept reminding myself that I must heave the load of sin off me, as I had been urging poor Mrs. Stokes to do. For surely, all fear is sin, and one of the most oppressive sins from which the Lord came to save us.

After dinner I set out for Squire Tresham's. He was a rough but kindhearted elderly man. When I told him the story of the poor woman's misery, he was quite concerned at her suffering. When I produced the sovereign, he would not receive it at first, but requested me to take it back to her, and say she must keep it by way of an apology for his rudeness about her ginger beer—for I took care to tell him the whole story, thinking it might be a lesson to him too. But I begged him to take it, for it would, I thought, not only relieve her mind more thoroughly, but keep her from thinking lightly of the affair afterward. Of course, I could not tell him I had advanced the money, for that would have quite prevented him from receiving it.

I then returned straight to the cottage.

"Well, Mrs. Stokes," I said, "it's all over now. That's one good thing done. How do you feel yourself now?"

"I feel better now, Sir. I hope God will forgive me."

"God does forgive you. But there are more things you need forgiveness for. It is not enough to get rid of one sin. We must get rid of all our sins, you know. They're not nice things, are they, to keep in our hearts? It is just like shutting up nasty corrupting things, dead carcasses, under lock and key in our most secret drawers, as if they were precious jewels."

"I wish I could be good, like some people, but I wasn't made so. There's my husband now. I do believe he never do anything wrong in his life. But then, you see, he would let a child take him in."

"And far better too. Infinitely better to be taken in. Indeed there is no harm in being taken in—but there is awful harm in taking in."

She did not reply, and I went on. "You would feel a good deal better yet, if you would send for your daughter and her husband now, and make up with them."

"I will. I'm tired of having my own way. But I was made so."

"You weren't made to continue so, at all events. God gives us the necessary strength to resist what is bad in us. But you must give in to Him, else He cannot get on with it. I think it very likely He made you ill now, just that you might think, and feel that you had done wrong."

"I have been feeling that for many a year."

"That made it the more needful to make you ill, for you had been feeling your duty and yet not doing it, and that was worst of all. You know Jesus came to lift the weight of our sins, our very sins themselves, off our hearts, by forgiving them and helping us to cast them away from us. Everything that makes you uncomfortable must have sin in it somewhere, and He came to save you from it. Send for your daughter and her husband. And, when you have done that, you will think of something else to set right that's wrong."

"But there would be no end to that way of it, Sir."

"Certainly not, till everything was put right."

"But a body might have nothing else to do, that way."

"Well, that's the very first thing that has to be done. It is our business in this world. We were not sent here to have our own way and try to enjoy ourselves."

"That is hard on a poor woman that has to work for her bread."

"To work for your bread is not to take your own way, for it is God's way.

But you have wanted many things your own way. And because you would not trust Him with His own business, but took it into your hands, you have not enjoyed your own life. If you will but do His will, He will take care that you have a life to be very glad of and very thankful for. And the longer you live, the more blessed you will find it. But I will leave you with that for now, for I have talked long enough. I will come and see you again tomorrow, if you like."

"Please do. I shall be very grateful."

As I headed home, I thought, if the lifting of one sin off the human heart was like a resurrection, what would it be when every sin was lifted from every heart! Every sin, then, discovered in one's own soul, must be a pledge of renewed bliss in its removing. And when St. Paul's words came to me—"Whatsoever is not of faith is sin"—I thought what a weight of sin had to be lifted from the earth. But what could I do for it? I could just begin with myself, and pray to God for that inward light which is His Spirit.

THIRTY

The Gathering Storm

The weather cleared up again the next day, and for a fortnight it was lovely. In this region we saw less of the sadness of the dying year than in our own parish, for there being so few trees in the vicinity of the ocean, the autumn had nowhere to hang out her mourning flags. There the air is so mild, and the temperature so equable, that the bitterness of the season is almost unknown. That is, however, no guarantee against furious storms.

Turner paid us another visit, and brought good news from home. Everything was going on well. Weir was working as hard as usual, and everybody agreed that I could not have found a better man to take my place.

Connie was much improved, and was now able to turn a good way from one side to the other. Finding her health so steady, Turner encouraged her in making gentle and frequent use of her strength, impressing upon her, however, that everything depended upon avoiding a jerk or twist of any sort. I was with them when he said this. She looked up at him with a happy smile.

"I will do all I can, Mr. Turner," she said, "to get out of people's way. I want to help—and not be helped more than other people—as soon as possible. I will therefore be as gentle as Mamma and as brave as Papa, and see if I don't get well, Mr. Turner. I mean to have a ride on old Sprite next summer, I do," she added, nodding her pretty head up from the pillow, when she saw the glance the doctor and I exchanged. "Look here," she went on, poking the eiderdown quilt up with her foot.

"Magnificent," said Turner, "but mind, you must do nothing out of bravado. That won't do at all."

"I have done," said Connie, putting on a face of mock submission.

That day we carried her out for a few minutes, but it was to be the last time for many weeks.

One day I was walking home from a visit I had been paying to Mrs. Stokes. She was much better—indeed, on her way to recovery—and her mental health was improved as well. Her manner to me was certainly very different, and the tone of her voice, when she spoke to her husband especially, was changed—a certain roughness in it was much modified.

It was a cold and gusty afternoon. The sky eastward and overhead was tolerably clear when I set out from home, but when I left the cottage to return, I could see that some change was at hand. Shaggy vapors of light gray were blowing rapidly across the sky from the west. A wind was blowing fiercely up there, although the gusts down below came from the east. Away to the west, a great thick curtain of luminous yellow fog covered all the horizon. A surly secret seemed to lie in its bosom, though now and then I could discern the dim ghost of a vessel through it. I was glad when I seated myself comfortably by the drawing room fire and saw Wynnie making tea.

"It looks stormy, I think, Wynnie," I said.

Her eyes lightened, as she looked out to sea from the window.

"You seem to like the idea of it," I added.

"You told me I was like you, Papa, and you look as if you liked the idea of it too."

"In itself, certainly, a storm is pleasant to me. I should not like a world without storms any more than I should like that Frenchman's idea of the perfection of the earth, when all was to be smooth as a trim shaven lawn: rocks and mountains banished, and the sea breaking on the shore only in wavelets of ginger beer or lemonade, I forget which. But the older you grow, the more sides of a thing will present themselves to your contemplation. The storm may be grand and exciting, but you cannot help thinking of the people who are in it. Think for a moment of the multitude of vessels, great and small, which are gathered within the skirts of that angry vapor out there."

"But," said Wynnie, "you say *everybody* is in God's hands."

"Yes, surely, my dear, as much out in yon stormy haze as here beside the fire."

"Then we ought not to be miserable about them, even if there comes a storm, ought we?"

"No, surely. And, besides, I think if we could help any of them, the very persons that enjoyed the storm the most would be the busiest to rescue them from it. At least, I fancy so. But isn't the tea ready?"

"Yes, Papa. I'll just go and tell Mamma."

She returned with her mother, and the three children also joined us. Turner had just come in from a walk over the hills, and was now standing looking out at the sea.

"She looks uneasy, does she not?" I said.

"You mean the Atlantic?" he returned, looking round. "Yes, I think so. I am glad she is not a patient of mine. I fear she is going to be very feverish, probably delirious before morning. She won't sleep much, and will talk rather loudly when the tide comes in."

"You will not care to go out again. What shall we do this evening? Shall we go to Connie's room and have some Shakespeare?"

"I could wish nothing better. What play shall we have?"

"Let us have the *Midsummer Night's Dream*," said Ethelwyn.

"Oh, yes!" said Wynnie with a roguish look. "There is one reason why I like that play."

"I should think there might be more than one, Wynnie."

"But one reason is enough for a woman at once—isn't it, Papa?"

"I'm not sure of that. But what is your reason?"

"The fairies are not allowed to play any tricks with the women. *They* are true throughout."

"I might choose to say that was because they were not tried."

"And I might venture to answer that Shakespeare, being true to nature always, as you say, Papa, knew very well how absurd it would be to represent a woman's feelings as under the influence of the juice of a paltry flower."

"Capital, Wynnie!" said her mother, and Turner and I chimed in with our approbation.

So we sat in Connie's room, delighting ourselves with the reflex of the poet's fancy, while the sound of the rising tide kept mingling with the fairy talk and the foolish rehearsal.

"Musk roses," said Titania—and the first of the blast, going round south to west, rattled the window.

"Good hay, sweet hay, hath no fellow," said Bottom—and the roar of the waves was in our ears.

"So doth the woodbine the sweet honeysuckle gently entwist," said Titania—and the blast poured the rain in a spout against the window.

"Slow in pursuit, but matched in mouth like bells," said Theseus—and the wind whistled shrill through the chinks of the bark house.

We drew the curtains closer, made up the fire higher, and read on. It was time for supper before we finished, and when we left Connie to go to sleep, it was with the hope that through all the rising storm, she would dream of breeze-haunted summer woods.

THIRTY-ONE
The Gathered Storm

I woke in the middle of the night and the darkness to hear the wind howling. It was wide awake now and up with intent. It seized the house and shook it furiously, and the rain kept pouring, only I could not hear it save in the *rallentando* passages of the wind. But through all the wind, I could hear the roaring of the big waves on the shore. I did not wake my wife, but put on my dressing gown and went softly to Connie's room to see whether she was awake. I feared if she were, she would be frightened, even though Wynnie was with her, for Wynnie always slept in a little bed in the same room.

I opened the door very gently, and peeped in. The fire was burning, for Wynnie was an admirable stoker and could generally keep the fire wakeful all night. There was just light enough to see that Connie was fast asleep, and that her dreams were not of storms. But as I turned to leave the room, Wynnie's voice called me in a whisper. Approaching her bed, I saw her eyes, like the eyes of the darkness, for I could scarcely see anything of her face.

"Awake, darling?" I said.

"Yes, Papa. I have been awake a long time. But isn't Connie sleeping delightfully? She does sleep so well! Sleep is surely very good for her."

"It is the best thing for us all, next to God's Spirit, I sometimes think, my dear. But are you frightened by the storm? Is that what keeps you awake?"

"No, but sometimes the house shakes so that I do feel a little nervous. I don't know how it is. I never felt afraid of anything natural before."

"What our Lord said about not being afraid of anything that could only hurt the body applies here. In all the terrors of the night, think about Him."

"I do try, Papa. But don't you stop—you will get cold. It is a dreadful storm, is it not? Suppose there should be people drowning out there now!"

"There may be, my love. People are dying every moment on the face of the earth, and drowning is only an easy way of dying. Mind, they are all in God's hands."

"Yes, Papa. I will turn round and shut my eyes, and fancy that His hand is over them, making them dark with His care."

"And it will not be fancy, my darling, if you do. Good night."

Dark, dank, weeping, the morning dawned. All dreary was the earth and sky, and the wind was still hunting the clouds across the heavens. It lulled a little as we sat at breakfast, but soon the storm was up again, and the wind raved. I went out, and the wind caught me and shook me as if with invisible human hands. I fought with it, and made my way into the deserted streets of the village. Not a man or horse was to be seen, no doors were open, and the little shops looked as if nobody had crossed their thresholds for a week.

One child came out of the baker's with a big loaf in her apron, and the wind threatened to blow the hair off her head, or her into the canal. I took her by the hand, and she led me to her home while I kept her from being carried away by the wind. Having landed her safely inside her mother's door, I went on, climbed the heights above the village, and looked abroad over the Atlantic.

What a waste of aimless tossing to and fro! Gray mist above full of falling rain—gray, wrathful waters underneath, foaming and bursting as billow broke upon billow. The tide was ebbing now, but almost every other wave swept the breakwater. They burst on the rocks at the other end of it, and rushed in shattered spouts and clouds of spray far into the air over their heads.

The solitary form of a man stood at some distance gazing, as I was, out upon the ocean. I walked toward him, suspecting who this might be who loved Nature so well that he did not shrink from her, even in her most uncompanionable moods. I soon found I was right—it was Percivale.

"What a clashing of waterdrops!" I said. "They are but waterdrops, after all, that make this great noise upon the rocks, only there are a great many of them."

"Yes," said Percivale. "But look out yonder. You see a single sail, close-reefed, away in the mist there? As soon as you think of the human struggle with the elements, as soon as you know that hearts are in the midst of it, it is a clashing of waterdrops no more. It is an awful power, which the will and all that it rules have to fight for the mastery, or at least for freedom."

"Surely you are right. But as I have now seen how matters are with the elements, and have had a good pluvial bath as well, I think I will go home and change my clothes."

"I have hardly had enough of it yet," returned Percivale. "I shall have a stroll along the heights here. And when the tide has fallen a little way from the foot of the cliffs, I shall go down on the sands, and watch a while there. But I will go with you as far as the village, and then turn and take my way along the downs for a mile or two. I don't mind being wet."

"I didn't once."

We reached the brow of the heights, and here we parted. A fierce blast of wind rushed at me, and I hastened down the hill. How dreary the streets did look—how much more dreary than the stormy down! I saw no living creature as I returned but a terribly draggled dog, a cat that seemed to have a bad conscience, and a lovely little-girl face flattening the tip of its nose against a windowpane. Every rain pool was a mimic sea, and had a mimic storm within its own narrow bounds. The water went hurrying down the kennels like a long brown snake anxious to get to its hole and hide from the tormenting wind; and every now and then the rain came in full rout before the conquering blast.

When I got home I peeped in at Connie's door, and saw that she was raised a little more than usual—that is, the end of the couch against which she leaned was at a more acute angle. She was sitting staring (rather than gazing) out at the wild tumult. Her face was paler and keener than usual.

"Why, Connie, who set you up so straight?"

"Mr. Turner, Papa. I wanted to see out, and he raised me himself. He says I am so much better, I may have it in the seventh notch as often as I like."

"But you look too tired for it. Hadn't you better lie down again?"

"It's only the storm, Papa."

"The more reason you should not see it if it tires you so."

"It does not tire me, Papa. Only I keep constantly wondering what is going to come out of it. It looks as if *something* must follow."

"You didn't hear me come into your room last night, Connie. The storm was raging then as loud as it is now, but you were out of its reach, fast asleep. Now it is too much for you. You must lie down."

"Very well, Papa."

I lowered the support, and when I returned from changing my wet garments she was already looking much better.

After dinner I went to my study. Then evening began to fall, and I went out again, for I wanted to see how the sexton and his wife were faring. The wind had already increased in violence, and threatened to blow a hurricane. The old mill shook its foundations as I passed through it to reach the lower part where they lived. When I peeped in from the bottom of the stair, I saw no one; but, hearing steps overhead, I called out.

Agnes answered, as she descended an inner stair which led to the bedrooms above, "Mother's gone to church."

"Gone to church!" I said, a vague pang darting through me as I thought I had forgotten some service. But the next moment I recalled the old woman's preference for the church during a storm.

"Oh, yes, Agnes! I remember," I said. "Your mother thinks the weather bad enough to take to the church, does she? How do you come to be here now? And where is your husband?"

"He'll be here in an hour or so. He don't mind the wet. You see, we don't like the old people to be left alone when it blows what the sailors call 'great guns.' "

"And what becomes of his mother then?"

"There don't be any sea out there. Leastways," she added with a quiet smile, and stopped.

"You mean, I suppose, Agnes, that there is never any perturbation of the elements out there?"

She laughed, for she understood me well enough. The temper of Joe's mother was proverbial.

"But really," she said, "she don't mind the weather a bit. And though we don't live in the same cottage with her, for Joe wouldn't hear of that, we see her far oftener than we see my mother, you know."

"I'm sure it's quite fair, Agnes. Is Joe very sorry that he married you, now?"

She hung her head, blushing deeply, and replied, "I don't think he be, Sir. I do think he gets better. He's been working very hard the last week or two, and he says it agrees with him."

"And how are you?"

"Quite well, thank you."

I had never seen her look half so well. Life was evidently a very different thing to both of them now. I left her and took my way to the church.

When I reached the churchyard, there in the middle of the rain and the gathering darkness was the old man busy with the duties of his calling. A certain headstone stood right under a drip from the roof, and this drip had caused the mold at the foot of the stone to sink, so that there was a considerable crack between the stone and the soil. The old man had cut some sod from another part of the churchyard, and was now standing, with the rain pouring on him from the roof, beating this sod down in the crack. He was sheltered from the wind by the church, but was as wet as could be.

"This will never do, Coombes," I said. "You will get your death of cold. You must be as full of water as a sponge. Old man, there's rheumatism in the world!"

"It be only my work, Sir, but I believe I ha' done now for a night. I think he'll be a bit more comfortable now. The very wind could get at him through that hole."

"Do go home, then," I said, "and change your clothes. Is your wife in the church?"

"She be, Sir. This door—this door," he added, as he saw me going round to the usual entrance. "You'll find her in there."

I lifted the great latch and entered. I could not see her at first, for it was much darker inside the church. It felt very quiet in there somehow, although the place was full of the noise of winds and waters. Mrs. Coombes was sitting at the foot of the chancel rail, knitting as usual.

Her sweet old face, lighted up by a moonlike smile, and seen in the middle of the ancient dusk filled with the sounds (but only the sounds) of tempest, gave me a sense of one dwelling in the secret place of the Most High.

"How long do you mean to stay here, Mrs. Coombes?" I asked. "Not all night?"

"No, not all night, surely. But I hadn't thought o' going yet for a bit."

"Why, there's Coombes out there, wet to the skin, and I'm afraid he'll go on pottering at the churchyard bedclothes till he gets his bones as full of rheumatism as they can hold."

"Deary me! I didn't know as my old man was there. He tould me he had them all comfortable for the winter a week ago. But to be sure there's always some mendin' to do."

I heard Joe speaking outside, and the next moment he came into the church. After speaking to me he turned to Mrs. Coombes.

"You be comin' home with me, Mother. This will never do. Father's wet as a mop. I ha' brought something for your supper, and Aggy's a-cookin' of it, and we're going to be comfortable over the fire, and have a chapter of the New Testament to keep down the noise of the sea. There! Come along."

The old woman drew her cloak over her head, put her knitting carefully in her pocket, and stood aside for me to lead the way.

"No, no," I said, "I'm the shepherd and you're the sheep, so I'll drive you before me—at least you and Coombes. Joe here will be offended if I take on me to say I am *his* shepherd."

"Nay, nay, don't say that. You've been a good shepherd to me, when I was a very sulky sheep. But if you'll please to go, I'll lock the door behind, for you know in them parts the shepherd goes first, and the sheep follow the shepherd. And I'll follow like a good sheep," he added laughing.

"You're right, Joe," I said, and took the lead without more ado. I was struck by his saying *them parts,* which indicated a habit of pondering on the places as well as circumstances of the Gospel story.

Coombes joined us at the door, and we all walked to his cottage, Joe taking care of his mother-in-law, and I taking what care I could of Coombes by carrying his tools for him. But as we went, I feared I had done ill in that, for the wind blew so fiercely that I thought the thin feeble little man would have got on better if he had been more heavily weighted against it. But I made him take hold of my arm, and so we got in. When we opened the inner door, the welcome of a glowing fire burst up the stair, and I went down with them. Coombes departed to change his clothes, and the rest of us stood round the fire where Agnes was busy cooking something like white puddings for their supper.

"Did you hear," said Joe, "that the coast guard is off to the Goose-pot? There's a vessel ashore there, they say. I met them on the road with the rocket cart."

"How far off is that, Joe?"

"Some five or six miles, I suppose, along the coast nor'ards."

"What sort of vessel is she?"

"That I don't know. Some say she be a schooner, others a brigantine. The coast guard didn't know themselves."

"Poor things!" said Mrs. Coombes. "If any of them come ashore, they'll be sadly knocked to pieces on the rocks in a night like this." She had caught a little infection of her husband's mode of thought.

"It's not likely to clear up before morning, I fear, is it, Joe?"

"I don't think so. There's no likelihood."

"Will you condescend to sit down and take a share with us, Sir?" said the old woman.

"There would be no condescension in that, Mrs. Coombes. I will another time with all my heart. But in such a night I ought to be at home with my own people. They will be more uneasy if I am away."

"Of coorse, of coorse."

"So I'll bid you good-night. I wish this storm were well over."

I buttoned my greatcoat, pulled my hat down on my head, and set out. The roaring of the waves on the shore was terrible. All I could see of them now was the whiteness of their breaking, but they filled the earth and the air with their furious noises.

I found the whole household full of the storm. The children kept pressing their faces to the windows trying to pierce as by force of will through the darkness, and discover what the wild thing out there was doing. They could see nothing—all was one mass of blackness and dismay and ceaseless roaring. I ran up to Connie's room, and found that she was left alone. She looked restless, pale, and frightened. The house quivered, and still the wind howled and whistled through the adjoining bark hut.

"Connie, darling, have they left you alone?"

"Only for a few minutes, Papa. I don't mind it."

"Don't be frightened at the storm, my dear. He who could walk on the Sea of Galilee and still the storm of that little pool, can rule the Atlantic just as well. Jeremiah says, 'He divideth the sea when the waves thereof roar.' "

The same moment Dora came running into the room. "Papa!" she cried. "The spray—such a lot of it—came dashing on the windows. Will it break them?"

"I hope not, my dear. Stay with Connie while I run down."

"O Papa! I do want to see."

"What do you want to see, Dora?"

"The storm, Papa."

"It is as black as pitch. You can't see anything."

"Oh, but I want to—to—be beside it."

"Well, you shan't stay with Connie, if you are not willing. Go along, and ask Wynnie to come here."

The child was so possessed by the commotion outside that she did not seem even to see my rebuke, much less feel it. She ran off, and Wynnie presently came. I left her with Connie and went down. The dining room was dark, for they had put out the lights that they might see better from the windows. The children and some of the servants were there looking out.

There came a lull in the wind, and I thought I heard a gun. I listened, but heard nothing more. When I went up to the drawing room, I found that Percivale had joined our party. He and Turner were talking together at one of the windows.

"Did you hear a gun?" I asked them.

"No. Was there one?"

"I'm not sure. I half fancied I heard one, but no other followed. There will be a good many fired tonight though, along this awful coast."

"I suppose they keep the lifeboat always ready," said Turner.

"No lifeboat, I fear, would live in such a sea," I said.

"They would try, though, I suppose," said Turner.

"I do not know," said Percivale, "for I don't know the people. But I have seen a lifeboat out in as bad a night—whether in as bad a sea, I cannot tell."

Then Wynnie joined us, and I asked her, "How is Connie, now, my dear?"

"Very restless and excited, Papa. I came down to say that if Mr. Turner didn't mind, I wish he would go up and see her."

"Of course, instantly," said Turner, and moved to follow Wynnie.

But the same moment, as if it had been beside us in the room, so clear, so shrill was it, we heard Connie's voice shrieking, "Papa! Papa! There's a great ship ashore down there. Come, come!"

Turner and I rushed from the room toward the narrow stairs that led directly up to the bark hut. The door at the top of it was open, as was the door from Connie's room. Enough light shone in to show a figure by the farthest window with its face pressed against the glass. "Papa! Papa! Quick, quick! The waves will knock her to pieces!"

It was Connie standing there.

THIRTY-TWO
The Shipwreck

Turner and I both rushed at the stair, though there was not room for more than one upon it. I was first, but stumbled on the lowest step and fell. Turner put his foot on my back, jumped over me, sprang up the stair, and when I reached the top, he was meeting me with Connie in his arms, carrying her back to her room. But she kept crying, "Papa, Papa! The ship, the ship!"

My duty woke in me—Turner could attend to Connie far better than I could. I made one spring to the window. The moon was not to be seen, but the clouds were thinner, and enough light was soaking through them to show a wave-tormented mass some little way out in the bay, and in that moment a shriek pierced the howling of the wind like a knife. I rushed bareheaded from the house and flew straight to the sexton's, snatched the key from the wall, crying only, "Ship ashore!" and rushed to the church.

My hand trembled so that I could hardly get the key into the lock, but I opened the door, felt my way to the tower, knelt before the keys of the hammer bells, opened the chest, and struck them wildly, fiercely. An awful jangling, out of tune and harsh, burst into the storm-vexed air. I struck repeatedly at the keys, wanting noise, outcry, *reveille.*

In a few minutes I heard voices and footsteps. From some parts of the village, out of sight of the shore, men and women gathered to the summons. Through the door of the church, which I had left open, came voices in hurried question. "Ship ashore!" was all I could answer.

I wondered that so few appeared at the cry of the bells. After those first nobody came for what seemed a long time. I believe, however, I was beating the alarm for only a few minutes altogether. Then a hand was laid on my shoulder.

"Who is there?" I said, for it was far too dark to know anyone.

"Percivale. What is to be done? The coast guard is away. Nobody seems to know anything. It is no use to go on ringing more. Everybody is out, even to the maidservants. Come down to the shore and you will see."

"But is there no lifeboat?"

"Nobody seems to know anything about it, except that 'it's no manner of use to go trying *that* with such a sea on.' "

"But someone must be in command of it," I said.

"Yes," returned Percivale. "But none of the crew are amongst the crowd. All the sailor-like fellows are going about with their hands in their pockets."

"Let us make haste, then," I said. "Perhaps we can find out. Are you sure the coast guard have nothing to do with the lifeboat?"

"I believe not. They have enough to do with their rockets."

"Roxton has far more confidence in his rockets than in anything a lifeboat could do, on this coast at least."

While we spoke, we came to the bank of the canal. To my surprise, the canal itself was in a storm, heaving and tossing and dashing over its banks.

"Percivale!" I exclaimed. "The gates are gone! The sea has torn them away."

"Yes, I suppose so. Would God I could get six men to help me. I have been doing what I could, but I have no influence amongst them."

"What do you mean?" I asked. "What could you do if you had a thousand men at your command?"

He made no answer for a few moments, during which we were hurrying on for the bridge over the canal. Then he said, "They regard me only as a meddling stranger, I suppose, for I have been able to get no useful answer. They are all excited, but nobody is doing anything."

"They must know about it a great deal better than we," I returned, "and we must not do them the injustice of supposing they are not ready to do all that can be done."

All this time the ocean was raving in our ears, and the awful tragedy was going on in the dark behind us. The wind was almost as loud as ever, but the rain had quite ceased, and when we reached the bridge the moon had succeeded in pushing the clouds aside. There was little shore left, for the waves had rushed up almost to the village. The sand and the roads, every garden wall, every window that looked seaward—all were crowded with gazers. But it seemed a wonderfully quiet crowd, for the noise of the wind and the waves filled the whole vault, and what was spoken was heard only in the ear to which it was spoken.

Out there in the moonlight lay a mass of something, made discernible by the flashing waves bursting over it. She was far above the low-water mark, nearer the village by a furlong than the spot where we had taken our last dinner on the shore. It was strange to think that yesterday the spot lay bare to human feet, where now so many men and women were isolated in a howling waste of angry waters. The cries came plainly to our ears, and we were helpless to save them.

Percivale went about hurriedly, talking to this one and that one, as if he still thought something might be done. He turned to me. "Do try, Mr. Walton, and find the captain of the lifeboat."

I turned to a sailor-like man who stood at my elbow and asked him.

"It's no use, I assure you," he answered. "No boat could live in such a sea. It would be throwing away the men's lives."

"Do you know where the captain lives?" Percivale asked.

"If I did, I tell you it is of no use."

"Are you the captain yourself?" returned Percivale.

"What is that to you?" he answered, surly now. "I know my own business."

The same moment several of the crowd nearest the edge of the water made a simultaneous rush into the surf and laid hold of the body of a woman—alive or dead I could not tell. I could just see the long hair hanging from the white face as they bore her up the bank.

"Run, Percivale," I said, "and fetch Turner. She may not be dead yet."

"I can't," answered Percivale. "You had better go yourself, Mr. Walton."

He spoke hurriedly, and I saw he must have some reason for answering me so abruptly. He was talking to Jim Allen, one of the village's most dissolute young fellows, and as I turned to go they strode away together.

I sped home as fast as I could, for it was easier to get along now that the moon shone. I found that Turner had given Connie a composing draught, and she was asleep exhausted. In her sleep she kept on talking about the ship.

We hurried back to see if anything could be done for the woman. As we went up the side of the canal, we perceived dark shadows before us—a body of men hauling something along. Yes, it was the lifeboat, afloat on the troubled waves of the canal, each man seated in his own place, his hands quiet upon his oar, his cork jacket braced about him, his feet out before him, ready to pull the moment they should pass beyond the broken gates of the lock out on the awful tossing waves. They sat very silent, and the men on the path towed them swiftly along. The moon uncovered the faces of two of the rowers.

"Percivale! Joe!" I cried.

"Right, Sir!" said Joe.

"I've nothing to lose," Percivale called out, "but Joe has his wife."

"I've everything to win," Joe returned. "The only thing that makes me feel a bit fainthearted is that I'm afraid it's not my duty that drives me to it, but the praise of men, leastaways, a woman. What would Aggy think of me if I was to let them drown out there and go to my bed and sleep? I must go. And it's the first chance I've had of returning thanks for her. Please God, I shall see her again tonight."

"That's good, Joe. Trust in God, my men, whether you sink or swim."

"Ay, ay, Sir," they answered as one man.

"This is your doing, Percivale," I said, turning and walking alongside of the boat for a little way.

"It's more Jim Allen's," said Percivale. "Without him I couldn't have done anything."

"God bless you, Jim," I said. "You'll be a better man after this."

"Donnow, Sir," returned Jim, cheerily. "That's harder work than pulling an oar."

And even the captain himself was on board. Percivale had persuaded Jim Allen, and the two had gone about in the crowd until they had found almost all the crew. The captain, protesting against the folly of it, at last gave in; and once having yielded, he was, like a true Englishman, as much in earnest as any of them. Two missing men were replaced by Percivale and Joe.

"God bless you, my men!" I called after them, and turned again to follow the doctor. I found Turner in the little public house whither they had carried the body. The woman was quite dead.

"It is an emigrant vessel," he said. "Look at the body."

It was that of a woman about twenty, tall and finely formed. The face was very handsome, but it did not need the evidence of the hands to prove that she was one of our sisters who have to labor for their bread.

"What should such a girl be doing on board ship but going out to America or Australia? To her lover, perhaps," said Turner. "You see she has a locket on her neck. I hope nobody will dare take it off. Some of these people are not far derived from those who thought a wreck a godsend."

A sound of many feet was at the door just as we turned to leave the house. They were bringing another body, that of an elderly woman—dead, quite dead. Turner had ceased examining her, and we were going out together when, through all the tumult of the winds and waves, a fierce hiss—vindictive, wrathful—tore the air over our heads. Far up seaward, something like a fiery snake shot from the high ground on the right side of the bay, over the vessel, and into the water beyond it.

"Thank God! That's the coast guard," I cried.

We rushed through the village and up onto the heights where they had planted their rocket apparatus. How dismal the sea looked in the struggling moonlight! I approached the cliff and saw down below the great mass of the vessel's hulk, with the waves breaking every moment upon her side. Now and then there would come a lull in the wild sequence of rolling waters, and then I saw how she rocked on the bottom. Her masts had all gone by the board, and a perfect chaos of cordage floated and swung in the waves that broke over her. But her bowsprit remained entire, and shot out into the foamy dark, crowded with human beings.

The first rocket missed, and its trailing lifeline fell uselessly to the water. They prepared to fire another. Roxton stood by with his telescope, ready to watch the result.

"This is a terrible job," he said when I approached him. "I doubt if we shall save one of them."

"There's the lifeboat!" I cried, as a dark spot approached the vessel from the other side.

"The lifeboat!" he returned with contempt. "You don't mean to say they've got *her* out! She'll only add to the mischief. We'll have to save her too."

She was still some way from the vessel, and in comparatively smooth water; but between her and the hull the sea raved in madness. The billows rode over each other in pursuit of some invisible prey. Another hiss, as of concentrated hatred, and the second rocket was shooting its parabola through the dusky air. Roxton raised his telescope to his eye the same moment.

"Over her starn!" he cried. "There's a fellow getting down from the cathead to run aft—Stop, stop!" he shouted. "There's an awful wave on your quarter!"

His voice was swallowed in the roaring of the storm. A dark something shot from the bow toward the stern, but then the huge wave fell upon the wreck. The same moment Roxton exclaimed—so cooly as to amaze me, forgetting how men must come to regard familiar things without discomposure—"He's gone! I said so. The next'll have better luck, I hope."

(That man came ashore alive, though, for I was to hear his story later.)

But now my attention was fixed on the lifeboat in the wildest of the broken water. At one moment she was down in a huge cleft, the next balanced like a beam on the knife edge of a wave, tossed about as the waves delighted in mocking the rudder. As yet she had shipped no water, but then a huge wave rushed up, towered over her, toppled, and fell upon her with tons of water. The boat vanished. The next moment, there she was, floating helplessly about like a living thing stunned by the blow of the falling wave. The struggle was over. As far as I could see, every man was in his place, but the boat drifted away before the storm shoreward, and the men let her drift. Were they all killed as they sat? I thought of my Wynnie, and turned to Roxton.

"That wave has done for them," he said. "I told you it was no use. There they go."

"But what is the matter?" I asked. "The men are sitting every man in his place."

"I think so," he answered. "Two were swept overboard, but they caught the ropes and got in again. But don't you see they have no oars?"

That wave had broken every one of them off at the rowlocks, and now they were helpless.

I turned and ran. Before I reached the brow of the hill another rocket was fired and fell wide shoreward, partly because the wind blew with fresh fury at that very moment. I heard Roxton say, "She's breaking up. It's no use. That last did for her." I hurried off for the other side of the bay, to see what became of the lifeboat. I heard a great cry from the vessel as I reached the brow of the hill, and so turned for a parting glance. The dark mass had vanished, and the waves were rushing at will over the space.

The crowd was less on the shore, and many were running toward the other side, anxious about the lifeboat. I hastened after them, for Percivale and Joe filled my heart. The crowd led the way to the little beach in front of the parsonage, where it would be well for the crew if they were driven ashore, for it was the only spot where they could escape being dashed on the rocks.

There was a crowd before the garden wall, a bustle, and great confusion of speech. The people, men and women, boys and girls, were all gathered about the crew of the lifeboat, which already lay exhausted on the grass.

"Percivale!" I cried, making my way through the crowd.

There was no answer.

"Joe!" I cried again, searching with eager eyes amongst the crew, to whom everybody was talking.

Still there was no answer, and from the disjointed phrases I heard, I could gather nothing. All at once I saw Wynnie looking over the wall, despair in her face, her wide eyes searching wildly through the crowd. I could not look at her till I knew the worst. The captain was talking to Old Coombes, but as soon as he saw me, he gave me his attention.

"Where is Mr. Percivale?" I asked, with all the calmness I could assume.

He took me by the arm, and drew me nearer to the mouth of the canal. He pointed in the direction of the Castle Rock. "If you mean the stranger gentleman—"

"And Joe Harper, the blacksmith," I interposed.

"They're there."

"You don't mean those two—just those two—are drowned?" I said.

"No, I don't say that, but God knows they have little chance."

I could not help thinking that God might know they were not in the smallest danger. However, I only begged him to tell me where they were.

"Do you see that schooner there, just between you and Castle Rock? The gentleman you mean and Joe Harper too are on board the schooner."

"No," I answered, "I can't say I see it. Is she aground?"

"Oh, dear no. She's a light craft, and can swim there well enough. If she'd be aground, she'd ha' been ashore in pieces hours ago. But whether she'll ride it out, God only knows, as I said afore."

"How ever did they get aboard of her? I never saw her from the heights opposite."

"You were all taken up with the ship ashore, you see. And she don't make much show in this light. But there she is, and they're aboard of her."

He gave me his part of the story, and the rest of it I was able to piece together later. Two men had been swept overboard, as Roxton said—one of them was Percivale—but they had got on board again, to drift, oarless, with the rest, now in a windless valley, and now aloft on a tempest-swept hill of water.

A little out of the full force of the current, and not far from the channel of the small stream, lay the little schooner, where it had been driven into the bay. The master, however, knew the ground well. The current carried him a little out of the wind, and would have thrown him upon the rocks next, but he managed to drop anchor just in time. The cable held and there the little schooner hung in the skirts of the storm, with the jagged teeth of the rocks within an arrow flight. In the excitement of the great wreck, no one had observed the danger of the little coasting bird. If their cable held till the tide went down, and the anchor did not drag, she would be safe. If not, she would surely be dashed to pieces.

In the schooner were two men and a boy: two men had been washed overboard an hour or so before they reached the bay. When they had dropped their anchor, they lay exhausted on the deck. Indeed they were so worn out that they had been unable to drop their sheet anchor, and were holding on only by their best bower. Had they not been a good deal out of the wind, this would have been useless. Even if it held, she was in danger of having her bottom stove in by bumping against the sands as the tide went out, but that they had not to think of yet. The moment they lay down, they fell asleep in the middle of the storm, and while they slept it increased in violence.

Suddenly one of them awoke, and thought he saw a vision of angels. For over his head faces looked down upon him from the air—that is, from the top of a great wave. The same moment he heard a voice, two of the angels dropped on the deck beside him, and the rest vanished. Those angels were Percivale and Joe. And angels they were, for they came just in time, as all angels do—the schooner *was* dragging her anchor.

But it did not take them many minutes now to drop their strongest anchor, and they were soon riding in perfect safety.

I thanked the captain, and returned to the garden wall, for I could do nothing by staring out in the direction of the schooner. Only one little group of the crowd remained, and at its center stood a woman. Wynnie had disappeared. The woman who remained was Agnes Harper.

"Agnes," I said, "the storm is breaking up."

"Yes, Sir," she answered, and looked up as if waiting for a command. There was no color in her cheeks or in her lips—at least it seemed so in the moonlight—only in her eyes. But she was perfectly calm. She was leaning against the low wall, with her hands clasped and hanging quietly down before her. Then, after just a moment's pause, in the same still tone, she spoke out her heart. "Joe's at his duty?"

"Yes," I returned. "At all events, he's not taking care of his own life. And if one is to go wrong, I would ten thousand times rather err on that side. But I am sure Joe has been doing right, and nothing else."

"Then there's nothing to be said, is there?" she returned, with a sigh of relief.

I presume some of the surrounding condolers had been giving her Job's comfort by blaming her husband.

"Do you remember, Agnes, what the Lord said to His mother when she reproached Him with having left her and His father?'

"I can't remember anything at this moment," was her touching answer.

"Then I will tell you. He said, 'Why did you look for Me? Didn't you know that I must be about something My Father had given Me to do?' Now Joe was and is about his Father's business, and you must not be anxious about him. There could be no better reason for not being anxious."

Without a word Agnes took my hand and kissed it. I did not withdraw my hand, for I knew that would be to rebuke her love for Joe.

"Will you come in and wait?" I asked.

"No, thank you. I must go to my mother. God will look after Joe, won't He?"

"As sure as there is a God, Agnes," I said, and she went away without another word.

I put my hand on the top of the wall and jumped over, and almost alighted on a woman lying there, my own Wynnie.

She had not fainted, but was lying with her handkerchief stuffed into her mouth to keep from screaming. She rose, and without looking at me, walked away toward the house, straight to her own room, and shut the door. I found her mother with Connie who was now awake, pale, and frightened. I told Ethelwyn that Percivale and Joe were on board the little schooner, that Wynnie was in terror about Percivale, that I had found her lying on the wet grass, and that she must get her into a warm bath and to bed.

We went together to Wynnie's room. She was standing in the middle of the floor, with her hands pressed against her temples.

"Wynnie," I said, "our friends are not drowned. I think you will see them quite safe in the morning. Pray to God for them."

She did not hear a word.

"Leave her with me," said Ethelwyn, proceeding to undress her, "and tell Nurse to bring up the large bath. There is plenty of hot water in the boiler: I gave orders to that effect, not knowing what might happen."

Wynnie shuddered as her mother said this, but I waited no longer, for when Ethelwyn spoke, everyone felt her authority. I obeyed her and then went to Connie's room.

"Do you mind being left alone a little while?" I asked her.

"No, Papa. Only—are they all drowned?" she said with a shudder.

"I hope not, my dear. But be sure of the mercy of God, whatever you fear. You must rest in Him, my love, for He is Life, and He will conquer death both in the soul and in the body."

Dora and the boys were all fast asleep, for it was very late. Telling Nurse to be on the watch because Connie was alone, I went again to the beach. I called first, however, to inquire after Agnes. I found her quite composed, sitting with her parents by the fire, none of them doing anything, scarcely speaking, only listening intently to the sounds of the storm now beginning to die away.

I next went to the place where I had left Turner. Five bodies lay there, and he was busy with a sixth. The surgeon of the place was with him, and they quite expected to recover this man.

The morning began to dawn with a pale ghastly light, and the sea raged on, although the wind had gone down. There were many strong men about, with two surgeons and all the coast guard, and the houses along the shore were at the disposal of any who wanted aid. The parsonage was at some distance, and I was glad to think there was no necessity for carrying thither any of those whom the waves cast on the shore.

When I reached home and found Wynnie quieter, and Connie again asleep, I walked out along our own downs till I could see the little schooner still safe at anchor. She was clearly out of all danger now, and if Percivale and Joe were safe on board, we might confidently expect to see them before many hours were past. I went home with the good news.

For a few moments I doubted whether I should tell Wynnie, for I could not know with any certainty that Percivale was in the schooner. But I reflected that we have no right to modify God's facts for fear of what may be to come. A little hope founded on a present appearance, even if that hope should never be realized, may be the very means of enabling a soul to bear the weight of a sorrow past the point at which it would otherwise break down. I would therefore tell Wynnie, and let her share my expectation.

I think she had been half asleep, for when I entered her room, she started up in a sitting posture, looking wild, and put her hands to her head.

"I have brought you good news, Wynnie," I said. "The little schooner is quite safe."

"What schooner?" she asked listlessly, and lay down again, her eyes still staring unappeased.

"Why the schooner they say Percivale got on board."

"He isn't drowned then!" she cried with a choking voice, and she put her hands to her face and burst into tears.

"Wynnie," I said, "everybody but you has known all night that Percivale and Joe Harper are probably quite safe. They may be ashore in a couple of hours."

"But you don't know it. He may be drowned yet."

"Of course, there is room for doubt—but none for despair. See what a poor helpless creature hopelessness makes you."

"But how can I help it, Papa?" she asked piteously. "I am made so." But as she spoke, the dawn was clear upon the height of her forehead.

"You are not made yet, as I am always telling you. And God has ordained that you shall have a hand in your own making. You have to consent, to desire that what you know for a fault shall be set right by His loving will and Spirit."

"I don't know God, Papa."

"Ah, my dear! That is where it all lies. You do not know Him, or you would never be without hope."

"But what am I to do to know Him?" she asked, rising on her elbow.

The saving power of hope was already working in her. She was once more turning her face toward the Life.

"Read as you have never read before about Christ Jesus, my love. Read with the express object of finding out what God is like, that you may know Him and trust Him. And give yourself to Him, and He will give you peace."

"What are we to do," I said to my wife later, "if Percivale continues silent? For even if he be in love with her, I doubt if he will speak."

"We must leave all that, Harry," she answered.

She was turning on me the counsel I had given Wynnie. It is strange how easily we can tell our brother what he ought to do, and yet do ourselves precisely as we rebuked him for doing. I lay down and fell fast asleep.

THIRTY-THREE
The Funeral

It was a lovely morning when I woke once more. The sun was flashing back from the sea which was still tossing, but no longer furiously, only as if it wanted to turn itself every way to flash the sunlight about. The madness of the night was over and gone; the light was abroad; and the world was rejoicing. And there was the schooner lying dry on the sands, her two cables and anchors stretching out yards behind her. But halfway between the two sides of the bay rose a mass of something shapeless, drifted over with sand. It was all that remained together of the great ship. The wind had ceased altogether, only now and then a little breeze arose which murmured, "I am very sorry," and lay down again. And I knew that in the houses on the shore, there lay at least fifteen dead men and women.

I went down to the dining room. The three youngest children were busy at their breakfast, but neither Ethelwyn, Wynnie, nor Turner had yet appeared. I made a hurried meal and was just rising to go and inquire further into the events of the night, when the door opened and in walked Percivale, looking very solemn, but in perfect health and well-being.

I grasped his hand warmly. "Thank God," I said, "that you are returned to us, Percivale!"

"I doubt if that is much to give thanks for," he said.

"We are the judges of that," I rejoined. "Tell me about it."

Percivale's account of the matter was that as they drifted helplessly along, he suddenly saw, from the top of a huge wave, the little vessel below him. They were, in fact, almost upon the rigging, and the wave on which they rode swept the quarterdeck of the schooner.

Percivale said the captain of the lifeboat called out, "Aboard!" even though the captain said he remembered nothing of the sort—if he did, he must have meant the men on the schooner to board the lifeboat. But Percivale, fancying the captain meant them to board the schooner, sprang at her foreshrouds. When the wave swept along the schooner's side, Joe sprang on the mainshrouds, and so they dropped on the deck together.

While he was narrating the events, Wynnie entered. She started, turned pale and then very red, and for a moment hesitated in the doorway.

"Here is another to rejoice at your safety, Percivale," I said.

Thereupon he stepped forward to meet her, and she gave him her hand with evident emotion, looking more lovely than I had ever seen her. Then she sat down and began to busy herself with the teapot, though her hand trembled. I requested Percivale to begin his story once more, and excused myself to go to the village. As I left, he was recounting to her—with evident enjoyment—the adventures of the night.

I went first to the mill to see how Joe was, but there was no one there but the old woman.

She greeted me with a beaming face. "Oh Sir! My Willie's come home!"

"Home? In this storm?"

"Did ye see that schooner there last night aridin' out the weather? He were on it, he were, though two on 'em were swept o'er and drowned, and two men o' the lifeboat had to come out to rescue 'em. Only drenched, he were, and wore out a bit, and now he's out wi' his Mary for a walk, and right glad she were to see him too."

I rejoiced with her, and told her the rest of the story, and how Percivale and Joe had come from the wet sky like sea-angels to deliver her Willie. "And where are Joe and Agnes?" I concluded.

"You see, Sir, Joe had promised a little job of work to be ready today, and so he couldn't stop. He did say Agnes needn't go with him, but she thought she couldn't part with him so soon, you see."

"She had received him too from the dead—raised to life again," I said. "It was most natural. But that Joe—will nothing make him lay aside his work?"

"I tried to get him to stop, saying he had done quite enough last night for all next day. But he told me it was his business to get the tire put on Farmer Wheatstone's cartwheel today just as much as it was his business to go in the lifeboat yesterday. So he would go, and Aggy wouldn't stay behind."

"Fine fellow, Joe!" I said, and took my leave of the happy woman.

As I drew near the village, I heard the sound of hammering and sawing, and apparently everything at once in the way of joinery, for they were making coffins in the joiner's shops.

The county magistrate sent a notice of the loss of the vessel to the Liverpool papers, requesting those who might wish to identify or claim any of the bodies, to appear within four days at Kilkhaven. As this threw the fourth day upon Saturday, and it was clear that the dead must not remain above ground over Sunday, I therefore arranged that they should be buried late on the Saturday night.

On the Friday morning, a young woman and an old man (unknown to each other) arrived by the coach from Barnstaple. They had come to look, if they might, at the shadow left behind by the departing souls of their friends. That afternoon, with the approbation of the magistrate, I had all the bodies removed to the church. Some in their coffins, others on stretchers, they were laid in front of the Communion rail. In the evening the two visitors went to see them, and I took care to be present.

The old man soon found his son. I was at his elbow as he walked between the rows of the dead. He turned to me and said quietly, "That's him. He was a good lad. God rest his soul. He's with his mother, and if I'm sorry, she's glad."

With that he smiled, or tried to smile. I could only lay my hand on his arm. He walked out of the church, sat down upon a stone, and stared at the mold of a new-made grave in front of him. It was well to see with what a sober sorrow the dignified old man bore his grief—as if he felt that the loss of his son was only for a moment.

But the young woman had taken on the hue of the corpse she had come to seek. Her eyes were sunken as if with the weight of the light she cared not for, and her cheeks had already pined away as if to be ready for the grave. She never even told us whom she came seeking, and after one involuntary question, which simply received no answer, I was very careful not to even approach another. I do not think the form she sought was there, and she may have left the church with the lingering hope that, after all, that one had escaped.

But God had them in His teaching, and all I could do was to ask them to be my guests till the funeral and the following Sunday were over. To this they kindly consented, and I took them to my wife who received them like herself, and had in a few minutes made them at home with her.

The next morning a Scotchman appeared, seeking the form of his daughter, and so I went with him to the church. He was a tall, gaunt, bony man, with long arms and huge hands, a rugged granitelike face, and a slow ponderous utterance which I had some difficulty in understanding. He treated the object of his visit with a certain hardness (and at the same time lightness) which I also had some difficulty in understanding.

"You want to see the—" I said, and hesitated.

"Ow ay—the boadies," he answered. "She winna be there, I daursay, but I jist like to see, for I wadna like her to be beeried gin sae be 'at she was there, wi'oot biddin' her good-by like."

When we reached the church, I opened the door and entered. An awe fell upon me fresh and new, for the beautiful church had become a tomb. Solemn, grand, ancient, it rose as a memorial of the dead who lay in peace before her altar rail, as if they had fled for sanctuary from a sea of troubles. And by the vestry door sat Mrs. Coombes, like an angel watching the dead, with her sweet solemn smile, and her constant ministration of knitting.

He glanced at one and another of the dead and passed on. He had looked at ten or twelve ere he stopped, and stood gazing on the face of the beautiful form which had been the first to come ashore. He stooped, and stroked the white cheeks, taking the dead in his great rough hands, and smoothing the brown hair tenderly, saying, as if he had quite forgotten that she was dead, "Eh, Maggie! Hoo cam ye here, Lass?"

Then, as if for the first time the reality had grown comprehensible, he put his hands before his face, and burst into tears. His huge frame was shaken with sobs for one long minute, while I stood looking on with awe and reverence. He ceased suddenly, pulled a blue cotton handkerchief from his pocket, rubbed his face with it as if drying it with a towel, put it back, turned, and said, without looking at me, "I'll awa' hae."

"She came ashore with a locket on," I said. "Would you like to take it with you, or would you rather she be laid away with it on?"

"Gin ye please," he said softly, "it wur her own mother's, and I wadna like to beery it too."

I gently unfastened the locket and laid it on the palm of his huge hand. He opened it, gazed inside at whatever picture was there, and then put it silently and tenderly in his pocket.

"Would you like a piece of her hair as well?" I asked.

"Gin ye please," he answered gently, as if his daughter's form had been mine now, and her effects and hair were mine to give.

I turned to Mrs. Coombes. "Have you a pair of scissors there?" I asked.

"Yes, to be sure," she answered, rising, and lifting a huge pair by the string suspending them from her waist.

"If you please, cut off a nice piece of her beautiful hair for her father," I said.

She lifted the lovely head, chose, and cut off a long piece, and handed it respectfully to him.

He took it without a word, sat down on the step before the Communion rail, and began to smooth out the wonderful sleave of dusky gold. He drew it out a yard long, passing his big fingers through and through it tenderly, as if it had been still growing on the live lovely head, and stopping every moment to pick out the bits of seaweed and shells, and shake out the sand that had been wrought into its mass. He sat thus for nearly half an hour, and we stood looking on with something closely akin to awe. At length he folded it up, drew from his pocket an old black leather book, laid it carefully in the innermost pocket, and rose. I led the way from the church, and he followed me.

Outside the church, he laid his hand on my arm, and said, groping with his other hand in his trousers pocket, "She'll hae putten ye to some expense—for the coffin an' sic like."

"We'll talk about that afterward," I answered. "Come home with me now, and have some refreshment."

"Na, I thank ye. I hae putten ye to eneuch o' tribble already. I'll jist awa' hame."

"We are going to lay them down this evening. You won't go before the funeral. Indeed, I think you can't get away till Monday morning. My wife and I will be glad of your company till then."

"I'm no company for gentle fowk, Sir."

"Come and show me in which of these graves you would like to have her laid," I said.

He yielded and followed me.

Coombes had not dug many spadefuls before he saw that ten such men as he could not dig the graves in time. But there was plenty of help to be had from the village and the neighboring farms, and most of the graves were ready now. The brown hillocks lay about the churchyard—the moleheaps of burrowing death.

The stranger looked around him and his face grew critical. He stepped a little hither and thither, and at length turned and said, "I wadna like to be greedy, but gin ye wad lat her lie next the kirk there—i' that neuk—I wad tak' it kindly. And syne gin ever it cam' aboot that I cam' here again, I wad kne whaur she was. Could ye get a sma' bit heidstane putten up? I wad leave the siller wi' ye to pay for't."

"To be sure I can. What will you have on the stone?"

"Ow jist—lat me see—'Maggie Jamieson'—nae Marget, but jist Maggie. She was aye Maggie at hame. 'Maggie Jamieson, frae her father.' It's the last thing I can gie her. Maybe ye micht put a verse o' Scripter aneath't, ye ken."

"What verse would you like?"

He thought for a while. "Isna there a text that says, 'The deid shall hear His voice'?"

"Yes. 'The dead shall hear the voice of the Son of God.' "

"Ay. That's it. Weel, jist put that on. They canna do better than hear His voice."

I led the way home, and he accompanied me without further objection or apology. After dinner, I proposed that we should all go on the downs, for the day was warm and bright. We sat on the grass. I felt that I could not talk to them as from myself. I knew nothing of the possible gulfs of sorrow in their hearts. To me their forms seemed each like a hill in whose unseen bosom lay a cavern of dripping waters, perhaps with a subterranean torrent of anguish raving through its hollows and tumbling down hidden precipices, whose voice only God heard, and only God could still. I would speak no words of my own. The Son of God had spoken words of comfort to His mourning friends, when He was the present God and they were the forefront of humanity. I would read some of the words He spoke. From them the human nature in each would draw what comfort it could.

I took my New Testament from my pocket and said, without any preamble, "When our Lord was going to die, He knew that His friends loved Him enough to be very wretched about it. He knew that they would be overwhelmed for a time with trouble. He knew too that they could not believe that glad end of it all, to which end He looked across the awful death that awaited Him—a death to which that of our friends in the wreck was ease itself. I will just read to you what He said."

I read from the fourteenth to the seventeenth chapter of John's Gospel. I knew there were words of meaning in the words into which I could hardly hope any of them would enter. But I knew likewise that the best things are just those from which the humble will draw the truth they are capable of seeing. Therefore I read as for myself, and left it to them to hear for themselves. Nor did I add any word of comment, fearful of darkening counsel by words without knowledge, for the Bible is awfully set against what is not wise.

When I had finished, I closed the book, rose from the grass, and walked toward the brow of the shore. They rose likewise and followed me. Little of any sort was said. The sea lay still before us, knowing nothing of the sorrow it had caused. We wandered a little way along the cliff.

The bell began to toll, and we went to church for the burial service. My companions placed themselves near the dead, while I went into the vestry till the appointed hour. I thought, as I put on my surplice, how in all religions but the Christian, the dead body was a pollution to the temple. Here the church received it as a holy thing, for a last embrace ere it went to the earth.

As the dead were already in the church, the usual form could not be carried out. I therefore stood by the Communion table and began to read. " 'I am the resurrection and the life,' saith the Lord; 'he that believeth in Me, though he were dead, yet shall he live: and whosoever liveth and believeth in Me shall never die.' "

I advanced as I read, till I came outside the rails and stood before the dead. There I read the psalm, "Lord, Thou hast been our refuge," and the glorious lesson, "Now is Christ risen from the dead, and become the firstfruits of them that slept." Then the men of the neighborhood came forward, and in long solemn procession bore the bodies out of the church, each to its grave. At the church door I stood and read, "Man that is born of woman," then went from one to another of the graves and read over each, as the earth fell on the coffin lid, "Forasmuch as it hath pleased Almighty God of His great mercy." Then I went back to the church door and read, "I heard a voice from heaven," and so to the end of the service.When I returned to the house, I found that one of the surviving sailors wished to see me—the very man, in fact, who had been washed from the deck before my eyes, and cast up on the shore with a broken leg. I went, and found him very pale and worn.

"I think I am going," he said, "and I wanted to see you before I die."

"Trust in Christ, and do not be afraid," I returned.

"I prayed to Him to save me when I was hanging to the rigging, and if I wasn't afraid then, I'm not going to be afraid now, dying quietly in my bed. But just look here."

He took from under his pillow something wrapped up in paper, unfolded the envelope, and showed a lump of something—I could not at first tell what. He put it in my hand, and then I saw that it was part of a Bible, with nearly the upper half of it worn or cut away, and the rest partly in a state of pulp.

"That's the Bible my mother gave me when I left home first," he said. "I don't know how I came to put it in my pocket, but I think the rope that cut through them when I was lashed to the shrouds would a'most have cut through my ribs if it hadn't been for it."

"Very likely," I returned. "The body of the Bible has saved your bodily life: may the spirit of it save your spiritual life."

"I think I know what you mean," he panted out. "My mother was a good woman, and I know she prayed to God for me."

"We will pray for you in church today, and I will come in afterward and see how you are."

I knelt and offered the prayers for the sick. He thanked me, and I took my leave.

As for my own family, Turner insisted on Connie's remaining in bed for two or three days. She looked worse in face—pale and worn—but it was clear, from the way she moved in bed, that the fresh power called forth by the shock had not vanished with the moment. Wynnie was quieter, almost, than ever, but there was a constant secret light in her eyes. Percivale was at the house every day, always ready to make himself useful.

THIRTY-FOUR
Changed Plans

In a day or two Connie was permitted to take to her couch once more. It seemed strange that she should look so much worse, and yet be so much stronger. Whenever they carried her, she begged to be allowed to put her feet to the ground. Turner yielded, though without quite ceasing to support her. He was satisfied, however, that she could have stood upright for a moment at least. He would not, of course, risk it.

The time of his departure was nearing, and he seemed anxious. Connie continued worn-looking and pale, and her smile, though ever ready to greet me when I entered, had lost much of its light. She had arranged the curtain of her window to shut out the sea, and I said something to her about it once. Her reply was "Papa, I can't bear it. I was so fond of the sea when I came down. It lay close to my window, with a friendly smile ready for me every morning when I looked out. I daresay it is all from want of faith, but I can't help it. It looks so far away now, like a friend that had failed me, and I would rather not see it."

I saw that the struggling life within her was grievously oppressed, and that the things which surrounded her were no longer helpful. Her life had been driven to its innermost cave, and now when it had been enticed to venture forth and look abroad, a sudden pall had descended upon Nature. I could not help thinking that the good of our visit to Kilkhaven had come, and that evil, from which I hoped we might escape, was following. I left her, and sought Turner.

"It strikes me, Turner," I said, "that the sooner we leave, the better it will be for Connie."

"I agree. The very prospect of leaving the place would do something to restore her."

"Would it be safe to move her?"

"Far safer than to let her remain. At the worst, she is now far better than when she came. Try her. Hint at the possibility of going home, and see how she will take it."

"Well," I said, "I shan't like to be left alone, but if she goes, they must all go, except, perhaps, I might keep Wynnie. But I don't know how her mother would get on without her."

"I don't see why you should stay behind. Mr. Weir would be as glad to come as you would be to go, and it can make no difference to Mr. Shepherd."

It seemed a very sensible suggestion. Certainly it was a desirable thing for both my sister and her husband. They had no such reasons as we had for disliking the place, and it would enable Martha to avoid the severity of yet another winter. I said as much to Turner, and went back to Connie's room.

The light of a lovely sunset was lying outside her window, but she was sitting so that she could not see it. I asked, without any preamble, "Would you like to go back to Marshmallows, Connie?"

Her countenance flashed into light. "Oh! Dear Papa! Do let us go," she said. "That would be delightful."

"Well, I think we can manage it, if you will only get a little stronger for the journey. The weather is not as good for travel as when we came down."

"No. But I am ever so much better, you know, than I was then."

The poor girl was already stronger from the mere prospect of going home again. She moved restlessly on her couch, half mechanically put her hand to the curtain, pulled it aside, looked out, faced the sun and the sea, and did not draw it back.

I left her and went to find Ethelwyn. She heartily approved of the proposal for Connie's sake, and said that it would be scarcely less agreeable to herself. I could see a certain troubled look above her eyes, however.

"You are thinking of Wynnie," I said.

"Yes. It is hard to make one sad for the sake of the rest."

"True. But it is one of the world's recognized necessities."

"No doubt."

"Besides, you don't suppose Percivale can stay here the whole winter. They must part sometime."

"Of course. Only they did not expect it so soon."

But here my wife was mistaken.

I went to my study to write to Weir. I had hardly finished my letter when Walter came to say that Mr. Percivale wished to see me.

I said as he was shown in, "I am just writing home to say that I want my curate to change places with me here, which I know he will be glad enough to do. I see Connie had better go home."

"You will all go then, I presume," returned Percivale.

"Yes, of course."

"Then I need not regret that I can stay no longer. I came to tell you that I must leave tomorrow."

"Ah! Going to London?"

"Yes. I don't know how to thank you for all your kindness. You have made my summer something like a summer."

"We have had our share of the advantage, and that a large one. We are all glad to have made your acquaintance, Mr. Percivale. Now, we shall be passing through London within a week or ten days, in all probability. Perhaps you will allow us the pleasure of looking at some of your pictures then?"

His face flushed. What did the flush mean? It was not one of mere pleasure, for there was confusion and perplexity in it. But he answered at once, "I will show you them with pleasure. I fear, however, you will not care for them."

Would this fear account for his embarrassment? I hardly thought it would, but I could not for a moment imagine that he had any serious reason for shrinking from a visit.

"I shall be sure to pay you a visit. But you will dine with us today, of course?" I said.

"With pleasure," he answered, and took his leave.

I finished my letter to Weir and went out for a walk. I wandered on the downs till I came to the place where a solitary rock stands upon the top of a cliff looking seaward, in the suggested shape of a monk praying. I seated myself, and looked out over the Atlantic. How faded the ocean appeared! It seemed as if all the sunny dyes of summer had been diluted and washed with the fogs of the coming winter.

The thought of seeing my own people again filled me with gladness. I would leave those I had here learned to love with regret, yet trusting I had taught them something. They had taught me much, and therefore there could be no end in our relation in the Lord, who alone gives security to any tie. I should not, therefore, sorrow as if I were to see their faces no more.

I took my farewell of that sea and those cliffs. I should see them often enough ere we went, but I should not feel so near them again. Even this parting said that I must "sit loose to the world," an old Puritan phrase. I could gather up only its uses, treasure its best things, and let all the rest go; those things I called mine—earth, sky and sea, home, books, the treasured gifts of friends—had all to leave me, belong to others and help to educate them. I should not need them. I should have my people, my souls, my beloved faces, and could well afford to part with these.

So my thoughts went on as I turned from the sea.

I found Wynnie looking very grave when I went into the drawing room. Her mother was there too, and Mr. Percivale. It seemed rather a moody party. They wakened up a little, however, after I entered, and before dinner was over, we were chatting together merrily.

"How is Connie?" I asked Ethelwyn.

"Better already," she answered.

"Everybody seems better," I said. "The very idea of going home seems reviving to us all."

Wynnie darted a quick glance at me, caught my eye (which was more than she had intended), and blushed. She sought refuge in a bewildered glance at Percivale, caught his eye in turn, and blushed yet deeper. He plunged instantly into conversation, not without a certain involuntary sparkle in his eyes.

"Did you go see Mrs. Stokes this morning?" he asked.

"No," I answered. "She does not want much visiting now. She is going about her work, apparently in good health. Her husband says she is not the same woman, and I hope he means that in more senses than one."

I did my best to keep up the conversation, but every now and then it fell like a wind that would not blow. I withdrew to my study. Percivale and Wynnie went out for a walk. The next morning he and Turner left by the early coach.

Wynnie did not seem very much dejected. I thought that perhaps the prospect of meeting Percivale again in London kept her up.

THIRTY-FIVE
The Studio

I will not linger over our preparations or leave-takings. The two boys, who had wanted to bring down the chest, now wanted to take home two or three boxes filled with pebbles, great oyster shells, and seaweed.

Weir was also quite pleased to make the unexpected exchange. Before he came, I went about among the people to tell them a little about my successor, that he might not appear among them quite as a stranger.

It was a bright cold morning when we started, and the first part of our railway journey was very pleasant. But as we drew near London we entered a thick fog, and before we arrived, a small dense November rain was falling. Connie looked a little dispirited, partly from weariness, but no doubt from the change in the weather.

"Not very cheerful, this, Connie, my dear," I said.

"No, Papa," she answered, "but we *are* going home, you know."

Going home. I lay back in the carriage and thought how this November London fog was like the valley of the shadow of death we had to pass through on the way *home.* A shadow like this would fall upon me, and the world would grow dark and life grow weary—but I should know it was the last of the way home.

As the thought of water is to the thirsty soul, such is the thought of home to the wanderer in a strange country. And my own soul had always felt the discomfort of strangeness in the very midst of its greatest blessedness. In the closest contact of one human soul with another, when all the atmosphere of thought was rosy with love, again and yet again on the far horizon, the dim, lurid flame of unrest would shoot for a moment through the enchanted air, and the soul would know that she was not yet home. But did I know where or what that home was?

I lifted my eyes, and saw those of my wife and Connie fixed on mine, as if they were reproaching me for saying in my soul that I could not be quite at home with them. Then I said in my heart, "Come home with me, Beloved; there is but one home for us all. When we find that home we shall be gardens of delight to each other, little chambers of rest, galleries of pictures, wells of water."

Again, what was this home? God Himself. His thoughts, His will, His love, His judgments, are man's home. To think His thoughts, to choose His will, to love His loves, to judge His judgments, and thus to know that He is in us—this is to be at home. It is the father, the mother, that make for the child his home. Indeed, I doubt if the *home* idea is complete to the parents of a family themselves, when they remember that their fathers and mothers have vanished.

At this point something rose in me seeking utterance.

"Won't it be delightful, Ethelwyn," I began, "to see our fathers and mothers such a long way back in heaven?"

But her face betrayed that I had pained her, and I felt at once how dreadful a thing it was not to have had a good father or mother. I do not know what would have become of me but for a good father. I wonder how anybody ever can be good who has not had a good father. Every father or mother who is not good makes it just as impossible to believe in God as it can be made. But He is our one good Father and does not leave us, even when our fathers and mothers have forsaken us and left Him without a witness.

Then the evil odor of brick-burning invaded my nostrils, and I knew that London was about us. A few moments after, we reached the station where a carriage was waiting to take us to our hotel.

Dreary was the change from the stillness and sunshine of Kilkhaven to the fog and noise of London. But Connie slept better that night than she had for a good many nights before.

After breakfast the next morning, I said to Wynnie, "I am going to see Mr. Percivale's studio, my dear. Have you any objection to going with me?"

"No, Papa," she answered, blushing. "I have never seen an artist's studio in my life."

"Get your bonnet and come along then."

She ran off and was ready in a few minutes. We gave the cab driver directions, and set out. It was a long drive, but at length we stopped in front of a very common-looking house on a very dreary street, in which no man could possibly identify his own door except by the number. I knocked under the number given on Percivale's card. A woman who looked at once dirty and cross (the former probably the cause of the latter) opened the door and gave bare assent to my question whether Mr. Percivale was at home. Then she withdrew with the words "Second floor," and left us to find our own way up the stairs.

We knocked at the door of the front room. A well-known voice cried, "Come in," and we entered. Percivale, in a short velvet coat, with his palette on his thumb, advanced to meet us. His face wore a slight flush, which I attributed solely to pleasure, and nothing to any awkwardness in receiving us in such a poor place as he occupied.

I cast my eyes round the room. Any romantic notions Wynnie might have indulged concerning the marvels of a studio must have paled considerably at the first glance around Percivale's room. It was plainly the abode, if not of poverty then of self-denial, although I suspected both. It was a common room, with no carpet save a square in front of the fireplace; no curtains except a piece of something like a drugget nailed flat across the lower half of the window to make the light fall from upward; two or three horsehair chairs, nearly worn out; a table in a corner, littered with books and papers; a horrible lay figure, at the present moment dressed apparently for a scarecrow; and a large easel, on which stood a half-finished oil painting. These constituted almost the whole furniture of the room.

With his pocket handkerchief, Percivale dusted one chair for Wynnie and another for me. Standing before us, he said, "This is a very shabby place to receive you in, Miss Walton, but it is all I have."

"A man's life consists not in the abundance of the things he possesses," I ventured to say.

"Thank you," said Percivale. "I hope not. It is well for me it should not."

"It is well for the richest man in England that it should not," I returned. "If it were not so, the man who could eat most would be the most blessed."

"Have you been very busy since you left us, Mr. Percivale?" asked Wynnie.

"Tolerably," he answered, "but I have not much to show for it. That on the easel is all. I hardly like to let you look at it, though."

"Why?" asked Wynnie.

"First, because the subject is painful. Next, because it is so unfinished."

"But why should you paint subjects you do not like people to look at?"

"I very much want people to look at them."

"Why not us, then?" said Wynnie.

"Because you do not need to be pained."

"Are you sure it is good for you to pain anybody?" I said.

"Good is done by pain, is it not?" he asked.

"Undoubtedly. But whether *we* are wise enough to know when and where and how much is the question."

"Of course, I do not make the pain my object."

"If it comes only as a necessary accompaniment, that may alter the matter greatly," I said. "But still I am not sure that anything in which the pain predominates can be useful in the best way."

"Perhaps not," he returned. "Will you look at the daub?"

"With much pleasure," I replied, and we rose and stood before the easel. Percivale made no remark, but left us to find out what the picture meant. Nor had I long to look before I understood it—in a measure at least.

It represented a wretchedly ruinous garret. The plaster had come away in several places, and between the laths in one spot hung the tail of a great rat. In a dark corner lay a man dying. A woman sat by his side with his hand in hers. Her eyes were fixed not on his face, but on the open door, where in the gloom you could just see the struggles of two undertaker's men to get the coffin past the turn of the landing toward the door. Through the window there was one peep of the blue sky, whence a ray of sunlight fell on the one scarlet blossom of a geranium in a broken pot on the windowsill outside.

"I do not wonder you did not like to show it," I said. "How can you bear to paint such a dreadful picture?"

"It is a true one. It only represents a fact."

"Not all facts have a right to be represented."

"Surely you would not get rid of painful things by huddling them out of sight?"

"No, nor yet by gloating upon them."

"You will believe me that it gives me anything but pleasure to paint such pictures, as far as the subject goes," he said with some discomposure.

"Of course. I know you well enough by this time to know that. But no one could hang it on his wall who would not either gloat on suffering or grow callous to it. Whence then would come the good in painting the picture? If it had come into my possession, I would—"

"Put it in the fire," suggested Percivale, with a strange smile.

"No. Still less would I sell it. I would hang it up with a curtain before it, and only look at it now and then when I thought my heart was in danger of growing hardened to the sufferings of my fellowmen and forgetting that they need the Saviour."

"I could not wish it a better fate. That would answer my end."

"Would it now? Is it not rather those who care little or nothing about such matters that you would like to influence? Would you be content with one solitary person like me? And, remember, I wouldn't buy it. I would rather not have it, and could hardly bear to know it was in my house. I am certain you cannot do people good by showing them *only* the painful. Make it as painful as you will, but put some hope into it, something to show that action is worth taking in the affair. People will turn away from mere suffering, and you cannot blame them. Every show of it, without hinting at some door of escape, only urges them to forget it all. Why should they be pained if it can do no good?"

"For the sake of sympathy, I should say," answered Percivale.

"They would rejoin, 'It is only a picture. Come along.' No. Give people hope, if you would have them act at all, in anything."

"I was almost hoping you would read the picture rather differently. There is a bit of blue sky up there, and a bit of sunshiny scarlet in the window." He looked at me curiously as he spoke.

"I have read it so for myself. But you only put in the sky and the scarlet to heighten the perplexity and make the other look more terrible."

"Now I know that as an artist I have succeeded, however I may have failed otherwise. I did so mean it. But knowing you would dislike the picture, I almost hoped, in my cowardice, that you would read your own meaning into it."

Wynnie had not said a word. As I turned away from the picture, I saw that she was quite distressed, but whether by the picture, or the freedom with which I had remarked upon it, I do not know. My eyes fell upon a little sketch in sepia, and I began to examine it, in the hope of finding something more pleasant to say. It was nearly the same thought, however, only treated in a gentler and more poetic mode. A girl lay dying on her bed, as a youth held her hand. A torrent of summer sunshine fell through the window, and made a lake of glory upon the floor.

I turned away.

"You like that better, don't you, Papa?" said Wynnie, tremulously.

"It is beautiful, certainly," I answered. "And if it were only one, I should enjoy it, as a mood. But coming after the other, it seems but the same thing more weakly embodied."

I confess I was a little vexed. I was much interested in Percivale, for his own sake, as well as for my daughter's, and I had expected better things from him. But I saw that I had gone too far.

"I beg your pardon, Mr. Percivale," I said. "I fear I have been too free in my remarks. I know, likewise, that I am a clergyman and not a painter, and therefore incapable of giving the praise which I have little doubt your art at least deserves."

"I trust that honesty cannot offend me, however much and justly it may pain me."

"But now I have said my worst, I should much like to see what else you have at hand to show me."

"Unfortunately, I have too much at hand. Let me see."

He strode to the other end of the room where several pictures were leaning with their faces against the wall. From these he chose one and fitted it into an empty frame, then brought it forward and set it on the easel.

In it a dark hill rose against the evening sky which shone through a few thin pines on its top. Along a road on the hillside, four squires bore a dying knight—a man past middle age. One behind carried his helm, and another led his horse whose fine head only appeared in the picture. The head and countenance of the knight were very noble, telling of many a battle, and ever for the right. The last had doubtless been gained, for one might read victory as well as peace in the dying look. The party had just reached the edge of a steep descent, and in the valley below, the last of the harvest was just being reaped, while the shocks stood all about the fields under the face of the sunset. There was no gold left in the sky, only a little dull saffron, but plenty of that lovely liquid green of the autumn sky, divided with a few streaks of pale rose. The sky overhead (which could not be seen in the picture) was mirrored in a piece of water in the center of the valley.

"My dear fellow!" I cried. "Why did you not show me this first, and save me from saying so many unkind things? Here is a picture to my own heart. It is glorious. Look here, Wynnie," I went on. "It is evening, and the sun's work is done—he has set in glory, leaving his good name behind him in a lovely harmony of color. The old knight's work is done too—his day has set in the storm of battle, and he is lying lapt in the coming peace. They are bearing him home to his couch and his grave, mourning for and honoring the life that is ebbing away. But he is gathered to his fathers like a shock of corn fully ripe, and so the harvest stands golden in the valley beneath. The picture would not be complete, however, if it did not tell us of the deep heaven overhead, the symbol of that heaven where the knight is bound. What a lovely idea to represent it by means of the water, the heaven embodying itself in the earth, as it were, that we may see it! And that dusky hillside, and those tall slender mournful-looking pines, with that sorrowful sky between, lead the eye and point the heart upward toward that heaven. It is indeed a grand picture, full of feeling, a picture and a parable."

I looked at the girl. Her eyes were full of tears called forth either by the picture or by the pleasure of finding something of Percivale's work appreciated by me, who had spoken so hardly of his other pictures.

"I cannot tell you how glad I am that you like it," she said.

"Like it!" I returned. "I am simply delighted with it—more than I can express—so much delighted that, if I could have this alongside of it, I should not mind hanging that other, that hopeless garret, on the most public wall I have."

"Then," said Wynnie bravely, though in a tremulous voice, "you confess, don't you, Papa, that you were too hard on Mr. Percivale at first?"

"Not too hard on his picture, my dear, and that was all he had given me to judge by. No man should paint a picture like that. You are not bound to disseminate hopelessness, for where there is no hope, there can be no sense of duty."

"But surely, Papa, Mr. Percivale has *some* sense of duty," said Wynnie, in an almost angry tone.

"Assuredly, my love. Therefore I argue that he has some hope, and therefore again that he has no right to publish such a picture."

At the word *publish* Percivale smiled. But Wynnie went on with her defense.

"But you see, Papa, that Mr. Percivale does not paint such pictures only. Look at the other."

"Yes, my dear. But pictures are not like poems, lying side by side in the same book, so that the one can counteract the other. The one of these might go to the stormy Hebrides, and the other to the vale of Avalon. But even then, I should be strongly inclined to criticize the poem that had nothing, positively nothing, of the aurora in it."

"He could refuse to let the one go without the other," said Wynnie.

"He might sell them together, but the owner would part them." I turned to Percivale. "If you would allow me, I will come and see your other pictures another time. I do hope, however, that we can persuade you to dine with us this evening."

We could, and he did. But though our meal was pleasant, the soon-to-be-fulfilled promise of home lay close to our hearts. We left early the next day, then, and the last segment of the journey to Marshmallows was accomplished in a rain and fog that could not dampen our spirits.

THIRTY-SIX
Home Again

Oldcastle Hall opened wide to welcome us. We laid Connie once more in her own room, and then I left the others to explore while I went up to my study. The familiar faces of my books welcomed me. I threw myself in my reading chair, and gazed around me with pleasure. I felt it so *homey* here. All my old friends—whom somehow I hoped to see someday—were present there in the spirit ready to talk with me any moment when I was in the mood, making no claim upon my attention when I was not! I felt as if I should like, when the hour should come, to die in that chair, and pass into the society of the witnesses in the presence of the tokens they had left behind.

I heard shouts on the stairs, and in rushed the two boys.

"Papa! Papa!" they were crying together.

"What is the matter?"

"We've found the big chest just where we left it!"

"Well, did you expect it would have taken itself off?"

"But there's everything in it just as we left it."

"Were you afraid that it would turn itself upside down, and empty all its contents on the floor the moment you turned your backs?"

"Well, Papa, we did not think anything about it, but—but—there everything is as we left it."

With this triumphant answer, they turned and hurried a little abashed out of the room. But not many more moments elapsed before the sounds that arose from them sufficiently reassured me of the state of their spirits.

When they were gone, I forgot my books in the attempt to penetrate and understand my boys' thoughts. And soon I came to see that they were right and I was wrong. Theirs was the wonder of the discovery of the existence of *law.* There was nothing that they had experienced, until now, that would lead them to believe that any such thing should remain where it was left. There *was* a reason in the nature of God, but as far as the boys had previously understood, no one could expect to find anything where he had left it. I began to see yet further into the truth—even the laws of nature reveal the character of God, being of necessity fashioned after His own being and will.

I rose and went down to see if everybody was getting settled, and how the place looked. Ethelwyn was already going about the house as if she had never left it, and as if we all had just returned from a long absence, and she had to show us home hospitality.

Wynnie had vanished, but I soon found her in her mother's favorite old haunt—beside the little pond called Bishop's Basin, for the fascination and horror of this mysterious spot had laid hold on Wynnie. The frost lay thick in the hollow when I went down there, and the branches, lately clothed with leaves, stood bare and icy around her.

I resolved that night to tell Wynnie, in her mother's presence, all the legend of the place, and the whole story of how I won her mother. But for now I left her there. I was so pleased to be at home again that I could not rest, but went wandering everywhere, into places even which I had not entered for ten years at least, and found fresh interest in everything. For this was home, and here I was.

EPILOGUE

And with our return to Marshmallows, our adventures in the Seaboard Parish came to an end.

And what has happened in the years that have followed after? Perhaps I have roused curiosity without satisfying it, but out of a life one cannot always cut complete portions and serve them up in nice shapes. I am well aware that I have not told the *fate* of any of my family. This I cannot relate, for their *fates* are not yet determined.

Harry has gone home, but Charlie is a barrister of the Middle Temple. And Dora puts up with the society of her old father and mother, and is something else than unhappy.

Nor did we leave our Kilkhaven friends entirely behind us. The Scotchman and the young lady, who were our guests for the funeral after the shipwreck, have since come to visit us here at Oldcastle Hall. And the seaman I went to see, he who had survived that same shipwreck by the protection of his mother's Bible—he did not die but recovered as I expected—and came after us to Marshmallows, where he still works for us in our garden and stables.

But of Wynnie and Mr. Percivale and Connie and Connie's baby? Ah! The rest of their story is long and must be left for another volume and another author. My hand is tired, and I promised my Ethelwyn an evening walk.

The story that began in *A Quiet Neighborhood* and continued in *The Seaboard Parish* concludes with *The Vicar's Daughter.*

The Vicar's Daughter

Contents

PROLOGUE

My name is Ethelwyn, and my father is the Vicar Walton who wrote *A Quiet Neighborhood* and *The Seaboard Parish.* Ten days ago he came up to London from Marshmallows to pay us a visit, and brought with him Mr. Sutton, his publisher. Mr. Blackstone, a clergyman and friend, was also present.

Mr. Sutton looked at me with a twinkle in his eye, and asked, "Do you keep a diary?"

"I would rather keep a rag and bottle shop," I answered, at which Mr. Blackstone burst into one of his splendid infectious roars of laughter. If ever a man could laugh like a Christian who believed the world was in a fair way after all, that man was Mr. Blackstone.

"I mean," I continued, "that it would be a more profitable employment to keep the one than the other."

"I suppose you think," said Mr. Blackstone, "that the lady who keeps a diary is in the same danger as the old woman who prided herself in keeping a strict account of her personal expenses. It was always correct. Whenever she could not make it balance, she brought it right by putting the remainder down as *charity.*"

"That's just what I mean."

"But," resumed Mr. Sutton, "I did not mean a diary of your feelings, but of the events of the days and hours."

"Which are never in themselves worth putting down," I said. "All that is worth remembering will find for itself some convenient cranny to sleep in till it is wanted, without being made a poor mummy of in a diary."

"If you have such a memory, that is even better for my purpose."

"For your purpose!" I repeated in surprise. "I beg your pardon, but what designs can you have upon my memory?"

"I will be straightforward: I want you to make up the sum of words your father owes me. He has provided me two books, but another story is required to complete the trilogy. He has left me in the lurch with an unfinished story, not to say an incomplete series. I have waited for the third for many years, and pressed him many times—but all I receive in return are excuses about the difficulties of growing older through the years, and failing judgments and all that. The upshot of it is that now he says I will have to get the third book from you."

I laughed, for the very notion of writing a book seemed preposterous. "You don't say you mean it! The thing is perfectly impossible. I never wrote a book in my life."

"Nor had I, my dear," said my father, "before I wrote my first one."

"But you grew up to it by degrees!"

"That will make it easier for you."

"It is perfectly absurd to suppose me capable of finishing anything my father has begun."

"I think, Wynnie, as everyone appears to wish it, you might as well try."

"If you will write a dozen pages or so," said Mr. Sutton, "I shall be able to judge by those well enough, and I will take the responsibility after that. Besides, my readers want to know about you and your sisters, and little Theodora."

They were all silent, and I began to feel as if I had behaved ungraciously. There was more talk, and in the end I agreed to try.

So I must start somewhere, and I will look at *The Seaboard Parish* to see how it ends. We had just returned from Kilkhaven to Marshmallows, but that was ten years ago. Can it be so long? So many things have happened, and I will try to give them in their right order.

ONE
After Kilkhaven

In the year after our return from Kilkhaven, my mother and father had a good many talks about me and Percivale, and sometimes they took different sides. One conversation, as I have since been told, went like this:

"But Harry," my mother said, "I am afraid they are too like each other to make a suitable match. For instance, Mr. Percivale does not seem, by all I can make out, a bit nearer believing in anything than poor Wynnie herself."

"Well," continued my father, "at least he doesn't fancy he believes when he does not, as so many do—and consider themselves superior persons in consequence. I don't know that it did you any great harm, Miss Ethelwyn, to have made my acquaintance when I was in the worst of my doubts concerning the truth of things. Allow me to tell you that I was nearer making shipwreck of my faith at a certain period than I ever was before or have been since."

"What period was that?"

"Just the little while when I had lost all hope of ever marrying you—unbeliever as you counted yourself."

"You don't mean to say you would have ceased to believe in God, if He hadn't given you your own way?"

"No, my dear. I firmly believe that had I never married you, I should have come in the end to say, 'Thy will be done,' and to believe that it must be all right, however hard to bear. But, oh, what a terrible thing it would have been, and what a frightful valley I should have had to go through first!"

My mother said nothing more just then, but let my father have it all his own way for a while.

"You see," continued my father, "Percivale attributes to Christianity doctrines which, if I supposed they actually belonged to it, would make me reject it at once as ungodlike and bad. This may be the case with him. I think his difficulty comes mainly from seeing so much suffering in the world, so that he cannot imagine the presence and rule of a good God. Therefore he sides with religion rather than with Christianity as yet. The only thing that will ever make him able to believe in a God at all is meditation on the Christian idea of God—I mean the idea of God *in* Christ reconciling the world to Himself—not that pagan corruption of Christ in God reconciling Him to the world. He will then see that suffering is neither wrath nor neglect, but purehearted love and tenderness. But we must give Percivale time.

"And as to trusting him with Wynnie, he seems to be as good as she is. I should have more apprehension in giving her to one who might be called a thoroughly religious man, for not only would the unfitness be greater, but such a man would be more likely to confirm her in doubt. How should they be able to love one another if they were not fit to be married to each other? The fitness seems inherent to the fact."

"But," interposed my mother, "many a two love each other, who would have loved each other a good deal more if they hadn't been married."

"Then it was most desirable they should find out that what they thought a grand affection was not worthy of the name. But I don't think there is much fear of that between those two. And love is the one great instructor. When Wynnie sees the troubled face of Percivale, she will know that he is suffering, and sympathy being thus established between them, the least word of the one will do more to help the other than oceans of argument."

"But I don't like her going from home for the help that lies at her very door. And then," added my mother, "if you will have them married, will you say how on earth you expect them to live? He just makes both ends meet now."

"Ah, yes!" agreed my father, "That is a consideration. There will be difficulty there, for Percivale is far too independent to let us do anything for him."

"And you couldn't do much, if he would. Really, they oughtn't to marry yet."

"We must leave it to them. When Percivale considers himself prepared to marry, and Wynnie thinks he is right, you may be sure they will have seen their way to a livelihood without running in hopeless debt to their tradespeople. And a little poverty and struggling would be a most healthy and healing thing for Wynnie. It hasn't done Percivale much good yet, for he is far too indifferent to his own comforts to mind it. But it will be quite another thing when he has a young wife and perhaps children depending upon him."

It may seem odd that my parents should be taking such opposite sides to those they had taken when we were in Kilkhaven, and Percivale and I had just met. But engagement and marriage are two different things, and although my mother was the first to recognize the possible good of our being engaged, she became frightened when it came time to consider marriage.

But then Percivale began to have what his artist friends called a run of luck, and sold one picture after another in a very extraordi-nary and hopeful manner. Percivale said it was his love for me which enabled him not only to see more deeply into things, but also to see much better the bloom that hangs about everything, and so to paint better pictures than before. He said he felt he now had a hold, where before he had only a sight. My mother, however, believed it was my father's good advice to Percivale (concerning the sort of pictures he painted) that brought his increased sales—and in consequence our marriage—about.

At any rate, he got on very well through the winter. In the very early spring he wrote, at last, that if I was willing to share his poverty, it would not be absolute starvation.

I, of course, was perfectly content. My father and mother made no objection. They had worked their way through many discussions, on one side or the other, had come to be of one mind about Mr. Percivale and me, and at last were quite agreed that marriage would be the best thing for both of us.

We fixed a date in early summer. In the spring, my mother went up to London—at Percivale's request—to help him get together a few things absolutely needful for the barest housekeeping.

She came back satisfied with the little house he had taken. It had not been easy to get one to suit us, for he required a large room to paint in, with a good north light.

"You will find things very different from what you have been used to, Wynnie," said my mother.

"Of course, Mamma," I answered. "I hope I am prepared to meet it. If I don't like it, I shall have no one to blame but myself, and I don't see what right people have to expect what they have been used to."

"There is just this advantage," said my father, "in having been used to nice things, that it ought to be easier to keep from sinking into sordid circumstances."

In the days after that, I found that leaving the place where I had been born was like forsaking the laws and order of the nature I knew. How could one who has been used to our bright sun and our pale modest moon, with our soft twilights, and far, mysterious skies of night, be willing to fall in with the order of things in a different planet with three or four suns, one red and another green and another yellow? I found it a great wrench to leave the dear old place, and of course loved it more than I ever had. But I would get all my crying about that over beforehand. It would be bad enough afterward to have to part with my father and mother and Connie and the rest. Only it wasn't like leaving them, for you can't leave hearts like you do rooms. Those you love only come nearer to you when you go away from them.

The night before my wedding, my last to spend in my father's house as just his daughter and not as Mrs. Percivale, my father had taken me and my mother into the octagon room, and there knelt down with us, and prayed for me in such a wonderful way that I was perfectly astonished and overcome. He was not favorable to extemporaneous prayer in public, or even in the family, and indeed had often seemed willing to omit prayers for what I could not always count sufficient reason. He had a horror of their getting to be a matter of course and form, for then, he said, they ceased to be worship at all, and were a mere pagan rite and far better left alone.

The first thing I did the morning of my wedding was to have a good cry. And after that it became very hard to get up and dress. I seemed to have grown very fond of my own bed and the queer old crows—as I had called them from my babyhood—on the chintz curtains, and the Chinese paper on the walls with the strangest birds and creeping things on it. It was a lovely spring morning and the sun was shining gloriously. I knew that the rain of the last night must be glittering on the grass and the young leaves, and I heard the birds singing as if they knew far more than mere human beings, and believed a great deal more than they knew.

Dora and the boys were making a great chatter under my window, like a whole colony of sparrows. Still, I felt as if I had twenty questions to settle before I could get up comfortably, and so lay on and on till the breakfast bell rang; and I was not more than half dressed when my mother came to see why I was late. She comforted me as nobody but a mother can comfort her child. And indeed, that morning, I felt more like her child than a woman about to become a man's wife.

TWO
The Wedding

My father, of course, gave me away, and my uncle, Mr. Weir, married us. We decided we should have no wedding journey, for we all liked the old-fashioned plan of the bride going straight from her father's house to her husband's.

After the wedding we spent the time as we should have done any other day, wandering about in groups, or sitting and reading, only that we were more smartly dressed. Then it was time for an early dinner, after which we drove to the station, accompanied only by my father and mother.

After our train left, my husband did not speak to me for nearly an hour. I knew why, and I was very grateful. He would not show his new face in the midst of my old loves, but would give me time to accustom myself to the new arrangement and bring him in when all was ready for him. When at last I had things a little tidier inside me, I held out my hand to him, and then I knew that I was his wife.

In London, instead of my father's nice carriage, we got into a jolting, lumbering, horrid cab, with my five boxes and Percivale's little portmanteau perched on the top of it, and drove away to Camden Town, a part of it near Regent's Park. It was indeed a change from a fine old house in the country; but, after what I had been told to expect, I was surprised at the prettiness of the little house. It was stuck like a swallow's nest onto the end of a great row of commonplace houses, nearly a quarter of a mile in length, though our nest itself was not the work of one of those wretched builders. It had been built by a painter for himself, in the Tudor style, and though Percivale said the idea was not very well carried out, I liked it.

It was, however, dreary and empty inside. The sitting room had just a table and two or three old-fashioned chairs, and not even a carpet on the floor. The bedroom and dressing room were as scantily furnished.

"Don't be dismayed, my darling," said my husband. "Look here," he continued, showing me a bunch of bank notes, "we shall go out tomorrow and buy all we want—as far as this will go—and then wait for the rest. It will be such a pleasure to buy the things with you, and see them come home, and have you appoint their places. You will make the carpets, won't you? And I will put them down, and we shall be like birds building their nest."

"We have only to line it—the nest is built already."

"Well, neither do the birds build the tree," he replied. "It is the only pretty house I know in all London," he went on, "with a studio at the back of it. I have had my eye on it for a long time, but there seemed no sign of a migratory disposition in the bird who had occupied it for three years past. All at once he spread his wings and flew. I count myself very fortunate."

"So do I. But now you must let me see your studio," I said. "I hope I may sit in it when you've got nobody there."

"As much as ever you like, my love," he answered. "Only I don't want to paint all my women like you, as I've been doing for the last two years."

He led me to the back of the little hall where he opened a small cloth-covered door. There yawned before me, below me, and above me, a great wide lofty room. Down into it led an almost perpendicular stair.

"So you keep a little private precipice here," I said.

"No, my dear," he returned. "It is a Jacob's ladder—or will be in one moment more."

He gave me his hand, and led me down.

"This is quite a banqueting hall, Percivale!" I cried, looking round me.

"It shall be, the first time I get a thousand pounds for a picture," he returned.

"How grand you talk!" I said, looking up at him with some wonder, for big words rarely came out of his mouth.

"Well," he answered merrily, "I had two hundred and seventy five for the last."

"That's a long way off a thousand," I returned, with a silly sigh.

"Quite right. And, therefore, this study is a long way off a banqueting hall."

There was literally nothing inside the seventeen-foot cube except one chair, one easel, a horrible thing like a huge doll with no end of joints (called a lay figure, but Percivale called it his bishop), a number of pictures leaning their faces against the walls in attitudes of grief that their beauty was despised and no man would buy them, a few casts of legs and arms and faces, a half dozen murderous-looking weapons, and a couple of yards square of the most exquisite tapestry I ever saw.

"Will you shut your eyes for one minute," he went on, "and whatever I do, not open them till I tell you?"

"You mustn't hurt me then, or I may open them without being able to help it, you know," I said, closing my eyes tight.

"Hurt you!" he repeated, with a tone I would not put on paper if I could, and the same moment I found myself in his arms, being carried like a baby.

But it was only for a few yards, and he laid me down somewhere and told me to open my eyes.

I was lying on a couch in a room, small, indeed, but beyond exception the loveliest I had ever seen. At first I was only aware of an exquisite harmony of color. Light came from a soft lamp hung in the middle, and when my eyes went up to see where it was fastened, I found the ceiling marvelous in deep blue, with a suspicion of green—just like some of the shades of a peacock's feathers—with a multitude of gold and red stars upon it. The walls were covered with pictures and sketches, and against one wall was a lovely little set of bookshelves filled with books. On a little carved table stood a vase of white hothouse flowers, with one red camellia. One picture had a curtain of green silk before it, and by its side hung the picture of the wounded knight whom his friends were carrying home to die.

"O my Percivale!" I cried, and could not say more.

"Do you like it?" he asked quietly, but with shining eyes.

"Like it?" I repeated. "Shall I like Paradise when I get there? But what a lot of money it must have cost you!"

"Not much," he answered. "Not more than thirty pounds or so. Every spot of paint there is from my own brush."

"O Percivale!"

"The carpet was the only expensive thing. That must be as thick as I could get it, for the floor is of stone and must not come near your pretty feet. You would never guess that the place was a shed before, in which the sculptor used to keep his wet clay and blocks of marble."

"Seeing is hardly believing," I said. "Is it to be my room? I know you mean it for my room, where I can ask you to come when I please, and where I can hide when anyone comes you don't want me to see."

"That is just what I meant it for, and to let you know what I *would* do for you if I could."

He made me shut my eyes again, and carried me into the study.

"Now," he said, "find your way to your own room."

I looked about me, but could see no sign of a door. He took up a tall stretcher with a canvas on it, and revealed the door. The canvas, as he turned it over, showed a likeness of myself at the top of the Jacob's ladder, as he called it, with one foot on the first step, and the other half way to the second. The light came from the window on my left, which he had turned into a western window, in order to get certain effects from a supposed sunset. I was represented in a white dress, tinged with the rose of the west—and he had managed to suggest one rosy wing behind me, with just the shoulder-root of another wing visible.

"There!" he said. "It is not finished yet, but that is how I saw you one evening as I was sitting here all alone in the twilight."

"But you didn't really see me like that!" I said.

"I was dreaming about you, and there I saw you, standing at the top of the stair, smiling to me as if to say, 'Have patience. My foot is on the first step. I'm coming.' I turned at once to my easel, and before the twilight was gone had sketched the vision."

The next morning we set out on our furniture hunt. We did not agree about the merits of everything by which one or the other was attracted; but an objection by the one always turned the other, and we bought nothing we were not agreed about. Yet that evening the hall was piled with things sent home to line our nest. Percivale, as I have said, had saved up some money for the purpose, and I had a hundred pounds my father had given me before we started, which, never having had more than ten of my own at one time, I was eager enough to spend. So we found plenty to do for the fortnight, during which time my mother had promised to say nothing to her friends in London of our arrival. Percivale also kept out of the way of his friends, and so everybody thought we were on the Continent, or somewhere else, and left us to ourselves. And as he had sent in his pictures to the Academy, he was able to take a rest—which consisted in working hard at all sorts of upholstery, not to mention painters' and carpenters' work, so that we soon got the little house made into a very warm and very pretty nest.

Percivale was particularly pleased with a cabinet I bought for him on the sly, to stand in his study and hold his paints and brushes and sketches. There were all sorts of drawers in it, and some that it took us a good deal of trouble to find out, though he was more clever than I, and suspected them from the first. That cabinet is just like him, for I have been going on finding out things in him that I had no idea were there when I married him.

THREE

Mrs. Morley's Visit

The very first morning after the expiry of the fortnight, when I was in the kitchen with our cook and housekeeper, Sarah, giving her instructions about a certain dish as if I had made it twenty times, whereas I had only just learned how from a shilling cookery book, there came a double knock at the door. I guessed who it must be.

"Run, Sarah," I said, "and show Mrs. Morley into the drawing room."

When I entered, there she was—Mrs. Morley, alias Cousin Judy.

"Well, Cozzie!" she cried, as she kissed me three or four times, "I'm glad to see you gone the way of womankind—wooed and married and a'! Fate, child! Inscrutable fate!" And she kissed me again.

She always calls me Little Coz, though I am a head taller than herself. She was as good as ever, quite as brusque, and at the first word apparently more overbearing. After a little trifling talk, which is sure to come first when people are more than ordinarily glad to meet, I asked after her children. I forget how many there were, but they were then pretty far into the plural number. All the little Morleys were full of life and eagerness. The fault in them was that they wouldn't take petting, and what's the good of a child that won't be petted? They lacked that something which makes a woman feel motherly.

"When did you arrive, Cozzie?" she asked.

"A fortnight ago yesterday."

"Ah, you sly thing! What have you been doing with yourself a' the time?"

"Furnishing."

"What? You came to an empty house?"

"Not quite that, but nearly."

"It is very odd that I should never have seen your husband."

"Not so *very* odd, seeing he has been my husband only a fortnight."

"What is he like?"

"Like nothing but himself."

"Is he tall?"

"Yes."

"Is he stout?"

"No."

"Very clever, I believe."

"Not at all." (For my father had taught me to look down on that word.)

"Why did you marry him then?"

"I didn't. He married me."

"What did you marry him for then?"

"For love."

"What did you love him for?"

"Because he was a philosopher."

"That's the oddest reason I ever heard for marrying a man."

"I said for loving him, Judy."

Her bright eyes were twinkling with fun. "Come, Cozzie," she said, "give me a proper reason for falling in love with this husband of yours."

"Well, I'll tell you, then," I said, "only you mustn't tell anybody: he has such a big shaggy head, just like a lion's."

"And such a big foot, just like a bear's?"

"Yes, and such great huge hands! Why, the two of them go quite around my waist! And such big eyes, that they look right through me. And such a big heart, that if he saw me doing anything wrong, he would kill me, and bury me in it."

"Well, I must say, it is the most extraordinary description of a husband I have ever heard. It sounds to me very like an ogre."

"The description is rather ogrish. But then he's poor, and that makes up for a good deal."

"How does that make up for anything?"

"Because if he is a poor man, he isn't a rich man, and therefore not so likely to be a stupid."

"How do you make that out?"

"Because, first of all, the rich man doesn't know what to do with his money, whereas my ogre knows what to do without it. Then the rich man wonders in the morning which waistcoat he shall put on, while my ogre has but one, besides his Sunday one. Then supposing the rich man has slept well, and has done a fair stroke or two of business, he wants nothing but a well-dressed wife, a well-dressed dinner, a few glasses of his favorite wine, and the evening paper, all well diluted with a sleep in his easy chair, to be perfectly satisfied that this world is the best of all possible worlds. Now my ogre, on the other hand—"

She interrupted me, saying with an odd tone of voice, "You are satirical, Cozzie. He's not the worst sort of man you've just described. A woman might be very happy with him."

It flashed upon me that, without the least intention, I had been giving a very fair portrait of Mr. Morley. I felt my face grow as red as fire.

"I had no intention of being satirical, Judy," I replied. "I was only describing a man the very opposite of my husband."

"You don't know mine yet," she said. "You may think—"

She actually broke down and cried. I had never in my life seen her cry, and I was miserable at what I had done. Here was a nice beginning of social relations in my married life!

I knelt down, put my arms round her, and looked up in her face.

"Dear Judy," I said. "I never thought of Mr. Morley when I said that. How should I have dared to say such things if I had? He is a most kind, good man, and Papa and everyone are glad when he comes to see us. I dare say he does like to sleep well—I know Percivale does—and I don't doubt he likes to get on with what he's at. Percivale does, for he's ever so much better company when he has got on with his picture, and I know he likes to see me well-dressed. I wish Percivale cared a little more for his dinner, for then it would be easier to do something for him. As to the newspaper, there I fear I must give him up, for I have never yet seen him with one in his hand. He's *so* stupid about some things!"

"Oh, you've found that out, have you? Men *are* stupid. There's no doubt of that. But you don't know my Walter yet."

I looked up, and, behold, Percivale was in the room! His face wore such a curious expression that I could hardly help laughing. And no wonder. For here was I on my knees, clasping my first visitor, and to all appearances pouring out the woes of my wedded life in her lap, woes so deep that they drew tears from her as she listened. All this flashed upon me as I started to my feet, but I could give no explanation: I could only make haste to introduce my husband to my cousin Judy.

He behaved, of course, as if he had heard nothing. But I fancy Judy caught a glimpse of the awkward position, for she plunged into the affair at once.

"Here is my cousin, Mr. Percivale—abusing my husband to my face, calling him rich and stupid, and I don't know what all. I confess he is so stupid as to be very fond of me, but that's all I know against him." And her handkerchief went once more to her eyes.

"Dear Judy!" I expostulated, "you know I didn't say one word about him."

"Of course I do, you silly coz!" she cried, and burst out laughing. "But I won't forgive you except you make amends by dining with us tomorrow."

Thus for the time she carried it off; but I believe that she had really mistaken me at first, and been much annoyed. And as glad as I had been to see her, how I longed to see the last of her! The moment she was gone, I threw myself into Percivale's arms, and told him how it came about. He laughed heartily.

"I *was* a little puzzled," he said, "to hear you informing a lady I had never seen that I was so very stupid."

"But I wasn't telling a story, either, for you know you are ve-e-e-ry stupid, Percivale. You don't know a leg from a shoulder of mutton, and you can't carve a bit. How you draw as you do is a marvel to me, when you know nothing about the shapes of things. It was very wrong to say it, even for the sake of covering poor Morley, but it was quite true."

"Perfectly true, my love," he said, "and I mean to remain so, in order that you may always have something to fall back upon when you get yourself into a scrape by forgetting that other people have husbands too."

FOUR
Good Society

We had agreed, rather against our inclinations, to dine the next evening with the Morleys. We should have preferred our own society, but could not refuse.

"They will be talking to me about my pictures," said my husband, "and that is just what I hate. People who know nothing of art, who can't distinguish purple from black, will yet parade their ignorance, and expect me to be pleased."

"Mr. Morley is a well-bred man, Percivale," I said.

"That's the worst of it—they do it for good manners. I know the kind of people perfectly. I hate to have my pictures praised. It is as bad as talking to one's face about the nose upon it."

I wonder if all ladies keep their husbands waiting. I did that night, I know, and, I am afraid, a good many times after; but not since Percivale told me very seriously that being late for dinner was the only fault of mine the blame of which he would not take on his own shoulders.

When we reached Bolivar Square, we found the company waiting; and, as if for a rebuke to us, the butler announced dinner the moment we entered. I was seated between Mr. Morley and a friend of his, Mr. Baddeley, a portly gentleman with an expanse of snowy shirt from which flashed three diamond studs. A huge gold chain reposed upon his front, and on his finger shone a brilliant diamond of great size. Everything about him seemed to say, "Look how rich I am! Nothing shoddy about me!" His hands were plump and white, and looked as if they did not know what dust was. His talk sounded very rich, and yet there was no pretense in it. His wife looked less of a lady than he a gentleman, for she betrayed conscious importance. I found afterwards that he was the only son of a railway contractor, who had himself handled the spade, but at last had died enormously rich. He spoke blandly, but with a certain authority which I disliked.

"Are you fond of the opera, Mrs. Percivale?" he asked me in order to make talk.

"I have never been to the opera," I answered.

"Never been to the opera? Are you not fond of music?"

"Did you ever know a lady that wasn't?"

"Then you must go to the opera."

"But it is just because I fancy myself fond of music that I don't think I should like the opera."

"You can't hear such music anywhere else."

"An artist's wife must do without such expensive amusements, except her husband's pictures be very popular indeed. I might as well cry for the moon. The cost of a box at the opera for a single night would keep my little household for a fortnight."

"Ah, well! But you should see *The Barber,*" he said.

"Perhaps if I could hear without seeing, I should like it better," I answered.

He fell silent, busying himself with his fish, and when he spoke again turned to the lady on his left. I went on with my dinner. I knew that our host had heard what I said, for I saw him turn rather hastily to his butler.

Mr. Morley is a man difficult to describe, stiff in the back, and long and loose in the neck, reminding me of those toy birds that bob head and tail up and down alternately. When he agrees with anything you say, down comes his head with a rectangular nod. When he does not agree with you, he is so silent and motionless that he leaves you in doubt whether he has heard a word of what you have been saying. His face is hard, and was to me then inscrutable, while what he said always seemed to have little or nothing to do with what he was thinking. I had not then learned whether he had a heart or not. His features were well formed, but they and his head and face were too small for his body. He had been very successful in business, and always looked full of schemes.

"Have you been to the Academy yet?" he asked.

"No. This is only the first day of it."

"Are your husband's pictures well hung?"

"As high as Haman," I answered, "skied, in fact."

"I would advise you to avoid slang, my dear cousin, *professional* slang especially, and to remember that in London there are no professions after six o'clock."

"Indeed!" I returned. "As we came along in the carriage I saw no end of shops open."

"I mean in society—at dinner—amongst friends."

"My dear Mr. Morley, you have just done asking me about my husband's pictures. And, if you will listen a moment, you will hear that lady next to my husband talking to him about Leslie and Turner, and I don't know who more, all in the trade."

"Hush! Hush! I beg you," he almost whispered, looking agonized. "That's Mrs. Baddeley. Her husband, next to you, is a great picture buyer.

That's why I asked him to meet you."

"I thought there were no professions in London after six o'clock."

"I am afraid I have not made my meaning quite clear to you. We'll have a talk about it another time."

"With pleasure."

It rather irritated me that he should talk to me, a married woman, as to a little girl who did not know how to behave herself, but his patronage of my husband displeased me far more. I was on the point of committing the terrible blunder of asking Mr. Baddeley if he had any poor relations, but I checked myself in time, and prayed to know whether he was a member of Parliament. He answered that he was not at present, and asked in return why I had wished to know. I answered that I wanted a bill brought in for the punishment of fraudulent milkmen, for I couldn't get a decent pennyworth of milk in all Camden Town. He laughed, and said it would be a very desirable measure, only too great an interference with the liberty of the subject. I told him that kind of liberty was just what the law in general owed its existence to, and was there on purpose to interfere with, but he did not seem to see it.

The fact is, I was very silly. Proud of being the wife of an artist, I resented the social injustice which I thought gave artists no place but one of sufferance. Proud also of being poor for Percivale's sake, I made a show of my poverty before people whom I supposed, rightly enough in many cases, to be proud of their riches. But I knew nothing of what poverty really meant, and was as yet only playing at being poor. I was thus wronging the dignity of my husband's position, and complimenting wealth by making so much of its absence. Poverty or wealth ought to have been in my eyes such a trifle that I never thought of publishing whether I was rich or poor.

I suspect also, now that I think of it, that I looked down on my cousin Judy because she had a mere man of business for her husband, forgetting that our Lord had found a collector of conquered taxes—a man, I presume, with little enough of the artistic about him—one of the fittest in his nation to bear the message of redemption to the hearts of his countrymen. It is his loves and his hopes, not his visions and intentions, by which a man is to be judged.

"Is Mrs. Percivale a lady of fortune?" asked Mr. Baddeley of my cousin Judy when we were gone, for we were the first to leave.

"Certainly not. Why do you ask?"

"Because, from her talk, I thought she must be."

Cousin Judy told me this the next day, and I could see she thought I had been bragging of my family. So I recounted all the conversation I had had with him, as nearly as I could recollect, and set down the question to an impertinent irony. But I have since changed my mind; I now judge that he could not believe any poor person would joke about poverty.

FIVE

A Refuge From the Heat

Our house boasted a little garden by the studio. One side was enclosed by the house, another by the studio, and the remaining two by walls, evidently built for the nightly convenience of promenading cats. One pear tree in a grass plot occupied the center, and a few small fruit trees (which, I may now safely say, never bore anything) around the walls. The last occupant had cared for his garden, but if you stop thinking about a garden, it begins at once to go bad.

Although I had been used to great wide lawns and parks and gardens and wilderness, the tiny enclosure soon became to me the type of the boundless universe. The streets roared about me with ugly omnibuses and uglier cabs, fine carriages, huge earthshaking drays, and (worse far) the cries of all the tribe of costermongers. Suburban London was roaring about me, and I was confined to a few square yards of grass and gravel walk and flower plot. But above was the depth of the sky, and at night the hosts of heaven looked in upon me with a calm assured glance, and there the moon would come, and cast her lovely shadows. There was room enough to feel alone and to try to pray.

And, strangely, the space seemed greater (for the loneliness was gone) when my husband walked up and down in it with me. True, the greater part of the walk seemed to be the turnings, for they always came just when you wanted to go on and on. But even with the scope of the world for your walk, you must turn and come back some time. At first, when he was smoking his great brown meerschaum, he and I would walk in opposite directions, passing each other in the middle, and so make the space double the size, for he had all the garden to himself, and I had it all to myself. That is how by degrees I grew able to bear the smoke of tobacco, for I had never been used to it, and found it a small trial at first. But now I like it, and greet a stray whiff from the study like a message from my husband.

There was in the garden a little summer house. Knowing my passion for the flower, Percivale had surrounded it with a multitude of sweet peas, which he had trailed over the trelliswork of its sides. To sit there in a warm evening, when the moth-airs just woke and gave two or three wafts of their wings and ceased, was like sitting in the midst of a small gospel.

The summer had come and the days were very hot, so hot and changeless, with their unclouded skies and their glowing center, that they seemed to grow stupid with their own heat. Like a hen brooding over her chickens, the day, brooding over its coming harvests, grew dull and sleepy, living only in what was to come. I began to long for a wider horizon, whence some wind might come and blow upon me, and wake me up, not merely to live, but to know that I lived.

One afternoon I left my little summer seat, where I had been sitting at work, and went through the house, and down the precipice into my husband's study.

"It is so hot," I said, "I will try my little grotto. It may be cooler."

He opened the door for me, and, with his palette on his thumb, and a brush in his hand, sat down for a moment beside me.

"This heat is too much for you, Darling," he said.

"I do feel it. I wish I could get from the garden into my nest without going up through the house and down the Jacob's ladder," I said. "It is so hot! I never felt heat like it before."

He sat silent for a while, and then said, "I've been thinking I must get you into the country for a few weeks. It would do you no end of good."

"I suppose the wind does blow somewhere," I returned. "But—"

"You don't want to leave me?"

"I don't. And with that ugly portrait on hand you can't go with me."

He happened to be painting a portrait of a plain red-faced lady in a delicate lace cap (a very unfit subject for art) much needing to be made over again first, it seemed to me. Only there she was, with a right to have her portrait painted if she wished it. And there was Percivale, with time on his hands and room in his pockets, and the faith that whatever God had thought worth making could not be unworthy of representation. Hence he had willingly undertaken her likeness, to be finished within a certain time, and was now working at it as conscientiously as if it had been the portrait of a lovely young duchess or peasant girl. (I was only afraid he would make it too like her to please the lady herself!) His time was now getting short, and he could not leave home before fulfilling his engagement.

"But," he returned, "why shouldn't you go to the Hall for a week or two without me? I will take you down, and come and fetch you."

"You want to get rid of me!" I said. I did not in the least believe it, and yet I was on the edge of crying.

"You know better than that, my Wynnie," he answered gravely. "You want your mother to comfort you. And there must be some air in the country. So tell Sarah to put up your things, and I'll take you down tomorrow evening. When I get this portrait done, I will come and stay a few days, if they will have me, and then take you home."

The thought of seeing my mother and my father and the old place came over me with a rush, and I felt all at once as if I had been absent for years instead of weeks. I cried in earnest now, with delight though, and there is no shame in that. So it was all arranged, and the next evening I was lying on a couch in the yellow drawing room, with my mother seated beside me. Connie sat in an easy chair by the open window, through which came every now and then such a sweet wave of air as bathed me with hope, and seemed to wash all the noises from my brain.

Yet, glad as I was to be once more at home, I felt, when Percivale left me the next morning to return by a third-class train to his ugly portrait, that the idea of home was already leaving Oldcastle Hall, and flitting back to the suburb of London.

But soon I felt better, for here there was plenty of shadow and in the hottest days my father could always tell where any wind would be stirring, for he knew every out and in of the place like his own pockets.

One forenoon in particular was most oppressive. I was sitting under a tree, trying to read, when he came up to me. There was a wooden gate, with open bars near. He went and set it wide, saying, "There, my love! You will fancy yourself cooler if I leave the gate open."

His words went deep to my heart, and I seemed to know God better for it ever after. A father is a great and marvelous truth, and one you can never get at the depth of, try how you may.

My mother was, if possible, yet more to me than my father. I could tell her anything and everything without fear, while I confess to a little dread of my father still. He is too like my conscience for me to be quite confident with him.

SIX
Connie

The worst of some illnesses (especially some small ones) is that they make you think a great deal too much about yourself. My sister Connie's illness (which was a great and terrible one) never made her do so.

She was now a thin, pale, delicate-looking girl, not handsome, but lovely. Some people said her eyes were too big for her face. She had been early ripened by the hot sun of suffering, and by the self-restraint which pain had taught her. Patience had mossed her over, and made her warm and soft and sweet. She never looked for attention, but accepted all that was offered with a smile. She was not confined to her sofa now, though she needed to lie down often, but could walk about pretty well—only you had to give her time. You could always make her merry by saying she walked like an old woman, and it was the only way we could get rid of the sadness of seeing it. And so we laughed her sadness away from us.

She was always forgetting herself in her interest about others, and now she would watch me with her gentle, dovelike eyes, and seemed to know at once, without being told, what was the matter with me. She never asked me what I should like, but went and brought something—and, if she saw that I didn't care for it, she wouldn't press me or offer anything instead, but chat for a minute or two, carry it away, and return with something else. My heart was like to break at times with the swelling of the love that was in it.

Once, as I lay on a couch on the lawn, she came toward me carrying a bunch of grapes from the greenhouse—a great bunch, each individual grape ready to burst with the sunlight bottled up in its swollen purple skin.

"They are too heavy for you, old lady," I cried.

"Yes, I *am* an old lady," she answered. "Think what good use of my time I have made compared with you! I have gone ever so far before you—I've nearly forgotten how to walk!"

The tears gathered in my eyes as she left the bunch with me—for how could one help being sad to think of the time when she used to bound like a slender fawn over the grass? She turned to say something and, perceiving my emotion, came slowly back.

"Dear Wynnie," she said, "you wouldn't have me back with my old foolishness, would you? Believe me, life is ten times more precious than it was before. I feel and enjoy and love so much more! I often thank God for what befell me."

And I believe she had a special affection for poor Sprite, the pony which threw her, regarding him as in some sense the angel which had driven her out of paradise into a better world. If ever he got loose and Connie was anywhere about, he was sure to find her. He was an omnivorous animal, and she always had something he would eat when his favorite apples were unobtainable. More than once she had been roused from her sleep on the lawn by the lips and the breath of Sprite on her face. Although she usually started at the least noise or sudden discovery of a presence, she never started at the most unexpected intrusion of Sprite, any more than at the voice of my father or mother.

There was one more whose voice or presence never startled her. The relation between that one and her was lovely to see. Turner was a fine, healthy, broad-shouldered fellow, of bold carriage and frank manners, above the middle height, with rather large features, keen black eyes, and great personal strength. Yet to such a man, poor little wan-faced, big-eyed Connie assumed imperious airs, mostly—but perhaps not entirely—for the fun of it, while he looked only enchanted every time she honored him with a little tyranny.

"There! I'm tired," she would say, holding out her arms like a baby. "Carry me in."

And he would stoop, and take her carefully, and carry her in as lightly and gently and steadily as if she had been but the baby whose manners she had for the moment assumed. This began, of course, when she was unable to walk, but it did not stop then, for she would occasionally tell him to carry her after she was quite capable of crawling at least. They had now been engaged for some months, and in front of me—a newly married woman—they did not mind talking a little.

One day she was lying on a rug on the lawn, with him on the grass beside her, leaning on his elbow, and looking down into her sky-like eyes. She lifted her hand, and stroked his mustache with a forefinger.

"Poor, poor man!" she said, and from the tone I knew the tears had begun to gather in those eyes.

"Why do you pity me, Connie?" he asked.

"Because you will have such a wretched little creature for a wife someday—or perhaps never."

"If you will allow me my choice," he answered cheerily, "I prefer just such a wretched little creature to anyone else in the world."

"And why, pray? Give a good reason, and I will forgive your bad taste."

"Because she won't be able to hurt me much when she beats me."

"A better reason, or she will."

"Because I can punish her if she isn't good by taking her up in my arms, and carrying her about until she gives in."

"A better reason, or I shall be naughty directly."

"Because I shall always know where to find her."

"Ah, yes! She must leave you to find her. But that's a silly reason. If you don't give me a better, I'll get up and walk into the house."

"Because there won't be any waste of me. Will that do?"

"What do you mean?" she asked.

"I mean that I shall be able to lay not only my heart but my brute strength at her feet. I shall be her beast of burden, to carry her whither she would."

"There! Take me, take me!" she said, stretching up her arms to him. "How good you are! I don't deserve such a great man one bit. But I will love him. Take me directly, for there's Wynnie listening and laughing at us."

I was crying, and the creature knew it. Turner brought her to me, and held her down for me to kiss, then carried her in.

I believe the country people round considered our family far gone on the inclined plane of degeneracy. First my mother, the heiress, had married a clergyman of no high family, and they had given their eldest daughter to a poor artist. And now Connie was engaged to a country practitioner, a man who made up his own prescriptions. Connie and I talked and laughed over certain remarks of the kind that reached us, and compared our two with the gentlemen about us—in no way to the advantage of any of the latter, you may be sure. It was silly work, but we were only two loving girls, with the best possible reasons for being proud of the men who had honored us with their love.

SEVEN
Connie's Baby

Theodora, our orphan, was now nearly four years old and a very pretty, dark-skinned, lithe-limbed, wild little creature. She was not like a lady's child, and neither did she look like the child of working people. She had a certain tinge of the savage about her, specially manifest in a certain furtive look of her black eyes, with which she seemed now and then to be measuring you, and her prospects in relation to you.

I have seen children stare at a stranger in the most persistent manner, never withdrawing their eyes, as if they would pierce to his soul. I have also seen their sidelong glance of sly merriment, or loving shyness, or small coquetry. But I have never, in any other child, seen *that* look of self-protective speculation; and it used to make me uneasy, for, of course, like everyone else in the house, I loved Theodora. She was a wayward, often unmanageable creature, but affectionate. She would take an unaccountable preference for someone of the family or household, at one time for the housekeeper, at another for the stableboy, at another for one of us. In these fits of partiality she would always turn a blind and deaf side on everyone else, actually seeming to imagine she showed the strength of her love to the one by the paraded exclusion of the others.

I cannot tell how much of this was natural to her, and how much the result of the foolish and injurious jealousy of the servants. I say servants, because I know such an influencing was all but impossible in the family itself. If my father heard anyone utter such a phrase as, "Don't you love me best?" or, "better than such a one?" or, "Ain't I your favorite?"—well, you would have been astonished, and perhaps at first bewildered as well, by the look of indignation that flashed from his eyes. He was not the gentle, all-excusing man some fancy him. He was gentle even to tenderness when he had time to think a moment, and in any quiet judgment he always took as much the side of the offender as was possible with any likelihood of justice.

Theodora was subject to attacks of the most furious passion, especially when anything occurred to thwart the indulgence of her partiality. Then, wherever she was, she would throw herself down on the floor, on the walk or lawn, or, as happened on one occasion, in the water, and kick and scream. At such times she cared nothing even for my father, of whom generally she stood in considerable awe—a feeling he rather encouraged.

"She has plenty of people about her to represent the Gospel," he said once. "I will keep the department of the law, without which she will never appreciate the Gospel. My part will, I trust, vanish in due time, and the law turn out to have been, after all, only the imperfect Gospel, just as the leaf is the imperfect flower. But the Gospel is no Gospel till it gets into the heart, and it sometimes wants a torpedo to blow the gates of that open."

For no torpedo, however, did Theodora care at such times. After repeated experience, my father gave orders that when a fit occurred, everyone, without exception, should not merely leave her alone, but go out of sight and out of her hearing, that she might know she had driven her friends far from her, and be brought to a sense of loneliness and need. I am pretty sure that if she had been one of his own, he would have taken sharper measures with her. But he said we must never attempt to treat other people's children as our own, for they are not. We did not love them enough, he said, to make severity safe either for them or for us.

The plan worked so far well that, after a time, varied in length according to causes inscrutable, she would always reappear smiling. But, as to any conscience of wrong, she seemed to have no more than Nature herself, who looks out with her smiling face after hours of thunder, lightning, and rain. Although this treatment brought her out of her attacks sooner, the fits themselves came quite as frequently as before.

But she had another habit, more alarming, and more troublesome as well—she would vanish and have to be long sought, for in such cases she never reappeared of herself. What made it so alarming was that there were dangerous places about our house. Yet she would generally be found seated, perfectly quiet, in some out-of-the-way nook where she had never been before, playing not with any of her toys, but with something she had picked up and appropriated, finding in it some shadowy amusement which no one understood but herself.

She was very fond of bright colors, especially in dress. If she found a brilliant or gorgeous fragment of any substance, she would be sure to hide it away in some hole or corner. Her love of approbation was strong, and her affection demonstrative, but she had not yet learned to speak the truth. She must, we thought, have come of wild parentage, for so many of her ways were like those of a forest animal.

In our design of training her for a maid to Connie, we seemed already likely enough to be frustrated. She had some sort of aversion to Connie, amounting almost to dread, and we could rarely persuade her to go near her. Perhaps it was a dislike to her helplessness—some vague impression that lying all day on the sofa indicated an unnatural condition of being.

Those of us who had the highest spirits, the greatest exuberance of animal life, were evidently those whose society was most attractive to her. Connie tried all she could to conquer Theodora's dislike and entice the wayward thing to her heart, but nothing would do. Sometimes she would seem to soften for a moment—but all at once, with a wriggle and a backward spasm in the arms of the person who carried her, she would manifest a fresh access of repulsion, and wailing, would be borne off hurriedly. I have seen Connie cry because the child treated her so.

You could not interest Theodora so much in a story that if the buzzing of a fly or the flutter of a bird reached her eye or ear, away she would dart on the instant, leaving the discomfited narrator in lonely disgrace. External nature and almost nothing else had free access to her mind; at any sudden sight or sound, she was alive on the instant. She was a most amusing and sometimes almost bewitching little companion, but the delight in her would be not unfrequently quenched by some altogether unforeseen outbreak of heartless petulance or turbulent rebellion.

Her resistance to authority grew as she grew older, and occasioned all of us no little anxiety. Even Charley and Harry would stand with open mouths, contemplating aghast the unheard-of atrocity of resistance to the will of the unquestioned authorities. Such resistance was almost always accompanied by storm and tempest, and the treatment which carried away the latter, generally carried away the former with it. After the passion had come and gone, she would obey. Had it been otherwise—had she been sullen and obstinate as well—I do not know what would have come of it, or how we could have got on at all. Miss Bowdler would have had a very satisfactory crow over Papa.

I have seen him sit in silent contemplation of the little puzzle, trying, no doubt, to fit her into his theories or, as my mother said, to find her a three-legged stool and a corner somewhere in the kingdom of heaven. We were certain something or other would come out of that pondering, though whether the same night or a twelvemonth after, no one could tell. I believe the main result of his thinking was that he did less and less with her.

"Why do you take so little notice of the child?" my mother said to him one evening. "It is all your doing that she is here, you know. You mustn't cast her off now."

"Cast her off!" exclaimed my father. "What *do* you mean, Ethel?"

"You never speak to her now."

"Oh, yes I do, sometimes!"

"Why only sometimes?"

"I believe I am a little afraid of her. I don't know how to attack the small enemy. She seems to be bombproof, and generally impregnable."

"But you mustn't therefore make *her* afraid of you."

"I suspect that is my only chance with her. She wants a little of Mount Sinai, in order that she may know where the manna comes from. But indeed I am laying myself out only to catch the little soul. I am watching and pondering how to reach her. I am biding my time to come in with my small stone for the building up of this temple of the Holy Ghost."

The moon was rising in the last fold of the twilight, and at that moment the nurse came through the darkening air, her figure hardly distinguishable from the dusk, saying, "Please, Ma'am, have you seen Miss Theodora?"

"I don't want you to call her *Miss,*" said my father.

"I beg your pardon, Sir," said the nurse, "I forgot."

"I have not seen her for an hour or more," said my mother.

"I declare," said my father, "I'll get a retriever pup and train him to find Theodora. He will be capable in a few months, and she will be foolish for years."

On that occasion the truant was found in the apple-loft, sitting in a dark corner upon a heap of straw. She was discovered only by the munching of her little teeth—she had found some wizened apples, and was busily devouring them.

My father actually did what he had said—a favorite spaniel had pups a few days after, and he took one of them in hand. Soon the long-drawn nose of Wagtail had learned to track Theodora to whatever retreat she might have chosen, and it was very amusing to watch the course of the proceedings. Someone would come running to my father with the news that Theo was hiding. Then my father would give a peculiar whistle, and Wagtail would come bounding to his side. My father himself would lay him on the scent, for he would heed directions from no one else. It was not necessary to follow him, however; after his tortuous and fatiguing pursuit, a joyous barking would be heard, always kept up until the ready pursuers were guided by the sound to the place. There Theo was certain to be found, hugging the animal, without the least notion of the traitorous character of his blandishments. It was long before she began to discover that there was danger in that dog's nose.

EIGHT
The Foundling and Wagtail

One evening during this first visit to my home, we had gone to take tea with the widow of an old servant—Connie and I in the pony carriage, and my father and mother on foot. It was quite dark when we returned, for the moon was late. Connie and I got home first, though we had a good round to make, and the path across the fields was but a third of the distance. My father and mother were lovers, and sure to be late when left out by themselves. When we arrived, there was no one to take the pony, and when I rang the bell, no one answered. I could not leave Connie in the carriage to go and look, so we waited and waited till we were getting very tired, and were glad indeed to hear the voices of my father and mother as they came through the shrubbery. My mother went to the rear to make inquiry, and came back with the news that Theo was missing, and that they had been searching for her in vain for nearly an hour. My father instantly called Wagtail, and sent him after her. We then got Connie in and laid her on the sofa, where I kept her company while the rest went in different directions, listening from what quarter would come the welcome voice of the dog. This was so long delayed, however, that my father began to get alarmed. At last he whistled very loudly, and in a little while Wagtail came creeping to his feet, with his tail between his legs—no wag left in it—clearly ashamed of himself.

My father was now thoroughly frightened, and began questioning the household. One of the servants then remembered that a strange-looking woman had been seen about the place in the morning, a tall, dark woman, with a gypsy look. She had come begging, but nothing had been given her, and she had gone away in anger. As soon as he heard this, my father ordered his horse, and told two of the men to get ready to accompany him. In the meantime, he came to us in the little drawing room, trying to look calm but evidently in much perturbation. He said he had little doubt that the woman had taken her.

"Could it be her mother?" said my mother.

"Who can tell?" returned my father. "It is more likely that the deed was prompted by revenge."

"If she be a gypsy's child—" said my mother.

"The gypsies," interrupted my father, "have always been more given to taking other people's children than forsaking their own. But one of them might have had reason for being ashamed of her child, and, dreading the severity of her family, abandoned it, with the intention of repossessing it herself, and passing it off as the child of gentlefolks. If we should fail in finding her tonight, the police all over the country can be apprised of the fact in a few hours, and the thief can hardly escape."

"But if she *should* be the mother?" suggested my mother.

"She would have to *prove* that."

"And then?"

"What then?" returned my father, and began pacing up and down the room, stopping now and then to listen for the horses.

"Would you give her up?" persisted my mother.

Still my father made no reply. He was evidently much agitated—more, I fancied, by my mother's question than by the present trouble. He left the room, and presently his whistle for Wagtail pierced the still air. A moment more, and we heard them all ride out of the paved yard. I had never known him to leave my mother without an answer.

There was not a dry eye amongst the women. Harry was in floods of tears and Charley was howling. We could not send them to bed in such a state, so we kept them with us in the drawing room. They soon fell fast asleep, one in an easy chair, the other on a sheepskin mat. Connie lay quite still, and my mother talked so sweetly and gently that she soon made me quiet and drowsy too. But I was haunted with the idea that it was somehow a child of my own lost out in the dark night, and that I could not anyhow reach her. I cannot explain the odd feeling—as if a dream had wandered out of the region of sleep, and half-possessed my waking brain. Every now and then my mother's voice would bring me back to my senses, and I would understand it all perfectly; but in a few moments I would be involved once more in a hazy search after my own child. Mother sought to quiet our hearts, helping us to trust in the great love of God that never ceases to watch. And she did make us quiet. But the time glided so slowly past that it seemed immobile.

When twelve struck, we heard in the stillness every clock in the house, and it seemed as if they would never have done.

Still the time went on, and there was no sound of horses or anything to break the silence, except the faint murmur which now and then the trees will make in the quietest night, as if they are dreaming and talking in their sleep. Only this and the occasional cry of an owl broke the silent flow of the undivided moments. We seldom spoke, and at length the house within seemed possessed by the silence from without, but we were all ears.

My mother at length started up, saying, "I hear them! They're coming!"

Then we too heard the sound of horses, and my mother hurried down to the hall. I would have stayed with Connie, but she begged me to go, and come back as soon as I knew the result. As I descended the stairs, I could see the dim light of the low-burning lamp on the heads of the listening, anxious groups—my mother at the open door with the housekeeper and her maid, and the menservants visible through the door in the moonlight beyond.

The first news that reached me was my father's shout the moment he rounded the sweep that brought him in sight of the house.

"All right! Here she is!" he cried.

And, ere I could reach the stair to run up to Connie, Wagtail was jumping on me and barking furiously. He rushed up before me with the scramble of twenty feet, licked Connie's face all over in spite of her efforts at self-defense, then rushed at Dora and the boys one after the other, and woke them all up. He was satisfied enough with himself now, and his tail was doing the wagging of forty. There was no tucking it away now, no drooping of the head in mute confession of conscious worthlessness; he was a dog self-satisfied because his master was well pleased with him.

My father cantered up to the door, followed by the two men. My mother hurried to meet him and only then saw the lost little lamb asleep in his bosom. He gave her up, and my mother ran in with her. He dismounted, and walked merrily but wearily up the stair after her. The first thing he did was to quiet the dog; the next to sit down beside Connie; the third to say, "Thank God!" and the next, "God bless Wagtail!" My mother was already undressing the little darling, and the maid was gone to fetch her night things. Tumbled hither and thither, she did not wake, but was carried off stone-sleeping to her crib.

As soon as he had had a bit of supper, my father began to tell us the whole story.

As they had ridden out of the gate, one of the menservants—Burton—rode up alongside of my father, and told him that there was an encampment of gypsies on the moor about five miles away. My father thought, in the absence of other indication, they ought to follow that direction and told Burton to guide them to the place as rapidly as possible. After half an hour's sharp riding, they came to the rising ground behind which lay the camp.

The other servant, Sim, was an old man who had been whipper-in to a baronet in the next county, and knew much of the ways of wild animals. It was his turn now to address my father, who had halted for a moment to think what ought to be done next.

"She can't well have got here before us, Sir, with that child to carry, but I think I had better have a peep over the brow first. She may be there already, or she may not; but, if we find out, we shall know better what to do."

"I'll go with you," said my father.

"No, Sir—excuse me—that won't do. You can't creep like a serpent. I can. They'll never know I'm stalking them. No more you couldn't show fight if need was, you know, Sir."

"How did you find that out, Sim?" asked my father, a little amused, notwithstanding the weight at his heart.

"Why, Sir, they do say a clergyman mustn't show fight."

"Who told you that, Sim?" he persisted.

"Well, I can't say, Sir. Only it wouldn't be respectable, would it, Sir?"

"There's nothing respectable but what's right, Sim, and what's right always is respectable, though it mayn't *look* so one bit."

"Suppose you was to get a black eye, Sir?"

"Did you ever hear of the martyrs, Sim?"

"Yes, Sir. I've heard you talk on 'em in the pulpit, Sir."

"Well, they didn't get black eyes only, they got black all over, you know—burnt black. And what for, do you think, now?"

"Don't know, Sir, except it was for doing right."

"That's just it. Was it any disgrace to them?"

"No, sure, Sir."

"Well, if I were to get a black eye for the sake of the child, would that be any disgrace to me, Sim?"

"None that I knows on, Sir. Only it'd *look* bad."

"Yes, no doubt. People might think I had got into a row at the Griffin. And yet I shouldn't be ashamed of it. I should count my black eye the more respectable of the two. I should also regard the evil judgment much as another black eye, and wait till they both came round again. Lead on, Sim."

They left their horses with Burton, and went toward the camp. But when they reached the slope behind which it lay, my father—much to Sim's discomfiture—my father, instead of lying down at the foot of it and creeping up the side of it, walked right up over the brow and straight into the camp with Wagtail.

There was nothing going on, neither tinkering nor cooking, and all seemed asleep. But presently, out of two or three of the tents—the dingy squalor of which no moonshine could silver over—came three or four men, half undressed, demanding of my father in no gentle tones what he wanted there.

"I'll tell you all about it," he answered. "I'm the parson of this parish, and therefore you're my own people, you see."

"We don't go to *your* church, Parson," said one of them.

"I don't care. You're my own people, for all that, and I want your help."

"Well, what's the matter? Whose cow's dead?" said the man.

"This evening," returned my father, "one of my children is missing; and a woman who might be one of your clan—mind, I say *might be*—I don't know, and I mean no offense, but such a woman was seen about the place. All I want is the child, and if I don't find her, I shall have to raise the county. I should be very sorry to disturb you, but I am afraid, in that case, whether the woman be one of you or not, the place will be too hot for you. I'm no enemy to honest gypsies; but you know there is a set of tramps that call themselves gypsies, who are nothing of the sort, only thieves. Tell me what I had better do to find my child. You know all about such things."

The men turned to each other, and began talking in undertones in a language my father could not understand. At length the spokesman of the party addressed him again.

"We'll give you our word, Sir, if that will satisfy you," he said more respectfully than he had spoken before, "to send the child home directly if anyone should bring her to our camp. That's all we can say."

My father saw that his best chance lay in accepting the offer. "Thank you," he said. "Perhaps I may have an opportunity of serving you someday."

They in their turn thanked him politely enough, and my father and Sim left the camp.

Upon this side the moor was bordered by a deep trench, the bottom of which was full of young firs. As the moon was now up, my father resolved to halt for a time, and watch the moor from the shelter of the firs, on the chance of the woman making her appearance.

They had lain in the firs for about half an hour when suddenly Wagtail rushed into the underwood and vanished. In a few moments they heard his joyous bark, followed, however, by a howl of pain. Before they had gained many yards in pursuit, Wagtail came cowering to my father's feet, who, patting his side, found it bleeding. He bound his handkerchief round him, and, fastening the lash of Sim's whip to his collar that he might not go too fast for them, told him to find Theodora. Instantly he pulled away through the brushwood, giving a little yelp now and then as some broken twig or stem hurt his wounded side.

Before he reached the spot for which he was making, however, my father heard a rustling nearer to the outskirts of the wood, and the same moment Wagtail turned and tugged fiercely in that direction. The figure of a woman rose up against the sky, and began to run for the open space beyond.

"Mount and head her, Sim. Mount, Burton. Ride over everything," cried my father, as he slipped Wagtail, who shot through the underwood like a bird. Wagtail reached her just as she reached the trench, and in an instant had her by the gown. My father saw something gleam in the moonlight, and again a howl broke from Wagtail, who was evidently once more wounded. But he held on. And now the horsemen were approaching her in front, and my father was hard upon her from behind. She gave a peculiar cry—half a shriek, and half a howl—clasped the child to her bosom, and stood rooted like a tree, evidently in the hope that her friends, hearing her signal, would come to her rescue.

But it was too late. The dog held her by the poor ragged skirt, and the horses snorted on the bank above her. She heaved the child over her head, either in appeal to Heaven, or to dash her to the earth. Then my father caught both her uplifted arms with his, so that she could not lower them, and Burton flung himself from his horse and took Theodora from them. Then my father called off Wagtail, and the poor woman sunk down in the bottom of the trench amongst the young firs without a sound, and there lay. My father went up to her, but she only stared at him with big blank black eyes, and yet such a lost look on her young, handsome, yet gaunt face, as almost convinced him she was the mother of the child. But, whatever might be her rights, she could not be allowed to recover possession, without those who had saved and tended the child having a word in the matter.

As he was thinking what he could say to her, Sim's voice reached his ear. "They're coming up over the brow, Sir—five or six from the camp. We'd better be off."

"The child is safe," he said, as he turned to leave her.

"From *me,*" she rejoined, in a pitiful tone, and this ambiguous utterance was all that fell from her.

My father mounted, took the child from Burton, and rode away, followed by the two men and Wagtail. Through the green rides they galloped in the moonlight, and were soon beyond all danger of pursuit. When they slackened pace, my father instructed Sim to find out all he could about the gypsies, to learn their names and to what tribe or community they belonged. Sim promised to do what was in his power, but said he did not expect much success.

. The children had listened to the story wide awake. Wagtail was lying at my father's feet, licking his wounds—which were not very serious, and had stopped bleeding.

"It is all your doing, Wagtail," said Harry, patting the dog.

"I think he deserves to be called *Mr.* Wagtail," said Charley.

And from that day he was Mr. Wagtail, much to the amusement of visitors, who, hearing the name gravely uttered, saw the owner of it approach on all fours with a tireless pendulum in his rear.

NINE
Home Again

My father took every means in his power to find out something about the woman and the gang of gypsies. But, the very next day, he heard that they had already vanished, and all his inquiries were of no avail. I believe he was dissatisfied with himself in what had occurred, thinking he ought to have discovered at the time whether she was indeed the mother, and, in that case, to do for her what he could. Had he done so, he might only have heaped difficulty upon difficulty. As it was, if he was saved from trouble, he was not delivered from uneasiness. Clearly, however, the child must not be exposed to the danger of the repetition of the attempt. By now the whole household was so fully alive to the necessity of not losing sight of her for a moment, that her danger was far less than it had been at any time before.

I continued at the hall for six weeks, during which my husband came several times to see me, and, at the close of that period, took me back with him to my dear little home. The rooms, all but the study, looked very small after those I had left, but I felt, notwithstanding, that the place was my home. I was at first a little ashamed of the feeling—for why should I be anywhere more at home than in the little house of parents such as mine? There is a certain amount of the queenly element in every woman, so that she cannot feel perfectly at ease without something to govern, however small and however troublesome her queendom may be. At my father's, I had every ministration and all comforts, but no responsibilities and no rule. I could not help feeling idle.

Besides, I could not be at all sure that my big bear was properly attended to. He was most independent of personal comforts, and should not be left to his own neglect. I still have to rack my brains for weeks before my bear's birthday comes round, to think of something that will in itself have a chance of giving him pleasure. Of course, it would be comparatively easy if I had plenty of money to spare, and hadn't "to muddle it all away" in paying butchers and bakers and such.

So home I went, to be queen again.

My father often used to say that the commonest things in the world were the loveliest—like the sky and water and grass. Now I found that the commonest feelings of humanity—for what feelings could be commoner than those which now made me blessed amongst women?—are those that are fullest of the divine. For simply because the life of the world was moving on toward its unseen goal, and I knew it and had a helpless share in it, I felt as if God was with me.

The winter passed slowly away, fog, rain, frost, snow, thaw, succeeding one another in all the seeming disorder of the season. A good many things happened, I believe, but I don't remember any of them. My mother wrote, offering me Dora for a companion in my growing need, but somehow I preferred being without her.

My father came to see me several times, and was all himself to me, but I could not feel quite comfortable with him: it indicates something very wrong in me somewhere. But he seemed to understand me, and always, the moment he left me, the tide of confidence began to flow afresh in the ocean that lay about the little island of my troubles. Then I knew he was my own *father*—something that even my husband could not be, and would not wish to be to me.

In the month of March, my mother came to see me, and that was all pleasure. My father did not always see when I was not able to listen to him, though he was most considerate when he did. But my mother—why, there is nothing better for a woman than to be with her own mother when she is awaiting a child. She brought with her a young Irish woman to take Sarah's place as cook for Sarah was now to be the child's nurse. Jemima had been kitchenmaid in a small family of my mother's acquaintance, and had a good character for honesty and plain cooking. I should have been perfectly satisfied with my mother's choice, even if I had not been so indifferent at the time to all that was going on in the lower regions of the house. But while my mother was there, I knew well enough that nothing could go wrong, and my housekeeping mind had never been so much at ease since we were married. It was very delightful not to be accountable; for the present, I felt exonerated from all responsibilities.

I woke one morning, after a sound sleep, recalling a very odd dream. I thought I was a hen, strutting about amongst ricks of corn, picking and scratching, followed by a whole brood of chickens, toward which I felt exceedingly benevolent and attentive. Suddenly I heard the scream of a hawk in the air above me, and tried to fetch the little creatures under my wings. They came scurrying to me as fast as their legs could carry them—all but one, which wouldn't mind my cry, although I kept repeating it again and again. Meantime the hawk kept screaming—and I felt as if I didn't care for any of those that were safe under my wings, but only for the solitary creature that kept pecking away as if nothing was the matter. I grew so terribly anxious that I woke with a cry of misery and terror.

I opened my eyes, and there was my mother standing beside me. The room was so dark that I thought for a moment what a fog there must be—but the next, I forgot everything at hearing a little cry, which I verily believe, in my stupid dream, I had taken for the voice of the hawk. It was the cry of my first chicken, which I had not yet seen, but which my mother now held in her grandmotherly arms, ready to hand her to me. I dared not speak for I felt very weak, and was afraid of crying from delight. I looked in my mother's face, and she folded back the clothes, and laid the baby down beside me, with its little head resting on my arm.

"Draw back the curtain a little bit, Mother dear," I whispered, "and let me see what it is like."

I believe I said *it,* for I was not quite a mother yet. My mother did as I requested, and a ray of clear spring light fell upon the face of the little white thing by my side—for white she was, my Ethel, though most babies are red—and if I dared not speak before, I could not now. My mother went away, and sat down by the fireside, leaving me with my baby. Never shall I forget the unutterable content of that hour. It was not gladness, nor was it thankfulness that filled my heart, but a certain absolute contentment—just on the point (but for my want of strength) of blossoming into unspeakable gladness and thankfulness. Somehow, too, there was mingled with it a sense of dignity, as if I had vindicated for myself a right to a part in the creation. Besides, the state of perfect repose after what had passed was in itself bliss. The very sense of weakness was delightful, for I had earned the right to be weak, to rest as much as I pleased, to be important, and to be congratulated.

I was listening to the gentle talk about me in the darkened room—not listening, indeed, only aware that loving words were spoken. Whether I was dozing, I do not know, but something touched my lips. I only opened my eyes, and there was my great big huge bear looking down on me, with something in his eyes I had never seen there before. But even his presence could not ripple the waters of my deep rest. I gave him a half-smile—I knew it was but a half-smile, but I thought it would do—closed my eyes and sank again, not into sleep, but into that same blessed repose. I remember wondering if I should feel anything like that for the first hour or two after I was dead.

This was all but the beginning of endlessly varied pleasures. First I began to wash and dress my baby myself. One who has not tried that kind of amusement cannot know what endless pleasure it affords. I do not doubt that to the paternal spectator it appears monotonous, unproductive, and unprogressive. But then he, looking on it from the outside, and regarding the process with a speculative compassion and not with sympathy, cannot know the communion with the baby into which it brings you.

Next I began to order the dinners, and the very day in which I first ordered the dinner, I took my place at the head of the table. I saw it all through the rose mists of my motherhood, but I am nevertheless bold to assert that my husband was happy, and that my mother was happy. And if there was one more guest at the table concerning whom I am not prepared to assert that he was happy, I can confidently affirm that he was merry and gracious and talkative, originating three parts of the laughter of the evening.

To watch him with the baby was a pleasure even to the heart of a mother, anxious as she must be when anyone, especially a gentleman, more especially a bachelor, and most especially a young bachelor, takes her precious little doll in his arms, and pretends to know all about the management of such. It was he indeed who introduced her to the dining room; leaving the table during dessert, he returned bearing her in his arms, to my astonishment, and even mild maternal indignation at the liberty. Resuming his seat, and pouring out for his charge, as he pretended, a glass of old port, he said, in the soberest voice:

"Charles Percivale, with all the solemnity suitable to the occasion, I, the old moon, with the new moon in my arms, propose the health of Miss Percivale on her first visit to this boring bullet of a world. By the way, what a mercy it is that she carries her atmosphere with her!"

Here I, stupidly thinking he reflected on the atmosphere of baby, rose to take her from him with suppressed indignation—for why should a man, who assumes a baby unbidden, be so very much nicer than a woman who accepts her as given, and makes the best of it? But he declined giving her up.

"I'm not pinching her," he said.

"No, but I am afraid that you find her disagreeable."

"On the contrary, she is the nicest of little ladies, for she lets you talk all the nonsense you like, and never takes the least offense."

I sat down again directly.

"I propose her health," he repeated, "coupled with that of her mother, to whom I, for one, am more obliged than I can explain, for at length convincing me that I belong no more to the youth of my country, but am an uncle with a homuncle in his arms."

"Wifie, your health! Baby, yours too!" said my husband, and the ladies drank the toast in silence.

It is time I explained who this fourth—or should I say fifth?—person in our family party was. He was the younger brother of my Percivale, by name, Roger, and still more unsuccessful than he. He was of similar trustworthiness, but less equanimity, for he was subject to sudden elevations and depressions of the inner barometer. And so my daughter began her acquaintance with him.

TEN

My First Dinner Party

We had not yet seen much company in our little house. My husband disliked parties, eschewed evening parties utterly, and never accepted an invitation to dinner except to the house of a friend, and there were not many, even among his artist acquaintances, whom he cared to visit. Altogether, I feared he passed for an unsociable man. I am certain he would have sold more pictures if he had accepted what invitations came his way. But to hint at such a thing would, I knew, crystallize his dislike into a resolve.

One day after I had got quite strong again, I proposed that we should ask some friends to dinner. Instead of objecting to the procedure upon general principles, which I confess I had half anticipated, he only asked me whom I thought of inviting. When I mentioned the Morleys, he made no reply, but went on with his painting as if he had not heard me. I knew then, of course, that the proposal was disagreeable to him.

"You see, we have been twice to dine with them," I said.

"Well, don't you think that enough for a while?"

"I'm talking of asking them here now."

"Couldn't you go and see your cousin some morning instead?"

"It's not that I want to see my cousin particularly. I want to ask them to dinner."

"Oh!" he said, as if he couldn't in the least make out what I was after. "I thought people asked people because they desired their company."

"But, you see, we owe them a dinner."

"Owe them a dinner! Did you borrow one, then?"

"Do you consider yourself under no obligation to people who ask you to dinner?"

"None in the least—if I accept the invitation. That is the natural acknowledgment of their kindness. Surely my company is worth my dinner. It is far more trouble to me to put on black clothes and a white choker and go to their house, than it is for them to ask me or, in a house like theirs, to have the necessary preparations made for receiving me in a manner befitting their dignity. I do violence to my own feelings in going—is not that enough? You know how much I prefer a chop alone with my wife to the grandest dinner the grandest of her grand relations could give me."

"Now, don't you make game of my grand relations. I'm not sure that you haven't far grander relations yourself, only you say so little about them, they might all have been jailed for housebreaking. Don't you think it natural, if a friend asks you to dinner, that you should ask him again?"

"Yes, if it would give him any pleasure. But just imagine your Cousin Morley dining at our table. Do you think he would enjoy it?"

"Of course, we must have somebody in to help Jemima."

"And somebody to wait, I suppose?"

"Yes, of course, Percivale."

"And what Thackeray calls cold balls handed about?"

"Well, I wouldn't have them cold."

"But they would be."

I was by this time so nearly crying, that I said nothing here.

"My love," he continued, "I object to the whole thing. It's all false. I have not the least disinclination to asking a few friends who would enjoy being received in the same style as your father or my brother—namely, to one of our better dinners, and perhaps something better to drink than I can afford every day. But just think with what uneasy compassion Mr. Morley would regard our poor ambitions, even if you had an occasional cook and an undertaker's man. And what would he do without his glass of dry sherry after his soup, and his hock and champagne later, not to mention his fine claret or tawny port afterwards? I don't know how to get things good enough for him without laying in a stock. And that, you know, would be as absurd as it is impossible."

"Oh, you gentlemen always think so much of the wine!"

"Believe me, it is as necessary to Mr. Morley's comfort as the dainties you would provide him with. Indeed, it would be cruelty to ask him. He would not and could not enjoy it."

"If he didn't like it, he needn't come again," I said, cross with the objections of which I could not but see the justice.

"Well, I must say you have an odd notion of hospitality," said my bear. "You may be certain that a man so well aware of his own importance will take it far more as a compliment that you do not presume to invite him to your house, but are content to enjoy his society when he asks you to his."

"I don't choose to take such an inferior position," I said.

"You can't help it, my dear," he returned. "Socially considered, you *are* his inferior. You cannot give dinners he would regard with anything better than a friendly contempt, combined with a certain mild indignation at your having presumed to ask him. It is far more graceful to accept the small fact, and let him have his whim, which is not a subversive one or at all dangerous to the community, being of a sort easy to cure. Ha! Ha! Ha!"

"May I ask what you are laughing at?" I said with severity.

"I was only fancying how such a man must feel—if what your blessed father believes is true—when he is stripped all at once of every possible source of consequence. Stripped of position, funds, house, including cellar, clothes, body, including stomach—"

"There, there! Don't be vulgar. It is not like you, Percivale."

"Don't be vexed with me, Wynnie," he said.

"I don't like not to be allowed to pay my debts."

"Back to the starting point, like a hunted hare! A woman's way," he said merrily, hoping to make me laugh, for he could not doubt I should see the absurdity of my position with a moment's reflection. But I was out of temper, and chose to pounce upon the liberty taken with my sex, and regard it as an insult. Without a word I rose, pressed my baby to my bosom as if her mother had been left a widow, and swept away. Percivale started to his feet. I did not see, but I knew he gazed after me for a moment. Then I heard him sit down to his painting as if nothing had happened—but, I knew, with a sharp pain inside his great chest. For me, I found the ladder very subversive of my dignity—for when a woman has to hold a baby in one arm, and with the hand of the other lift up the front of her skirt in order to walk up an almost perpendicular staircase, it is quite impossible for her to *sweep* anymore.

When I reached the top, the picture he had made of me (with the sunset coming through the window) flashed upon my memory. All dignity forgotten, I bolted through the door at the top, flung my baby into the arms of her nurse, turned, almost tumbled headlong down the precipice, and altogether tumbled down at my husband's chair. I couldn't speak, but could only lay my head on his knees.

"Darling," he said, "you shall ask the great Pan Jan with his button atop, if you like. I'll do my best for him."

Between crying and laughing, I nearly lost my composure altogether. "I was very naughty, Percivale," I said. "I will give a dinner party, and it shall be such as you shall enjoy, and I won't ask Mr. Morley."

"Thank you, my love," he said, "and the next time Mr. Morley asks us I will go without a grumble, and make myself as agreeable as I can."

Now I have had a good many servants, but Jemima seems a fixture. How this has come about, it would be impossible to say in ever so many words. She has by turns every fault under the sun—I say *faults.* She will struggle with one for a day, and succumb to it for a month, while the smallest amount of praise is sufficient to render her incapable of deserving a word of commendation for a week. It was long an impossibility to make her see, or at least own, that she was to blame for anything. If the dish she had last cooked to perfection made its appearance the next time inedible, she would lay it all to the silly oven, which was too hot or too cold, or the silly pepper pot, the top of which fell off as she was using it. She had no sense of the value of proportion and would insist, for instance, that she had made the cake precisely as she had been told, but suddenly betray that she had not weighed the flour, which *could* be of no consequence, seeing she had weighed everything else.

"Please, 'm, could you eat your dinner now? It's all ready," she came saying an hour before dinnertime, the very first day after my mother left. Even now her desire to be punctual is chiefly evidenced by absurd precipitancy, to the danger of doing everything to either a pulp or a cinder. Yet here she is, and here she is likely to remain, so far as I see, till death or some other catastrophe do us part. The reason of it is that with all her faults—and they are innumerable—she has some heart. Yes, after deducting all that can be laid to the account of a certain cunning perception that she is well off, she has yet a good deal of genuine attachment left, and is a jealous partisan to her master and mistress.

There was nothing more said about the dinner party until my father came to see us in July, commissioned by my mother to arrange for my going to Marshmallows the next month.

As soon as I had shown my father to his little room, I ran down to Percivale. "Papa is come," I said.

"I am delighted to hear it," he answered, laying down his palette and brushes. "Where is he?"

"Gone upstairs," I answered. "I wouldn't disturb you till he came down again."

"I haven't quite finished my pipe—I will go on till he comes down."

Although he laid it on his pipe, I knew well enough it was just that little bit of paint he wanted to finish, and not the residue of tobacco in the black and red bowl.

"And now we'll have our dinner party," I said.

I do believe that, for all the nonsense I had talked about returning invitations, the real thing at my heart even then was an impulse toward hospitable entertainment, and the desire to see my husband merry with his friends, under the protecting wing of his wife. For, as mother of the family, the wife has to mother her husband also, to consider him as her firstborn, and look out for what will not only give him pleasure but be good for him. My bear has fully given in to this.

"And who are you going to ask?" he said. "Mr. and Mrs. Morley to begin with, and—"

"No, no," I answered. "We are going to have a jolly evening of it, with nobody present who will make you either anxious or annoyed. Mr. Blackstone—and Miss Clare, I think, for I must have one lady to keep me in countenance with so many gentlemen, you know.

"Mr. Blackstone I know. And being a clergyman, he would get on well with your father. But who is Miss Clare?"

"I met her at Cousin Judy's. I have a reason for asking her, which I would rather you should find out by yourself. Do you mind?"

"Not in the least, if you don't think she will spoil the fun."

"I am sure she won't. Then there's your brother Roger."

"Of course. Who more?"

"I think that will do. There will be six of us then—quite a large enough party for our little dining room."

"Why shouldn't we dine here in the studio? It wouldn't be so hot, and we should have more room."

I liked the idea. So the night before the dinner, Percivale arranged not only his paintings but all his properties to be accessory to a picturesque effect. And when the table was laid and adorned with flowers, the bird's-eye from the top of the Jacob's ladder was a very pretty one indeed.

Resolved that Percivale should have no cause of complaint as regarded the simplicity of my arrangements, I gave orders that our little Ethel (who at that time of the evening was always asleep) should be laid on the couch in my room off the study, with the door ajar, so that Sarah, who was now her nurse, might wait with an easy mind. The dinner was brought in by the outer door of the study, to avoid the awkwardness and possible disaster of the private precipice.

The principal dish, a small sirloin of beef, was at the foot of the table and a couple of boiled fowls were (I thought) before me. But when the covers were removed, to my surprise I found they were roasted.

"What have you got there, Percivale?" I asked. "Isn't it a sirloin?"

"I'm not adept in such matters," he replied. "I should say it was."

My father gave a glance at the joint. Something seemed to be wrong. I rose and went to my husband's side. Powers of cuisine! Jemima had roasted the fowls and boiled the sirloin. My exclamation was the signal for an outbreak of laughter, led by my father. I was trembling in the balance between mortification on my own account and sympathy with the evident amusement of my father and Mr. Blackstone. But the thought that Mr. Morley might have been and was not of the party came with such a pang and such a relief as to settle the point, and I burst out laughing.

"I dare say it's all right," said Roger. "Why shouldn't a sirloin be boiled as well as roasted? I venture to assert that it is all a whim, and we are on the verge of a new discovery to swell the number of those which already owe their being to blunders."

"Let us all try a slice, then," said Mr. Blackstone, "and compare results."

This was agreed to—and a solemn silence followed, during which each sought acquaintance with the new dish.

"I am sorry to say," remarked my father, finally, "that Roger is all wrong, and we have only made the discovery that custom is right. It is plain enough why sirloin is always roasted."

"I yield myself convinced," said Roger.

"And I am certain," said Mr. Blackstone, "that if the loin set before the king, whoever he was, had been boiled, he would never have knighted it."

Thanks to the loin, the last possible touch of constraint had vanished, and the party grew a very merry one. The apple pudding which followed was declared perfect and eaten up, and Percivale produced some good wine from somewhere. But a tiny whimper called me away, and Miss Clare accompanied me. The gentlemen insisted that we should return as soon as possible, and bring the homuncle, as Roger called the baby, with us.

When we returned, the two clergymen were in close conversation, and the other two gentlemen were chiefly listening. My father was saying, "My dear sir, I don't see how any man can do his duty as a clergyman who doesn't visit his parishioners."

"In London it is simply impossible," returned Mr. Blackstone. "In the country *you* are welcome wherever you go. Any visit I might pay would most likely be regarded either as an intrusion or as giving the right to pecuniary aid, of which evils the latter is worse. There are portions of every London parish which clergymen and their coadjutors have so degraded, by the practical teaching of beggary, that they have blocked up every possible door to a healthy spiritual relation between them and the pastor."

"Would you not give alms at all, then?"

"One thing, at least, I have made up my mind on—alms from any hand but the hand of a personal friendship tend to evil, and will, in the long run, increase misery."

"What, then, do you suppose the proper relation is between a London clergyman and his parishioners?"

"One, I am afraid, which does not at present exist—one which it is his first business perhaps to bring about. I confess I regard with a repulsion amounting to horror the idea of walking into a poor man's house, except either I have business with him, or desire his personal acquaintance."

"But if our office—"

"My business is to serve, not to force service upon them. I will not say how far intimacy may justify you in immediate assault upon a man's conscience, but I shrink from any plan that seems to take it for granted that the poor are more wicked then the rich. Why don't we send missionaries to Belgravia? The outside of the cup and platter may sometimes be dirtier than the inside."

"Your missionary could hardly force his way through the servants to the boudoir or drawing room."

"And the poor have no servants to defend them."

"Don't you think, Sir," Miss Clare said, addressing my father, "that the help one can give to another must always depend on the measure in which one is free oneself?"

My father was silent, thinking. We were all silent. With marked deference and solemnity he answered at length, "I have little doubt you are right, Miss Clare. That puts the question upon its own eternal foundation. The mode used must be of infinitely less importance than the person who uses it."

As he spoke, he looked at her with attentive regard. Indeed, the eyes of all the company seemed to be scanning the small woman. But she bore the scrutiny well, if indeed she was not unconscious of it, and my husband began to find out one of my reasons for asking her, which was simply that he might see her face. At this moment it was in one of its higher phases. It was, at its best, a grand face; at its worst, a suffering face. It was a little too large, perhaps, for the small body which it crowned with a flame of soul, but while you saw her face you never thought of the rest of her.

"But," my father went on, looking at Mr. Blackstone, "I am anxious, from the clergyman's point of view, to know what my friend here thinks he must try to do in his very difficult position."

"I think the best thing I could do," returned Mr. Blackstone, laughing, "would be to go to school under Miss Clare."

"I shouldn't wonder," my father responded.

"But, in the meantime, I should prefer the chaplaincy of a suburban cemetery."

"Certainly your charge would be a less troublesome one. Your congregation would be quiet enough, at least," said Roger.

"Then are they glad because they be quiet," said my father, as if unconsciously uttering his own reflections. But he was a little cunning, and would say things like that when, fearful of irreverence, he wanted to turn the current of the conversation.

"But surely," said Miss Clare, "a more active congregation would be quite desirable."

She had one fault—no—defect; she was slow to enter into the humor of a thing. It seemed almost as if the first aspect of any bit of fun presented to her was that of something wrong. A moment's reflection, however, almost always ended in a sunny laugh, partly at her own stupidity, as she called it.

"You mistake my meaning," said Mr. Blackstone. "My chief, almost sole, attraction to the regions of the grave is the sexton, and not the placidity of the inhabitants—though perhaps Miss Clare might value that more highly if she had more experience of how noisy human nature can be."

Miss Clare gave a little smile, but she said nothing.

"My first inquiry," he went on, "before accepting such an appointment, would be as to the character and mental habits of the sexton. If I found him a man capable of regarding human nature from a standpoint of his own, I should close with the offer at once. If, on the contrary, he was a commonplace man, who made faultless responses, and cherished the friendship of the undertaker, I should decline. In fact, I should regard the sexton as my proposed master, and whether I should accept the place or not would depend altogether on whether I liked him or not. Think what revelations of human nature a real man in such a position could give me: 'Hand me the shovel. You stop a bit—you're out of breath. Sit down on that stone there, and light your pipe—here's some tobacco. Now tell me the rest of the story. How did the old fellow get on after he had buried his termagant wife?' That's how I should treat him, and I should get, in return, such a succession of peeps into human life and intent and aspirations as, in the course of a few years, would send me to the next vicarage a sadder and wiser man, Mr. Walton."

"I don't doubt it," said my father. But whether in sympathy with Mr. Blackstone, or in latent disapproval of a tone judged unbecoming to a clergyman, I could not tell.

Miss Clare was the first to leave.

"What a lovely countenance that is!" said my husband, the moment she was out of hearing.

"She is a very remarkable woman," said my father.

"I suspect she knows a good deal more than most of us," said Mr. Blackstone. "Did you see how her face always lighted up before she said anything? You can never come nearer to seeing a thought than in her face just before she speaks."

"What is she?" asked Roger.

"Can't you see what she is?" returned his brother. "She's a saint—Saint Clare."

"But what does she do?"

"Why should you think that she does anything?" I asked.

"She looks as if she had to earn her own living."

"She does. She teaches music."

"Why didn't you ask her to play?"

"Because this is the first time she has been to the house."

"Does she go to church, do you suppose?"

"I have no doubt of it, but why do you ask?"

"Because she looks as if she didn't want it. I never saw such an angelic expression upon a countenance."

"You must take me to call upon her," said my father.

"I will with pleasure," I answered.

This was easier promised than performed, for I had asked her by word of mouth at Cousin Judy's, and had not the slightest idea where she lived. Of course I applied to Judy, but she had mislaid her address, and, promising to ask her for it, forgot more than once. So my father had to return home without seeing Miss Clare again.

ELEVEN

Pictures and Rumors

For some time I was fully occupied with a new life to tend and cultivate. I marveled that God should entrust me with such a charge, that He did not keep the lovely creature in His own arms, and refuse her to any others. Then I would realize that He had not sent her out of His own arms, for I too was a child in His arms, holding and tending my live doll, until she should grow something like me, only ever so much better.

But I feared lest my love for my baby should make me neglect my husband. The fear first arose in me one morning as I sat with her half-dressed on my knees. I was dawdling over her in my fondness (as I used to dawdle over the dressing of my doll) when suddenly I became aware that never once since her arrival had I sat with my husband in his study. A pang of dismay shot through me. "Is this to be a wife?" I said to myself, "to play with a live love like a dead doll, and forget her husband!" I caught up a blanket from the cradle, wrapped it round the treasure, which was shooting its arms and legs in every direction like a polypus feeling after its food, and rushed downstairs and down the precipice into the study. Percivale started up in terror, thinking something fearful had happened, and I was bringing him all that was left of the child.

"What—what—what's the matter?" he gasped.

"I've brought you the baby to kiss," I said, unfolding the blanket and holding up the sprawling little goddess toward the face that towered above me.

"Was it dying for a kiss, then?" he asked, taking her, blanket and all, from my arms.

The end of the blanket swept across his easel, and smeared the face of the baby in his picture of "The Three Kings."

"O Percivale!" I cried. "You've smeared your baby!"

"But this is a real live baby—she may smear anything she likes."

"Except her own face and hands, please, then, Percivale."

"Or her blessed frock," said Percivale. "She hasn't got one, though. Why hasn't the little angel got her feathers on yet?"

"I was in such a hurry to bring her."

"To be kissed?"

"No, not exactly. It wasn't her I was in a hurry to bring—it was myself."

"Ah! You wanted to be kissed, did you?"

"No, I didn't want to be kissed, but I did so want to kiss you, Percivale."

"Isn't it all the same, though, Darling?"

"Sometimes, Percivale, you are so very stupid! It's not the same at all. There's a world of difference between the two, and you ought to know it, or be told it, if you don't."

"I shall think it over as soon as you leave me," he said.

"But I'm not going to leave you for a long time. I haven't seen you paint for weeks and weeks, not since this little troublesome thing came poking in between us."

"But she's not dressed yet."

"That doesn't signify. She's well wrapped up, and quite warm."

He put me in a chair where I could see his picture without catching the shine of the paint. I took the baby from him, and he went on with his work.

"You don't think I am going to sacrifice all my privileges to this little tyrant, do you?" I asked.

"It would be rather hard for me, at least," he rejoined.

"You did think I was neglecting you, then, Percivale?"

"Not for a moment."

"Then you didn't miss me?"

"I did, very much."

"And you didn't grumble?"

"No."

"Do I disturb you?" I asked, after a little pause. "Can you paint just as well when I am here as when you are alone?"

"Better. I feel warmer to my work somehow."

I was satisfied, and held my peace. When I am best pleased, I don't want to talk. But Percivale, perhaps not having found this out yet, looked anxiously in my face. As at the moment my eyes were fixed on his picture, I thought he wanted to find out whether I liked the design.

"I see it now!" I cried. "I could not make out where the Magi were."

He had taken for the scene of his picture an old farm kitchen, or yeoman's hall, with its rich brown rafters, its fire on the hearth, and its red brick floor. A tub half full of bright water stood on one side, and the mother was bending over her baby which, undressed for the bath, she was holding out for the admiration of the Magi. Immediately behind the mother stood, in the garb of a shepherd, my father, leaning upon the ordinary shepherd's crook. My mother, like a peasant woman in her Sunday best, with a white handkerchief crossed upon her bosom, stood beside him, and both were gazing with a chastened yet profound pleasure on the lovely child.

In front stood two boys and a girl, between the ages of five and nine, each gazing with a peculiar wondering delight. The youngest boy, with a great spotted wooden horse in his hand, was approaching to embrace the infant in such a fashion as made the toy look dangerous, and the left hand of the mother was lifted with a motion of warning and defense. The little girl, the next youngest, had, in her absorption, dropped her gaudily dressed doll at her feet, and stood sucking her thumb, her big blue eyes wide with contemplation. The eldest boy had brought his white rabbit to give to the baby, but had forgotten all about it, so full was his heart of his new brother. An expression of mingled love and wonder and perplexity had already begun to dawn on the face, but it was yet far from finished. He stood behind the other two peeping over their heads.

"Were you thinking of that Titian in the Louvre, with the white rabbit in it?" I asked Percivale.

"I did not think of it until after I had put in the rabbit," he replied. "And it shall remain, for it suits my purpose, and Titian would not claim all the white rabbits because of that one."

"Did you think of the black lamb in it, then, when you laid that black kitten on the hearth?" I asked.

"Black lamb?" he returned.

"Yes," I insisted. "A black lamb, in the dark background—such a very black lamb, and in such a dark background, that it seems you never discovered it."

"Are you sure?" he persisted.

"Absolutely certain," I replied. "I pointed it out to Papa in the picture itself in the Louvre. He had not observed it before either."

"I am very glad to know there is such a thing there. I need not answer your question, you see. It is odd enough I should have put in the black cat. Upon some grounds I might argue that it is better than Titian's lamb."

"What grounds? Tell me."

"If the painter wanted a contrast, a lamb—be he as black as ever paint could make him—must still be a more Christian animal than a cat as white as snow. Under what pretense could a cat be used as a Christian symbol?"

"What do you make of her playfulness?"

"I should count that a virtue, were it not for the fatal objection that it is always exercised at the expense of other creatures."

"A ball of string, or a reel, or a bit of paper is enough for an uncorrupted kitten."

"But you must not forget that it serves only in virtue of the creature's imagination representing it as alive. If you do not make it move, she will herself set it in motion as the initiative of the game. If she cannot do that, she will take no notice of it."

"Yes, I see. I give in."

All this time he had been painting diligently. But then a knock came to the study door and, remembering baby's unpresentable condition, I cuddled her up, climbed the stair again, and finished the fledging of my little angel in a very happy frame of mind.

I descended with the baby to find that Cousin Judy had called and was waiting for me. I remembered that I must again ask her for Miss Clare's address, so, as soon as she had kissed and admired the baby, I said, "Have you found out yet where Miss Clare lives, Judy?"

"I don't choose to find out," she answered. "I am sorry to say I have had to give her up. It is a disappointment, I confess."

"What do you mean?" I said. "I thought you considered her a very good teacher."

"I have no fault to find with her on that score. She was always punctual, and I must allow she played well and taught the children delightfully. But I have heard such questionable things about her! Very strange things indeed!"

"What are they?"

"I can't say I've been able to fix on more than one thing directly against her character, but—"

"Against her character!" I exclaimed.

"Yes, indeed. She lives by herself in lodgings, and the house is not at all a respectable one."

"But have you made no further inquiry?"

"I consider that quite enough. I had already met more than one person, however, who seemed to think it very odd that I should have her teach music in my family."

"Did they give any reason for thinking her unfit?"

"I did not choose to ask them. One was Miss Clarke—you know her. She smiled in her usual supercilious manner, but in her case I believe it was only because Miss Clare looks so dowdy. But nobody knows anything about her except what I've just told you."

"And who told you that?'

"Mrs. Jefferson."

"She is a great gossip."

"Else she wouldn't have heard it. But that doesn't make it untrue. In fact, she convinced me of its truth, for she knows the place she lives in, and assured me it was at great risk of infection to the children that I allowed her to enter the house. So, of course, I felt compelled to let Miss Clare know that I didn't require her services any longer."

"There must be some mistake, surely!" I said.

"Oh, no! Not in the least, I am sorry to say."

"How did she take it?"

"Very sweetly indeed. She didn't even ask me why, which was just as well, seeing I should have found it awkward to tell her. But I suppose she knew too many grounds herself to dare the question."

I was dreadfully sorry, but I could not say much more then. I only expressed my conviction that there could not be any charge to bring against Miss Clare herself. Judy, however, insisted that what she had heard was reason enough for at least ending the engagement—indeed, that no one was fit for such a situation of whom such things could be said, whether they were true or not.

When she left me, I gave the baby to her nurse, and went straight to the studio, peeping in to see if Percivale was alone, for I had heard another voice.

He caught sight of me, and called to me to come down. "It's only Roger," he said.

I was always pleased to see Roger. He was a strange creature, one of those gifted men who are capable of anything, if not everything, and yet carry nothing within sight of proficiency. He whistled like a starling, and accompanied his whistling on the piano, but never played. He could copy a drawing to a hair's breadth, but never drew. He could engrave well on wood and, although he had often been employed in that way, he had always got tired of it after a few weeks. He was forever wanting to do something other than what he was at, and the moment he tired of a thing, he would work at it no longer, for he had never learned to drive himself. He would come every day to the study for a week to paint in backgrounds, or make a duplicate and then, perhaps, we wouldn't see him for a fortnight. At other times he would work, say, for a month, modeling or carving marble for a sculptor friend, from whom he might have had constant employment if he had pleased. He had given lessons in various branches, for he was an excellent scholar, and had the finest ear for verse, as well as the keenest appreciation of the loveliest of poetry.

I could not help liking him. There was a half-plaintive playfulness about him, alternated with gloom, and occasionally wild merriment, which made him interesting even when one felt most inclined to quarrel with him. The worst was that he considered himself a generally misunderstood—if not ill-used—man, who could not only distinguish himself but render valuable service to society, if only society would do him the justice to give him a chance. Were it only, however, for his love to my baby, I could not but be ready to take up his defense. When I mentioned what I had just heard about Miss Clare, Percivale looked both astonished and troubled. But before he could speak, Roger, with the air of a man of the world whom experience enabled to come at once to a decision, said, "Depend upon it, Wynnie, there is falsehood there somewhere. You will always be nearer the truth if you believe nothing, than if you believe the half of what you hear."

"That's very much what Papa says," I answered. "He affirms that he never searched into an injurious report in his own parish without finding it so nearly false as to deprive it of all right to go about."

"Besides," said Roger, "look at that face! How I should like to model it. She's a good woman that, depend upon it."

I was delighted with his enthusiasm.

"I wish you would ask her again, as soon as you can," said Percivale, who always tended to embody his conclusions in acts rather than in words. "Your cousin Judy is a jolly good creature, but from your father's description of her as a girl, she must have grown a good deal more worldly since her marriage. Respectability is an awful snare."

"I should be very glad to," I said, "but how can I? I haven't learned where she lives. It was asking Judy for her address that brought it all out. I certainly didn't insist, but if she didn't remember it before, you may be sure she could not have given it to me then."

"It's very odd," said Roger, stroking his long mustache, the sole ornament of the kind he wore. "It's very odd," he repeated thoughtfully, and then paused again.

"What's so very odd, Roger?" asked Percivale.

"The other evening," answered Roger, "happening to be in Tottenham Court Road, I walked for some distance behind a young woman carrying a brown beer jug in her hand. You understand that I sometimes amuse myself in the street by walking persistently behind someone, devising the unseen face in my mind, until the person looks round and gives me the opportunity of comparing the two—I mean the face I had devised and the real one. When the young woman at length turned her head, it was only my astonishment that kept me from addressing her as Miss Clare. My surprise, however, gave me the time to see how absurd it would have been. Presently she turned down a yard and disappeared."

"Don't tell my cousin Judy," I said. "She would believe it *was* Miss Clare."

"There isn't much danger," he returned. "Even if I knew your cousin, I should not be likely to mention such an incident in her hearing."

"Could it have been she?" said Percivale thoughtfully.

"Absurd!" said Roger. "Miss Clare is a lady, wherever she may live."

"I don't know," said his brother thoughtfully. "Who can tell? It mightn't have been beer she was carrying."

"I didn't say it was beer," returned Roger. "I only said it was a beer jug—one of those brown, squat, stone jugs, with a dash of gray."

"Brown jug or not, I wish I could get a few sittings from her. She would make a lovely St. Cecilia," said my husband.

"Brown jug and all?" asked Roger.

"If only she were a little taller," I objected.

"And had an aureole," said my husband. "But I might succeed in omitting the jug as well as adding the aureole and another half-foot of stature, if only I could get that lovely countenance on the canvas, so full of life and yet of repose."

"Don't you think it a little hard?" I ventured to say.

"I think so," said Roger.

"I don't," said my husband. "I know what in it looks like hardness, but I think it comes of the repression of feeling."

"You have studied her well for your opportunities," I said.

"I have. And I am sure, whatever Mrs. Morley may say, if there be any truth at all in those reports, there is some satisfactory explanation. I wish we knew anybody else who knew her. Do try to find one who does, Wynnie."

"I should be only too glad, but I don't know how to set about it."

"I will try," said Roger.

And try he did. One evening he came in late from a dinner at Lady Bernard's.

"Whom do you think I took down to dinner?" he asked, almost before he was seated.

"Lady Bernard?" I said, flying high.

"Her dowager aunt?" said Percivale.

"No, no—Miss Clare."

"Miss Clare!" we both repeated.

"Yes, Miss Clare."

"Did you ask her if it was she you saw carrying the jug of beer in Tottenham Court Road?" said Percivale.

"Did you ask her address?" I said. "That is a question more worthy of an answer."

"Yes, I did. I believe I did. I think I did."

"What is it, then?"

"Upon my word, I haven't the slightest idea."

"So, Mr. Roger! You have had a perfect opportunity, and have let it slip! You are a man to be trusted indeed!"

"I don't know how it could have been. I distinctly remember approaching the subject more than once or twice, and now I discover that I never asked the question. Or if I did, I am certain I got no answer."

"Bewitched!"

"Yes, I suppose so."

"Or," suggested Percivale, "she did not choose to tell you. She saw the question coming, and led you away from it, never let you ask it."

"I have heard that ladies can keep one from saying what they don't want to hear. But she shan't escape me so a second time."

"Indeed, you don't deserve another chance," I said. "You're not half so clever as I took you to be, Roger."

"When I think of it, though, it wasn't a question so easy to ask, or one you would like to be overheard asking."

"Clearly bewitched," I said. "But for that I forgive you. Did she sing?"

"No. I don't suppose anyone there ever thought of asking such a dingy-feathered bird to sing."

"You had some music?"

"Oh, yes! Pretty good, and very bad. Miss Clare's forehead was crossed by no end of flickering shadows as she listened."

"It wasn't for want of interest in her you forgot to find out where she lived! You had better take care, Master Roger."

"Take care of what?"

"Why, you don't know her address."

"What has that to do with taking care?"

"That you won't know where to find your heart if you should happen to want it."

"Oh! I am past that kind of thing long ago. You've made an uncle of me."

And so on, with a good deal more nonsense, but no news of Miss Clare's retreat.

I had before this remarked to my husband that it was odd she had never called since dining with us. But he made little of it, saying that people who gained their own livelihood ought to be excused from attending to rules which had their origin with another class. I thought no more about it, save in disappointment that she had not given me that opportunity of improving my acquaintance with her.

TWELVE

A Discovery

One Saturday night when my husband happened to be out (an event of rare occurrence), Roger called. I asked him to go with me to Tottenham Court Road. It was not far from the region where we lived, and I did a great part of my small shopping there. Several of the shops were shut, and we walked a long way down the street, looking for some place likely to supply what I required.

"It was just here I came up with the girl and the brown jug," said Roger, as we reached the large dissenting chapel. "She was so like Miss Clare! I can't get the one face clear of the other. When I met her at Lady Bernard's, the first thing I thought of was the brown jug."

"Were you as much pleased with her conversation as at our house?" I asked.

"Even more," he answered. "I found her ideas of art so wide, as well as just and accurate, that I was puzzled to think where she had had opportunity of developing them. I questioned her about it, and found she was in the habit of going, as often as she could spare time, to the National Gallery. Her custom was, she said, not to pass from picture to picture, but keep to one until it formed itself in her mind, until she seemed to know what the painter had set himself to do, and why this was and that was—which she could not at first understand. Clearly, without ever having taken a pencil in her hand, she has educated herself to a keen perception of what is demanded of a true picture. Of course the root of it lies in her musical development—There!" he cried suddenly, as we came opposite a paved passage. "That is the place I saw her go down."

"Then you do think the girl with the beer jug was Miss Clare, after all?"

"Not in the least."

"But where, then, does Miss Clare live? Nobody seems to know."

"You never asked anyone but Mrs. Morley."

"You have yourself, however, given me reason to think she avoids the subject. If she did live anywhere hereabout, she would have some cause to avoid it."

I stopped to look down the passage.

"Suppose," said Roger, "someone were to come past now, and see Mrs. Percivale, the wife of the celebrated painter, standing in Tottenham Court Road beside the swing door of a corner public house, talking to a young man."

"Yes, it might give occasion for scandal," I said. "To avoid it, let us go down the court and see what it is like."

"It's not a fit place for you to go into."

"If it were in my father's parish, I should have known everybody in it. Come, and let us see what the place is like," I insisted.

He gave me his arm and down the court we went, past the flaring gin shop, and into the gloom beyond. The houses had once been occupied by people in better circumstances than their present inhabitants. Indeed, they all looked decent enough until, turning two right angles, we came upon another sort. They were still as large, and had plenty of windows but, in the light of a single lamp at the corner, they looked very dirty and wretched and dreary. A little shop, with dried herrings and bull's-eyes in the window, was lighted by a tallow candle set in a ginger-beer bottle, with a card of "Kinahan's LL Whiskey" for a reflector.

The houses had sunken areas, just wide enough for a stair, and the basements seemed full of tenants. There was a little wind blowing, so that the atmosphere was tolerable, notwithstanding a few stray leaves of cabbage, suggestive of others in a more objectionable condition not so far off.

A confused noise of loud voices, calling and scolding, now reached our ears. The place took one turn more, and at the farther end of the passage a lamp shone upon a group of men and women in altercation which had not yet come to blows. It might, including children, have numbered twenty, of which some seemed drunk, and all more or less excited. Roger turned to go back the moment he caught sight of them, but I felt inclined to linger a little. Should any danger offer, it would be easy to gain the open thoroughfare.

"It's not at all a fit place for a lady," he said.

"Certainly not," I answered. "It hardly seems a fit place for human beings. These are human beings, though. Let us go through it."

He still hesitated, but as I went on, he could only follow me. I wanted to see what the attracting center of the little crowd was. A good many superterrestrial spectators looked down from the windows upon the disputants, whose voices now and then lulled for a moment only to break out in fresh dispute.

A slight parting of the crowd revealed its core to us. It was a little woman, without bonnet or shawl, whose back was toward us. She turned from side to side, now talking to one, and now to another of the surrounding circle. At first I thought she was setting forth her grievances in hope of sympathy or justice, but her motions were too calm for that. Sometimes the crowd would speak altogether, sometimes keep silent for a full minute while she went on talking. When she turned her face toward us, Roger and I turned ours and stared at each other. The face was disfigured by a swollen eye, evidently from a blow; but clearly enough, if it was not Miss Clare, it was the young woman of the beer jug.

Neither of us spoke, but turned once more to watch as the argument settled down to an almost amicable conference. After a few more grumbles and protestations, the group began to break up into twos and threes. These the young woman set herself to break up again. Here, however, an ill-looking fellow like a costermonger, with a broken nose, came up to us; and with a strong Irish accent and offensive manner, but still with a touch of Irish breeding, requested to know what our business was. Roger asked if the place wasn't a thoroughfare.

"Not for the likes o' you," he answered, "as comes pryin' after the likes of us. We manage our own affairs down here, we do. You'd better be off, my lady."

I have my doubts what sort of reply Roger might have returned if he had been alone, but he certainly spoke in a very conciliatory manner which, however, the man did not seem to appreciate, for he called it blarney. The young woman caught sight of our little group and approached us. She had come within a yard of us, when suddenly her face brightened, and she exclaimed, in a tone of surprise, "Mrs. Percivale! You here?"

It was indeed Miss Clare. Without the least embarrassment, she held out her hand to me, but I am afraid I did not take it very cordially. Roger, however, behaved to her as if they stood in a drawing room, and this brought me to a sense of propriety.

"I don't look very respectable, I fear," she said, putting her hand over her eye. "I have had a blow, and it will look worse tomorrow. Were you coming to find me?"

I forget what lame answer either of us gave.

"Will you come in?" she said.

I declined. For all my fine talk to Roger, I shrunk from the idea of entering one of those houses. I can only say, in excuse, that I was bewildered.

"Can I do anything for you, then?" she asked, in a tone slightly marked with disappointment, I thought.

"Thank you, no," I answered, hardly knowing what my words were.

"Then good night," she said, and, nodding kindly, turned and entered one of the houses.

We also turned in silence, and walked out of the court.

"Why didn't you go with her?" said Roger, as soon as we were in the street.

"I didn't think you wanted to go, Roger, but—"

"I think you might have gone, seeing I was with you," he said.

"I don't think it would have been at all a proper thing to do, without knowing more about her," I answered, a little hurt. "You can't tell what sort of a place it may be."

"It's a good place wherever she is, or I am much mistaken," he returned. "You would have gone if I hadn't been with you?"

"Certainly, if she had asked me, which is not very likely."

"And you lay the disappointment of missing a glimpse into the sweet privacy of such a home to my charge?"

It was a spiteful speech, and Roger's silence made me feel it was. With the rather patronizing opinion I had of Roger, I found it not a little galling. So I too kept silence, and nothing beyond a platitude had passed between us when I found myself at my own door, my shopping utterly forgotten, and something acid on my mind.

"Don't you mean to come in?" I said. "My husband will be home soon, if he has not come already. You needn't be bored with my company—you can sit in the study."

"I think I had better not," he answered.

"I am very sorry, Roger, if I was rude to you," I said, "but how could you wish me to be hand-in-glove with a woman who visits people who she is well aware would not think of inviting her if they had a notion of her surroundings. That can't be right, I am certain. I protest I feel just as if I had been reading an ill-invented story, an unnatural fiction."

"There must be some accounting for it," said Roger. "You may be wrong in supposing that the people at whose houses she visits know nothing about her habits."

"My cousin dispensed with her services as soon as she came to the knowledge of certain facts concerning these very points."

"Excuse me—certain rumors—very uncertain facts."

When you are cross, the slightest play upon words is an offense. I knocked at the door in dudgeon, then turned and said, "My cousin Judy, Mr. Roger—"

But here I paused, for I had nothing ready. Anger makes people cleverer for the moment, but when I am angry I am always stupid. Roger finished the sentence for me.

"Your cousin Judy is, you must allow, a very conventional woman," he said.

"She is very good-natured, anyhow. And what do you say to Lady Bernard?"

"She hasn't repudiated Miss Clare's acquaintance."

"But, answer me, do you believe Lady Bernard would invite her to meet her friends if she knew at all?"

"Depend upon it, Lady Bernard knows what she is about. People of her rank can afford to be unconventional."

This irritated me yet more, for it implied that I was influenced by the conventionality which both he and my husband despised. Sarah opened the door, and I stepped in without even saying good-night. Before she closed it, however, I heard my husband's voice and ran out again to welcome him.

He and Roger had already met in the little front garden. They did not shake hands—they never did—they always met as if they had just parted only an hour ago.

"What were you and my wife quarreling about, Roger?" I heard Percivale ask. I paused on the middle of the stair to hear his answer.

"How do you know we were quarreling?" returned Roger gloomily.

"I heard you from the very end of the street," said my husband.

"That's not so far," said Roger.

"Too far to hear a wife and brother, though," returned Percivale jocosely.

It stung me to the quick. Here I had been regarding, not even with contempt, only with disgust, the quarrel in which Miss Clare was mixed up. And yet half an hour after, my own voice was heard in dispute with my husband's brother from the other end of our own street!

I rushed down the steps, and kissed Roger before I kissed my husband.

"Come in," interposed Percivale, "and refer the cause in dispute to me."

We did go in, and we did refer the matter to him. By the time he had the facts of the case, however, the point in dispute between us appeared to have grown hazy, and neither of us cared to say anything more about it. Percivale insisted that there was no question before the court.

At length Roger, turning from me to his brother, said, "It's not worth mentioning, Charley, but what led to our quarrel was this: I thought Wynnie might have accepted Miss Clare's invitation to walk in and pay her a visit. Wynnie thought me, I suppose, too ready to sacrifice her dignity to the pleasure of seeing a little more of Miss Clare."

My husband turned to me and said, "Mrs. Percivale, do you accept this as a correct representation of your difference?"

"Well," I answered, hesitating, "yes, on the whole. All I object to is the word *dignity.*"

"I retract it," cried Roger, "and accept any substitute you prefer."

"Let it stand," I returned. "It will do as well as a better. I only wish to say that it was not exactly my dignity—"

"No, no, your sense of propriety," said my husband, who then sat silent for a minute or two, pondering like a judge. At length he said, "Wife, you might have gone with your brother, I think, but I understand your disinclination. At the same time, a more generous judgment of Miss Clare might have prevented any difference of feeling in the matter."

"But," I said, greatly inclined to cry, "I only postponed my judgment concerning her." And I only postponed my crying, for I was very much ashamed of myself.

Later, of course, my husband and I talked a good deal more about what I ought to have done, and I saw clearly enough that I ought to have run any risk there might be in accepting her invitation. I had been foolishly taking more care of myself than was necessary. I told him I would write to Roger, and ask him when he could take me there again.

"I will tell you a better plan," he said. "I will go with you myself."

"But would that be fair to Roger? Miss Clare would think I didn't like going with him, and I would go with Roger anywhere. It was I who did not want to go. He did."

"My plan, however, will pave the way for a full explanation or confession. The next time you can go with Roger, and then you will be able to set him right in her eyes."

The plan seemed unobjectionable. But just then Percivale was very busy, and I was as much occupied with my baby, so day after day and week after week passed, during which our duty to Miss Clare was not forgotten, but only unfulfilled.

One afternoon I was surprised by a visit from my father. He not unfrequently surprised us.

"Why didn't you let us know, Papa?" I said. "A surprise is very nice, but an expectation is much nicer, and lasts so much longer."

"I might have disappointed you."

"Even if you had, I should have already enjoyed the expectation. That would be safe."

"There's a good deal to be said in excuse of surprises," he rejoined, "but in the present case, I have a special one to offer. I was taken with a sudden desire to see you. It was very foolish no doubt, and you are quite right in wishing I weren't here, only going to come tomorrow."

"Don't be so cruel, Papa. Scarcely a day passes in which *I* do not long to see *you*. My baby makes me think more about my home than ever."

"Then she's a very healthy baby, if one may judge her influences. But you know, if I had had to give you warning I could not have been here before tomorrow. And surely you will acknowledge, that, however nice expectation may be, presence is better."

"Yes, Papa. We will make a compromise, if you please. Every time you think of coming to me, you must either come at once, or let me know you are coming. Do you agree to that?"

"I agree," he said.

So I have the pleasure of a constant expectation. Any day he may walk in unheralded, or by any post I may receive a letter with the news that he is coming at such a time.

As we sat at dinner that evening, he asked if we had lately seen Miss Clare.

"I've seen her only once, and Percivale not at all, since you were here last, Papa," I answered.

"How's that?" he asked again, a little surprised. "Haven't you got her address yet? I want very much to know more of her."

"So do we. I haven't got her address, but I know where she lives."

"What do you mean, Wynnie? Has she taken to dark sayings of late, Percivale?"

I told him the whole story of my adventure with Roger, and the reports by which Judy had prejudiced my judgment. He heard me through in silence, for it was a rule with him never to interrupt a narrator. He used to say, "You will generally get at more, and in better fashion, if you let any narrative take its own devious course, without the interruption of requested explanations. By the time it is over, you will find the questions you wanted to ask mostly vanished."

"Describe the place to me, Wynnie," he said, when I had ended. "I must go and see her. I have a suspicion—almost a conviction—that she is one whose acquaintance ought to be cultivated at any cost."

"I don't think I could describe the place to you so that you would find it. But if Percivale wouldn't mind my going with you instead of with him, I should be only too happy to accompany you. May I, Percivale?"

"Certainly. It will do just as well to go with your father as with me. I only stipulate that, if you are both satisfied, you take Roger with you next time."

"Of course I will."

"Then we'll go tomorrow evening," said my father.

So it was arranged. My father went about some business in the morning. We dined early, and set out about six o'clock.

My father was getting an old man, and if any protection had been required, he could not have been half so active as Roger, and yet I felt twice as safe with him. I am satisfied that the deepest sense of safety, even in respect of physical dangers, can spring only from moral causes. I believe what made me so courageous was the undeveloped forefeeling that if any evil should overtake me in my father's company, I should not care; it would be all right then, anyhow. The repose was in my father himself, and not in his strength nor his wisdom. The former might fail, the latter might mistake; but so long as I was with him in what I did, no harm worth counting harm could come to me.

It was a cold evening in the middle of November. The light, which had been scanty enough all day, had vanished in a thin penetrating fog. Round every lamp in the street was a colored halo. The shops gleamed like jewel caverns of Alladin hollowed out of the darkness, and the people who hurried or sauntered along looked inscrutable. Where could they live? Had they anybody to love them? Were their hearts quiet under their dingy cloaks and shabby coats?

"Yes," returned my father, to whom I had said something to this effect, "what would not one give for a peep into the mysteries of all these worlds that go crowding past us. If we could but see through the opaque husk of them, some would glitter and glow like diamond mines. Others perhaps would look mere earthy holes, some of them forsaken quarries, with a great pool of stagnant water in the bottom, some like vast coalpits of gloom, into which you dared not carry a lighted lamp for fear of explosion. Some would be mere lumber rooms, and others ill-arranged libraries, without a poet's corner anywhere. But what a wealth of creation they show, and what infinite room for hope it affords!"

"But don't you think, Papa, there may be something of worth lying even in the earth-pit, or at the bottom of the stagnant water in the forsaken quarry?"

"Indeed I do, though I *have* met more than one in my lifetime concerning whom I felt compelled to say that it wanted keener eyes than mine to discover the hidden jewel. But then there *are* keener eyes than mine, for there are more loving eyes. I have myself been able to see good very clearly where some could see none, and shall I doubt that God can see good where my mole eyes can see none? Just as He is keen-eyed for the evil in His creatures in order to destroy it, He would, if it were possible, be yet keener-eyed for the good to nourish and cherish it. If men would only side with the good that is in them, and that the seed should grow and bring forth fruit!"

THIRTEEN
Miss Clare's Home

We arrived at the passage where the gin shop flared through the fog. A man in a fustian jacket came out of the shop and walked slowly down before us, with brickfield clay clinging to him as high as the leather straps which confined his trousers, garterwise, under the knee. The place was quiet. We and the brickmaker seemed the only people in it. When we turned the last corner, he was walking in at the very door where Miss Clare had disappeared. When I told my father that was the house, he called after the man, who came out again and, standing on the pavement, waited until we came up.

"Does Miss Clare live in this house?" my father asked.

"She do," answered the man curtly.

"First floor?"

"No. Nor yet the second, nor the third. She live nearer heaven then 'ere another in the house 'cep' myself. I live in the attic, and so do she."

He was a rough, lumpish young man, with good but dull features—only his blue eyes were clear. He looked my father full in the face, and I thought I saw a dim smile about his mouth.

"You know her, then, I suppose?"

"Everybody in the house knows *her.* There ain't many the likes o' her as lives wi' the likes of us. You go right up to the top. I don't know if she's in, but a'most anyone'll be able to tell you. I ain't been home yet."

My father thanked him, and we entered the house, and began to ascend. The stair was very much worn and rather dirty, and some of the bannisters were broken away, but the walls were tolerably clean. Halfway up we met a little girl with tangled hair and tattered garments, carrying a bottle.

"Do you know, my dear," said my father to her, "whether Miss Clare is at home?"

"I dunno," she answered. "I dunno who you mean. I been mindin' the baby. He ain't well. Mother says his head's bad. She's a-going up to tell

Grannie, and see if she can't do suthin' for him. You better ast mother—Mother!" she called out—"Here's a lady an' a gen'lem."

"You go about yer business, and be back direckly," cried a gruff voice from somewhere above.

"That's Mother," said the child, and ran down the stair.

When we reached the second floor, there stood a big fat woman on the landing, with her face red, and her hair looking like that of a doll poorly stuck on. She did not speak, but stood waiting to see what we wanted.

"I'm told Miss Clare lives here," said my father. "Can you tell me, my good woman, whether she's at home?"

"I'm neither a good nor bad woman," she returned in an insolent tone.

"I beg your pardon," said my father, "but you see I didn't know your name."

"An' ye don't know it yet."

"All I wanted to trouble you about was whether Miss Clare was at home or not."

"I don't know no one o' that name. If it's Grannie you mean, she's at home, I know, though it's not much reason I've got to care whether she's at home or not. I don't care what you call her. I dare say it'll be all one, come judgment. You'd better go up till you can't go no further, an' knocks yer head agin the tiles, and then you may feel about for a door, and knock at that, and see if the party as opens is the party you wants."

So saying, she turned in at a door behind her, and shut it. But we could hear her still growling and grumbling.

"It's very odd," said my father, with a bewildered smile. "I think we'd better do as she says, and go up till we knock our heads against the tiles."

We climbed two stairs more—the last one very steep and so dark that when we reached the top we found it necessary to follow the woman's directions literally and feel about for a door. But we had not to feel long or far, for there was one close to the top of the stair. My father knocked. There was no reply, but we heard the sound of a chair and presently someone opened it. The only light being behind her, I could not see her face, but the size and shape were those of Miss Clare.

She did not leave us in doubt, however; for, without a moment's hesitation, she held out her hand, saying to me, "This *is* kind of you, Mrs. Percivale," then to my father, "I'm very glad to see you, Mr. Walton. Will you walk in?"

We followed her into the room. It was not very small, for it occupied nearly the breadth of the house. On one side the roof sloped so nearly to the floor that there was not height enough to stand erect. On the other side the sloping part was partitioned off, evidently for a bedroom. But what a change it was from the lower part of the house! By the light of a single candle, I saw that the floor was as clean as old boards could be scrubbed. The two dormer windows were hung with white dimity curtains. Back in the angle of the roof, between the windows, stood an old bureau.

There was little more than room between the top of it and the ceiling for a little plaster statuette with bound hands and a strangely crowned head. A few books on hanging shelves were on the opposite side by the door to the other room, and the whitewashed walls were a good deal covered with engravings or etchings or lithographs, none of them framed.

There was a fire cheerfully burning in the gable, and opposite that a tall old-fashioned cabinet piano, in faded red silk. On the music rest lay Handel's "Verdi Prati." A few wooden chairs, and one very old-fashioned easy chair covered with striped chintz, from which not glaze only but color had almost disappeared, with an oblong table of deal, completed the furniture of the room. She made my father sit down in the easy chair, placed me one in front of the fire, and took another at the corner opposite my father. A moment of awkward silence followed. But my father never allowed awkwardness to accumulate.

"I had hoped to have been able to call upon you long ago, Miss Clare, but there was some difficulty in finding out where you lived."

"You are no longer surprised at that difficulty, I presume," she returned with a smile.

"But," said my father, "if you will allow an old man to speak to you freely—"

"Say what you please, Mr. Walton. I promise to answer *any* question *you* think proper to ask me."

"My dear Miss Clare, I had not the slightest intention of catechising you. What I meant to say might indeed have taken the form of a question, but as such could have been intended only for you to answer to yourself whether, namely, it was wise to place yourself at such a disadvantage as living in this quarter must be to you."

"If you were acquainted with my history, you would perhaps hesitate, Mr. Walton, before you said I *placed myself* at such disadvantage."

Here a thought struck me. "I fancy, Papa, it is not for her own sake Miss Clare lives here."

"I hope not," she interposed.

"I believe," I went on, "she has a grandmother, who probably has grown accustomed to the place, and is unwilling to leave it."

She looked puzzled for a moment, then burst into a merry laugh. "I see!" she exclaimed. "How stupid I am! You have heard some of the people in this house talk about *Grannie:* That's me! I am known in the house as Grannie, and have been for a good many years now—I can hardly, without thinking, tell for how many."

Again she laughed heartily, and my father and I shared her merriment.

"How many grandchildren have you then, pray, Miss Clare?"

"Let me see." She thought for a while. "There are about thirty-five in this house, but unfortunately the name has been caught up in the neighboring houses, and I cannot with certainty say how many grandchildren I have. I think I know them all, however, and I fancy that is more than many an English grandmother, with children in America, India, or Australia, can say for herself."

Certainly she was not older than I was. While hearing her merry laugh, and seeing her young face overflowing with smiles, which appeared to come sparkling out of her eyes as out of two well-springs, one could not help feeling puzzled how, even in jest, she could have got the name of Grannie.

"Would you like to hear," she said, when our merriment had a little subsided, "how I have so easily arrived at the honorable name of Grannie?"

"I should be delighted," said my father.

"You don't know what you are pledging yourself to when you say so," she rejoined, again laughing. "You will have to hear the whole of my story from the beginning."

"Again I say I shall be delighted," returned my father, confident that her history could be the source of nothing but pleasure to him.

FOURTEEN
Miss Clare's Story

Thereupon Miss Clare began.

"My mother died when I was very young, and I was left alone with my father, for I was his only child. He was a studious and thoughtful man. He supported us by literary work of, I presume, a secondary order. He would spend all his mornings for many weeks in the library of the British Museum, reading and making notes, after which he would sit writing at home. I should have found it very dull during the former of these times, had he not discovered that I had some capacity for music, and provided instruction for me. I believe he could not have found me a better teacher in all Europe. Her character was lovely, and her music the natural outcome of its harmony. I went to her, then, almost every day for a time.

"What my father wrote I cannot tell. How gladly would I now read the shortest sentence I knew to be his! He never told me for what journals or publishers he wrote. I fancy it was work in which his brain was more interested than his heart, and which he was always hoping to exchange for something more to his mind. After his death I could discover scarcely a scrap of his writings, and not a hint to guide me to what he had written.

"My happiest times were when my father asked me to play to him while he wrote, and I sat down to my old cabinet Broadwood—the one you see there is as like it as I could find—and played anything and everything I liked, for I never forgot what I learned.

"Even though we went to church on Sunday mornings, my father rarely talked much to me about religion. When he did, it was with evident awe in his spirit, and reverence in his demeanor. Waking one night after I had been asleep for some time, I saw him on his knees by my bedside. I did not move or speak, for fear of disturbing him, and when he lifted his head I caught a glimpse of a pale, tearful face. It is no wonder that the virtue of the sight should never have passed away. He was in the habit of reading chapters of the New Testament to me, but the consolations of religion were not yet mine, for I had not yet begun to think of God in any relation to myself.

"We lived then near the Museum where I would linger about looking at things, sometimes for hours, before my father came to me. He always came at the very minute he had said, though, and always found me at the appointed spot.

"One afternoon I was waiting as usual, but my father did not come at the time appointed. I waited on and on till it grew dark, and the hour for closing arrived, and I was forced to go home without him. I found he had been seized with some kind of fit in the reading room and had been carried home . . . and after that I was alone in the world.

"Our landlady was very kind to me, at least until she found that my father had left no money. All our little effects were sold for less than half their value, in consequence of that conspiracy of the brokers which they call *knocking out.* I was especially miserable at losing my father's books, which I greatly valued, more miserable even than at seeing my beloved piano carried off.

"When the sale was over, I sat down on the floor, amidst the dust and bits of paper and straw and cord, without a single idea in my head as to what was to become of me, or what I was to do next. I didn't cry, but I doubt if in all London there was a more wretched child than myself just then, in the twilight of a November afternoon. While I sat on the floor, the landlady and someone else came into the room. They, not seeing me, talked about me, reflecting severely on my father, and announcing the decree that I must go to the workhouse. The moment they left me alone, I got up, glided down the stairs, and ran from the house.

"Within a few yards I ran up against Mrs. Conan, an old Irishwoman who did all the little charring we wanted. I broke out in sobs, and told her I was running away because they were going to send me to the workhouse. She burst into a torrent of Irish indignation, and assured me that such should never be my fate while she lived. She led me away to a large house in a square—the largest house I had ever been in, though it was rather desolate. Except in one little room below, where she had scarcely more than a bed and a chair, a slip of carpet and a frying pan, there was not an article of furniture in the whole place. She had been put there when the last tenant left, to take care of the place until another tenant should appear to turn her out. She had her houseroom and a trifle a week besides for her services, beyond which she depended entirely on what she could make by charring. When she had no house to live in on the same terms, she took a room somewhere.

"Here I lived for several months, and was able to be of use. Mrs. Conan was bound to be there at certain times to show anyone over the house who brought an order from the agent, and this necessarily took up a good part of her working time. But as I could open the door and walk about the place as well as another, she willingly left me in charge as often as she had a job elsewhere.

"I found it very dreary indeed, for few people called, and she would not infrequently be absent the whole day. I had not my piano, and only a single book and what do you think that was? An odd volume of the *Newgate Calendar*. It moved me, indeed, to the profoundest sympathy, not with the crimes of the malefactors, but with the malefactors themselves, and their mental condition after the deed was actually done. But it made me feel almost as if I had committed every crime. It was not until long afterward that I was able to understand that a man's actions are not the man, but may be separated from him. His character may be changed while he yet holds the same individuality—the man was blind though he now sees. And though the deeds may continue to be his, all stain of them may yet be washed out of him.

"I cannot think that the study of the *Newgate Calendar* could do an innocent child harm. Even familiarity with vice is not necessarily pollution. There cannot be many women of my age as familiar with it in every shape as I am, and I do not regard it with one atom less of absolute abhorrence, although I neither shudder at the mention of it, nor turn with disgust from the person in whom it dwells. I believe that volume threw down the first deposit of soil, from which afterward sprung what grew to be almost a passion for getting the people about me clean—a passion which might have done as much harm as good, if its companion, patience, had not been sent me to guide and restrain it. In a word, I came at length to understand, in some measure, the last prayer of our Lord for those who crucified Him, and the ground on which He begged from His Father their forgiveness—that they knew not what they did.

"The house was in an old square, built in the reign of Queen Anne but fallen far from its first high estate. No one would believe, to look at it from the outside, what a great place it was. The whole of the space behind it, corresponding to the small gardens of the other houses, was occupied by a large music room, under which was a low-pitched room of equal extent, while all under that were cellars, connected with the sunken story in front by a long vaulted passage, corresponding to a wooden gallery above, which formed a communication between the drawing room floor and the music room. Most girls of my age, knowing these vast empty spaces about them, would have been terrified at being left alone there, even in midday. But I was, I suppose, too miserable to be frightened. Sometimes Mrs. Conan was later than usual, and the night came down, and I had to sit, perhaps for hours, in the dark—for she would not allow me to have a candle, for fear of fire. I used to cry a good deal, although I did my best to hide the traces of it, because I knew it would annoy my kind old friend. She showed me a great deal of rough tenderness, and you may be sure I learned to love her dearly.

"One rainy winter evening I have a particular cause to remember, both for itself, and because of something that followed many years after. I was in the drawing room on the first floor, a double room with folding doors and a small cabinet behind communicating with a back stair. The stairs were double all through the house, adding much to the eeriness of the place. I had been looking out of the window all the afternoon upon the silent square—there were no tradesmen there, and no children playing in the garden. A gray cloud of fog and soot hung from the whole sky. A score of yellow leaves yet quivered on the trees, and the statue of Queen Anne stood bleak and disconsolate among the bare branches.

"I gazed at it all drearily without interest. I brooded over the past, not dreaming of looking forward. I had no hope, and it never occurred to me that things might grow better. I was dull and wretched.

"I think this experience enabled me to understand the peculiar misery of the poor in our large towns—they have no hope, no impulse to look forward, nothing to expect. They live but in the present, and the dreariness of that soon shapes the whole atmosphere of their spirits to its own likeness. Perhaps the first thing one who would help them has to do is to aid the birth of some small vital hope in them, for that is better than a thousand gifts.

"But it began to grow dark. Tired of standing, I sat down upon the floor, until long after it was quite dark. All at once a surge of self-pity arose in my heart. I burst out wailing and sobbing, and cried aloud, 'God has forgotten me altogether!' I was really thinking that I could do nothing for anybody. My little ambition had always been to be useful. I knew I was of some use to my father, for I kept the rooms tidy for him, and dusted his pet books oh, so carefully, for they were like household gods to me. I had also played for him, and I knew he enjoyed that—he said so, many times. And I had begun to think, just before he left me, how I should be able to help him better by and by. For I saw that he worked very hard, so hard that it made him silent. I knew that my music mistress made her livelihood, partly at least, by giving lessons; and I thought that I might, by and by, be able to give lessons too, and then papa would not be required to work so hard, for I too should bring money home.

"But now I was of use to nobody. I could not help even poor Mrs. Conan. I did not earn a penny of our living. I only gave the poor old thing time to work harder, that I might eat up her earnings! I always thought of myself as a lady, for was not Papa a gentleman, let him be ever so poor? Shillings and sovereigns in his pocket could not determine whether a man was a gentleman or not! And if he was a gentleman, his daughter must be a lady. But how could I be a lady if I was content to be a burden to a poor charwoman, instead of earning my own living, and something besides with which to help her? For I had the notion that position depended on how much a person was able to help other people, and here I was, worse than useless to anybody! 'I am of no use,' I cried, 'and God has forgotten me altogether!' And I went on weeping until I fell fast asleep on the floor.

"I have no theory about dreams and visions, but surely if one falls fast asleep without an idea in one's head, and a whole dismal world of misery in one's heart, and wakes up quiet and refreshed, without the misery and with an idea, there can be no great fanaticism in thinking that God may have had something—or everything—to do with it. Certainly, if it had a physical source, it wasn't that I was more comfortable, for I was hungrier than ever, and cold enough, having slept on the bare floor without anything to cover me on Christmas Eve—for Christmas Eve it was.

"The way Mrs. Conan kept Christmas Day was to comfort her old bones in bed until the afternoon, and then to have a good tea with a chop. So, as soon as I had washed up the few breakfast things, I dressed myself as neatly as I could, and set out to look for work.

"In a nearby shop I had seen a piano standing, and a girl of about my own age watching. I found the shop, although it was shut up, and knocked at the door. A stout matron opened it, and asked me what I wanted. I told her I wanted work. She seemed amused at the idea, but asked what I could do. I told her I could teach her daughter music. She asked me what made me come to her, and I told her. But how was she to know, she asked, that I could teach her properly? I told her I would let her hear me play; whereupon she led me into the shop, took down a shutter, and managed to clear me a passage through a crowd of furniture to the instrument. With a struggle I squeezed through and reached it; but at the first chord I struck, I gave a cry of dismay. In some alarm she asked what was the matter, calling me Child very kindly. I told her it was so dreadfully out of tune that I couldn't play on it at all; but, if she would get it tuned, I should show her that I could do what I professed. She told me she could not afford to have it tuned, and if I could not teach Bertha on it as it was, she couldn't help it. This, I assured her, was utterly impossible; and then, with some show of offense, she reached over a chest of drawers, and shut down the cover. I believe she doubted whether I could play at all, and had not been merely amusing myself at her expense. Nothing was left but to thank her and walk out of the house, dreadfully disappointed.

"Unwilling to go home at once, I wandered about the neighborhood, through street after street, and found myself in front of a pianoforte firm, and a thought came into my head. The next morning I returned, and asked to see the master, Mr. Perkins, who was amused with my story. If I had asked him for money, he would probably have got rid of me quickly enough. But to my request that he would spare a man to tune Mrs. Lampeter's piano, he replied at once that he would, provided I could satisfy him as to my efficiency. Thereupon he took me to a grand piano in the shop and told me to play. I could not help trembling a good deal, but I tried my best. In a few moments, however, the tears were dropping on the keys, and when he asked me what was the matter, I told him it was months since I had touched a piano. He asked very kindly how that was, and I had to tell him my whole story. Then he not only promised to have the piano tuned for me at once, but told me I might come and practice in his shop as often as I pleased, so long as I was a good girl, and did not take up with bad company. Imagine my delight! Then he sent for a tuner, and I suppose told him a little about me, for the man spoke very kindly to me as we went to the broker's.

"Mr. Perkins has been a good friend to me ever since.

"For six months I continued to give Bertha Lampeter lessons. Her mother introduced me to several families, and I found five or six new pupils.

"When the house was let, Mrs. Conan took a room in the neighborhood, that I might keep up my connection. Then I was first introduced to the scenes and experiences with which I am now familiar. Mrs. Percivale might well recoil if I were to tell her half the wretchedness, wickedness, and vulgarity I have encountered. For two years or so we changed about, at one time in an empty house, at another in a hired room, sometimes better, sometimes worse off, as regarded our neighbors. When Mrs. Conan came to the conclusion that it would be better for her to confine herself to charring, we at last settled down here, where I have now lived for many years.

"I had never thought of going back to Miss Harper, my former music mistress, until Mr. Perkins asked me one day who had taught me. I resolved to go and see her. She welcomed me with more than kindness, with tenderness, and told me I had caused her much uneasiness by not letting her know what had become of me. She looked quite aghast when she learned in what sort of place and with whom I lived. But I told her Mrs. Conan had saved me from the workhouse, and was as much of a mother to me as possible, that we loved each other, and that it would be very wrong of me to leave her now, especially since she was not so well as she had been. I believe she then saw the thing as I saw it. She made me play to her, was pleased—indeed surprised—until I told her how I had been supporting myself, and she insisted on my resuming my studies with her, which I was only too glad to do. I now, of course, got on much faster.

"Then Mrs. Conan fell ill, and we indeed had hard work of it. Had it not been for the kindness of the neighbors, we should sometimes have been in want of bread; and when I hear hard things said of the poor, I often think that surely improvidence is not so bad as selfishness.

"Miss Harper said I must raise my terms, but I told her that would be the loss of my pupils. Then she said she must see what could be done for me, only no one she knew was likely to employ a child. One morning, however, within a week, a note came from Lady Bernard asking me to go and see her.

"I went, and found—a mother. You do not know her, I think? But you must one day. Good people like you must come together. She awed me at first—I was not much more than thirteen then—but with the awe came a certain confidence which was far better then ease. The immediate result was that she engaged me to go and play for an hour, five days a week, at a hospital for sick children in the neighborhood, which she partly supported. For she had a strong belief that there was in music a great healing power, and I do think that good has been and is the result of my playing to those children. I go still, though not quite so often, and it is music to me to watch my music thrown back in light from some of those sweet, pale, suffering faces.

"Lady Bernard was too wise to pay me much at first. She inquired how much I was already earning, asked me on how much I could support Mrs. Conan and myself, and then made up that amount. At the same time, however, she sent many things to warm and feed the old woman, so that my mind was set at ease about her. Mrs. Conan continued to suffer so much from rheumatism that she was quite unfit to go out charring anymore, and we removed ourselves to this place. It was a good while before the inmates of this house and I began to know each other. They regarded us from the first with disapproval. The little girls would make grimaces at me, and the bigger girls would pull my hair, slap my face, and even occasionally push me downstairs, while the boys made themselves far more terrible in my eyes. But with time and a few events, things began to grow better.

"And this is not by any means one of the worst parts of London. I could take Mr. Walton to houses in the East End, where the manners are indescribable. We are all earning our bread here. Some have an occasional attack of drunkenness, and idle about, but they are sick of it again after a while. I remember asking a woman once if her husband would be present at a little entertainment to which Lady Bernard had invited them. She answered that he would be there if he was drunk, but if he was sober he couldn't spare the time.

"My main stay and comfort was an old woman who then occupied the room opposite to this. She was such a good creature! She was nearly blind, yet I never saw a speck of dust on that chest of drawers, which was hers then. Her floor and her little muslin window curtains, her bed, and everything about her were as clean as a lady could desire. She was very pleased when I asked her to pay a visit to Mrs. Conan, and I think she did us both good. I wish you could picture her coming in at that door, with the broad borders of her white cap waving, and her hands stretched out before her. The most remarkable thing to me was the calmness with which she looked forward to her approaching death, although without the expectation which so many good people seem to have in connection with their departure. Her belief amounted to this—that she had never known beforehand what lay round the next corner, or what was going to happen to her, but under Providence things always turned out right and good for her, and she did not doubt she would find it so when she came to the last turn.

"I also kept my rooms as clean and tidy as I could—indeed, the sight of the blind woman's room was a constant reminder. I also was able to get a few more articles of furniture and a bit of carpet. I whitewashed the walls myself, and after a while began to whitewash the walls of the landing as well, and all down the stair. Before long some of the other tenants began to whitewash their rooms also, and contrive to keep things a little tidier. Soon this one and that began to apply to me for help in various difficulties that arose. But they didn't call me Grannie then—they called the blind woman Grannie, and the name got associated with the top of the house. After her death, the name settled down upon me, and I came to be called Grannie by everybody in the house.

"By and by I got a few music pupils amongst tradespeople of a more superior class, and I both asked and obtained double my former fee, so that our financial situation grew gradually better. Some of Lady Bernard's friends engaged me to teach their children as well.

"Having come once or twice to see Mrs. Conan, Lady Bernard discovered that we were gaining a little influence over the people in the house; and it occurred to her, as she told me afterward, that the virtue of music might be tried there with a moral end in view. Hence I was astonished and delighted one evening by the arrival of a piano—not that one, for I wore the other out. First I asked some of the children to come and listen while I played. Even the least educated children are made for music: whatever the street organs may be to poets and mathematicians, they are certainly a godsend to the children of our courts and alleys. The only condition I made was that they should come with clean hands and faces and tidy hair. Considerable indignation was at first manifested by some parents whose children I refused to admit, but the grumbling passed away while the condition gathered weight. After a while I began to invite the mothers to join us, and at length it came to be understood that every Saturday evening, whoever chose to be tidy would be welcome to an hour or two of my music. Some of the husbands even began to come.

"There was another point. Never since my father's death had I attended public worship, and I hardly know what induced me one evening to step into a chapel of which I knew nothing. There was not even Sunday to account for it. I believe, however, it had to do with my feeling tired. I only felt empty all through—I felt that something was not right with me, that something was required of me which I was not rendering. I entered the chapel and found about a dozen people present and singing. Something in the air of the place, meagre and waste as it looked, yet induced me to remain. An address followed from a pale-faced, weak-looking man of middle age, who had no gift of person, voice, or utterance to recommend what he said. But there dwelt a powerful enforcement in him, that of earnestness. I went again and again, and slowly the sense of life and its majesty grew upon me.

"To one hungering for bread, it is of little consequence in what sort of platter it is handed him. This was a dissenting chapel—of what order, it was long before I knew—and my father had accustomed me to the church services. And now, although a communicant of the Church of England, I do not prefer one over against the other.

"I gathered from this good man one practical thought which was the main fruit—the fruit by which I know that he was good. If all the labor of God was to bring sons into glory, lifting them out of the abyss of evil bondage up to the rock of His pure freedom, the only worthy end of life must be to work in the same direction—to be a fellow worker with God. Might I not, then, do such in my own small way? The urging, the hope, grew in me. Then my teacher taught me that the way for *me* to help others was not to tell them of their duty, but myself to learn of Him who bore our griefs and carried our sorrows. As I learned of Him, I should be able to help them. I have never had any theory since then but just to be their friend—to do for them the best I can. When I feel I may, I tell them what has done me good, but I never urge any belief of mine upon their acceptance.

"And so I remain where I am. I was sixteen when Mrs. Conan died. Then my friends, including Lady Bernard and Miss Harper, expected me to move. Indeed, Lady Bernard said she knew precisely the place for me. When I told her I should remain where I was, she was silent, and soon left me—offended, I thought. I wrote to her at once, explaining why I chose my part here, saying that I would not hastily alter anything that had been appointed me; that I loved the people; that they called me Grannie; that they came to me with their troubles; that there were few changes in the house now; that the sick looked to me for help, and the children for teaching; that they seemed to be steadily rising in the moral scale; and that I knew some of them were trying hard to be good. So I put it to her whether, if I were to leave them in order merely to better myself, I should not be forsaking my post, almost my family. If I was at all necessary to them, I knew they were yet more necessary to me.

"I have a burning desire to help in the making of the world clean, if it be only by sweeping one little room in it. I want to lead some poor stray sheep home—not home to the church, Mr. Walton. I would not be supposed to curry favor with you. I never think of what they call the church. I only care to lead them home to the bosom of God, where alone man is true man.

"I could talk to you all night about what Lady Bernard has been to me since, and what she has done for me and my grandchildren. But I have said enough to explain how it is that I am in such a questionable position."

FIFTEEN
A Few More Facts

A silence followed. My father had scarcely interrupted, and I had not spoken a word, for her story moved us deeply. My father sat perfectly composed, betraying his emotion in silence alone. I had a great lump in my throat, but in part from the shame which mingled with my admiration. The silence had not lasted more than a few seconds, when I yielded to a struggling impulse, rose, and kneeling before her, put my hands on her knees, and said, "Forgive me," and could say no more. She put her hand on my shoulder, whispered, "My dear Mrs. Percivale!" bent down her face, and kissed me on the forehead.

"How could you help being shy of me?" she said. "Perhaps I ought to have come to you and explained it all, but I shrink from self-justification—at least before a fit opportunity makes it comparatively easy."

"That is the way to give it all its force," remarked my father.

"You see, Mr. Walton, it is not in the least as if, living in comfort, I had taken notice of the misery of the poor for the want of such sympathy and help as I could give them, and had therefore gone to live amongst them that I might so help them. It is quite different from that. If I had done so, I might be in danger of magnifying not merely my office but myself. On the contrary, I have been trained to it in such slow and continuous ways, that it would be a far greater trial to me to forsake my work than it has ever been to continue it."

My father said no more, but I knew he had his own thought. I remained kneeling, and understood for the first time what had led to saint worship.

"Won't you sit, Mrs. Percivale?" she said, as if merely expostulating with me for not making myself comfortable.

"Have you forgiven me?" I asked.

"How can I say I have, when I never had anything to forgive?"

"Well then, I must go unforgiven, for I cannot forgive myself," I said.

"O Mrs. Percivale! If you think how the world is flooded with forgiveness, you will just dip in your cup, and take what you want."

I rose, humbled, and took my seat.

The work to which Miss Clare had given herself seemed more like that of the Son of God than any other I knew. For she was not helping her friends from afar, but as one of themselves; nor with money, but with herself. She was not condescending to them, but finding her highest life in companionship with them. It seemed at least more like what His life must have been before He was thirty, than anything else I could think of. At length I ventured to remind her of something she seemed to have forgotten.

"When you were telling us, Miss Clare," I said, "of the help that came to you that dreary afternoon in the empty house, you mentioned that something which happened afterward made it still more remarkable."

"Oh, yes!" she answered. "I forgot about that. I did not carry my history far enough to be reminded of it again.

"About five years ago, Lady Bernard asked me to give an entertainment to my friends, and to as many of the neighbors as I pleased, to the number of about a hundred. She wanted to put the thing entirely in my hands, and it should be my entertainment, she claiming only the privilege of defraying expenses. I told her I should be delighted to convey *her* invitation, but that the entertainment must not pretend to be mine.

"She had bought a large house to be a home for young women out of employment, and she proposed the entertainment be given in it. There were a good many nice young women there who would help us to wait upon our guests. The idea was carried out, and the thing succeeded admirably. We had music and games, the latter such as the children were mostly acquainted with, only producing more merriment and conducted with more propriety than was usual in the court or the streets. Had these been children of the poorest sort, we should have had to teach them, for one of the saddest things is that they, in London at least, do not know how to play.

"In one of the games, I was seated on the floor with a handkerchief tied over my eyes, waiting, I believe, for some gentle trick to be played upon me, that I might guess who played it. There was a delay of only a few seconds, long enough, however, for a sudden return of that dreary December afternoon in which I sat on the floor too miserable even to think that I was cold and hungry. It was not the picture of it that came back to me first, but the sound of my voice calling aloud in the ringing echo of desolate rooms that I was of no use to anybody, and that God had forgotten me utterly.

"Then I jumped to my feet, and tore the bandage from my eyes. I stared about the room, convinced that it was the very room in which I had so sat in desolation and despair. I hurried into the back room—and there was the cabinet beyond! In a few moments more I was absolutely satisfied that this was indeed the house in which I had first found refuge. I sat down in the corner, and cried for joy. Someone went for Lady Bernard, whom I told that there was nothing the matter but a little too much happiness, and, that if she would come into the cabinet, I would tell her all about it. She did so, and a few words made her a hearty sharer in my pleasure. She insisted that I should tell the company all about it, 'for,' she said, 'you do not know how much it may help some poor creature to trust in God.' I promised I would. Then she left me alone for a little while, and after that I was able to join in the games again.

"At supper I stood up, and gave them all a little sketch of my history, and told what had happened that evening. Many of the simpler hearts about me received it without question, as a divine arrangement for my comfort and encouragement. But presently a man stood up—one who thought more than the rest of them, perhaps because he was blind—a man at once conceited, honest, and skeptical. Silence was made for him, and he began to speak, 'Ladies and gentlemen,' as if he had been addressing a public meeting, 'you've all heard what Grannie has said. It's very kind of her to give us so much of her history. It's a very remarkable one, *I* think, and she deserves to have it. As to what upset her this very night as is—and I must say for her, I've knowed her now for six years, and I never knowed her upset afore—and as to what upset her, all I can say is, it may or may not ha' been what phylosophers call a coincydence. But at the same time, if it wasn't a coincydence, and if the Almighty had a hand in it, it were no more than you might expect. He would look at it in this light, you see, that maybe she was wrong to fancy herself so down on her luck as all that, but she was a good soul, notwithstandin,' and He would let her know He hadn't forgotten her. And so He set her down in that room there for a minute, jest to put her in mind o' what had been, and what she had said there, an' how it was all so different now. In my opinion, it were no wonder as she broke down, God bless her. I beg leave to propose her health.'

"So they drank my health in lemonade and ginger beer. Then we had more music and singing; and a clergyman, who knew how to be neighbor to them that had fallen among thieves, read a short chapter and a collect or two, and said a few words to them. Then Grannie and her children went home together, all happy, but Grannie the happiest of them all."

"Strange and beautiful!" said my father. "But," he added, after a pause, "you must have met with many strange and beautiful things in such a life as yours, for such a life must open to the entrance of all simple wonders. Conventionality and routine and arbitrary law banish their very approach."

"I believe," said Miss Clare, "that every life has its own private experience of the strange and beautiful. But I have sometimes thought that perhaps God took pains to bar out such things of the sort as we should be no better for. The reason why Lazarus was not allowed to visit the brothers of Dives was, that the repentance he would have urged would not have followed, and they would have been only the worse in consequence."

"Admirably said," remarked my father.

Before we took our leave, I had engaged Miss Clare to dine with us while my father was in town.

SIXTEEN
Lady Bernard

When Miss Clare came we had no other guests, and so had plenty of talk with her. Before dinner I showed her my husband's pictures, and she was especially pleased with that which hung in the little room off the study with a curtain before it. My father has described it in *The Seaboard Parish:* a pauper lies dead, and they are bringing in his coffin. She said it is no wonder it had not been sold, notwithstanding its excellence and force, and asked if I would allow her to bring Lady Bernard to see it.

Percivale succeeded in persuading her to sit for him—but not, however, before I had joined my entreaties with his, and my father had insisted that her face was not her own, but belonged to all her kind.

The very next morning she came with Lady Bernard. I wish I could give a photograph of that lady. She was slight and appeared taller than she was, being rather stately than graceful, with a commanding forehead and blue eyes. She gave at first the impression of coldness, with a touch of haughtiness. She said she knew my husband well by reputation and had, before our marriage, asked him to her house, but had not been fortunate enough to possess sufficient attraction. Percivale was much taken with her, for when her eyes lighted up, her seeming coldness vanished in the light that flashed into her eyes and the smile that illumined her face. She was much pleased with some of his pictures, criticizing freely and with evident understanding. She bought both the pauper picture and that of the dying knight.

"But I am sorry to deprive your lovely room of such treasures, Mrs. Percivale," she said, with a kind smile.

"Of course I shall miss them," I returned, "but the thought that you have them will console me. Besides, it is good to have a change and there are only too many lying in the study, from which he will let me choose another."

"Will you let me come and see which you have chosen?" she asked.

"With the greatest pleasure."

"And will you come and see me? Do you think you could persuade your husband to bring you to dine with me?"

I told her I could promise the one with more than pleasure, and had little doubt of being able to do the other, now that my husband had seen her.

A reference to my husband's dislike to fashionable society followed, and I had occasion to mention his feeling about being asked without me. Of the latter, Lady Bernard expressed the warmest approval; and of the former, she said that it would have no force in respect of her parties, for they were not at all fashionable.

This was the commencement of a friendship for which we have much cause to thank God. (Nor did we forget that it came through Miss Clare.)

Lady Bernard interested me in many of her schemes of helping the poor. Some of the programs were for providing them with work in hard times, but more for giving them an interest in life itself, without which no one would begin to inquire into its relations and duties. She felt that one ought not, where avoidable, give them anything they *ought* to provide for themselves, such as food or clothing or shelter. But she heartily approved of making them an occasional present of something they could not be expected to procure for themselves—flowers, for instance. "You would not imagine," I have heard her say, "how they delight in flowers. I am sure they prize and enjoy them far more than most people with gardens and greenhouses do. A gift of that sort can only do them good. I would rather give a workman a gold watch than a leg of mutton. By a present you mean a compliment, and none feel more grateful for such an acknowledgment of your human relation to them than those who look up to you as their superior."

If ever there was a woman who lived this outer life for the sake of others, it was she. Her inner life was sufficient for herself and found its natural outward expression in blessing others. I believe no one, not even Miss Clare, knew half the munificent things she did, or what an immense proportion of her large income she spent upon other people. But, as she said herself, no one understood the worth of money better, and no one liked better to have the worth of it. Therefore, she always administered her charity with some view to the value of the probable return, with some regard to the amount of good likely to result to others from the aid given to one. She always took into consideration whether the good was likely to be propagated, or to die with the receiver.

It was some time after our encounter with Lady Bernard that I judged I might give another little dinner party. I now knew Lady Bernard sufficiently well to know also that she would willingly accept an invitation from me, and would be pleased to bring Miss Clare with her.

I proposed the dinner and Percivale consented to it. My main object was the glorification of Miss Clare, who had more engagements of one kind or another than anybody I knew; so I first invited her, asking her to fix her own day. Next I invited Mr. and Mrs. Morley, and next Lady Bernard. Then I invited Mr. Blackstone, and Roger—for I was much interested in his meeting Miss Clare. He had been absent from London for some time, and had not seen her since he and I had quarreled.

On the evening, Roger arrived first, then Mr. Blackstone. Lady Bernard brought Miss Clare, and Mr. and Mrs. Morley came last. There were several introductions to be gone through, and I failed to observe how the presence of Miss Clare affected Mr. and Mrs. Morley. But my husband told me that Judy turned red, and that Mr. Morley bowed to her with studied politeness. I took care that Mr. Blackstone should take her down to dinner, which was served in the studio as before.

The conversation was broken and desultory at first, but eventually centered around Lady Bernard and my husband at the foot of the table.

"Then you do believe," my husband was saying, "in the importance of birth and descent—of *havage,* as some call it?"

"I believe that descent involves very important considerations," Lady Bernard returned.

"No one," interposed Mr. Morley, "can have a better right than your ladyship to believe that."

"One cannot have a better right than another to believe a fact, Mr. Morley," she answered with a smile. "It is but a fact that you start better or worse according to the position of your starting point."

"Undeniably," said Mr. Morley. "And for all the growth of leveling notions in this country, it will be many generations before a profound respect for birth is eradicated from the feelings of the English people."

He drew in his chin with a jerk, and devoted himself again to his plate. He was not permitted to eat in peace, however.

"No growth of nations," said Mr. Blackstone, "will blot love, honesty, and kindness out of the human heart."

"Then," said Lady Bernard archly, "am I to understand, Mr. Blackstone, that you don't believe it of the least importance to come of decent people?"

"Your ladyship puts it well," said Mr. Morley, laughing mildly, "and with authority. The longer the decent—"

"The more doubtful," interrupted Lady Bernard, laughing. "One can hardly have come of decent people all through. Let us only hope, without inquiring too closely, that their number preponderates in our own individual cases."

Mr. Morley stared for a moment, and then tried to laugh, but unable to determine where he stood, returned to his glass of sherry.

"On the contrary," Mr. Blackstone rejoined, "it must be a serious fact to anyone like myself who believes that the sins of the fathers are visited on the children."

"I can't imagine you believing such a manifest injustice," objected Roger. "I must either disbelieve that, or disbelieve in a God."

"But don't you see it is a fact? Don't you see children born with the sins of their parents nestling in their very bodies?"

"Wouldn't you rather *not* believe in a God than in an unjust one?"

"An unjust god," said Mr. Blackstone, with the honest evasion of one who will not answer an awful question hastily, "must be a false god—that is, no god. But I will go further on my original statement. I will assert that it is an honor to us to have the sins of our fathers laid upon us. For thus it is given into our power to put a stop to them, so that they shall descend no further."

"I would differ from you in only one thing," said Lady Bernard. "The chain of descent is linked in such a complicated pattern that the choices of one link, or of many links, cannot break the transmission of qualities."

"If I understand you rightly, Lady Bernard," said Roger, "it is the personal character of your ancestors, and not their social position, that you regard as of importance."

"It was of their character alone I was thinking."

"Then we are all equally descended," I remarked, "for we have each had about the same number of ancestors, with characters of some sort or other, whose faults and virtues have to do with ours."

"Certainly," returned Lady Bernard. "And it is impossible to say in whose descent the good or the bad may predominate. I cannot tell, for instance, how much of the property I inherit has been honestly come by, or is the spoil of rapacity and injustice."

"You are doing the best you can to atone for such a possible fact, then, by its redistribution," said my husband.

"I have no right to throw up my stewardship, for that was none of my seeking, and I do not know anyone who has a better claim to it—but I count it only a stewardship. I am not at liberty to throw my orchard open, for that would result not only in its destruction, but in a renewal of the fight for its possession. However, I will try to distribute my apples properly to the poor and needy. I have not the same right to give away that I have to keep wisely."

"For my part," said Mr. Morley, "I don't see what is to be done. The poor go on increasing."

"It cannot be denied," said Lady Bernard, "whoever may be to blame for it, that the separation between rich and poor has greatly widened of late. Or perhaps we have become more aware of the breadth and depth of the gulf. Certainly the rich withdraw themselves from the poor. Instead of helping them to bear their burdens, they leave the still struggling poor of whole parishes to sink into hopeless want, under the weight of those who have already sunk beyond recovery. At all events, he that hates his brother is a murderer."

"But there is no question of hating here," objected Mr. Morley.

"I am not certain that absolute indifference to one's neighbor is not as bad. It came to pretty nearly the same thing in the case of the priest and the Levite, who passed by on the other side," said Mr. Blackstone.

"Still," said Mr. Morley, in all the self-importance of one who prided himself on the practical, "I do not see that anyone has proposed a remedy. What is to be *done?* What can *I* do?"

"I will not dare to answer what *you* can do. I can only speak of what principles I have discovered. But until a man begins to behave to those with whom he comes into personal contact as partakers of the same nature—to recognize, for instance, between himself and his tradespeople a bond superior to that of supply and demand—I cannot imagine how he is to do anything toward the drawing together of the edges of the gaping wound in the social body."

"But," persisted Mr. Morley, who, I began to think, showed some real desire to come at a practical conclusion, "suppose a man finds himself incapable of that sort of thing—for it wants some rare qualification or other to be able to converse with an uneducated person—"

"Especially amongst those of the trades," interposed Mr. Blackstone, "there are many who think a great deal more than most of the so-called educated. There is a truer education to be got in the pursuit of a trade than in the life of a mere scholar. But I beg your pardon, Mr. Morley."

"Suppose," resumed Mr. Morley, accepting the apology without disclaimer, "suppose I find I can do nothing of that sort—is there nothing I can do?"

"Nothing of the best sort, I firmly believe," answered Miss Clare, "for the genuine recognition of the human relationship can alone give value to whatever else you may do, and indeed can alone guide you to what might serve toward the filling up of the gulf between the classes."

"Well, will not all kindness shown to the poor by persons in a superior station tend in that direction?"

"I maintain that you can do nothing for them in the way of kindness that shall not result in more harm than good, except you do it from and with genuine charity of soul—with some of that love, in short, which is the heart of religion. Except what is done for them is so done as to draw out their trust and affection, and so raise them consciously in the human scale, it can only tend either to hurt their feelings and generate indignation, or to encourage fawning and beggary. But—"

"I am entirely of your mind," said Mr. Blackstone. "But do go on."

"I was going to add," said Miss Clare, "that while no other charity than this can touch the sore, a good deal might yet be effected by bare justice. It seems to me high time that we dropped talking about charity and took up the cry of justice.

"Is it just in the nation," she continued, "to abandon those who can do nothing to help themselves, to be preyed upon by bad landlords, railway companies, and dishonest tradespeople with their false weights, balances, and measures, and adulterations to boot—from all of which their more wealthy brethren are completely safe? Does not a nation exist for the protection of its parts? Have these no claims on the nation? Would you call it just in a family to abandon its less gifted to any moral or physical spoiler who might be bred within it?

"To say a citizen must take care of himself *may* be just in those cases where he *can* take care of himself, but *cannot* be just wherever that is impossible. A thousand causes, originating mainly in the neglect of their neighbors, have combined to sink the poor into a state of moral paralysis. Are we to say the paralyzed may be run over in our streets with impunity? *Must* they take care of themselves? Have we not to awake them to the very sense that life is worth caring for? I cannot but feel that the bond between such a neglected class, and any nation in which it is to be found, is only little stronger than that between slaves and their masters. Who could preach to them their duty to the nation, except on grounds which such a nation acknowledges only with the lips?"

"You have to prove, Miss Clare," said Mr. Morley, in a tone that seemed intended to imply that he was not in the least affected by mistimed eloquence, "that the relation is that of a family."

"I believe," she returned, "that it is closer than the mere human relation of the parts of any family. But, at all events, until we *are* their friends, it is worse then useless to pretend to be such. And until they feel that we are their friends, it is worse than useless to talk to them about God and religion. They will have none of it from our lips."

"Will they from any lips? Are they not already too far sunk toward the brutish to be capable of receiving any such rousing influence?" suggested Mr. Blackstone with a smile, evidently wishing to draw Miss Clare yet further.

"You turn me aside, Mr. Blackstone. I wanted to urge Mr. Morley to go into Parliament as spiritual member for the poor of our large towns. Besides, I know you don't think as your question would imply. As far as my experience guides me, I am bound to believe that there is a spot of soil in every heart sufficient for the growth of a gospel seed. And I believe, moreover, that not only is he a fellow worker with God who sows that seed, but that he also is one who opens a way for that seed to enter the soil. If such preparation were not necessary, the Saviour would have come the moment Adam and Eve fell, and would have required no Baptist to precede Him."

A good deal followed which I would gladly record, but I fear I have already given too much conversation.

SEVENTEEN

The End of the Evening

A special delight during the evening was the marked attention, and the serious look in the eyes, with which Roger listened. It was not often that he did look serious. He preferred, if possible, to get a joke out of a thing; but when he did enter into an argument, he was always fair.

Mr. Morley, on the other hand, seemed an insoluble mass, incapable of receiving impressions from other minds. He regarded any suggestion of his own mind as reasonable and right, and was more than ordinarily prejudiced in his own favor. The day after they thus met at our house, Miss Clare had a letter from him, in which he took the high hand with her, rebuking her solemnly for her presumption in saying, as he represented it, that no good could be done except after the fashion she had laid down, and assuring her that she would thus alienate valuable assistance for any scheme to ameliorate the condition of the lower classes. It ended with the offer of a yearly subscription of five pounds to any project of the wisdom of which she would take the trouble to convince him. She replied, thanking him both for his advice and his offer, but saying that, as she had no scheme on foot requiring such assistance, she could not at present accept the offer. However, should anything show itself for which that sort of help was desirable, she would take the liberty of reminding him of it.

When the ladies rose, Judy took me aside, and said, "What does it all mean, Wynnie?"

"Just what you hear," I answered.

"You asked us, just to have a triumph over me, you naughty thing."

"Well, partly—if I am to be honest—but far more to make you do justice to Miss Clare. You being my cousin, she had a right to that at my hands."

"Does Lady Bernard know as much about her as she seems?"

"She knows everything about her, and visits her too, in her very questionable abode. You see, Judy, a report may be a fact and yet be untrue."

"I'm not going to be lectured by a chit like you. But I should like to have a little talk with Miss Clare."

"I will make you an opportunity."

I did so, and could not help overhearing a very pretty apology, to which Miss Clare replied that she feared she only was to blame, inasmuch as she ought to have explained the peculiarity of her circumstances before accepting the engagement. It had not appeared to her necessary, she said; but now she would make a point of explaining before she accepted any fresh duty of the kind, for she saw it would be fairer to both parties. It was no wonder such an answer should entirely disarm cousin Judy, who forthwith begged she would, if she had no objection, resume her lessons with the children at the commencement of the next quarter.

"But I understand from Mrs. Percivale," objected Miss Clare, "that the office is filled to your satisfaction."

"Yes, the lady I have is an excellent teacher, but the engagement was only for a quarter."

"If you have no other reason for parting with her, I could not think of stepping into her place. It would be a great disappointment to her, and my want of openness with you would be the cause of it. If you should part with her for any other reason, I should be very glad to serve you again."

Judy tried to argue with her, but Miss Clare was immovable.

"Will you let me come and see you, then?" said Judy.

"With all my heart," she answered. "You had better come with Mrs. Percivale, though, for it would not be easy for you to find the place."

We went up to the drawing room to tea, passing through the study, and taking the gentlemen with us. Miss Clare played to us, and sang several songs.

When my husband would have put her into Lady Bernard's carriage, as they were leaving, she said she should prefer walking home; and, as Lady Bernard did not press her to the contrary, Percivale could not remonstrate. "I am sorry I cannot walk with you, Miss Clare," he said. "I must not leave my duties, but—"

"There's not the slightest occasion," she interrupted. "I know every yard of the way. Good night."

The carriage drove off in one direction, and Miss Clare tripped lightly along in the other. Percivale darted into the house and told Roger, who snatched up his hat and bounded after her. Already she was out of sight; but he, following lightfooted, overtook her in the crescent. It was, however, only after persistent entreaty that he prevailed on her to allow him to accompany her.

"You do not know, Mr. Roger," she said pleasantly, "what you may be exposing yourself to, in going with me. I may have to do something you wouldn't like to have a share in."

"I shall be only too glad to have the humblest share in anything you draw me into," said Roger.

As it fell out, they had not gone far before they came upon a little crowd, chiefly of boys who ought to have been in bed long before, gathered about a man and woman. The man was forcing his company on a woman who was evidently annoyed that she could not get rid of him.

"Is he your husband?" asked Miss Clare, making her way through the crowd.

"No, Miss," the woman answered. "I never saw him afore. I'm only just come in from the country."

She looked more angry than frightened. Roger said her black eyes flashed dangerously, and she felt about the bosom of her dress—for a knife, he was certain.

"You leave her alone," he said to the man, getting between him and her.

"Mind your own business," returned the man, in a voice that showed he was drunk.

For a moment Roger was undecided what to do, for he feared involving Miss Clare in a row. But when the fellow pushed past him suddenly and laid his hand on Miss Clare and shoved her away, Roger gave him a blow that sent him staggering into the street. Whereupon, to his astonishment, Miss Clare left the woman, followed the man, and laid her hand on his arm and spoke to him, but in a voice so low and gentle that Roger could not hear a word. For a moment or two the man seemed to try to listen, but his condition was too much for him; and he rose and began to follow the woman again, who was now walking wearily away. Roger again interposed.

"Don't strike him, Mr. Roger," cried Miss Clare. "He's too drunk for that. But keep him back if you can, while I take the woman away. If I see a policeman, I will send him."

The man heard her last words, and they roused him to fury. He rushed at Roger, who only dodged and again confronted him, engaging his attention until help arrived. He was, however, by this time so fierce and violent, that Roger felt bound to assist the policeman.

As soon as the man was locked up, Roger went to Lime Court. The moon was shining and the narrow passage lay bright beneath her. Along the street people were going and coming, though it was past midnight, and the court was very still. He walked into it as far as the spot where we had together seen Miss Clare. The door at which she had entered was open, but he knew nothing of the house or its people, and feared to compromise her by making inquiries. He walked several times up and down, somewhat anxious, but gradually persuading himself that in all probability no further annoyance had befallen her, and at last he felt able to leave the place. He came back to our house, where, finding his brother at his final pipe in the study, he told him all about their adventure.

EIGHTEEN
My First Terror

I will pass lightly over the next two years—not because nothing of importance happened, but because what came after was of greater importance and still looms large in my heart.

On the fourth anniversary of our marriage, Percivale took a holiday in order to give me one, and we went to spend it at Richmond. We wanted to enjoy it thoroughly, and so left our children at home. (As precious as children are, not *every* pleasure is enhanced by their company!) I say *children,* for Ethel's brother Roger (named after Percivale's father) was now nearly a year old.

It was a lovely day, with just a sufficient number of passing clouds to glorify the sunshine, and a gentle breeze, which itself seemed to be taking a holiday, for it blew just when you wanted it, and then only enough to make you think of that wind which, blowing where it lists, always blows where it is wanted. We took the train to Hammersmith, for my husband wished to row me from there to Richmond. How gay the riverside looked, with its fine broad landing stage and the numberless boats ready to push off on the swift water! Percivale hired his boat at a certain builder's shed, that I might see the shed—such a picture of loveliest gloom—as if it had been the cave where the twilight abode its time! You could not tell whether to call it light or shade—that diffused presence of a soft elusive brown. But is what we call shade anything but subdued light?

Not having been used to boats, I felt nervous as we got into the long, sharp-nosed, hollow fish which Percivale made shoot out on the rising tide. Then the slight fear vanished almost the moment we were afloat. Ignorant as I was of the art of rowing, I could not help seeing how perfectly Percivale was at home in it. The oars in his hands were like knitting needles in mine, so deftly, so swimmingly, so variously, did he wield them. Only once my fear returned, when he stood up in the swaying thing—a mere length without breadth—to pull off his coat and waistcoat. But he stood steady, sat down gently, took his oars quietly, and the same instant we were shooting so fast through the rising tide that it seemed as if *we* were pulling the water up to Richmond.

How merrily the water rippled in the sun and the wind! And so responsive were our feelings to the play of light and shade around us, that more than once when a cloud crossed us, I saw its shadow turn almost into sadness on the countenance of my companion, to vanish the next moment when the one sun above and the thousand mimic suns below shone out in universal laughter. Percivale suffered me to steer us, and so when a steamer came in sight, or announced its approach by the far-heard sound of its beating paddles, it brought with it a few moments of almost awful responsibility. But I found that the presence of danger and duty together enabled me to concentrate on getting the head of the boat as nearly possible at right angles with the waves from the paddles, for Percivale had told me that if one of any size struck us on the side, it would most probably capsize us.

I will say nothing more of the delights of that day. They were such a contrast to its close, and I could not rid myself of the foolish feeling that our enjoyment had been somehow to blame for what was happening at home while we were thus reveling in blessed carelessness.

When we returned to our little nest, rather late in the evening, I found to my annoyance that the front door was open. It had been a fault of which I thought I had cured the cook—to leave it thus when she ran out to fetch anything. Percivale went down to the study, and I walked into the drawing room, about to ring the bell in anger. There, to my surprise and further annoyance, I found Sarah seated on the sofa with her head in her hands, and little Roger wide awake on the floor.

"What *does* this mean?" I cried. "The front door open! Master Roger still up!"

"O Ma'am!" she almost shrieked as she rose. "Have you found her, Ma'am?"

"Found whom?" I returned in alarm. Her face was very pale, and her eyes were red with crying.

"Miss Ethel," she answered in a cry choked with a sob, and dropping again on the sofa, she hid her face once more between her hands.

I rushed to the study door, and called Percivale, then returned to question the girl. I wonder now that I did nothing outrageous, but fear kept down folly and made me unnaturally calm.

"Sarah," I said, as quietly as I could, while I trembled all over, "tell me what has happened. Where is the child?"

"Indeed it's not my fault, Ma'am. I was busy with Master Roger, and Miss Ethel was downstairs with Jemima."

"Where is she?" I repeated sternly.

"I don't know no more than the man in the moon, Ma'am."

"Where's Jemima? Run out to look for her? How long have you missed her?"

"An hour, or perhaps two hours. I don't know, my head's in such a whirl. I can't remember when I saw her last. O Ma'am! What *shall* I do?"

Percivale had come up and was standing beside me. When I looked round, he was as pale as death, and at the sight of his face, I nearly dropped on the floor. But he caught hold of me and said, in a voice so dreadfully still that it frightened me more than anything, "Come, my love—don't give way, for we must go to the police at once." Then, turning to Sarah, "Have you searched the house and garden?"

"Yes, Sir. Every hole and every corner. We've looked under every bed, and into every cupboard and chest—the coal cellar, the boxroom—everywhere."

"Have there been any tramps about the house since we left?" Percivale asked.

"Not that I know of, but the nursery window looks into the garden, you know, Sir. Jemima didn't mention it."

"Come, my dear," said my husband, and he led me away to the nearest cabstand. He glanced calmly along the line and chose the horse whose appearance promised the best speed. In a few minutes we were telling the inspector at the police station in Albany Street what had happened. He asked one question after another about her age, appearance, and dress, and wrote down our answers. He then gave the paper and some words of direction to another man.

"The men are now going on their beats for the night," he said, turning again to us. "They will all hear the description of the child."

"Thank you," said my husband. "Which station had we better go to next?"

"The news will be at the farthest before you can reach the nearest," he answered. "We shall telegraph to the suburbs first."

"Then what more can we do?" asked Percivale.

"Nothing," said the inspector, "except you find out whether any of the neighbors saw her, and when and where. It would be something to know in what direction she was going. Have you any ground for suspicion? Have you ever discharged a servant? Were any tramps seen about the place?"

"I know who it is!" I cried. "It's the woman that took Theodora! It's Theodora's mother! I know it is!"

Percivale explained what I meant.

"That's what people get, you see, when they take on themselves other people's business," returned the inspector. "That child ought to have been sent to the workhouse. But I have your address," he continued. "The child shall be brought back to you the moment she's found."

"Where are you going now?" I said to my husband, as we left the station to reenter the cab.

"I don't know," he answered, "except we go home and question all the shops in the neighborhood."

"Let us go to Miss Clare first," I said.

"By all means," he answered, and soon we were at the entrance of Lime Court.

When we turned the corner, we heard the sound of a piano. We entered the house and ascended the stairs in haste, hearing now the sounds of dancing as well as of music. In a moment, with our load of gnawing fear and helpless eagerness, we stood in the midst of a merry assembly of men, women and children, who filled Miss Clare's room to overflowing.

They made way for us, and Miss Clare left the piano, and came to meet us with a smile on her beautiful face. But when she saw our faces, hers fell.

"What *is* the matter, Mrs. Percivale?" she asked in alarm.

"We've lost Ethel," said my husband quietly.

"What do you mean? You don't—"

"No, no: she's gone—stolen. We don't know where she is," he answered with faltering voice. "We've just been to the police."

Miss Clare turned white. But, instead of making any remark, she called out to some of her friends whose good manners were making them leave the room.

"Don't go, please—we want you." Then turning to me, she asked, "May I do as I think best?"

"Yes, certainly," answered my husband.

"My friend, Mrs. Percivale," she said, addressing the whole assembly, "has lost her little girl."

A murmur of dismay and sympathy arose.

"What can we do to find her?" she went on.

They fell to talking among themselves. Then two men came up to us—one a keen-faced, elderly man, with iron-gray whiskers and clean-shaved chin, the other a young bricklayer. The elder addressed my husband, while the other listened without speaking.

"Tell us what she's like, Sir, and how she was dressed—though that ain't much use. She'll be different by this time."

The words shot a keen pang to my heart. My darling stripped of her nice clothes and covered with dirty, perhaps infected garments!

My husband repeated the description he had given the police, loud enough for the whole room to hear.

"Tell them also, please, Mr. Percivale, about the child Mrs. Percivale's father and mother found and brought up. That may have something to do with this."

My husband told them all the story, adding that the mother of the child might have found out who we were, and taken ours as a pledge for the recovery of her own.

Here one of the women spoke. "That dark woman you took in one night—two years ago, Miss Clare—she say something. I was astin' of her on the mornin' what her trouble was, for that trouble *she* had on *her* mind was plain to see, and she come over something, halfway like, about losin' of a child. But whether it were dead or strayed or stolen or what, I couldn't tell—and no more, I believe, she wanted me to."

Here another woman spoke. "I'm most sure I saw her—the same woman—two days ago, and no furrer off than Gower Street," she said. "You're too good by half, Miss," she went on, "to the likes of sich. They ain't none of them respectable."

"Perhaps you'll see some good come out of it before long," said Miss Clare in reply.

The words sounded like a rebuke, for all this time I had hardly sent a thought upward for help. The image of my child had so filled my heart, that there was no room left for the thought of duty, or even of God.

Miss Clare went on, still addressing the company, and her words had a tone of authority. "I will tell you what you must do, every one of you. Run and tell everybody you know, and tell everyone to tell everybody else. No time should be lost in making it as quickly and as widely known as possible. Go, please."

In a few moments the room was empty of all but ourselves. The rush on the stairs was tremendous for a single minute, and then all was still. Even the children had rushed out to tell what other children they could find.

"What must we do next?" said my husband.

"I would go and tell Mr. Blackstone," Miss Clare said. "It is a long way from here, but whoever has taken the child would not be likely to linger in the neighborhood. It is best to try everything."

"Right," said my husband. "Come, Wynnie."

We parted instantly, and drove to Mr. Blackstone's. What a long way it was! Down Oxford Street and Holborn we rattled and jolted, and then through many narrow ways, emerging at length in a broad road with many poor and a few fine old houses in it. We found the parsonage, and Mr. Blackstone in his study. The moment he heard our story he went to the door and called his servant. "Run, Jabez," he said, "and tell the sexton to ring the church bell. I will come to him directly I hear it."

About ten minutes passed, during which little was said. When the first boom of the big bell filled the little study in which we sat, I gave a cry and jumped up from my chair: it sounded in my ears like the knell of my lost baby, for at the moment I was thinking of her as once when a baby she lay for dead in my arms. Mr. Blackstone got up and left the room. It was a dreadful half hour before he returned; to sit doing nothing, not even being carried somewhere to do something, was frightful.

"I've told them all about it," he said. "I couldn't do better than follow Miss Clare's example. But my impression is that if the woman you suspect be the culprit, she would make her way out to the open as quickly as possible. Such people are most at home on the commons. They are of a less gregarious nature than the wild animals of the town. What shall you do next?"

"That is just what I want to know," answered my husband. He never asked advice except when he did not know what to do, and never except from one whose advice he meant to follow.

"Well," returned Mr. Blackstone, "I should put an advertisement into every one of the morning papers."

"But the offices will all be closed," said Percivale.

"Yes, the publishing, but not the printing offices. I know one or two of them, and the people there will tell us the rest."

"Then you mean to go with us?"

"Of course I do—that is, if you will have me. You don't think I would leave you to go alone?"

So we all left, and found a cab outside.

"Are you sure," said my husband, "that they will take an advertisement at the printing office?"

"I think they will. The circumstances are pressing. They will see that we are honest people, and will help us."

"We must pay, though," said Percivale, putting his hand in his pocket, and taking out his purse. "There! Just as I feared! No money—two—three shillings—and sixpence!"

Mr. Blackstone stopped the cab. "I've got as much," he said. "But it's of no consequence. I'll borrow five pounds at the Blue Posts."

"Let me do it, then," said Percivale. "You shouldn't be seen going into a public house."

"Pooh!" said Mr. Blackstone. "Do you think my character won't stand that much? Besides, they wouldn't do it for you."

We drove on to the Blue Posts. He got out, and returned in one minute with five sovereigns.

"What will people say to your borrowing five pounds at a public house?" said Percivale.

"If they say what is right, it won't hurt me."

"But if they say what is wrong?"

"That they can do any time, and that won't hurt me either."

"But what will the landlord think himself?"

"I have no doubt he feels grateful to me for being so friendly. You can't oblige a man more than by asking a *light* favor of him."

"Do you think it well in your position to be obliged to a man in his?" asked Percivale.

"I do. I am glad of the chance. It will bring me into friendly relations with him. I have done quite a stroke of business in borrowing that money of him."

Mr. Blackstone laughed, and the laugh sounded frightfully harsh in my ears.

"A man"—my husband went on, who was surprised that a clergyman should be so liberal—"a man who sells drink! In whose house so many of your parishioners will tomorrow night get too drunk to be in church the next morning!"

"I wish having been drunk were what *would* keep them from being in church. Drunk or sober, it would be all the same. Few of them care to go. They are turning out better, however, than when I first came. As for the publican, who knows what chance of doing him a good turn it may put in my way?"

"You don't expect to persuade him to shut up shop?"

"No. He must persuade himself to do that. But you can't tell what good may or may not come out of it, any more than you can tell which of your efforts, or which of your helpers, may this night be the means of restoring your child."

"What, then, do you mean to tell him?" asked Percivale.

"The truth, the whole truth, and nothing but the truth," said Mr. Blackstone. "I shall go in tomorrow morning, just at the time when there will probably be far too many people in the bar—a little after noon. I shall return him his five sovereigns, ask for a glass of ale, and tell him the whole story—how my friend, the celebrated painter, came with his wife, and the rest of it, adding, I trust, that the child is all right, and at the moment probably going out for a walk with her mother, who won't let her out of her sight for a moment."

He laughed again, and again I thought him heartless, but I understood him better now. I wonder too that Percivale *could* go on talking, and yet I found that their talk did make the time go a little quicker. At length we reached the printing office of *The Times*, where an overseer agreed to find the best place in the morning paper for our advertisement.

We spent the greater part of the night in driving from one printing office to another. Mr. Blackstone declared he would not leave us until we had found her.

"You have to preach twice tomorrow," said Percivale. It was then three o'clock.

"I shall preach all the better," he returned. "I shall give them *one* good sermon tomorrow."

"The man talks as if the child were found already!" I thought, with indignation. "It's a pity he hasn't a child of his own. He would be more sympathetic." At the same time, if I had been honest, I should have confessed to myself that his confidence and hope helped to keep me up.

At last, having been to the printing office of every daily paper in London, we were on our dreary way home.

Oh, how dreary it was, and the more dreary that the cool, sweet light of a spring dawn was growing in every street, no smoke having yet begun to pour from the chimneys to sully its purity! From misery and want of sleep, my soul and body both felt like a gray foggy night. Every now and then the thought of my child came with a fresh pang. I pictured her little face—white with terror and misery and smeared with the dirt of the pitiful hands that rubbed the streaming eyes. They might have beaten her! She might have cried herself to sleep in some wretched hovel, or worse, in some fever-stricken and crowded lodging house, with horrible sights about her and horrible voices in her ears! Or she might at that moment be dragged wearily along a country road, farther and farther from her mother! I could have shrieked, and torn my hair. What if I should never see her again? She might be murdered, and I never know it!

At that thought a groan escaped my lips. My husband laid his hand on my arm, and Mr. Blackstone's voice was in my ear.

"Do you think God loves the child less than you do? Or do you think He is less able to take care of her than you are? When the disciples thought themselves sinking, Jesus rebuked them for being afraid. Be still, and you will see the hand of God in this. Good you cannot foresee will come out of it."

I could not answer him, but I felt both rebuked and grateful. Then all at once I thought of Roger. What would he say when he found that his pet was gone, and we had never told him?

"Roger!" I said to my husband. "We've never told him!"

"Let us go now," he returned.

When we arrived, Percivale rushed up the stairs and returned with Roger. They got into the cab, and a great talk followed. Roger was very indignant with his brother for having been out all night without him to help.

"I never thought of you, Roger," said Percivale.

"So much the worse!" said Roger.

"No," said Mr. Blackstone. "A thousand things make us forget. I dare say your brother all but forgot God in the first misery of his loss. To have thought of you—and not to have told you—would have been another thing."

A few minutes after, we stopped at our desolate house, where only a dim light was burning in the drawing room. Percivale took his passkey and opened the front door. I hurried in, and went straight to my own room, for I longed to be alone that I might weep, but not only weep. I fell on my knees by the bedside, buried my face and sobbed and tried to pray. But I could not collect my thoughts and, overwhelmed by a fresh access of despair, I started again to my feet.

Could I believe my eyes? What was that on the bed? Trembling in terror lest the vision vanish, I stooped toward it. It was my darling fast asleep, without one trace of suffering on her angelic loveliness! They tell me I gave a great cry and fell on the floor. When I came to, I was lying on the bed, my husband bending over me, and Roger and Mr. Blackstone both in the room. I could not speak, but my husband understood me.

"Yes, yes, my love," he said quietly, "she's all right—safe and sound, thank God!"

And I did thank God.

Mr. Blackstone came to the bedside, with a look and a smile that seemed to my conscience to say, "I told you so." I held out my hand to him, but could only weep.

Then I remembered how we had vexed Roger, and I called to him. "Dear Roger," I said, "forgive me, and go and tell Miss Clare."

I had some reason to think this the best amends I could make him.

"I will go at once," he said. "She will be anxious."

"And I will go to my sermon," said Mr. Blackstone, with the same quiet smile.

They shook hands with me, and went away. And my husband and I rejoiced over our firstborn.

NINETEEN
The Aftermath

Later we found that my darling had been recovered by the police, and not through Miss Clare's injunctions or Mr. Blackstone's bell ringing. A woman had been walking steadily westward, carrying the child asleep in her arms, when a policeman stopped her at Turnham Green. She betrayed no fear, only annoyance, and offered no resistance, only begged he would not wake the child, or take her from her. He brought them in a cab to the station house, whence the child was sent home. As soon as Ethel arrived, Sarah gave her a warm bath and put her to bed, but she scarcely opened her eyes.

Jemima had run about the streets till midnight, and then fallen asleep on the doorstep, where the policeman found her when he brought the child. (For a week she went about like one dazed, and the blunders she made were marvelous. She ordered a brace of cod from the poulterer, and a pound of anchovies at the crockery shop. One day at dinner, we could not think how the chops were so pulpy, and why we got so many bits of bone in our mouth: she had powerfully beaten them, as if they had been steaks. She sent up melted butter for bread sauce, and stuffed a hare with sausages.)

After breakfast, Percivale walked to the police station to thank the inspector, pay what expenses had been incurred, and see the woman. I was not well enough to go with him and I suggested that he should take Miss Clare. She accompanied him willingly, and recognized the woman as the one she had befriended.

Percivale told the magistrate he did not wish to punish her, but that there were certain circumstances which made him desirous of detaining her until a gentleman who could identify her should arrive. The magistrate therefore remanded her.

The next day but one my father came. When he saw the woman, he had little doubt she was the same who had carried off Theo. He told the magistrate the whole story, saying that if she should prove the mother of the child, he was most anxious to do what he could for her. The magistrate expressed grave doubts whether he would find it possible to befriend her to any effectual degree.

Now came the benefit of the kindness Miss Clare had shown the woman. I doubt if anyone else could have got the truth from her. Even she found it difficult, for to tell her that if she was Theo's mother she should not be punished, might be only to tempt her to lie. All Miss Clare could do was to assure her of the kindness of everyone concerned, and to urge her to disclose her reasons for doing such a grievous wrong as to steal another woman's child.

"*They* stole *my* child," she blurted out at last, when the cruelty of the action was pressed upon her.

"Oh, no!" said Miss Clare. "You left her to die in the cold."

"No, no!" she cried. "I wanted somebody to hear her and take her in. I wasn't far off, and was just going to take her again, when I saw a light, and heard them searching for her. Oh, dear! Oh, dear!"

"Then how can you say they stole her? You would have had no child at all, but for them. She was nearly dead when they found her. And in return you go and steal their grandchild!"

"They took her from me afterward. They wouldn't let me have my own flesh and blood. I wanted to let them know what it was like to have *their* child taken from them."

"How could they tell she was your child, when you stole her away like that? It might, for anything they knew, be some other woman stealing her, as you stole theirs the other day. What would have become of you if it had been so?"

To this reasoning she made no answer, but only moaned, "I want my child—I want my child. I shall kill myself if I don't get my child! O, Lady, you don't know what it is to have a child and not have her! I shall kill myself if they don't let me have her back. They can't say I did their child any harm. I was as good to her as if she had been my own."

"They know that quite well, and don't want to punish you. Would you like to see your child?"

She clasped her hands above her head, fell on her knees at Miss Clare's feet, and looked up in her face without uttering a word.

"I will speak to Mr. Walton," said Miss Clare, and left her.

The next morning the woman was discharged with the warning that, if ever she came to the attention of the law again, this would be brought up against her, and she would have the severest punishment the law could inflict. It may be right to pass a first offense, and wrong to pass a second.

My husband brought her home with him. Sympathy with the mother-passion in her bosom had melted away my resentment. She was a fine young woman, about twenty-five, though her weather-browned complexion made her look much older. With the help of the servants, I persuaded her to have a bath, during which they removed her clothes and substituted others. She objected to putting them on—seemed half-frightened at them, as if they might involve some shape of bondage, and begged to have her own again. At last Jemima (who, although so sparingly provided with brains, is not without genius) prevailed upon her, insisting that her little girl would turn away from her if she wasn't well dressed, for she had been used to seeing ladies about her. With a deep sigh, she yielded, begging, however, to have her old garments restored to her.

She had brought with her a small bundle tied up in a cotton handkerchief, and from it she now took a scarf of red silk, and twisted it up with her black hair in a fashion I had never seen before. In this headdress she had almost a brilliant look, while her carriage had a certain dignity. My husband admired her even more than I did, and made a very good sketch of her. Her eyes were large and dark—unquestionably fine—and if there was not much of the light of thought in them, they had a certain wildness which in a measure made up for want. She had a Spanish rather than an Eastern look, I thought, with an air of defiance that prevented me from feeling at ease with her. In the presence of Miss Clare she seemed humbler, and answered her questions more readily than ours. If Ethel was in the room, her eyes would be constantly wandering after her, with a wistful, troubled, eager look. Surely, the mother-passion must have infinite relations and destinies.

As I was unable to leave home, my father persuaded Miss Clare to accompany him and help him to take charge of her. I confess it was a relief to me when she left the house; for though I wanted to be as kind to her as I could, I felt considerable discomfort in her presence.

When Miss Clare returned, the next day but one, I found she had learned the main points of the woman's history, fully justifying my father's previous conjectures.

She belonged to one of the principal gypsy families in this country. The fact that they had no settled habitation but lived in tents, like Abraham and Isaac, had nothing to do with poverty. The silver buttons on her father's coat were, she had said, worth nearly twenty pounds. When friends of any distinction came to tea with them, they spread a tablecloth of fine linen on the grass, and set out upon it the best of china, and a tea service of hallmarked silver. She said her friends scorned stealing, and affirmed that no real gypsy would "risk his neck for his belly," except he were driven by hunger. All her family could read, she said, and they carried a big Bible with them.

One summer they were encamped (as was their custom) for several months in the neighborhood of Edinburgh, making horn spoons and baskets, and some of them working in tin. There they were visited by a clergyman, who talked and read the Bible to them and prayed with them. But all their visitors were not of the same sort. One young fellow of loose character, a clerk in the city, was attracted by her appearance and prevailed upon her to meet him often. She was not then eighteen. Any aberration from the paths of modesty is exceedingly rare among the gypsies, and regarded with severity. Therefore, her father gave her a terrible punishment with the whip he used in driving his horses. In terror of what would follow when the worst came to be known, she ran away. She was soon forsaken by her so-called lover, and wandered about, a common vagrant, until her baby was born—under the stars on a summer night, in a field of long grass.

For some time she wandered up and down, longing to join a tribe of her own people, but dreading unspeakably the disgrace of her motherhood. At length, having found a home with our family for her child, she associated herself with a gang of gypsies of inferior character, amongst whom she had many hardships to endure. Although she had no intention of carrying off her child to share her present lot, the urgings of mere mother-hunger drove her to the Hall for a sight of her child. When she had succeeded in enticing her out of sight of the house, however, the longing to possess her grew fierce and—braving all consequences, or unable to weigh them—she did carry her away. Foiled in this attempt, and seeing that her chances of future success in any similar one were diminished by it, she sought some other plan. Learning that one of the family had married and moved to London, she succeeded, through gypsy acquaintances who lodged occasionally near Tottenham Court Road, in finding out where we lived. Then she arrived off Ethel with the vague intent, as we had conjectured, of using her to recover her own child.

Theodora was now about seven years of age and almost as wild as ever. Miss Clare was present with my father and the rest of the family when the mother and daughter met. They were all more than curious to see how the child would behave, and whether there would be any instinct to draw her to her parent. In this, however, they were disappointed.

It was a fine warm forenoon when she came running onto the lawn where they were assembled, the gypsy mother with them.

"There she is!" said my father to the woman. "Make the best of yourself you can."

Miss Clare said the poor creature turned very pale, but her eyes glowed with such a fire!

With the cunning of her race, she knew better than to bound forward and catch up the child in her arms. She walked away from the rest and stood watching the little damsel romp merrily with Mr. Wagtail. They thought she recognized the dog and was afraid of him. She had put on a few silver ornaments which she had either kept or managed to procure, notwithstanding her poverty. The glittering of these in the sun, and the glow of her red satin scarf in her dark hair, along with the strangeness of her whole appearance, attracted the child who approached to look at her. Then the mother took from her pocket a large gilded ball and rolled it gleaming along the grass. Theo and Mr. Wagtail bounded after it with a shriek and a bark. The child examined it for a moment and threw it again along the lawn, and this time the mother, lithe as a leopard and fleet as a savage, joined in the chase, caught it first, and again sent it spinning away, farther from the assembled group. Once more all three followed in swift pursuit, but this time the mother allowed the child to seize the treasure. After the sport had continued a little while, a general consultation of mother, child, and dog took place over the bauble, and presently the watchers saw that Theo was eating something.

"I trust," said my mother, "she won't hurt the child with any nasty stuff."

"She will not do so wittingly," said my father, "you may be sure. Anyhow, we must not interfere."

In a few minutes more the mother approached them with a subdued look of triumph, and her eyes overflowed with light, carrying the child in her arms. Theo was playing with some foreign coins which adorned her hair, and with a string of coral and silver beads round her neck.

For the rest of the day they were left to do much as they pleased—only everyone kept watch.

In the joy of recovering her child, the mother seemed herself to have gained a new and childlike spirit. She hastened to do what was requested of her, as if she fully acknowledged the right of authority in those now around her. Whether this would last when the novelty of the new experience had worn off, whether jealousy would not then come in for its share in the ordering of her conduct, remained to be shown; but in the meantime the good in her was uppermost.

She was allowed to spend a whole fortnight in making friends with her daughter, before a word was spoken about the future, for the design of my father was to win the mother through the child. (Certain people considered him not eager enough to convert the wicked. Whatever apparent indifference he showed in that direction arose from his utter belief in the guiding of God, and his dread of outrunning His designs. He would *follow* the operations of the Spirit. "Your forced hothouse fruits," he would say, "are often finer to look at than those which have waited for God's wind and weather, but what are they worth in respect of all for the sake of which fruit exists?")

Until an opportunity, then, was thrown his way, he would hold back. But when it was clear to him that he had to minister, then he was thoughtful, watchful, instant, and unswerving. You might have seen him during this time, as the letters of Connie informed me, often standing for a time watching the mother and daughter, and pondering in his heart concerning them. The fortnight had not passed before, to all appearance, the unknown mother had become the greatest favorite of the child.

One twilight, he overheard the following talk between them. When they came near where he sat, Theodora, carried by her mother, and pulling at her neck with her arms, was saying, "Tell me! Tell me! Tell me!" in the tone of one who would compel an answer to a question repeatedly asked in vain.

"What do you want me to tell you?" said the mother.

"You know well enough. Tell me your name."

In reply she uttered a few words my father did not comprehend. The child shook her petulantly and with violence crying, "That's nonsense. I don't know what you say, and I don't know what to call you."

My father had desired the household, if possible, to give no name to the woman in the child's hearing.

"Call me Ma'am, if you like."

"But you're not a lady, and I won't say Ma'am to you," said Theo, rude as a child will sometimes be when she least intends offense.

Her mother set her down and gave a deep sigh. Was it only that the child's restlessness and roughness tired her? My father thought otherwise.

"Tell me! Tell me!" the child persisted, beating her with her little clenched fist. "Take me up again, and tell me, or I will make you."

My father thought it time to interfere. As he stepped forward, the mother started with a little cry and caught up the child.

"Theo," said my father, "I cannot allow you to be rude, especially to one who loves you more than anyone else loves you."

The woman set her down again, dropped on her knees, and caught and kissed his hand. The child stared, but she stood in awe of my father, and perhaps the more that she had none for anyone else. When her mother lifted her once more she was carried away in silence.

The difficulty was solved by telling the child to call the woman *Nurse.*

My father was now sufficiently satisfied with immediate results to carry out the remainder of his contingent plan, of which my mother heartily approved. The gardener and his wife were elderly and without family, and therefore did not require the whole of their cottage, which was within a short distance of the house. My mother arranged their spare room for the gypsy, and there she was housed, with free access to her child, and the understanding that when Theo liked to sleep with her, she was at liberty to do so.

But before long her old habits were working in her and making her restless. She was pining after the liberty of her old wandering life, with sun and wind, space and change, all about her. It was spring, and the reviving life of nature was rousing in her the longing for motion and room and variety. My father had foreseen the probability, and had already thought over what could be done for her if the wandering passion should revive too powerfully. He reasoned that there was nothing bad in such an impulse—one doubtless felt by Abraham himself—however much its indulgence might place her at a disadvantage in the midst of a settled social order. He saw too that the love of her child could, like an elastic but infrangible cord, gradually tame her down to a more settled life.

He proposed, therefore, that she go and visit her parents and let them know of her welfare. She looked alarmed.

"Your father will show you no unkindness, I am certain, after the lapse of so many years," he added. "Think it over, and tell me tomorrow how you feel about it. You shall go by train to Edinburgh, and once there you may find them. The child will be safe with us till you come back."

So she went, found her people, spent a fortnight with them, and returned. The rest of that year she remained quietly at home, stilling her desires by frequent and long rambles with her child. Mr. Wagtail alone accompanied them, for my father thought it better to run the risk of her escaping than to force the thought on her by appearing not to trust her. She no doubt suspected that the dog was there to prevent, or at least expose, any such imprudence. The following spring she went on a second visit to her friends, but was back within a week, and the next year did not go at all.

My father continued to do what he could to teach her, presenting every truth as something it was necessary she should teach her child. With this duty, he said, he always baited the hook with which he fished for her.

What will be the final result, who dares to prophesy? At my old home she still resides—grateful, and in some measure useful, idolizing, but not altogether spoiling her child, who understands the relation between them and now calls her Mother.

Dora teaches Theo, and the mother comes in for what share she inclines to appropriate. She does not take much to reading, but she is fond of listening, and is a regular and devout attendant at public worship. Above all, they have sufficing proof that her conscience is awake, and that she gives some heed to what it says.

Mr. Blackstone was right when he told me that good would result from the loss which then drowned me in despair.

TWENTY
Troubles

In the beginning of the following year, the lady who filled Miss Clare's music-teaching position with the Morleys was married, and Miss Clare resumed the teaching of Judy's children.

In the spring, great trouble fell upon the Morleys. One of the children was taken with scarlet fever, and then another and another in such rapid succession—until five of them were lying ill together. Cousin Judy would accept no assistance in nursing them, beyond that of her own maids. But then her strength gave way, and she contracted the infection herself in the form of diphtheria, and was compelled to take to her bed.

There she lay moaning, with her eyes shut, when a hand was laid in hers and Miss Clare's voice came in her ear. She had come to give her usual lesson to one of the girls who had as yet escaped the infection, and when she heard that Mrs. Morley had been taken ill, she walked straight to her room.

"Go away!" said Judy. "Do you want to die too?"

"Dear Mrs. Morley," said Miss Clare, "I will just run home and make a few arrangements, and then come back and nurse you."

"Never mind me," said Judy. "The children! The children! What shall I do?"

"I am quite able to look after you all, if you will allow me to bring a young woman to help me."

"You are an angel!" said poor Judy. "But there is no occasion to bring anyone with you. My servants are quite competent."

"I must have everything in my own hands," said Miss Clare, "and therefore must have someone who will do exactly as I tell her. This girl has been with me now for some time, and I can depend upon her."

"Do whatever you like, you blessed creature," said Judy. "If any one of my servants behaves improperly to you, or neglects your orders, she shall go as soon as I am up again."

"I would rather give them as little opportunity as I can of running the risk. If I may bring this friend of my own, I shall soon have the house under hospital regulations."

She had hardly left the room before Judy fell asleep. Ere she awoke, Miss Clare was in a cab on her way back to the Morley residence on Bolivar Square, with her friend and two carpetbags. Within an hour, she had entrenched herself in a spare bedroom, lighted a fire, arranged all the medicines on a chest of drawers, made the rounds of the patients (who were all in adjoining rooms) and the rounds of the house to see that the disinfectants were fresh and active, added to their number, and then gone to await the arrival of the medical attendant in Mrs. Morley's room.

"Dr. Brand might have been a little more gracious," said Judy, "but I thought it better not to interrupt him by explaining that you were not the professional nurse he took you for."

"Indeed, there was no occasion," answered Miss Clare. "I should have told him so myself, had it not been that I have done a nurse's regular work in St. George's Hospital. Anyhow, I understood every word he said."

Meeting Mr. Morley in the hall, the doctor advised him not to go near his wife, diptheria being so infectious, but comforted him with the assurance that the nurse appeared an intelligent young person who would attend to all his directions. He added, "I could have wished that she had been older, but there is a great deal of illness about, and experienced nurses are scarce."

Miss Clare was a week in the house before Mr. Morley saw her, or knew she was there. One evening, needing brandy for medicine, she ran down to the dining room where he sat over his lonely glass of Madeira, and went straight to the sideboard. As she turned to leave the room, he recognized her and said, in some astonishment, "You need not trouble yourself, Miss Clare. The nurse can get what she wants from Hawkins. Indeed, I don't see—"

"Excuse me, Mr. Morley. If you wish to speak to me, I will return in a few minutes, but I have a good deal to attend to now."

She left the room and, as he had said nothing in reply, she did not return.

Two days after, about the same hour, whether suspecting the fact, or for some other reason, he requested the butler to send the nurse to him.

"The nurse from the nursery, Sir, or the young person as teaches the young ladies the piano?" asked Hawkins.

"I mean the sick-nurse," said his master.

In a few minutes Miss Clare entered the dining room and approached Mr. Morley.

"How do you do, Miss Clare?" he said stiffly, for to anyone in his employment he was gracious only now and then. "Allow me to say that I doubt the propriety of your being here so much. You cannot fail to carry the infection. I think your lessons had better be postponed until *all* your pupils are able to benefit by them. I have just sent for the nurse, and, if you please—"

"Yes. Hawkins told me you wanted me," said Miss Clare.

"I did not want you. He must have been mistaken."

"I *am* the nurse, Mr. Morley."

"Then I *must* say it is not with my approval!" he returned, rising from his chair in anger. "I was given to understand that a properly qualified person was in charge of my wife and family. This is no ordinary case, where a little coddling is all that is wanted."

"I am perfectly qualified, Mr. Morley."

He walked up and down the room several times, and said, "I must speak to Mrs. Morley about this."

"I entreat you will not disturb her. She is not well this afternoon."

"How *is* this, Miss Clare? Pray explain to me how you have come to take a part in the affairs of this family so very different from that arranged between Mrs. Morley and yourself."

"It is but an illustration of the law of supply and demand," answered Miss Clare. "A nurse was wanted, Mrs. Morley had strong objections to a hired nurse, and I was very glad to be able to set her mind at rest."

"It was very obliging of you, no doubt," he returned, "but—but—"

"Let us leave it thus for the present, if you please, for while I am nurse, I must mind my business. Dr. Brand expresses himself quite satisfied with me, and it is better for the children, not to mention Mrs. Morley, to have someone they are used to."

She left the room without waiting for further parley.

When a terrible time of anxiety was at length over, during which one after another, and especially Judy herself, had been in great danger, Dr. Brand assured Mr. Morley that, but for the vigilance and intelligence of Miss Clare, he did not believe he could have brought Mrs. Morley through.

Judy and the little Morleys had recovered so far that they were to set out the next morning for Hastings, when Mr. Morley sent for Miss Clare once more.

"I hope you will accompany them, Miss Clare," he said. "By this time you must be in no small need of a change yourself."

"The best change for me will be Lime Court," she answered, laughing. "I am anxious about my friends there. I fear they have not been getting on quite so well without me. A Bible woman and a Roman Catholic have been quarreling dreadfully, I hear."

Mr. Morley compressed his lips. It *was* annoying to be so indebted to one who, from whatever motives, called such people her friends.

"Oblige me, then," he said loftily, taking an envelope from the mantle piece, and handing it to her, "by opening that at your leisure."

"I will open it now, if you please," she returned.

It contained a bank note for a hundred pounds. Mr. Morley, though a hard man, was not by any means stingy. She replaced it in the envelope, and laid it again upon the chimney piece.

"You owe me nothing, Mr. Morley," she said.

"Owe you nothing! I owe you more than I can ever repay."

"Then don't try it, please. You are *very* generous—but indeed I could not accept it."

"You must oblige me. You *might* take it from *me,*" he added, almost pathetically, as if the bond was so close that money was nothing between them.

"You are the last—one of the last—I *could* take money from, Mr. Morley."

"Why?"

"Because you think so much of it, and yet would look down on me all the more if I accepted it."

He bit his lip, rubbed his forehead with his hand, threw back his head, and turned away from her.

"I should be very sorry to offend you," she said, "and, believe me, there is hardly anything I value less than money. I have enough, and could have plenty more if I liked. I would rather have your friendship than all the money you possess. But that cannot be, so long as—"

"So long as what?"

"So long as you are a worshiper of mammon," she answered, and left the room.

This she told me later, saying, "I am afraid it was very wrong, and very rude as well. But just think—there was a generous heart, clogged up with self-importance and wealth! As he stood there on the hearthrug, he was a most pitiable object, with an impervious wall betwixt him and the kingdom of heaven! He seemed like a man in a terrible dream, from which I *must* awake him by calling aloud in his ear! Alas! The dream was not terrible to him, only to me! If he had been one of my poor friends, guilty of some plain fault, I should have told him so without compunction—and why not, being what he was? There he stood, a man of estimable qualities, of benevolence, if not bounty, no miser, nor consciously unjust, yet a man whose heart the moth and rust were eating into a sponge. A man who went to church every Sunday, and who had many friends, not one of whom, not even his own wife, would tell him that he was a mammon-worshiper and losing his life. It may have been useless, and it may have been wrong, but I felt driven to it by bare human pity."

Strange tableau—a young and poor woman, prophetlike, rebuking a wealthy London merchant on his own hearthrug, as a worshiper of mammon!

And no one can tell what effects the words may have had upon him. I do not believe he ever mentioned the circumstance to his wife. At all events, there was no change in her manner to Miss Clare. Indeed, I could not help fancying that a little halo of quiet reverence now encircled the love in every look Judy cast upon her.

She firmly believed that Miss Marion Clare had saved her life, and that of more than one of her children. Nothing, she said, could equal the quietness and tenderness and tirelessness of her nursing. She was never flurried, never impatient, and never frightened. Even when the tears would be flowing down her face, the light never left her eyes nor the music her voice. And when she had the nursery piano brought out on the landing in the middle of the sickrooms, and there played and sang to them, it was, she said, like the voice of an angel, come fresh to the earth with the same old news of peace and goodwill.

But even so, Miss Clare came out of it very pale and a good deal worn. The day the Morleys set off for Hastings, she returned to Lime Court. The next day she resumed her lessons, and soon recovered her usual appearance. A change of work, she always said, was the best restorative. But before a month was over, I succeeded in persuading her to accept my mother's invitation to spend a week at the Hall, and from this visit she returned quite invigorated.

TWENTY-ONE
Mr. Morley

As soon as my cousin Judy returned from Hastings, I called to see her, and found them all well restored except Amy, a child between eight and nine. There was nothing very definite the matter with her, but she was white and thin, and looked wistful; the blue of her eyes had grown pale, and her fair locks had nearly lost the curl which had so well suited her rosy cheeks. She had been her father's pride for her looks, and her mother's for her sayings—at once odd and simple.

Judy that morning reminded me of how, one night, when Amy was about three years old, she had gone to bed, and some time after had called out for her mother. There had been jam-making that day, and Judy feared Amy had been having more than the portion which on such an occasion fell to her share. But Amy only begged to be taken up that she might say her prayers over again. Amy accordingly kneeled by the bedside in her nightgown and, having gone over all her petitions from beginning to end, paused a moment before the final word, and inserted the following special and peculiar request: "And please, God, give me some more jam tomorrow-day, forever and ever. Amen."

(I remember my father being quite troubled when he heard that the child had been rebuked for offering what was probably her very first genuine prayer. The rebuke, however, had little effect on the petitioner, for she was fast asleep a moment after it.)

"There is one thing that puzzles and annoys me," said Judy. "I can't think what it means. My husband tells me that Miss Clare was so rude to him the day before we left for Hastings, that he would rather not be aware of it any time she was in the house. Those were his very words. 'I will not interfere with your doing as you think proper,' he said, 'seeing you consider yourself under such obligation to her. And I should be very sorry to deprive her of the advantage of giving lessons in a house like this, but I wish you to be careful that the girls do not copy her manners. She has not by any means escaped the influence of the company she keeps.' I was utterly astonished, you may well think, but I could get no further explanation from him. He only said that when I wished to have her society of an evening, I must let him know, because he would then dine at his club.

"I said that he must have misunderstood her. 'Not in the least,' he said. 'I have no doubt she is to you everything amiable, but she has taken some unaccountable aversion to me, and loses no opportunity of showing it. And I *don't* think I deserve it.' I told him I was so sure he did not deserve it, that I must believe there was some mistake. But he only shook his head and raised his newspaper. You must help me, little coz."

"How am I to help you, Judy dear?" I returned. "I can't interfere between husband and wife, you know. If I dared such a thing, he would quarrel with me too—and rightly."

"No, no," she said, laughing. "I don't want your intercession. I only want you to find out from Miss Clare whether she knows how she has so mortally offended my husband. I believe she knows nothing about it. Help me, now, there's a dear!"

I promised I would, and hence came the story I have already given. But Miss Clare was so distressed at the result of her words, and so anxious that Judy should not be hurt, that she begged me to avoid disclosing the matter, especially seeing Mr. Morley himself judged it too heinous to impart to his wife.

How to manage it I could not think, but at length we arranged it between us. I told Judy that Miss Clare confessed to having said something which had offended Mr. Morley, that she was very sorry, and hoped she need not say that such had not been her intention; and that, as Mr. Morley evidently preferred what had passed between them to remain unmentioned, to disclose it would be merely to swell the mischief. It would be better for them all, she requested me to say, that she should give up her lessons for the present, and therefore she hoped Mrs. Morley would excuse her. When I gave the message, Judy cried and said nothing. When the children heard that Miss Clare was not coming for a while, Amy cried, the other girls looked very grave, and the boys protested. Judy insisted that I should let Mr. Morley hear Miss Clare's message.

"But the message is not to Mr. Morley," I said. "Miss Clare would never have thought of sending one to him."

"But if I ask you to repeat it in his hearing, you will not refuse?"

To this I consented, but I fear she was disappointed in the result. Her husband only smiled sarcastically, drew in his chin, and showed himself a little more cheerful than usual.

One morning, about two months after that, as I was sitting in the drawing room with my baby on the floor beside me, I was surprised to see Judy's brougham pull up at the little gate. When she got out, I saw that something was amiss, and I ran to open the door. Her eyes were red, her cheeks were ashy, and the moment we reached the drawing room, she sunk on the couch and burst into tears.

"Judy!" I cried, "what *is* the matter? Is Amy worse?"

"No, no, Cozzy dear, but we are ruined. We haven't a penny in the world. The children will be beggars."

And there were the gay little horses champing their bits at the door, and the coachman sitting in all his glory, erect and impassive!

I did my best to quiet her. With difficulty she managed to let me understand that her husband had been speculating, and had failed. I could hardly believe myself awake. Mr. Morley was the last man I should have thought capable either of speculating or of failing in it if he did.

Judy said he had not been like himself for months; but it was only on the previous night he had told her they must give up their house in Bolivar Square, and take a small one in the suburbs. For anything he could see, he said, he must look out for a situation.

"Still you may be happier than ever, Judy. I can tell you that happiness does not depend on riches," I said, though I could not help crying with her.

"It's a different thing though, after you've been used to them," she answered. "But the question is of bread for my children, not of putting down my carriage."

She rose hurriedly.

"Where are you going? Is there anything I can do for you?" I asked.

"Nothing," she answered. "I left my husband at Mr. Baddeley's. He is as rich as Croesus, and could write him a check that would float him."

When she reached Mr. Baddeley's, her husband was gone. Having driven to his counting house, and been shown into his private room, she found him there with his head between his hands. The great man had declined doing anything for him, and had even rebuked him for his imprudence, without wasting a thought on the fact that every penny he himself possessed was the result of the boldest speculation on the part of his father.

And now only a very few days would elapse before the falling due of certain bills would disclose the state of his affairs.

As soon as she left me, I put on my bonnet, and went to find Miss Clare. I must tell *her* everything that caused me either joy or sorrow; and besides, she had all the right that love could give to know of Judy's distress.

I told her my sad news and after a pause, she asked, "Is there anything to be done?"

"I know of nothing," I answered.

Again she sat silent for a few minutes. "One can't move without knowing all the circumstances and particulars," she said at length. "And how to get at them? He wouldn't make a confidante of *me*," she said, smiling sadly. "It will be best," she continued, "to go to Mr. Blackstone. He has a wonderful acquaintance with business for a clergyman, and knows many of the city people."

"What could any clergyman do?" I returned. "Mr. Morley would not accept even consolation at his hands."

"The time for that is not come yet," said Miss Clare. "We must try to help him some other way first. We will, if we can, make friends with him by means of the very Mammon that has all but ruined him. Mr. Blackstone can find out for me what Mr. Morley's liabilities are, and how much would serve to tide him over the bar of his present difficulties. I suspect he has few friends who would risk anything for him. You believe him an honorable man, do you not?" she asked abruptly.

"It never entered my head to doubt it," I replied.

"Then let us go see Mr. Blackstone now!" she said, and we descended and found a cab to drive us to Mile End.

"I fear I can't go with you so far, Marion," I said. "I must go home. I don't know what you intend, but *please* don't let anything come out. I can trust *you*, but—"

"If you can trust me, I can trust Mr. Blackstone. He is the most cautious man in the world. Shall I get out, and take another cab?"

"No. You can drop me at Tottenham Court Road, and I will go home by omnibus. But you must let me pay the cab."

"No, no—I am richer than you: I have no children. What fun it is to spend money for Mr. Morley, and lay him under an obligation he will never know!" she said, laughing.

As a result of her endeavors, Mr. Blackstone, by a circuitous succession of introductions, reached Mr. Morley's confidential clerk who, satisfied concerning the object in desiring the information, made a full disclosure of the condition of affairs, and stated what sum would be sufficient to carry them over their difficulties. The clerk added, though, that the greatest care, and every possible reduction of expenditure for some years, would be indispensible to their complete restoration.

Mr. Blackstone carried his discoveries to Miss Clare and she to Lady Bernard.

"My dear Marion," said Lady Bernard, "this is a serious matter you suggest. The man may be honest, and yet it may be of no use trying to help him. I don't want to bolster him up for a few months in order to see my money go after his. That's not what I have to do with my money. No doubt I could lose as much as you mention, without being crippled by it. I hope it's no disgrace in me to be rich, as it's none in you to be poor. But I hate waste, and I will *not* be guilty of it. If Mr. Morley will convince me that there is good probability of his recovering himself by means of it, then, and not till then, I shall feel justified in risking the amount. For, as you say, it would prevent much misery to many besides that good-hearted creature, Mrs. Morley, and her children. It is worth doing if it can be done, but not worth trying if it can't."

The same evening Lady Bernard's shabby one-horse brougham stopped at Mr. Morley's door. Without circumlocution, she told him that if he would lay his affairs before her and a certain accountant she named, to use their judgment in the hope of finding it possible to serve him, they would wait upon him for that purpose at any time and place he pleased. Mr. Morley expressed his obligation—not very warmly, she said—repudiating, however, the slightest objection to her ladyship's knowing now what all the world must know the next day but one.

Early the following morning Lady Bernard and the accountant met Mr. Morley at his place in the city, and by three o'clock in the afternoon fifteen thousand pounds were handed into his account at his bank.

At Miss Clare's earnest entreaty, no one told either Mr. or Mrs. Morley of the share she had had in saving his credit and social position.

Immediately after that, the carriage was put down; the butler, one of the footmen, and the lady's maid were dismissed; and household arrangements fitted to a different scale. The whole family drew yet more closely and lovingly together, and I must say for Judy that, after a few weeks of what she called poverty, her spirits seemed in no degree the worse for the trial.

But that it was not all the trial needful for Mr. Morley was soon apparent. His favorite Amy began to pine more rapidly, and Judy saw that except some change speedily took place, they could not have her with them for long. The father, however, refused to admit the idea that she was in danger. I suppose he felt that if he were once to allow the possibility of losing her, from that moment there would be no stay between her and the grave—it would be a giving of her over to death. When the chills of autumn drew near, her mother took her to Ventnor, but little change followed, and before the new year she was gone. It was the first death, beyond that of an infant, they had had in their family, and took place at a time when business obligations rendered it impossible for her father to be out of London. He could only go to lay her in the earth, and bring back his wife.

Judy had never seen him weep before. Certainly I never saw such a change in a man. He was literally bowed with grief, as if he bore a material burden on his back. The best feelings of his nature, unimpeded by any jar to his self-importance or his prejudices, had been able to spend themselves on the lovely little creature, and I do not believe any other suffering than the loss of such a child could have brought into play that in him which was purely human.

He was at home one morning, ill for the first time in his life, when Miss Clare called on Judy. While she waited in the drawing room, he entered. He turned the moment he saw her, but had not taken two steps toward the door when he turned again and approached her. She went to meet him, and he held out his hand.

"She was very fond of you, Miss Clare," he said. "She was talking about you the very last time I saw her. Let bygones be bygones between us."

"I was rough and rude to you, Mr. Morley, and I am very sorry," said Miss Clare.

"But you spoke the truth," he rejoined. "I thought I was above being spoken to like a sinner, but now I don't know why."

He sat down on a couch, and leaned his head on his hand. Miss Clare took a chair near him, but could not speak.

"It is very hard," he murmured at length.

"Whom the Lord loveth He chasteneth," said Miss Clare.

"That may be true in some cases, but I have no right to believe it applies to me. He loved the child, I believe—for I dare not think of her either as having ceased to be, or as alone in the world to which she has gone. You do think, Miss Clare, do you not, that we shall know our friends in another world?"

"I believe," answered Miss Clare, "that God sent you that child for the express purpose of enticing you back to Himself. And if I believe anything at all, I believe that the gifts of God are without repentance."

At this point Judy came in. Seeing them together she would have withdrawn again, but her husband called her with more tenderness in his voice than Miss Clare could have imagined belonging to it.

"Come, my dear. Miss Clare and I were talking about our little angel. I didn't think ever to speak of her again, but I fear I am growing foolish. All the strength is out of me, and I feel so tired, so weary of everything!"

She sat down beside him and took his hand, and Miss Clare crept away to the children. An hour after, Judy found her in the nursery, with the youngest on her knee and the rest all about her. She was telling them that we were sent into this world to learn to be good, and then to go back to God from whom we came, like little Amy.

"When I go out tomowwow," said one little fellow, about four years old, "I'll look up in the sky vewy hard, wight up, and then I shall see Amy, and God saying to her, 'Hushaby, poo' Amy! You bette' now, Amy?' Shan't I, Mawion?"

She had taught them to call her Marion.

"No, my pet. You might look and look, all day long and every day, and never see God or Amy."

"Then they *ain't* there!" he exclaimed indignantly.

"God is there, anyhow," she answered, "only you can't see Him that way."

"I don't care about seeing God," said the next elder. "It's Amy I want to see. Do tell me, Marion, how we are to see Amy?"

"I will tell you the only way I know. When Jesus was in the world, He told us that all who had clean hearts should see God. That's how Jesus Himself saw God. And how can you see Amy if you can't even see God? If Amy be in God's arms, the first thing, in order to find her, is to find God. To be good is the only way to get near to anybody. When you're naughty, Willie, you can't get near your mamma, can you?"

"Yes, I can. I can get close up to her."

"Is that near enough? Would you be quite content with that? Even when she turns away her face and won't look at you?"

The little boy was silent.

"Did you ever see God, Marion?" asked one of the girls.

She thought for a moment before giving her answer. "No," she said. "I've seen things just after He has done them, and I think I've heard Him speak to me, but I've never seen Him yet."

"Then you're not good, Marion," said the freethinker of the group.

"No—that's just it. But I hope to be good someday, and then I *shall* see Him."

"How do you grow good, Marion?" asked the girl.

"God is always trying to make me good," she answered, "and I try not to interfere with Him."

"But sometimes you forget, don't you?"

"Yes, I do."

"And what do you do then?"

"Then I'm sorry and unhappy, and begin to try again."

"And God don't mind much, does He?"

"He minds very much until I mind, but after that He forgets it all, takes all my naughtiness and throws it behind His back, and won't look at it."

"That's very good of God," said the reasoner, but with such a self-satisfied air in his approval, that Miss Clare thought it time to stop.

She came straight to see me and told me, with a perfectly radiant face, of the alteration of Mr. Morley's behavior to her, and, what was of much more consequence, the evident change that had begun to be wrought in him.

He has not, as yet, shown a very shining light, but some change is evident. The eternal wind must now be able to get in through the chink which the loss of his child has left behind. And if the changes were not going on, surely he would by now have returned to his wallowing in the mire of Mammon, for his former fortune is all but restored to him.

I fancy his growth in goodness is measured by his progress in appreciating Marion. He still regards her as extreme in her notions, but it is curious to see how, as they gradually sink into his understanding, he comes to adopt them as, and even to mistake them for, his own.

TWENTY-TWO

Percivale

I should say a few words concerning my husband, if possible, because women differ much in the degree and manner in which their feelings will permit them to talk about their husbands. I have known women who set a whole community against their husbands by the way in which they trumpet their praises; and I have known one woman who set everybody against herself by the way in which she published her husband's faults. I find it difficult to believe either sort. To praise one's husband is so much like praising one's self that it seems immodest and subject to suspicion; while to blame one's husband, even justly and openly, seems to border upon treachery.

My father had long been concerned about Percivale's opinions. Now my father is large-minded, but I am not certain that he has done Percivale justice—although Percivale is partly to blame himself, for he never took pains to show my father what he was. Had he done so, my father of all men would have understood him.

My husband left the impression on my father's mind that he had some definite repugnance to Christianity itself. I, however, had soon been satisfied (perhaps from Percivale being more open with me) that certain representations of Christianity, coming to him with authority, had cast discredit on the whole idea. We had had many talks, and I was astonished at the things he imagined to be acknowledged essentials of Christianity, but which have no place whatever in the New Testament. There was little or no outward difference to be perceived in him as he came to see his misconceptions, but I could clearly distinguish an undercurrent of thought and feeling setting toward the faith which Christianity preaches. He said little or nothing, for he was almost morbidly careful not to seem to know anything he did not know or to appear to be what he was not.

I remember one occasion, some time before we began to go to Marion's on Sunday evenings, when I had asked him to go with me to a certain little chapel in the neighborhood—the very chapel, in fact, into which Marion had stepped on that evening so miserable to her.

"What!" he said merrily, "the daughter of a clergyman being seen going to a conventicle?"

"If I went, I would be seen doing it," I answered.

"Don't you know that the man is no conciliator, or even mild dissenter, but a decided enemy to church and state and all that?" pursued Percivale.

"I don't care," I replied. "He's a poet and a prophet both in one, and he stirs up my heart within me and makes me long to be good. He is no studied orator, as you profess such a great aversion to, yet he often breaks into eloquence."

"I don't mind going if you wish. I suppose he believes what he says, at least."

"Not a doubt of it, else he could not speak as he does."

"Do you mean he is *sure* of everything—is he *sure* that the story of the New Testament is, in the main, actual fact? I should be very sorry to trouble your faith, but—"

"My father says," I interrupted, "that a true faith is like the pool of Bethesda—it is when it is troubled that it shows its healing power."

"That may depend on where the trouble comes from," said Percivale.

"It is only that which cannot be shaken that shall remain."

"Well, here is a common sense difficulty: how is anyone to be *sure* of the things recorded? I cannot imagine a man of our time absolutely certain of them. If you tell me I have testimony, I answer that the testimony itself requires testimony. I never even saw the people who bear it, so I have just as good reason to doubt their existence as I do His. I have no means of verifying their testimony, and have so little confidence in what is called 'evidence,' knowing how it can be twisted, that I distrust any conclusion I should come to on one side or the other. If the thing were of God, He would have made it possible for an honest man to place a hearty confidence in its record."

He had never talked to me so openly, and I felt it a serious matter to answer him, for how could I have any better assurance of that external kind than Percivale himself? For a short time I was silent, while he regarded me with a look of concern, fearful, I fancied, lest he should have involved me in his own perplexity.

"Isn't it possible, Percivale," I said "that God may not care so much for beginning at that end? A man might believe every fact concerning our Lord, and yet not have the faith that God wishes him to have."

"Yes, certainly. But is the converse true? Will you say a man may have the faith God cares for without the faith you say He does not care for?"

"I didn't say that God does not care about our assurance of the facts. I only expressed a doubt whether He cares that we should have that assurance first. Perhaps He means it to be the result of that higher kind of faith which rests in the will."

"How can the higher faith precede the lower?"

"What is the test of discipleship the Lord laid down? Is it not obedience?

'If you love Me, keep My commandments.' Suppose a man feels in himself that he must have some Saviour or perish—suppose he feels drawn by conscience, admiration, or early memories to Jesus, dimly seen through the mists of ages. Suppose he cannot be sure there ever was such a Man, but reads about Him, and ponders over the words attributed to Him, until he feels they are the right thing, whether He said them or not, and that if he could be sure there were such a Being, he would believe in Him with heart and soul. Suppose also that he comes upon the words, 'If any man is willing to do the will of My Father, he shall know whether I speak of Myself or He who sent Me.' Suppose the man then says to himself, 'I cannot tell whether all this is true, but I know nothing else that seems half so good, and I will try to do the will of the Father in the hope of the promised knowledge.' Do you think God would, or would not, count that to the man for faith?"

I had no more to say. After a pause of some duration, Percivale said, "I will go with you, my dear," and that was all his answer.

When we came out of the little chapel, we walked homeward in silence and reached our own door ere a word was spoken.

But Percivale followed me into our room and said, "Whether that man is *certain* of the fact or not, I cannot tell, but I am perfectly satisfied he believes in the manner of which you were speaking—that of obedience, Wynnie. He must believe with his heart and will and life."

"If so, he can well afford to wait for what light God will give him on things that belong to the intellect and judgment."

"I would rather think," he returned, "that purity of life must react on the judgment, so as to make it likewise clear, and enable it to recognize the true force of the evidence."

"That is how my father came to believe," I said.

"But your father seems to me to rest his conviction more upon external proof."

"Only because it is easier to talk about. He told me once that he was never able to estimate the force and weight of the external arguments until after he had believed for the very love of the eternal truth he saw in the story. His heart, he said, had been the guide of his intellect."

"That is just what I would fain believe. But O Wynnie! The pity of it if that story should not be true after all!"

"That very word makes me surer than ever that it cannot but be true! Let us go on putting it to the hardest test. Let us try it until it crumbles in our hands. Let us try it by the touchstone of action founded on its requirements."

"There may be no other way," said Percivale, "of becoming capable of recognizing the truth. It may be beyond the grasp of all but the mind that has thus yielded to it. Such a conviction, then, could neither be forestalled nor communicated. Its very existence must remain doubtful until it asserts itself."

And so we went on to other things.

TWENTY-THREE
A Strange Text

For some time after the events last related, things went on pretty smoothly with us for several years. What with my children and the increase of social duty resulting from the growth of acquaintance—occasioned in part by my success in persuading Percivale to mingle a little more with his fellow painters—my heart and mind and hands were all pretty fully occupied. But I still managed to see Miss Clare two or three times a week, sometimes alone, sometimes with her friends as well. Her society did much to keep my heart open, and to prevent it from becoming selfishly absorbed in its cares for husband and children. For love which is *only* concentrating its force—that is, not widening its circle—is itself doomed, and for its objects is ruinous, be those objects ever so sacred. God Himself could never be content that His children should love Him only, nor has He allowed the few to succeed who have tried after it; perhaps their divinest success has been their most mortifying failure. Indeed, for exclusive love, sharp suffering is often sent as the needful cure.

For some time I had seen a considerable change in Roger, reaching even to his dress. Hitherto, when got up for dinner, he was what I was astonished to hear my boy call "a howling swell"; but at other times he did not even escape remark, not for the oddity merely, but for the slovenliness of his attire. He had worn (for more years than I dare guess) a brown coat of some rich-looking stuff, whose long pile was stuck together in so many places with spots and dabs of paint that he looked like our long-haired Bedlington terrier toward the end of a muddy week. This coat was now discarded—so far at least as to be hung up in his brother's study, to be at hand when he did anything for him there. It was replaced by a more civilized garment of tweed, of which he actually showed himself a little careful. While his necktie *was* red, it was of a very deep and rich red, and he had seldom worn one at all before. His brigand-looking felt hat was exchanged for one of half the altitude, which he did not crush on his head with quite as many indentations as its surface could hold. He also began to go to church with us sometimes.

But there was a greater and more significant change than any of these. We found that he was sticking more steadily to work. I can hardly say *his* work, for he was jack-of-all-trades. His forte was engraving on wood, and my husband said that if he could do so well with so little practice as he had had, he must be capable of becoming an admirable engraver. To our delight, then, we discovered, all at once, that he had been working steadily for three months for the Messrs. Danby, whose place was not far from our house. He had said nothing about it to his brother, probably from having good reason to fear that he would regard it only as a *spurt*. Having now, however, executed a block which greatly pleased himself, he had brought a proof impression to show Percivale. He, more pleased with it than even Roger himself, gave him a hearty congratulation, and told him it would be a shame if he did not bring his execution in that art to perfection, from which, judging by the present specimen, he said it could not be far off. The words brought into Roger's face an expression of modest gratification which it rejoiced me to behold. He accepted Percivale's approbation more like a son than a brother, with a humid glow in his eyes and hardly a word on his lips. It seemed to me that the child in his heart had begun to throw off the swaddling clothes which foolish manhood had wrapped around it, and the germ of his being was about to assert itself. Indeed, I have seldom seen Percivale look so pleased.

"Do me a dozen as good as that," he said, "and I'll have the proofs framed in silver gilt."

(It *has* been done, but the proofs had to wait longer for the frames than Percivale for the proofs.)

But he need have held out no such bribe of brotherly love, for there was another love already at work in himself more than sufficing to the affair. Roger always took a half holiday on Saturdays, and now generally came to us. On one of these occasions I said to him, "Wouldn't you like to come and hear Marion play to her friends this evening, Roger?"

"Nothing would give me greater pleasure," he answered, and we went.

It was delightful, for Marion is a real artist. While she uttered from herself, she heard with her audience, and while she played and sang with her own fingers and mouth, she at the same time listened with their ears, knowing what they must feel, as well as what she meant to utter. And hence it was, I think, that she came into such vital contact with them, even through her piano.

As we returned home, Roger said, after some remark of mine, "Does she never try to teach them anything, Wynnie?"

"She is constantly teaching them, whether she tries or not," I answered. "If you can make anyone believe that there is something somewhere to be trusted, is not that the best lesson you can give them? That can be taught only by being such that people can but trust you."

"I don't need to be told that," he answered. "I want to know whether or not she ever teaches them by word of mouth, by an ordinary and inferior mode, if you will."

"If you had ever heard her, you would not call hers an ordinary or inferior mode," I returned. "Her teaching is the outcome of her life, the blossom of her being, and therefore has the whole force of her living truth to back it. She teaches them every Sunday evening, and I never heard anything like it."

"Could you take me with you sometime?" he asked, in an assumed tone of ordinary interest, out of which, however, he could not keep a slight tremble.

"I don't know. I don't quite see why I shouldn't. And yet—"

"Men do go," urged Roger, as if it were a mere half-indifferent suggestion.

"Oh, yes! You would have plenty to keep you in countenance! Men enough—and worth teaching too—some of them, at least!"

"Then, I don't see why she should object to me for another."

"I don't know that she would. You are not exactly of the sort, you know, that—"

"I see no essential difference. I am in want of teaching as much as any of them. And, if she stands on circumstances, I am a workingman as much as any of them, perhaps more than most of them. Few of them work after midnight, as I do not unfrequently."

"Still, all admitted, I should hardly like—"

"I didn't mean you were to take me without asking her," he said. "I should never have dreamed of that."

"And if I were to ask her, I am certain she would refuse. But," I added, thinking over the matter a little, "I will take you without asking her. Come with me tomorrow night. I don't think she will have the heart to send you away."

"I will," he answered, with more gladness in his voice than he intended.

We arranged that he should call for me at a certain hour. I told Percivale, and he pretended to grumble that I was taking Roger instead of him.

"It was Roger, and not you, that made the request," I returned. "If you really want to go, I don't see why you shouldn't. It's ever so much better than going to any church I know of—except one. But we must be prudent. I can't take more than one the first time. We must get the thin edge of the wedge in first."

"And you count Roger the thin edge?"

"Yes."

"I'll tell him so."

"Do. The thin edge, mind, without which the thicker rest is useless! But, seriously, I quite expect to take you there too, the Sunday after."

Roger and I went. Intending to be a little late, we found that the class had already begun. When we reached the last stair we could hear her saying, "I will now read to you the chapter of which I spoke."

The door was open, and we could hear well enough, although she was sitting where we could not see her. We would not show ourselves until the reading was ended—so much, at least, we might overhear without offense.

Before she had read many words, Roger and I began to cast strange looks to each other. For this was the chapter she read:

"And Joseph, wheresoever he went in the city, took the Lord Jesus with him, where he was sent for to work, to make gates or milk pails, or sieves, or boxes. And as often as Joseph had anything in his work to make longer or shorter, or wider or narrower, the Lord Jesus would stretch His hand toward it. And presently it became as Joseph would have it. And he had no need to finish anything with his own hands, for he was not very skillful at his carpenter's trade.

"On a certain time the king of Jerusalem sent for him, and said, 'I would have thee make me a throne of the same dimensions with that place in which I commonly sit.' Joseph obeyed, and forthwith began with the work, and continued two years in the king's palace before he finished. And when he came to fix it in its place, he found it wanted two spans on each side of the appointed measure. Which, when the king saw, he was very angry with Joseph, and Joseph, afraid of the king's anger, went to bed without his supper, taking not anything to eat. Then the Lord Jesus asked him what he was afraid of. Joseph replied, 'Because I have lost my labor in the work which I have been about these two years.' Jesus said to him, 'Fear not, neither be cast down. Do thou lay hold on one side of the throne, and I will the other, and we will bring it to its just dimensions.' And when Joseph had done as the Lord Jesus said, and each of them had with strength drawn his side, the throne obeyed, and was brought to the proper dimensions of the place. They who stood by saw this miracle, and were astonished, and praised God. The throne was made of the same wood which was in being in Solomon's time, namely, wood adorned with various shapes and figures."

Her voice ceased, and a pause followed.

"We must go in now," I whispered.

"Now, what do you think of it?" asked Marion in a meditative tone.

We crept within the scope of her vision, and stood. A voice (which I knew) was at that moment replying to her question.

"I don't think it's much of a chapter, that, Grannie."

The speaker was the keen-faced, elderly man with iron-gray whiskers, who had helped us search for little Ethel. He sat near the door, between two respectable-looking women who had been listening to the chapter as devoutly as if it had been of the true Gospel.

"Sure, Grannie, that ain't out o' the Bible?" said another voice, from somewhere farther off.

"We'll talk about that presently," answered Marion. "I want to hear what

Mr. Jarvis has to say. He's a carpenter himself, you see."

All the faces in the room were now turned toward Jarvis.

"Tell me why you don't think much of it, Mr. Jarvis," said Marion.

" 'Tain't a bit likely," he answered.

"What isn't likely?"

"First and foremost, 'tain't a bit likely the old man 'ud ha' been sich a duffer."

"Why not? There must have been stupid people then as well as now."

"Well, it ain't likely sich a workman 'ud ha' stood so high i' the trade that the king of Jerusalem would ha' sent for *him* of all the tradesmen in the town to make his new throne for him. No more it ain't likely—and let him be as big a duffer as ever was, to be a jiner at all—that he'd ha' been two years at work on that there throne—an' a carvin' of it in figures too—and never found out it was four spans too narrer for the place it had to stand in. Do ye 'appen to know now, Grannie, how much is a span?"

"I don't know. Do you know, Mrs. Percivale?"

The sudden reference took me very much by surprise, but I had not forgotten, happily, the answer I received to the same question, when anxious to realize the monstrous height of Goliath.

"I remember my father telling me," I replied, "that it was as much as you could stretch between your thumb and little finger."

"There!" cried Jarvis triumphantly, parting the extreme members of his right hand against the back of the woman in front of him. "That would be seven or eight inches! Four times that? Two foot and a half at least! Think of that!"

"I admit the force of both your objections," said Marion. "And what do you think of the way He got His father out of his evil plight?"

Before Jarvis had time to make any reply, the blind man struck in.

"*I* make more o' that pint than the t' other," he said. "A man as is a duffer may well make a mull of a thing, but a man as knows what he's up to can't. I don't make much o' them miracles, you know, Grannie—but what I'm sure of is this here one thing—that man or boy as *could* work a miracle, you know, Grannie, wouldn't work no miracle as there wasn't no good working of."

"It was to help His father," suggested Marion.

Here Jarvis broke in almost with scorn. "To help him to pass for a clever fellow, when he was as great a duffer as ever broke bread!"

"I'm quite o' your opinion, Mr. Jarvis," said the blind man. "It'ud ha' been more like Him to tell His father what a duffer he was, and send him home to learn his trade."

"He couldn't do that, you know," said Marion gently. "He *couldn't* use such words to His father, if he were ever so stupid."

"I think, though," said Jarvis, "for as hard as He'd ha' found it, it would ha' been more like Him to set up to work and teach His father, than to scamp up his mulls."

"Certainly," acquiesced Marion. "To hide any man's faults, and leave him not only stupid but, in all probability, obstinate and self-satisfied, would not be like *Him.* What do you think our Lord would have done?"

"He'd ha' done all He could to make a man of him," answered Jarvis.

"Wouldn't He have set about making him comfortable then, in spite of his blunders?" said Marion.

A significant silence followed this question.

"Well, no, not first thing, I don't think," returned Jarvis at length. "He'd ha' got him some good first, and gone in to make him comfortable after."

"Then I suppose you would rather be of some good and uncomfortable, than of no good and comfortable?" said Marion.

"I hope so, Grannie," answered Jarvis, and "I would," "Yes," and "That I would" came from several voices in the little crowd.

"Then," she said—and I saw by the light which rose in her eyes that she was now coming to the point—"then, surely it must be worth our while to bear discomfort in order to grow of some good! Mr. Jarvis has truly said that if Jesus had had such a father, He would have made him of some good before He made him comfortable. That is just the way your Father in heaven is acting with you. Not many of you would say you are of much good yet, but you would like to be better. And yet, put it to yourselves: do you not grumble at everything that comes to you that you don't like, and call it bad luck, and worse—yes, even when you know it comes of your own fault? You think if you only had this or that to make you comfortable, you would be content. You forget that to make you comfortable as you are would be the same as to pull out Joseph's misfitted thrones and doors, and make his misshapen buckets over again for him. And that you think so absurd that you can't believe the story a bit. Yet you would wish to be helped out of all *your* troubles, even those you bring on yourselves, not thinking what the certain consequence would be, namely, that you would grow of less and less value, until you were of no good, either to God or man.

"When, for instance, are you most willing to do right? When are you most ready to hear about good things? When are you most inclined to pray to God? When you have plenty of money in your pockets, or when you are in want? When you have had a good dinner, or when you have not had enough to get one? When you are in jolly health, or when the life seems ebbing out of you in misery and pain? If suffering drives you to God, that is its end and there will be an end of it.

"Now, however, that we have got a lesson from a false gospel, we may as well get one from the true."

As she spoke, she turned to her New Testament which lay beside her. But Jarvis interrupted her.

"Where did you get that stuff you was a readin' of to us, Grannie?" he asked.

"The chapter I read to you," she answered, "is part of a pretended gospel called *The First Gospel of the Infancy of Jesus Christ.* Very early in the history of the church, there were some people who indulged themselves in inventing things about Jesus, who had no idea of the importance of keeping to facts—of speaking and writing only the truth. It is long before some people learn to speak the truth, even after they know it is wicked to lie. Perhaps, however, they did not expect their stories to be received as facts, intending them only as a sort of recognized fiction about Him—an amazing presumption at the best."

"Did anybody, then, believe the likes of that, Grannie?" asked Jarvis.

"Yes. What I read to you seems to have been believed within a hundred years after the death of the apostles. There are several such writings, with a great deal of nonsense in them, which were generally accepted by Christian people for many hundreds of years.

"One comfort is, that such a story is sure not to be consistent with itself. It is sure to show its own falsehood to anyone who is good enough to doubt it, and who will look into it and examine it well. You don't, for instance, want any other proof than the things themselves to show you that what I have just read to you can't be true."

"Then don't you think it likely this much is true, Grannie," said Jarvis, "that He worked with His father, and helped him in his trade?"

"I do indeed," answered Marion. "I believe that to be the one germ of truth in the whole story. Is it likely that He, who came down for the express purpose of being a true man, would see His father toiling to feed Him and His mother and His brothers and sisters, and go idling about, instead of putting in His hand to help him? Would that have been like Him?"

"Certainly not," said Mr. Jarvis.

"Mr. Jarvis, will you tell me whether you think the work of the carpenter's Son would have been in any way distinguishable from that of another man?"

"Well, I don't know, Grannie. He wouldn't want to be putting of a private mark upon it. He wouldn't want to be showing of it off, would He? He'd use His tools like another man, anyhow."

"We may be certain of that. But do you suppose you would have been able to distinguish His work from that of any other carpenter?"

A silence followed. Jarvis was thinking, and at last his face brightened.

"Well, Grannie," he said, "I think it would be very difficult in anything easy, but very easy in anything difficult." Then he laughed, for he had not perceived the paradox before uttering it.

"Explain yourself, if you please, Mr. Jarvis. I am not sure that I understand you," said Marion.

"I mean that in an easy job, which any fair workman could do well enough, it would not be easy to tell His work. But, where the job was difficult, His would be so much better done that it would not be difficult to see the better hand in it."

"Then the chief distinction would lie in the quality of the work—that whatever He did, he would do in such a thorough manner that, over the whole of what He turned out, the perfection of the work would be a striking characteristic. Is that it?"

"That is what I do mean, Grannie."

"And that is just the conclusion I had come to myself."

"I should like to say just one word to it, Grannie," said the blind man. "Mr. Jarvis, he say as how the jiner-work done by Jesus Christ would be better done than e'er another man's—tip-top fashion—and there would lie the difference. Now, it do seem to me as I've got no call to come to that 'ere conclusion. For the works o' God—there ain't one on' em as I can see downright well managed—tip-top jiner's work, as I may say. We ha' got most uncommon bad weather more'n at times, and the walnuts they turns out, every now an' then, full o' mere dirt, an' the oranges awful. There ain't been a good crop o' hay, they tells me, for many's the year. An' i' furren parts, what wi' earthquakes an' wolcanies an' lions an' tigers, an' savages as eats their wisiters, an' chimley-pots blowin' about, an' ships goin' down, an' fathers o' families choked an' drownded an' burnt i' coal pits by the hundreds—it do seem to me that if His jinerin' hadn't been tip-top, it would ha' been but like the rest on it. There, Grannie! Mind, I mean no offense, an' I don't doubt you ha' got somethink i' your weskit pocket as'll turn it all topsy-turvy in a moment. Anyhow, I won't purtend to nothink, and that's how it looks to me."

"I admit," said Marion, "that the objection is a reasonable one. Allow me just to put a question or two to Mr. Jarvis, because he's a joiner himself, and that's a great comfort to me tonight. What would you say, Mr. Jarvis, of a master who planed the timber he used for scaffolding, and tied the crosspieces with ropes of silk?"

"I should say he was a fool, Grannie, not only for losin' his money and his labor, but for weakenin' of his scaffoldin'."

"What's the object of a scaffold, Mr. Jarvis?"

"To get at something else by means of—say, to build a house."

"Then, so long as the house was going up all right, the probability is there wouldn't be much amiss with the scaffold?"

"Certainly, provided it stood till it was taken down."

"If you saw a scaffold," said Marion, "would you mistake it for a permanent erection?"

"Nobody wouldn't be such a fool," he answered. "The look of it would tell you that."

"You wouldn't complain, then, if it should be a little out of the square, and if there should be no windows in it?"

Jarvis only laughed.

"Mr. Evans," Marion went on, turning to the blind man, "do you think the design of this world was to make men comfortable?"

"If it was, it don't seem to ha' succeeded," answered Evans.

"And you complain of that, don't you?"

"Well, yes, rather," said the blind man.

"You think, perhaps, that God, having gone so far to make this world a pleasant and comfortable place to live in, might have gone farther and made it quite pleasant and comfortable for everybody?"

"Whoever could make it at all could ha' done that, Grannie."

"Then, as He hasn't done it, the probability is He didn't mean to do it?"

"Of course. That's what I complain of."

"Then He meant to do something else?"

"It looks like it."

"The whole affair has an unfinished look, you think?"

"I just do."

"What if it were not meant to stand, then? What if it were meant only for a temporary assistance in carrying out something finished and lasting, and of unspeakably more importance? Suppose God were building a palace for you, and had set up a scaffold, upon which He wanted you to help Him. Would it be reasonable for you to complain that you didn't find the scaffold at all a comfortable place to live in? Or that it was draughty and cold? This world is that scaffold, and if you were busy carrying stones and mortar for the palace, you would be glad of all the cold to cool the glow of your labor.

"But what will all the labor of a workman who does not fall in with the design of the builder come to? Instead of working away at the palace, like men, will you go on tacking bits of matting and old carpet about the corners of the scaffold to keep the wind off, while that same wind keeps tearing them away and scattering them? You keep trying to live in a scaffold, which not all eternity would make a house of. God wants to build you a house whereof the walls shall be *goodness*. You want a house with walls of *comfort*. But God knows that such walls cannot be built—that that kind of stone crumbles away in the foolish workman's hands. He would make you comfortable, but neither is that His first object, nor can it be gained without the first, which is to make you good. He loves you so much that He would infinitely rather have you good and uncomfortable—for then He could take you to His heart as His own children—than comfortable and not good, for then He could not come near you, or give you anything He counted worth having."

"So," said Jarvis, "you've just brought us 'round, Grannie, to the same thing as before."

"I believe so," returned Marion. "It comes to this, that when God would build a palace for Himself to dwell in with His children, He does not want His scaffold so constructed that they shall be able to make a house of it for themselves, and live like apes instead of angels.

"You see, then, it is not inconsistent with the apparent imperfections of the creation around us, that Jesus should have done the best possible carpenter's work, for those very imperfections are actually through their imperfections the means of carrying out the higher creation God has in view, and at which He is working all the time.

"Now let me read you what King David thought upon this question."

She read Psalm 107. Then they had some singing, and Roger and I slipped out. We had agreed it would be best to make no apology, but just vanish, and come again with Percivale the following Sunday.

The greater part of the way home we walked in silence.

"What do you think of that, Roger?" I asked at length.

"Quite Socratic as to method," he answered, and said no more.

I sent a full report of the evening to my father, who was delighted with it, although, of course, much was lost in the reporting of the mere words, not to mention the absence of her sweet face and shining eyes, and of her quiet, earnest, musical voice.

TWENTY-FOUR

My Second Terror

"Please, Ma'am, is Master Fido to carry Master Zohrab about?" said Jemima, in indignant appeal one afternoon late in November, bursting into the study where I sat with my husband.

Fido was our Bedlington terrier which, having been reared by Newcastle colliers and taught to draw a badger, had a passion for burrowing after anything buried. Swept away by the current of the said passion, he had unearthed poor Zohrab, the tortoise, who had ensconced himself (he thought) for the winter in the earth at the foot of a lilac tree. Now, much to his jeopardy, he was being triumphantly borne about the garden in Fido's jaws.

Alarmed at the danger to the poor powerless animal, Percivale threw down his palette and brushes and ran out the door.

"Do put on your coat and hat, Percivale!" I cried, but he was gone.

Cold as it was, he had been sitting in the light blouse he had worn at his work all summer. The stove was red-hot, and the room like an oven, while outside a dank fog filled the air. I hurried after him with his coat, and found him pursuing Fido about the garden. The brute declined to obey his call or to drop the tortoise. Percivale was equally deaf to my call, and not until he had chastised the dog did he return with the rescued tortoise in his hands. The consequences were serious—first the death of Zohrab, and next a terrible illness to my husband. A cold settled into his lungs and passed into bronchitis.

It was a terrible time for me, for I had no doubt that he was dying. The measures taken seemed thoroughly futile.

It is an awful moment when first Death looks in at the door. The positive recognition of his presence is so different from any vividest imagination of it! For the moment I believed nothing—felt only the coming blackness of absolute loss. I cared neither for my children, nor for my father or mother. Nothing appeared of any worth anymore. I had conscience enough left to try to pray, but no prayer would rise from the frozen depths of my spirit. I could only move about in mechanical and hopeless ministration to one whom it seemed of no use to go on loving any more. For what was nature but a soulless machine, the constant clank of whose motion sounded only, "Dust to dust, dust to dust," forevermore?

But my husband caught a glimpse of my despair, motioned me to him with a smile as of sunshine upon snow, and whispered in my ear, "I am afraid you haven't much more faith than myself, after all, Wynnie."

It stung me into life, not for the sake of my professions, not even for the honor of our Heavenly Father, but by waking in me the awful thought of my beloved passing through the shadow of death with no one beside him to help or comfort him, in absolute loneliness and uncertainty. For a moment I wished he might die suddenly, and so escape the vacuous despair of a conscious lingering betwixt life and the something or the nothing beyond it.

"But I cannot go with you!" I cried, and forgetting all my duty as a nurse, I wept in agony.

"Perhaps another will, my Wynnie—One who knows the way," he whispered, for he could not speak aloud, and closed his eyes.

It was as if an arrow of light had slain the python coiled about my heart. If *he* believed, *I* could believe also. If *he* could encounter the vague dark, *I* could endure the cheerless light. I was myself again and, with one word of endearment, left the bedside to do what had to be done.

At length a faint hope began to glimmer in the depths of my cavernous fear, though it was long ere it swelled into confidence. For a whole week I did not once undress, and for weeks I was half-awake all the time I slept. The softest whisper would rouse me thoroughly, and it was only when Marion took my place that I could sleep at all.

I am afraid I neglected my poor children dreadfully, but then I knew that they were well attended to. Friends were very kind— especially Judy—in taking them out, and Marion's daily visits were like those of a mother. (Indeed, she was able to mother anything human except a baby, to whom she felt no attraction, any more than to animals, for which she had little regard. She would hurt no creature that was not hurtful, but she had scarcely an atom of kindness for dog or cat, or anything that is petted of woman. It is the only defect I am aware of in her character.)

My husband slowly recovered, but it was months before he was able to do anything he would call work. But, even in labor, success is not only to the strong. Working a little at the short best time of the day, he managed, long before his full recovery, to paint a small picture which better critics than I have thought worthy of Fra Angelico. I will attempt to describe it.

Through the lighted windows of a great hall, the spectator catches broken glimpses of a festive company. At the head of the table, pouring red wine, he sees One like unto the Son of man, upon whom all eyes are turned. At the other end of the hall, seated high in a gallery, with rapt looks and quaint yet homely angelic instruments, he sees the orchestra pouring out their souls through their strings and trumpets. The hall is filled with a jewelly glow, the radiating center is the red wine on the table. Mingled wings of all gorgeous splendors hovering in the dim height are suffused and harmonized by the molten ruby tint that pervades the whole.

Outside, in the drizzly darkness, stands a lonely man. He stoops, listening with one ear laid almost against the door. His half-upturned face catches a ray of the light reflected from a muddy pool in the road. It discloses features wan and wasted with sorrow and sickness, but glorified with the joy of the music. He is like one who has been four days dead, to whose body the music has recalled the soul. Down by his knee he holds a violin, fashioned like those of the orchestra within and, as he listens, he is tuning to their pitch.

The origin of all this was a poem of Dr. Donne's—"Hymn to God, My God in My Sickness." I had read some verses of it to him in his convalescence, and having heard them once, he requested them often again. The first stanza runs thus:

> Since I am coming to that holy room
> Where with the choir of saints forevermore
> I shall be made Thy musique, as I come,
> I tune the instrument here at the door;
> And what I must do then, think here before.

The painting is almost the only one he has yet refused to let me see before it was finished, but when it was, he hung it up in my own little room off the study, and I became thoroughly acquainted with it. I think I love it more than anything else he has done. I got him, without telling him why, to put a touch or two to the listening figure, which made it really like himself.

During this period of recovery, I often came upon him reading his Greek New Testament, which he would shove aside when I entered. At length, one morning, I said to him, "Are you ashamed of reading the New Testament, Percivale? One would think it was a bad book from the way you try to hide it."

"No, my love," he said. "It is only that I am jealous of appearing to do that from suffering and weakness only, which I did not do when I was strong and well. But sickness has opened my eyes a good deal, I think, and I am sure of this much, that, whatever truth there is here, I want it all the same whether I am feeling the want or not. I had no idea what there was in this Book."

"Would you mind telling me," I said, "what made you take to reading it?"

"I will try. When I thought I was dying, a black cloud seemed to fall over everything. It was not so much that I was afraid to die—although I did dread the final conflict—as that I felt so forsaken and lonely. It was of little use saying to myself that I mustn't be a coward, and that it was the part of a man to meet his fate, whatever it might be, with composure; for I saw nothing worth being brave about. The heart had melted out of me. There was nothing to give me joy, nothing for my life to rest upon, no sense of love at the heart of things. Didn't you feel something the same that terrible day?"

"I did," I answered. "For one fearful moment the skeleton of Death seemed to swell and grow till he blotted out the sun and the stars, and the life beyond was too shadowy to show behind him. And so Death was victorious, until the thought of your loneliness in the dark valley broke the spell, and for your sake I hoped in God again."

Percivale then continued, "And I asked myself if God would set His children down in the dark, and leave them to cry aloud in anguish at the terrors of the night? Would He not make the very darkness light about them? Or, if they must pass through such tortures, would He not at least let them know that He was with them? Then arose in my mind all at once the old story how, in the person of His Son, God Himself had passed through the darkness now gathering about me, had gone down to the grave, and had conquered death by dying. If this was true, this was to be a God indeed. Well might He call us to endure, who had Himself borne the far heavier share. If there were an Eternal Life who would perfect my life, I could be brave, I could endure what He chose to lay upon me, I could go whither He led."

"And were you able to think all that when you were so ill, my love?" I said.

"Something like it," he answered. "It kept growing in my mind, coming and going, and gathering clearer in shape. If there was a God, He certainly knew that I would give myself to Him if I could—that if I knew Jesus to be verily and really His Son, however it might seem strange to believe in Him and hard to obey Him—I would try to do so. Then the verse about the smoking flax and the bruised reed came into my head, and a great hope arose in me. I do not know if it was what the good people would call faith, but I had no time and no heart to think about words. I wanted God and His Christ. A fresh spring of life seemed to burst up in my heart. All the world grew bright again, and I seemed to love you and the children twice as much as before. A calmness came down upon my spirit which seemed to me like nothing but the presence of God; and, although I dare say you did not then perceive a change, I am certain that the same moment I began to recover."

The little money we had in hand rapidly vanished during Percivale's illness. While he was making nothing, the expenses of the family went on as usual, and the doctor was yet to pay. Even up to the time when he had been taken ill, we had been doing little better than living from hand to mouth, for as often as we thought income was about to get a few yards ahead in the race with expense, something invariably happened to disappoint us.

While Percivale was ill, not a picture had been disposed of, and even after he was able to work a little, I could not encourage visitors. He was fatigued, and he shrunk with irritability from seeing anyone. I watched my little stock—which was bodily in my hand, for we had no banking account—rapidly approach its final evanishment.

Some may think that, with parents in the position of mine, a temporary difficulty need have caused me no anxiety.

In the first place, my husband could not feel toward my father as I felt. Percivale had married me as a poor man who yet could keep a wife, and I knew it would be a bitter humiliation to him to ask my father for money, on the ground that he had given his daughter.

In the second place, even I, in my fullest freedom, could not have asked help from my father just at this time. He had taken upon himself to pay some two thousand pounds of injudicious debts incurred by my eldest brother—incurred through no other vice beyond that of thoughtlessness and folly. Indeed, he had to borrow part of the money on a fresh mortgage in order to clear him. Some lawyer told him that he was not bound to pay, but my father said that although such creditors deserved no protection of the law, he was not bound to give them a lesson in honesty at the expense of weakening the bond between himself and his son, for whose misdeeds he acknowledged a large share of responsibility. On the other hand, he was bound to give his son the lesson of the suffering he brought on his family by his selfishness, and therefore would pay the money—if not gladly, yet willingly. How the poor boy got through the shame and misery of it, I can hardly imagine. But this I can say for him, that it was purely of himself that he accepted a situation in Ceylon, with the intention of repaying my father. If he succeeds in doing so, he will doubtless make a fairer start the second time—because of the discipline—than if he had gone out with money in his pocket.

It was natural, then, that in such circumstances a daughter should shrink from adding her troubles to those caused by a son. My father had also of late been laying out a good deal in building cottages for the laborers on his farms, and the land itself was not entirely freed from the mortgages my mother had inherited with it.

Percivale continued so weak that for some time I could not bring myself to say a word to him about money. But to keep the household debts as low as possible did not prevent them from accumulating, and the servants' wages were on the point of coming due. I had been careful to keep the milkman paid and, if the worse came to the worst, there was plenty of furniture in the house to pay the rest of the tradesmen. Still, of all burdens, next to sin, that of debt must be heaviest.

"What *is* the matter, my darling?" asked Percivale.

I took a half crown out of my pocket, and held it out on the palm of my hand.

"That's all I've got, Percivale," I said.

"Oh! That's all, is it?" he returned lightly.

"Yes, isn't that enough?" I said with some indignation.

"Certainly, for tonight," he answered, "seeing the shops are shut. But is that all that's troubling you?"

"It seems to me quite enough," I said again, "and if you had the housekeeping to do, and the bills to pay, you would think a solitary half crown quite enough to make you miserable."

"Never mind, so long as it's a good one," he said. "I'll get you more tomorrow."

"How can you do that?" I asked.

"Easily," he answered. "You'll see. Don't you trouble your dear heart about it for a moment."

I felt relieved, and asked him no more questions.

The next morning, when I went into the study to speak to him, he was not there. I guessed that he had gone to town to get the money, for he had not been out before since his illness, at least not without me. But I hoped of all things he was not going to borrow it of a moneylender, of which I had a great and justifiable horror. I would have sold three-fourths of the things in the house rather. But as I turned to leave the study, anxious both about himself and his proceedings, I thought something was different, and soon discovered that a certain favorite picture was missing from the wall. It was clear he had gone either to sell it or raise money upon it.

He soon returned and put two five-pound notes into my hands, although with a look of forced cheerfulness.

"Is that all you got for that picture?" I said.

"That is all Mr. Spencer would advance me," he answered. "I thought he had made enough by me to have risked a little more than that, but the picture dealers—well, never mind. That is enough to give time for twenty things to happen."

And no doubt twenty things did happen, but none of them of the sort he meant. The ten pounds sank through my purse like water through gravel. I paid a number of small bills at once, for they pressed the more heavily upon me that I knew the money was wanted, and by the end of another fortnight we were as badly off as before, with an additional trouble.

Jemima gave warning, for it was out of my power to pay her wages, and there was no sign of her yielding.

I tried to pray to God to deliver us, but a whole day would sometimes pass under a weight of care that amounted often to misery, and not until its close would I see that I had been all the weary hours without God. Even when more hopeful, I would keep looking and looking for the impossibility of something to happen of itself, instead of looking for some good and perfect gift to come down from the Father of lights.

It was, indeed, a miserable time. There was, besides, one definite thought that always choked my prayers: I could not say in my conscience that I had been sufficiently careful either in my management or my expenditures. "If," I thought, "I could be certain that I had done my best, I should be able to trust in God for all that lies beyond my power. But now He may mean to punish me for my carelessness." Then why should I not endure it calmly and without complaint? Alas! It was not I alone that thus would be punished, but my children and my husband as well.

Sometimes, however, in more faithful moods, I would reason with myself that God would not be hard upon me, even if I had not been so saving as I ought. My father had taken his son's debts on himself, and would not allow him to be disgraced more than could be helped. And, if an earthly parent would act thus for his child, would our Father in heaven be less tender with us?

Things went on, and grew no better.

Percivale at length asked Roger if he had any money by him to lend him a little. Roger gave him all he had, amounting to six pounds, a wonderful amount for Roger to have accumulated. The next step I had in view was to take my little valuables to the pawnbroker's—amongst them a watch, whose face was encircled with a row of good-sized diamonds. It had belonged to my great-grandmother, and my mother had given it to me when I was married.

Percivale had gone out, and I was sitting in the drawing room, lost in anything but a blessed reverie, with the children chattering amongst themselves beside me, when Jemima entered, looking subdued.

"If you please, ma'am, this is my day," she said.

"Have you got a place, then, Jemima?" I asked, for I had been so much occupied with my own affairs that I had thought little of the future of the poor girl to whom I could have given but a lukewarm recommendation for anything prized amongst housekeepers.

"No, Ma'am. Please, Ma'am, mayn't I stop?"

"No, Jemima. I am very sorry, but I can't afford to keep you. I shall have to do all the work myself when you are gone."

Jemima burst into an Irish wail, mingled with sobs and tears, crying between the convulsions of all three, "I thought there was something wrong, Mis'ess. You and master looked so scared-like. Please, Mis'ess, don't send me away."

"I never wanted to send you away, Jemima. You wanted to go yourself."

"No, Ma'am, *that* I didn't. I only wanted you to ask me to stop. Wirra! Wirra! It's myself is sorry I was so rude. It's not me—it's my temper, Mis'ess. I do believe I was born with a devil inside me."

I could not help laughing, partly from amusement, partly from relief.

"But you see I can't ask you to stop," I said. "I've no money, not even enough to pay you today."

"I don't want no money, Ma'am. Let me stop, and I'll cook for yez, and wash and scrub for yez, to the end o' my days. An' I'll eat no more than'll keep the life in me. Please 'm, I ha' got fifteen pounds in the savings bank. I'll give ye all of that, if ye'll let me stop wid ye."

"Thank you very much, Jemima," I said, as soon as I could speak. "I won't take your money, for then you would be as poor as I am. But if you would like to stop with us, you shall, and I won't pay you till I'm able."

The poor girl was profuse in her thanks, and left the room sobbing in her apron.

It was a gloomy, drizzly, dreary afternoon. The children were hard to amuse, and I was glad when their bedtime arrived. It was getting late before Percivale returned. He looked pale, and I found afterward that he had walked home. He had got wet, and had to change some of his clothes. When I related to him what had passed with Jemima, he laughed merrily and was evidently a good deal relieved. Then I asked him where he had been.

"To the city," he answered.

"Have you sold another picture?" I asked. As much as we wanted the money, I could ill bear the thought of his pictures going for the price of mere potboilers.

"No," he replied. "The last picture is blocking the way. Mr. Tait has been advertising it as a bargain for a hundred and fifty. But he hasn't sold it yet, and can't—he says—risk ten pounds more on another. What's to come of it, I don't know. But meantime it's a comfort that Jemima can wait for *her* money."

Later I thought I saw a look on Percivale's face which I had never seen there before. After a long pause, during which we had been both looking into the fire, he said, "Wynnie, I'm going to paint a better picture than I've ever painted yet. I can, and I will."

"But how are we to live in the meantime?" I said.

His face fell, and I saw with shame what a Job's comforter I was. Instead of sympathizing with his ardor, I had quenched it. What if my foolish remark had ruined a great picture! Anyhow, it had wounded a great heart, which had turned to labor as its plainest duty, and would thereby have been strengthened to endure and to hope. It was too cruel of me. I knelt by his knee, and told him I was both ashamed and sorry I had been so faithless and unkind. He made little of it, and even tried to be merry over it. But I could see well enough that I had let a gust of the foggy night into his soul, and I was thoroughly vexed with myself. We went to bed gloomy, but slept well and awoke more cheerful in the morning.

TWENTY-FIVE

The Rays of Sunshine

As we were dressing, it came into my mind that I had forgotten to give Percivale a black-bordered letter which had arrived the night before. It looked like a business letter, and I feared it might be a demand for the overdue rent of the house. By this time I dreaded opening any letter if I did not recognize the writing.

"Here is a letter, Percivale," I said. "I'm sorry I forgot to give it to you last night."

"Who is it from?" he asked, talking through his towel from his dressing room.

"I don't know. I didn't open it. It looks like something disagreeable."

He came in, opened it, and read it. Then suddenly his arms were around me and his cheek on mine.

"Read that," he said, putting the letter into my hand.

It was from a lawyer in Shrewsbury, informing him that his godmother, with whom he had been a great favorite when a boy, had died, and had left him three hundred pounds.

Death itself may sometimes be a release, but the gift out of this woman's death was a reprieve to us. I could only weep and thank God, once more believing in my Father in heaven. But it was a humbling thought that, if He had not thus helped me, I might have ceased to believe in Him. I saw plainly that my own faith was but a wretched thing. It is all very well to have noble theories about God; but where is the good of them except we actually trust in Him as a real, present, living, loving Being, who counts us of more value than many sparrows, and will not let one of them fall to the ground without Him?

"I thought, Wynnie, if there was such a God as you believed in, and with you to pray to Him, we shouldn't be long without a hearing," said my husband.

But our troubles weren't nearly over yet. Percivale wrote, acknowledging the letter, and requesting the money as he was in immediate want of it.

The reply was that the trustees were not bound to pay the legacies for a year, but that possibly they might stretch a point in his favor if he applied to them. Percivale did so, but received a very curt answer, with little encouragement to expect anything but the extreme of legal delay. He received the money, however, about four months after, lightened, to the great disappointment of my ignorance, of thirty pounds legacy duty.

In the meantime, although our minds were much relieved, and Percivale was working away at his new picture with great energy and courage, the immediate pressure of circumstances was nearly as painful as ever. It was a comfort, however, to know that we might borrow on the security of the legacy but, greatly grudging the loss of the interest which that would involve, I would have persuaded Percivale to ask a loan of Lady Bernard. He objected, on the ground that it would be disagreeable to Lady Bernard to be repaid the sum she had lent us! He would have finally consented, however, I have little doubt, had the absolute necessity for borrowing arrived.

About a week or ten days after the blessed news, he had a note from Mr. Tait, whom he had authorized to part with the picture for thirty guineas. (How much this was under its value, it is not easy to say, but, if the fairy godmother's executors had paid her legacy at once, that picture would not have been sold for less than five times the amount. The last time it changed hands, it fetched five hundred and seventy pounds.)

Mr. Tait wrote that he had an offer of five and twenty for it, desiring to know whether he might sell it for that sum. Percivale at once gave his consent, and the next day received a check for eleven pounds and some odd shillings, the difference being the borrowed amount upon it, its interest, the commission charged on the sale, and the price of a small picture frame.

The next day, Percivale had a visitor at the studio—no less a person than Mr. Baddeley, with his shirtfront in full blossom, and his diamond wallowing in light on his fifth finger. His hands were as huge as they were soft and white—hands descended of generations of laborious ones, but which had never themselves done any work beyond paddling in money.

He greeted Percivale with a jolly condescension and told him that, having seen and rather liked a picture of his the other day, he had come to inquire whether he had one that would do for a pendant to it, as he should like to have it, provided he did not want a fancy price for it.

Percivale felt as if he were setting out his children for sale, as he invited him to look about the room, and turned round a few from against the wall. The great man flitted hither and thither, spying at one after another through the cylinder of his curved hand, Percivale going on with his painting as if no one were there.

"How much do you want for this sketch?" asked Mr. Baddeley, at length, pointing to one of the most highly finished paintings in the room.

"I put three hundred on it at the Academy Exhibition," answered

Percivale. "My friends thought it too little, but as it has been on my hands a long time now, and pictures don't rise in price in the keeping of the painter, I shouldn't mind taking two for it."

"Two tens, I suppose you mean," said Mr. Baddeley.

Percivale gave him a look, and I know what kind of phenomenon that look must have been.

"Come, now," Mr. Baddeley went on, perhaps misinterpreting the look, for it was such as a man of his property was not in the habit of receiving. "You mustn't think I'm made of money, or that I'm a green hand in the market. I know what your pictures fetch, and I'm a pretty sharp man of business, I believe. What do you really mean to say and stick to? Ready money, you know."

"Three hundred," said Percivale coolly.

"Why, Mr. Percivale!" cried Mr. Baddeley, drawing himself up with the air of one who knew a trick worth two of that, "I paid Mr. Tait fifty pounds, neither more nor less, for a picture of yours yesterday—a picture, allow me to say, worth—"

He turned again to the one in question with a critical air, as if about to estimate to a fraction its value as compared with the other.

"Worth three of that, some people think," said Percivale.

"The price of this, then, joking aside, is—?"

"Three hundred pounds," answered Percivale quietly.

"I understood you wished to sell it," said Mr. Baddeley, beginning, for all his good nature, to look offended, as well he might.

"I do wish to sell it. I happen to be in want of money."

"Then I'll be liberal, and offer you the same I paid for the other. I'll send you a check this afternoon for fifty—with pleasure."

"You cannot have that picture under three hundred."

"Why!" said the rich man, puzzled. "You offered it for two hundred, not five minutes ago."

"Yes, and you pretended to think I meant two tens."

"Offended you, I fear."

"At all events, you betrayed so much ignorance of painting, that I would rather not have a picture of mine in your house."

"You're the first man who ever presumed to tell me I was ignorant of painting," said Mr. Baddeley, now thoroughly indignant.

"You have heard the truth, then, for the first time," said Percivale, and resumed his work.

Mr. Baddeley walked out of the study.

I am not sure that he was so very ignorant. He had been buying popular pictures for some time, paying thousands for certain of them. I suspect he had eye enough to see that my husband's would probably rise in value, and, with the true huckster spirit, was ambitious of boasting how little he had given compared with what they were really worth.

Percivale in this case was doubtless rude. He had an insuperable aversion to men of Mr. Baddeley's class—men who could have no position but for their money, and who yet presumed upon it, as if it were their gifts and graces, genius and learning, judgment and art, all in one.

Before long, through Lady Bernard, he sold a picture at a fair price, and soon after, seeing in a shop window the one Mr. Tait had sold to Mr. Baddeley, marked ten pounds now, went in and bought it. Within the year he sold it for a hundred and fifty.

By working day and night almost, he finished his new picture in time for the Academy—and, as he had himself predicted, it proved the best that he had ever painted. It was bought at once for three hundred pounds, and never since then have we been in want of money.

TWENTY-SIX
Lady Bernard Again

I have not mentioned Marion in these troubles. I could not bring myself to tell her of them, partly because she was in some trouble herself, from strangers who had taken rooms in the house and made mischief between her and her grandchildren, and partly because I knew she would insist on going to Lady Bernard. Although I should not have minded it myself, I knew that nothing but seeing the children hungry would have driven my husband to consent to it.

One evening, after it was all over, I told Lady Bernard the story. She allowed me to finish it without saying a word. When I had ended, she still sat silent for a few moments. Then laying her hand on my arm, she said, "My dear child, you were very wrong, as well as very unkind. Why did you not let me know?"

"Because my husband would never have allowed me," I answered.

"Then I must have a talk with your husband," she said.

"I wish you would," I replied, "for I can't help thinking Percivale too severe about such things."

The very next day she called, and did have a talk with him in the study.

"I have come to quarrel with you, Mr. Percivale," said Lady Bernard.

"I'm sorry to hear it," he returned. "You're the last person I should like to quarrel with, for it would imply some unpardonable fault in me."

"It does imply a fault—and a great one," she rejoined, "though I trust not an unpardonable one. That depends on whether you can repent of it."

She spoke with such a serious air that Percivale grew uneasy, and began to wonder what he could possibly have done to offend her.

When she saw him troubled, she smiled.

"Is it not a fault, Mr. Percivale, to prevent one from obeying the divine law of bearing another's burden?"

"But," said Percivale, "I read as well, that every man shall bear his own burden."

"Ah!" returned Lady Bernard, "but I learn that two different Greek words are used there, which we translate only by the English *burden.* I cannot tell you what they are. I can only tell you the practical result. We are to bear one another's burdens of pain or grief or misfortune or doubt—whatever weighs one down is to be borne by another. But the man who is tempted to exalt himself over his neighbors is taught to remember that he has his own load of grace to bear and answer for. It is just a weaker form of the lesson of the mote and the beam. You cannot get out at that door, Mr. Percivale. I beg you will read the passage in your Greek Testament, and see if you have not misapplied it. You *ought* to have let me bear your burden."

"Well, you see, my dear Lady Bernard," returned Percivale, at a loss to reply to such a vigorous assault, "I knew how it would be. You would have come here and bought pictures you didn't want, and I, knowing all the time you did it only to give me the money, should have had to talk to you as if I were taken by it, and I really could *not* stand it."

"There you are altogether wrong. Besides depriving me of the opportunity of fulfilling a duty, and of the pleasure and the honor of helping you to bear your burden, you have deprived me of the opportunity of indulging a positive passion for pictures. I am constantly compelled to restrain it lest I should spend too much of the money given me for the common good on my own private tastes. But here was a chance for me! I might have had some of your lovely pictures in my drawing room now, with a good conscience and a happy heart, if you had only been friendly. It was too bad of you, Mr. Percivale! I am not pretending in the least when I assert that I am really and thoroughly disappointed."

"I haven't a word to say for myself," returned Percivale.

"You couldn't have said a better word, then," rejoined Lady Bernard. "I hope you will never have to say it again."

"That I shall not. If ever I find myself in any difficulty worth speaking of, I will let you know at once."

"Thank you. Then we are friends again. And now I do think I am entitled to a picture—at least, I think it will be pardonable if I yield to the *very* strong temptation I am under at this moment to buy one. Let me see, what have you in the slave market, as your wife calls it?"

She bought *The Street Musician,* as Percivale had named that first picture he painted after his illness. I was more miserable than I ought to have been when I found he had parted with it, but it was a great consolation to think it had gone to Lady Bernard's. She was the only one, except my mother or Miss Clare, I could bear to think of as its possessor.

Percivale had asked her what I thought a very low price for it, and I judge that Lady Bernard thought the same. But after what had passed between them, she would not have ventured to expostulate. With such a man as my husband, I fancy, she thought it best to let well enough alone. Anyhow, one day soon after this, her servant brought him a little box, containing a fine brilliant.

"The good lady's kindness is longsighted," said my husband, as he placed it on his finger. "I shall be hard up, though, before I part with this. Wynnie, I've actually got a finer diamond than Mr. Baddeley! It *is* a beauty, if ever there was one!"

My husband, with all his carelessness of dress and adornment, has almost a passion for stones. It is delightful to hear him talk about them, but he had never possessed a single gem before Lady Bernard made him this present. I believe he is child enough to be happier for all his life.

TWENTY-SEVEN

Mrs. Cromwell Comes

The moment the legacy was paid and all our liabilities discharged, my husband took us all to Hastings. I had never before been to any other seacoast town where the land was worthy of the sea, except Kilkhaven. Assuredly, there is no place within easy reach of London to compare with Hastings. The immediate shore with its earthy cliffs is vastly inferior to the magnificent rock about Tintagel, but there is no outlook on the sea that I know more satisfying than that from the heights of Hastings, especially East Hill. From the west side you may, when weary of the ocean, look straight down on the ancient port, with its old houses and fine, multiform red roofs, through the gauze of blue smoke which at eve of a summer day fills the narrow valley, softening the rough goings-on of life with the gentleness of sea and shore, field and sky.

On the brow of East Hill, just where it begins to sink towards Ecclesbourne Glen, stands a small, old, rickety house in the midst of the sweet grass of the downs. This house my husband was fortunate in finding to let, and took for three months. It was there I made the acquaintance of Mrs. Cromwell.

One bright day, about noon, a rather fashionable maid ran up to our little garden, begging for some water for her mistress. Sending her on with water, I followed myself with a glass of sherry.

The door in our garden house opened immediately on a green hollow in the hill, sloping toward the glen. As I stepped from the little gate onto the grass, I saw, to my surprise, that a white fog was blowing in from the sea. The heights on the opposite side of the glen, partially obscured thereby, looked more majestic than was their wont, and were mottled with patches of duller and brighter color as the drifts of the fog were heaped or parted here or there. Far down, at the foot of the cliffs, the waves of the rising tide caught and threw back what sunlight reached them, and thinned with their shine the fog between. It was all so strange and fine, and had come on so suddenly, that I stood for a moment or two and gazed, almost forgetting why I was there.

Then I saw, in the sheltered hollow before me, a lady seated in a curiously shaped chair, a kind of litter. It was plain she was an invalid from her paleness and the tension of the skin on her face which revealed the outline of the bones beneath. Her features were finely formed, but rather small, and her forehead low—a Greeklike face with large, pale blue eyes that reminded me of little Amy Morley. She smiled very sweetly when she saw me and shook her head at the wine.

"I only wanted a little water," she said. "This fog stifles me."

"It has come on very suddenly," I said. "Perhaps it is the cold of it that affects your breathing. You don't seem very strong, and any sudden change of temperature—"

"I am not the most vigorous of mortals," she answered with a sad smile. "But the day seemed of such indubitable character that, after my husband had brought me here in the carriage, he sent it home, and left me with my maid, while he went for a long walk across the downs. When he sees the change in the weather, though, he will turn directly."

"It won't do to wait him here," I said. "We must get you in at once! Would it be wrong to press you to take a little of this wine, just to counteract a chill?"

"I daren't touch anything but water," she replied. "It would make me feverish at once."

"Run and tell the cook," I said to the maid, "that I want her here. You and she could carry your mistress in, could you not?"

"There's no occasion for that, Ma'am. She's as light as a feather," was the whispered answer.

"I am quite ashamed of giving you so much trouble," said the lady, either hearing or guessing at our words. "My husband will be very grateful to you."

"It is only an act of common humanity," I said.

But, as I spoke, her fair brow clouded a little, as if she was not accustomed to common humanity, and the word sounded harsh in her ear. The cloud, however, passed so quickly that I doubted whether it had really been there.

Jemima and her own maid lifted her with the utmost ease and bore her gently towards the house. The garden gate was just wide enough to let the chair through, and in a minute more she was on the sofa. Then a fit of coughing came on which shook her dreadfully. When it had passed she lay quiet, with closed eyes, and a smile hovering about her sweet, thin-lipped mouth. By and by she opened her eyes and looked at me with a pitiful expression.

"I fear you are far from well," I said.

"I'm dying," she returned quietly.

"I hope not," was all I could answer.

"Why should you hope not?" she returned. "I desire to depart. For me to die will be all gain."

"But your friends?" I ventured to suggest, feeling my way, and not quite relishing either the form or tone of her utterance.

"I have none but my husband."

"Then your husband?" I persisted.

"Ah!" she said mournfully, "He will miss me, no doubt, for a while. But it *must* be a weight off him, for I have been a sufferer so long!"

At this moment I heard a heavy, hasty step in the passage. Then the door opened, and in rushed a burly man, clumsy and active, wiping his face with his hand. He carried an umbrella, and was followed by a great, lumbering Newfoundland dog.

"Down, Polyphemus!" he said to the dog, which crept under a chair. He, taking no notice of my presence, hurried up to his wife.

"My love! My little dove!" he said eagerly. "Did you think I had forsaken you to the cruel elements?"

"No, Alcibiades," she answered with a sweet little drawl. "But you do not observe that I am not the only lady in the room." Then, turning to me, "This is my husband, Mr. Cromwell," she said. "I cannot tell him *your* name."

"I am Mrs. Percivale," I returned, almost mechanically.

"I beg your pardon, Ma'am," said Mr. Cromwell, bowing. "Permit my anxiety about my poor wife to cover my rudeness. I had climbed the other side of the glen before I saw the fog, and it is no such easy matter to get up and down these hills of yours. I am greatly obliged to you for your hospitality. You have doubtless saved her life, for she is a frail flower, shrinking from the least breath of cold."

The lady closed her eyes again, and the gentleman took her hand and felt her pulse. He seemed about twice her age—she not thirty, he well past fifty, the top of his head bald, and his gray hair sticking out fiercely over his good-natured red cheeks. He laid her hand gently down, put his hat on the table and his umbrella in a corner, wiped his face again, drew a chair near the sofa, and took his place by her side. I thought it better to leave them.

When I reentered after a while, I saw from the seaward window that the wind had risen, and was driving great, thick, white masses of seafog landwards. It was the storm wind of that southwest coast which dashes the pebbles over the Parade, and the heavy spray against the houses. Mr. Alcibiades Cromwell was sitting as I had left him, silent, by the side of his wife, whose blue-veined eyelids had apparently never been lifted from her large eyes.

"Is there anything I could offer Mrs. Cromwell?" I said. "Could she not eat something?"

"It is very little she can take," he answered, "but you are very kind. If you could let her have a little beef tea? She generally has a spoonful or two about this time of day."

"I am sorry we have none," I said, "and it would be far too long for her to wait. I have a nice chicken, though, ready for cooking. If she could take a little chicken-broth, that would be ready in a very little while."

"Thank you a thousand times, Ma'am," he said heartily. "Nothing could be better. She might even be induced to eat a mouthful of the chicken. But I am afraid your extreme kindness prevents me from being so thoroughly ashamed as I ought to be at putting you to so much trouble for perfect strangers."

"It is a pleasure to be of service to anyone in want of it," I said.

Mrs. Cromwell opened her eyes and smiled gratefully.

I left the room to give orders about the chicken. When I returned, Mr. Cromwell had open in his hand a little hymnbook of mine, and his wife was saying to him, "That is lovely! Thank you, Husband. How can it be I never saw it before? I am quite astonished."

She little knows what multitudes of hymns there are! I thought. My father's collection had given me some idea of the extent of that department of religious literature.

"This is a hymnbook we are not acquainted with," said Mr. Cromwell, addressing me.

"It is not much known," I answered. "It was compiled by a friend of my father's for his own schools."

"And this," he went on, "is a very beautiful hymn. You may trust my wife's judgment, Mrs. Percivale. She lives on hymns."

In telling them a few of the facts connected with the hymn, I presume I had manifested my admiration with some degree of fervor.

"Ah!" said Mrs. Cromwell, opening her eyes very wide, and letting the rising tears fill them, "Ah! Mrs. Percivale! You are—you must be one of us!"

"You must tell me first who you are," I said.

She held out her hand, and I gave her mine. She drew me toward her, and whispered almost in my ear—though why the secrecy I can only imagine—the name of a certain small and exclusive sect.

"No," I answered, speaking with the calmness of self-compulsion, for I confess I felt repelled. "I am not one of you, except as we all belong to the Church of Christ."

She gave a little sigh of disappointment, closed her eyes for a moment, opened them again with a smile and said, with a pleading tone, "But you do believe in personal religion?"

"I don't see," I returned, "how religion can be anything but personal."

Again she closed her eyes in a way that made me think how convenient bad health must be—conferring not only the privilege of passing into retirement at any desirable moment, but of doing so in such a ready and easy manner as the mere dropping of the eyelids.

I rose to leave the room once more. Mr. Cromwell, who had made way for me to sit beside his wife, stood looking out the window, against which came sweeping the great volumes of mist. Not only was the sea invisible, but even the brow of the cliffs.

When he turned toward me, I saw that his face had lost much of its rubicund hue, and looked troubled and anxious.

"There is nothing for it," I said to myself, "but to keep them all night." I did not much like it, I confess, for I was not much interested in either of them, while the sect to which she belonged was the narrowest and most sectarian in Christendom. It was a pity she had sought to claim me by a would-be closer bond than that of the body of Christ. At the same time I did feel some curiosity concerning the oddly yoked couple, and wondered whether the lady was really so ill as she would appear. She might be using her illness both as an excuse for self-indulgence, and as a means of keeping her husband's interest. I did not like the wearing of her religion on her sleeve, nor the mellifluous drawl in which she spoke.

When the chicken broth was ready, she partook daintily, but before she ended had made a very good meal, including a wing and a bit of the breast, after which she fell asleep.

"There seems little chance of the weather clearing," said Mr. Cromwell in a whisper, as I approached the window where he once more stood.

"You must remain here for the night," I said.

"My dear Madam, I couldn't think of it," he returned. "She requires so many little comforts and peculiar contrivances to entice repose, that I must get her home."

"Where do you live?" I asked, not sorry to find his intention of going so fixed.

"We have a house in Warrior Square," he answered. "We live in London, but have been here all the past winter. I doubt if she improves, though."

He said the last words in a yet lower and more mournful whisper. Then, with a shake of his head, he turned and gazed again through the window.

A peculiar little cough from the sofa made us both look round. Mrs. Cromwell was awake and searching for her handkerchief. Her husband understood her movements and hurried to her assistance. When she took the handkerchief from her mouth, there was a red spot against the white. Mr. Cromwell's face turned the color of lead, but his wife looked up at him and smiled a sweet, consciously pathetic smile.

"He has sent for me," she said. "The messenger has come."

Her husband made no answer. His eyes seemed starting from his head.

"Who is your medical man?" I asked.

He told me, and I sent off my housemaid to fetch him. It was a long hour before he arrived. As often as I peeped in, I saw Mr. Cromwell sitting silent, and holding her head, until the last time, when I found him reading a hymn to her. She was apparently once more asleep.

When the doctor came, he proceeded to examine her with much care, and averred in her hearing that he found nothing serious. But he told her husband apart that there was considerable mischief, and assured me afterward that her lungs were all but gone, and that she could not live beyond a month or two. She had better be removed to her own house, he said, as speedily as possible.

"But it would be cruelty to send her out in a day like this," I returned.

"Yes, yes. I did not mean that," he said. "But tomorrow, perhaps. You'll see what the weather is like. Is Mrs. Cromwell an old friend?"

"I have never seen her until today," I replied.

"Ah!" he remarked, and said no more.

It was a week before she got up again, and a month before she was carried down the hill, during which time her husband sat up with her or slept on a sofa in the room beside her, every night. During the day I took a share in the nursing, which was by no means oppressive, for she did not suffer much, and required little. Her chief demand was for hymns, and the only annoyance was that she often wished me to admire with her such as I could only half like, and occasionally such as were thoroughly distasteful to me. Her husband had brought her own collection from Warrior Square—volumes of hymns in manuscript, copied by her own hand, many of them strange to me. None of those I read were altogether devoid of literary merit, and some of them were lovely both in feeling and form. But all, even the best, belonged to one class—a class breathing a certain tone difficult to describe. What pleased me in them was their full utterance of personal devotion to the Saviour, and what displeased me was a sort of sentimental regard of self in the matter—an implied special, and thus partially exclusive, preference of the Saviour for the individual making use of them. It was a certain fundamental want of humility, therefore, although the forms of speech in which they were cast might be laboriously humble. They also not unfrequently manifested a great leaning to the forms of earthly show as representative of the glories of that kingdom which the Lord says is *within us.*

One morning, the fine weather returned in all its summer glory, and Mrs. Cromwell was lying on a couch in her own room near the window, where she could gaze on the expanse of sea below. This morning it was streaked with the most delicate gradations of distance, sweep beyond sweep, line and band and ribbon of softly varying hue, leading the eyes on and on into the infinite. There may have been some atmospheric illusion ending off the show, for the last reaches so mingled with the air that you saw no horizon line, only a great breadth of border—no spot you could assign with certainty either to sea or sky, while here and there was a vessel appearing to pursue its path in the sky, and not upon the sea. It was a still, gray forenoon, with a film of cloud over all the heavens, and many horizontal strata of deeper but varying density near the horizon.

Mrs. Cromwell had lain for some time with her large eyes fixed on the farthest confusion of sea and sky.

"I have been sending out my soul," she said at length, "to travel all across those distances, step by step, on to the gates of pearl. Who knows but that may be the path I must travel to meet the Bridegroom?"

"The way is wide," I said. "What if you should miss Him?"

I spoke almost involuntarily. The style of her talk was very distasteful to me, and I had just been thinking of what I had once heard my father say, that at no time were people in more danger of being theatrical than when upon their deathbeds.

"No," she returned, with a smile of gentle superiority. "No, that cannot be. Is He not waiting for me? Has He not chosen me, and called me for His own? Is not my Jesus mine? I shall *not* miss Him. He waits to give me my new name and clothe me in the garments of righteousness."

As she spoke, she clasped her thin hands and looked upward with a radiant expression. Far as it was from me to hint, even in my own soul, that the Saviour was not hers, yet tenfold more hers than she was able to think, I doubted whether her heart and soul and mind were as close to Him as she thought. She could not be wrong in trusting Him, but could she be right in her notion of the measure to which her union with Him had been perfected? A little fear, soon to pass into reverence, might be to her a salutary thing. The fear would heighten and deepen the love, and purify it from that self which haunted her whole consciousness, and of which she had not yet sickened, as one day she certainly must.

"My lamp is burning," she said. "I feel it burning. I love my Lord. It would be false to say otherwise."

"Are you sure you have oil enough in your vessel as well as in your lamp?" I said.

"Ah, you are one of the doubting!" she returned kindly. "Don't you know that sweet hymn about feeding our lamps from the olive trees of Gethsemane? The idea is taken from the lamp the Prophet Zechariah saw in his vision, into which two olive branches, through two golden pipes, emptied the golden oil out of themselves. If we are thus one with the olive tree, the oil cannot fail us. It is not as if we had to fill our lamps from a cruse of our own. This is the cruse that cannot fail."

"True, true," I said, "but ought we not to examine our own selves whether we are in the faith?"

"Let those examine who doubt," she replied, and I could not but yield in my heart that she had had the best of the argument.

For I knew that the confidence in Christ which prevents us from thinking of ourselves, and makes us eager to obey His Word, leaving all the care of our feelings to Him, is a true and healthy faith. Hence I could not answer her, although I doubted for several reasons whether her peace came from such confidence. One, that she seemed full of herself. Another, that she seemed to find no difficulty with herself in any way, and surely, she was too young for all struggle to be over! I perceived no reference to the will of God in regard of anything she had to do, only in regard of what she had to suffer, and especially in regard of that smallest of matters, when she was to go. Here I checked myself, for what could she *do* in such a state of health? But then she never spoke as if she had any anxiety about the welfare of other people. That, however, might be from her absolute contentment in the will of God.

But why did she always look to the Saviour through a mist of hymns, and never go straight back to the genuine old Good News, or to the mighty thoughts and exhortations with which the first preachers of that news followed them up and unfolded the grandeur of their goodness?

But I had no right to say anything, and to be uneasy about her was to distrust Him whose it was to teach her, and who would perfect that which He had certainly begun in her. For her heart, however poor and faulty and flimsy its faith might be, was yet certainly drawn toward the object of faith. I, therefore, said nothing. My plain duty was to serve her as one of those least whom the Saviour set forth as representing Himself. I would do it to her as unto Him.

My children were out the greater part of the day, and Dora was with me, so that I had more leisure than I had had for a long time. I therefore set myself to wait upon her as a kind of lady's maid in things spiritual. Her own maid, understanding her ways, was sufficient for things temporal. I resolved to try to help her after her own fashion, and not after mine, for however strange the nourish-ment she preferred, it must at length be of the kind she could best assimilate. My care should be to give her her gruel as good as I might, and her beef tea strong, with chicken broth instead of barley water and delusive jelly.

I could set myself to find fitting pabulum for her and that of her chosen sort. This was possible for me in virtue of my father's collection of hymns, and the aid he could give me. I therefore sent him a detailed description of what seemed to me her condition, and what I thought I might do for her. His answer arrived in the shape of a box of books, each bristling with paper marks, many of them inscribed with some fact concerning, or criticism upon, the hymn indicated. And he wrote that he quite agreed with my notion of the right mode of serving her.

I judged that in all of my father's hymns there was something she must appreciate, although the main drift of several would be entirely beyond her apprehension. Accordingly, the next time she asked me to read from her collection, I made the request that she would listen to some of which I believed she did not know, but would, I thought, like. She consented with eagerness, was astonished to find she knew none of them, expressed much approbation of some, and showed herself delighted with others.

That she must have had some literary faculty seems evident from the genuine pleasure she took in simple, quaint, sometimes odd hymns of her own peculiar kind. But the very best of another sort she could not appreciate.

However, my endeavors were crowned with success insofar that she accepted better specimens of the sort she liked than any she had, and I think they must have had a good influence upon her.

She seemed to have no fear of death, contemplating the change she believed at hand, not with equanimity merely, but with expectation. She even wrote hymns about it—sweet, pretty, and weak, always with herself and the love of her Saviour for *her* in the foreground.

One of my conversations with her took place the evening before her departure for her own house. Her husband had gone to make some final preparations. For one who expected to be unclothed that she might be clothed upon, she certainly made a tolerable to-do about the garment she was so soon to lay aside, especially seeing she often spoke of it as an ill-fitting garment—never with peevishness or complaint, only, as it seemed to me, with far more interest than it was worth. Perhaps I should have been considerably less bewildered with her conduct had I suspected that she was not half so near death as she chose to think, and that she had as yet suffered little.

That evening, the stars just beginning to glimmer through the warm flush that lingered from the sunset, we sat together in the drawing room looking out on the sea. My patient appearing, from the light in her eyes, about to go off into one of her ecstatic moods, I hastened to forestall it.

"It seems like turning you out to let you go tomorrow, Mrs. Cromwell," I said, "but, you see, our three months are up two days after that, and I cannot help it."

"You have been very kind," she said, half abstractedly.

"And you are really much better. Who would have thought three weeks ago to see you so well today?"

"Ah, you congratulate me, do you?" she rejoined, turning her big full eyes upon me. "Congratulate me that I am doomed to be still a captive in the prison of this vile body? Is it kind? Is it well?"

"At least, you must remember, if you are doomed, who dooms you."

"Oh, that I had the wings of a dove!" she cried, avoiding my remark, of which I doubt she saw the drift. "Think, dear Mrs. Percivale, the society of saints and angels—all brightness and harmony and peace! Is it not worth forsaking this world to inherit a kingdom like that? Wouldn't *you* like to go? Don't you wish to fly away and be at rest?"

She spoke as if expostulating and reasoning with one she would persuade to some kind of holy emigration.

"Not until I am sent for," I answered.

"*I* am sent for," she returned, and then recited,

> Here all my labor is so poor!
> Here all my love so faint!
> But when I reach the heavenly door,
> I cease the weary plaint.

I couldn't help wishing she would cease her plaint a little sooner.

"But suppose," I ventured to say, "it were the will of God that you should live many years yet."

"That cannot be. And why should you wish it for me? Is it not better to depart and be with Him? What pleasure could it be to a weak, worn creature like me to go on living in this isle of banishment?"

"But suppose you were to recover your health? Would it not be delightful to *do* something for His sake? If you would think of how much there is to be done in the world, perhaps you would wish less to die and leave it."

"Do not tempt me," she returned reproachfully. And then she quoted a passage of application, which to her own case appeared to me so irreverent that I felt I could bear with her no longer.

She did leave the next day, and I breathed more freely than since she had come.

I concluded that Mrs. Cromwell was but a spoiled child, who would, somehow or other, be brought to her senses before all was over. I was ashamed of my impatience with her, and believed if I could have learned her history, it would have explained the rare phenomenon of one apparently able to look death in the face with so little of the really spiritual to support her; for she seemed to me to know Christ only after the flesh. But had she indeed ever looked death in the face?

TWENTY-EIGHT

Mrs. Cromwell Goes

I heard nothing more of Mrs. Cromwell for about a year. A note or two passed between us, and then all communication ceased. This, I am happy to think, was not immediately my fault; not that it mattered much, for we were not then fitted for much communion—we had too little in common.

We could not commune, that is, with any heartiness. The Saviour of whom she spoke so often, and evidently thought so much, was in a great measure a being of her own fancy. She manifested no desire to find out who the Christ was who had spent thirty-three years making a revelation of Himself to the world. The knowledge she had about Him was not even secondhand, but at many removes. She did not study His words or His actions to learn His thought or His meanings, but lived in a kind of dreamland of her own, which could be interesting only to the dreamer. She did not take the trouble to "know Him and the power of His resurrection." Therefore we had scarcely enough common ground to meet upon. I could not help contrasting her religion with that of Marion Clare.

At length I had a note from her, begging me to go and see her at her house in Richmond, and apologizing for not coming to me, on the score of her health. I felt it my duty to go, but sadly grudged the loss of time, for I expected neither pleasure nor profit from the visit. Percivale went with me, and left me at the door to have a row on the river, and to call for me at a certain hour.

The house and grounds were both luxurious and lovely—two qualities often dissociated. She could have nothing to desire of this world's gifts, I thought. But the moment I saw her, I was shocked at the change. She was in a widow's cap, and disease and coming death were plain on every feature. The face I had held in my memory was healthy in contrast.

"My dear Mrs. Cromwell!" I gasped.

"You see," she said, and sitting down on a straight-backed chair, looked at me with lusterless eyes.

Death had been hovering about her windows before, but had entered at last—not to take the sickly young woman longing to die, but the hale man who would have clung to the last edge of life.

"He is taken and I am left," she said abruptly.

Her drawl had vanished. Pain and grief had made her simple. *Then,* I thought with myself, *she did love him!* But I could say nothing. She took my silence for the sympathy it was, and smiled a heartrending smile, so different from that little sad smile she used to have—really pathetic now, and with hardly a glimmer in it of the old self-pity. I rose, put my arms about her, and kissed her on the forehead. She laid her head on my shoulder and wept.

"Whom the Lord loveth He chasteneth," I faltered out, for her sorrow filled me with new respect.

"Yes," she returned, as gently as hopelessly. "And whom He does not love, as well."

"You have no grounds for saying so," I answered. "The Apostle does not."

"My lamp is gone out," she said, "gone out in darkness, utter darkness. You warned me, and I did not heed the warning. I thought I knew better, but I was full of self-conceit. And now I am wandering where there is no way and no light. My iniquities have found me out."

I did not say what I saw plain enough—that her lamp was just beginning to burn. Neither did I try to persuade her that her iniquities were small.

"But the Bridegroom," I said, "is not yet come. There is time to go and get some oil."

"Where am I to get it?" she returned, in a tone of despair.

"From the Bridegroom Himself," I said.

"No," she answered. "I have talked and talked and talked, and you know He says He abhors talkers. I am one of those to whom He will say, 'I know you not.' "

"And you will answer Him that you have eaten and drunk in His presence, and cast out devils, and—?"

"No, no. I will say that He is right—that it was all my own fault, and that I thought I was something when I was nothing, but that I know better now."

A dreadful fit of coughing interrupted her. As soon as it was over, I said, "And what will the Lord say to you, do you think, when you have said so to Him?"

"Depart from Me," she answered in a hollow, forced voice.

"No," I returned. "He will say, 'I know you well. You have told Me the truth. Come in.' "

"*Do* you think so?" she cried. "You never used to think well of me."

"Those who were turned away," I said, avoiding her last words, "were trying to make themselves out better than they were. They trusted not in the love of Christ but in what they thought their worth and social standing. Perhaps, if their deeds had been as good as they thought them, they would have known better than to trust in them. If they had told Him the truth, if they had said, 'Lord, we are workers of iniquity. Lord, we used to be hypocrites, but we speak the truth now—forgive us,' do you think He would have them turned away? No, surely. If your lamp is gone out, make haste and tell Him how careless you have been. Tell Him all, and pray Him for oil and light, and see whether your lamp will not straightway glimmer—glimmer first, then glow."

"Ah, Mrs. Percivale!" she cried. "I would *do* something for His sake now if I might, but I cannot. If I had but resisted the disease in me for the sake of serving Him, I might have been able now. But my chance is over: I cannot now—I have too much pain. And death looks such a different thing now! I used to think of it only as a kind of going to sleep, easy though sad—sad, I mean, in the eyes of mourning friends. But I have no friends, now that my husband is gone! I never dreamed of him going first. He loved me—indeed he did, though I always took it as a matter of course. I never saw how beautiful and unselfish he was till he was gone. I have been selfish and stupid and dull, and my sins have found me out. A great darkness has fallen upon me, and although weary of life, instead of longing for death, I shrink from it with horror. My cough will not let me sleep, and there is nothing but weariness in my body, and despair in my heart. Oh, how black and dreary the nights are! I think of the time in your house as an earthly paradise. But where is the heavenly paradise I used to dream of then?"

"Would it content you," I asked, "to be able to dream of it again?"

"No, no. I want something very different now. Those fancies look so uninteresting and stupid now! All I want now is to hear God say, 'I forgive you.' And my husband—I must have troubled him sorely. You don't know how good he was, Mrs. Percivale. *He* made no pretenses like silly me. Do you know," she went on, lowering her voice, and speaking with something like horror in its tone, "do you know, I cannot *bear* hymns?"

As she said it, she looked up in my face, half-terrified with the anticipation of the horror she expected to see manifested there. I could not help smiling. The case was not one for argument of any kind. I thought for a moment, then merely repeated a verse:

When the law threatens endless death,
Upon the awful hill,
Straightway, from her consuming breath,
My soul goeth higher still—
Goeth to Jesus, wounded, slain,
And maketh Him her home again,
And where Death cannot come.

"Ah! That is good," she said. "If only I could get to Him. But I cannot. He is so far off! He seems to be—nowhere."

I think she was going to say *nobody,* but changed the word.

"If you felt for a moment how helpless and wretched I feel, especially in the early morning," she went on, "how there seems nothing to look for, and no help to be had—you would pity rather than blame me, though I know I deserve blame. I feel as if all the heart and soul and strength and mind, with which we are told to love God, has gone out of me, or rather, as if I had never had any. I doubt if I ever had. I tried very hard for a long time to get a sight of Jesus, to feel myself in His presence, but it was of no use, and I have quite given it up now."

I made her lie on the sofa, and I sat down beside her.

"Do you think," I said, "that anyone, before He came, could have imagined such a visitor to the world as Jesus Christ?"

"I suppose not," she answered listlessly.

"Then, no more can you come near Him now by trying to imagine Him. You cannot represent to yourself the reality, the Being who can comfort you. You cannot take Him into your heart. Only He knows Himself, and only He can reveal Himself to you. And not until He does can you find any certainty or any peace."

"But He doesn't—He won't reveal Himself to me."

"Suppose you had forgotten what some friend of your childhood was like—say, if it were possible, your own mother. Suppose you could not recall a feature of her face or the color of her eyes. And suppose that while you were very miserable about it, you remembered all at once that you had a portrait of her in an old desk you had not opened for years. What would you do?"

"Go and get it," she answered like a child at the Sunday School.

"Then why shouldn't you do so now? You have such a portrait of Jesus, far truer and more complete than any other kind of portrait can be—the portrait His own deeds and words give us of Him."

"I see what you mean, but that is all about long ago, and I want Him now. That is in a book, and I want Him in my heart."

"How are you to get Him into your heart? How could you have Him there, except by knowing Him? But perhaps you think you do know Him?"

"I am certain I do not know Him—at least, as I want to know Him," she said.

"No doubt," I went on, "He can speak to your heart without the record and, I think, is speaking to you now in this very want of Him you feel. But how could He show Himself to you otherwise than by helping you to understand the revelation of Himself which cost Him such labor? If the story were millions of years old, so long as it were true, it would be all the same as if it had been only yesterday; for, being what He represented Himself, He can never change. To know what He was then is to know what He is now."

"But, if I knew Him so, that wouldn't be to have Him with me."

"No, but in that knowledge He might come to you. It is by the door of that knowledge that His Spirit, which is Himself, comes into the soul. You would at least be more able to pray to Him. You would know what kind of a being you had to cry to. *You* would thus come nearer to Him, and no one ever drew nigh to Him whom He did not also draw nigh. If you would but read the story as if you had never read it before, as if you were reading the history of a man you heard of for the first time—"

I ceased, and for some moments she sat silent. Then she said feebly, "There's a Bible somewhere in the room."

I found it and read the story of the woman who came from behind Him in terror, and touched the hem of His garment. I could hardly read it for the emotion it caused in myself, and when I ceased I saw her weeping silently.

A servant entered with the message that Mr. Percivale had called for me.

"I cannot see him today," she sobbed.

"Of course not," I replied. "I must leave you now, but I will come again—come as often as you like."

"You are as kind as ever!" she returned, with a fresh burst of tears. "Will you come and be with me when—when—?"

She could not finish for sobs.

"I will," I said, knowing well what she meant.

And I know her story now. When her husband died suddenly, of apoplexy, she was stunned for a time, gradually awaking to a miserable sense of unprotected loneliness, so much the more painful for her weakly condition and the overcare to which she had been accustomed. Left thus without shelter, like a delicate plant whose house of glass has been shattered, she speedily recognized her true condition. With no one to heed her whims, and no one capable of sympathizing with the genuine misery which supervened, her disease gathered strength rapidly, her lamp went out, and she saw no light beyond—for the smoke of that lamp had dimmed the windows at which the stars would have looked in. She saw that she was poor and miserable and blind and naked, that she had never had faith fit to support her.

But out of this darkness dawned at least a twilight, gradual, slow. She became aware of a deeper and simpler need than hitherto she had known—the need of life in herself, the life of the Son of God.

I went to see her often, going every other day and sometimes oftener, for her end seemed to be drawing nigh. Her weakness had greatly increased: she could but just walk across the room, and was constantly restless. She had no great continuous pain, but oft-returning sharp fits of it. She looked genuinely sad, and her spirits never recovered themselves. She seldom looked out of the window, for the daylight seemed to distress her. Flowers were the only links between her and the outer world—wild ones, for the scent of greenhouse flowers, and even that of most garden ones, she could not bear. She had been very fond of music, but could no longer endure her piano—every note seemed to strike on a nerve. But she was generally quiet in her mind and often peaceful. The more her body decayed, the more her spirit seemed to come alive. It was the calm of a gray evening, not so lovely as a golden sunset or a silvery moonlight, but more sweet than either. She talked little of her feelings, but evidently longed after the words of our Lord. As she listened to some of them, I could see the eyes, which had now grown dim with suffering, gleam with the light of holy longing and humble adoration.

She often referred to her coming departure, and confessed that she feared death—not so much what might be on the other side, as the dark way itself, the struggle, the torture, the fainting. But by degrees her allusions to it became rarer, and at length ceased almost entirely.

Once I said to her, "Are you afraid of death still, Eleanor?"

"No, not much," she replied, after a brief pause. "He may do with me whatever He likes."

Knowing so well what Marion could do to comfort and support, and therefore desirous of bringing them together, I took her one day with me. Before we left, it was plain that Marion had a far more soothing influence upon her than I had myself. She looked eagerly to her next visit, and my mind was now more at peace concerning her.

One evening, after listening to some stories from Marion about her friends, Mrs. Cromwell said, "Ah, Miss Clare! To think I might have done something for *Him* by doing it for *them!* Alas! I have led a useless life, and am dying out of this world without having borne any fruit! Ah, me, me!"

"You are doing a good deal for Him now," said Marion, "and hard work too! Harder far than mine."

"I am only dying," she returned, so sadly.

"You are enduring chastisement," said Marion. "The Lord gives one person one thing to do, and another person another. We have no right to wish for other work than He gives us. It is rebellious and unchildlike, whatever it may seem. Neither have we any right to wish to be better in *our* way; we must wish to be better in *His*.

"And what is the will of God? Is it not your sanctification? And why did He make the Captain of our salvation perfect through suffering? Was it not that He might in like manner bring many sons into glory? Then, if you are enduring, you are working with God for the perfection through suffering of one more. You are working for God in yourself, that the will of God may be done in you, that He may have His very own way with you. It is the only work He requires of you now; do it not only willingly, then, but contentedly. To make people good is all His labor. Be good, and you are a fellow worker with God in the highest region of labor. He does not want you for other people—yet."

One evening, when we were both with her, it had grown very sultry and breathless.

"Isn't it very close, dear Mrs. Percivale?" she said.

I rose to get a fan, and Marion, leaving the window as if moved by a sudden resolve, went and opened the piano. Mrs. Cromwell made a hasty motion, as if she must prevent her. But, such was my faith in my friend's soul as well as her heart, in her divine taste as well as her human faculty, that I laid my hand on Mrs. Cromwell's. It was enough for sweetness like hers; she yielded instantly and lay still, evidently nerving herself to suffer. But the first movement stole so "soft and soullike" on her ear, trembling as it were on the borderland between sound and silence, that she missed the pain she expected and found only the pleasure she looked not for. Marion's hands made the instrument sigh and sing, not merely as with a human voice, but as with a human soul. Marion's voice next stole its way into her heart, to set first one chord then another vibrating, until the whole soul was filled with responses.

Where she got the song she then sang, she always avoids telling me. I had told her all I knew and understood concerning Mrs. Cromwell and have my suspicions. This was her song:

I fancy I hear a whisper
As of leaves in a gentle air:
Is it wrong, I wonder, to fancy
It may be the tree up there?
The tree that heals the nations,
Growing amidst the street,
And dropping, for who will gather,
Its apples at their feet?

I fancy I hear a rushing
As of waters down a slope:
Is it wrong, I wonder, to fancy
It may be the river of hope?
The river of crystal waters
That flows from the very throne,
And runs through the street of the city
With a softly jubilant sound?

I fancy a twilight around me,
And a wandering of the breeze,
With a hush in that high city,
And a going in the trees.
But I know there will be no night there—
No coming and going day;
For the holy face of the Father
Will be perfect light alway.

I could do without the darkness,
And better without the sun;
But, oh, I should like a twilight

After the day was done!
Would He lay His hand on my forehead,
On His hair as white as wool,
And shine one hour through His fingers,
Till the shadow had made me cool?

But the thought is very foolish:
If that face I did but see,
All else would be forgotten—
River and twilight and tree;
I should seek, I should care, for nothing,
Beholding His countenance;
And fear only to lose one glimmer
By one single sideway glance.

'Tis but again a foolish fancy
To picture the countenance so,
Which is shining in all our spirits,
Making them white as snow.
Come to me, shine in me, Master,
And I care not for river or tree—
Care for no sorrow or crying,
If only Thou shine in me.

I would lie on my bed for ages,
Looking out on the dusty street,
Where whisper nor leaves nor waters,
Nor anything cool and sweet;
At my heart this ghastly fainting,
And this burning in my blood—
If only I knew Thou wast with me—
Wast with me and making me good.

When Marion rose from the piano, Mrs. Cromwell stretched out her hand for hers, and held it for some time, unable to speak. Then she said, "That has done me good, I hope. I will try to be more patient, for I think *He* is teaching me."

She died, at length, in my arms. I cannot linger over the last time. She suffered a good deal, but went without a struggle. The last words I heard her utter were, "Yes, Lord," after which she breathed but once. A half-smile came over her face, which froze upon it and remained as the coffin lid covered it. But I shall see it, I trust, a whole smile some day.

TWENTY-NINE

Double, Double, Toil and Trouble

I had for a day or two fancied that Marion was looking less bright than usual, as if some little shadow had fallen upon the morning of her life. She must now have been twenty-seven or twenty-eight. Unwilling at once to assert the ultimate privilege of friendship, I asked her if anything was amiss with her friends. She answered that all was going on well, at least so far that she had no special anxiety about any of them. Encouraged by a half-conscious and more than half-sad smile, I ventured a little further.

"I am afraid there is something troubling you," I said.

"There is," she replied, "Something is troubling me a good deal, but I hope it will pass away soon."

The sigh which followed, however, seemed to indicate a fear that the trouble might not pass away so very soon.

"I am not to ask you any questions, I suppose," I returned.

"Better not at present," she answered. "I am not quite sure that—" She paused several moments before finishing her sentence, then added, "—that I am at liberty to tell you about it."

"Then don't say another word," I rejoined. "Only when I can be of service to you, you *will* let me know, won't you?"

The tears rose to her eyes. "I'm afraid it may be some fault of mine," she said. "I can't tell. I don't understand such things."

She sighed again, and held her peace.

It was enigmatic enough, but I held my peace, and in a few minutes Marion went, with a more affectionate leave-taking than usual.

I pondered, but it was not of much use. Of course, the first thing that suggested itself was, Could my angel be in love? And with some mere mortal? Being a woman, she *might* be in love, but the two ideas, *Marion* and *love,* refused to coalesce. And again, was it likely that she, her mind occupied with so many other absorbing interests, would fall in love unprovoked, unsolicited? That was not likely. Then if solicited, she but returned love for love, why was she sad? The new experience might trouble her greatly. She would not know what to do with it, nor where to accommodate her new inmate so as to keep him from meddling with affairs he had no right to meddle with. It was easy enough to fancy him troublesome in a house like hers. But surely of all women *she* might be able to meet her own liabilities. And if this were all, why should she have said she hoped it would soon pass? That might, however, mean only that she hoped soon to get her guest brought amenable to her existing household economy.

Yet another conjecture seemed to suit the case better. If Marion knew little of what is commonly called love, there was no one who knew more of the tenderness of compassion than she, and was it not possible someone might be wanting to marry her, to whom she could not give herself away?

This at least covered the facts in my possession. But who was there to dare offer love to my saint? Roger? Pooh! Pooh! Mr. Blackstone? Ah! I had seen him lately looking at her with an expression of more than ordinary admiration. But what man who knew anything of her could help looking at her with such admiration? If it was Mr. Blackstone why—*he* might dare—yes, why should he not dare to love her? Especially if he couldn't help it, as, of course, he couldn't. Was he not one whose love, simply because he was a *true* man from the heart to the hands, would honor any woman, even Saint Clare—as she must become when the church has learned to do its business without the pope?

If it were Mr. Blackstone, certainly I knew no man who could understand her better, or whose modes of thinking and working would more thoroughly fall in with her own. True, he was peculiar—that is, he had kept the angles of his individuality, for all the grinding of the social mill. His manners were too abrupt, and drove at the heart of things too directly, seldom suggesting a by-your-leave to those whose prejudices he overturned. True also that his person, though dignified, was somewhat ungainly, with an ungainliness, however, which I could well imagine a wife learning absolutely to love. On the whole, the thing was reasonable. Only what would become of her friends? There, I could hardly doubt, there lay the difficulty!

Let no one think, when I say we went to Mr. Blackstone's church, that it had anything to do with these speculations. We often went there on the first Sunday of the month.

"What's the matter with Blackstone?" said my husband as we came home.

"What do *you* think is the matter with him?" I returned.

"I don't know. He wasn't himself."

"I thought he was more than himself," I rejoined, "for I never heard even *him* read the litany with such fervor."

"In some of the petitions," said Percivale, "it amounted to a suppressed agony of supplication. I am certain he is in trouble."

I told him my suspicions.

"Likely—very likely," he answered, and became thoughtful.

"But you don't think she refused him?" he said at length.

"If he ever asked her," I returned, "I fear she did, for she is plainly in trouble too."

"She'll never stick to it," he said.

"You mustn't judge Marion by ordinary standards," I replied. "You must remember she has not only found her vocation, but for many years has proved it. I never knew her to turn aside from what she made up her mind to. I can hardly imagine her forsaking her friends to keep house for any man, even if she loved him with all her heart. She is dedicated as irrevocably as any nun, and will, with St. Paul, cling to the right of self-denial."

"Yet what great difficulty would there be in combining the two sets of duties, especially with such a man as Blackstone? Of all the men I know, he comes the nearest to her in his devotion to the well-being of humanity, especially of the poor. Did you ever know a man with such a plentiful lack of condescension?"

"That may be. He is the same all through and—I had almost said—worthy of Saint Clare. Well, they must settle it for themselves. We can do nothing."

"We can do nothing," he assented, and, although we repeatedly reverted to the subject on the way home, we carried no conclusions to a different result.

Toward evening, Roger came to accompany us, as I thought, to Marion's gathering. But, as it turned out, he only told me he couldn't go. I expressed my regret, and asked him why. He gave me no answer, and his lip trembled. A sudden conviction seized me. I laid my hand on his arm, but could only say, "Dear Roger!" He turned his head aside and, sitting down on the sofa, laid his forehead on his hand.

"I'm so sorry!" I said.

"She has told you then?" he murmured.

"No one has told me anything."

He was silent. I sat down beside him. It was all I could do. After a moment he rose, saying, "There's no good whining about it, only she might have made a man of me. But she's quite right. It's a comfort to think I'm so unworthy of her. That's all the consolation left me, but there's more in that than you think."

He attempted to laugh, but made a miserable failure of it, then rose and caught up his hat to go. I rose also.

"Roger," I said, "I can't leave you miserable. We'll go somewhere else—anywhere you please, only you mustn't leave us."

"I don't want to go somewhere else. I don't know the place," he added, with a feeble attempt at his usual gaiety.

"Stop at home, then, and tell me all about it. It will do you good to talk. You shall have your pipe, and you shall tell me just as much as you like, and keep the rest to yourself."

I ran to Percivale, gave him a hint of how it was, and demanded his pipe, telling him he must be content with a cigar.

I returned to Roger, who took it and began to fill it mechanically, but not uncarefully. I sat down, laid my hands in my lap, and looked at him without a word. When the pipe was filled I rose and got him a light. Having whiffed a good many whiffs in silence, he took his pipe from his mouth, and said, "I've made a fool of myself, Wynnie."

"Not more than a gentleman had a right to do, I will pledge myself," I returned.

"She *has* told you, then?" he said once more, looking rather disappointed than annoyed.

"No one has mentioned your name to me, Roger. I only guessed it from what Marion said when I questioned her about her sad looks."

"Her sad looks?"

"Yes."

"What did she say?"

"She only confessed she had had something to trouble her, and said she hoped it would soon be over."

"I dare say!" returned Roger dryly, looking gratified however, for a moment.

"You see, Wynnie," he said, with pauses, and puffs at his pipe, "I don't mean I'm a fool for falling in love with Marion. Not to have fallen in love with her would have argued me a beast. Being a man, it was impossible for me to help it, after what she's been to me. But I was worse than a fool to open my mouth on the subject to an angel like her. Only there again, I couldn't, that is, I hadn't the strength to help it. I beg, however, you won't think me such a downright idiot as to fancy myself worth her. In that case, I should have deserved as much scorn as she gave me kindness. If you ask me how it was, then, that I dared to speak to her on the subject, I can only answer that I yielded to the impulse common to all kinds of love to make itself known. If you love God, you are not content with His knowing it even, but you must tell Him as if He didn't know it. You may think from this cool talk of mine that I am very philosophical about it; but there are lulls in every storm, and I am in one, else I shouldn't be sitting here with you."

"Dear Roger!" I said, "I am very sorry for your disappointment. I can't be sorry you should love Marion. That can do you nothing but good, and in itself must raise you above yourself. And how could I blame you that you wanted her to know it? But come, now, if you can trust me, tell me all about it, and especially what she said to you. I dare not give you any hope, for I am not in her confidence in this matter. It is well that I am not, for then I might not be able to talk to you about it with any freedom. To confess the real truth, I do not see much likelihood, knowing her as I do, that she will recall her decision."

"It could hardly be called a decision," said Roger. "You would have thought, from the way she took it, there was nothing to decide about. No more there was, and I thought I knew it, only I couldn't be quiet. To *think* you know a thing and to *know* it are two very different matters, however."

I was not moved by sympathetic curiosity alone, but also by the vague desire of rendering some help beyond comfort. What he had now said greatly heightened my opinion of him, and thereby, in my thoughts, lessened the distance between him and Marion.

And he did tell me the whole, and I learned more afterward from Marion.

THIRTY
Roger and Marion

During an all but sleepless night, Roger had made up his mind to go and see Marion—not, certainly, for the first time, for he had again and again ventured to call upon her. But hitherto he had always had some pretext sufficient to veil his deeper reason; and sufficient also to prevent her, in her more ordinary simplicity with regard to such matters, from suspecting one under it.

She was at home, and received him with her usual kindness. Feeling that he must not let an awkward silence intervene, he spoke at once.

"I want to tell you something, Miss Clare," he said as lightly as he could.

"Well?" she returned, with the sweet smile which graced her every approach to communication.

"Did my sister-in-law ever tell you what an idle fellow I used to be?"

"Certainly not. I never heard her say one word of you that wasn't kind."

"That I am sure of. But there would have been no unkindness in saying that, for an idle fellow I was, and idle because I was conceited enough to believe I could do anything. I actually thought at one time I could play the violin. I made an impertinent attempt in your presence one evening, years and years ago. I wonder if you remember it. Anyhow, I caught a look on your face that cured me of that conceit. I have never touched the creature since."

"I am very sorry, indeed I am. I don't remember—do you think you could have played a false note?"

"Nothing more likely."

"Then, I dare say I made an ugly face. One can't always help it, you know, when something unexpected happens. Do forgive me."

"Forgive *you,* you angel!" cried Roger, but instantly checked himself, afraid of reaching his mark before he had gathered sufficient momentum to pierce it. "I thought you would see what a good thing it was for me. I wanted to thank you for it."

"It's such a pity you didn't go on, though. Progress is the real cure for an overestimate of ourselves."

"The fact is, I was beginning to see what small praise there is in doing many things ill and nothing well. I wish you would take my violin. I could teach you the ABC's—how you would make it talk! That *would* be something to live for, to hear *you* play the violin."

"I have no time. I should have been delighted to be your pupil, but I am sorry to say it is out of the question."

"Of course it is. Only I wish—well, never mind. I only wanted to tell you something. I was leading a life then that wasn't worth leading, for where's the good of being just what happens—one time full of right feeling and impulse, and the next a prey to all wrong judgments and falsehoods? It was you who made me see it. I've been trying to get put right for a long time now. You and your Sunday evenings have waked me up to know what I am, and what I ought to be. I *am* a little better. I work hard now. I used to work only by fits and starts. Ask Wynnie."

"Dear Mr. Roger, I don't need to ask Wynnie about anything you tell me. I can take your word for it just as well as hers. I am very glad if I have been of any use to you. It is a great honor to me."

"But the worst of it is, I couldn't be content without letting you know, and making myself miserable."

"I don't understand you. Surely there can be no harm in letting me know what makes me very happy! How it should make you miserable, I can't imagine."

"Because I can't stop there. I'm driven to say what may offend you. I can't help loving you—dreadfully—and it's such impudence! To think of you and me in one thought! And yet I can't help it. O Miss Clare, don't drive me away from you."

He fell on his knees as he spoke, and laid his head on her lap, sobbing like a child who had offended his mother. Marion started to her feet in confusion—almost in terror, for she had never seen such emotion in a man—but the divine compassion of her nature conquered, and she sat down again, took his head in her hands, and began stroking his hair as if she were indeed a mother seeking to soothe and comfort her troubled child. She was the first to speak again, for Roger could not command himself.

"I'm very sorry, Roger," she said. "I must be to blame somehow."

"To blame!" he cried, lifting up his head. "*You* to blame! It would be downright stupidity not to love you with all my soul."

"Hush! Hush!" said Marion. "You *couldn't* love me with all your soul if you would. God *only* can be loved with all the power of the human soul."

"If I love Him at all, Marion, it is you who have taught me. Do not drive me from you."

"I will not drive you from me. Why should I?"

"Then I may come and see you again?"

"Yes, when you please."

"You *don't* mean I may come as often as I like?"

"Roger," said Marion, pale as death, and rising also—for, alas! The sunshine of her kindness had caused hopes to blossom whose buds she had taken only for leaves. "I thought you understood me! I am not my own to keep or to give away. I belong to these people—my friends. To take personal and private duties upon me would be to abandon them. You don't know what it would result in, or you would not dream of it. Were I to do such a thing, I should hate and despise and condemn myself with utter reprobation. And then what a prize you would have, my poor Roger!"

But even these were such precious words to hear from her lips! He fell again on his knees before her as she stood, caught her hands and, hiding his face in them, poured forth in a torrent, "Marion, do not think me so selfish as not to have thought about that. It should be only the better for them all. I can earn quite enough for you and me too, and so you would have the more time to give to them. I should never have dreamed of asking you to leave them."

Deeply moved by the unselfishness of his love, Marion could not help a pressure of her hands against the face which had sought refuge within them. Roger fell to kissing them wildly.

But Marion was a woman—and women, I think, look forward and round about, more than men do, and therefore Marion saw other things. Marion saw that as a married woman, she might be compelled to forsake her friends more or less, for there might arise other and paramount claims on her self-devotion. If she were to have children, she would have no choice in respect to whose welfare should constitute the main business of her life, and it even became a question whether she would have a right to place them in circumstances so unfavorable for growth and education. Therefore, to marry might be tantamount to forsaking her friends.

But where was the need of any such mental parley? Of course, she couldn't marry Roger. How could she marry a man she couldn't look up to? And look up to him she certainly did not, and could not.

"No, Roger," she said, this last thought large in her mind, and withdrew her hands. "It mustn't be. It is out of the question. I can't look up to you," she added, as simply as a child.

"I should think not," he burst out. "That *would* be a fine thing! If you looked up to a fellow like me, I think it would almost cure me of looking up to you, and what I want is to look up to you, only I can do that whether you let me or not."

"But I don't choose to have a—a friend to whom I can't look up."

"Then I shall never be even a friend," he returned sadly. "But I would have tried hard to be less unworthy of you."

At this precise moment, Marion caught sight of a pair of great round blue eyes, wide open under a shock of red hair, about three feet from the floor, staring as if they had not winked for the last ten minutes. The child looked so comical that Marion, reading perhaps in her looks the reflex of her own position, could not help laughing. Roger started up in dismay but, beholding the apparition, laughed also.

"Please, Grannie," said the urchin, "Mother's took bad and wants ye."

"Run and tell your mother I shall be with her directly," answered Marion, and the child departed.

"You told me I might come again," pleaded Roger.

"Better not. I didn't know what it would mean to you when I said it."

"Let it mean what you meant by it, only let me come."

"But I see now it can't mean that. No, but I will write to you. At all events, you must go now, for I can't stop with you—"

"Don't make me wretched, Marion. If you can't love me, don't kill me. Don't say I'm not to come and see you. I *will* come on Sundays, anyhow."

The next day he received the following letter:

"Dear Mr. Roger—

"I am very sorry, both for your sake and my own, that I did not speak more plainly yesterday. I was so distressed for you, and my heart was so friendly toward you that I could hardly think of anything at first but how to comfort you. I fear I allowed you, after all, to go away with the idea that what you wished was not altogether impossible. But indeed it is. If even I loved you in the way you love me, I should yet make everything yield to the duties I have undertaken. In listening to you, I should be undermining the whole of my past labors, and the idea of becoming less of a friend to my friends is horrible to me.

"But as much as I esteem you, and as much pleasure as your society gives me, the idea you brought before me yesterday was absolutely startling. The peculiarities of my position should convince you that it could never become a familiar one to me. All that friendship can do or yield, you may ever claim of me, and I thank God if I have been of the smallest service to you. But I should be quite unworthy of that honor, were I even to think of abandoning the work which has been growing up around me for so many years, and is so peculiarly mine that it could be transferred to no one else.

"Believe me yours most truly,

"Marion Clare"

That same Sunday evening as we sat together, after telling me the greater part of the story, Roger handed me this very letter.

I read it and returned it to him. "It seems final, Roger?"

"Of course it is," he replied. "How could any honest man urge his suit after that, after she says that to grant it would be to destroy the whole of her previous life, and ruin her self-respect? But I'm not so miserable as you may think me, Wynnie. Though I couldn't quite bring myself to go tonight, I don't feel cut off from her. She's not likely, if I know her, to listen to anybody else so long as the same reasons hold which wouldn't give me a chance. She can't help me loving her, and I'm sure she'll let me help her when I've the luck to find a chance. You may be sure I shall keep a sharp lookout. If I can be her servant, that will be something. Though she won't give herself to me, she can't prevent me from giving myself to her. So long as I may love her, and see her as often as I don't doubt I may, and things continue as they are, I shan't be downhearted."

Here he started, and hurriedly pulled out his watch. "I declare, there's time yet!" he cried, and sprung to his feet. "Let's go and hear what she's got to say tonight."

"Should you? Won't you put her out?"

"If I understand her at all," he said, "she will be more put out by my absence, for she will fear I am wretched, caring only for herself, and not what she has taught me. You may come or stay—*I'm* off. You've done me so much good, Wynnie!" he added, looking back in the doorway. "Thank you a thousand times. There's no comforter like a sister."

Percivale and I followed as quickly as we could. When we reached Lime Court, there was Roger sitting in the midst, intent on her words, and Marion speaking with all her natural composure.

When she shook hands with him after the service, a slight flush washed the white of her face with a delicate warmth, nothing more. I said to myself, however, as we went home, and afterward to my husband, that his case was not a desperate one.

"But what's to become of Blackstone?" asked Percivale.

I know how afterward Mr. Blackstone seemed to me to have fared, but I have no information concerning his supposed connection with this part of my story. I cannot even be sure that he was in love with Marion. Troubled he certainly was, at this time, and Marion continued so for a while—more troubled, I think, than her words with Roger will quite account for. If, however, she had to make two men miserable in one week, that might well cover the case.

Before the week was over, my husband received a note from Mr. Blackstone, informing him that he was just about to start for a few weeks on the Continent. When he returned I was satisfied from his appearance that a notable change had passed upon him: a certain indescribable serenity seemed to have taken possession of his whole being, and every look and tone indicated a mind that knew more than tongue could utter—a heart that had had glimpses into a region of content. I thought of the words, "He that dwelleth in the secret place of the Most High," and my heart was at rest about him. He had fared, I thought, as the child who has had a hurt, but is taken up in his mother's arms and comforted. What hurt would not such comforting outweigh to the child? And who but he that has had the worst hurt man can receive, and the best comfort God can give, can tell what either is?

I was present the first time he met Marion after his return. She was a little embarrassed: he showed a tender dignity, a respect as if from above, like the love of a wise angel for such a woman. For the moment I felt as if Mr. Blackstone were a step above Marion. Plainly, I had no occasion to be troubled about either of them.

On the supposition that Marion had refused him, I argued with myself that it could not have been on the ground that she was unable to look up to him. And I was satisfied that anyone she felt she could help to be a nobler creature must have a greatly better chance of rousing all the woman in her, than one whom she must regard as needing no aid from her. All her life had been spent in serving and sheltering human beings whose condition she regarded with hopeful compassion. Could she now help adding Roger to her number of such? If she once looked upon him thus tenderly, was it not at least possible that, in some softer mood, a feeling hitherto unknown to her might surprise her consciousness with its presence, floating to the surface of her sea from its strange depths, and leaning toward him with the outstretched arms of embrace?

But I dared not think what might become of Roger should his divine resolves fail—should the frequent society of Marion prove insufficient for the solace and quiet of his heart.

As the days went on, though, I saw no sign of failure or change in Roger. He was steady at his work, and came to see us as constantly as before. He never missed a chance of meeting Marion, and at every treat she gave her friends, Roger was always at hand for service and help. Still, I was uneasy, for might there not come a collapse, especially if some new event were to destroy the hope which he still cherished, and which I feared was his main support? Would his religion then prove of a quality and power sufficient to keep him from drifting away with the receding tide of his hopes and imaginations? In this anxiety perhaps I regarded too exclusively the faith of Roger, and thought too little about the faith of God. However this may be, I could not rest, but thought and thought, until at last I made up my mind to go and tell Lady Bernard all about it.

THIRTY-ONE
Some Final Words

"And you think Marion likes him?" asked Lady Bernard, when she had in silence heard my story.

"I am sure she *likes* him. But you know he is so far inferior to her in every way."

"How do you know that? Questions are involved there which no one but God can determine. You must remember that both are growing. What matter if any two are unequal at a given moment, seeing their relative positions may be reversed twenty times in a thousand years? Besides, I doubt very much if any one who brought his favors with him would have the least chance with Marion. Poverty, to turn into wealth, is the one irresistible attraction for her—and, however duty may compel her to act, my impression is that she will not escape *loving* Roger."

I was gratified to find Lady Bernard's conclusion from Marion's character running parallel with my own.

"But what can come of it?" I said.

"Why, marriage, I hope."

"But Marion would as soon think of falling down and worshiping Baal and Ashtoreth as of forsaking her grandchildren."

"Doubtless. But there would be no occasion for that. Where two things are both of God, it is not likely they will be found mutually obstructive."

"Roger does declare himself quite ready to go and live amongst her friends, and do his best to help her."

"That is all as it should be, so far as he—as both of them are concerned, but there are contingencies: how would that do in regard of their children?"

"If I could imagine Marion consenting," I said, "I know what she would answer to that question. She would ask why her children should be better off than the children about them? She would say that the children must share the life and work of their parents."

"And I think she would be right, though the obvious rejoinder would be,

'You may waive your own social privileges, and sacrifice yourselves to the good of others, but have you a right to sacrifice your children, and heap disadvantages on their future?' "

"Now give us the answer on the other side, seeing you think Marion would be right after all."

"Marion's answer would be, I think, that their children would be God's children, and He couldn't desire better for them than to be born in lowly conditions, and trained from the first to give themselves to the service of their fellows, seeing that insofar their history would resemble that of His own Son, our Saviour. In sacrificing their earthly future, as men would call it, their parents would but be furthering their eternal good."

"But how would her new position affect her ministrations?"

"There can be no doubt," Lady Bernard replied, "that what her friends would lose thereby—I mean, what amount of her personal ministrations would be turned aside from them by the necessities of her new position—would be far more than made up to them by the presence among them of a whole well-ordered and growing family, instead of a single woman only. But all this yet leaves something for her more personal friends to consider, as regards their duty in the matter. I will turn the thing over in my mind, and let you know what comes of it."

The result of Lady Bernard's cogitations is, so far, to be seen in the rapid rise of a block of houses at no great distance from London on the Northwestern railway, planned under the instructions of Marion Clare. The design provides accommodation for all Marion's friends, with room to add largely to their number. Lady Bernard has also secured ground sufficient for great extension of the present building, should it prove desirable. Each family is to have the same amount of accommodation it has now—only far better—at the same rent it pays now, with the privilege of taking an additional room or rooms at a much lower rate. Marion has undertaken to collect the rents, and believes that she will thus in time gain an additional hold of the people for their good, although the plan may at first expose her to misunderstanding. From thorough calculation she is satisfied she can pay Lady Bernard five percent for her money, lay out all that is necessary for keeping the property in thorough repair, and accumulate a fund besides to be spent on building more houses. The removal of so many will also make a little room for the accommodation of the multitudes constantly driven from their homes by the wickedness of those who, either for the sake of railways or fine streets, pull down crowded houses, and drive into other courts and alleys their poor inhabitants, to double the wretchedness already there from overcrowding.

In the center of the building is a house for Marion, where she will have her own private advantage in the inclusion of large space primarily for the entertainment of her friends. I believe Lady Bernard intends to give her a hint that a married couple would, in her opinion, be far more useful in such a position than a single woman.

If the scheme should answer, what a strange reversion it will be to something like a right reading of the feudal system!

Of course, it will be objected that, should it succeed ever so well, it will all go to pieces at Marion's death. But such a work as hers can never be lost, for the world can never be the same as if she had not lived, while in any case there will be more room for her brothers and sisters who are now being crowded out of the world by the stronger and richer. It would be sufficient answer, however, that the work is worth doing for its own sake and its immediate result. Surely it will receive a "Well Done" from the Judge of us all. And while His idea of right remains above hers, as high as the heavens are above the earth, His approbation will be all that either Lady Bernard or Marion will seek.

If but a small proportion of those who love the right and have means to spare would, like Lady Bernard, use their wealth to make up to the poor for the wrongs they receive at the hands of the rich—let me say, to defend the Saviour in their persons from the tyranny of Mammon—how many of the poor might they not lead with them into the joy of the Lord!

There are many more things to say, of my own family and those of my friends, but words have already multiplied too abundantly, and there is no time left to say it all. And what better thing, in the end, can I say except that we all live in hope of the glory of God!

AFTERWORD

MacDonald's England can still be found, if you look closely enough, and know the thin disguises he applied to his settings. He did not invent his settings, people, or situations—his works were written from life, and reflect his deep insight into the natures of God, fallen man, and redeemed man. The places and people were largely taken from places and people around him—the things near at hand, the things he knew best.

"Marshmallows" is MacDonald's name for the village of Arundel, situated directly south of London and only a few miles north of the English Channel.

Arundel was the scene of MacDonald's first pastorate, from 1850 to 1853. He was the minister of a small Congregational assembly, whose chapel still stands (though disused) only a hundred yards or so from the larger Anglican church. MacDonald's years there held both pleasure and turmoil; in Arundel he was married, he first contracted the tuberculosis that would so torture and shape the rest of his life, and his first child was born. Those years ended on a less than happy note: the elders of his congregation, unhappy with certain aspects of his theology, halved his salary and ultimately forced him from the pulpit.

When MacDonald took up his pen a few years later to write *A Quiet Neighborhood*, he carried forward a number of Arundelian memories: Old Rogers and the mill, the bridge over the River Arun, the Anglican church with its stone walls and the poor graves near the church door, and the mysterious old hall at the edge of the village.

Old Rogers is indeed the name and image of one of MacDonald's Arundel flock—a man who attended services regularly in his round frock, red cotton handkerchief, and tall beaver hat. The mill once stood near the bridge, but both the mill and the bridge are gone. A chemist's shop (drug store) stands where the mill stood, and a newer (though still elegant) stone bridge has replaced the old one where MacDonald did, in truth, first meet his Old Rogers.

Oldcastle Hall is patterned after the main part of the huge castle which overshadows all Arundel. A lover of castles and staircases (as MacDonald was) could not but take away strong memories of that imposing, sprawling structure. (I suspect that the very name "Oldcastle Hall" is a private joke, for one might refer to the living quarters at Arundel castle as "the old castle hall.")

And the Anglican church itself nestles in the walls that surround the castle. The side door is still there, which Walton used as a private exit—and the path from that door yet wanders among quiet graves whose quiet is that of patient and enduring hope in Christ.

Kilkhaven was MacDonald's name for Bude, a town on the northern Cornish coast where MacDonald and his family spent the summer of 1867. (MacDonald's son Greville recollected the family's time in the area of Bude as among the happiest of his childhood—and largely because his father was more involved in the lives and play of his children then than at any other time within his memory.)

My wife and I visited Bude in the summer of 1984, and found much of it exactly as described—the marvelous cobbled breakwater protecting the harbor from the daily ravages of the sea; the curious cottages at the end of the quay near the canal; and even the ornate boathouse—not the one used now (at the head of the canal) but the one which still stands a few hundred yards away from the sea.

Tintagel—a plausible candidate for King Arthur's seat of power—is exactly as MacDonald saw it, except that wide stone steps with sturdy handrails ease the climb to the top, making an otherwise perilous ascent possible even for the visitors (such as myself) who have no head for heights. The stone arch through which Connie saw the sea still affords an unparalleled view of the waves crashing between the cliffs hundreds of feet below. Merlin's Cave burrows under the peninsula where the castle stands, and the old church and graveyard still huddle atop the land's edge overlooking the castle ruins. St. Nectan's Glen, a few miles away, is also preserved as a tourist stop and tea garden.

London is accurately portrayed in *The Vicar's Daughter* as well. The Tottenham Court area of London (where Percivale and Wynnie lived) still contains traces and memories of MacDonald's world.

MacDonald and his family lived briefly at 18 Queen Square, a short walk northeast of the British Museum; the house was soon after torn down for the construction of a children's hospital. This house presumably served as the model for the house of Marion Clare's memories. The square is still there with its statue, labeled now as Queen Charlotte, with a notice that in the previous century it had been thought to be Queen Anne.

The Blue Posts Pub continues, though greatly modernized, southwest of the British Museum on Tottenham Court Road.

And Lady Bernard is based upon a very real person and dear friend of the MacDonalds—Lady Noel Byron, widow of Lord Byron, the poet. The generosity and warmth of Lady Bernard reflect Lady Byron's generosity and warmth to the MacDonald family.

The clues are there. The diligent reader and traveler may find more that we have missed.